KU-133-290

DICK FRANCIS

DICK FRANCIS

REFLEX

BANKER

PROOF

Reflex first published in Great Britain in 1980
by Michael Joseph Ltd
Banker first published in Great Britain in 1982
by Michael Joseph Ltd
Proof first published in Great Britain in 1984
by Michael Joseph Ltd

This omnibus edition first published in Great Britain in 1988
exclusively for Marks and Spencer plc
by Michael Joseph Ltd,
27 Wrights Lane,
London W8

ISBN 0 1408 7285 X

Typeset by Cambrian Typesetters, Frimley, Surrey
Printed in Great Britain by
Richard Clay Ltd, Bungay, Suffolk

CONTENTS

REFLEX
1
BANKER
241
PROOF
501

REFLEX

My thanks to the Photographers
Bernard Parkin
and
David Hastings
and especially
RON MASSEY
who made me the puzzles.

ONE:

Winded and coughing, I lay on one elbow and spat out a mouthful of grass and mud. The horse I'd been riding raised its weight off my ankle, scrambled untidily to its feet and departed at an unfeeling gallop. I waited for things to settle: chest heaving, bones still rattling from the bang, sense of balance recovering from a thirty-mile-an-hour somersault and a few tumbling rolls. No harm done. Nothing broken. Just another fall.

Time and place: sixteenth fence, three-mile steeplechase, Sandown Park racecourse, Friday, November, in thin, cold, persistent rain. At the return of breath and energy I stood wearily up and thought with intensity that this was a damn silly way for a grown man to be spending his life.

The thought itself was a jolt. Not one I'd ever thought before. Riding horses at high speed over various jumps was the only way I knew of making a living, and it was a job one couldn't do if one's heart wasn't in it. The chilling flicker of disillusion nudged like the first twinge of toothache, unexpected, unwelcome, an uneasy hint of possible trouble.

I repressed it without much alarm. Reassured myself that I loved the life, of course I did, the way I always had. Believed quite easily that nothing was wrong except the weather, the fall, the lost race . . . minor, everyday stuff, business as usual.

Squelching uphill to the stands in paper-thin racing boots unsuitable for hiking, I thought only and firmly about the horse I'd started out on, sorting out what I might and might not say to its trainer. Discarded 'How do you expect it to jump if you don't school it properly?' in favour of 'The experience will do him good.' Thought better of 'useless, panicky, hard-mouthed, underfed dog', and decided on 'might try him in blinkers'. The trainer, anyway, would blame me for the fall and tell the owner I'd misjudged the pace. He was that sort of trainer. Every crash was a pilot error.

I thanked heaven in a mild way that I didn't ride often for that stable, and had been engaged on that day only because

Steve Millace, its usual jockey, had gone to his father's funeral. Spare rides, even with disaster staring up from the form books, were not lightly to be turned down. Not if you needed the money, which I did. And not if, like me, you needed your name up on the number boards as often as possible, to show you were useful and wanted and *there*.

The only good thing, I supposed, about my descent at the fence was that Steve Millace's father hadn't been there to record it. George Millace, pitiless photographer of moments all jockeys preferred to ignore, was safe in his box and approximately at that moment being lowered underground to his long sleep. And good riddance, I thought uncharitably. Goodbye to the snide sneering pleasure George got from delivering to owners the irrefutable evidence of their jockeys' failings. Goodbye to the motorised camera catching at three and a half frames per second one's balance in the wrong place, one's arms in the air, one's face in the mud.

Where other sports photographers played fair and shot you winning from time to time, George trafficked exclusively in ignominy and humiliation. George was a natural-born dragger-down. Newspapers might mourn the passing of his snigger-raising pictures, but there had been little sorrow in the changing room the day Steve told us his father had driven into a tree.

Out of liking for Steve himself, no one had said much. He had listened to the silence, though, and he knew. He had been anxiously defending his father for years; and he knew.

Trudging back in the rain it seemed odd to me still that we wouldn't actually be seeing George Millace again. His image, too familiar for too long, rose sharply in the mind: bright clever eyes, long nose, drooping moustache, twisted mouth sourly smiling. A terrific photographer, one had to admit, with an exceptional talent for anticipation and timing, his lens always pointing in the right direction at the right moment. A comic, too, in his way, showing me less than a week ago a black and white glossy of me taking a dive, nose to ground, bottom up, with a caption written on the back, 'Philip Nore, arse high to a grasshopper.' One would have laughed but for the genuine ill-will which had prompted his humour. One might always have at least tolerated his debunking approach but for the cruelty sliding out of his eyes. He had been a mental thrower of banana skins, lying in wait to scoff at the hurt; and he would be missed with thankfulness.

When I finally reached the shelter of the verandah outside the weighing room, the trainer and owner were waiting there with the expected accusing expressions.

'Misjudged things pretty badly, didn't you?' said the trainer aggressively.

'He took off a stride too soon.'

'Your job to put him right.'

No point in saying that no jockey on earth could get every horse to jump perfectly always, and particularly not a badly schooled rogue. I simply nodded, and smiled a shade ruefully at the owner.

'Might try him in blinkers,' I said.

'*I'll* decide about that,' said the trainer sharply.

'Not hurt, are you?' asked the owner timidly.

I shook my head. The trainer brusquely stamped on this humane jockey-orientated enquiry and wheeled his money-source away from the danger that I might say something truthful about why the horse wouldn't jump when asked. I watched them go without rancour and turned towards the weighing room door.

'I say,' said a young man, stepping in front of me, 'Are you Philip Nore?'

'That's right.'

'Well . . . could I have a word with you?'

He was about twenty-five, tall as a stork and earnest, with office-coloured skin. Charcoal flannel suit, striped tie, no binoculars, and no air of belonging where he stood, in the business-only section of the racecourse.

'Sure,' I said. 'If you'll wait while I check with the doctor and get into something dry.'

'Doctor?' He looked alarmed.

'Oh . . . routine. After a fall. I shan't be long.'

When I went out again, warmed and in street clothes, he was still waiting; and he was more or less alone on the verandah, as nearly everyone else had gone to watch the last race, already in progress.

'I . . . er . . . my name is Jeremy Folk.' He produced a card from inside the charcoal jacket and held it out to me. I took it, and read: *Folk, Langley, Son and Folk.*

Solicitors. Address in St Albans, Hertfordshire.

'That last Folk,' said Jeremy, pointing diffidently, 'Is me.'

'Congratulations,' I said.

He gave me an anxious half smile and cleared his throat.

'I've been sent . . . er . . . I've come to ask you to . . . er . . .' He stopped, looking helpless and not in the least like a solicitor.

'To what?' I said encouragingly.

'They said you wouldn't like . . . but well . . . I've been sent to ask you . . . er . . .'

'Do get on with it,' I said.

'To come and see your grandmother.' The words came out in a nervous rush, and he seemed relieved to be rid of them.

'No,' I said.

He scanned my face and seemed to take heart from its calmness.

'She's dying,' he said. 'And she wants to see you.'

Death all around, I thought. George Millace and my mother's mother. Negative grief in both cases.

'Did you hear?' he said.

'I heard.'

'Now, then? I mean, today?'

'No,' I said. 'I'm not going.'

'But you must.' He looked troubled. 'I mean . . . she's old . . . and she's dying . . . and she wants you . . .'

'Too bad.'

'And if I don't persuade you, my uncle . . . that's Son . . .' he pointed to the card again, getting flustered. 'Er. Folk is my grandfather and Langley is my great-uncle, and . . . er . . . they sent me . . .' He swallowed. 'They think I'm frightfully useless, to be honest.'

'And that's blackmail,' I said.

A faint glint in his eyes told me that he wasn't basically as silly as he made out.

'I don't want to see her,' I said.

'But she is dying.'

'Have you yourself seen her . . . dying?'

'Er . . . no . . .'

'I'll bet she isn't. If she wants to see me, she would say she was dying just to fetch me, because she'd guess nothing else would.'

He looked shocked. 'She's seventy-eight, after all.'

I looked gloomily out at the non-stop rain. I had never met my grandmother and I didn't want to, dying or dead. I didn't approve of death-bed repentances, last minute insurances at the gates of hell. It was too damned late.

'The answer,' I said, 'is still no.'

He shrugged dispiritedly and seemed to give up. Walked a few steps out into the rain, bareheaded, vulnerable, with no umbrella. Turned round after ten paces and came tentatively back again.

'Look . . . she really needs you, my uncle says.' He was as earnest, as intense, as a missionary. 'You can't just let her die.'

'Where is she?' I said.

He brightened. 'In a nursing home.' He fished in another pocket. 'I've got the address. But I'll lead you there, straight away, if you'll come. It's in St Albans. You live in Lambourn, don't you? So it isn't so terribly far out of your way, is it? I mean, not a hundred miles, or anything like that.'

'A good fifty, though.'

'Well . . . I mean . . . you always do drive around an awful lot.'

I sighed. The options were rotten. A choice between meek capitulation or a stony rejection. Both unpalatable. That she had dished out to me the stony rejection from my birth gave me no excuse, I supposed, for doing it to her at her death. Also I could hardly go on smugly despising her, as I had done for years, if I followed her example. Irritating, that.

The winter afternoon was already fading, with electric lights growing brighter by the minute, shining fuzzily through the rain. I thought of my empty cottage; of nothing much to fill the evening, of two eggs, a piece of cheese and black coffee for supper, of wanting to eat more and not doing so. If I went, I thought, it would at least take my mind off food, and anything which helped with the perennial fight against weight couldn't be wholly bad. Not even meeting my grandmother.

'All right,' I said, resignedly, 'lead on.'

The old woman sat upright in bed staring at me, and if she was dying it wasn't going to be on that evening, for sure. The life force was strong in the dark eyes and there was no mortal weakness in her voice.

'Philip,' she said, making it a statement and looking me up and down.

'Yes.'

'Hah.'

The explosive sound contained both triumph and contempt and was everything I would have expected. Her ramrod will had devastated my childhood and done worse damage to her own daughter, and there was to be, I was relieved to see, no maudlin plea for forgiveness. Rejection, even if in a moderated form, was still in operation.

'I knew you'd come running,' she said, 'When you heard about the money.' As a cold sneer it was pretty unbeatable.

'What money?'

'The hundred thousand pounds, of course.'

'No one,' I said, 'has mentioned any money.'

'Don't lie. Why else would you come?'

'They said you were dying.'

She gave me a startled and malevolent flash of the eyes and a baring of teeth which had nothing to do with smiling. 'So I am. So are we all.'

'Yeah,' I said, 'and all at the same rate. One day at a time.'

She was no one's idea of a sweet little pink-cheeked grannie. A strong stubborn face with disapproval lines cut deep around the mouth. Iron grey hair still vigorous, clean and well shaped. Blotchy freckles of age showing brown on an otherwise pale skin, and dark ridged veins on the backs of the hands. A thin woman, almost gaunt; and tall, as far as I could judge.

The large room where she lay was furnished more as a sitting room with a bed in it than as a hospital, which was all of a piece with what I'd seen of the place on the way in. A country house put to new use: hotels with nurses. Carpets everywhere, long chintz curtains, armchairs for visitors, vases of flowers. Gracious dying, I thought.

'I instructed Mr Folk,' she said, 'to make you the offer.'

I reflected. 'Young Mr Folk? About twenty-five? Jeremy?'

'Of course not.' She was impatient. 'Mr Folk, my solicitor. I told him to get you here. And he did. Here you are.'

'He sent his grandson.'

I turned away from her and sat unasked in an armchair. Why, I wondered, had Jeremy not mentioned a hundred thousand pounds? It was the sort of trifle, after all, that one didn't easily forget.

My grandmother stared at me steadily with no signs of affection, and I stared as steadily back. I disliked her certainty that she could buy me. I was repelled by her contempt, and mistrusted her intentions.

'I will leave you a hundred thousand pounds in my will, upon certain conditions,' she said.

'No, you won't,' I said.

'I beg your pardon?' Icy voice, stony look.

'I said no. No money. No conditions.'

'You haven't heard my proposition.'

I said nothing. I felt in fact the first stirrings of curiosity, but I was definitely not going to let her see it. Since she seemed in no hurry, the silence lengthened. More stocktaking on her part, perhaps. Simple patience, on mine. One thing my haphazard upbringing had given me was an almost limitless capacity for waiting. Waiting for people to come, who didn't; and for promises to be fulfilled, that weren't.

Finally she said, 'You're taller than I expected. And much tougher.'

I waited some more.

'Where is your mother?' she said.

My mother, her daughter. 'Scattered on the winds,' I said.

'What do you mean?'

'I think she's dead.'

'*Think*!' She looked more annoyed than anxious. 'Don't you *know*?'

'She didn't exactly write to me to say she'd died; no.'

'Your flippancy is disgraceful.'

'Your behaviour since before my birth,' I said, 'gives you no right to say so.'

She blinked. Her mouth opened, and stayed open for fully five seconds. Then it shut tight with rigid muscles showing along the jaw, and she stared at me darkly in a daunting mixture of fury and ferocity. I saw, in that expression, what my poor young mother had had to face, and felt a great uprush of sympathy for the feckless butterfly who'd borne me.

There had been a day, when I was quite small, that I had been dressed in new clothes and told to be exceptionally good as I was going with my mother to see my grandmother. My mother had collected me from where I was living and we had travelled by car to a large house, where I was left alone in the hall, to wait. Behind a white painted closed door there had been a lot of shouting. Then my mother had come out, crying, and had grabbed me by the hand, and pulled me after her to the car.

'Come on, Philip. We'll never ask her for anything, ever again. She wouldn't even see you. Don't you ever forget, Philip, that your grandmother's a hateful *beast*.'

I hadn't forgotten. I'd thought of it rarely, but I still clearly remembered sitting in the chair in the hall, my feet not touching the ground, waiting stiffly in my new clothes, listening to the shouting.

I had never actually lived with my mother, except for a traumatic week or two now and then. We had had no house, no address, no permanent base. Herself always on the move, she had solved the problem of what to do with me by simply dumping me for varying periods with a long succession of mostly astonished married friends, who had been, in retrospect, remarkably tolerant.

'Do look after Philip for me for a few days, darling,' she would say, giving me a push towards yet another strange lady. 'Life is so unutterably *cluttered* just now and I'm at my wits' end to know what to do with him, you know how it is, so, darling Deborah . . . (or Miranda, or Chloe, or Samantha, or anyone else under the sun) . . . do be an absolute *sweetie*, and I'll pick him up on Saturday, I promise.' And mostly she would have soundly kissed darling Deborah or Miranda or Chloe or Samantha and gone off with a wave in a cloud of Joy.

Saturdays came and my mother didn't, but she always turned up in the end, full of flutter and laughter and gushing thanks, retrieving her parcel, so to speak, from the left luggage office. I could remain uncollected for days or for weeks or for months: I never knew which in advance, and nor, I suspect, did my hosts. Mostly, I think, she paid something towards my keep, but it was all done with a giggle.

She was, even to my eyes, deliciously pretty, to the extent that people hugged her and indulged her and lit up when she was around. Only later, when they were left literally holding the baby, did the doubts creep in. I became a bewildered silent child forever tip-toeing nervously around so as not to give offence, perennially frightened that someone, one day, would abandon me altogether out in the street.

Looking back, I knew I owed a great deal to Samantha, Deborah, Chloe, *et al.* I never went hungry, was never ill-treated, nor was ever, in the end, totally rejected. Occasionally people took me in twice or three times, sometimes with welcome, mostly with resignation. When I was three or four someone in long hair and bangles and an ethnic smock taught me to read and write, but I never stayed anywhere long enough to be formally sent to school. It was an extraordinary, disorientating and rootless existence from which I emerged at twelve, when I was dumped in my first long-stay home, able to do almost any job around the house and unable to love.

She left me with two photographers, Duncan and Charlie,

standing in their big bare-floored studio that had a darkroom, a bathroom, a gas ring and a bed behind a curtain.

'Darlings, look after him until Saturday, there's a sweet pair of lambs . . .' And although birthday cards arrived, and presents at Christmas, I didn't see her again for three years. Then when Duncan departed she swooped in one day and took me away from Charlie, and drove me down to a racehorse trainer and his wife in Hampshire, telling those bemused friends, 'It's only until Saturday, darlings, and he's fifteen and strong, he'll muck out the horses for you, and things like that . . .'

Cards and presents arrived for two years or so, always without an address to reply to. On my eighteenth birthday there was no card, and no present the following Christmas, and I'd never heard from her again.

She must have died, I had come to understand, from drugs. There was a great deal, as I grew older, that I'd sorted out and understood.

The old woman glared across the room, as unforgiving and destructive as ever, and still angry at what I'd said.

'You won't get far with me if you talk like that,' she said.

'I don't want to get far.' I stood up. 'This visit is pointless. If you wanted to find your daughter you should have looked twenty years ago. And as for me . . . I wouldn't find her for you, even if I could.'

'I don't want you to find Caroline. I dare say you're right, that she's dead.' The idea clearly caused her no grief. 'I want you to find your sister.'

'My . . . *what*?'

The hostile dark eyes assessed me shrewdly. 'You didn't know you had a sister? Well, you have. I'll leave you a hundred thousand pounds in my will if you find her and bring her here to me. And don't think,' she went on caustically, before I had time to utter, 'that you can produce any little imposter and expect me to believe it. I'm old but I'm far from a fool. You would have to prove to Mr Folk's satisfaction that the girl was my grandchild. And Mr Folk would not be easy to convince.'

I scarcely heard the acid words, but felt only a curiously intense thrust of shock. There had been only one of me. One single fruit of the butterfly. I felt an unreasonable but stinging jealously that she had had another. She had been mine alone, and now I had to share her: to revise and share her memory. I thought in confusion that it was ridiculous to be experiencing at thirty the displacement emotions of two.

'Well?' my grandmother said sharply.

'No,' I said.

'It's a lot of money,' she snapped.

'If you've got it.'

She was again outraged. 'You're insolent!'

'Oh, sure. Well, if that's all, I'll be going.' I turned and went towards the door.

'Wait,' she said urgently. 'Don't you even want to see her picture? There's a photograph of your sister over there on the chest.'

I glanced over my shoulder and saw her nodding towards a chest of drawers across the room. She must have seen the hesitation that slowed my hand on the doorknob because she said with more confidence 'Just look at her, then. Why don't you look?'

Without positively wanting to but impelled by undeniable curiosity I walked over to the chest and looked. There was a snapshot lying there, an ordinary postcard-size family-album print. I picked it up and tilted it towards the light.

A little girl, three or four years old, on a pony.

The child, with shoulder-length brown hair, wore a red and white striped T-shirt and a pair of jeans. The pony was an unremarkable Welsh grey, with clean-looking tack. Photographed in what was evidently a stable yard, they both looked contented and well fed, but the photographer had been standing too far away to bring out much detail in the child's face. Enlargement would help to some extent.

I turned the print over, but there was nothing on the back of it to indicate where it had come from, or who had held the camera.

Vaguely disappointed, I put it down again on the chest and saw, with a wince of nostalgia, an envelope lying there addressed in my mother's handwriting. Addressed to my grandmother, Mrs Lavinia Nore, at the old house in Northamptonshire where I'd had to wait in the hall.

In the envelope, a letter.

'What are you doing?' said my grandmother in alarm.

'Reading a letter from my mother.'

'But I . . . That letter shouldn't be out. Put it down at once. I thought it was in the drawer.'

I ignored her. The loopy, extravagant, extrovert writing

came as freshly to me off the paper as if she'd been there in the room, gushing and half laughing, calling out as always for help.

That letter, dated only October 2nd, was no joke.

Dear Mother,

I know I said I would never ask you for anything ever again but I'm having one more try because I still hope, silly me, that one day you might change your mind. I am sending you a photograph of my daughter Amanda, your granddaughter. She is very sweet and darling and she's three now, and she needs a proper home and to go to school and everything, and I know you wouldn't want a child around but if you'd just give her an allowance or even do one of those covenant things for her, she could live with some perfectly angelic people who love her and want to keep her but simply can't afford everything for another child as they've three of their own already. If you could pay something regularly into their bank account you wouldn't even notice it and it would mean your granddaughter was brought up in a happy home and I am so desperate to get that for her that I'm writing to you now.

She hasn't the same father as Philip, so you couldn't hate her for the same reasons, and if you'd see her you'd love her, but even if you won't see her, please, Mother, look after her. I'll hope to hear from you soon. Please, please, Mother, answer this letter.

Your daughter,
Caroline.

Staying at Pine Woods Lodge,
Mindle Bridge, Sussex.

I looked up and across at the hard old woman.

'When did she write this?'

'Years ago.'

'And you didn't reply,' I said flatly.

'No.'

I supposed it was no good getting angry over so old a tragedy. I looked at the envelope to try to see the date of the letter from the postmark, but it was smudged and indecipherable. How long, I wondered, had she waited at Pine Woods Lodge, hoping and caring and desperate. Desperation, of course, when it concerned my mother, was always a relative term. Desperation was a laugh and an outstretched hand – and the Lord (or Deborah or Samantha or Chloe) would provide. Desperation wouldn't be grim and gritty: but it must have been pretty deep to make her ask her own mother for help.

I put the letter, the envelope and the photograph in my jacket pocket. It seemed disgusting to me that the old woman had kept them all these years when she had ignored their plea, and I felt in an obscure way that they belonged to me, not to her.

'So you'll do it,' she said.

'No.'

'But you're taking the photograph.'

'Yes.'

'Well, then.'

'If you want . . . Amanda . . . found, you should hire a private detective.'

'I did,' she said impatiently. 'Naturally. Three detectives. They were all useless.'

'If three failed, she can't be found,' I said. 'There's no way I could succeed.'

'More incentive,' she said triumphantly. 'You'll try your damnedest, for that sort of money.'

'You're wrong.' I stared bitterly at her across the room and from her pillow-piled bed she stared as unsmilingly back. 'If I took any money from you I'd vomit.'

I walked over to the door and this time opened it without hesitation.

To my departing back she said, 'Amanda shall have my money . . . if you find her.'

TWO:

When I went back to Sandown Park the following day the letter and photograph were still in my pocket but the emotions they had engendered had subsided. The unknown half-sister could be contemplated without infantile rage, and yet another chunk of the past had fallen into place.

It was the present, in the shape of Steve Millace, which claimed everyone's attention. He came steaming into the changing room half an hour before the first race with drizzle on his hair and righteous fury in his eyes.

His mother's house, he said, had been burgled while they were all out at his father's funeral.

We sat in rows on the benches, half changed into riding clothes, listening with shock. I looked at the scene – jockeys in all stages of undress, in underpants, bare-chested, in silks and pulling on nylon tights and boots, and all of them suddenly still, as if in suspended animation, listening with open mouths and eyes turned towards Steve.

Almost automatically I reached for my Nikon, twiddled the controls, and took a couple of photographs: and they were all so accustomed to me doing that sort of thing that no one took any notice.

'It was awful,' Steve said. 'Bloody disgusting. She'd made some cakes and things, Mum had, for the aunts and everyone, for when we got back from the cremation, and they were all thrown around the place, squashed flat, jam and such, onto the walls, and stamped into the carpet. And there was more mess everywhere, in the kitchen . . . bathroom . . . It looked as if a herd of mad children had rampaged round the whole house making it as filthy as they could. But it wasn't children . . . children wouldn't have stolen all that was taken, the police said.'

'Your mother have a load of jewels, did she?' said someone, teasing.

One or two laughed and the first tension was broken, but the sympathy for Steve was genuine enough, and he went on talking about it to anyone who cared to listen: and I did listen, not only because his peg at Sandown was next to mine, which gave me little choice, but also because we always got on well together in a day-to-day, superficial way.

'They stripped Dad's darkroom,' he said. 'Just ripped everything out. And it was senseless . . . like I told the police . . . because they didn't just take things you could sell, like the enlarger and the developing stuff, but all his work, all those pictures taken over all those years, they're all gone. It's such a bloody shame. There's Mum with all that mess, and Dad dead, and now she hasn't even got what he spent his life doing. Just *nothing*. And they took her fur jacket and even the scent Dad gave her for her birthday, that she hadn't opened, and she's just sitting there crying . . .'

He stopped suddenly and swallowed, as if it was all too much for him. At twenty-three, although he no longer lived with them, he was still very much his parents' child, attached to them with a difficult loyalty most people admired. George Millace himself might have been widely disliked, but he had never been belittled by his son.

Small-boned, slight in build, Steve had bright dark eyes and ears that stuck out widely, giving him an overall slightly comic look: but in character he was more intense than humorous, and was apt, even without so much cause as on that day, to keep on returning obsessively to things which upset him.

'The police said that burglars do it for spite,' Steve said '. . . mess up people's houses and steal their photographs. They told Mum it's always happening. They said to be thankful there wasn't urine and shit over everything, which there often was, and she was lucky she didn't have the chairs and settee slashed and all the furniture scratched.' He went on compulsively talking to all comers, but I finished changing and went out to ride in the first race, and more or less forgot the Millace burglary for the rest of the afternoon.

It was a day I had been looking forward to, and trying not to, for nearly a month. The day that Daylight was to run in the Sandown Handicap Pattern 'Chase. A big race, a good horse, moderate opposition, and a great chance of winning. Such combinations came my way rarely enough to be prized, but I never liked to believe in them until I was actually on my way down to the post. Daylight, I'd been told, had arrived at the course safe and sound, and for me there was just the first race, a novice hurdle, to come back unscathed from, and then, perhaps, I would win the big Pattern 'Chase and half a dozen people would fall over themselves to offer me the favourite for the Gold Cup.

Two races a day was about my usual mark, and if I ended a season in the top twenty on the jockeys' list, I was happy. For years I'd been able to kid myself that the modesty of my success was due to being taller and heavier than was best for the job. Even with constant semi-starvation I weighed ten stone seven stripped, and was cut off, consequently, from the countless horses running at ten stone or less. Most seasons I rode in about two hundred races with forty or so winners, and knew that I was considered 'strong', 'reliable', 'good over fences', and 'not first class in a close finish'.

Most people think, when they're young, that they're going to the top of their chosen world, and that the climb up is only a formality. Without that faith, I suppose, they might never start. Somewhere on the way they lift their eyes to the summit and know they aren't going to reach it; and happiness then is looking down and enjoying the view they've got, not envying the one they haven't. At around twenty-six I'd come to terms with the view I'd reached, and with knowing I wasn't going any further: and oddly, far from depressing me, the realisation had been a relief. I'd never been graspingly ambitious, but only willing to do anything as well as I could. If I couldn't do better, well, I couldn't, and that was that. All the same, I'd no positive objection to having Gold Cup winners thrust upon me, so to speak.

On that afternoon at Sandown I completed the novice hurdle in an uneventful way ('useful but uninspired'), finishing fifth out of eighteen runners. Not too bad. Just the best that I and the horse could do on the day, same as usual.

I changed into Daylight's colours and in due course walked out to the parade ring, feeling nothing but pleasure for the coming race. Daylight's trainer, for whom I rode regularly, was waiting there, and also Daylight's owner.

Daylight's owner waved away my cheerful opener about it being splendid the drizzle had stopped and said without preamble, 'You'll lose this one today, Philip.'

I smiled. 'Not if I can help it.'

'Indeed you will,' he said sharply. 'Lose it. My money's on the other way.'

I don't suppose I kept much of the dismay and anger out of my face. He had done this sort of thing before, but not for about three years, and he knew I didn't like it.

Victor Briggs, Daylight's owner, was a sturdily built man in his forties, about whose job and background I knew almost nothing. Unsociable, secretive, he came to the races with a closed unsmiling face, and never talked to me much. He wore always a heavy navy-blue overcoat, a black broad-brimmed hat, and thick black leather gloves. He had been, in the past, an aggressive gambler, and in riding for him I had had the choice of doing what he said or losing my job with the stable. Harold Osborne, the trainer, had said to me plainly, soon after I'd joined him, that if I wouldn't do what Victor Briggs wanted, I was out.

I had lost races for Victor Briggs that I might have won. It was a fact of life. I needed to eat and to pay off the mortgage on the cottage. For that I needed a good big stable to ride for, and if I had walked out of the one that was giving me a chance I might easily not have found another. There weren't so very many of them, and apart from Victor Briggs the Osborne set-up was just right. So, like many another rider in a like fix, I had done what I was told, and kept quiet.

Back at the beginning Victor Briggs had offered me a fair-sized cash present for losing. I'd said I didn't want it: I would lose if I had to, but I wouldn't be paid. He said I was a pompous young fool, but after I'd refused his offer a second time he'd kept his bribes in his pocket and his opinion of me to himself.

'Why don't you take it?' Harold Osborne had said. 'Don't forget you're passing up the ten per cent you'd get for winning. Mr Briggs is making it up to you, that's all.'

I'd shaken my head, and he hadn't persevered. I thought that probably I was indeed a fool, but somewhere along the line it seemed that Samantha or Chloe or the others had given me this unwelcome uncomfortable conviction that one should pay for one's sins. As for three years or more I'd been let off the dilemma it was all the more infuriating to be faced with it again.

'I can't lose,' I protested. 'Daylight's the best of the bunch. Far and away. You know he is.'

'Just do it,' Victor Briggs said. 'And lower your voice, unless you want the Stewards to hear you.'

I looked at Harold Osborne. He was busy watching the horses plod round the ring and pretending not to listen to what Victor Briggs was saying.

'Harold,' I said.

He gave me a brief unemotional glance. 'Victor's right. The

money's on the other way. You'll cost us a packet if you win, so don't.'

'Us?'

He nodded. 'Us. That's right. Fall off, if you have to. Come in second, if you like. But not first. Understood?'

I nodded. I understood. Back in the old pincers, three years on.

I cantered Daylight down to the start with reality winning out over rebellion, as before. If I hadn't been able to afford to lose the job at twenty-three, still less could I at thirty. I was known as Osborne's jockey. I'd been with him seven years. If he chucked me out, all I'd get would be other stables' odds and ends; ride second string to other jockeys; be on a one-way track to oblivion. He wouldn't say to the Press that he'd got rid of me because I wouldn't any longer lose to order. He would tell them (regretfully, of course) that he was looking for someone younger . . . had to do what was best for the owners . . . terribly sad, but an end came to every jockey's career . . . naturally sorry, and all that, but time marches on, don't you know?

God damn it, I thought. I didn't want to lose that race. I hated to be dishonest . . . and the ten per cent I would lose this time was big enough to make me even angrier. Why the bloody hell had Briggs gone back to this caper, after this long time? I'd thought that he'd stopped it because I'd got just far enough as a jockey for him to think it likely I would refuse. A jockey who got high enough on the winners' list was safe from that sort of pressure, because if his own stable was silly enough to give him the kick, another would welcome him in. And maybe he thought I'd gone past that stage now that I was older, and was back again in the danger area: and he was right.

We circled around while the starter called the roll, and I looked apprehensively at the four horses ranged against Daylight. There wasn't a good one among them. Nothing that on paper could defeat my own powerful gelding; which was why people were at that moment staking four pounds on Daylight to win one.

Four to one on . . .

Far from risking his own money at those odds, Victor Briggs in some subterranean way had taken bets from other people, and would have to pay out if his horse won. And so, it seemed, would Harold also: and however I might feel I did owe Harold some allegiance.

After seven years of a working relationship that had a firmer base than many a trainer-jockey alliance, I had come to regard him if not with close personal warmth at least with active friendship. He was a man of rages and charms, of black moods and boisterous highs, of tyrannical decisions and generous gifts. His voice could out-shout and out-curse any other on the Berkshire Downs, and stable lads with delicate sensibilities left his employ in droves. On the first day that I rode work for him his blistering opinion of my riding could be heard fortissimo from Wantage to Swindon, and, in his house immediately afterwards, at ten in the morning, he had opened a bottle of champagne, and we had drunk to our forthcoming collaboration.

He had trusted me always and entirely, and had defended me against criticism where many a trainer would not. Every jockey, he had said robustly, had bad patches; and he had employed me steadily through mine. He assumed that I would be, for my part, totally committed to himself and his stable, and for the past three years that had been easy.

The starter called the horses into line, and I wheeled Daylight round to point his nose in the right direction.

No starting stalls. They were never used for jump racing. A gate of elastic tapes instead.

In cold angry misery I decided that the race, from Daylight's point of view, would have to be over as near the start as possible. With thousands of pairs of binoculars trained my way, with television eyes and patrol cameras and perceptive pressmen acutely focused, losing would be hard enough anyway, and practically suicidal if I left it until it was clear that Daylight would win. Then, if I just fell off in the last half mile for not much reason, there would be an enquiry and I might lose my licence; and it would be no comfort to know that I deserved to.

The starter put his hand on the lever and the tapes flew up, and I kicked Daylight forward into his business. None of the other jockeys wanted to make the running, and we set off in consequence at a slow pace, which compounded my troubles. Daylight, with all the time in the world, wouldn't stumble at any fence. A fluent jumper always, he hardly ever fell. Some horses couldn't be put right on the approach to a fence: Daylight couldn't be put wrong. All he accepted were the smallest indications from his jockey, and he would do the rest himself. I had ridden him many times. Won six races on him. Knew him well.

Cheat the horse. Cheat the public.

Cheat.

Damn it, I thought. *Damn and damn and damn.*

I did it at the third fence, on the decline from the top of the hill, round the sharpish bend, going away from the stands. It was the best from the credibility angle as it was the least visible to the massed watchers, and it had a sharp downhill slope on the approach side: a fence that claimed many a victim during the year.

Daylight, confused by getting the wrong signals from me, and perhaps feeling some of my turmoil and fury in the telepathic way that horses do, began to waver in the stride before take-off, putting in a small jerky extra stride where none was needed.

God, boy, I thought, I'm bloody sorry, but down you go, if I can make you: and I kicked him at the wrong moment and twitched hard on the bit in his mouth while he was in mid-air, and shifted my weight forward in front of his shoulder.

He landed awkwardly and stumbled slightly, dipping his head down to recover his balance. It wasn't really enough . . . but it would have to do. I whisked my right foot out of the stirrup and over his back, so that I was entirely on his left side, out of the saddle, clinging onto his neck.

It's almost impossible to stay on, from that position. I clung to him for about three bucking strides and then slid down the chest, irrevocably losing my grip and bouncing onto the grass under his feet. A flurry of thuds from his hooves, and a roll or two, and the noise and the galloping horses were gone.

I sat on the quiet ground and unbuckled my helmet, and felt absolutely wretched.

'Bad luck,' they said briefly in the weighing room. 'Rotten luck'; and got on with the rest of the day. I wondered if any of them guessed, but maybe they didn't. No one nudged or winked or looked sardonic. It was my own embarrassed sense of shame which kept me staring mostly at the floor.

'Cheer up,' Steve Millace said, buttoning some orange and blue colours. 'Its not the end of the world.' He picked up his whip and his helmet. 'Always another day.'

'Yeah.'

He went off to ride and I changed gloomily back into street clothes. So much, I thought, for the sense of excitement in which I'd arrived. So much for winning, for half a dozen mythical trainers climbing over themselves to secure my services for the Gold Cup. So much for a nice boost to the finances, which were wilting a bit after buying a new car. On all fronts, depression.

I went out to watch the race.

Steve Millace, with more courage than sense, drove his horse at leg-tangling pace into the second last fence and crashed on landing. It was the sort of hard fast fall which cracked bones, and one could see straight away that Steve was in trouble. He struggled up as far as his knees, and then sat on his heels with his head bent forward and his arms wrapped round his body, as if he was hugging himself. Arm, shoulder, ribs . . . something had gone.

His horse, unhurt, got up and galloped away, and I stood for a while watching while two first aid men gingerly helped Steve into an ambulance. A bad day for him, too, I thought, on top of all his family troubles. What on earth made us do it? Whatever drove us to persist, disregarding injury and risk and disappointment? What lured us continually to speed, when we could earn as much sitting in an office?

I walked back to the weighing room feeling the bits of me that Daylight had trodden on beginning to stiffen with bruises. I'd be crimson and black the next day, which was nothing but usual. The biffs and bangs of the trade had never bothered me much and nothing I'd so far broken had made me frightened about the next lot. I normally had, in fact, a great feeling of physical well-being, of living in a strong and supple body, of existing as an efficient coordinated athletic whole. Nothing obtrusive. It was there. It was health.

Disillusion, I thought, would be the killer. If the job no longer seemed worth it, if people like Victor Briggs soured it beyond acceptance, at that point one would give up. But not yet. It was still the life I wanted; still the life I was far from ready to leave.

Steve came into the changing room in boots, breeches, undervest, clavicle rings, bandage and sling, with his head inclined stiffly to one side.

'Collar bone,' he said crossly. 'Bloody nuisance.' Discomfort was making his thin face gaunt, digging hollows in his cheeks and round his eyes, but what he clearly felt most was annoyance.

His valet helped him to change and dress, touching him with the gentleness of long practice, and pulling off his boots smoothly so as not to jar the shoulder. A crowd of other jockeys around us jostled and sang and made jokes, drank tea and ate fruit cake, slid out of colours and pulled on trousers, laughed and cursed and hurried. Knocking-off time, the end of the working week, back again Monday.

'I suppose,' Steve said to me, 'You couldn't possibly drive me home?' He sounded tentative, as if not sure if our friendship stretched that far.

'Yes, I should think so,' I said.

'To my mother's house? Near Ascot?'

'OK.'

'I'll get someone to fetch my car tomorrow,' he said. 'Sodding nuisance.'

I took a photograph of him and his valet, who was pulling off the second boot.

'What do you ever do with all them snaps?' the valet said.

'Put them in a drawer.'

He gave a heaven-help-us jerk of the head. 'Waste of time.'

Steve glanced at the Nikon. 'Dad said once he'd seen some of your pics. You would put him out of business one of these days, he said.'

'He was laughing at me.'

'Yeah. Maybe. I don't know.' He inched one arm into his shirt and let the valet fasten the buttons over the other. 'Ouch,' he said, wincing.

George Millace had seen the pictures I'd had in my car, catching me looking through them as I sat in the car park at the end of a sunny spring day, waiting for the friend I'd given a lift to, to come out of the racecourse.

'Proper little Cartier Bresson' George had said, faintly smiling. 'Let's have a look.' He'd put his arm through the open window and grasped the stack, and short of a tug-o'-war I couldn't have prevented him. 'Well, well,' he said, going through them methodically. 'Horses on the Downs, coming out of a mist. Romantic muck.' He handed them back. 'Keep it up, kid. One of these days you might take a photograph.'

He'd gone off across the car park, the heavy camera bag hanging from his shoulder, with him hitching it from time to time to ease its weight: the only photographer I knew with whom I didn't feel at home.

Duncan and Charlie, in the three years I'd lived with them, had patiently taught me all I could learn. No matter that when I was first dumped on them I was only twelve: Charlie had said from the start that as I was there I could sweep the floors and clean up in the darkroom, and I'd been glad to. The rest had come gradually and thoroughly, and I'd finished by regularly doing all of Duncan's printing, and the routine half of Charlie's. 'Our lab assistant' Charlie called me. 'He mixes our chemicals,' he would say. 'A dab hand with a hypodermic. Mind now, Philip, only one point four millilitres of benzol alcohol.' And I'd suck the tiny amounts accurately into the syringe and add them to the developer, and feel as if I were perhaps of some use in the world after all.

The valet helped Steve into his jacket and gave him his watch and wallet, and we went at Steve's tender pace out to my car.

'I promised to give Mum a hand with clearing up that mess, when I got back. What a bloody hope.'

'She's probably got neighbours.' I eased him into the modern Ford and went round to the driving seat. Started up in the closing dusk, switched on the lights and drove off in the direction of Ascot.

'I can't get used to the idea of Dad not being there,' Steve said.

'What happened?' I asked. 'I mean, you said he drove into a tree . . . '

'Yes.' He sighed. 'He went to sleep. At least, that's what everyone reckons. There weren't any other cars, nothing like that. There was a bend, or something, and he didn't go round it. Just drove straight ahead. He must have had his foot on the accelerator . . . The front of the car was smashed right in.' He shivered. 'He was on his way home from Doncaster. Mum's always warned him about driving on the motorway at night when he's had a long day, but this wasn't the motorway . . . he was much nearer home.'

He sounded tired and depressed, which no doubt he was, and in brief sideways glances I could see that for all my care the car's motion was hurting his shoulder.

'He'd stopped for half an hour at a friend's house,' Steve said. 'And they'd had a couple of whiskies. It was all so stupid. Just going to sleep . . .'

We drove for a long way in silence, he with his problems, and I with mine.

'Only last Saturday,' Steve said. 'Only a week ago.'

Alive one minute, dead the next . . . the same as everybody.

'Turn left here,' Steve said.

We turned left and right and left a few times and came finally to a road bordered on one side by a hedge and on the other by neat detached houses in shadowy gardens.

In the middle distance along there things were happening. There were lights and people. An ambulance with its doors open, its blue turret flashing on top. A police car. Policemen. People coming and going from one of the houses, hurrying. Every window uncurtained, spilling out light.

'My *God,*' Steve said. 'That's *their* house. Mum's and Dad's.'

I pulled up outside, and he sat unmoving, staring, stricken.

'It's Mum,' he said. 'It must be. It's Mum.'

There was something near cracking point in his voice. His face was twisted with terrible anxiety and his eyes in the reflected light looked wide and very young.

'Stay here,' I said practically. 'I'll go and see.'

THREE:

His mum lay on the sofa in the sitting room, quivering and coughing and bleeding. Someone had attacked his mum pretty nastily, splitting her nose and mouth and eyelid and leaving her with bright raw patches on cheek and jaw. Her clothes were torn here and there, her shoes were off, and her hair stuck out in straggly wisps.

I had seen Steve's mother at the races from time to time: a pleasant well-dressed woman nearing fifty, secure and happy in her life, plainly proud of her husband and son. As the grief-stricken, burgled, beaten-up person on the sofa, she was unrecognisable.

There was a policeman sitting on a stool beside her, and a policewoman, standing, holding a bloodstained cloth. Two ambulance men hovered in the background, with a stretcher propped upright against one wall. A neighbourly looking woman stood around looking grave and worried. The room itself was a shambles, with papers and smashed furniture littering the floor. On the wall, the signs of jams and cakes, as Steve had said.

When I walked in the policeman turned his head. 'Are you the doctor?'

'No . . .' I explained who I was.

'Steve!' His mother said. Her mouth trembled, and her hands. 'Steve's hurt.' She could hardly speak, yet the fear for her son came across like a fresh torment, overshadowing anything she'd yet suffered.

'It's not bad, I promise you,' I said hastily. 'He's here, outside. It's just his collar bone. I'll get him straight away.'

I went outside and told him, and helped him out of the car. He was hunched and stiff, but seemed not to feel it.

'Why?' he said, uselessly, going up the path. 'Why did it happen? What for?'

The policeman indoors was asking the same question, and others as well.

'You were just saying, when your son came home, that

there were two of them, with stockings over their faces. Is that right?'

She nodded slightly. 'Young' she said. The word came out distorted through her cut, swollen lips. She saw Steve and held her hand out to him, to hold his own hand tight. He himself, at the sight of her, grew still paler and even more gaunt.

'White youths or black?' the policeman said.

'White.'

'What were they wearing?'

'Jeans.'

'Gloves?'

She closed her eyes. The cut one looked puffed and angry. She whispered 'Yes.'

'Mrs Millace, please try to answer,' the policeman said. 'What did they want.'

'Safe,' she said, mumbling.

'What?'

'Safe. We haven't got a safe. I told them.' A pair of tears rolled down her cheeks. 'Where's the safe, they said. They hit me.'

'There isn't a safe here,' Steve said furiously. 'I'd like to kill them.'

'Yes, sir,' the policeman said. 'Just keep quiet, sir, if you wouldn't mind.'

'One . . . smashed things,' Mrs Millace said. 'The other just hit me.'

'Bloody *animals*,' Steve said.

'Did they say what they wanted?' the policeman asked.

'Safe.'

'Yes, but is that all? Did they say they wanted money? Jewellery? Silver? Gold coins? What exactly did they say they wanted, Mrs Millace?'

She frowned slightly, as if thinking. Then forming the words with difficulty, she said, 'All they said was "where is the safe?" '

'I suppose you do know,' I said to the policeman, 'that this house was also burgled yesterday?'

'Yes, I do, sir. I was here yesterday myself.' He looked at me assessingly for a few seconds and turned back to Steve's mother.

'Did these two young men in stocking masks say anything about being here yesterday? Try to remember, Mrs Millace.'

'I don't . . . think so.'

'Take your time,' he said. 'Try to remember.'

She was silent for a long interval, and two more tears appeared. Poor lady, I thought. Too much pain, too much grief, too much outrage: and a good deal of courage.

At last she said, 'They were . . . like bulls. They shouted. They were rough. Rough voices. They . . . shoved me. Pushed. I opened the front door. They shoved in. Pushed me . . . in here. Started . . . smashing things. Making this mess. Shouting . . . where is the safe. Tell us, where is the safe . . . Hit me.' She paused. 'I don't think . . . they said anything . . . about yesterday.'

'I'd like to *kill* them,' Steve said.

'Third time,' mumbled his mother.

'What was that, Mrs Millace?' the policeman said.

'Third time burgled. Happened . . . two years ago.'

'You can't just let her lie here,' Steve said violently. 'Asking all these questions . . . Haven't you got a doctor?'

'It's all right, Steve dear,' the neighbourly woman said, moving forward as if to give comfort. 'I've rung Dr Williams. He said he would come at once.' Caring and bothered, she was nonetheless enjoying the drama, and I could envisage her looking forward to telling it all to the locals. 'I was over here helping your mother earlier, Steve dear' she said rushing on, 'but of course I went home – next door, as you know, dear – to get tea for my family, and then I heard all this shouting, and it seemed all wrong, dear, so I was just coming back to see, and calling out to your mother to ask if she was all right, and those two dreadful young men just burst out of the house, dear, just *burst* out, so of course I came in here . . . and well . . . your poor mother . . . so I rang for the police and for the ambulance, and Dr Williams . . . and everybody.' She looked as if she would like at least a pat on the back for all this presence of mind, but Steve was beyond such responses.

The policeman was equally unappreciative. He said to her, 'And you still can't remember any more about the car they drove off in?'

Defensively she said, 'It was dark.'

'A lightish-coloured car, medium sized. Is that all?'

'I don't notice cars much.'

No one suggested that this was a car she could have noticed. Everyone thought it.

I cleared my throat and said diffidently to the policeman, 'I don't know if it would be of any use, and of course you may want your own man or something, but I've a camera in my car, if you could do with any photographs of all this.'

He raised his eyebrows and considered and said yes: so I fetched both cameras and took two sets of pictures, in colour and in black and white, with close-ups of the damaged face and wide-angle shots of the room. Steve's mother bore the flashlight without complaint, and none of it took very long.

'Professional, are you sir?' the policeman said.

I shook my head. 'Just had a lot of practice.'

He told me where to send the photographs when they were printed, and the doctor arrived.

'Don't go yet,' Steve said to me, and I looked at the desperation in his overstretched face, and stayed with him through all the ensuing bustle, sitting on the stairs out in the hall.

'I don't know what to do,' he said, joining me there. 'I can't drive like this, and I'll have to go and see that she's all right. They're taking her to hospital for the night. I suppose I can get a taxi . . .'

He didn't actually ask it, but the question was there. I stifled a small sigh and offered my services, and he thanked me as if I'd thrown him a lifebelt.

I found myself finally staying the night, because when we got back from the hospital he looked so exhausted that one simply couldn't drive away and leave him. I made us a couple of omelettes as by that time, ten o'clock, we were both starving, neither of us having eaten since breakfast; and after that I picked up some of the mess.

He sat on the edge of the sofa looking white and strained and not mentioning that his fracture was hurting quite a bit. Perhaps he hardly felt it, though one could see the pain in his face. Whenever he spoke it was of his mother.

'I'll kill them,' he said. 'Those *bastards*.'

More guts than sense, I thought; same as usual. By the sound of things, if nine-stone-seven Steve met up with the two young bulls, it would be those bastards who'd do the killing.

I started at the far end of the room, picking up a lot of magazines, newspapers, and old letters, and also the base and lid of a flat ten-by-eight-inch box which had once held photographic printing paper. An old friend.

'What shall I do with all this?' I asked Steve.

'Oh, just pile it anywhere,' he said vaguely. 'Some of it came out of that rack over there by the television.'

A wooden-slatted magazine rack, empty, lay on its side on the carpet.

'And that's Dad's rubbish box, that battered old orange thing. He kept it in that rack with the papers. Never threw it away. Just left it there, year after year. Funny really.' He yawned. 'Don't bother too much. Mum's neighbour will do it.'

I picked up a small batch of oddments; a transparent piece of film about three inches wide by eight long, several strips of 35 mm colour negatives, developed but blank, and an otherwise pleasant picture of Mrs Millace spoilt by splashes of chemical down the hair and neck.

'Those were in Dad's rubbish box, I think,' Steve said, yawning again. 'You might as well throw them away.'

I put them in the wastepaper basket, and added to them a nearly black black-and-white print which had been torn in half, and some more colour negatives covered in magenta blotches.

'He kept them to remind himself of his worst mistakes,' Steve said. 'It doesn't seem *possible* that he isn't coming back.'

There was another very dark print in a paper folder, showing a shadowy man sitting at a table. 'Do you want this?' I asked.

He shook his head. 'Dad's junk.'

I put some feminine magazines and a series on woodwork back in the magazine rack, and piled the letters on the table. The bulk of the mess left on the floor seemed to be broken china ornaments, the remnants of a spindly-legged sewing box which had been thoroughly smashed, and a small bureau, tipped on its side, with cascades of writing paper falling out of the drawers. None of the damage seemed to have had any purpose beyond noise and speed and frightening power, all of a piece with the pushing, shoving and shouting that Mrs Millace had described. A rampage designed to confuse and bewilder: and when they got no results from attacking her possessions, they'd started on her face.

I stood the bureau up again and shovelled most of the stuff back into it, and collected together a heap of scattered tapestry patterns and dozens of skeins of wool. One began at last to see clear stretches of carpet.

'*Bastards*', Steve said. 'I hate them. I'll kill them.'

'Why would they think your mother had a safe?'

'God knows. Perhaps they just go round ripping off new widows, screaming "safe" at them on the off-chance. I mean, if she'd had one, she'd have told them where it was, wouldn't she? After losing Dad like that. And yesterday's burglary, while we were at the funeral. Such dreadful shocks. She'd have told them. I know she would.'

I nodded.

'She can't take any more,' he said. There were tears in his voice, and his eyes were dark with the effort of trying not to cry. It was he, I thought, who was closest to the edge. His mother would be tucked up with sympathy and sedation.

'Time for bed,' I said abruptly. 'Come on. I'll help you undress. She'll be better tomorrow.'

I woke early after an uneasy night and lay watching the dingy November dawn creep through the window. There was a good deal about life that I didn't want to get up and face; a situation common, no doubt, to the bulk of mankind. Wouldn't it be marvellous, I thought dimly, to be pleased with oneself, to look forward to the day ahead, to not have to think about mean-minded dying grandmothers and one's own depressing dishonesty. Normally fairly happy-go-lucky, a taking-things-as-they-come sort of person, I disliked being backed into uncomfortable corners from which escape meant action.

Things had happened to me, had arrived, all my life. I'd never gone out looking. I had learned whatever had come my way, whatever was there. Like photography, because of Duncan and Charlie. And like riding, because of my mother dumping me in a racing stable: and if she'd left me with a farmer I would no doubt be making hay.

Survival for so many years had been a matter of accepting what I was given, of making myself useful, of being quiet and agreeable and no trouble, of repression and introversion and self-control, that I was now, as a man, fundamentally unwilling to make a fuss or fight.

I had taught myself for so long not to want things that weren't offered to me that I now found very little to want. I had made no major decisions. What I had, had simply come.

Harold Osborne had offered me the cottage, along with the job of stable jockey. I'd accepted. The bank had offered a mortgage. I'd accepted. The local garage had suggested a certain car. I'd bought it.

I understood why I was as I was. I knew why I just drifted

along, going where the tide took me. I knew why I was passive, but I felt absolutely no desire to change things, to stamp about and insist on being the master of my own fate.

I didn't want to look for my half-sister, and I didn't want to lose my job with Harold. I could simply drift along as usual doing nothing very positive . . . and yet for some obscure reason that instinctive course was seeming increasingly *wet.*

Irritated, I put my clothes on and went downstairs, peering in at Steve on the way and finding him sound asleep.

Someone had perfunctorily swept the kitchen floor since the funeral-day burglary, pushing into a heap a lot of broken crockery and spilled groceries. The coffee and sugar had turned out the evening before to be down there in the dust, but there was milk along with the eggs in the refrigerator, and I drank some of that. Then, to pass the time, I wandered round the downstairs rooms, just looking.

The room which had been George Millace's darkroom would have been far and away the most interesting, had there been anything there: but it was in there that the original burglary had been the most thorough. All that was left was a wide bench down one side, two large deep sinks down the other, and rows of empty shelves across the end. Countless grubby outlines and smudges on the walls showed where the loads of equipment had stood, and stains on the floor marked where he'd stored his chemicals.

He had, I knew, done a lot of his own colour developing and printing, which most professional photographers did not. The development of colour slides and negatives was difficult and exacting, and it was safer, for consistent results, to entrust the process to commercial large-scale labs. Duncan and Charlie had sent all their colour developing out: it was only the printing from negatives, much easier, which they had done themselves.

George Millace had been a craftsman of the first order. Pity about his unkind nature.

From the looks of things he had had two enlargers, one big and one smaller, enlargers being machines which held the negatives in what was basically a box up a stick, so that a bright light could shine through the negative onto a baseboard beneath.

The head of the enlarger, holding the light and the negative, could be wound up and down the stick. The higher one wound the head above the baseboard, the larger one saw the picture.

The lower the head, the smaller the picture. An enlarger was in fact a projector, and the baseboard was the screen.

To take a print from a negative one wound the enlarger head up or down to get the size required, then sharpened the focus, then in darkness put a piece of photographic paper on the base-board, then shone the light through the negative onto the photographic paper for a few seconds, then put the photographic paper through developer, fixer, washer and stabilizer, and hey presto, if one hadn't stuck thumb marks all over it, one ended with a clear print, enlarged to the size one wanted.

Besides the enlargers, George would have had an electric box of tricks for regulating the length of exposures, and a mass of developing equipment, and a drier for drying the finished prints. He would have had dozens of sheets of various types of photographic paper in different sizes, and light-tight dispensers to store them in. He would have had rows of files holding all his past work in reference order, and safe-lights and measuring jugs and paper-trimmers and filters.

The whole lot, every scrap, had gone.

Like most serious photographers he had kept his unexposed films in the refrigerator. They too had gone, Steve had said, and were presumably at the root of the vandalism in the kitchen.

I went aimlessly into the sitting room and switched on the lights, wondering how soon I could decently wake Steve and say I was going. The half-tidied room looked cold and dreary, a miserable sight for poor Mrs Millace when she got home. From habit and from having nothing else to do I slowly carried on from where I'd stopped the night before, picking up broken scraps of vases and ornaments and retrieving reels of cotton and bits of sewing from under the chairs.

Half under the sofa itself lay a large black light-proof envelope, an unremarkable object in a photographer's house. I looked inside, but all it seemed to contain was a piece of clear thickish plastic about eight inches square, straight cut on three sides but wavy along the fourth. More rubbish. I put it back in the envelope and threw it in the wastepaper basket.

George Millace's rubbish box lay open and empty on the table. For no reason in particular, and certainly impelled by nothing more than photographic curiosity, I picked up the wastepaper basket and emptied it again on the carpet. Then I put all of George's worst mistakes back in the box where he'd kept them, and returned the broken bits of glass and china to the waste basket.

Why, I wondered, looking at the spoiled prints and pieces of film, had George ever bothered to keep them. Photographers, like doctors, tended to be quick to bury their mistakes, and didn't usually leave them hanging around in magazine racks as permanent mementoes of disasters. I had always been fond of puzzles. I thought it would be quite interesting to find out why such an expert as George should have found these particular things interesting.

Steve came downstairs in his pyjamas looking frail and hugging his injured arm, wanly contemplating the day.

'Good Lord,' he said. 'You've tidied the lot.'

'Might as well.'

'Thanks, then.' He saw the rubbish box on the table, with all its contents back inside. 'He used to keep that lot in the freezer,' he said. 'Mum told me there was a terrible fuss one day when the freezer broke down and all the peas and stuff unfroze. Dad didn't care a damn about the chickens and things and all the pies she'd made which had spoiled. All he went on and on about, she said, was that some ice-cream had melted all over his rubbish.' Steve's tired face lit into a remembering smile. 'It must have been quite a scene. She thought it was terribly funny, and when she laughed he got crosser and crosser . . .' He broke off, the smile dying. 'I can't believe he isn't coming back.'

'Did your father often keep things in the freezer?'

'Oh sure. Of course. Masses of stuff. You know what photographers are like. Always having fits about colour dyes not being permanent. He was always raving on about his work deteriorating after twenty years. He said the only way to posterity was through the deep freeze and even that wasn't certain.'

'Well . . . ' I said. 'Did the burglars also empty the freezer?'

'Good Lord.' He looked startled. 'I don't know. I never thought of that. But why should they want his films?'

'They stole the ones that were in the darkroom.'

'But the policeman said that that was just spite. What they really wanted was the equipment, which they could sell.'

'Um,' I said. 'Your father took a lot of pictures which people didn't like.'

'Yes, but only as a joke.' He was defending George, the same as ever.

'We might look in the freezer,' I suggested.

'Yes. All right. It's out at the back, in a sort of shed.'

He picked a key out of the pocket of an apron hanging in the kitchen and led the way through the back door into a small covered yard, where there were dustbins and stacks of logs and a lot of parsley growing in a tub.

'In there,' Steve said, giving me the key and nodding to a green painted door set into a bordering wall; and I went in and found a huge chest freezer standing between a motor lawn mower and about six pairs of gum boots.

I lifted the lid. Inside, filling one end and nestling next to joints of lamb and boxes of beefburgers, was a stack of three large grey metal cash boxes, each one closely wrapped in transparent polythene sheeting. Taped to the top one was a terse message:

DO NOT STORE ICE CREAM NEAR THESE BOXES

I laughed.

Steve looked at the boxes and the message and said, 'There you are. Mum said he went berserk when it all melted, but in the end nothing of his was really damaged. The food was all spoilt, but his best transparencies were O.K. It was after that that he started storing them in these boxes.'

I shut the lid, and we locked the shed and went back into the house.

'You don't really think,' Steve said doubtfully, 'That the burglars were after Dad's pictures? I mean, they stole all sorts of things. Mum's rings, and his cuff-links, and her fur coat, and everything.'

'Yes . . . so they did.'

'Do you think I should mention to the police that all that stuff's in the freezer? I'm sure Mum's forgotten it's there. We never gave it a thought.'

'You could talk it over with her,' I said. 'See what she says.'

'Yes, that's best.' He looked a shade more cheerful. 'One good thing, she may have lost all the indexes and the dates and places saying where all the pictures were taken, but she has at least still got some of his best work. It hasn't all gone. Not all of it.'

I helped him to get dressed and left soon afterwards, as he said he felt better, and looked it; and I took with me George Millace's box of disasters, which Steve had said to throw in the dustbin.

'But you don't mind if I take it?' I said.

'Of course not. I know you like messing about with films, the same as he does . . . same as he did. He liked that old rubbish. Don't know why. Take it, if you want, by all means.'

He came out into the drive and watched me stow the box in the boot, alongside my two camera bags.

'You never go anywhere without a camera, do you?' he said. 'Just like Dad.'

'I suppose not.'

'Dad said he felt naked without one.'

'It gets to be part of you.' I shut the boot and locked it from long habit. 'It's your shield. Keeps you a step away from the world. Makes you an observer. Gives you an excuse not to feel.'

He looked extremely surprised that I should think such things, and so was I surprised, not that I'd thought them, but that I should have said them to him. I smiled to take the serious truth away and leave only an impression of satire, and Steve, photographer's son, looked relieved.

I drove the hour from Ascot to Lambourn at a Sunday morning pace and found a large dark car standing outside my front door.

The cottage was one of a terrace of seven built in the Edwardian era for the not-so-rich and currently inhabited, apart from me, by a schoolteacher, a horsebox driver, a curate, a vet's assistant, sundry wives and children, and two hostelsful of stable lads. I was the only person living alone. It seemed almost indecent, among such a crowd, to have so much space to myself.

My house was in the centre: two up, two down, with a modern kitchen stuck on at the back. A white painted brick front, nothing fancy, facing straight out onto the road, with no room for garden. A black door, needing paint. New aluminium window frames replacing the original wood, which had rotted away. An old thing patched up. Not impressive, but home.

I drove slowly past the visiting car and turned into the muddy drive at the end of the row, continuing round to the back and parking under the corrugated plastic roof of the carport next to the kitchen. As I went I caught a glimpse of a man getting hastily out of the car, and knew he had seen me; and for my part thought only that he had no business to be pursuing me on a Sunday.

I went through the house from the back and opened the front door. Jeremy Folk stood there, tall, thin, physically awkward, using earnest diffidence as a lever, as before.

'Don't solicitors sleep on Sundays?' I said.

'Well, I say, I'm awfully sorry . . .'

'Yeah,' I said. 'Come on in, then. How long have you been waiting?'

'Nothing to . . . ah . . . worry about.'

He stepped through the door with a hint of expectancy and took the immediate disappointment with a blink. I had rearranged the interior of the cottage so that what had once been the front parlour was now divided into an entrance hall and dark-room, and in the hall section there was only a filing cabinet and the window which looked out to the street. White walls, white floor tiles; uninformative.

'This way,' I said amused, and led him past the darkroom to what had once been the back kitchen but was now mostly bathroom and in part a continuation of the hall. Beyond lay the new kitchen, and to the left, the narrow stairs.

'Which do you want,' I said. 'Coffee or talk?'

'Er . . . talk.'

'Up here, then.'

I went up the stairs, and he followed. I used one of the two original bedrooms as the sitting room, because it was the largest room in the house and had the best view of the Downs; and the smaller room next to it was where I slept.

In the sitting room, white walls, brown carpet, blue curtains, track lighting, bookshelves, sofa, low table and floor cushions. My guest looked around with small flickering glances, making assessments.

'Well?' I said neutrally.

'Er . . . that's a nice picture.' He walked over to take a closer look at the only thing hanging on the wall, a view of pale yellow sunshine falling through some leafless silver birches onto snow. 'It's . . . er . . . a print?'

'It's a photograph,' I said.

'Oh! Is it really? It looks like a painting.' He turned away and said, 'Where would you live if you had a hundred thousand pounds?'

'I told her I didn't want it.' I looked at the angular helpless way he was standing there, dressed that day not in working charcoal flannel but in a tweed jacket with decorative leather patches on the elbows. The brain under the silly ass act couldn't be totally disguised, and I wondered vaguely whether he had developed that surface because he was embarrassed by his own acuteness.

'Sit down,' I said, gesturing to the sofa, and he folded his long legs as if I'd given him a gift. I sat on a bean-bag floor cushion and said, 'Why didn't you mention the money when I saw you at Sandown?'

He seemed almost to wriggle. 'I just . . . ah . . . thought I'd try you first on blood-stronger-than-water, don't you know?'

'And if that failed, you'd try greed?'

'Sort of.'

'So that you would know what you were dealing with?'

He blinked.

'Look,' I sighed. 'I do understand thoughts of one syllable, so why don't you just . . . drop the waffle?'

His body relaxed for the first time into approximate naturalness and he gave me a small smile that was mostly in the eyes.

'It gets to be a habit,' he said.

'So I gathered.'

He cast a fresh look around the room, and I said, 'All right, say what you see.'

He did so, without squirming and without apology. 'You like to be alone. You're emotionally cold. You don't need props. And unless you took that photograph, you've no vanity.'

'I took it.'

'Tut tut.'

'Yes,' I said. 'So what did you come for?'

'Well, obviously, to persuade you to do what you don't want to.'

'To try to find the half-sister I didn't know I had?'

He nodded.

'Why?'

After a very short pause into which I could imagine him packing a lot of pros and cons he said, 'Mrs Nore is insisting on leaving a fortune to someone who can't be found. It is . . . unsatisfactory.'

'Why is she insisting?'

'I don't know. She instructs my grandfather. She doesn't take his advice. He's old and he's fed up with her, and so is my uncle, and they've shoved the whole mess onto me.'

'Three detectives couldn't find Amanda.'

'They didn't know where to look.'

'Nor do I,' I said.

He considered me. 'You'd know.'

'No.'

'Do you know who your father is?' he said.

FOUR:

I sat with my head turned towards the window, looking out at the bare calm of the Downs. A measurable silence passed. The Downs would be there for ever.

I said, 'I don't want to get tangled up in a family I don't feel I belong to. I don't like their threads falling over me like a web. That old woman can't claw me back just because she feels like it, after all these years.'

Jeremy Folk didn't answer directly, and when he stood up some of the habitual gaucheness had come back into his movements, though not yet into his voice.

'I brought the reports we received from the three firms of detectives,' he said. 'I'll leave them with you.'

'No, don't.'

'It's useless,' he said. He looked again around the room. 'I see quite plainly that you don't want to be involved. But I'm afraid I'm going to plague you until you are.'

'Do your own dirty work.'

He smiled. 'The dirty work was done about thirty years ago, wasn't it? Before either of us was born. This is just the muck floating back on the tide.'

'Thanks a bunch.'

He pulled a long bulging envelope out of the inside pocket of his country tweed and put it carefully down on the table. 'They're not very long reports. You could just read them, couldn't you?'

He didn't expect an answer, or get one. He just moved vaguely towards the door to indicate that he was ready to leave, and I went downstairs with him and saw him out to his car.

'By the way,' he said, pausing awkwardly halfway into the driving seat, 'Mrs Nore really is dying. She has cancer of the spine. Secondaries, they say. Nothing to be done. She'll live maybe six weeks, or maybe six months. They can't tell. So . . . er . . . no time to waste, don't you know?'

* * *

I spent the bulk of the day contentedly in the darkroom, developing and printing the black-and-white shots of Mrs Millace and her troubles. They came out clear and sharp so that one could actually read the papers on the floor, and I wondered casually just where the borderline fell between positive vanity and simple pleasure in a job efficiently done. Perhaps it had been vanity to mount and hang the silver birches . . . but apart from the content the large size of the print had been a technical problem, and it had all come out right . . . and what did a sculptor do, throw a sack over his best statue?

Jeremy Folk's envelope stayed upstairs on the table where he'd put it; unopened, contents unread. I ate some tomatoes and some muesli when I grew hungry, and cleared up the darkroom, and at six o'clock locked my doors and walked up the road to see Harold Osborne.

Sundays at six o'clock he expected me for a drink, and each Sunday from six to seven we talked over what had happened in the past week and discussed plans for the week ahead. For all his unpredictable up-and-down moods Harold was a man of method and he hated anything to interrupt these sessions, which he referred to as our military briefings. His wife during that hour answered the telephone and took messages for him to ring back as requested, and they had once had a blazing row with me there because she had burst in to say their dog had been run over and killed.

'You could have told me in twenty minutes,' he yelled. 'Now how the hell am I going to concentrate on Philip's orders for the Schweppes?'

'But the dog,' she wailed.

'Damn the dog.' He'd ranted at her for several minutes and then he'd gone out into the road and wept over the body of his mangled friend. Harold, I supposed, was everything I wasn't: moody, emotional, flamboyant, bursting with peaks of feeling, full of rage and love and guile and gusto. Only in our basic belief in getting things right were we alike, and that tacit agreement stuck us together in underlying peace. He might scream at me violently, but he didn't expect me to mind, and because I knew him well, I didn't. Other jockeys and trainers and several pressmen had said to me often in varying degrees of exasperation or humour, 'I don't know how you put up with it,' and the answer was always the true one . . . 'Easily.'

On that particular Sunday the sacrosanct hour had been interrupted before it could begin, because Harold had a visitor. I walked through his house from the stable entrance and went into the comfortable cluttered sittingroom–office, and there in one of the armchairs was Victor Briggs.

'Philip!' Harold said, welcoming and smiling. 'Pour yourself a drink. We're just going to run through the video tape of yesterday. Sit down. Are you ready? I'll switch on.'

Victor Briggs gave me several nods of approval and a handshake. No gloves, I thought. Cold pale dry hands with nothing aggressive in the grasp. Without the broadbrimmed hat he had thick glossy straight black hair which was receding slightly above the eyebrows to leave a centre peak: and without the heavy navy overcoat, a plain dark suit. Indoors he still wore the close-guarded expression as if afraid his thoughts might show, but there was overall a distinct air of satisfaction. Not a smile, just an atmosphere.

I opened a can of Coca-Cola and poured some into a glass.

'Don't you drink?' Victor Briggs asked.

'Champagne,' Harold said. 'That's what he drinks, don't you, Philip?' He was in great good humour, his voice and presence amplifying the warm russet colours of the room, resonant as brass.

Harold's reddish-brown hair sprang in wiry curls all over his head, as untamable as his nature. He was fifty-two at that time and looked ten years younger, a big burly six feet of active muscle commanded by a strong but ambiguous face, his features more rounded than hawkish.

He switched on the video machine and sat back in his armchair to watch Daylight's débacle in the Sandown Pattern 'Chase, as pleased as if he'd won the Grand National. A good job no Stewards were peering in, I thought. There was no mistaking the trainer's joy in his horse's failure.

The recording showed me on Daylight going down to the start, and lining up, and setting off: odds-on favourite at four to one on, said the commentator; only got to jump round to win. Immaculate leaps over the first two fences. Strong and steady up past the stands. Daylight just in the lead, dictating the pace, but all five runners closely bunched. Round the top bend, glued to the rails . . . faster downhill. The approach to the third fence . . . everything looking all right . . . and then the screw in the air and the stumbling landing, and the figure in red and blue silks going over the horse's neck and down under the feet. A groaning roar from the crowd, and the commentator's unemotional voice, 'Daylight's down at that fence, and now in the lead is Little Moth . . . '

The rest of the race rolled on into a plodding undistinguished finish, and then came a re-run of Daylight's departure, with afterthought remarks from the commentator. 'You can see the horse try to put in an extra stride, throwing Philip Nore forward . . . the horse's head ducks on landing, giving his jockey no chance . . . poor Philip Nore clinging on . . . but hopeless . . . horse and jockey both unhurt.'

Harold stood up and switched the machine off. 'Artistic,' he said, beaming down. 'I've run through it twenty times. It's impossible to tell.'

'No one suspected,' Victor Briggs said, 'One of the Stewards said to me "what rotten bad luck".' There was a laugh somewhere inside Victor Briggs, a laugh not quite breaking the surface but quivering in the chest. He picked up a large envelope which had lain beside his gin and tonic, and held it out to me. 'Here's my thank you, Philip.'

I said matter-of-factly, 'It's kind of you, Mr Briggs. But nothing's changed. I don't like to be paid for losing . . . I can't help it.'

Victor Briggs put the envelope down again without comment, and it wasn't he who was immediately angry, but Harold.

'Philip,' he said loudly, towering above me. 'Don't be such a bloody prig. There's a great deal of money in that envelope. Victor's being very generous. Take it and thank him, and shut up.'

'I'd . . . rather not.'

'I don't care what you'd bloody rather. You're not so squeamish when it comes to committing the crime, are you, it's just the thirty pieces of silver you turn your pious nose up at. You make me sick. And you'll take that bloody money if I have to ram it down your throat.'

'Well, you will,' I said.

'I will what?'

'Have to ram it down my throat.'

Victor Briggs actually laughed, though when I glanced at him his mouth was tight shut as if the sound had escaped without his approval.

'And,' I said slowly, 'I don't want to do it any more.'

'You'll do what you're bloody told,' Harold said.

Victor Briggs rose purposefully to his feet, and the two of them, suddenly silent, stood looking down at me.

It seemed that a long time passed, and then Harold said in a quiet voice which held a great deal more threat than his shouting, 'You'll do what you're told, Philip.'

I stood up in my turn. My mouth had gone dry, but I made my voice sound as neutral, as calm, as unprovoking as possible.

'Please . . . don't ask me for a repeat of yesterday.'

Victor Briggs narrowed his eyes. 'Did the horse hurt you? He trod on you . . . you can see it on the video.'

I shook my head. 'It's not that. It's the losing. You know I hate it. I just . . . don't want you to ask me . . . again.'

More silence.

'Look,' I said. 'There are degrees. Of course I'll give a horse an easy race if he isn't a hundred per cent fit and a hard race would ruin him for the next time. Of course I'll do that, it only makes sense. But no more like Daylight yesterday. I know I used to . . . but yesterday was the last.'

Harold said coldly, 'You'd better go now, Philip. I'll talk to you in the morning,' and I nodded, and left, and there were none of the warm handshakes which had greeted my arrival.

What would they do, I wondered. I walked in the windy dark down the road from Harold's house to mine as I had on hundreds of Sundays, and wondered if it would be for the last time. If he wanted to he could put other jockeys up on his horses from that day onwards. He was under no obligation to give me rides. I was classed as self-employed, because I was paid per race by the owners, and not per week by the trainer; and there was no such thing as 'unfair dismissal' enquiries for the self-employed.

I suppose it was too much to hope that they would let me get away with it. Yet for three years they had run the Briggs horses honestly, so why not in future? And if they insisted on fraud, couldn't they get some other poor young slob just starting his career, and put the squeezers on him when they wanted a race lost? Foolish wishes, all of them. I'd put my job down at their feet like a football and at that moment they were probably kicking it out of the ground.

It was ironic. I hadn't known I was going to say what I had. It had just forced its own way out, like water through a new spring.

All those races I'd thrown away in the past, not liking it, but doing it . . . Why was it so different now? Why was the revulsion so strong now that I didn't think I *could* do a Daylight again, even if to refuse meant virtually the end of being a jockey?

When had I changed . . . and how could it have happened without my noticing? I didn't know. I just had a sense of having already travelled too far to turn back. Too far down a road where I didn't want to go.

I went upstairs and read the three detectives' reports on Amanda because it was better, on the whole, than thinking about Briggs and Harold.

Two of the reports had come from fairly large firms and one from a one-man outfit, and all three had spent a lot of ingenuity padding out very few results. Justifying their charges, no doubt. Copiously explaining what they had all spent so long not finding out: and all three, not surprisingly had not found out approximately the same things.

None of them, for a start, could find any trace of her birth having been registered. They all expressed doubt and disbelief over this discovery, but to me it was no surprise at all. I had discovered that I myself was unregistered when I tried to get a passport, and the fuss had gone on for months.

I knew my name, my mother's name, my birth date, and that I'd been born in London. Officially, however, I didn't exist. 'But here I am,' I'd protested, and I'd been told, 'Ah yes, but you don't have a piece of paper to prove it, do you?' There had been affidavits by the ton and miles of red tape, and I'd missed the race I'd been offered in France by the time I got permission to go there.

The detectives had all scoured Somerset House for records of Amanda Nore, aged between ten and twenty-five, possibly born in Sussex. In spite of the fairly unusual name, they had all completely failed.

I sucked my teeth, thinking that I could do better than that about her age.

She couldn't have been born before I went to live with Duncan and Charlie, because I'd seen my mother fairly often before that, about five or six times a year, and often for a week at a time, and I would have known if she'd had a child. The people she left me with used to talk about her when they thought I wasn't listening, and I gradually understood what I remembered them saying, though sometimes not for years afterwards: but none of them, ever, had hinted that she was pregnant.

That meant that I was at least twelve when Amanda was born; and consequently she couldn't at present be older than eighteen.

At the other end of things she couldn't possibly be as young as ten. My mother, I was sure, had died sometime between Christmas and my eighteenth birthday. She might have been desperate enough at that time to write to her own mother and send her the photograph. Amanda in the photograph had been three . . . so Amanda, if she was still alive, would be at least fifteen.

Sixteen or seventeen, most likely. Born during the three years when I hadn't seen my mother at all, when I'd lived with Duncan and Charlie.

I went back to the reports . . .

All three detectives had been given the last known address of Caroline Nore, Amanda's mother: Pine Woods Lodge, Mindle Bridge, Sussex. All three had trekked there 'to make enquiries'.

Pine Woods Lodge, they rather plaintively reported, was not as the name might suggest a small private hotel complete with guest register going back umpteen years, forwarding addresses attached. Pine Woods Lodge was an old Georgian mansion going to ruin and due to be demolished. There were trees growing in what had been the ballroom. Large sections had no roof.

It was owned by a family which had largely died out twenty-five years earlier, leaving distant heirs who had no wish and no money to keep the place up. They had let the house at first to various organisations (list attached, supplied by Estate Agents) but of latter years it had been inhabited by squatters and vagrants. The dilapidation was now so advanced that even such as they moved out, and the five acres the house was built on were to come up for auction within three months; but as whoever bought the land was going to have to demolish the mansion, it was not expected to fetch much of a price.

I read through the list of tenants, none of whom had stayed long. A nursing home. A sisterhood of nuns. An artists' commune. A boys' youth club adventure project. A television film company. A musicians cooperative. Colleagues of Supreme Grace. The Confidential Mail Order Corporation.

One of the detectives, persevering, had investigated the

tenants as far as he could, and had added unflattering comments.

Nursing home	–	euthanasia for all. Closed by council.
Nuns	–	disbanded through bitchiness.
Artists	–	left disgusting murals.
Boys	–	broke everything still whole.
T.V.	–	needed a ruin to film.
Musicians	–	fused all the electricity.
Colleagues	–	religious nutters.
Mail order	–	perverts' delights.

There were no dates attached to the tenancies, but presumably if the Estate Agents could still furnish the list, they would have kept some other details. If I was right about when my mother had written her desperate letter, I should at least be able to find out which bunch of kooks she had been staying with.

If I wanted to, of course.

Sighing, I read on.

Copies of the photograph of Amanda Nore had been extensively displayed in public places (newsagents' shop windows) in the vicinity of the small town of Mindle Bridge, but no one had come forward to identify either the child or the stable yard or the pony.

Advertisements had been inserted (accounts attached) in various periodicals and one national Sunday newspaper (for six weeks) stating that if Amanda Nore wished to hear something to her advantage she should write to Folk, Langley, Son and Folk, solicitors, of St Albans, Herts.

One of the detectives, the one who had persisted with the tenants, had also enterprisingly questioned the Pony Club, but to no avail. They had never had a member called Amanda Nore. He had furthermore written to the British Show Jumping Association, with the same result.

A canvass of schools in a wide area round Mindle Bridge had produced no one called Amanda Nore on the registers, past or present.

She had not come into council care in Sussex. She was on no official list of any sort. No doctor or dentist had heard of her.

She had not been confirmed, married, buried or cremated within the county.

The reports came to the same conclusions: that she had been, or was being, brought up elsewhere (possibly under a different name), and was no longer interested in riding.

I shuffled the typed sheets together and returned them to the envelope. They had tried, one had to admit. They had also indicated their willingness to continue to search through each county in the land, if the considerable expenditure should be authorised: but they couldn't in any way guarantee success.

Their collective fee must already have been fearful. The authorisation, anyway, seemed not to have been forthcoming. I wondered sardonically if the old woman had thought of me to look for Amanda because it would cost so much less. A promise, a bribe . . . no foal, no fee.

I couldn't understand her late interest in her long ignored grandchildren. She'd had a son of her own, a boy my mother had called 'my hateful little brother'. He would have been about ten when I was born, which made him now about forty, presumably with children of his own.

Uncle. Cousins. Half-sister. Grandmother.

I didn't want them. I didn't want to know them or be drawn into their lives. I was in no way whatever going to look for Amanda.

I stood up with decision and went down to the kitchen to do something about cheese and eggs: and to stave off the thought of Harold a bit longer I fetched George Millace's box of trash in from the car and opened it on the kitchen table, taking out the items and looking at them one by one.

On a closer inspection it still didn't seem to make much sense that he should have kept those particular odds and ends. They didn't have the appearance of interesting or unique mistakes. Sorting my way through them I concluded with disappointment that it had been a waste of time after all to bring them home.

I picked up the folder which contained the dark print of a shadowy man sitting at a table and thought vaguely that it was odd to have bothered to put such an over-exposed mess into a mount.

Shrugging, I slid the dark print out onto my hand . . . and it was then that I found George's private pot of gold.

FIVE:

It was not, at first sight, very exciting.

Sellotaped onto the back of the print there was an envelope made of the special sort of sulphur-free paper used by careful professionals for the long-term storage of developed film. Inside the envelope, a negative.

It was the negative from which the print had been made, but whereas the print was mostly black and elsewhere very dark greys, the negative itself was clear and sharp with many details and highlights.

I looked at the print and at the negative, side by side.

I had no quickening of the pulse. No suspicions, no theories, merely curiosity. As I also had the means and the time, I went back into the darkroom and made four five-by-four inch prints, each at a different exposure, from one second to eight seconds.

Not even the longest exposure looked exactly like George's dark print, so I started again with the most suitable exposure, six seconds, and left the photograph in the developer too long, until the sharp outlines first went dark and then mostly disappeared, leaving a grey man sitting at a table against blackness. At that point I lifted the paper from the tray of developer and transferred it to the one containing fixer; and what I had then was another print almost exactly like George's.

Leaving a print too long in the developing fluid had to be one of the commonest mistakes on earth. If George's attention had been distracted and he'd left a print too long in developer, he'd simply have cursed and thrown the ruin away. Why, then had he kept it? And mounted it. And stuck the clear sharp negative onto the back?

It wasn't until I switched on a bright light and looked more closely at the best of the four original exposures I'd made that I understood why: and I stood utterly still in the darkroom, taking in the implications in disbelief.

With something approaching a whistle I finally moved. I

switched off the white light, and, when my eyes had accustomed themselves again to the red safelight, I made another print, four times as large, and on higher contrast grade of paper, to get as clear a result as I could possibly manage.

I switched on the white light again and fed the finished print through the drier, and then I looked at what I'd got.

What I'd got was a picture of two people talking together who had sworn on oath in a court of law that they had never met.

There wasn't the slightest possibility of a mistake. The shadowy man was now revealed as a customer sitting at a table outside a café somewhere in France. The man himself was a Frenchman with a moustache who had merely happened to be sitting there, a plate and a glass by his hand. The café had a name: Le Lapin d'Argent. There were advertisements for beer and lottery tickets in its half-curtained window, and a waiter in an apron standing in the doorway. A woman some way inside was sitting at a cash desk in front of a mirror, looking out to the street. The detail was sharp throughout, with remarkable depth of focus. George Millace at his usual expert best.

Sitting together at a table outside the café window were two men, both of them facing the camera but with their heads turned towards each other, unmistakably deep in conversation. A wine glass stood in front of each of them, half full, with a bottle to one side. There were coffee cups also, and an ashtray with a half-smoked cigar balanced on the edge. All the signs of a lengthy meeting.

Both men had been involved in an affair which had shaken the racing world like a thunderclap eighteen months earlier. Elgin Yaxley, the one on the left of the photograph, had owned five expensive steeplechasers which had been trained in Lambourn. At the end of the 'chasing season all five had been sent to a local farmer for a few weeks' summer break out at grass; and then, out in the fields, they had all been shot dead with a rifle. Terence O'Tree, the man on the right in the photograph, had shot them.

Some smart police work (aided by two young boys out at dawn when their parents thought them safe in bed) had tracked down and identified O'Tree, and brought him to court.

All five horses had been heavily insured. The insurance company, screeching with disbelief, had tried their damnedest to prove that Yaxley himself had hired O'Tree to do the killing, but both men had consistently denied it, and no link between them had been found.

O'Tree, saying he'd shot the horses just because he'd felt like it . . . 'for a bit o' target practice, like, your honour, and how was I to know they was valuable racehorses' . . . had been sent to jail for nine months with a recommendation that he should see a psychiatrist.

Elgin Yaxley, indignantly proclaiming his virtue and threatening to sue the insurance company for defamation of character if they didn't instantly pay up, had wrung out of them the whole insured amount and had then faded out of the racing scene.

The insurance company, I thought, would surely have paid George Millace a great deal for his photograph, if they had known it existed. Probably ten per cent of what they would not have had to pay Yaxley. I couldn't remember the exact sums, but I knew the total insured value of the five horses had been getting on for a hundred and fifty thousand pounds. It had been, in fact, the very size of the pay-out which had infuriated the insurers into suspecting fraud.

So why hadn't George asked for a reward . . . and why had he so carefully hidden the negative . . . and why had his house been burgled three times? For all that I'd never liked George Millace, it was the obvious answer to those questions that I disliked even more.

In the morning I walked up to the stables and rode out at early exercise as usual. Harold behaved in his normal blustery fashion, raising his voice over the scouring note of the November wind. The lads scowled and sulked as the vocal lash landed, and one or two, I reckoned, would be gone by the week's end. When lads left any stable nowadays they tended simply not to turn up one morning, nor ever again. They would sidle off to some other stable and the first news their old masters would have would be requests for references from the new. Notice, for many of the modern breed of lads, was something they never gave. Notice led to arguments and aggro, and who wanted that, man, when ducking out was so much easier? The lad population washed in and out of British stables like a swirling endless river, with long-stayers being an exception rather than the rule.

'Breakfast,' Harold bellowed at me at one point. 'Be there.'

I nodded. I usually went home for breakfast even if I were

riding out second lot, which I did only on non-racing days, and not always even then. Breakfast, in Harold's wife's view, consisted of a huge fry-up accompanied by mountains of toast served on the big kitchen table with generosity and warmth. It always smelled and looked delicious, and I always fell.

'Another sausage, Philip?' Harold's wife said, lavishly shovelling straight from the pan. 'And some hot fried potatoes?'

'You're destroying him, woman,' Harold said, reaching for the butter.

Harold's wife smiled at me in her special way. She thought I was too thin; and she thought I needed a wife. She told me so, often. I disagreed with her on both counts, but I dare say she was right.

'Last night,' Harold said. 'We didn't discuss the week's plans.'

'No.'

'There's Pamphlet at Kempton on Wednesday,' he said. 'In the two mile hurdle; and Tishoo and Sharpener on Thursday . . .'

He talked about the races for some time, munching vigorously all the while, so that I got my riding instructions out of the side of his mouth accompanied by crumbs.

'Understood?' he said finally.

'Yes.'

It appeared that after all I had not been given the instant sack, and for that I was relieved and grateful, but it was clear all the same that the precipice wasn't all that far away.

Harold glanced across the big kitchen to where his wife was stacking things in the dishwasher and said, 'Victor doesn't like your attitude.'

I didn't answer.

Harold said, 'The first thing one demands from a jockey is loyalty.'

That was rubbish. The first thing one demanded from a jockey was value for money.

'My Fuehrer, right or wrong?' I said.

'Owners won't stand for jockeys passing moral judgements on them.'

'Owners shouldn't defraud the public, then.'

'Have you finished eating?' he demanded.

I sighed regretfully. 'Yes.'

'Then come into the office.'

He led the way into the russet-coloured room which was

filled with chill bluish Monday morning light and had no fire yet in the grate.

'Shut the door,' he said.

I shut it.

'You'll have to choose, Philip,' he said. He stood by the fireplace with one foot on the hearth, a big man in riding clothes, smelling of horses and fresh air and fried eggs.

I waited non-committally.

'Victor will eventually want another race lost. Not at once, I grant you, because it would be too obvious. But in the end, yes. He says if you really mean you won't do it, we'll have to get someone else.'

'For those races only?'

'Don't be stupid. You're not stupid. You're too bloody smart for your own good.'

I shook my head. 'Why does he want to start this caper again? He's won a lot of prize money playing it straight these last three years.'

Harold shrugged. 'I don't know. What does it matter? He told me on Saturday when we got to Sandown that he'd laid his horse and that I was on to a big share of the profit. We've all done it before . . . why not again? Just what has got into you Philip, that you're swooning over a little fiddle like a bloody virgin?'

I didn't know the answer. He swept on anyway before I'd thought of a reply. 'Well, you just work it out, boy. Whose are the best horses in the yard? Victor's. Who buys good new horses to replace the old? Victor. Who pays his training bills on the nose, bills for usually five horses? Victor. Who owns more horses in this yard than anyone else? Victor. And which owner can I least afford to lose, particularly as he has been with me for more than ten years and has provided me with a large proportion of the winners I've trained in the past, and is likely to provide most of those I train in the future. Just who, do you think, my business most depends on?'

I stared at him. I suppose that I hadn't realised until then that he was in perhaps the same position as myself. Do what Victor wanted, or else.

'I don't want to lose you, Philip,' he said. 'You're a prickly bastard, but we've got on all right all these years. You won't go on for ever, though. You've been racing . . . what . . . ten years?'

I nodded.

'Three or four more, then. At the most, five. Pretty soon you won't bounce back from those falls the way you do now. And at any time a bad one might put you out of action for good. So look at it straight, Philip. Who do I need most in the long term, you or Victor?'

In a sort of melancholy we walked into the yard, where Harold shouted, but half-heartedly, at a couple of dawdling lads.

'Let me know,' he said, turning towards me.

'All right.'

'I want you to stay.'

I was surprised, but also pleased.

'Thanks,' I said.

He gave me a clumsy buffet on the shoulder, the nearest he'd ever come to the slightest show of affection. More than all the threatening and screaming on earth it made me want to agree to do what he asked; a reaction, I acknowledged flickeringly, as old as the hills. It was often kindness that finally broke the prisoner's spirit, not torture. One's defences were always defiantly angled outward to withstand aggression: it was kindness which crept round behind and stabbed you in the back, so that your will evaporated into tears and gratitude. Defences against kindness were much harder to build. And not the defences I would ever have thought I needed against Harold.

I sought instinctively to change the subject, and came up with the nearest thought to hand, which was George Millace and his photograph.

'Um,' I said, as we stood a shade awkwardly, 'Do you remember those five horses of Elgin Yaxley's, that were shot?'

'What?' He looked bewildered. 'What's that got to do with Victor?'

'Nothing at all,' I said. 'I was just thinking about them, yesterday.'

Irritation immediately cancelled out the passing moment of emotion, which was probably a relief to us both.

'For God's sake,' he said sharply. 'I'm serious. Your career's at stake. You can do what you damn well like. You can bloody well go to hell. It's up to you.'

I nodded.

He turned away abruptly and took two purposeful steps. Then he stopped, looked back, and said, 'If you're so bloody interested in Elgin Yaxley's horses, why don't you ask Kenny?'

He pointed to one of the lads, who was filling two buckets by the tap. 'He looked after them.'

He turned his back again and firmly strode away, outrage and anger thumping down with every foot.

I walked irresolutely over to Kenny, not sure what questions I wanted to ask, or even if I wanted to ask questions at all.

Kenny was one of those people whose defences were the other way round: impervious to kindness, open to fright. Kenny was a natural near-delinquent who had been treated with so much understanding by social workers that he could shrug off pleasant approaches with contempt.

He watched me come with an expression wilfully blank to the point of insolence, his habitual expression. Skin reddened by the wind; eyes slightly watering; spots.

'Mr Osborne said you used to work for Bart Underfield,' I said.

'So what?'

The water splashed over the top of the first bucket. He bent to remove it, and kicked the second one forward under the tap.

'And looked after some of Elgin Yaxley's horses?'

'So what?'

'So were you sorry when they were shot?'

He shrugged. 'Suppose so.'

'What did Mr Underfield say about it?'

'Huh?' His gaze rested squarely on my face. 'He didn't say nothing.'

'Wasn't he angry?'

'Not as I noticed.'

'He must have been,' I said.

Kenny shrugged again.

'At the very least,' I said, 'He was five horses short, and no trainer with his size stable can afford that.'

'He didn't say nothing.' The second bucket was nearly full, and Kenny turned off the tap. 'He didn't seem to care much about losing them. Something cheesed him of a bit later, though.'

'What did?'

Kenny looked uninterested and picked up the buckets.

'Don't know. He was right grumpy. Some of the owners got fed up and left.'

'So did you,' I said.

'Yeah.' He started walking across the yard with water

sloshing gently at each step. I went with him, warily keeping a dry distance. 'What's the point of staying when a place is going down the drain?'

'Were Yaxley's horses in good shape when they went off to the farm?' I asked.

'Sure.' He looked slightly puzzled. 'Why are you asking?'

'No real reason. Someone mentioned those horses . . . and Mr Osborne said you looked after them. I was just interested.'

'Oh.' He nodded. 'They had the vet in court, you know, to say the horses were fine the day before they died. He went to the farm to give one of them some anti-tetanus jabs, and he said he looked them all over, and they were O.K.'

'Did you go to the trial?'

'No. Read it in the *Sporting Life*.' He reached the row of boxes and put the buckets down outside one of the doors. 'That all, then?'

'Yes. Thanks, Kenny.'

'Tell you something . . .' He looked almost surprised at his own sudden helpfulness.

'What?'

'That Mr Yaxley,' he said. 'You'd've thought he'd been pleased getting all that lolly, even if he had lost his horses, but he came into Underfield's yard one day in a right proper rage. Come to think of it, it was after that that Underfield went sour. And Yaxley, of course, he buggered off out of racing and we never saw no more of him. Not while I was there, we didn't.'

I walked thoughtfully home, and when I got there the telephone was ringing.

'Jeremy Folk,' a familiar voice said.

'Oh, not again,' I protested.

'Did you read those reports?'

'Yes, I did. And I'm not going looking for her.'

'Be a good fellow,' he said.

'No.' I paused. 'To get you off my back, I'll help you a bit. But you must do the looking.'

'Well . . .' He sighed. 'What sort of help?'

I told him my conclusions about Amanda's age, and also suggested he should get the dates of the various tenancies of Pine Woods Lodge from the estate agents.

'My mother was probably there thirteen years ago,' I said. 'And now it's all yours.'

'But I *say* . . .' he almost wailed. 'You simply can't stop there.'

'I simply can.'

'I'll get back to you.'

'Just leave me alone,' I said.

I drove into Swindon to take the colour film to the processors, and on the way thought about the life and times of Bart Underfield.

I knew him in the way one got to know everyone in racing if one lived long enough in Lambourn. We met occasionally in the village shops and in other people's houses, as well as at the races. We exchanged 'Good mornings' and 'Hard lucks' and a variety of vague nods. I had never ridden for him because he had never asked me; and he'd never asked me, I thought, because he didn't like me.

He was a small busy man full of importance, given to telling people confidentially what other more successful trainers had done wrong. 'Of course Walwyn shouldn't have run such-and-such at Ascot' he would say. 'The distance was all wrong, one could see it a mile off.' Strangers thought him very knowledgeable. Lambourn thought him an ass.

No one had suggested, however, that he was such an ass as to deliver his five best horses to the slaughter. Everyone had undoubtedly felt sorry for him, particularly as Elgin Yaxley had not spent the insurance money on buying new and equal animals, but had merely departed altogether, leaving Bart a great deal worse off.

Those horses, I reflected, had undoubtedly been good, and must always have earned more than their keep, and could have been sold for high prices. They had been insured above their market value, certainly, but not by impossible margins if one took into account the prizes they couldn't win if they were dead. It was the fact that there seemed to be little profit in killing them that had finally baffled the suspicious insurers into paying up.

That . . . and no trace of a link between Elgin Yaxley and Terence O'Tree.

In Swindon the processors, who knew me well, said I was lucky, they were just going to feed a batch through, and if I cared to hang about I could have my negatives back in a couple of hours. I did some oddments of shopping and in due course picked up the developed films, and went home.

In the afternoon I printed the coloured versions of Mrs Millace, and sent them off with the black-and-white lot to the police; and in the evening I tried – and failed – to stop thinking in uncomfortable circles about Amanda and Victor Briggs and George Millace.

By far the worst was Victor Briggs and Harold's ultimatum. The jockey life suited me fine in every way, physically, mentally, financially. I'd put off for years the thought that one day I would have to do something else: the 'one day' had always been in the mists of the future, not staring me brutally in the face.

The only thing I knew anything about besides horses was photography, but there were thousands of photographers all over the place . . . everyone took photographs, every family had a camera, the whole western world was awash with photographers . . . and to make a living at it one had to be exceptionally good.

One also had to work exceptionally hard. The photographers I knew on the racecourse were always running about: scurrying from the start to the last fence and from there up to the unsaddling enclosure before the winner got there, and then down the course again for the next race, and six times, at least, every afternoon, five or six days a week. Some of their pictures they rushed off to news agencies who might offer them to newspapers, and some they sent to magazines, and some they flogged to the owners of the horses, and some to sponsors handing over cups.

If you were a racing photographer the pictures didn't come to you, you had to go out looking. And when you'd got them, the customers didn't flock to your door, you had to go out selling. It was all a lot different from Duncan and Charie, who had mostly done still-life things like pots and pans and clocks and garden furniture for advertisements.

There were very few full-time successful racing photographers. Fewer than ten, probably. Of those perhaps four were outstanding; and one of those four had been George Millace.

If I tried to join their ranks the others wouldn't hinder me, but they wouldn't help me either. I'd be out there on my own, stand or fall.

I wouldn't mind the running about, I thought: it was the selling part that daunted. Even if I considered my pictures good enough, I couldn't push.

And what else?

Setting up as a trainer was out. I hadn't the capital, and training racehorses was no sort of life for someone who liked stretches of silent time and being alone. Trainers talked to people from dawn to bedtime and lived in a whirl.

What I wanted, and instinctively knew that I would always need, was to continue to be self-employed. A regular wage packet looked like chains. An illogical feeling, but overwhelming. Whatever I did, I would have to do it on my own.

The habit of never making decisions would have to be broken. I could drift, I saw, into jobs which had none of the terrific satisfactions of being a jockey. I had been lucky so far, but if I wanted to find contentment in the next chapter I would have for once to be positive.

Damn Victor Briggs, I thought violently.

Inciting jockeys to throw races was a warning-off offence, but even if I could manage to get Victor Briggs warned-off the person who would most suffer would be Harold. And I'd lose my job anyway, as Harold would hardly keep me on after that, even if we didn't both lose our licences altogether because of the races I'd thrown in the past. I couldn't prove Victor Briggs's villainy without having to admit Harold's and my own.

Cheat or retire. A stark choice . . . absolutely bloody.

Nothing changed much on the Tuesday, but when I went to Kempton on Wednesday to ride Pamphlet the weighing-room was electric with two pieces of gossip.

Ivor den Relgan had been made a Member of the Jockey Club, and Steve Millace's mother's house had burned down.

SIX:

'Ivor den Relgan!' I heard the name on every side, repeated in varying tones of astonishment and disbelief. 'A Member of the Jockey Club! Incredible!'

The Jockey Club, that exclusive and gentlemanly body, had apparently that morning voted into its fastidious ranks a man they had been holding at arm's lengths for years, a rich self-important man from no one knew where, who had spread his money about in racing and done a certain amount of good in a way that affronted the recipients.

He was supposed to be of Dutch extraction. Extraction, that is, from some unspecified ex-Dutch colony. He spoke with an accent that sounded like a mixture of South African, Australian and American, a conglomerate mid-globe amalgam of vowels and consonants which could have been attractive but came out as patronising. He, the voice seemed to say, was a great deal more sophisticated than the stuffy British upper crust. He sought no favours from the entrenched powers, but admiration. It was they, he implied, who would prosper if they took his advice. He offered it to them free, frequently, in letters to the *Sporting Life*.

Until that morning the Jockey Club had indeed observably taken his advice on several occasions while steadfastly refusing to acknowledge he had given it. I wondered fleetingly what had brought them to such a turnaround; what had caused them suddenly to embrace the anathema.

Steve Millace was in the changing room, waiting by my peg.

The strain in him that was visible from the doorway was at close quarters overpowering. White-faced, vibrating, he stood with his arm in a black webbing sling and looked at me from sunken desperate eyes.

'Have you heard?' he said.

I nodded.

'It happened on Monday night. Well, yesterday morning, I suppose . . . about three o'clock. By the time anyone noticed the whole place had gone.'

'Your mother wasn't there?'

'They'd kept her in hospital. She's still there. It's too much for her. I mean . . .' He was trembling, '. . . too much.'

I made some sincerely sympathetic noises.

'Tell me what to do,' he said; and I thought, he's elected me as some sort of elder brother, an unofficial advice bureau.

'Didn't you say something about aunts?' I asked. 'At the funeral?'

He shook his head impatiently. 'They're Dad's sisters. Older sisters. They've never liked Mum.'

'All the same . . .'

'They're *cats,*' he said, exploding. 'I rang them . . . they said what a shame.' He mimicked their voices venomously. ' "Tell poor dear Marie she can get quite a nice little bungalow near the seaside with the insurance money." They make me sick.'

I began taking off my street clothes to change into colours, aware that to Steve the day's work was irrelevant.

'Philip,' he said imploringly. 'You saw her. All bashed about . . . and without Dad . . . and now the whole house . . . Please . . . *please* . . . help me.'

'All right,' I said resignedly. What else could one say? 'When I've finished riding, we'll work something out.'

He sat down on the bench as if his legs wouldn't hold him and just stayed there staring into space while I finished changing and went to weigh out.

Harold was by the scales as usual, waiting to take my saddle when I'd been weighed. Since Monday he'd made no reference to the life-altering decision he'd handed me, and perhaps he took my silence not for spirit-tearing indecision but tacit acceptance of a return to things past. At any rate it was with a totally normal manner that he said, as I put the saddle over his arm, 'Did you hear who's been elected to the Jockey Club?'

'Yeah.'

'They'll take Genghis Khan next.'

He walked out with the saddle to go and put it on Pamphlet, and in due course I joined him in the parade ring, where the horse walked nonchalantly round and his pop-star owner bit his nails with concentration.

Harold had gleaned some more news. 'I hear that it was the Great White Chief who insisted on den Relgan joining the Club.'

'Lord White?' I was surprised.

'Old Driven Snow himself.'

Pamphlet's youngish owner flicked his fingers and said 'Hey, man, how's about a little sweet music on this baby?'

'A tenner each way,' Harold suggested, having learnt the pop-star's language. The pop-star was using the horse for publicity and would only let it run when its race would be televised: and he was, as usual, wholly aware of the positions of the cameras, so that if they should chance to point his way he would not be carelessly obscured behind Harold or me. I admired his expertise in this respect, and indeed his whole performance, because off-stage, so to speak, he was apt to relapse into middle-class suburban. The jazzed-up working-class image was all a fake.

He had come to the races that day with dark blue hair. The onset of a mild apoplexy could be observed in the parade ring all about us, but Harold behaved as if he hadn't noticed, on the basis that owners who paid their bills could be as eccentric as they liked.

'Philip, darling,' said the pop-star, 'Bring this baby back for Daddy.'

He must have learned it out of old movies, I thought. Surely not even pop musicians talked like that any more. He reverted to biting his nails and I got up on Pamphlet and rode out to see what I could do about the tenner each way.

I was not popularly supposed to be much good over hurdles, but maybe Pamphlet had winning on his mind that day as much as I did. He soared round the whole thing with bursting joie-de-vivre, even to the extent of passing the favourite on the run-in, and we came back to bear hugs from the blue hair (for the benefit of television) and an offer to me of a spare ride in the fifth race, from a worried-looking small-time trainer. Stable jockey hurt . . . would I mind? I wouldn't mind, I'd be delighted. Fine, the valet has the colours, see you in the parade ring. Great.

Steve was still brooding by my peg.

'Was the shed burnt?' I asked.

'What?'

'The shed. The deep freeze. Your Dad's photos.'

'Oh, well, yes it was . . . but Dad's stuff wasn't in there.'

I stripped off the pop-star's orange and pink colours and went in search of the calmer green and brown of the spare ride.

'Where was it, then?' I said, returning.

'I told Mum what you said about people maybe not liking Dad's pictures of them, and she reckoned that you thought all the burglaries were really aimed at the photos, not at her fur and all that, and that if so she didn't want to leave those transparencies where they could still be stolen, so on Monday she got me to move them next door, to her neighbours. And that's where they are now, in a sort of outhouse.'

I buttoned the green and brown shirt, thinking it over.

'Do you want me to visit her in the hospital?' I said.

Almost on my direct route home. No great shakes. He fell on it, though, with embarrassing fervour. He had come to the races, he said, with the pub-keeper from the Sussex village where he lived in digs near the stable he rode for, and if I would visit his mother he could go home with the pub-keeper, because otherwise he had no transport, because of his collarbone. I hadn't exactly meant I would see Mrs Millace alone, but on reflection I didn't mind.

Having shifted his burden Steve cheered up a bit and asked if I would telephone him when I got home.

'Yes,' I said absently. 'Did your father often go to France?'

'France?'

'Ever heard of it?' I said.

'Oh . . .' He was in no mood to be teased. 'Of course he did. Longchamps, Auteuil, St Cloud. Everywhere.'

'And round the world?' I said, packing lead into my weight-cloth.

'Huh?' He was decidedly puzzled. 'What do you mean?'

'What did he spend his money on?'

'Lenses, mostly. Telephotos as long as your arm. Anything new.'

I took my saddle and weight-cloth over to the trial scales and added another flat pound of lead. Steve got up and followed me.

'What do you mean, what did he spend his money on?'

I said 'Nothing. Nothing at all. Just wondered what he liked doing, away from the races.'

'He just took pictures. All the time, everywhere. He wasn't interested in anything else.'

In time I went out to ride the green-and-brown horse and it was one of those days, which happened so seldom, when absolutely everything went right. In unqualified euphoria I dismounted once again in the winners' enclosure, and thought that I couldn't possibly give up the life; I couldn't *possibly*. Not when winning put you higher than heroin.

My mother had likely died of heroin.

Steve's mother lay alone in a glass-walled side-ward, isolated but indecently exposed to the curious glances of any stranger walking past. There were curtains which might have shielded her from public gaze, but they were not pulled across. I hated the system which denied privacy to people in hospital: who on earth, if they were ill or injured, wanted their indignities gawped at?

Marie Millace lay on her back with two flat pillows under her head and a sheet and a thin blue blanket covering her. Her eyes were shut. Her brown hair, greasy and in disarray, straggled on the pillow. Her face was dreadful.

The raw patches of Saturday night were now covered by extensive dark scabs. The cut eyelid, stitched, was monstrously swollen and black. The nose was crimson under some shaping plaster-of-paris, which had been stuck onto forehead and cheeks with white sticky tape. Her mouth, open and also swollen, looked purple. All the rest showed deep signs of bruising: crimson, grey, black and yellow. Fresh, the injuries had looked merely nasty: it was in the healing process that their true extent showed.

I'd seen people in that state before, and worse than that, damaged by horses' galloping hooves; but this, done out of malice to an inoffensive lady in her own home, was differently disturbing. I felt no sympathy but anger: Steve's 'I'll kill the bastards' anger.

She heard me come in, and opened her less battered eye a fraction as I approached. What I could see of an expression looked merely blank, as if I was the last person she would have expected.

'Steve asked me to come,' I said. 'He couldn't get here because of his shoulder. He can't drive . . . not for a day or two.'

The eye closed.

I fetched a chair from against the wall and put it by the bed, to sit beside her. The eye opened again; and then her hand, which had been lying on the blanket, slowly stretched out towards me. I took it, and she gripped me hard, holding on fiercely, seeking, it seemed, support and comfort and re-assurance. The spirit of need ebbed after a while, and she let go of my hand and put her own weakly back on the blanket.

'Did Steve tell you,' she said, 'about the house?'

'Yes, he did. I'm so sorry.' It sounded feeble. Anything sounded feeble in the face of such knocks as she'd taken.

'Have you seen it?' she said.

'No. Steve told me about it at the races. At Kempton, this afternoon.'

Her speech was slurred and difficult to understand, as she moved her tongue as if it were stiff inside the swollen lips.

'My nose is broken,' she said, fluttering her fingers on the blanket.

'Yes,' I said. 'I broke mine once. They put a plaster on me, too, just like yours. You'll be as good as new in a week.'

Her silent response couldn't be interpreted as anything but dissent.

'You'll be surprised,' I said.

There was the sort of pause that occurs at hospital bed-sides. Perhaps it was there that the ward system scored, I thought: when you'd run out of platitudes you could always discuss the gruesome symptoms in the next bed.

'George said you took photographs, like him,' she said.

'Not like him,' I said. 'George was the best.'

No dissent at all, this time. Discernibly the intentions of a smile.

'Steve told me you'd had George's boxes of transparencies moved out before the fire,' I said. 'That was lucky.'

Her smile, however, disappeared, and was slowly replaced by distress.

'The police came today,' she said. A sort of shudder shook her, and her breathing grew more troubled. She could get no air through her nose so the change was audible and rasped in her throat.

'They came here?' I asked.

'Yes. They said . . . Oh God . . .' Her chest heaved and she coughed.

I put my hand flatly over hers on the blanket and said urgently, 'Don't get upset. You'll make everything hurt worse. Just take three slow deep breaths. Four or five, if you need them. Don't talk until you can make it cold.'

She lay silent for a while until the heavy breathing slackened. I watched the tightened muscles relax under the blanket, and eventually she said, 'You're much older than Steve.'

'Eight years,' I agreed, letting go of her hand.

'No. Much . . . much older.' There was a pause. 'Could you give me some water?'

There was a glass on the locker beside her bed. Water in the glass, angled tube for drinking. I steered the tube to her mouth, and she sucked up a couple of inches.

'Thanks.' Another pause, then she tried again, this time much more calmly. 'The police said . . . The police said it was arson.'

'Did they?'

'You're not . . . surprised?'

'After two burglaries, no.'

'Paraffin,' she said. 'Five gallon drum. Police found it in the hall.'

'Was it your paraffin?'

'No.'

Another pause.

'The police asked . . . if George had any enemies.' She moved her head restlessly. 'I said of course not . . . and they asked . . . if he had anything someone would want . . . enough . . . enough . . . oh . . .'

'Mrs Milace,' I said matter-of-factly. 'Did they ask if George had any photographs worth burglary and burning?'

'George wouldn't . . .' she said intensely.

George had, I thought.

'Look,' I said slowly, 'You might not want me to . . . you might not trust me . . . but if you like I could look through those transparencies for you, and I could tell you if I thought there were any which could possibly come into the category we're talking about.'

After a while she said only, 'Tonight?'

'Yes, certainly. Then if they're O.K. you can tell the police they exist . . . if you want to.'

'George isn't a blackmailer,' she said. Coming from the swollen mouth the words sounded extraordinary, distorted but passionately meant. She was not saying 'I don't want to believe George could blackmail anyone,' but 'George didn't.' Yet she hadn't been sure enough to give the transparencies to the police. Sure but not sure. Emotionally sure. Rationally unsure. In a nonsensical way, that made sense.

She hadn't much left except that instinctive faith. It was beyond me entirely to tell her it was misplaced.

I collected the three metal boxes from the neighbour, who had been told, it appeared, that they contained just odds and ends the burglars had missed, and I was given by her a conducted tour of the burned mess next door.

Even in the dark one could see that there was nothing to salvage. Five gallons of paraffin had made no mistake. The house was a shell, roofless, windowless, acrid and creaking: and it was to this savage destruction of her nest that Marie would have to return.

I drove home with George's life's work and spent the rest of the evening and half of the night projecting his slides onto the flat white wall of my sitting room.

His talent had been stupendous. Seeing his pictures there together, one after the other, and not scattered in books and newspapers and magazines across a canvas of years, I was struck continually by the speed of his vision. He had caught life over and over and over again at the moment when a painter would have composed it: nothing left out, nothing disruptive let in. An absolute master.

The best of his racing pictures were there, some in colour, some in black and white, but there were also several stunning series on unexpected subjects like card players and alcoholics and giraffes and sculptors in action and hot Sundays in New York. These series stretched back almost to George's youth, the date and place being written on each mount in tiny fine-nibbed letters.

There were dozens of portraits of people: some posed in a studio, mostly not. Again and again he had caught the fleeting expression which exposed the soul, and even if he had originally taken twenty shots to keep but one, the ones he had kept were collectively breathtaking.

Pictures of France, Paris, St Tropez, cycle racing, fish docks. No pictures of people sitting outside cafes, talking to whom they shouldn't.

When I'd got the end of the third box I sat for a while thinking of what George hadn't photographed, or hadn't in any case kept.

No war. No riots. No horrors. No mangled bodies or starving children or executions or bombed-apart cars.

What had yelled from my wall for hours had been a satirical baring of the essence under the external; and perhaps George had felt the external satire of violence left him nothing to say.

I was rather deeply aware that I was never going to see the world in quite the same way again: that George's piercing view of things would intrude when I least expected it and nudge me in the ribs. But George had had no compassion. The pictures were brilliant. Objective, exciting, imaginative and revealing; but none of them kind.

None of them either, in any way that I could see, could have been used as a basis for blackmail.

I telephoned to Marie Millace in the morning, and told her so. The relief in her voice when she answered betrayed the existence of her doubts, and she heard it herself and immediately began a cover-up.

'I mean,' she said, 'Of course I knew George wouldn't . . .'

'Of course,' I said. 'What shall I do with the pictures?'

'Oh dear, I don't know. No one will try to steal them now though, will they?' The mumbling voice was even less distinct over the wire. 'What do you think?'

'Well,' I said. 'You can't exactly advertise that although George's pictures still exist no one needs to feel threatened. So I do think they may still be at risk.'

'But that means . . . that means . . .'

'I'm terribly sorry. I know it means that I agree with the police. That George did have something which someone desperately wanted destroyed. But please don't worry. Please don't. Whatever it was has probably gone with the house . . . and it's all over.' And God forgive me, I thought.

'Oh dear . . . George didn't . . . I know he didn't . . .'

I could hear the distress rising again in the noise of her breathing.

'Listen,' I said quickly. 'About those transparencies. Are you listening?'

'Yes.'

'I think the best thing for now would be to put them into a cold store somewhere. Then when you feel better, you could get an agent to put on an exhibition of George's work. The collection is marvellous, it really is. An exhibition would celebrate his talent, and make you a bit of money . . . and also reassure anyone who might be worrying that there was nothing to . . . er . . . worry about.'

There was a silence, but I knew she was still there, because of the breathing.

'George wouldn't use an agent,' she said at last. 'How could I find one?'

'I know one or two. I could give you their names.'

'Oh . . .' She sounded weak and there was another long pause. Then she said, 'I know . . . I'm asking such a lot . . . but could you . . . put those transparencies into store? I'd ask Steve . . . but you seem to know . . . what to do.'

I said that I would, and when we had disconnected I wrapped the three boxes in their polythene sheets and took them along to the local butcher, who already kept a box of my own in his walk-in freezer room. He cheerfully agreed to the extra lodgers, suggested a reasonable rental, and gave me a receipt.

Back home I looked at the negative and the print of Elgin Yaxley talking to Terence O'Tree, and wondered what on earth I should do with them.

If George had extorted from Elgin Yaxley all the profits from the shot-horse affair – and it looked as if he must have done, because of Bart Underfield's gloominess and Yaxley's own disappearance from racing – then it had to be Elgin Yaxley who was now desperate to find the photograph before anyone else did.

If Elgin Yaxley had arranged the burglaries, the beating-up and the burning, should retribution not follow? If I gave the photograph to the police, with explanations, Elgin Yaxley would be in line for prosecution for most crimes on the statutes, not least perjury and defrauding an insurance company of a hundred and fifty thousand.

If I gave the photograph to the police I was telling the world that George Millace had been a blackmailer.

Which would Marie Millace prefer, I thought: never to know who had attacked her, or to know for sure that George had been a villain . . . and to have everyone else know it too.

There was no doubt about the answer.

I had no qualms about legal justice. I put the negative back where I'd found it, in its envelope stuck onto the back of the dark print in its paper mount. I put the mount back into the box of rubbish which still lay on the kitchen dresser, and I put the clear big print I'd made into a folder in the filing cabinet in the hall.

No one knew I had them. No one would come looking. No one would burgle or burn my house, or beat me up. Nothing at all would happen from now on.

I locked my doors and went to the races to ride Tishoo and Sharpener and to agonise over that other thorny problem, Victor Briggs.

SEVEN:

Ivor den Relgan was again the big news, and what was more, he was there.

I saw him immediately I arrived, as he was standing just outside the weighing room door talking to two pressmen. I was a face among many to him, but to me, as to everyone else whose business was racing, he was as recognisable as a poppy in corn.

He wore, as he often did, an expensively soft camel-coloured coat, buttoned and belted, and he stood bareheaded with greying hair neatly brushed, a stocky slightly pugnacious-looking man with an air of expecting people to notice his presence. A lot of people considered it a plus to be in his favour, but for some reason I found his self-confidence repellent, and his strong gravitational pull was something I instinctively resisted.

I would have been more than happy never to come into his focus, but as I was passing them one of the pressmen shot out a hand and fastened it on my arm.

'Philip,' he said, 'You can tell us. You're always on the business end of a camera.'

'Tell you what?' I said, hovering in mid-stride, and intending to walk on.

'How do you photograph a wild horse?'

'Point and click,' I said pleasantly.

'No, Philip,' he said, exasperated. 'You know Mr den Relgan, don't you?'

I inclined my head slightly and said 'By sight.'

'Mr den Relgan, this is Philip Nore. Jockey, of course.' The pressman was unaccustomedly obsequious: I'd noticed den Relgan often had that effect. 'Mr den Relgan wants photographs of all his horses, but one of them rears up all the time when he sees a camera. How would you get him to stand still?'

'I know one photographer,' I said, 'Who got a wild horse to stand still by playing a tape of a hunt in full cry. The horse just stood and listened. The pictures were great.'

Den Relgan smiled superciliously as if he didn't want to hear good ideas that weren't his own, and I nodded with about as much fervour and went on into the weighing room thinking that the Jockey Club must have been mad. The existing members of the Jockey Club were for the most part forward-looking people who put good will and energy into running a huge industry fairly. That they were also self-electing meant in practice that the members were almost all aristocrats or upper class, but the ideal of service bred into them worked pretty well for the good of racing. The old autocratic change-resistant bunch had died out, and there were fewer bitter jokes nowadays about bone-heads at the top. All the more surprising that they should have beckoned to a semi-phoney like den Relgan.

Harold was inside the weighing room talking to Lord White, which gave me a frisson like seeing a traffic warden standing next to one's wrongly parked car: but it appeared that Lord White, powerful Steward of the Jockey Club, was not enquiring into the outcome of the Sandown Pattern 'Chase, nor into any other committed sins. He was telling Harold that there was a special trophy for Sharpener's race, and, should he happen to win it, both Harold and I, besides the owner, would be required to put in an appearance and receive our gifts.

'It wasn't advertised as a sponsored race,' Harold said, surprised.

'No . . . but Mr den Relgan has generously made this gesture. And incidentally it will be his daughter who does the actual presentations.' He looked directly at me. 'Nore, isn't it?'

'Yes, sir.'

'You heard all that? Good. Fine.' He nodded, turned, and left us, crossing to speak to another trainer with a runner in the same race.

'How many trophies does it take,' Harold said under his breath, 'To buy your way into the Jockey Club?' And in a normal voice he added, 'Victor's here.'

I said anxiously, 'But Sharpener will do his best.'

Harold looked amused. 'Yes, he will. This time. Win that pot if you can. It would really give Victor a buzz, taking Ivor den Relgan's cup. They can't stand each other.'

'I didn't know they knew . . .'

'Everyone knows everyone,' Harold said, shrugging. 'I think they belong to the same gaming club.' He lost interest and went out of the weighing room, and I stood for a few aimless moments watching Lord White make his way towards yet another trainer to pass on the instructions.

Lord White, in his fifties, was a well-built good-looking man with thick light-grey hair progressively turning the colour of his name. He had disconcertingly bright blue eyes and a manner that disarmed anyone advancing on him with a grievance; and it was he, although not Senior Steward, who was the true leader of the Jockey Club, elected not by votes but by the natural force born in him.

An upright man, widely respected, whose nickname Driven Snow (spoken only behind his back) had been coined, I thought, only partly through admiration and mostly to poke fun at the presence of so much noticeable virtue.

I went off to the changing room and on into the business of the day, and was guiltily relieved to find Steve Millace had not made the journey. No beseeching eyes and general helplessness to inveigle me into yet another round of fetching and carrying and visiting the sick. I changed into Tishoo's colours and thought only about the race he was due to start in, which was for novices over hurdles.

In the event there were no great problems but no repeat either of the previous day's joys. Tishoo galloped willingly enough into fourth place at the finish, which pleased his woman owner, and I carried my saddle to the scales to be weighed-in, and so back to my changing-room peg to put on Victor Briggs's colours for Sharpener. Just another day's work. Each day unique in itself, but in essence the same. On two thousand days, or thereabouts, I had gone into changing rooms and put on colours and passed the scales and ridden the races. Two thousand days of hope and effort and sweat and just and unjust rewards. More than a job: part of my fabric.

I put on a jacket over Victor Briggs's colours, because there were two other races to be run before Sharpener's, and went outside for a while to see what was happening in general: and what was happening in particular was Lady White with a scowl on her thin aristocratic face.

Lady White didn't know me especially, but I, along with most other jump jockeys, had shaken her hand as she stood elegantly at Lord White's side at two parties they had given to the racing world. The parties had been large everyone-invited affairs three or four years apart, held at Cheltenham racecourse during the March meeting; and they had been Lord White's own idea, paid for by him, and given, one understood, because of his belief that everyone in jump racing belonged at heart to a brotherhood of friends, and should meet as such to enjoy themselves. Old Driven Snow at his priceless best, and like everyone else I'd gone to the parties and enjoyed them.

Lady White was hugging her mink around her and almost glaring forth from under a wide-brimmed brown hat. Her intensity was such that I followed her gaze and found it fixed on her paragon of a husband, who was himself talking to a girl.

Lord White was not simply talking to the girl but revelling in it, radiating flirtatious fun from his sparkling eyes to his gesturing fingertips. I looked sardonically back from this picture telling the old old story and found Lady White's attention still balefully fixed on it and I thought in amusement 'Oh dear', as one does. The pure white lord, that evening, would be in for an unaristocratic ticking off.

Ivor den Relgan was still holding court to a clutch of journalists, among whom were two racing writers and three gossip columnists from the larger daily papers. Ivor den Relgan was definitely a gossip man's man.

Bart Underfield was loudly telling an elderly married couple that Osborne should know better than to run Sharpener in a three mile 'chase when any fool knew that the horse couldn't go further than two. The elderly couple nodded, impressed.

I gradually became aware that a man standing near me was also, like Lady White, intently watching Lord White and the girl. The man near me was physically unremarkable; an ordinary average man, no longer young, not quite middle-aged, with dark thinning hair and black-framed glasses. Grey trousers, olive green jacket, suede, not tweed, well-cut. When he realised that I was looking at him he gave me a quick annoyed glance and moved away: and I thought no more about him for another hour.

Victor Briggs, when I joined him in the parade ring before Sharpener's race, was heavily pleasant and made no reference to the issue hanging between us. Harold had boosted himself into a state of confidence and was standing with his long legs apart, his hat tipped back on his head, and his binoculars swinging rhythmically from one hand.

'A formality,' he was saying. 'Sharpener's never been better, eh, Philip? Gave you a good feel on the Downs, didn't he? Worked like a train.' His robust voice floated easily over several nearby owner-trainer-jockey groups who were all suffering from their own pre-race tension and could have done without Harold's.

'Jumping out of his skin,' Harold said, booming. 'Never been better. He'll run the legs off 'em, today, eh, Victor?'

The only good thing one could say about Harold's bursts of over-confidence was that if in the event they proved to be misplaced he would not relapse into acrimony and gloom. Failures were apt to be expansively forgiven with 'it was the weight that beat him, of course' and were seldom held to be the jockey's fault, even when they were.

Sharpener himself reacted to Harold's optimism in a thoroughly positive way, and encouraged also perhaps by my confidence left over from the two winners the day before, ran a faultless race with energy and courage, so that for the third time at that meeting my mount returned to applause.

Harold was metaphorically by this time two feet off the ground, and even Victor allowed his mouth a small smile.

Ivor den Relgan manfully shaped up to the fact that his fancy trophy had been won by a man he disliked, and Lord White fluttered around the girl he'd been talking to, clearing a passage for her through the throng.

When I'd weighed-in and handed my saddle to the valet, and combed my hair and gone out to the prizegiving, the scene had sorted itself out into a square table with a blue cloth bearing one large silver object and two smaller ones surrounded by Lord White, the girl, Ivor den Relgan, Victor and Harold.

Lord White said through a hand microphone to the small watching crowd that Miss Dana den Relgan would present the trophies so kindly given by her father: and it cannot have been only in my mind that the cynical speculation arose. Was it the Dad that Lord White wanted in the Jockey Club, or Dad's daughter? Perish the thought. Lord White with a girl friend? Impossible.

At close quarters it was clear that he was attracted beyond sober good sense. He touched her continually under the guise of arranging everyone suitably for the presentations, and he was vivacious where normally staid. It all remained just within the acceptable limits of roguishly avuncular behaviour, but discreet it was not.

Dana den Relgan was enough, I supposed, to excite any man she cared to respond to: and to Lord White she was responding with sweetness. Slender and graceful and not very tall, she had a lot of blonde-flecked hair curling casually onto her shoulders. There was also a curving mouth, very wide-apart eyes and excellent skin, and a quality of being not all dolly-bird in the brain. Her manner was observably more restrained than Lord White's, as if she didn't dislike his attentions but thought them too obvious, and she presented the trophies to Victor and Harold and myself without much conversation attached.

To me she said merely 'Well done,' and gave me the small silver object (which turned out to be a saddle-shaped paper-weight) with the bright surface smile of someone who isn't really looking at you and is going to forget you again within five minutes. Her voice, from what I heard of it, held the same modified American accent as her father's, but in her it lacked the patronising quality and was, to me at least, attractive. A very pretty girl, but not mine. Life was full of them.

While Victor and Harold and I compared trophies the average-looking man in spectacles reappeared, walking quietly up to Dana den Relgan's shoulder and speaking softly into her ear. She turned away from the presentation table and began slowly to move off with him, nodding and smiling a little, and listening to what he was saying.

This apparently harmless proceeding had the most extra-ordinary effect upon den Relgan, who stopped looking fatuously pleased with himself in one five-hundredth of a second and flung himself into action. He almost ran after his daughter, gripped the inoffensive-looking man by the shoulder and threw him away from her with such force that he staggered and went down on one knee.

'I've told you to keep away from her,' den Relgan said, looking as if kicking a man when he was down was something he had no reservations about; and Lord White muttered, 'I say' and 'Oh dear' and looked uncomfortable.

'Who is that man?' I asked of no one in particular, and it was Victor Briggs, surprisingly, who answered.

'Film director. Fellow called Lance Kinship.'

'And why the fuss?'

Victor Briggs knew the answer, but it took a fair amount of internal calculation before he decided to part with it. 'Cocaine,' he said finally. 'White powder, for sniffing straight up the nose. Very fashionable. All these stupid little girls . . . their noses will collapse when the bone dissolves, and then where will they be?'

Both Harold and I looked at him with astonishment, as it

was the longest speech I'd ever heard him make, and certainly the only one containing any private opinion.

'Lance Kinship supplies it,' he said. 'He gets asked to the parties for what he takes along.'

Lance Kinship was up on his feet and brushing dirt off his trousers; setting his glasses firmly on his nose and looking murderous.

'If I want to talk to Dana, I'll talk to her,' he said.

'Not while I'm there, you won't.'

Den Relgan's Jockey Club manners were in tatters and the bedrock under the camouflage was plainly on view. A bully, I thought; a bad enemy, even if his cause was just.

Lance Kinship seemed unintimidated. 'Little girls don't always have their daddies with them,' he said nastily; and den Relgan hit him; a hard sharp efficient crunch on the nose.

Noses bleed easily, and there was a good deal of blood. Lance Kinship tried to wipe it away with his hands and succeeded only in smearing it all over his face. It poured down on his mouth and chin, and fell in big splashing drops on his olive suede jacket.

Lord White, hating the whole thing, stretched out an arm towards Kinship and held out a huge white handkerchief as if in tongs. Kinship grabbed it without thanks and soaked it scarlet as he tried to staunch the flow.

'First aid room, don't you think?' Lord White said, looking round. 'Er . . . Nore,' he said, his gaze alighting. 'You know where the first aid room is, don't you? Take this gentleman there, would you? Awfully good of you . . .' He waved me towards the errand, but when I put a hand out towards the olive green sleeve, to guide Kinship in the direction of cold compresses and succour, he jerked away from me.

'Bleed, then,' I said.

Unfriendly eyes behind the black frames glared out at me, but he was too busy mopping to speak.

'I'll show you,' I said. 'Follow if you want.'

I set off past the parade ring towards the green-painted hut where the motherly ladies would be waiting to patch up the damaged, and not only did Kinship follow, but den Relgan also. I heard his voice as clearly as Kinship did, and there was no doubt about the message.

'If you come near Dana again, I'll break your neck.'

Kinship again didn't answer.

Den Relgan said, 'Did you hear, you vicious little ponce?'

We had gone far enough for there to be plenty of people blocking us from the view of the group outside the weighing room. I heard a scuffle behind me and looked over my shoulder in time to see Kinship aim a hard karate kick at den Relgan's crutch and land deftly on target. Kinship turned back to me and gave me another unfriendly stare over the reddening handkerchief, which he had held uninterruptedly to his nose.

Den Relgan was making choking noises and clutching himself. The whole fracas was hardly what one expected as the outcome of a decorous racecourse presentation on a Thursday afternoon.

'In there,' I said to Kinship, jerking my head, and he gave me a final reptilian glance as the first aid room opened its doors. Den Relgan said 'Aah . . .' and walked round in a small circle half doubled over, one hand pressed hard under the lower front of his camel-hair coat.

A pity George Millace had gone to his fathers, I thought. He of all people would have relished the ding-dong, and he, unlike everyone else, would have been here with his lens sharply focused, pointing the right way and taking inexorable notes at three point five frames a second. Den Relgan could thank George's couple of scotches and a tree in the wrong place that he wouldn't find his tangle with Kinship illustrating in the daily papers the edifying news of his elevation to the Jockey Club.

Harold and Victor Briggs were still where I'd left them, but Lord White and Dana den Relgan had gone.

'His lordship took her off to calm her nerves,' Harold said dryly. 'The old goat's practically dancing round her, silly fool.'

'She's pretty,' I said.

'Wars have been fought for pretty girls,' said Victor Briggs.

I looked at him with renewed astonishment and received in return the usual stonewall closed-in expression. Victor might have unexpected hidden depths, but that was just what they still were, hidden.

When I went out of the weighing room later to set off for home I was apologetically intercepted by the tall loitering figure of Jeremy Folk.

'I don't believe it,' I said.

'I did . . . er . . . warn you.'

'So you did.'

'Could I . . . um . . . have a word with you?'
'What do you want?'
'Ah yes . . . well . . .'
'The answer's no,' I said.
'But you don't know what I'm going to ask.'
'I can see that it's something I don't want to do.'
'Um,' he said. 'Your grandmother asks you to visit her.'
'Absolutely not,' I said.

There was a pause. People around us were going home, calling goodnights. It was four o'clock. Goodnights started early in the racing world.

'I went to see her,' Jeremy said, 'I told her you wouldn't look for your sister for money. I told her she would have to give you something else.'

I was puzzled. 'Give me what?'

Jeremy looked vaguely around from his great height and said, 'You could find her, couldn't you, if you really tried?'

'I don't think so.'

'But you might.'

I didn't answer and his attention came gently back to my face.

'Your grandmother agreed,' he said, 'That she had a flaming row with Caroline . . . your mother . . . and chucked her out when she was pregnant.'

'My mother,' I said, 'was seventeen.'

'Um. That's right.' He smiled. 'Funny, isn't it, to think of one's mother being so *young*.'

Poor defenceless little butterfly . . . 'Yes,' I said.

'Your grandmother says . . . has agreed . . . that if you will look for Amanda she will tell you why she threw Caroline out. And also she will tell you who your father is.'

'My God!'

I took two compulsive steps away from him, and stopped, and turned, and stared at him.

'Is that what you said to her?' I demanded. 'Tell him who his father is, and he'll do what you want?'

'You don't know who your father is,' he said reasonably. 'But you'd want to know, wouldn't you?'

'No,' I said.

'I don't believe you.'

We practically glared at each other.

'You have to want to know,' he said. 'It's human nature.'

I swallowed. 'Did she tell you who he is?'

He shook his head. 'No. She didn't. She's apparently never told anyone. No one at all. If you don't go and find out, you'll never know.'

'You're a real bastard, Jeremy,' I said.

He wriggled his body with an embarrassment he didn't actually feel. The light in his eyes, which would have done a check-mating chess-player justice, was a far more accurate indicator of how he operated.

I said bitterly, 'I thought solicitors were supposed to sit behind desks and pontificate, not go tearing about manipulating old ladies.'

'This particular old lady is a . . . a challenge.'

I had an idea he had changed his sentence in mid-stride, but I said only, 'Why doesn't she leave her money to her son?'

'I don't know. She won't give reasons. She told my grandfather simply that she wanted to cancel her old will, which left everything to her son, and make a new one in favour of Amanda. The son will contest it, of course. We've told her that, but it makes no difference. She's . . . er . . . stubborn.'

'Have you met her son?'

'No,' he said. 'Have you?'

I shook my head. Jeremy took another long vague look around the racecourse and said, 'Why don't we get cracking on this together? We'd turn Amanda up in no time, wouldn't we? Then you could go back into your shell and forget the whole thing, if you want.'

'You couldn't forget . . . who your father was.'

His gaze sharpened instantly. 'Are you on, then?'

He would persevere, I thought, with or without my help. He would bother me whenever he wanted, catch me at the races any day he cared to read the programmes in the newspapers, and never let up, because he wanted, as he'd told me at the beginning, to prove to his grandfather and uncle that when he set his mind to sorting something out, it got sorted.

As for me . . . the mists round my birth were there for the parting. The cataclysm which had echoed like a storm receding over the horizon through my earliest memories could at last be explained and understood. I could know what the shouting had been about behind the white painted door, while I waited in the hall in my new clothes.

I might in the event detest the man who'd fathered me. I might be horrified. I might wish I hadn't been told anything about him. But Jeremy was right. Given the chance . . . one had to know.

'Well?' he said.

'All right.'

'Find her together?'

'Yes.'

He was visibly pleased. 'That's great.'

I wasn't so sure; but it was settled.

'Can you go this evening?' He said. 'I'll telephone and tell her you're coming.' He plunged lankily towards the public telephone box and disappeared inside with his eyes switched anxiously my way, watching all through his call to make sure I didn't go back on my decision and scram.

The call, however, gave him no joy.

'Blast,' he said, rejoining me. 'I spoke to a nurse. Mrs Nore had a bad day and they've given her an injection. She's asleep. No visitors. Ring tomorrow.'

I felt a distinct sense of relief, which he noticed.

'It's all very well for you,' I said. 'But how would you like to be on the verge of finding out that you owe your existence to a quickie in the bushes with the milkman?'

'Is that what you think?'

'Something like that. It has to be, doesn't it?'

'All the same . . .' he said doubtfully.

'All the same,' I agreed resignedly, 'One wants to know.'

I set off towards the car park thinking that Jeremy's errand was concluded, but it appeared not. He came in my wake, but slowly, so that I looked back and waited.

'About Mrs Nore's son,' he said. 'Her son James.'

'What about him?'

'I just thought you might visit him. Find out why he's been disinherited.'

'You just thought . . .'

'As we're working together,' he said hastily.

'You could go yourself,' I suggested.

'Er, no,' he said. 'As Mrs Nore's solicitor, I'd be asking questions I shouldn't.'

'And I can just see this James bird answering mine.'

He pulled a card out of his charcoal pocket. 'I brought his address,' he said, holding it out. 'And you've promised to help.'

'A pact is a pact,' I said, and took the card. 'But you're still a bastard.'

EIGHT:

James Nore lived in London, and since I was more than half way there I drove straight from the races to the house on Camden Hill. I hoped all the way there that he would be out, but when I'd found the street and the number and pressed the right bell, the door was opened by a man of about forty who agreed that James Nore was his name.

He was astounded, as well he might be, to find an unknown nephew standing unannounced on his mat, but with only a slight hesitation he invited me in, leading the way into a sitting room crammed with Victorian bric-a-brac and vibrant with colour.

'I thought Caroline had aborted you,' he said baldly. 'Mother said the child had been got rid of.'

He was nothing like my memories of his sister. He was plump, soft-muscled and small-mouthed, and had a mournful droop to his eyes. None of her giggly lightness or grace of movement or hectic speed could ever have lived in his flaccid body. I felt ill at ease with him on sight, disliking my errand more by the minute.

He listened with his small lips pouted while I explained about looking for Amanda, and he showed more and more annoyance.

'The old bag's been saying for months that she's going to cut me off,' he said furiously. 'Ever since she came here.' He glanced round the room, but nothing there seemed to me likely to alienate a mother. 'Everything was all right as long as I went to Northamptonshire now and then. Then she came *here*. Uninvited. The old bag.'

'She's ill now,' I said.

'Of course she is.' He flung out his arms in an exaggerated gesture. 'I suggest visiting. She says no. Won't see me. Pig-headed old crone.'

A brass clock on the mantelshelf sweetly chimed the half hour, and I took note that everything there was of fine quality and carefully dusted. James Nore's bric-a-brac wasn't just junk but antiques.

'I'd be a fool to help you find this wretched second by-blow of Caroline's, wouldn't I?' he said. 'If no one can find her the whole estate reverts to me anyway, will or no will. But I'd have to wait years for it. Years and years. Mother's just being spiteful.'

'Why?' I said mildly.

'She loved Noel Coward,' he said resentfully, meaning, by the sound of it, if she loved Noel Coward she should have loved *him*.

'The abstract,' I said, enlightened, 'isn't always the same as the particular.'

'I didn't want her to come here. It would have saved all this fuss if she hadn't.' He shrugged. 'Are you going now? There's no point in your staying.'

He began to walk towards the door, but before he reached it it was opened by a man wearing a plastic cooking apron and limply carrying a wooden spoon. He was much younger than James, naturally camp, and unmistakable.

'Oh, hello, dear,' he said, seeing me. 'Are you staying for supper?'

'He's just going,' James said sharply. 'He's not . . . er . . .'

They both stood back to leave me room to pass, and as I went out into the hall I said to the man in the apron, 'Did you meet Mrs Nore when she came here?'

'Sure did, dear,' he said ruefully, and then caught sight of James shaking his head vigorously at him and meaning shut up. I smiled halfheartedly at a point in the air near their heads, and went to the front door.

'I wish you bad luck,' James said. 'That beastly Caroline, spawning all over the place. I never did like her.'

'Do you remember her?'

'Always laughing at me and tripping me up. I was glad when she went.'

I nodded, and opened the door.

'Wait,' he said suddenly.

He came towards me along the hall, and I could see he had had an idea that pleased him.

'Mother would never leave *you* anything, of course,' he began.

'Why not?' I said.

He frowned. 'There was a terrible drama, wasn't there, when Caroline got pregnant? Frightful scenes. Lots of screaming. I remember it . . . but no one would ever explain.

All I do know is that everything changed because of you. Caroline went and Mother turned into a bitter old bag and I had beastly miserable years in that big house with her, before I left. She hated you . . . the thought of you. Do you know what she called you? "Caroline's disgusting foetus", that's what. Caroline's disgusting foetus.'

He peered at me expectantly, but in truth I felt nothing. The old woman's hatred hadn't troubled me for years.

'I'll give you some of the money, though,' he said, 'If you can prove that Amanda is dead.'

On Saturday morning Jeremy Folk telephoned.

'Will you be at home tomorrow?' he said.

'Yes, but . . .'

'Good. I'll pop over.' He put down his receiver without giving me a chance to say I didn't want him. It was an advance, I supposed, that he'd announced his visit and not simply turned up.

Also on Saturday I ran into Bart Underfield in the post office and in place of our usual unenthusiastic 'good mornings' I asked him a question.

'Where is Elgin Yaxley these days, Bart?'

'Hong Kong,' he said. 'Why?'

'For a holiday?' I said.

'Of course not. He lives there.'

'But he's over here now, isn't he?'

'No, he isn't. He'd have told me.'

'But he must be,' I said insistently.

Bart said irritably, 'Why must he be? He isn't. He's working for a bloodstock agency and they don't give him much time off. And what's it to do with you?'

'I just thought . . . I saw him.'

'You couldn't have. When?'

'Oh . . . last week. A week ago yesterday.'

'Well, you're wrong,' Bart said triumphantly. 'That was the day of George Millace's funeral, and Elgin sent me a cable . . .' He hesitated and his eyes flickered, but he went on, '. . . and the cable came from Hong Kong.'

'A cable of regrets, was it?'

'George Millace,' Bart said with venom, 'was a shit.'

'You didn't go to the funeral yourself, then?'

'Are you crazy? I'd have spat on his coffin.'

'Catch you bending with his camera, did he, Bart?'

He narrowed his eyes and didn't answer.

'Oh well,' I said, shrugging, 'I dare say a good many people will be relieved now he's gone.'

'More like down on their knees giving thanks.'

'Do you ever hear anything nowadays about that chap who shot Elgin's horses? What's his name . . . Terence O'Tree?'

'He's still in jail,' Bart said.

'But,' I said, counting with my fingers, 'March, April, May . . . he should be out by now.'

'He lost his remission,' Bart said. 'He hit a warder.'

'How do you know?' I asked curiously.

'I . . . er . . . heard.' He had suddenly had too much of this conversation, and began to move off, backing away.

'And did you hear also that George Millace's house had burned down?' I said.

He nodded. 'Of course. Heard it at the races.'

'And that it was arson?'

He stopped in mid-stride. 'Arson?' he said, looking surprised. 'Why would anyone want . . . ? Oh!' He abruptly at that point understood why; and I thought that he couldn't possibly have achieved that revelationary expression by art.

He hadn't known.

Elgin Yaxley was in Hong Kong and Terence O'Tree was in jail, and neither they nor Bart Underfield had burgled, or bashed, or burned.

The easy explanations were all wrong.

I had jumped, I thought penitently, to conclusions.

It was only because I'd disliked George Millace that I'd been so ready to believe ill of him. He had taken that incriminating photograph, but there was really nothing to prove that he'd used it, except that Elgin Yaxley had taken a paid job in Hong Kong instead of ploughing his insurance money back into racehorses. Any man had a right to do that. It didn't make him a villain.

Yet he had been a villain. He had sworn he'd never met Terence O'Tree; and he had. And it had to have been before the trial in February at least, since O'Tree had been in jail ever since. Not during the winter months just before the trial either, because it had been sitting-in-the-street weather; and there had been . . . I had unconsciously noticed and now remembered . . . there had been a newspaper lying on the table in front of the Frenchman, on which one might possibly see a date.

I walked slowly and thoughtfully home, and projected my big new print hugely onto the sitting room wall through an epidiascope.

The Frenchman's newspaper lay too flat on the table. Neither the date nor any useful headlines could be seen.

Regretfully I studied the rest of the picture for anything at all which might date it; and in the depths, beside Madame at her cash desk inside the cafe, there was a calendar hanging on a hook. The letters and numbers on it could be discerned by the general shape even if not with pin-sharp clarity, and they announced that it was Avril of the previous year.

Elgin Yaxley's horses had been sent out to grass late that April, and they had been shot on the fourth of May.

I switched off the projector and drove to Windsor races puzzling over the inconsistencies and feeling that I had gone round a corner in a maze confidently expecting to have reached the centre, only to find myself in a dead end and surrounded by ten foot hedges.

It was a moderate day's racing at Windsor, all the star names having gone to the more important meeting at Cheltenham, and because of the weak opposition one of Harold's slowest old 'chasers finally had his day. Half of the rest of the equally old runners obligingly fell, and my geriatric pal with his head down in exhaustion loped in first after three and a half miles of slog.

He stood with his chest heaving in the unsaddling enclosure as I, scarcely less tired, lugged at the girth buckles and pulled off my saddle, but the surprised delight of his faithful elderly lady owner made it all well worth the effort.

'I knew he'd do it one day,' she said enthusiastically. 'I knew he would. Isn't he a great old boy?'

'Great,' I agreed.

'It's his last season, you know. I'll have to retire him.' She patted his neck and spoke to his head. 'We're all getting on a bit, old boy, aren't we? Can't go on for ever, more's the pity. Everything ends, doesn't it old boy? But today it's been great.'

I went in and sat on the scales and her words came with me: everything ends, but today it's been great. Ten years had been great, but everything ends.

Most of my mind still rebelled against the thought of ending, particularly an ending dictated by Victor Briggs; but somewhere the frail seedling of acceptance was stretching its first leaf in the dark. Life changes, everything ends. I myself was changing.

I didn't want it, but it was happening. My long contented float was slowly drifting to shore.

Outside the weighing room one wouldn't have guessed it. I had uncharacteristically won four races that week. I was the jockey in form. I had brought a no-hoper home. I was offered five rides for the following week by trainers other than Harold. The success-breeds-success syndrome was coming up trumps. Everything on a high note, with smiles all around. Seven days away from Daylight, and seven leagues in mood.

I enjoyed the congratulations and thrust away the doubt, and if anyone had asked me in that moment about retiring I'd have said 'Oh yes . . . in five years' time.'

They didn't ask me. They didn't expect me to retire. Retire was a word in my mind, not in theirs.

Jeremy Folk arrived the following morning, as he'd said he would, angling his stork-like figure apologetically through my front door and following me along the kitchen.

'Champagne?' I said, picking a bottle out of the refrigerator.

'It's . . . er . . . only ten o'clock,' he said.

'Four winners,' I said, 'Need celebrating. Would you rather have coffee?'

'Er . . . actually . . . no.'

He took his first sip all the same as if the wickedness of it would overwhelm him, and I thought that for all his wily ways he was a conformist at heart.

He had made an effort to be casual in his clothes: wool checked shirt, woolly tie, neat pale blue sweater. Whatever he thought of my unbuttoned collar, unbuttoned cuffs and unshaven jaw, he didn't say. He let his gaze do its usual inventorial travel-around from a great height and as usual return to my face when he'd shaped his question.

'Did you see . . . ah . . . James Nore?'

'Yes, I did.'

I gestured to him to sit on the leather-covered corner bench round the kitchen table, and joined him, with the bottle in reach.

'He's cohabiting happily in Camden Hill.'

'Oh,' Jeremy said. 'Ah.'

I smiled. 'Mrs Nore visited his house unexpectedly one day. She hadn't been there before. She met James's friend, and she realised, I suppose for the first time, that her son was one hundred per cent homosexual.'

'Oh,' Jeremy said, understanding much.

I nodded. 'No descendants.'

'So she thought of Amanda.' He sighed and drank some pale gold fizz. 'Are you sure he's homosexual. I mean . . . did he say so?'

'As good as. But anyway, I'm used to homosexuals. I lived with two of them for a while. You get to know, somehow.'

He looked slightly shocked and covered it with a relapse into the silly ass waffle.

'Did you? I mean . . . are you . . .? Er . . . I mean . . . living alone . . .? I shouldn't ask. Sorry.'

'If I take someone to bed, she's female,' I said mildly. 'I just don't like permanence.'

He buried his nose and his embarrassment in his glass, and I thought of Duncan and Charlie who had hugged and kissed and loved each other all around me for three years. Charlie had been older than Duncan; a mature man in his forties, solid and industrious and kind. Charlie, to me, had been father, uncle, guardian, all in one. Duncan had been chatty and quarrelsome and very good company, and neither of them had tried to teach me their way.

Duncan had slowly grown less chatty, more quarrelsome and less good company, and one day he fell in love with someone else and walked out. Charlie's grief had been white-faced and desperately deep. He had put his arm round my shoulders and hugged me, and wept; and I'd wept for Charlie's unhappiness.

My mother had arrived within a week, blowing in like a whirlwind. Huge eyes, hollow cheeks, fluffy silk scarves.

'But you must see, Charlie darling,' she said. 'That I can't leave Philip with you now that Duncan's gone. Look at him, darling, he's hardly ugly, the way he's grown up. Darling Charlie, you must see that he can't stay here. Not any more.' She'd looked across at me, bright and more brittle than I remembered, and less beautiful. 'Go and pack, Philip darling. We're going down to the country.'

Charlie had come into the little box-like room he and Duncan had built for me in one corner of the studio, and I'd told him I didn't want to leave him.

'Your mother's right, boy,' he said. 'It's time you were off. We must do what she says.'

He'd helped me pack and given me one of his cameras as a

goodbye present, and from the old life I'd been flung straight into the new in the space of a day. That evening I learned how to muck out a horse-box, and the next morning I started to ride.

After a week I'd written to Charlie to say I was missing him, and he replied encouragingly that I'd soon get over it: and get over it I did, while Charlie himself pined miserably for Duncan and swallowed two hundred sleeping pills. Charlie made a will a week before the pills leaving all his possessions to me, including all his other cameras and darkroom equipment. He also left a letter saying he was sorry and wishing me luck.

'Look after your mother,' he wrote. 'I think she's sick. Keep on taking photographs, you already have the eye. You'll be all right, boy. So long now. Charlie.'

I drank some champagne and said to Jeremy, 'Did you get the list of the Pine Woods Lodge tenancies from the estate agents?'

'Oh gosh, yes,' he said, relieved to be back on firm ground. 'I've got it here somewhere.' He patted several pockets but stuck two fingers unerringly and only into the one where he'd stored the slip of paper he wanted: and I wondered how much energy he wasted each day in camouflage movements.

'Here we are . . .' He spread the sheet of paper out, and pointed. 'If your mother was there thirteen years ago, the people she was with would have been the boy scouts, the television company, or the musicians. But the television people didn't live there, the agents say. They just worked there during the day. The musicians did live there, though. They were . . . er . . . experimental musicians, whatever that means.'

'More soul than success.'

He gave me a quick bright glance. 'A man in the estate agents' says he remembers they ruined the electric wiring and were supposed to be high all the time on drugs. Does any of that sound . . . er . . . like your mother?'

I pondered.

'Boy scouts don't sound like her a bit,' I said. 'We can leave them out. Drugs sounds like her, but musicians don't. Especially unsuccessful musicians. She never left me with anyone unsuccessful . . . or anyone musical, come to that.' I thought some more. 'I suppose if she was really drug-dependent by that time, she mightn't have cared. But she liked comfort.' I paused again. 'I think I'd try the television company first. They could at least tell us what programme they were making then, and who worked on it. They're bound to have kept the credits somewhere.'

Jeremy's face showed a jumble of emotions varying, I thought, from incredulity to bewilderment.

'Er . . .' he said, 'I mean . . .'

'Look,' I interrupted. 'Just ask the questions. If I don't like them I won't answer.'

'You're so frantically direct,' he complained. 'All right, then. What do you mean about your mother leaving you with people, and what do you mean about your mother and drugs?'

I outlined the dumping procedure and what I owed to the Deborahs, Samathas and Chloes. Jeremy's shattered expression alone would have told me that this was not every child's experience of life.

'Drugs,' I said, 'Are more difficult, I didn't understand about the drugs until I grew up, and I only saw her once after I was twelve . . . the day she took me away from the homosexuals and put me in the racing stable. But certainly she was taking drugs for as long as I remember. She kept me with her for a week, sometimes, and there would be a smell, an acrid distinctive smell. I smelled it again years later . . . I must have been past twenty . . . and it was marihuana. Cannabis. I smoked it when I was little. One of my mother's friends gave it to me when she was out, and she was furious. She did try, you know, in her way, to see I grew up properly. Another time a man she was with gave me some acid. She was absolutely livid.'

'Acid,' Jeremy said. 'Do you mean L.S.D.?'

'Yeah. I could see all the blood running through my arteries and veins, just as if the skin was transparent. I could see the bones, like X-rays. It's extraordinary. You realise the limitations of our everyday senses. I could hear sounds as if they were three-dimensional. A clock ticking. Amazing. My mother came into the room and found me wanting to fly out of the window. I could see the blood going round in her, too.' I remembered it all vividly, though I'd been about five. 'I didn't know why she was so angry. The man was laughing, and she slapped him.' I paused. 'She did keep me away from drugs. She died from heroin, I think but she kept me free of even the sight of it.'

'Why do you think she died of heroin?'

I poured refills of champagne.

'Something the racing people said. Margaret and Bill. Soon

after I got there I went into the sitting room one day when they were arguing. I didn't realise at first that it was about me, but they stopped abruptly when they saw me, so then I did. Bill had been saying "his place is with his mother", and Margaret interrupted, "She's a heroin . . ." and then she saw me and stopped. It's ironic, but I was so pleased they should think my mother a heroine. I felt warmly towards them.' I smiled lop-sidedly. 'It wasn't for years that I realised what Margaret had really been going to say was "she's a heroin addict". I asked her later and she told me that she and Bill had known that my mother was taking heroin, but they didn't know, any more than I did, where to find her. They guessed, as I did, that she'd died, and of course, long before I did, they guessed why. They didn't tell me, to save me pain. Kind people. Very kind.'

Jeremy shook his head. 'I'm so sorry,' he said.

'Don't be. It was all long ago. I never grieved for my mother. I think perhaps now that I should have done, but I didn't.'

I had grieved for Charlie, though. For a short intense time when I was fifteen, and vaguely, sporadically, ever since. I used Charlie's legacy almost every day, literally in the case of photographic equipment and figuratively in the knowledge he'd given me. Any photograph I took was thanks to Charlie.

'I'll try the television people,' Jeremy said.

'O.K.'

'And you'll see your grandmother?'

I said without enthusiasm, 'I suppose so.'

Jeremy half smiled. 'Where else can we look? For Amanda, I mean. If your mother dumped you all over the place like that, she must have done the same for Amanda. Haven't you thought of that?'

'Yes, I have.'

'Well, then?'

I was silent. All those people. All so long in the past. Chloe, Deborah, Samantha . . . all shadows without faces. I wouldn't know any of them if they walked into the room.

'What are you thinking?' Jeremy demanded.

'No one I was left with had a pony. I would have remembered a pony. I was never left where Amanda was in the photograph.'

'Oh, I see.'

'And I don't think,' I said, 'that the same friends would be pressed into looking after a second child. I very rarely went back to the same place myself. My mother at least spread the load.'

Jeremy sighed. 'It's all so irregular.'

I said slowly, unwillingly, 'I might find one place I stayed. Perhaps I could try. But even then . . . there might be different people in the house after all this time, and anyway they're unlikely to know anything about Amanda . . .'

Jeremy pounced on it. 'It's a chance.'

'Very distant.'

'Well worth trying.'

I drank some champagne and looked thoughtfully across the kitchen to where George Millace's box of rubbish lay on the dresser: and a hovering intention suddenly crystallised. Well worth trying. Why not?

'I've lost you,' Jeremy said.

'Yes.' I looked at him. 'You're welcome to stay, but I want to spend the day on a different sort of puzzle. Nothing to do with Amanda. A sort of treasure hunt . . . but there may be no treasure. I just want to find out.'

'I don't . . .' he said vaguely: and I got up and fetched the box and put it on the table.

'Tell me what you think of that lot,' I said.

He opened the box and poked through the contents, lifting things out and putting them back. From expectancy his face changed to disappointment, and he said, 'They're just . . . nothing.'

'Mm.' I stretched over and picked out the piece of clear-looking film which was about two and a half inches across by seven inches long. 'Look at that against the light.'

He took the piece of film and held it up. 'It's got smudges on it,' he said. 'Very faint. You can hardly see them.'

'They're pictures,' I said. 'Three pictures on one-twenty roll film.'

'Well . . . you can't see them.'

'No,' I agreed. 'But if I'm careful . . . and lucky . . . we might.'

He was puzzled. 'How?'

'With intensifying chemicals.'

'But what's the point? Why bother?'

I sucked my teeth. 'I found something of great interest in that box. All those things were kept by a great photographer who was also an odd sort of man. I just think that maybe some more of those bits aren't the rubbish they look.'

'But . . . which ones?'

'That's the question. Which ones . . . if any.'

Jeremy took a gulp of champagne. 'Let's stick to Amanda.'

'You stick to Amanda. I'm better at photographs.'

He watched with interest, however, while I rummaged in one of the cupboards in the darkroom.

'This all looks frightfully workmanlike,' he said, doing the eye-travel round the enlargers and print processor. 'I'd no idea you did this sort of thing.'

I explained briefly about Charlie and finally found what I was looking for, a tucked away bottle that I'd acquired on an American holiday three years earlier. It said Negative Intensifier on the label, followed by instructions. Most helpful. Many manufacturers printed their instructions on separate flimsy sheets of paper, which got wet or lost. I carried the bottle across to the sink, where there was a water filter fixed under the tap.

'What's that?' Jeremy asked, pointing at its round bulbous shape.

'You have to use ultra-clean soft water for photographic processing. And no iron pipes, otherwise you get a lot of little black dots on the prints.'

'It's all mad,' he said.

'It's precise.'

In a plastic measure I mixed water and intensifier into the strength of solution that the instructions said, and poured it into the developing tray.

'I've never done this before,' I said to Jeremy. 'It may not work. Do you want to watch, or would you rather stay with the bubbly in the kitchen?'

'I'm . . . ah . . . absolutely riveted, as a matter of fact. What exactly are you going to do?'

'I'm going to contact-print this clear strip of film with the ultra-faint smudges onto some ordinary black-and-white paper and see what it looks like. And then I'm going to put the negative into this intensifying liquid, and after that I'm going to make another black-and-white print to see if there's any difference. And after that . . . well, we'll have to see.'

He watched while I worked in dim red light, peering into the developing tray with his nose right down to the liquid.

'Can't see anything happening,' he said.

'It's a bit trial-and-error,' I agreed. I tried printing the clear film four times at different exposures, but all we got on the prints was a fairly uniform black, or a uniform grey, or a uniform white.

'There's nothing there,' Jeremy said. 'It's useless.'

'Wait until we try the intensifier.'

With more hope than expectation I slid the clear film into the intensifying liquid and sloshed it about in there for a good deal longer than the required minimum time. Then I washed it and looked at it against the light: and the ultra-faint smudges were still ultra-faint.

'No good?' Jeremy asked, disappointed.

'I don't know. I don't really know what should happen. And maybe that intensifier is too old. Some photographic chemicals lose their power with age. Shelf life, and so on.'

I printed the negative again at the same variety of exposures as before, and as before we got a uniform black and a uniform dark grey, but this time on the light grey print there were patchy marks, and on the nearly white print, swirly shapes.

'Huh,' Jeremy said. 'Well, that's that.'

We retreated to the kitchen for thought and revivers.

'Too bad,' he said. 'Never mind, it was impossible to start with.'

I sipped a few bubbles and popped them around my teeth.

'I think,' I said reflectively, 'That we might get further if I print that negative not onto paper, but onto another film.'

'Print it onto a film? Do you mean the stuff you load into cameras? I didn't know it was possible.'

'Oh yes. You can print onto anything which has a photographic emulsion. And you can coat practically anything with photographic emulsion. I mean, it doesn't have to be paper, though that's the way everyone thinks of it, because of seeing snapshots in family albums, and all that. Or glass. Or wood. On the back of your hand, I dare say, if you'd like to stand around in darkness for a while.'

'Good gracious.'

'Black-and-white, of course,' I said. 'Not colour.'

I popped a few more bubbles.

'Let's have another go, then,' I said.

'You really love this sort of thing, don't you?' Jeremy said.

'Love it? Do you mean photography . . . or puzzles?'

'Both.'

'Well . . . I suppose so.'

I got up and went back to the darkroom, and he again followed to watch. In the dim red light I took a new roll of high-contrast Kodak 2556 film, pulling it off its spool into a long strip and cutting it into five pieces. Onto each separate piece I printed the almost-clear negative, exposing it under the white light of the enlarger for various exposure times: one second the shortest, up to ten seconds the longest. Each piece of high-contrast film after exposure went into the tray of developer, with Jeremy sloshing the liquid about and bending down to see the results.

The results, after taking each piece of film out of the developer at what looked like the best moment, and transferring it to the fixing tray, and finally washing it, were five new positives. From those positives I repeated the whole process, ending with negatives. Seen in bright light, all of the new negatives were much denser than the one I'd started with. On two of them there was a decipherable image . . . and the smudges had come alive.

'What are you smiling at?' Jeremy demanded.

'Take a look,' I said.

He held the negative strip I gave him up to the light and said, 'I can see that you've got much clearer smudges. But they're still smudges, all the same.'

'No they're not. They're three pictures of a girl and a man.'

'How can you tell?'

'You get used to reading negatives, after a while.'

'And you look smug,' Jeremy complained.

'To be honest,' I said, 'I'm dead pleased with myself. Let's finish the champagne and then do the next bit.'

'What next bit?' he said, as we again drank in the kitchen.

'Positive prints from the new negatives. Black-and-white pictures. All revealed.'

'What's so funny?'

'The girl's nude, more or less.'

He nearly spilt his drink. 'Are you sure?'

'You can see her breasts.' I laughed at him. 'They're the clearest parts of the negatives, actually.'

'What . . . I mean . . . about her face?'

'We'll see better soon. Are you hungry?'

'Good heavens. It's one o'clock.'

We ate ham and tomatoes and brown toast, and finished the bubbles: and then returned to the darkroom.

Printing onto paper from such faint negatives was still a critical business as again one had first to judge the exposure right and then stop the developing print at exactly the best instant and switch it to the fixer, or all that came out was a flat light or a dark grey sheet with no depth and no highlights. It took me several tries with each of the two best new strips to get truly visible results, but I finished with three pictures which were moderately clear, and more than clear enough to reveal what George had photographed. I looked at them with the bright lights on, and with a magnifying glass; and there was no chance of a mistake.

'What's the matter?' Jeremy said. 'They're wonderful. Unbelievable. Why aren't you blowing your trumpets and patting yourself on the back?'

I put the finished articles into the print drier, and silently cleared up the developing trays.

'What is it?' Jeremy asked. 'What's the matter?'

'They're bloody dynamite,' I said.

NINE:

I took Jeremy and the new pictures upstairs and switched on the epidiascope, which hummed slightly in its idiosyncratic way as it warmed up.

'What's that?' Jeremy said, looking at the machine.

'You must have seen one,' I said, surprised. 'It's pretty old, I know. I inherited it from Charlie. But all the same, they must still be around. You put things in here on this baseboard and their image is projected large and bright onto a screen – or in my case, a wall. You can project anything. Pages of books, illustrations, photographs, letters, dead leaves. All done by mirrors.'

The photograph of Elgin Yaxley and Terence O'Tree still lay in position, and at the flick of a switch came into sharp focus as before, calendar and dates and all.

I drew the curtains against the fading afternoon light and let the picture shine bright in the dark room. After a minute I unclamped it and took it out, and put in instead the best strip I'd made downstairs, adjusting the lens, and enlarging each third separately, showing each of the three pictures on its own.

Eventually in their unavoidably imperfect state, even in shades of white to dark grey, they pulsated off the wall. The first one showed the top half of a girl as far down as the waist, and also the head and shoulders of a man. They were facing each other, the girl's head higher than the man's. Neither of them wore clothes. The man had his hands under the girl's breasts, lifting them up, with his mouth against the nipple furthest away from the camera.

'Good heavens,' Jeremy said faintly.

'Mm,' I said. 'Do you want to see the others?'

'They didn't look so bad in snapshot size.'

I projected the second picture, which was of much the same pose, except that the camera had been at a different angle, showing less of the girl's front and nearly all of the man's face.

'It's just pornography,' Jeremy said.

'No, it isn't.'

I unclamped the second picture and showed the third, which was different entirely. Events had moved on. The girl, whose own face this time was clearly visible, seemed to be lying on her back. The picture now stretched down to her knees, which were apart. Over her lay the man, his head turned to one side, showing his profile. His hand cupped the one visible breast, and there wasn't much doubt about the activity they were engaged in.

There was nothing to indicate where the pictures had been taken. No distinguishable background. The faint smudges on the transparent film had turned into people, but behind them there was nothing but grey.

I switched off the epidiascope and put on the room lights.

'Why do you say it isn't pornography?' Jeremy said. 'What else is it?'

'I've met them,' I said. 'I know who they are.'

He stared.

'As you're a lawyer,' I said. 'You can tell me. What do you do if you find out after a man's death that he may have been a blackmailer while he was alive?'

'Are you serious?'

'Absolutely.'

'Well . . . ah . . . he can't be prosecuted, exactly.'

'So one does nothing?'

He frowned. 'Are you . . . um . . . going to tell me what you're on about?'

'Yes, I think so.'

I told him about George Millace. About the burglaries, the attack on Marie Millace, and the burning of their house. I told him about Elgin Yaxley and Terence O'Tree and the five shot horses: and I told him about the lovers.

'George very carefully kept those oddments in that box,' I said. 'I've deciphered two of them. What if some of the others are riddles? What if they all are?'

'And all . . . the basis for blackmail?'

'Heaven knows.'

'Heaven knows . . . and you want to find out.'

I slowly nodded. 'It's not so much the blackmail angle, but the photographic puzzles. If George made them, I'd like to solve them. Just to see if I can. You were quite right. I do enjoy that sort of thing.'

Jeremy stared at the floor. He shivered as if he were cold. He said abruptly, 'I think you should destroy the whole lot.'

'That's instinct, not reason.'

'You have the same instinct. You said . . . dynamite.'

'Well . . . someone burgled and burnt George Millace's house. When I found the first picture I thought it must have been Elgin Yaxley who'd done it, but he was in Hong Kong, and it doesn't seem likely . . . And now one would think the lovers did it . . . but it might not be them either.'

Jeremy stood up and moved restlessly around the room in angular uncoordinated jerks.

'I don't like the feel of it,' he said. 'It could be dangerous.'

'To me?'

'Of course to you.'

'No one knows what I've got,' I said. 'Except, of course, you.'

His movements grew even more disturbed, his elbows bending and flapping almost as if he were imitating a bird. Agitation in his mind, I thought: real agitation, not camouflage.

'I suppose . . .' he said. 'Um . . . ah . . .'

'Ask the question.'

He shot me a glance. 'Oh yes . . . Well . . . Was there any doubt . . . about the way George Millace died?'

'Dear . . . God,' I said. I felt as if he'd punched the air out of my lungs. 'I don't think so.'

'What happened exactly?'

'He was driving home from Doncaster, and he went to sleep and ran into a tree.'

'Is that all? Precisely all?'

'Um . . .' I thought back. 'His son said his father stopped at a friend's house for a drink. Then he drove on towards home. Then he hit a tree.'

Jeremy jerked around a little more and said, 'How did anyone know he had stopped at the friend's house? And how does anyone know he went to sleep?'

'These are true lawyers' questions,' I said. 'I don't know the answer to the first, and as to the second, of course nobody knows; it's just what everyone supposes. Going to sleep in the dark towards the end of a long drive isn't all that uncommon. Deadly. Tragic. But always happening.'

'Did they do an autopsy?' he said.

'I don't know. Do they usually?'

He shrugged. 'Sometimes. They'd have tested his blood for the alcohol level. They might have checked for heart attack or stroke, if he wasn't too badly damaged. If there were no suspicious circumstances, that would be all.'

'His son would have told me – have told everyone on the racecourse – if there had been any odd questions asked. I'm sure there weren't any.'

'Those burglaries must have made the police think a bit, though,' he said frowning.

I said weakly, 'The first serious burglary occurred actually during the funeral.'

'Cremation?'

I nodded. 'Cremation.' I pondered. 'The police might have wondered . . . in fact they did hint very broadly to Marie Millace, and upset her considerably . . . about George possessing photographs other people might not want found. But they don't *know* he had them.'

'Like we do.'

'As you say.'

'Give it up,' he said abruptly. 'Burn those pictures. Stick to looking for Amanda.'

'You're a lawyer. I'm surprised you want to suppress incriminating evidence.'

'You can damn well stop laughing,' he said. 'You could end up like George Millace. Splat on a tree.'

Jeremy left at six, and I walked along to the military briefing with Harold. He had six runners planned for me during the week, and with those and the five spare rides I'd been offered at Windsor I looked like having an exceptionally busy time.

'Don't come crashing down on one of those hyenas you've accepted,' Harold said. 'What you take them for when you've got all my horses to ride I don't know.'

'Money,' I said.

'Huh.'

He never liked me taking outside rides, although as I was self-employed he couldn't stop me. He never admitted that some of the biggest races I'd won had been for other stables. In those cases, he would point out if pressed, I had been riding those stables' second strings, which had confounded the trainer's assessments and won when they weren't expected.

'Next Saturday at Ascot I'm running two of Victor's,' he said. 'Chainmail . . . and Daylight.'

I glanced at him quickly, but he didn't meet my eyes.

'He didn't have a proper race at Sandown, of course,' he said. 'He's still at his peak.'

'He'll have a harder job at Ascot. Much stronger opponents.'

He nodded, and after a pause he said casually, 'Chainmail might be the best bet. Depends what's left in at the four day stage, of course. And there's the overnights . . . We'll see better what the prospects are on Friday.'

There was a silence.

'Prospects for winning?' I said at last. 'Or for losing?'

'Philip . . .'

'I'm not going to,' I said.

'But . . .'

'You tell me, Harold,' I said. 'Tell me early Saturday morning, if you've a feeling for me at all. I'll get acute stomach ache. Bilious. The trots. Won't be able to go racing.'

'But there's Daylight.'

I compressed my mouth and stifled the tremble of anger.

'We had four winners last week,' I said tightly. 'Isn't that enough for you?'

'But Victor . . .'

I said, 'I'll ride my bloody guts out for Victor as long as we're trying to win. You tell him that. Tell him just that.' I stood up, unable to sit calmly. 'And don't you forget, Harold, that Chainmail's still only four, and pretty wayward, for all that he's fast. He pulls like a train and tries to duck out at the hurdles, and he's not above sinking his teeth into any horse that bumps him. He's the devil of a hard ride, but he's brave and I like him . . . and I'm not going to help you ruin him. And you *will* damn well ruin him if you muck him about. You'll turn him sour. You'll make him a real rogue. Apart from dishonest, it's stupid.'

'Have you finished?'

'I guess so.'

'Then I agree with you about Chainmail. I'll say it all to Victor. But in the end it's Victor's horse.'

I stood without speaking. Anything I said, I thought, could prove too decisive. While I was still riding for the stable, there was hope.

'Do you want a drink?' Harold said; and I said yes, coke; and the fraught moment passed. We talked normally about the chances and plans for the other three runners, and only when I was leaving did Harold make any reference to the awaiting chasm.

'If necessary,' he said heavily. 'I'll give you time to get sick.'

At Fontwell races the next day I rode one horse for Harold, which fell three from home, and two for other people, resulting in a second place and a third, and faint congratulatory noises but no avalanches of further work. An average sort of day; better than some. The fall had been slow and easy: a bruise but no damage.

No hot gossip in the weighing room.

Not unseemly fighting between newly elected Jockey Club members and cocaine-pushing film directors. No elderly Lords drooling over delectable dollies. Not even any worried broken-collarboned jockeys agonising over battered mothers.

No heavy blue-overcoated owners putting pressure on their going-straight jockeys.

A quiet day at the office.

Tuesday, with no racing engagements, I rode out both lots with Harold's string and schooled some of the horses over training jumps. It was a raw damp morning, the sort to endure, not enjoy, and even Harold seemed to take no pleasure in the work. The mood of the Downs, I thought, walking my mount back through Lambourn, infected the whole village. On days like this the inhabitants scarcely said good morning.

From twelve o'clock onwards the day was my own.

Eating some muesli I contemplated George Millace's box of riddles, but felt too restless for another long spell in the dark-room.

Thought of my promised visit to my grandmother, and hastily sought a reason for postponing it.

Decided to placate the accusing image of Jeremy Folk by seeing if I could find the house in my childhood. A nice vague expedition with no expectation of success. A drift-around day; undemanding.

I set off accordingly to London and cruised up and down a whole lot of little streets between Chiswick and Hammersmith. All of them looked familiar to me in a way: rows of tidy terraces of mostly three storeys and a basement, bow-fronted townhouses for middle-income people, misleadingly narrow frontages stretching far back to small enclosed gardens. I had lived in several houses like that at some time or another, and I couldn't remember even the name of a road.

The years, too, had brought a host of changes. Whole streets had obviously disappeared with the building of bigger roads. Little remaining blocks of houses stood in lonely islands, marooned. Cinemas had closed. Asian shops had moved in. The buses looked the same.

Bus routes.

The buses triggered the memory. The house I was looking for had been three or four from the end of the road, and just round the corner there had been a bus-stop. I had been on the buses often, catching them at that stop.

Going to where?

Going to the river, for walks.

The knowledge drifted quietly back across twenty-plus years. We'd gone down to the river in the afternoons, to look at the houseboats and the seagulls and the mud when the tide was out; and we'd looked across the gardens at Kew.

I drove down to Kew Bridge and reversed, and started from there, following buses.

A slow business, because I stopped when the bus did. Unproductive also, because none of the stops anywhere seemed to be near the corners of roads. I gave it up after an hour and simply cruised around, resigned to not finding anything I recognised. Probably I'd got even the district wrong. Probably I should be looking at Hampstead, where I knew I'd been also.

It was a pub that finally orientated me. The Willing Horse. An old pub. Dark brown paint. Frosted glass in the windows with tracery patterns round the edges. I parked the car round the corner and walked back to the chocolate doors, and simply stood there, waiting.

After a while I seemed to know which way to go. Turn left, walk three hundred yards, cross the road, first turning on the right.

I turned into a street of bow-fronted terraced houses, three storeys high, narrow and neat and typical. Cars lined both sides of the street, with many front gardens converted to parking places. There were a few bare-branched trees growing from earth-patches near the edge of the pavement, and hedges and shrubs by the houses. Three steps up to a small flat area outside each front door.

I crossed that road and walked slowly up it, but the impetus had gone. Nothing told me whether I was in the right place, or which house to try. I walked more slowly, indecisively, wondering what to do next.

Four houses from the end I went up the short footpath, and up the steps, and rang the doorbell.

A woman with a cigarette opened the door.

'Excuse me,' I said. 'Does Samantha live here?'

'Who?'

'Samantha?'

'No.' She looked me up and down with the utmost suspicion, and closed the door.

I tried six more houses. Two no answers, one 'clear off', one 'no dear, I'm Popsy, like to come in?', one 'we don't want no brushes', and one 'is that a cat?'

At the eighth an old lady told me I was up to no good, she'd watched me go from house to house, and if I didn't stop it she would call the police.

'I'm looking for someone called Samantha,' I said. 'She used to live here.'

'I'm watching you,' she said. 'If you try to climb in through any windows, I'll call the police.'

I walked away from her grim little face and she came right out into the street to watch me.

It wasn't much good, I thought. I wouldn't find Samantha. She might be out, she might have moved, she might never have lived in that street in the first place. Under the old woman's baleful gaze I tried another house where no one answered, and another where a girl of about twenty opened the door.

'Excuse me,' I said, 'Does anyone called Samantha live here?' I'd said it so often it now sounded ridiculous. This is the last one, I thought. I may as well give it up and go home.

'Who?'

'Samantha?'

'Samantha what? Samantha who?'

'I'm afraid I don't know.'

She pursed her lips, not quite liking it.

'Wait a moment,' she said. 'I'll go and see.' She shut the door and went away. I walked down the steps to the front garden where a small red car stood on some tarmac. Hovered, waiting to see if the girl returned, aware of the old woman beadily watching from along the road.

The door behind me opened as I turned. There were two people there, the girl and an older woman. When I took a step towards them the woman made a sharp movement of the arm, to keep me away. Raising her voice she said, 'What do you want?'

'Well . . . I'm looking for someone called Samantha.'

'So I hear. What for?'

'Are you,' I said slowly, 'Samantha?'

She looked me up and down with the suspicion I was by now used to. A comfortably sized lady, grey-brown wavy hair to her shoulders.

'What do you want?' she said again, unsmiling.

I said, 'Would the name Nore mean anything to you? Philip Nore, or Caroline Nore?'

To the girl the names meant nothing, but in the woman there was a fast sharpening of attention.

'What exactly do you want?' she demanded.

'I'm . . . Philip Nore.'

The guarded expression turned to incredulity. Not exactly to pleasure, but certainly to acknowledgement.

'You'd better come in,' she said. 'I'm Samantha Bergen.'

I went up the steps and through the front door, and didn't have, as I'd half expected, the feeling of coming home.

'Downstairs,' she said, leading the way and looking over her shoulder, and I followed her through the hall and down the stairs which in all those London houses led to the kitchen and the door out to the garden. The girl followed after me, looking mystified and still wary.

'Sorry not to have been more welcoming,' Samantha said, 'but you know what it is these days. So many burglaries. You have to be careful. And strange young men coming to the door asking for Samantha . . .'

'Yes,' I said.

She went through a doorway into a large room which looked more like a country kitchen than most kitchens in the country. A row of pine-covered fitments on the right. A big table, with chairs. A red-tiled floor. French windows to the garden. A big basket-chair hanging on a chain from the ceiling. Beams. Inglenook with gas fire. Bits of gleaming copper.

Without thinking I walked across the red floor and sat in the hanging basket chair, beside the inglenook, tucking my feet up under me, out of sight.

Samantha Bergen stood there looking astounded.

'You are!' she said. 'You are Philip. Little Philip. He always used to sit there like that, with his feet up. I'd forgotten. But seeing you do it . . . Good gracious heavens.'

'I'm sorry,' I said, half stammering and standing up again, steadying the swinging chair. 'I just . . . did it.'

'My dear man,' she said. 'It's all right. It's extraordinary to see you, that's all.' She turned to the girl but said still to me, 'This is my daughter, Clare. She wasn't born when you stayed here.' And to her daughter she said, 'I looked after a friend's child now and then. Heavens . . . it must be twenty-two years since the last time. I don't suppose I ever told you.'

The girl shook her head but looked less mystified and a good deal more friendly. They were both of them attractive in an unforced sort of way, both of them wearing jeans and sloppy jerseys and unpainted Tuesday afternoon faces. The girl was slimmer and had darker and shorter hair, but they both had large grey eyes, straight noses, and unaggressive chins. Both were self-assured; and both undefinably intelligent.

The work I had interrupted lay spread out on the table. Galley proofs and drawings and photographs, the makings of a book. When I glanced at it Clare said 'Mother's cookery book' and Samantha said 'Clare is a publishers' assistant,' and they invited me to sit down again.

We sat round the table, and I told them about looking for Amanda, and the off-chance which had brought me to their door.

Samantha regretfully shook her head. 'An off-chance is all it was,' she said. 'I never saw Caroline after she took you away the last time. I didn't even know she had a daughter. She never brought her here.'

'Tell me about her,' I said. 'What was she like?'

'Caroline? So pretty you wanted to hug her. Full of light and fun. She could get anyone to do anything. 'But . . .' she stopped.

'But what?' I said. 'And please do be frank. She's been dead for twelve years, and you won't hurt my feelings.'

'Well . . . she took drugs.' Samantha looked at me anxiously, and seemed relieved when I nodded. 'Cocaine, L.S.D. Cannabis. Almost anything. Poppers and uppers and downers. She tried the lot. She told me she didn't want you around when she and her friends were all high. She begged me to look after you for a few days . . . it always turned into a few weeks . . . and you were such a quiet little mouse . . . you were quite good company, actually. I never minded, when she brought you.'

'How often?' I said slowly.

'How often did she bring you? Oh . . . half a dozen times. You were about four the first time . . . and about eight at the end, I suppose. I told her I couldn't take you again, as Clare was imminent.'

'I've always been grateful to you,' I said.

'Have you?' She seemed pleased. 'I wouldn't have thought you'd remember . . . but I suppose you must have done, as you're here.'

'Did you know anyone called Chloe or Deborah or Miranda?' I said.

'Deborah Baederbeck? Went to live in Brussels?'

'I don't know.'

Samantha shook her head dubiously. 'She wouldn't know anything about your Amanda. She must have been in Brussels for . . . oh . . . twenty-five years.'

Clare made some tea and I asked Samantha if my mother had ever told her anything about my father.

'No, nothing,' she said positively. 'An absolutely taboo subject, I gathered. She was supposed to have an abortion, and didn't. Left it too late. Just like Caroline, absolutely irresponsible.' She made a comical face. 'I suppose you wouldn't be here if she'd done what she'd promised her old dragon of a mother.'

'She made up for it by not registering my birth.'

'Oh God.' She chuckled with appreciation. 'I must say that's typical Caroline. We went to the same school. I'd known her for years. We'd not long left when she got landed with you.'

'Did she take drugs then? At school?'

'Heavens, no.' She frowned, thinking. 'Afterwards. We all did. I don't mean she and I together. But our generation . . . we all tried it, I should think, some time or other, when we were young. Pot mostly.'

Clare looked surprised, as if mothers didn't do that sort of thing.

I said, 'Did you know the friends she got high with?'

Samantha shook her head. 'Never met any of them. Caroline called them friends in the plural, but I always thought of it as one friend, a man.'

'No,' I said. 'Sometimes there were more. People lying on floor cushions half asleep, with the room full of haze. All enormously peaceful.'

They were the people with words like 'skins' and 'grass' and 'joints', which never seemed to mean what my childish brain expected; and it was one of those who had given me a cigarette and urged me to suck in the smoke. Suck it into your lungs, he'd said, and then hold your breath while you count ten. I'd coughed all the smoke out before I'd counted two, and he'd laughed and told me to try again. Three or four small drags, I'd had.

The result, which I'd dreamed of occasionally afterwards rather than actively remembered, was a great feeling of tranquillity. Relaxed limbs, quiet breathing, slight lightness of head. My mother had come home and slapped me, which put paid to all that. The friend who'd initiated me never re-appeared. I hadn't met hash again until I was twenty, when I'd been given a present of some greeny-yellow Lebanese resin to sprinkle like an OXO cube onto tobacco.

I'd smoked some, and given some away, and never bothered again. The results, to me, weren't worth the trouble and expense. They would have been, a doctor friend had told me, if I'd had asthma. Cannabis was terrific for asthmatics, he'd said, sadly. Pity they couldn't smoke it on the National Health.

We drank the tea Clare had made, and Samantha asked what I did in the way of a job.

'I'm a jockey.'

They were incredulous. 'You're too tall,' Samantha said, and Clare said, 'People just aren't jockeys.'

'People are,' I said. 'I am. And steeplechase jockeys don't have to be small. Six-footers have been known.'

'Extraordinary thing to be,' Clare said. 'Pretty pointless, isn't it?'

'Clare!' Samantha said, protesting.

'If you mean,' I said equably, 'That being a jockey contributes nothing useful to society, I'm not so sure.'

'Proceed,' Clare said.

'Recreation gives health. I provide recreation.'

'And betting?' she demanded. 'Is that healthy?'

'Sublimation of risk-taking. Stake your money, not your life. If everyone actually set out to climb Everest, just think of the rescue parties.'

She started to smile and converted it into a chewing motion with her lips. 'But you yourself . . . take the risks.'

'I don't bet.'

'Clare will tie you in knots,' her mother said. 'Don't listen to her.'

Clare however shook her head. 'I would think your little Philip is as easy to tie in knots as a stream of water.'

Samantha gave her a surprised glance and asked me where I lived.

'In Lambourn. It's a village in Berkshire. Out on the Downs.'

Clare frowned and looked at me with sharpened concentration.

'Lambourn . . . isn't that the village where there are a lot of racing stables, rather like Newmarket?'

'That's right.'

'Hm.' She thought for a minute. 'I think I'll just ring up my boss. He's doing a book on British villages and village life. He was saying this morning the book's still a bit thin – asked me if I had any ideas. He has a writer chap doing it. Going to villages, staying a week and writing a chapter. He's just done one on a village that produces its own operas . . . Look, do you mind if I give him a call?'

'Of course not.'

She was on her feet and going across to a telephone extension on the kitchen worktop before I'd even answered. Samantha gave her a fond motherly look, and I thought how odd it was to find Samantha in her late forties, when I'd always imagined her perpetually young. From under the unrecognisable exterior, though, the warmth, the directness, the steady values and the basic goodness came across to me as something long known: and I was reassured to find that those half-buried impressions had been right.

'Clare will bully you into things,' she said. 'She bullied me into doing this cookery book. She's got more energy than a power station. She told me when she was about six that she was going to be a publisher, and she's well on her way. She's already second-in-command to the man she's talking to. She'll be running the whole firm before they know where they are.' She sighed with pleased resignation, vividly illuminating the trials and prides of mothering a prodigy.

The prodigy herself, who looked normal enough, finished talking on the telephone and came back to the table nodding.

'He's interested. He says we'll both go down and look the place over, and then if it's O.K. he'll send the writer, and a photographer.'

I said diffidently, 'I've taken pictures of Lambourn . . . If you'd like to . . .'

She interrupted with a shake of the head. 'We'd need

professional work. Sorry and all that. But my boss says if you don't mind we'll call at your digs or whatever, if you'd be willing to help us with directions and general info.'

'Yes . . . I'd be willing.'

'That's great.' She gave me a sudden smile that was more like a pat on the back than a declaration of friendship. She knows she's bright, I thought. She's used to being brighter than most. She's not as good as Jeremy Folk at concealing that she knows it.

'Can we come on Friday?' she said.

TEN:

Lance Kinship was wandering around at the head of a retinue of cameramen, sound recordists and general dogsbodies when I arrived at Newbury racecourse on the following day, Wednesday. We heard in the changing room that he was taking stock shots for a film with the blessing of the management and that jockeys were asked to cooperate. Not, it was said, to the point of grinning into the camera lens at every opportunity, but just to not treading on the crew if one found them underfoot.

I slung my Nikon round my neck inside my raincoat and unobtrusively took a few pictures of the men taking pictures.

Technically speaking, cameras were not welcome at race meetings except in the hands of recognised photographers, but most racecourses didn't fidget unduly about the general public taking snaps anywhere except in the Members' enclosure. Most racecourse managers, because I'd been doing it for so long, looked tolerantly upon my own efforts and let me get on with it. Only at Royal Ascot was the crack-down on amateurs complete: the one meeting where people had to park their shooters at the entrance, like gunslingers riding into a bullet-free town.

Lance Kinship looked as if he had tried hard not to look like a film director. In place of his olive suede jacket, now presumably having its bloodstains removed at the cleaners, he wore a brownish tweed suit topped by a brown trilby set at a conservative angle and accompanied by checked shirt, quiet tie, and race-glasses. He looked, I thought, as if he'd cast himself as an uppercrust extra in his own film.

He was telling his crew what to do with pomposity in his voice and with indecisive gestures. It was only in the tenseness with which they listened to him, their eyes sliding his way every time he spoke, that one saw any authority. I took a couple of shots of that reaction; the eyes all looking towards him from averted heads. I reckoned that when printed those pictures might quite clearly show men obeying someone they didn't like.

At one point, round by the saddling boxes, where the crew were filming the trainers fitting on the saddles before the first race, Lance Kinship turned his head in the instant I pressed the button, and stared straight into my lens.

He strode across to me, looking annoyed.

'What are you doing?' he said, though it must have been obvious.

'I was just interested,' I said inoffensively.

He looked at my boots, my white breeches and the red and yellow shirt which I wore under the raincoat.

'A jockey,' he said, as if to himself. He peered through his black framed spectacles at my camera. 'A Nikon.' He raised his eyes to my face and frowned with half-recognition.

'How's the nose?' I said politely.

He grunted, finally placing me.

'Don't get into shot,' he said. 'You're not typical. I don't want Nikon-toting jocks lousing up the footage. Right?'

'I'll be careful,' I said.

He seemed on the point of telling me to go away altogether, but he glanced from side to side and took note that a few racegoers were listening, and decided against it. With a brief dissaproving nod he went back to his crew, and presently they moved off and began taking shots of the saddled horses walking into the parade ring.

The chief cameraman carried his big movie camera on his shoulder and mostly operated it from there. An assistant walked one step behind, carrying a tripod. One sound recorder carried the charcoal sausage-shaped boom and a second fiddled endlessly with knobs on an electric box. A young man with frizzy hair operated a clapper board, and a girl took copious notes. They trailed round all afternoon getting in everyone's way and apologising like mad so that no one much minded.

They were down at the start when I lined up on a scatty novice 'chaser for Harold, and thankfully absent from the eighth fence, where the novice 'chaser put his fore-feet into the open ditch on the take-off side and crossed the birch almost upside down. Somewhere during this wild somersault I fell out of the saddle, but by the mercy of heaven when the half-ton of horse crashed to the ground I was not underneath it.

He lay prostrate for a few moments, winded and panting, giving me plenty of time to grasp hold of the reins and save his lad the frustrating job of catching him loose. Some horses I loved: and some I didn't. This was a clumsy stubborn delinquent with a hard mouth, just starting what was likely to be a long career of bad jumping. I'd schooled him at home several times and knew him too well. If he met a fence right, he was safe enough, but if he met it wrong he ignored signals to change his stride; and every horse met a fence wrong now and then, however skilful his rider. I reckoned every time he completed a race, I'd be lucky.

Resignedly I waited until he was on his feet and prancing about a bit, then remounted him and trotted him back to the stands, and made encouraging remarks to the downcast owner and honest ones to Harold.

'Tell him to cut his losses and buy a better horse.'

'He can't afford it.'

'He's wasting the training fees.'

'I dare say,' Harold said, 'but we're not telling him, are we?'

I grinned at him. 'No, I guess not.'

I took my saddle into the weighing-room and Harold went off to join the owner in a consolatory drink. Harold needed the training fees. I needed the riding fees. The owner was buying a dream and kidding himself. It happened every day, all the time, in racing. It was only occasionally that the dream came superbly, soul-fillingly true, and when that happened you saw points of light like stars in the owner's eyes. Thank God for the owners, I thought. Without them racing wouldn't exist.

When I was changing back into street clothes someone came and told me there was a man outside asking for the jockey with the camera.

I went to see, and found Lance Kinship trudging up and down and looking impatient.

'Oh there you are,' he said, as if I'd seriously kept him waiting. 'What's your name?'

'Philip Nore.'

'Well, Phil, what do you say? You took some photographs today. If they're any good I'll buy them from you. How's that?'

'Well . . .' I was nonplussed. 'Yes, if you like.'

'Good. Where's your camera? Get it then, get it. The crew is over by the winning post. Take some photographs of them shooting the finish of the next race. Right? Right?'

'Yes,' I said dazedly.

'Come on then. Come on.'

I fetched the camera from the changing room and found

him still waiting for me but definitely in a hurry. I would have to get over there and assess the best angles, he explained, and I'd only have one chance because the crew would be moving out to the car park presently to film the racegoers going home.

He had apparently tried to get the regular photographers to do the present job, but they had said they were too busy.

'I thought of you. Worth trying, I thought. With that camera, you at least have to be able to focus. Right?'

We were walking fast. He broke now and then into a sort of trotting stride, and his breathing gradually grew shorter. His mental energy however was unflagging.

'We need these pics for publicity. Right?'

'I see,' I said.

His words and manner were so much at variance with his appearance that the whole expedition seemed to me powerfully unreal. Urgent film producers (who might or might not provide cocaine for sniffing at parties) were surely not accustomed to look the country gentleman, nor tweeded country gentlemen to speak with slovenly vowels and glottal-stop consonants. The 'right?' he was so fond of was pronounced without its final 't'.

I would have thought, if he wanted publicity pictures, that he would have brought a photographer of his own; and I asked him.

'Sure,' he said. 'I had one lined up. Then he died. Didn't get around to it again. Then today, saw you. Reminded me. Asked the news photographers. No dice. Thought of you, right? Asked them about you. They said you were good, you could do it. You may be lousy. If your pics are no good, I don't buy, right?'

He panted across the course to the winning post on the far side, and I asked him which photographer had died.

'Fellow called Millace. Know him?'

'I knew him,' I said.

'He said he'd do it. Died in a car crash. Here we are. You get on with it. Take what you want. Got colour film in there, have you?'

I nodded and he nodded, and he turned away to give instructions to the crew. They again listened to him with the slightly averted heads, and I wandered away. Lance Kinship was not immediately likeable, but I again had a strong feeling that his crew felt positive discontent. He wouldn't buy photographs showing that response, I thought dryly, so I waited until the crew were not looking at him, and shot them absorbed in their work.

Lance Kinship's breathing returned to normal and he himself merged again into the racing background as if he'd been born there. An actor at heart, I thought: but unlike an actor he was dressing a part in real life, which seemed odd.

'What film are you making?' I asked.

'Stock shots,' he said uninformatively. 'Background.'

I left it, and walked round the crew looking for useful angles for pictures. The horses came out onto the course and cantered down to the start, and the frizzy-haired boy with the clapper board, who happened to be close to me, said with sudden and unexpected fierceness, 'You'd think he was God Almighty. You'd think this was an epic, the way he frigs about. We're making commercials. Half a second on screen, flash off. Huh!'

I half smiled. 'What's the product?'

'Some sort of brandy.'

Lance Kinship came towards me and told me it was important that he should be included in my photographs, and that I should take them from where he would be prominently in shot.

The frizzy haired boy surreptitiously raised his eyebrows into comical peaks, and I assured Lance Kinship with a trembling straight face that I would do my absolute best.

I did by good luck get one or two reasonable pictures, but no doubt George Millace with his inner eye and his motor-drive camera would have outstrpped me by miles. Lance Kinship gave ma a card with his address on and told me again that he would buy the pictures if he liked them, right?

He didn't say for how much, and I didn't like to ask.

I would never be a salesman.

Taking photographs for a living, I thought ruefully, would find me starving within a week.

Reaching home I switched on the lights and drew the curtains, and sat by the kitchen table going again through George Millace's rubbish box, thinking of his talents and his cruel mind, and wondering just how much profit he had made from his deadly photographs.

It was true that if he'd left any more pictures in that box I wanted to decipher them. The urge to solve the puzzles was overpowering. But if I learned any more secrets, what would I do with them . . . and what ought I to do with those I already had?

In a fairly typical manner I decided to do pretty well nothing. To let events take their course. To see what happened.

Meanwhile there were those tantalising bits that looked so pointless . . .

I lifted out the black plastic light-proof envelope which was of about the same size as the box and lying at the bottom of it, under everything else. I looked again at its contents, as I had in Steve Millace's house, and saw again the page-sized piece of clear plastic, and also, which hadn't registered before, two sheets of paper of about the same size.

I looked at them briefly and closed them again into their light-proof holder, because it had suddenly occurred to me that George might not have stored them like that unless it was necessary. That plastic and that paper might bear latent images . . . which I might already have destroyed by exposing them to light.

The piece of plastic and the sheets of paper didn't actually look to me like photographic materials at all. They looked like a piece of plastic and two sheets of typing paper.

If they bore latent images, I didn't know how to develop them. If they didn't, why had George kept them in a light-proof envelope.

I sat staring vaguely at the silent black plastic and thinking about developers. To bring out the image on any particular type of film or any type of paper one had to use the right type of developer, the matched mixture of chemicals made for the task. All of which meant that unless I knew the make and type of the plastic and of the two sheets of paper I couldn't get any further.

A little pensively I pushed the black envelope aside and took up the strips of blank negatives, which at least didn't have the built-in difficulty of being still sensitive to light. They had already been developed. They just looked as if when they had been developed there had been no latent images on them to bring out.

They were thirty-five millimetre colour film negatives, and there were a lot of them, some simply blank and others blank with uneven magenta blotches here and there. The negatives were in strips, mostly six to a strip. I laid them all out end to end and made the first interesting discovery.

All the plain blank negatives had come from one film, and those with magenta blotches from another. The frame numbers along the top of each strip ran consecutively from one to thirty-six in each case. Two films of thirty-six exposures each.

I knew what make of film they were, because each manufacturer placed the frame numbers differently, but I didn't suppose that that was important. What might be important, however, was the very nature of colour negatives.

While slide films – transparencies – appeared to the eye in their true lifelike colours, negative film appeared in the reciprocal colours: and to get back to the true colours one had of course to make a print from the negative.

The primary colours of light were blue, green, and red. The reciprocal colours, in which they appeared on a negative, were yellow, magenta and cyan. Negatives therefore would have looked like mixtures of yellow, deep pink (magenta) and greeny-blue (cyan), except that to get good whites and highlights all manufacturers gave their negatives an overall pale orange cast. Colour negatives therefore always looked a pale clear orange at the edges.

The overall orange colour also had the effect of masking the yellow sections so that they didn't show to the eye as yellow bits of negative, but as orange.

George Millace's negatives looked a pale clear transparent orange throughout.

Just suppose, I thought, that under the orange there was an image in yellow, which at the moment didn't show.

If I printed those negatives, the yellow would become blue.

An invisible yellow negative image could turn into a totally visible printed image in blue.

Worth trying, I thought. I went into the darkroom and mixed the developing chemicals, and set up the colour print processor. It meant waiting half an hour for the built-in thermostatic heaters to raise the various chemical baths to the correct temperatures, but after that the prints were conveyed automatically inside the closed processor from one bath to another on rollers, each sheet of photographic paper taking seven minutes to travel from entry to exit.

I found out almost at once, by making contact prints, that under the orange masking there was indeed blue: but not blue images. Just blue.

There were so many variables in colour printing that searching for an image on blank negatives was like walking blindfold through a forest, and although in the end I printed every negative separately and tried every way I knew, I was only partially successful.

I ended, in fact, with thirty-six solid blue oblongs, enlarged to four inches by five and printed four to a sheet, and thirty-six more with greenish blotches here and there.

The only thing one could say, I thought, as I let them wash thoroughly in running water, was that George wouldn't have taken seventy-two pictures of a blue oblong for nothing.

I dried some of the prints and looked at them closely, and it did seem to me that there were faint darker marks on some of them. Nothing one could see plainly see, but something.

When it dawned on me far too late what George had done I was too tired to start all over again. I cleaned up the processor and everything else, and went to bed.

Jeremy Folk telephoned early the next morning and asked if I'd been to see my grandmother.

Give me time, I said, and he said I'd had time, and did I remember I had promised?

'Well . . . I'll go,' I said. 'Saturday, after Ascot.'

'What have you been doing?' he asked plaintively. 'You could have gone any day this week. Don't forget she really is dying.'

'I've been working,' I said. 'And printing.'

'From that box?' he said suspiciously.

'Uh huh.'

'Don't do it,' he said, and then, 'What have you got?'

'Blue prints. Blue pictures.'

'What?'

'Blue as in blue. Pure deep blue. Forty-seven B.'

'*What* did you say? Are you sober?'

'I am awake and yawning,' I said. 'So listen. George Millace screwed a deep blue filter onto his camera and pointed it at a black and white picture, and he photographed the black and white picture through the blue filter onto colour negative film. Forty-seven B is the most intense blue filter you can buy, and I bet that's what he used.'

'You're talking Chinese.'

'I'm talking Millace. Crafty double Millace. Second cousin to double Dutch.'

'You really are drunk.'

'Don't be silly. As soon as I work out how to unscramble the blue, and do it, the next riveting Millace instalment will fall into our hands.'

'I seriously think you should burn the lot.'

'Not a chance.'

'You think of it as a game. It isn't a game.'

'No.'

'For God's sake be careful.'

I said I would. One says things like that so easily.

I went to Wincanton races in Somerset and rode twice for Harold and three times for other people. The day was dry with a sharp wind that brought tears to the eyes, tears which the standard of racing did nothing to dispel, since all the good horses had cried off and gone to Newbury or Ascot instead, leaving chances for the blundering majority. I fumbled and booted my way around five times in safety, and in the novice 'chase, owing to most of the field having fallen over each other at the first open ditch, found myself finishing in front, all alone.

My mount's thin little trainer greeted my return with a huge grin, tear-filled eyes and a blue dripping nose.

'By gum, lad, well done. By gum, it's bloody cold. Get thee in and weighed. Don't stand about. By gum, then, that was a bit of all right, wasn't it, all them others falling?'

'You'd schooled yours a treat,' I said, pulling off the saddle. 'He jumped great.'

His mouth nearly split its sides with pleasure. 'By gum, lad, he'd jump Aintree, the way he went today. Get thee in. Get thee in.'

I went in and weighed, and changed and weighed out, and raced, and returned, and changed and weighed . . .

There had been a time, when it was all new, that my heart had pumped madly every time I walked from the changing room to the parade ring, every time I cantered to the start. After ten years my heart pumped above normal only for the big ones, the Grand National and so on, and then only if my horse had a reasonable chance. The once fiendish excitement had turned to routine.

Bad weather, long journeys, disappointments and injuries had at first been shrugged off as 'part of the job'. After ten years I saw that they *were* the job. The peaks, the winners, those were the bonuses. Extras.

The tools of my trade were a liking for speed and a liking for horses, and the power to combine those two feelings. Also strong bones, an ability to bounce, and a tendency to mend quickly when I didn't.

None of these tools, except probably the liking for horses, would be of the slightest use to me as a photographer.

I walked irritably out to my car at the end of the afternoon. I didn't want to be a photographer. I wanted to remain a jockey. I wanted to stay where I was, in the known: not to step irrevocably into the future. I wanted things to go on as they were, and not to change.

Early the following morning Clare Bergen appeared on my doorstep accompanied by a dark young man whose fingertips in a handshake almost tingled with energy. Publishers, I had vaguely supposed, were portly father-figures. Another out-of-date illusion gone bust.

Clare herself had come in a bright woolly hat, bright scarf, Afghan sheepskin jacket, yellow satin ski-pants and huge fleece-lined boots. Ah well, I thought, she would only frighten half of the horses. The nervous half.

I drove them up onto the Downs in the Land Rover borrowed from Harold for the occasion, and we watched a few strings work. Then I drove them round the village, pointing out which trainers lived where. Then I took them back to the cottage for coffee and cogitation.

The publisher said he would like to poke round a little on foot, and walked off. Clare drank her second steaming cup and said how on earth did we bear it with a wind like that sawing everyone in half.

'It always seems to be windy here,' I agreed, thinking about it.

'All those naked hills.'

'Good for horses.'

'I don't think I've ever actually touched a horse.' She looked faintly surprised. 'Most of the people I know despise horse people.'

'Everyone likes to feel superior,' I said, uninsulted. 'Particularly when they aren't.'

'Ouch,' she said. 'That's a damned fast riposte.'

I smiled. 'You'd be surprised the sort of hate that gets aimed at horses. Anything from sneers to hysteria.'

'And you don't mind?'

'What those people feel is their problem, not mine.'

She looked at me straightly with the wide grey eyes.

'What hurts you?' she said.

'People saying I jumped overboard when I went down with the ship.'

'Er . . . what?'

'People saying I fell off when it was the horse which fell, and took me with it.'

'And there's a distinction?'

'Most important.'

'You're having me on,' she said.

'A bit.' I took her empty cup and put it in the dishwasher. 'So what hurts you?'

She blinked, but after a pause she answered. 'Being held to be a fool.'

'That,' I said, 'is a piercingly truthful reply.'

She looked away from me as if embarrassed, and said she liked the cottage and the kitchen and could she borrow the bathroom. She emerged from there shortly minus the woolly hat and plus some fresh lipstick and asked if the rest of the house was on a par.

'You want to see it?' I said.

'Love to.'

I showed her the sitting room, the bedroom, and finally the darkroom. 'And that's all,' I said.

She turned slowly from the darkroom to where I stood behind her in the hall.

'You said you took photographs.'

'Yes, I do.'

'But I thought you meant . . .' She frowned. 'Mother said I was short with you when you offered . . . but I'd no idea . . .'

'It doesn't matter,' I said. 'It's quite all right.'

'Well . . . can I see them?'

'If you like. They're in that filing cabinet over there.'

I pulled open one of the drawers and sorted through the folders. 'Here you are, Lambourn village.'

'What are all those others?' she said.

'Just pictures.'

'What of?'

'Fifteen years.'

She looked at me sharply as if I wasn't making sense, so I added, 'Since I owned my own camera.'

'Oh.' She looked along the tags on the folders, reading

aloud, 'America, France, children, Harold's place, Jockey's life . . . What's Jockey's life?'

'Just everyday living, if you're a jockey.'

'Can I look?'

'Sure.'

She eased the well-filled holder out of the drawer and peered inside. Then she carried it away towards the kitchen and I followed with the pictures of Lambourn.

She laid the folder she carried on the kitchen table, and opened it, and went through the bulky contents picture by picture, steadily and frowning.

No comments.

'Can I see Lambourn?' she said.

I gave her Lambourn, and she looked through those also in silence.

'I know they're not marvellous,' I said mildly. 'You don't have to rack your brains for something kind to say.'

She looked up at me fiercely. 'You're lying. You know damned well they're good.'

She closed the Lambourn file and drummed her fingers on it. 'I can't see why we can't use these,' she said. 'But it's not my decision, of course.'

She fished into her large brown handbag and came up with cigarettes and a lighter. She put a cigarette to her mouth and lit it, and I noticed with surprise that her fingers were trembling. What on earth, I wondered, could have made her nervous. Something had disturbed her deeply, because all the glittery extrovert surface had vanished, and what I saw was a dark-haired young woman concentrating acutely on the thoughts in her head.

She took several deep inhaling breaths of smoke, and looked unseeingly at her fingers, which went on trembling.

'What's the matter?' I said at last.

'Nothing.' She gave me a quick glance and looked away, and said, 'I've been looking for something like you.'

'Something?' I echoed, puzzled.

'Mm.' She tapped off some ash. 'Mother told you, didn't she, that I wanted to be a publisher?'

'Yes, she did.'

'Most people smile, because I'm still young. But I've worked in publishing for five years . . . and I know what I'm doing.'

'I don't doubt it.'

'No . . . but I need . . . I want . . . I need to make a book that will establish my own personal reputation in publishing. I need to be known as the person who produced such-and-such a book. A very successful book. Then my whole future in publishing will be assured. Do you understand?'

'Yes.'

'So I've been looking for that book for a year or two now. Looking and despairing, because what I want is exceptional. And now . . .' She took a deep breath, 'now I've found it.'

'But,' I said, puzzled, 'Lambourn's not news, and anyway I thought it was your boss's book . . .'

'Not that, you fool,' she said. 'This.' She put her hand on the Jockey's Life folder. 'The pictures in here. They don't need a text. They tell the story on their own.' She drew on the cigarette. 'Arranged in the right order . . . presented as a way of living . . . as an autobiography, a social comment, an insight into human nature . . . as well as how an industry works . . . it'll make a spectacular change from flowers and fish.'

'The flowers sold about two million copies, didn't they?'

'You don't believe me, do you?' she demanded. 'You simply don't see . . .' She broke of and frowned. 'You haven't had any of these photographs published before, have you? In papers or magazines, or anywhere?'

I shook my head. 'Nowhere. I've never tried.'

'You're amazing. You have this talent, and you don't use it.'

'But . . . everyone takes photographs.'

'Sure they do. But not everyone takes a long series of photographs which illustrate a whole way of life.' She tapped off the ash. 'It's all there, isn't it? The hard work, the dedication, the bad weather, the humdrum, the triumphs, the pain . . . I've only looked through these pictures once, and in no sort of order, and I know what your life's like. I know it *intimately*. Because that's how you've photographed it. I know your life from inside. I see what you've seen. I see the enthusiasm in those owners. I see their variety. I see what you owe to the stable-lads. I see the worry of trainers, it's everywhere. I see the laughter in jockeys, and the stoicism. I see what you've felt. I see what you've understood about people. I see people in a way I hadn't before, because of what you've seen.'

'I didn't know,' I said slowly, 'That those pictures were quite so revealing.'

'Look at this last one,' she said, pulling it out. 'This picture of a man in an overall pulling the boot off this boy with the broken shoulder . . . you don't need any words to say the man is doing it as gently as he can, or that it hurts . . . you can see it all, in every line of their bodies and faces.' She replaced the picture in the folder and said seriously, 'It's going to take me some time to set things up the way I want. Will you give me your assurance that you won't go straight off and sell these pictures to someone else?'

'Of course,' I said.

'And don't mention any of this to my boss when he comes back. I want this to be my book, not his.'

I half smiled. 'All right.'

'You may have no ambition,' she said sharply, 'but I have.'

'Yes.'

'And my ambitions won't do you any harm either,' she said. 'If the book's a seller . . . and it will be . . . you'll get royalties.' She paused. 'You can have an advance, anyway, as soon as the contracts are signed.'

'Contracts . . .'

'Contracts, naturally,' she said. 'And keep these pictures safe, will you? I'll come back for them soon, on my own.'

She thrust the folder into my hands and I replaced it in the filing cabinet, so that when her energetic young boss returned it was only the views of Lambourn that he saw. He said without too much excitement that they would do well enough, and shortly afterwards he and Clare bore them away.

When he'd gone I thought that Clare's certainty about her book would evaporate. She would remember that most of the people she knew despised horse people. She would work out that a book of pictures taken by a jockey about his life would have a very limited appeal, and she would write apologetically, or briskly, and say that after all, on reflection . . .

I shrugged. I had no expectations. When the letter came, that would be that.

ELEVEN:

I went into Swindon to collect the films I'd left there for processing on my way to Wincanton the previous morning, and spent the rest of that Friday printing the shots of Lance Kinship and his crew.

Apart from those showing clearly the crew's unease in his company, which I didn't intend in any case to show him, I thought that quite likely he might approve. I'd been fortunate in the way the crew had arranged themselves often into natural patterns, and there was Kinship himself looking frantically upper-class in his racing tweeds directing them with a conductor's gestures, and in one sequence the horses behind them were all coming head on satisfactorily towards the winning post.

There were also several close-ups of Kinship with the crew in blurred focus behind him, and a couple of slightly surrealistic views which I'd taken from directly behind the cameraman, in which the camera itself looked large with Kinship's sharply focussed figure standing in a stray shaft of sunlight in the middle field. The total effect, looking through them all, was a record of a substantial operator in command of his job, and that, I presumed, was what he'd wanted. No matter that the product had been two seconds in a commercial, the production itself looked an epic.

In the evening I captioned the dried prints with typed strips of thin paper sellotaped onto the backs, and feeling faintly foolish added the words *Copyright Philip Nore,* in the way I'd seen Charlie do, all those long years ago. Charlie seemed almost to be leaning over my shoulder, reminding me to keep control of my work.

Work.

The very word filled me with disquiet. It was the first time I'd actively thought of my photographs in those terms.

No, I thought, I'm a jockey.

When I woke early on Saturday morning I waited for Harold to telephone and tell me to get sick, and it wouldn't have been much trouble as I already felt sick with waiting.

He called at a quarter to ten.

'Are you well?' he said.

'Christ.'

'You'd better be,' he said. 'Victor rang just now. I didn't wait to hear what he meant to say. I told him straight away that Chainmail's future depended on his being handled right in all his races.'

'What happened?'

'Victor said an easy race wouldn't hurt him, so I told him what you said. Word for word. And I told him you'd said you would ride your bloody guts out for him as long as we're trying to win.' Harold's voice boomed down the wire with cheerfulness. 'And do you know what Victor said? He said tell that pious bastard that that's just what I'll expect.'

'Do you mean . . .?'

'I mean,' Harold bellowed, 'he's changed his mind. You can win on Chainmail if you can. In fact you'd better.'

'But Chainmail isn't . . .'

'Dammit, do you want to ride the horse or don't you?'

'I do.'

'Right, then. See you at Ascot.' He slammed the receiver down, informing me that he didn't think I'd been properly grateful for his efforts with Victor: but if he had promised Victor that Chainmail would win – and it seemed only too likely that he had – I would be in a worse fix than ever.

At Ascot I sought out Harold's head travelling lad, who had as usual come with the horses, and asked how Chainmail was feeling that day.

'Bucking and kicking fit to murder.'

'And Daylight?'

'Placid as an old cow.'

'Where have the lads put their money?'

He gave me a sharp sideways look. 'A bit on both of them. Why, shouldn't they?'

'Sure,' I said casually. 'They should. But you know how it is . . . sometimes the lads know more about a horse's chances than the trainer does.'

He grinned. 'I'll say. But today . . .' he shrugged. 'A bit on both. Not the week's wages, mind. Just some beer money, like.'

'Thanks.' I nodded and went off to the weighing room with

at least no added anxieties. The lads wouldn't be staking even beer money without what they considered to be good reason. The legs, stomachs and spirits of both horses could be held to be normal. One didn't ask more.

I saw Victor Briggs standing in a group of one on the area of grass outside the weighing room door. Always the same clothes: the broad-brimmed hat, the thick navy overcoat, the black leather gloves. Always the same expression: the wiped-clean slate. He saw me, and no doubt he also saw the falter in my stride as I wondered whether I could possibly walk right past him without speaking.

I couldn't.

'Good morning, Mr Briggs.'

'Morning.' His voice was curt, but no more. He didn't seem to want me to stop for conversation, so after a slight hesitation I went on towards the weighing room. As I passed him he said grittily, 'I'll see your guts.'

I stopped and turned my head. His face was still expressionless. His eyes looked cold and hard. I stopped myself from swallowing, and said merely 'All right', and went on again, wishing I'd never made that stupidly flamboyant promise.

Inside the changing room someone was telling a funny story about two statues, and Steve Millace was flexing his mending arm and complaining that the doctor wouldn't pass him fit to ride, and someone else was voicing the first rumours of a major racing upheaval. I took off my street clothes and listened to all three at once.

'So these two naked statues, the man and the woman, they had been standing looking at each other in this park for a hundred years . . .'

'I told him I'd got all the movement back. It's not fair . . .'

'Is it true the Jockey Club are forming a new committee . . .'

'So an angel comes to visit them, and says that as they've stood there patiently through such ages of summers and winters, they will be rewarded by half an hour of human life to do what they have been wanting to do most . . .'

'Look, I can swing my arm round in a circle. What do you think?'

'A committee for appointing paid Stewards, or something.'

'So these two statues come to life, and look at each other and laugh a bit, and say "Shall we?" and "Yes, let's", and then they nip off behind some bushes, and there's a lot of rustling . . .'

'I could hold any horse. I told him so, but the sod wouldn't listen.'

'. . . like paying the Senior Steward a salary.'

'After a quarter of an hour they come out from behind the bushes all hot and flustered and happy and the angel says they've only used half the time, why don't they start all over again . . .'

'How long do collar-bones usually take, anyway?'

'I heard Lord White has agreed to the scheme . . .'

'So the statues giggle a bit and the man statue says to the girl statue, "O.K. let's do it again, only this time we'll do it the other way round. I'll hold down the effing pigeon, and you shit on it." '

Amid the burst of laughter I heard the rumour man say '. . . and Ivor den Relgan is to be chairman.'

I turned to him. 'What did you say?'

'I don't know if it's true . . . one of the gossip writers told me Ivor den Relgan's been appointed to set up a committee to appoint paid Stewards.'

I frowned. 'That gives den Relgan an awful lot of power all of a sudden, doesn't it?'

He shrugged. 'Don't know.'

He might not, but others did. During the afternoon one could almost see the onward march of the rumour as uneasy surprise spread from one Jockey Club face to the next. The only group seeming unaffected by the general reaction were the ill-assorted bunch of people attracting the glances of everyone else.

Lord White. Lady White. Ivor den Relgan. Dana den Relgan.

They stood outside the weighing room in weak November sunshine, the women both dressed in mink. Lady White, always thin, looked gaunt and plain and unhappy. Dana den Relgan glowed with health, laughed with bright teeth, twinkled her eyes at Lord White, and cast patronising glances at his Lady.

Lord White basked in the light of Dana's smile, shedding years like snakeskins. Ivor den Relgan smirked at the world in general and smoked a cigar with proprietorial gestures, as if Ascot racecourse were his own. He wore again the belted camel overcoat and the swept back greyish hair, and commanded attention as his natural right.

Harold appeared at my elbow, following my gaze.

'Ghengis Khan,' he said, 'is setting out to rule the world.'

'This committee?'

'Wouldn't you say,' Harold asked acidly, 'That asking someone like den Relgan to chair a committee of his own choosing is a paint job?'

'Cosmetic . . . or camouflage?'

'Both. What they're really doing is saying to den Relgan "O.K. you choose anyone you like as Stewards, and we'll pay them." It's incredible.'

'Yes, it is.'

'Old Driven Snow,' Harold said, 'Is so besotted with that girl that he'll give her father *anything*.'

'Was it all Lord White's idea?'

Harold grimaced wolfishly. 'Be your age, Philip. Just who has been trying for years to muscle into the Jockey Club? And just who has a knock-out of a daughter who is now old enough to play up to old Driven Snow? Ivor den Relgan has at last got his lever into the door to power in racing, and once he's inside the citadel and making decisions the old guard will have a hopeless job trying to get him out.'

'You really care,' I said wonderingly.

'Of course I bloody do. This is a great sport, and at the moment, free. Who the hell wants the top management of racing to be carved up and manipulated and sold and *tainted* like some other sports we could mention. The health of racing is guaranteed by having unpaid aristocrats working for the love of it. Sure, they make stupid fuck-ups occasionally, but we get them put right. If den Relgan appoints paid Stewards, for whom do you think those Stewards will be working? For us? For racing? Or for the interests of Ivor den bloody Relgan?'

I listened to his passion and his conviction and felt the tremor of his extreme dismay.

'Surely,' I said, 'the Jockey Club won't let it happen.'

'It is happening. The ones at the top are all so used to being led by Lord White that they've agreed to his proposal for this committee without thinking it through. They take it for granted he's virtuous and well-meaning and dead honest. And so he is. But he's also infatuated. And that's damn bloody dangerous.'

We watched the group of four. Lord White made continual small gestures which involved laying his hand on Dana's arm, or across her shoulders, or against her cheek. Her father watched with an indulgent smile and a noticeable air of satisfaction: and poor Lady White seemed to shrink even further and more greyly into her mink. When she eventually walked away, not one of the others seemed to notice her go.

'Someone,' Harold said grimly, 'has got to do something to stop all this. And before it goes too far.'

He saw Victor Briggs standing as usual alone in the distance and strode off to join him, and I watched Lord White and Dana flirt together like two joyful humming birds, and thought that today she was responding to him with much less discretion than she had at Kempton.

I turned away, troubled, and found Lance Kinship coming slowly towards me, his gaze flicking rapidly from me to the den Relgans and back again. It struck me that he wanted to talk to me without den Relgan noticing he was there, and with an inward smile I went to meet him.

'I've got your pictures in the car,' I said. 'I brought them in case you were here.'

'Have you? Good, good. I want to talk to that girl.' He flicked another quick glance. 'Can you get near her? Give her a message? Without that man hearing. Without either of them hearing. Can you?'

'I might try,' I said.

'Right. Good. You tell her, then, that I'll meet her after the third race in one of the private boxes.' He told me the number. 'You tell her to come up there. Right?'

'I'll try,' I said again.

'Good. I'll watch you. From over there.' He pointed. 'When you've given her the message, you come and tell me. Right?'

I nodded, and with another quick peek at Dana he scuttled away. His clothes that day were much as they had been at Newbury, except that he'd ruined the overall true-blue impression with some pale green socks. A pathetic man, I thought. Making himself out to be what he wasn't. Neither a significant film producer nor bred in the purple. They asked him to parties, Victor Briggs had said, because of what he brings. A sad ineffectual man buying his way into the big time with little packets of white powder.

I looked from him to den Relgan, who was using Dana, instead, for much the same purpose. Nothing sad or pathetic, though, about Ivor den Relgan. A bully boy on the march, power hungry and complacent, a trampler of little men.

I went up to him, and in an ingratiating voice, which after years of buttering-up owners I could regrettably do quite convincingly, thanked him again for the gifts he had scattered at Kempton.

'The silver saddle . . . thought I must tell you,' I said. 'Great to have around, just to look at.'

'So glad,' he said, his gaze passing over me without interest. 'My daughter selected it.'

'Splendid taste,' Lord White said fondly, and I said directly to Dana, 'Thank you very much.'

'So glad,' she murmured also with an almost identical lack of interest.

'Please do tell me,' I said, 'whether it is unique, or whether it is one of many.'

I moved a step or two so that to answer she had to turn away from the two men, and almost before she had finished replying that it was the only one she'd seen, but she couldn't be certain . . . I said to her quietly, 'Lance Kinship is here, wanting to see you.'

'Oh.' She glanced quickly to the two men, returned Lord White's automatic smile with a dazzling one of her own, and softly said to me 'Where?'

'After the third race in a private box.' I gave her the number.

'So glad you liked the saddle,' she said clearly, turning back towards Lord White. 'Isn't it fun,' she said to him, 'to give pleasure?'

'My dear girl,' he said roguishly, 'you give pleasure just by being yourself.'

Enough to bring angels to tears, I thought.

I wandered away and by a roundabout route arrived at Lance Kinship's side.

'She got the message,' I said, and he said 'Good,' and we arranged for me to give him his pictures outside the weighing-room during the running of the last race.

Daylight's race was third on the card, and Chainmail's the fourth. When I went out for the third I was stopped on my way from weighing-room to parade-ring by a pleasant-mannered woman who I realised with delayed shock was Marie Millace.

Marie Millace with scarcely a trace showing of the devastation of her face. Mrs Millace on her feet, dressed in brown, pale and ill-looking, but healed.

'You said there wouldn't be a mark,' she said, 'and there isn't.'

'You look great.'

'Can I talk to you?'

I looked to where all the other jockeys I'd started out with were already filing into the parade ring. 'Well . . . how about later? How about . . . um . . . after the fourth race. After I've changed. In the warm somewhere.'

She mentioned a particular bar, and we agreed on it, and I went on to the ring where Harold and Victor Briggs waited. Neither of them said anything to me, nor I to them. Everything of importance had already been said and for the unimportant there was no appetite. Harold gave me a leg-up onto Daylight, and I nodded to him and Victor and got a grade-one blank Briggs stare in return.

There was no certainty that day that Daylight would win. With much stronger opponents, he wasn't even favourite, let alone odds-on.

I cantered down to the starting gate thinking about courage, which was not normally a word I found much in my mind. The process of getting a horse to go fast over jumps seemed to me merely natural, and something I very much liked doing. One knew theoretically that there would be falls and injuries, but the risk of them seldom affected the way I rode. I had no constant preoccupation with my own safety.

On the other hand I'd never been reckless, as some were, as Steve Millace was, and perhaps my aim had been a little too much to bring myself and the horse back together, and not enough to throw my heart over a fence and let the horse catch up if he could.

It was the latter style of riding that Victor Briggs would expect on that day. My own fault, I thought. And moreover I'd have to do it twice.

On Daylight it turned out to be fairly easy, as his jumping style held good even though I could see his surprise at the change of mental gears in his rider. The telepathic quality of horses, that remarkable extra sense, picked up instantaneously the strength of my intention, and although I knew horses did tune in in that way, it freshly amazed me. One got used to a certain response from horses, because it was to oneself they were responding. When one's own cast of mind changed radically, so did the horse's response.

Daylight and I therefore turned in what was for us a thoroughly uncharacteristic performance, leaving more to luck than judgement. He was accustomed to measure his distance from a fence and alter his stride accordingly; but infected by my urgency he began not to do that but simply to take-off when he was vaguely within striking distance of getting over. We hit the tops of three fences hard, which was unheard of for him, and when we came to the last and met it right we raced over it as if it had been but a shadow on the ground.

Hard as we tried, we didn't win the race. Although we persevered to the end, a stronger, faster, fitter, (whatever) horse beat us into second place by three lengths.

In the unsaddling enclosure I unbuckled the girths while Daylight panted and rocketed around in a highly excitable state which was a world away from his 'placid cow' image; and Victor Briggs watched without giving a thought surface life.

'Sorry,' I said to Harold, as he walked in with me to the scales.

He grunted, went into the changing room for a change of lead weights in the weight cloth, and returned to the scales to check out for Chainmail.

'Don't kill yourself,' Harold said, taking my saddle. 'It won't prove anything except that you're a bloody fool.'

I smiled at him. 'People die crossing the road.'

'What you're doing is no accident.'

He walked off with the saddle and I noticed that he had not in fact instructed me to return to a more sober style for his second runner. Perhaps he too, I reflected, wanted Victor to run his horse straight, and if this was the only way to achieve that, well . . . so be it.

With Chainmail things were different to the extent that the four-year-old hurdler was unstable to begin with, and what I was doing to him was much like urging a juvenile delinquent to go mugging. The rage within him, which made him fight against his jockey and duck out at the jumps and bite other horses, needed to be controlled by a calm mind and steady handling: or so I'd always thought.

On that day he didn't get it. He got a rider prepared to overlook every aggressive act except that of ducking out, and when he tried that at the third hurdle he got such a fierce slash from my whip that I could almost feel him thinking resentfully, 'Hey, that's not like you,'; and it wasn't.

He fought and scrambled and surged and flew. I went with him to his ultimate speed, to total disregard of good sense. I did without any reservation ride my bloody guts out for Victor Briggs.

It wasn't enough. Chainmail finished third in a field of

fourteen. Undisgraced. Better, probably, than one would realistically have expected. Beaten only by a length and a neck. But still third.

Victor Briggs unsmilingly watched me pull the saddle off his second stamping, tossing, hepped-up horse. I wrapped the girths round the saddle and paused for a moment face to face with him. He said nothing at all, and nor did I. We looked with equal blankness into each other's eyes for a space of seconds, and then I went on, past him, away to the scales.

When I had changed and come out again, he was nowhere in sight. I had needed two winners to save my job, and got none. Recklessness wasn't enough. He wanted winners. If he couldn't have certain winners, he'd want certain losers. Like before. Like three years ago. Like when I and my soul were young.

With a deep feeling of weariness I went to meet Marie Millace in the appointed bar.

TWELVE:

She was sitting in an armchair deep in conversation with another woman, whom I found to my surprise to be Lady White.

'I'll come back later,' I said, preparing to retreat.

'No, no,' Lady White said, standing up. 'I know Marie wants to talk to you.' She smiled with all her own troubles showing in lines of anxiety, her eyes screwed up as if in permanent pain. 'She tells me you've been so helpful.'

'Nothing,' I said, shaking my head.

'Not what she says.'

The two women smiled and kissed cheeks, and said goodbye, and Lady White with a nod and another vague smile for me made her way out of the bar. I watched her go; a thin defeated lady trying to behave as if the whole racing world were not aware of her discomfiture, and not altogether succeeding.

'We were at school together,' Marie Millace said. 'We shared a bedroom, in our last year there. I'm very fond of her.'

'You know about . . . er . . .?'

'About Dana den Relgan? Yes.' She nodded. 'Would you like a drink?'

'Let me get you one.'

I fetched a gin and tonic for her and some coke for me, and sat in the armchair Lady White had left.

The bar itself, an attractive place of bamboo furniture and green and white colours, was seldom crowded and often, as on that day, almost empty. Tucked away up on the stands far away from the parade ring and the bookmakers, it was a better place for talking than for following the horses, and as such was also warm where most of the stands were not. Semi-invalids tended to spend a lot of time there, with nephews and nieces scurrying backwards and forwards with Tote tickets.

Marie Millace said, 'Wendy . . . Wendy White . . . was asking me if I thought her husband's affair with Dana den Relgan would just blow over. But I don't know. I couldn't tell her. How could I tell her? I said I was sure it would . . .' She paused, and when I didn't answer, said, 'Do you think it will?'

'Not for a while, I wouldn't think.'

She gloomily swilled the ice around in her drink. 'Wendy says he's been away with her. He took her to some friends overnight. He told Wendy he was going to shoot, which she finds boring. She hasn't gone with him to shooting parties for years. But he took Dana den Relgan with him this week, and Wendy says when the party went out with the guns, her husband and Dana den Relgan stayed in the house . . . I suppose I shouldn't be telling you all this. She heard it from someone who was there. You're not to repeat what I've just said. You won't, will you?'

'Of course not.'

'It's so awful for Wendy,' Marie Millace said. 'She thought it was all over long ago.'

'All over? I thought it had just started.'

She sighed. 'Wendy says her husband fell like a ton of bricks for this Dana creature months ago, but then the wretched girl faded off the scene and didn't go racing at all, and Wendy thought that he'd stopped seeing her. And now she's back in full view and it's obvious to everyone. Wendy says that her husband is more overpoweringly in love than ever, and also *proud* of it. I'm so sorry for Wendy. It's all so horrid.' She looked genuinely sympathetic, and yet her own troubles, by any standard, were much worse.

'Do you know Dana den Relgan yourself?' I asked.

'No, not at all. George knew her, I think. Or at least he knew her by sight. He knew everyone. He said when we were in St Tropez last summer that he thought he'd seen her there one afternoon, but I don't know if he meant it, he was laughing when he said it.'

I drank some coke and asked her conversationally if she and George had enjoyed St Tropez, and if they had been there often. Yes they had loved it, and no, only once. George as usual had spent most of the time glued to his camera, but he and Marie had lain on their balcony looking out to sea every afternoon and had tanned marvellously . . .

'Anyway,' she said, 'That's not what I wanted to talk to you about. I wanted to thank you for your kindness and ask you about that exhibition you suggested . . . and about how I might make some money out of those photographs. Because

. . . and I know it's a sordid subject . . . I'm going to need . . . er . . .'

'Everyone needs,' I said comfortingly. 'But didn't George leave things like insurance policies?'

'Yes. Some. And I'll have the money for the house, though not its full value, unfortunately. But it won't be enough to live on, not with inflation and everything.'

'Didn't George,' I said delicately, 'have any . . . well . . . savings . . . in any separate bank accounts?'

Her friendly expression began to change to suspicion. 'Are you asking me the same sort of things as the police?'

'Marie . . . Think of the burglaries, and your face, and the arson.'

'He wasn't,' she said explosively. 'George wouldn't . . . I told you before. Don't you believe me?'

I sighed and didn't answer, and asked her if she knew which friend George had stopped for a drink with, on his way back from Doncaster.

'Of course I know. He wasn't a friend. Barely an acquaintance. A man called Lance Kinship. George rang me from Doncaster in the morning, as he often did when he stayed away overnight, and he mentioned he'd be half an hour or so late as he was calling at this man's house, as it was on his way home. This Lance Kinship wanted George to take some pictures of him working. He's a film director, or something. George said he was a pernicious self-deluding little egotist, but if he flattered him he'd pay well. That was almost the last thing he said to me.' She took a deep breath and tried to control the tears which stood suddenly in her eyes. 'I'm so sorry . . .' She sniffed and straightened her face with an effort, fishing in her pocket for a handkerchief.

'It's natural to cry,' I said. It was only three weeks, after all, since George had died.

'Yes, but . . .' she tried to smile. 'Not at the races.' She wiped the edge of the handkerchief along under her lower eyelids and sniffed again. 'The very last thing he said,' she said, trying too hard, 'was to ask me to buy some Ajax window cleaner. It's stupid, isn't it? I mean, except for saying "See you," the last thing George ever said to me was "get some liquid Ajax, will you?" and I don't even know . . .' She gulped. The tears were winning. 'I don't even know what he wanted it for.'

'Marie . . .' I held my hand out towards her and gripped it as fiercely as at the hospital.

'They say you always remember the last thing that someone you love says to you . . .' Her lips quivered hopelessly.

'Don't think about it now,' I said.

'No.'

She wiped her eyes again and held onto my hand, but presently the turmoil subsided and she loosened her grip and gave a small laugh of embarrassment: and I asked her if there had been an autopsy.

'Oh . . . alcohol, do you mean? Yes, they tested his blood. They said it was below the limit . . . he'd only had two small whiskies with that Kinship. The police asked him . . . Lance Kinship . . . after I told them about George planning to stop there. He wrote to me, you know, saying he was sorry. But it wasn't his fault. I'd told George over and over to be careful. He often got dozy when he'd been driving a long way.'

I told her how it had happened that it had been I who took the photographs of Lance Kinship that George had been going to do, and she was more interested than I had expected.

'George always said you'd wake up one day and pinch his market.' She produced a wavery smile to make it the joke it had undoubtedly been. 'I wish he knew. I wish . . . oh dear, oh dear.'

We just sat for a while until the fresh tears subsided, and she apologised again for them, and again I said one would expect them.

I asked for her address so that I could put her in touch with an agent for George's work, and she said she was staying with some friends who lived near Steve. She didn't know, she said forlornly, where she would be going from there. Because of the arson she had no clothes except the few new ones she was wearing. No furniture. Nothing to make a home of. Worse . . . much worse . . . she had no photograph of George.

By the time I left Marie Millace the fifth race had been run. I went straight out to the car to fetch Lance Kinship's pictures, and returned towards the weighing room to find Jeremy Folk standing outside the door on one leg.

'You'll fall over,' I said.

'Oh . . . er . . .' He put the foot down gingerly as if to stand on two legs made him more positively there. 'I thought . . . er . . .'

'You thought if you weren't here I might not do what you want.'

'Er . . . yes.'

'You may well be right.'

'I came here by train,' he said contentedly. 'So can you take me with you to St Albans?'

'I guess I'll have to.'

Lance Kinship, seeing me there, came over to collect his prints. I introduced him and Jeremy to each other out of habit, and added for Jeremy's sake that it was at Lance Kinship's house that George Millace had taken his last drink.

Lance Kinship, untucking the flap of the stiffened envelope, gave each of us a sharp glance followed by a sorrowful shake of the head.

'A great fellow, George,' he said. 'Too bad.'

He pulled the pictures out of the envelope and looked through them with his eyebrows rising even higher above his spectacle frames.

'Well, well,' he said. 'I like them. How much do you want?'

I mentioned a figure which I thought exorbitant but he merely nodded, pulled out a stuffed wallet, and paid me there and then in cash.

'Reprints?' he said.

'Certainly. They'd be less.'

'Get me two sets,' he said. 'Right?'

As before the last 't' of right stuck somewhere in his throat.

'Complete sets?' I said surprised. 'All of them?'

'Sure. All of them. Very nice, they are. Want to see?'

He flicked them invitingly at Jeremy, who said he'd like to see them very much: and he too inspected them with his eyebrows rising.

'You must be,' he said to Kinship, 'a director of great note.'

Kinship positively beamed and tucked his pictures back into the envelope. 'Two more sets,' he said. 'Right?'

'Right.'

He nodded and walked away, and before he'd gone ten paces he was pulling the pictures out again to show them to someone else.

'He'll get you a lot of work if you don't look out,' Jeremy said, watching.

I didn't know whether or not I wanted to believe him, and in any case my attention was caught by something much more extraordinary. I stood very still, and stared.

'Do you see,' I said to Jeremy, 'those two men over there, talking?'

'Of course I see them.'

'One of them is Bart Underfield, who trains in Lambourn. And the other is one of the men in that photograph of the French café. That's Elgin Yaxley . . . come home from Hong Kong.'

Three weeks after George's death, two weeks after the burning of his house; and Elgin Yaxley back on the scene.

I had jumped to conclusions before, but surely this time it was reasonable to suppose that Elgin Yaxley believed the incriminating photograph had safely gone up in smoke.

Reasonable to suppose, watching him standing there expansively smiling and full of confidence, that he felt freed and secure.

When a blackmailer and all his possessions were cremated, his victims rejoiced.

Jeremy said, 'It can't be coincidence.'

'No.'

'He looks pretty smug.'

'He's a creep.'

Jeremy glanced at me. 'You've still got that photo?'

'I sure have.'

We stood for a while looking on while Elgin Yaxley clapped Bart Underfield on the back and smiled like a crocodile and Bart Underfield looked happier than he had since soon after the trial.

'What will you do with it?'

'Just wait, I suppose,' I said, 'to see what happens.'

'I think I was wrong,' Jeremy said thoughtfully, 'to say you should burn all those things in the box.'

'Mm,' I smiled faintly. 'Tomorrow I'll have a go at the blue oblongs.'

'So you've worked out how?'

'Well, I hope so. Have to see.'

'How, then?'

He looked genuinely interested, his eyes switching from their customary scanning of the neighbourhood to a steady ten seconds in my direction.

'Um . . . do you want a lecture on the nature of light, or just the proposed order of events?'

'No lecture.'

'O.K. Then I think if I enlarge the orange negatives through blue light onto high contrast black and white paper I might get a picture.'

He blinked. 'In black and white?'

'With luck.'

'How do you get blue light?'

'That's rather where the lecture comes in,' I said. 'Do you want to watch the last race?'

We had a slight return of angular elbow movements and of standing on one leg and of hesitated waffle, all on account, I guessed, of squaring the solicitorial conscience with the condoning of gambling.

I had done him an injustice, however. When we were watching on the stands for the race to start he said, 'I did . . . ah . . . in point of fact . . . er . . . watch you ride . . . this afternoon.'

'Did you?'

'I thought . . . it, ah, might be instructive.'

'And how did it grab you?'

'To be honest,' he said, 'rather you than me.'

He told me, as we drove towards St Albans, about his researches into the television company.

'I got them to show me the credits, as you suggested, and I asked if they could put me in touch with anyone who worked on the play at Pine Woods Lodge. It was only a single play, by the way. The unit was there for only about six weeks.'

'Not very promising,' I said.

'No. Anyway, they told me where to find the director. Still working in television. Very dour and depressing man, all grunts and heavy moustache. He was sitting on the side of a road in Streatham watching some electricians holding a union meeting before they went on strike and refused to light the scene he wanted to shoot in a church porch. His mood, in a word, was vile.'

'I can imagine.'

'I'm afraid,' Jeremy said regretfully, 'That he wasn't much help. Thirteen years ago? How the hell did I expect him to remember one crummy six weeks thirteen years ago? How the hell did I expect him to remember some crummy girl with a crummy brat? And much more to that effect. The only positive thing he said was that if he'd been directing there would have been no crummy hangers on anywhere near Pine Woods Lodge. He couldn't stand outsiders hanging about when he was working, and would I, too, please get the hell out.'

'Pity.'

'After that I tracked down one of the main actors in the play, who is temporarily working in an art gallery, and got much the same answer. Thirteen years? Girl with small child? Not a chance.'

I sighed. 'I had great hopes of the television lot.'

'I could carry on,' Jeremy said. 'They aren't difficult to find. I just rang up a few agents, to get the actor.'

'It's up to you, really.'

'I think I might.'

'How long were the musicians there?' I said.

Jeremy fished out a by now rather worn-looking piece of paper, and consulted.

'Three months, give or take a week.'

'And after them?'

'The religious fanatics.' He grimaced. 'I don't suppose your mother was religious?'

'Heathen.'

'It's all so long ago.'

'Mm.' I said, 'Why don't we try something else? Why not publish Amanda's photograph in the *Horse and Hound,* and ask specifically for an identification of the stable. Those buildings are probably still standing, and looking just the same.'

'Wouldn't a big enough picture cost a lot?'

'Not compared with private detectives.' I reflected. 'I think *Horse and Hound* charges for space, not for what you put in it. Photographs cost no more than words. So I could make a good sharp black and white print of Amanda . . . and we could at least see.'

He sighed. 'O.K., then. But I can see the final expenses of this search costing more than the inheritance.'

I glanced at him. 'Just how rich is she . . . my grandmother?'

'She may be broke, for all I know. She's incredibly secretive. I dare say her accountant has some idea, but he makes a clam look sloppy.'

We reached St Albans and detoured around to the nursing home; and while Jeremy read old copies of *The Lady* in the waiting room I talked upstairs with the dying old woman.

Sitting up, supported by pillows, she watched me walk into her room. The strong harsh face was still full of stubborn life, the eyes as unrelentingly fierce. She said not something gentle like 'Hallo' or 'Good evening,' but merely 'Have you found her?'

'No.'

She compressed her mouth. 'Are you trying?'

'Yes and no.'

'What does that mean?'

'It means I've used some of my spare time looking for her but not my whole life.'

She stared at me with narrowed eyes, and presently I sat in the visitors' armchair and continued to stare back.

'I went to see your son,' I said.

Her face melted for a passing moment into an unguarded and revealing mixture of rage and disgust, and with a sense of surprise I saw the passion of her disappointment. I had already understood that a non-marrying non-child-producing son had essentially robbed her not of daughter-in-law and grand-children as such, to whom on known form she might anyway have behaved tyrannically, but of continuation itself: but I certainly hadn't realised that her search for Amanda sprang from obsession and not pique.

'Your genes to go on,' I said slowly. 'Is that what you want?'

'Death is pointless otherwise.'

I thought that life itself was pretty pointless, but I didn't say so. One woke up alive, and did what one could, and died. Perhaps she was in fact right . . . that the point of life was for genes to go on. Genes surviving, through generations of bodies.

'Whether you like it or not,' I said, 'your genes may go on through me.'

The idea still displeased her. The muscles tightened along her jaw, and it was in a hard unfriendly voice that at length she said, 'That young solicitor thinks I should tell you who your father was.'

I stood up at once, unable to stay calm. Although I had come to find out, I now didn't want to. I wanted to escape. To leave the room. Not to hear. I felt nervous in a way I hadn't done for years, and my mouth was sticky and dry.

'Don't you want to know?' she demanded.

'No.'

'Are you afraid?' She was scornful. Sneering.

I simply stood there, not answering, wanting to know and not wanting, afraid and not afraid: in an absolute muddle.

'I have hated your father since before you were born,' she said bitterly. 'I can hardly bear even now to look at you, because you're like him . . . like he was at your age. Thin . . . and physical . . . and with the same eyes.'

I swallowed, and waited, and felt numb.

'I loved him,' she said, spitting the words out as if they themselves offended her. 'I doted on him. He was thirty and I was forty-four. I'd been a widow for five years . . . I was lonely. Then he came. He lived with me . . . and we were going to marry. I adored him. I was stupid.'

She stopped. There really was no need to go on. I knew all the rest. All the hatred she had felt for me all those years was finally explained. So simply explained . . . and understood . . . and forgiven. Against all expectations what I suddenly felt for my grandmother was pity.

I took a deep breath. I said, 'Is he still alive?'

'I don't know. I haven't spoken to him or heard of him since.'

'And what . . . was his name?'

She stared at me straightly, nothing in her own persistent hatred being changed a scrap. 'I'm not going to tell you. I don't want you seeking him out. He ruined my life. He bedded my seventeen-year-old daughter under my own roof and he was after my money. That's the sort of man your father was. The only favour I'll do you is not to tell you his name. So be satisfied.'

I nodded. I made a vague gesture with one hand and said awkwardly, 'I'm sorry.'

Her scowl if anything deepened.

'Now find Amanda for me,' she said. 'That solicitor said you would, if I told you. So go away and do it.' She closed her eyes and looked immediately more ill, more vulnerable. 'I don't like you,' she said. 'So go away.'

'Well?' Jeremy said, downstairs.

'She told me.'

'The milkman?'

'Near enough.' I relayed to him the gist of it, and his reaction was the same as mine.

'Poor old woman.'

'I could do with a drink,' I said.

THIRTEEN:

In printing colour photographs one's aim was usually to produce a result that looked natural, and this was nowhere near as easy as it sounded. Apart from trifles like sharp focus and the best length and brightness of exposure, there was the matter of colour itself, which came out differently on each make of film, and on each type of photographic printing paper, and even on paper from two boxes of the same type from the same manufacturer: the reason for this being that the four ultra-thin layers of emulsion laid onto colour printing paper varied slightly from batch to batch. In the same way that it was almost impossible to dye two pieces of cloth in different dye baths and produce an identical result, so it was with light-sensitive emulsions.

To even this out and persuade all colours to look natural one used colour filters – pieces of coloured glass inserted between the bright light on the enlarger and the negative. Get the mixture of filters right, and in the finished print blue eyes came out blue and cherry lips, cherry.

In my enlarger, as on the majority worldwide, the three filters were the same colours as the colours of negatives: yellow, magenta, and cyan. Using all three filters together produced grey, so one only ever used two at once, and those two, as far as my sort of photographs were concerned, were always yellow and magenta. Used in delicate balance they could produce skin colours that were neither too yellow nor too pink for human faces, and it was a natural-looking skin colour that one normally geared one's prints.

However, if one put a square of magenta-coloured glass on a square of yellow-coloured glass, and shone a light through both together, one saw the result as red.

Shine a light through yellow and cyan, and you got green. And through magenta and cyan . . . a pure royal blue.

I had been confused when Charlie had first shown me, because mixing coloured light produced dramatically different results from mixing coloured paints. Even the primary colours were different. Forget paint, Charlie had said. This is light. You can't make blue by mixing other coloured paints, but you can with light.

'Cyan?' I'd said. 'Like cyanide?'

'Cyanide turns you blue,' he said. 'Cyan is a Greek word for blue. Kyanos. Don't forget. Cyan is greeny blue, and not surprisingly you get it by mixing blue light with green.'

'You do?' I'd said doubtfully, and he had shown me the six colours of light, and mixed them for me before my eyes until I got their relationship fixed in my head forever, until they were as basic in my brain as the shape of letters.

In the beginning were red, green, and blue . . .

I went into my darkroom on that fateful Sunday morning and adjusted the filters in the head of the enlarger so that the light which shone through the negatives would be that unheard-of combination for normal printing: full cyan and full magenta filtration, producing a deep clear blue.

I was going to print George's blank colour negatives onto black and white paper, which would certainly rid me of the blue of the oblongs: but all I might get instead were grey oblongs.

Black and white printing paper was sensitive only to blue light (which was why one could print in black and white in red safe-light). I thought that if I printed the blank-looking negatives through heavy pure filtration I might get a greater contrast between the yellow dye image on the negative and the orange mask covering it. Make the image, in fact, emerge from its surroundings.

I had a feeling that whatever was hidden by the mask would not itself be sharply black and white anyway . . . because if it had been it would have been visible through and in spite of the blue. What I was looking for would in itself be some sort of grey.

I set out the trays of developer and stop bath and fixer, and put all of the first thirty-six un-blotched negatives into a contact-printing frame. In this the negative was held directly against the printing paper when the light was passed through it, so that the print, when finished, was exactly the same size as the negative. The frame merely held all the negatives conveniently so that all thirty-six could be printed at once onto one eight-by-ten inch sheet of paper.

Getting the exposure time right was the biggest difficulty, chiefly because the heavy blue filtration meant that the light getting to the negatives was far dimmer than I was used to. I wasted about six shots in tests, getting useless results from grey to black, all the little oblongs still stubbornly looking as if there was nothing on them to see, whatever I did.

Finally in irritation I cut down the exposure time to far below what it was reasonable to think right, and came up with a print that was almost entirely white. I stood in the dim red light watching the white sheet lie in the developer with practically nothing happening except that the frame numbers of the negatives very palely appeared, followed by faint lines showing where the edges of the negatives had been.

Sighing with frustration I left it in the developer until nothing else emerged and then, feeling depressed, dipped it in the stop bath and then fixed it and washed it, and switched on the bright lights.

Five of the oblongs were not entirely white. Five of the little oblongs, scattered at random through the thirty-six, bore very pale grey geometric shapes.

I had found them.

I could feel myself smiling with ridiculous joy. George had left a puzzle, and I had almost solved it. If I was going to take his place, it was right that I should.

If I . . . My God, I thought. Where did thoughts come from? I had no intention of taking his place. No conscious intention. That thought had come straight from the subconscious, unbidden, unwanted.

I shivered slightly and felt vaguely alarmed, and without any smile at all wrote down the frame numbers of the five grey-patterned prints. Then I wandered round the house for a while doing mindless jobs like tidying the bedroom and shaking out the bean bags and stacking a few things in the dishwasher. Made a cup of coffee and sat down in the kitchen to drink it. Considered walking down to the village to fetch a Sunday paper, and instead went compulsively back to the dark-room.

It made all the difference knowing which negatives to look at, and roughly what to look for.

I took the first one numerically, which happened to be number seven, and enlarged it to the full size of the ten-by-eight inch paper. A couple more bad guesses at exposure times left me with unclear dark grey prints, but in the end I came up with one which developed into mid-grey on white; and I took it out of the developer as soon as it had reached its peak of contrast, and stopped it and fixed it and washed it, and carried it out to the daylight in the kitchen.

Although the print was still wet one could see exactly what it was. One could read it without difficulty. A typewritten letter starting 'Dear Mr Morton' and ending 'Yours sincerely, George Millace.'

A letter typed onto white paper with an old greyish ribbon, so that the typing itself looked pale grey. Pale grey, but distinct.

The letter said:

Dear Mr Morton,

I am sure you will be interested in the enclosed two photographs. As you will see, the first one is a picture of your horse Amber Globe running poorly in your colours in the two-thirty race at Southwell on Monday, May 12th.

As you will also see, the second picture is of your horse Amber Globe winning the four o'clock race at Fontwell on Wednesday, August 27th.

If you look closely at the photographs you will see that they are not of the same horse. Alike, but not identical.

I am sure that the Jockey Club would be interested in this difference. I will ring you shortly, however, with an alternative suggestion.

Yours sincerely,
George Millace.

I read it through about six times, not because I didn't take it in the first time, but simply as an interval for assimilation and thought.

There were some practical observations to be made, which were that the letter bore no heading and no date and no hand-written signature. There was an assumption to be drawn that the other four pale grey geometric patterns would also turn out to be letters; and that what I had found was George's idiosyncratic filing system.

Beyond those flat thoughts lay a sort of chaos: a feeling of looking into a pit. If I enlarged and read the other letters I could find that I knew things which would make 'waiting to see what happens' impossible. I might feel, as in the case of the grey-smudge lovers I already did feel, that doing nothing was weak and wrong. If I learned all George's secrets I would have to accept the moral burden of deciding what to do about them . . . and of doing it.

To postpone the decision I went upstairs to the sitting room and looked through the form books to find out in which year Amber Globe had won at Fontwell on August 27th; and it had been four years previously.

I looked up Amber Globe's career from start to finish, and what it amounted to on average was three or four poorer showings followed by an easy win at high odds, this pattern being repeated twice a season for four years. Amber Globe's last win had been the one on August 27th, and from then on he had run in no more races at all.

A supplementary search showed that the trainer of Amber Globe did not appear in the list of trainers for any subsequent years, and had probably gone out of business. There was no way of checking from those particular books whether 'Dear Mr Morton' had subsequently owned or run any more horses, although such facts would be stored in central official racing records.

Dear Mr Morton and his trainer had been running two horses under the name of Amber Globe, switching in the good one for the big gambles, letting the poor one lengthen the odds. I wondered if George had noticed the pattern and gone deliberately to take his photographs; or whether he had taken the photographs merely in the course of work, and then had noticed the difference in the horses. There was no way of knowing or even guessing, as I hadn't found the two photographs in question.

I looked out of the window at the Downs for a while, and wandered round a bit fingering things and doing nothing much, waiting for the arrival of a comfortable certainty that knowledge did not involve responsibility.

I waited in vain. I knew that it did. The knowledge was downstairs, and I would have to acquire it. I had come too far to want to stop.

Unsettled, fearful, but with a feeling of inevitability, I went down to the darkroom and printed the other four negatives one by one, and read the resulting letters in the kitchen.

With all five in the drier I sat for ages staring into space, thinking disjointed thoughts.

George had been busy.

The sly malice of George's mind spoke out as clearly as if I could hear his voice.

George's ominous letters must have induced fear and despondency in colossal proportions.

The second of them said:

Dear Bonnington Ford,

I am sure you will be interested in the enclosed series of photographs, which, as you will see, are a record of you entertaining in your training stables on Sunday afternoons a person who has been 'warned off'. I don't suppose I need to remind you that the racing authorities would object strongly to this continuous association, even to the extent of reviewing your licence to train.

I could of course send copies of these photographs to the Jockey Club. I will ring you shortly, however, with an alternative suggestion.

Yours sincerely,
George Millace.

Bonnington Ford was a third-rate trainer who by general consensus was as honest and trustworthy as a pickpocket at Aintree, and he trained in a hollow in the Downs at a spot where any passing motorist could glance down into his yard. It would have been no trouble at all for George Millace, if he had wanted to, to sit in his car at that spot and take telephoto pictures at his leisure.

Again I hadn't found the photographs in question, so there was nothing I could do about that particular letter, even if I had wanted to. George hadn't even mentioned the name of the disqualified person. I was let off any worrying choice.

The last three letters were a different matter, one in which the dilemma sharply raised its head: where did duty lie, and from how much could one opt out.

Of these three letters the first said:

Dear Elgin Yaxley,

I am sure you will be interested in the enclosed photograph. As you will see, it clearly contradicts a statement you recently made on oath at a certain trial.

I am sure that the Jockey Club would be interested to see it, and also the police, the judge, and the insurance company. I could send all of them copies simultaneously.

I will ring you shortly, however with an alternative suggestion.

Yours sincerely,
George Millace.

The one next to it on the film roll would have driven the nails right in. It said:

Dear Elgin Yaxley,

I am happily able to tell you that since I wrote to you yesterday there have been further developments.

Yesterday I also visited the farmer upon whose farm you boarded your unfortunate steeplechasers, and I showed him in confidence a copy of the photograph, which I sent to you. I suggested that there might be a full further enquiry, during which his own share in the tragedy might be investigated.

He felt able to respond to my promise of silence with the pleasing information that your five good horses were not after all dead. The five horses which died had been bought especially and cheaply by him (your farmer friend) from a local auction, and it was these which were shot by Terence O'Tree at the appointed time and place. Terence O'Tree was not told of the substitution.

Your farmer friend also confirmed that when the veterinary surgeon had given your good horses their anti-tetanus jabs and had left after seeing them in good health, you yourself arrived at the farm in a horsebox to supervise their removal.

Your friend understood you would be shipping them out to the Far East, where you already had a buyer.

I enclose a photograph of his signed statement to this effect.

I will ring you shortly with a suggestion.

Yours sincerely,
George Millace.

The last of the five prints was different from the others in that its letter was handwritten, not typed: but as it had been apparently written in pencil, it was still of the same pale grey.

It said:

Dear Elgin Yaxley,

I bought the five horses that T.O'Tree shot. You fetched your own horses away in a horsebox, to export them to the East. I am satisfied with what you paid me for this service.

Yours faithfully, David Parker.

I thought of Elgin Yaxley as I had seen him the previous day at Ascot, smirking complacently and believing himself safe.

I thought of right and wrong, and justice. Thought of Elgin

Yaxley as the victim of George Millace, and of the insurance company as the victim of Elgin Yaxley. Thought of Terence O'Tree who had gone to jail, and David Parker, who hadn't.

I couldn't decide what to do.

After a while I got up stiffly and went to the darkroom. I put all of the magenta-splashed set of negatives into the contact-printing frame, and made a nearly white print: and this time there were not five little oblongs with grey blocks on, but fifteen.

With a hollow feeling of horror I switched off all the lights, locked the doors, and walked up the road to my briefing with Harold.

'Pay attention,' Harold said sharply.

'Er . . . yes.'

'What's the matter?'

'Nothing.'

'I'm talking about Coral Key and Kempton on Wednesday, and you're not listening.'

I dragged my attention back to the matter in hand.

'Coral Key,' I said. 'For Victor Briggs.'

'That's right.'

'Has he said anything . . . about yesterday?'

Harold shook his head. 'We had a drink after the race, but if Victor doesn't want to talk you can't get a word out of him, and all he uttered were grunts. But until he tells me you're off his horses you're still on them.'

He gave me a glass and a can of coke, and poured a large whisky for himself.

'I haven't much for you this week,' he said. 'Nothing Monday or Tuesday. Pebble was going to run at Leicester but there's some heat in his leg . . . There's just Coral Key on Wednesday, Diamond Buyer and the mare Friday, and two on Saturday, as long as it doesn't rain. Have you any outside rides lined up?'

'A novice 'chaser at Kempton on Thursday.'

'I hope it can bloody jump.'

I went back to the quiet cottage and made prints from the fifteen magenta-splashed negatives, getting plain white and grey results as before, as the blotchy shapes were filtered out along with the blue.

To my relief they were not fifteen threatening letters: only the first two of them finished with the promise of alternative suggestions.

I had expected one on the subject of the lovers, and it was there. It was the second one which left me breathless and weakly laughing in the kitchen: and certainly it put me in a better frame of mind for any revelations to come.

The last thirteen prints, however, turned out to be George's own notes of where and when he had taken his incriminating pictures, and on what film, and at which exposures, and on what dates he had sent the frightening letters. I guessed he had kept his records in this form because it had turned out to be easy for him, and had seemed safer than leaving such damaging material lying legibly around on paper.

As a back up to the photographs and letters they were fascinating: but they all failed to say what the 'alternative suggestions' had been. There was no record of what monies George had extorted, nor of any bank, safe deposit, or hiding place where he could have stashed the proceeds. Even to himself, George on this subject had been reticent.

I went late to bed and couldn't sleep, and in the morning made some telephone calls.

One to the editor of *Horse and Hound*, whom I knew, begging him to include Amanda's picture in that week's issue, emphasising that time was short. He said dubiously that he would print it if I got it to his office that morning, but after that it would be too late.

'I'll be there,' I said. 'Two columns wide, photograph seven centimetres deep, with some wording top and bottom. Say eleven centimetres altogether. On a nice right-hand page near the front where no one can miss it.'

'Philip!' he protested, but then sighed audibly, and I knew he would do it. 'That camera of yours . . . If you've got any racing pics I might use, bring them along. I'll have a look anyway. No promises, mind, but a look. It's people I want, not horses. Portraits. Got any?'

'Well . . . yes.'

'Good. Soon as possible, then. See you.'

I telephoned Marie Millace for Lord White's home number, and then I telephoned Old Driven Snow at his home in the Cotswolds.

'You want to see me?' he said. 'What about?'

'About George Millace, sir.'

'Photographer? Died recently?'

'Yes, sir. His wife is a friend of Lady White.'

'Yes, yes,' he said, impatiently. 'I could see you at Kempton, if you like.'

I asked if I could call on him at his home instead, and although he wasn't overpoweringly keen he agreed to my taking half an hour of his time at five o'clock the next day. With slightly sweating palms I replaced the receiver and said 'Phew' and thought that all I had to do to back out was to ring him again and cancel.

After that I telephoned to Samantha, which was a great deal easier, and asked if I could take her and Clare out to dinner. Her warm voice sounded pleased.

'Tonight?' she said.

'Yes.'

'I can't go. But I'm sure Clare can. She'd like it.'

'Would she?'

'Yes, you silly man. What time?'

I said I would pick her up at about eight, and Samantha said fine and how was the search for Amanda going, and I found myself talking to her as if I'd known her all my life. As indeed, in a way, I had.

I drove to London to the *Horse and Hound* offices and fixed with the editor to print Amanda's picture captioned '*Where is this stable? Ten pounds reward for the first person – and particularly for the first child – who can telephone Philip Nore to tell him.*'

'Child?' said the editor, raising his eyebrows and adding my telephone number. 'Do they read this paper?'

'Their mothers do.'

'Subtle stuff.'

He said, looking through the folder I'd brought of racing faces, that they were starting a series on racing personalities, and he wanted new pictures that hadn't already appeared all over the place, and he could use some of mine, if I liked.

'Er . . . yes.'

'Usual rates,' he said casually, and I said fine: and only after a pause did I ask him what the usual rates were. Even to ask, it seemed to me, was a step nearer to caring as much for the income as for the photographs themselves. Usual rates were a commitment. Usual rates meant joining the club. I found it disturbing. I accepted them, all the same.

Samantha was out when I went to fetch Clare.

'Come in for a drink first,' Clare said, opening the door wide. 'It's such a lousy evening.'

I stepped in out of the wind and cold rain of late November and we went not downstairs to the kitchen but into the long, gently lit ground-floor sitting room, which stretched from the front to the back of the house. I looked around, seeing its comfort, but feeling no familiarity.

'Do you remember this room?' Clare said.

I shook my head.

'Where's the bathroom?' she said.

I answered immediately, 'Up the stairs, turn right, blue ba . . .'

She laughed. 'Straight from the subconscious.'

'It's so odd.'

There was a television set in one corner with a programme of talking heads, and Clare walked over and switched it off.

'Don't, if you're in the middle of watching,' I said.

'It was just another anti-drug lecture. All these pontificating so-called experts. How about that drink? What would you like? There is some wine . . .' She held up a bottle of white Burgundy, opened, so we settled on that.

'Some smug little presenter was saying,' she said, pouring into the glasses, 'That one in five women take tranquillisers, but only one in ten men. Implying that poor little women are so much less able to deal with life, the feeble little dears.' She handed me a glass. 'Makes you laugh.'

'Does it?'

She grinned. 'I suppose it never occurs to the doctors who write out the prescriptions that the poor feeble little women sprinkle those tranquillisers all over their husbands' dinner when he comes home from work.'

I laughed.

'They do,' she said. 'The ones with great hulking bastards who knock them about, and the ones who don't like too much sex . . . they mix the nice tasteless powder into the brute's meat and two veg, and lead a quiet life.'

'It's a great theory.'

'Fact,' she said.

We sat in a couple of pale velvet armchairs sipping the cool wine, she, in a scarlet silk shirt and black trousers, making a bright statement against the soft colouring of the room. A girl given to positive statements. A girl of decision and certainty and mental energy. Not at all like the gentle undemanding girls I occasionally took home.

'I saw you racing on Saturday,' she said. 'On television.'

'I didn't think you were interested.'

'Of course I am, since I saw your photos.' She drank a mouthful. 'You do take some frightful risks.'

'Not always like Saturday.' She asked why not, and rather to my surprise, I told her.

'But my goodness,' she said indignantly, 'that's not fair.'

'Life's not fair. Too bad.'

'What a gloomy philósophy.'

'Not really. Take what comes, but hope for the best.'

She shook her head. 'Go out looking for the best.' She drank and said, 'What happens if you're really smashed up by one of those falls?'

'You curse.'

'No, you fool. To your life, I mean.'

'Mend as fast as possible and get back in the saddle. While you're out of it, some other jockey is pinching your rides.'

'Charming,' she said. 'And what if it's too bad to mend?'

'You've got a problem. No rides, no income. You start looking at "sits vac".'

'And what happens if you're killed?'

'Nothing much,' I said.

'You don't take it seriously,' she complained.

'Of course not.'

She studied my face. 'I'm not used to people who casually risk their lives most days of the week.'

I smiled at her. 'The risk is less than you'd think. But if you're really unlucky, there's always the Injured Jockeys' Fund.'

'What's that?'

'The racing industry's private charity. It looks after the widows and orphans of dead jockeys and gives succour to badly damaged live ones, and makes sure no one pops off in old age for want of a lump of coal.'

'Can't be bad.'

We went out a little later and ate in a small restaurant determinedly decorated as a French peasant kitchen with scrubbed board tables, rushes on the floor, and dripping candles stuck in wine bottles. The food turned out to be as bogus as the surroundings, never having seen the light of anyone's *pot au feu*. Clare however seemed not to mind and we ate microwaved veal in a blanket white sauce, trying not to remember the blanquettes in France, where she too had been frequently, though for holidays, not racing.

'You race in France?'

'After Christmas, if it freezes here, there's always the chance of some rides at Cagnes sur Mer . . . down on the south coast.'

'It sounds marvellous.'

'It's still winter. And still work. But yes, not bad.'

She returned to the subject of photographs, and said she would like to come down to Lambourn again to go through the Jockey's Life file.

'Don't worry if you want to change your mind,' I said.

'Of course I don't.' She looked at me in seeming alarm. 'You haven't sold any to anyone else, have you? You did say you wouldn't.'

'Not those.'

'What, then?'

I told her about *Horse and Hound*, and about Lance Kinship, and how odd I found it that all of a sudden people seemed to be wanting to buy my work.

'I would think,' she said judiciously, 'that the word has gone round.' She finished her veal and sat back, her face serious with thought. 'What you need is an agent.'

I explained about having to find one for Marie Millace anyway, but she brushed that aside.

'Not *any* agent,' she said. 'I mean me.'

She looked at my stunned expression and smiled. 'Well?' she said. 'What does any agent do? He knows the markets and sells the goods. Your goods will sell . . . obviously. So I'll learn pretty damn quick what the markets are, that I don't know already. The sports side of it, I mean. And what if I got you commissions for illustrations for other books . . . on any subject . . . would you do them?'

'Yes, but . . .'

'No buts,' she said. 'There's no point in taking super pics if no one sees them.'

'But there are thousands of photographers.'

'Why are you so defeatist?' she said. 'There's always room for one more.'

The candlelight shone on the intent expression and lay in apricot shadows under cheekbone and skin. Her grey eyes looked steadily at a future I still shied away from. I wondered what she'd say if I said I wanted to kiss her, when her thoughts were clearly more practical.

'I could try,' she said, persuasively. 'I'd like to try. Will you let me? If I'm no good, I'll admit it.'

She'll bully you into things, Samantha had said.

Take what comes, and hope for the best.

I stuck to my old philosophy and said, 'All right,' and she said 'Great' as if she meant it: and later, when I delivered her to her doorstep and kissed her, she didn't object to that either.

FOURTEEN:

Four times on Tuesday morning I lifted the telephone to cancel my appointment with Lord White. Once I got as far as hearing the bell ring at the other end.

Four times I put the receiver down and decided I would have to go. I would have liked to have gone with more certainty that I was doing right; but anyway, I went.

Lord White's house in Gloucestershire turned out to be a weathered stone pile with more grandeur than gardeners. Noble windows raised their eyebrows above drifts of unswept leaves. A stubble of fawn stalks indicated lawn. A mat of dead weeds glued the gravel together. I rang the front doorbell and wondered about the economics of barony.

The third Baron White received me in a small sitting room which gave onto a view of straggly rosebushes and an unclipped hedge. Inside, everything was of venerable antiquity, dusted and gleaming. Holes in the chintz chair covers had been patched. Less money than was needed, I diagnosed briefly, but still enough to keep at bay a three-bedroomed semi.

Lord White shook hands and offered me a chair in a mixture of puzzlement and civility, waiting for me to say why I had come: and although I'd spent the whole journey inventing possible openings, I found it an agony to begin.

'Sir . . . I said. 'I'm sorry . . . very sorry, sir . . . but I'm afraid what I've come about may be a great shock to you.'

He frowned slightly. 'About George Millace?' he said. 'You said it was something about George Millace.'

'Yes . . . about some photographs he took.'

I stopped. Too late, I wished fervently that I hadn't come. I should after all have adhered to the lifetime habit of non-involvement, of wait and see. I should never have set out to use George's wicked arsenal. But I had. I was there. I had made the decision and acted on it. What I was there for . . . had to be done.

My errand was to give pain. Purposely to hurt. To go against all the instincts of compassion I owed to Samantha and Charlie and Margaret and Bill. To serve as a wrecker, with a brutal celuloid axe.

'Get on with it, Nore,' Lord White said comfortably, unsuspecting.

With foreboding I opened the large envelope I carried. I pulled out the first of the three pictures of the lovers, and put it into his outstretched hand: and for all that I thought he was behaving foolishly over Dana den Relgan, I felt deeply sorry for him.

His first reaction was of extreme anger. How dared I, he said, standing up and quivering, how dared I bring him anything so filthy and *disgusting*.

With the greatest difficulty, I thought; but he wouldn't have appreciated it. I took the second and third photographs out of the envelope and rested them picture-side-down on the arm of my chair.

'As you will see,' I said, and my voice was hoarse, 'The others are if anything worse.'

I reckoned it took him a lot of courage to pick up the other two pictures. He looked at them in desperate silence, and slowly sank down again in his chair.

His face told of his anguish. Of his disbelief. Of his horror.

The man making love to Dana was Ivor den Relgan.

'They say,' Lord White said, 'that they can fake pictures of anything.' His voice shook. 'Cameras do lie.'

'Not this one,' I said regretfully.

'It can't be true.'

I took from the envelope a print of the letter George Millace had written, and gave it to him. He had difficulty in bringing himself to read it, so physically shaking was his distress.

The letter, which I knew by heart, read:

Dear Ivor den Relgan,

I am sure you will be interested in the enclosed photographs, which I was happily able to take a few days ago in St Tropez.

As you will see, they show you in a compromising position with the young lady who is known as your daughter. (It is surely unwise to do this sort of thing on hotel balconies without making sure that one cannot be seen by telephoto lenses?)

There seem to be two possibilities here.

One. Dana den Relgan IS your daughter, in which case this is incest.

Two. Dana den Relgan is NOT your daughter, in which case why are you pretending she is? Can it have anything to do with the ensnaring of a certain member of the Jockey Club? Are you hoping for entry to the Club, and other favours?

I could of course send these photographs to the Lord in question. I will ring you shortly, however, with an alternative suggestion.

Yours sincerely,
George Millace.

Lord White became much older before my eyes, the glow that loving had given him shrinking greyly back into deepening wrinkles. I looked away. Looked at my hands, my feet, the spindly rose-bushes outside. Anywhere but at that devastated man.

After a very long time he said, 'Where did you get these?'

'George Millace's son gave me a box with some things of his father's in, after his father died. These photos were in it.'

He suffered through another silence, and said, 'Why did you bring them to me? For the sake of causing me . . . mortification?'

I swallowed and said as flatly as possible, 'You won't really have noticed, sir, but people are worried about how much power has been given recently to Ivor den Relgan.'

He shuddered slightly at the name but raised the blue eyes to give me a long unfriendly inspection.

'And you have taken it upon yourself to try to stop it?'

'Sir . . . yes.'

He looked grim, and as if seeking refuge in anger he said authoritatively, 'It's none of your business, Nore.'

I didn't answer at once. I'd had enough trouble in persuading myself that it *was* my business to last a lifetime. But in the end, diffidently, I said, 'Sir, if you are certain in your own mind that Ivor den Relgan's sudden rise to unheard-of-power is nothing whatever to do with your affection for Dana den Relgan, then I do most abjectly beg your pardon.'

He merely stared.

I tried again. 'If you truly believe that racing would benefit by Ivor den Relgan appointing paid Stewards, I apologise.'

'Please leave,' he said rigidly.

'Yes, sir.'

I stood up and walked over to the door, but when I reached it I heard his voice from behind me.

'Wait. Nore . . . I must think.'

I turned, hovering. 'Sir,' I said, 'You're so respected . . . and liked . . . by everyone. It's been no fun to watch what's been happening.'

'Will you please come back and sit down?' His voice was still stern, still full of accusation and judgment. Still full of defence.

I returned to the armchair, and he went and stood by the window with his back to me, looking out at the dead roses.

His thoughts took time. So would mine have done, in the same situation. The result of them was a deep change in his voice in both pitch and content, for when he finally spoke again he sounded not shattered nor furious, but normal. He spoke, however, without turning round.

'How many people,' he said, 'have seen these pictures?'

'I don't know how many George Millace showed them to,' I said. 'As for me, they've been seen only by one friend. He was with me when I found them. But he doesn't know the den Relgans. He doesn't often go racing.'

'So you didn't consult with anyone before you came here?'

'No, sir.'

Another long pause. I was good, anyway, at waiting. The house around us was very quiet: holding its breath, I thought fancifully, as I, in a way, held mine.

'Do you intend,' he said quietly, 'to make jokes about this on the racecourse?'

'No.' I was horrified. 'I do not.'

'And would you . . .' he paused, but went on, 'would you expect any reward, in service . . . or cash . . . for this silence?'

I stood up as if he had actually hit me, not delivered his thrust from six paces with his back turned.

'I would not,' I said. 'I'm not George Millace. I think . . . I think I'll go now.' And go I did, out of the room, out of the house, out of his weedy domain, impelled by a severe hurt to the vanity.

On Wednesday nothing much happened; less, in fact, than expected, as I was met when I went to ride out first lot with the news that Coral Key wouldn't be running that day at Kempton after all.

'Bloody animal got cast in its box during the night,' Harold said. 'I woke and heard him banging. God knows how long he'd been down; he was halfway exhausted. It won't please Victor.'

With the riding fee down the drain it wasn't worthwhile spending money on petrol to go spectating at the races, so I stayed at home and did Lance Kinship's reprints.

Thursday I set off to Kempton with only one ride, thinking it was a very thin week on the earning front; but almost as soon as I'd stepped through the gate I was grabbed by a fierce little man who said his guv'nor was looking for me, and if I wanted his spare rides I should shift my arse.

I shifted, and got the rides just before the trainer in question thought I wouldn't get there in time and gave them to someone else.

'Very annoying,' he said, puffing as if breathless, though I gathered he had been standing still waiting for me for fifteen minutes. 'My fellow said yesterday he'd no ill effects from a fall he'd had. And then this morning, cool as you please, he rings to say he's got 'flu.'

'Well . . . er . . .' I swallowed a laugh. 'I don't suppose he can help it.'

'Damned inconsiderate.'

His horses turned out to have better lungs than their master, but were otherwise no great shakes. I got one of them round into third place in a field of six, and came down on the other two fences from home; a bit of a crash but nothing broken in either him or me.

The third horse, the one I'd gone originally to ride, wasn't much better: a clumsy underschooled baby of a horse with guts about equal to his skill. I took him round carefully in the novice 'chase to try to teach him his job, and got no thanks from the trainer who said I hadn't gone fast enough to keep him warm.

'There were six or seven behind us,' I said mildly.

'And six or seven in front.'

I nodded. 'He needs time.' And patience, and weeks and months of jumping practice. He probably wouldn't get either, and I probably wouldn't be offered the mount again. The trainer would go for speed regardless, and the horse would crash at the open ditch, and it would serve the trainer right. Pity the poor horse.

The relief of the afternoon, as far as I was concerned, was the absence of Lord White.

The surprise of the afternoon was the presence of Clare.

She was waiting outside the weighing room when I'd changed back into street clothes and was leaving for home.

'Hullo,' she said.

'Clare!'

'Just thought I'd come and take a look at the real thing.' Her eyes smiled. 'Is today typical?'

I looked at the grey windy sky and the thin Thursday crowd, and thought of my three nondescript races.

'Pretty much,' I said. 'How did you get here?'

'By race-train. Very educational. And I've been walking around all afternoon all a-goggle. I never knew people actually *ate* jellied eels.'

I laughed. 'I've never looked one in the face. Er . . . what would you like? A drink? A cup of tea? A trip to Lambourn?'

She thought it over briefly. 'Lambourn,' she said. 'I can get a train back from there, can't I.'

I drove her to Berkshire with an unaccustomed feeling of contentment. It felt right to have her sitting there in the car. Natural. Probably, I thought, rationalising, because she was Samantha's daughter.

The cottage was dark and cold, but soon warmed. I went round switching on lights and heat and the kettle for tea; and the telephone rang. I answered it in the kitchen, which was where it happened to be plugged in, and had my ear-drum half-shattered by a piercing voice which shrieked, 'Am I first?'

'Um,' I said, wincing and holding the receiver away from my ear. 'Are you first what?'

'First!' A very young voice. A child. Female. 'I've been ringing every five minutes for *hours*. Honestly. So am I first? Do say I'm first.'

Realisation dawned. 'Yes,' I said. 'You're the first. Have you been reading *Horse and Hound*? It isn't published until tomorrow . . .'

'It gets to my auntie's bookshop on Thursdays.' She sounded as if anyone in their right mind would know things like that. 'I collect it for Mummy on my way home from school. And she saw the picture, and told me to ring you. So can I have the ten pounds? Can I really?'

'If you know where the stable is, yes, of course.'

'Mummy knows. She'll tell you. You'd better talk to her now, but you won't forget, will you?'

'I won't,' I said.

There were some background voices and clicks of the

receiver at the far end, and then a woman's voice, pleasant and far less excited.

'Are you the Philip Nore who rides in National Hunt races?'

'Yes,' I said.

It seemed to be enough of a reference, because she said without reservation, 'I do know where that stable is, but I'm afraid you'll be disappointed, because it isn't used for horses any longer. Jane, my daughter, is afraid you won't send her the ten pounds when you know that, but I expect you will.'

'I expect so,' I agreed, smiling. 'Where is it?'

'Not far from here. That's Horley, in Surrey. Near Gatwick Airport. The stable's about half a mile from our house. It's still called Zephyr Farm Stables, but the riding school has been closed for years and years.'

I sighed. 'And the people who kept it?'

'No idea,' she said. 'I suppose they sold it. Anyway, it's been adapted into living quarters. Do you want the actual address?'

'I guess so,' I said, 'and yours, too, please.'

She read them out to me and I wrote them down, and then I said, 'Do you happen to know the name of the people living there now?'

'Huh,' she said scornfully. 'They're a real pest. You won't get far with them, whatever it is you want, I'm afraid. They've got the place practically fortified to ward off furious parents.'

'To . . . what?' I said, mystified.

'Parents trying to persuade their children to come home. It's one of those commune things. Religious brainwashing, something like that. They call themselves Colleagues of Supreme Grace. All nonsense. Pernicious nonsense.'

I felt breathless.

'I'll send Jane the money,' I said. 'And thanks very much.'

'What is it?' Clare said, as I slowly replaced the receiver.

'The first real lead to Amanda.'

I explained about the *Horse and Hound* advertisement, and about the tenants of Pine Woods Lodge.

Clare shook her head. 'If these Supreme Grace people know where Amanda is, they won't tell you. You must have heard of them, haven't you? Or others like them? They're all gentle and smiling on the surface, and like steel rat-traps underneath. They lure people my age with friendliness and sweet songs and hook them into Believing, and once they're in the poor slobs never get out. They're in love with their prison. Their parents hardly stand a chance.'

'I've heard of something like it. But I've never seen the point.'

'Money,' Clare said crisply. 'All the darling little Colleagues go out with saintly faces and collecting boxes, and rake in the lolly.'

'To live on?'

'Sure, to live on. And to further the cause, or in other words, to line the pockets of our great leader.'

I made the tea and we sat by the table to drink it.

Amanda in a stable-yard at Horley; Caroline twenty miles away at Pine Woods Lodge. Colleagues of Supreme Grace at Pine Woods Lodge, Colleagues ditto at Horley. Too close a connection to be a coincidence. Even if I never found out precisely what, there had been a rational sequence of events.

'She's probably not still there,' I said.

'But you'll go looking?'

I nodded. 'Tomorrow, I think, after racing.'

When we'd finished the tea Clare said she wanted to see the Jockey's Life folder again, so we took it upstairs, and I showed some of the pictures blown up on the wall to amuse her, and we talked of her life and mine and of nothing in particular; and later in the evening we went to the good pub at Ashbury for a steak.

'A great day,' Clare said, smiling over the coffee. 'Where's the train?'

'Swindon. I'll drive you there . . . or you could stay.'

She regarded me levelly. 'Is that the sort of invitation I think it is?'

'I wouldn't be surprised.'

She looked down and fiddled with her coffee spoon, paying it a lot of attention. I watched the bent, dark, thinking head and knew that if it took her so long to answer, she would go.

'There's a fast train at ten thirty,' I said. 'You could catch it comfortably. Just over an hour to Paddington.'

'Philip . . .'

'It's all right,' I said easily. 'If one never asks, one never gets.' I paid the bill. 'Come on.'

She was distinctly quiet on the six-mile drive to the railway station, and she didn't share her thoughts. Not until I'd bought her a ticket (against her objections) and was waiting with her up on the platform did she give any indication of what was in her mind, and then only obliquely.

'There's a Board meeting in the office tomorrow,' she said.

'It will be the first I've been to. They made me a Director a month ago, at the last one.'

I was most impressed, and said so. It couldn't be often that publishing houses put girls of twenty-two on the Board. I understood, also, why she wouldn't stay. Why she might never stay. The regret I felt shocked me with its sudden intensity, because my invitation to her hadn't been a desperate plea but only a suggestion for a passing pleasure. I had meant it as a small thing, not a lifetime commitment. My sense of loss, on that railway platform, seemed out of all proportion.

The train came in and she climbed aboard, pausing with the door open to exchange kisses. Brief unpassionate kisses, no advance from Monday on the doorstep.

See you soon, she said, and I said yes. About contracts, she said. A lot to discuss.

'Come on Sunday,' I said.

'Let you know. Goodbye.'

'Goodbye.'

The impatient train ground away, accelerating fast, and I drove home to the empty cottage with a most unaccustomed feeling of loneliness.

Newbury races, Friday, late November.

Lord White was there, standing under the expanse of glass roof outside the weighing room, talking earnestly to two fellow Stewards. He looked the same as always, grey-white hair mostly hidden by trilby, brown covert coat over dark grey suit, air of benign good sense. Hard to imagine him high as a kite on love. Impossible, if one hadn't seen it.

As always in those areas I had to pass near him to reach the weighing-room door. He steadfastly continued his conversation with the Stewards, and only through the barest flicker of his eyes in my direction did he show he knew I was there.

If he didn't want to talk to me, I didn't mind. Less embarrassing all round.

Inside the weighing room stood Harold, expansively telling a crony about a good place for cut-price new tyres. Hardly pausing for breath he told me he'd wait for my saddle if I'd do him a favour and change and weigh quickly, and when I went back to him in colours he was still on about cross-ply and radials. The crony took the opportunity to depart, and Harold, taking my saddle and weightcloth, said with mischievous amusement, 'Did you hear that Ghengis Khan got the boot?'

I paid him sharp attention.

'Are you sure?' I said.

Harold nodded. 'Old Lanky . . .' he pointed to the disappearing crony, '. . . was telling me just before you arrived. He says they held an emergency-type meeting of the Jockey Club this morning in London. He was at it. Lord White asked them to cancel plans for a committee chaired by Ivor den Relgan, and as it was old Driven Snow's idea in the first place, they all agreed.'

'It's something, anyway,' I said.

'Something?' Harold swung towards exasperation, 'Is that all you think? It's the best about-turn since the Armada.'

He stalked off with my saddle, muttering and shaking his head, and leaving me, had he but known it, in a state of extreme relief. Whatever else my visit to Lord White had done, it had achieved its primary object. At least, I thought gratefully, I hadn't caused so much havoc in a man I liked for nothing at all.

I rode a novice hurdler which finished second, pleasing the owner mightily and Harold not much, and later a two-mile 'chase on a sensitive mare who had no real heart for the job and had to be nursed. Getting her round at all was the best to be hoped for, a successful conclusion greeted by Harold with a grunt. As we had also finished fourth I took it for a grunt of approval, but one could never be sure.

When I was changing back into street clothes a racecourse official stepped into the big bustling jockeys' room and shouted down the length of it, 'Nore, you're wanted.'

I finished dressing and went out into the weighing room, and found that the person who was waiting was Lord White.

'I want to talk to you,' he said. 'Come over here into the Stewards' room . . . and close the door, will you?'

I followed him into the room off the weighing room used by the Stewards for on-the-spot enquiries, and, as he asked, shut the door. He stood behind one of the chairs which surrounded the big table, grasping its back with both hands as if it gave him a shield, a barrier, the rampart of a citadel.

'I regret,' he said formally, 'What I imputed to you on Tuesday.'

'It's all right, sir.'

'I was upset . . . but it was indefensible.'

'I do understand, sir.'

'What do you understand?'

'Well . . . that when someone hurts you, you want to kick them.'

He half smiled. 'Poetically put, if I may say so.'

'Is that all, sir?'

'No, it isn't.' He paused, pondering. 'I suppose you've heard that the committee is cancelled?'

I nodded.

He drew a sober breath. 'I want to request den Relgan's resignation from the Jockey Club. The better to persuade him, I am of a mind to show him those photographs, which of course he has seen already. I think, however, that I need your permission to do so, and that is what I am asking.'

Talk about leverage, I thought; and I said, 'I've no objection. Please do what you like with them.'

'Are they . . . the only copies?'

'Yes,' I said, which in fact they were. I didn't tell him I also had the negatives. He would have wanted me to destroy them, and my instincts were against it.

He let go of the chair back as if no longer needing it, and walked round me to the door. His face, as he opened it, bore the firm familiar blameless expression of pre-Dana days. The cruel cure, I thought, had been complete.

'I can't exactly thank you,' he said civilly, 'but I'm in your debt.' He gave me a slight nod and went out of the room: transaction accomplished, apology given, dignity intact. He would soon be busy persuading himself, I thought, that he hadn't felt what he'd felt, that his infatuation hadn't existed.

Slowly I followed, satisfied on many counts, on many levels, but not knowing if he knew it. The profoundest gifts weren't always those explicitly given.

From Marie Millace I learned more.

She had come to Newbury to see Steve ride now that his collarbone had mended, though she confessed, as I steered her off for a cup of coffee, that watching one's son race over fences was an agony.

'All jockeys' wives say it's worse when their sons start,' I said. 'Daughters too, I dare say.'

We sat at a small table in one of the bars, surrounded by people in bulky overcoats which smelled of cold damp air and seemed to steam slightly in the warmth. Marie automatically stacked to one side the debris of cups and sandwich wrappers left by the last customers, and thoughtfully stirred her coffee.

'You're looking better,' I said.

She nodded. 'I feel it.'

She had been to a hairdresser, I saw, and had bought some more clothes. Still pale, with smudged grieving eyes. Still fragile, thin-shelled, inclined to sound shaky, tears under control but not far. Four weeks away from George's death.

She sipped the hot coffee and said, 'You can forget what I told you last week about the Whites and Dana den Relgan.'

'Can I?'

She nodded. 'Wendy's here. We had coffee earlier on. She's very much happier.'

'Tell me about it,' I said.

'Are you interested? I'm not prattling on?'

'Very interested,' I assured her.

'She said that last Tuesday, sometime on Tuesday, her husband found out something he didn't like about Dana den Relgan. She doesn't know what. He didn't tell her. But she said he was like a zombie all evening, white and staring and not hearing a word that was said to him. She didn't know what was the matter, not then, and she was quite frightened. He locked himself away alone all Wednesday, but in the evening he told her his affair with Dana was over, and that he'd been a fool, and would she forgive him.'

I listened, amazed that women so easily relayed that sort of gossip, and pleased they did.

'And after that?' I said.

'Aren't men extraordinary?' Marie Millace said. 'After that he began to behave as if the whole thing had never happened. Wendy says that now he has confessed and apologised, he expects her to go on as before, as if he'd never gone off and slept with the wretched girl.'

'And will she?'

'Oh, I expect so. Wendy says his trouble was the common one among men or fifty or so, wanting to prove to themselves they're still young. She understands him, you see.'

'So do you,' I said.

She smiled with sweetness. 'Goodness, yes. You see it all the time.'

When we'd finished the coffee I gave her a short list of agents that she might try, and said I'd give any help I could. After that I told her I'd brought a present for her. I had been going to give it to her, but as she was there herself, she could have it: it was in my bag in the changing room.

I fetched out and handed to her a ten-by-eight inch cardboard envelope which said 'Photographs. Do not Bend' along its borders.

'Don't open it until you're alone,' I said.

'I *must*,' she said, and opened it there and then.

It contained a photograph I'd taken once of George. George holding his camera, looking toward me, smiling his familiar sardonic smile. George in colour. George in a typically George-like pose, one leg forward with his weight back on the other one, head back, considering the world a bad joke. George as he'd lived.

There and then in full public view Marie Millace flung her arms round me and hugged me as if she would never let go, and I could feel her tears trickling down my neck.

FIFTEEN:

Zephyr Farm Stables was indeed fortified like a stockade, surrounded by a seven-foot high stout wooden fence and guarded by a gate that would have done credit to Alcatraz. I sat lazily in my car across the street from it, waiting for it to open.

I waited while the cold gradually seeped through my anorak and numbed my hands and feet. Waited while a few intrepid pedestrians hurried along the narrow path beside the fence without giving the gate a glance. Waited in the semi-suburban street on the outskirts of Horley, where the street lamps faltered to a stop and darkness lay beyond.

No one went in or out of the gate. It stayed obstinately shut, secretive and unfriendly, and after two fruitless hours I abandoned the chilly vigil and booked in to a local motel.

Enquiries brought a sour response. Yes, the receptionist said, they did sometimes have people staying there who were hoping to persuade their sons and daughters to come home from Zephyr Farm Stables. Hardly any of them ever managed it, because they were never allowed to see their children alone, if at all. Proper scandal, said the receptionist: and the law can't do a blind thing about it. All over eighteen, they are, see? Old enough to know their own minds. Phooey.

'I just want to find out if someone's there,' I said.

She shook her head and said I didn't have a chance.

I spent the evening drifting around hotels and pubs talking about the Colleagues to a succession of locals propping up the bars. The general opinion was the same as the receptionist's: anything or anyone I wanted from Zephyr Farm Stables, I wouldn't get.

'Do they ever come out?' I asked. 'To go shopping, perhaps?'

Amid a reaction of rueful and sneering smiles I was told that yes indeed the Colleagues did emerge, always in groups, and always collecting money.

'They'll sell you things,' one man said. 'Try to sell you bits o' polished stone and such. Just beggin' really. For the cause, they say. For the love of God. Bunk, I say. I tell 'em to be off to church, and they don't like that, I'll tell ye.'

'Ever so strict, they are,' a barmaid said. 'No smokes, no drinks, no sex. Can't see what the nitwits see in it, myself.'

'They don't do no harm,' someone said. 'Always smiling and that.'

Would they be out collecting in the morning, I asked. And if so, where?

'In the summer they hang about the airport all the time, scrounging from people going on holiday and sometimes picking someone up for themselves . . . recruits, like . . . but your best bet would be in the centre of town. Right here. Saturday . . . they're sure to be here. Sure to be.'

I thanked them all, and slept, and in the morning parked as near to the centre as possible and wandered about on foot.

By ten o'clock the town was bustling with its morning trade, and I'd worked out that I would have to leave by eleven-thirty at the latest to get back to Newbury, and even that was cutting it a bit fine. The first race was at twelve-thirty because of the short winter days, and although I wasn't riding in the first two, I had to be there an hour before the third, or Harold would be dancing mad.

I saw no groups of collecting Colleagues. No groups at all. No chanting people with shaven heads and bells, or anything like that. All that happened was that a smiling girl touched my arm and asked if I would like to buy a pretty paperweight.

The stone lay on the palm of her hand, wedge-shaped, greeny-brown, and polished.

'Yes,' I said. 'How much?'

'It's for charity,' she said. 'As much as you like.' She produced in her other hand a wooden box with a slit in the top but with no names of charities advertised on its sides.

'What charity?' I asked pleasantly, fishing for my wallet.

'Lots of causes,' she said.

I sorted out a pound note, folded it, and pushed it through the slit.

'Are there many of you collecting?' I asked.

She turned her head involuntarily sideways, and I saw from the direction of her eyes that there was another girl offering a stone to someone waiting at a bus stop, and on the other side of the road, another. All pretty girls in ordinary clothes, smiling.

'What's your name?' I asked.

She broadened the smile as if that were answer enough, and

gave me the stone. 'Thank you very much,' she said. 'Your gift will do so much good.'

I watched her move on down the street, pulling another stone from a pocket in her swirling skirt and accosting a kind-looking old lady. She was too old to be Amanda, I thought, though it wasn't always easy to tell. Especially not, I saw a minute later as I stood in the path of another stone-seller, in view of the other-worldly air of saintliness they wore like badges.

'Would you like to buy a paperweight?'

'Yes,' I said: and we went through the routine again.

'What's your name?' I asked.

'Susan,' she said. 'What's yours?'

I in my turn gave her the smile and shake of the head, and moved on.

In half an hour I bought four paperweights. To the fourth girl I said, 'Is Amanda out here this morning?'

'Amanda? We haven't got a . . .' She stopped, and her eyes, too, went on a giveaway trek.

'Never mind,' I said, pretending not to see. 'Thanks for the stone.'

She smiled the bright empty smile and moved on, and I waited a short while until I could decently drift in front of the girl she'd looked at.

She was young, short, smooth faced, curiously blank about the eyes, and dressed in an anorak and swirling skirt. Her hair was medium brown, like mine, but straight, not slightly curling, and there was no resemblance that I could see between our faces. She might or she might not be my mother's child.

The stone she held out to me was dark blue with black flecks, the size of a plum.

'Very pretty,' I said. 'How much?'

I got the stock reply, and gave her a pound.

'Amanda,' I said.

She jumped. She looked at me doubtfully. 'My name's not Amanda.'

'What then?'

'Mandy.'

'Mandy what?'

'Mandy North.'

I breathed very slowly, so as not to alarm her, and smiled, and asked her how long she had lived at Zephyr Farm Stables.

'All my life,' she said limpidly.

'With your friends?'

She nodded. 'They're my guardians.'

'And you're happy?'

'Yes, of course. We do God's work.'

'How old are you?'

Her doubts returned. 'Eighteen . . . yesterday . . . but I'm not supposed to talk about myself . . . only about the stones.'

The childlike quality was very marked. She seemed not exactly to be mentally retarded, but in the old sense, simple. There was no life in her, no fun, no awakening of womanhood. Beside the average clued-up teenager she was like a sleepwalker who had never known day.

'Have you any more stones then?' I asked.

She nodded and produced another one from her skirt. I admired it and agreed to buy it, and said while picking out another note, 'What was your mother's name, Mandy?'

She looked scared. 'I don't know. You mustn't ask things like that.'

'When you were little did you have a pony?'

For an instant her blank eyes lit with an uncrushable memory, and then she glanced at someone over my left shoulder, and her simple pleasure turned to red-faced shame.

I half turned. A man stood there; not young, not smiling. A tough looking man a few years older than myself, very clean, very neatly dressed, and very annoyed.

'No conversations, Mandy,' he said to her severely. 'Remember the rule. Your first day out collecting, and you break the rule. The girls will take you home now. You'll be back on housework, after this. Go along, they're waiting over there.' He nodded sharply to where a group of girls waited together, and watched as she walked leaden-footed to join them. Poor Mandy in disgrace. Poor Amanda. Poor little sister.

'What's your game?' the man said to me. 'The girls say you've bought stones from all of them. What are you after?'

'Nothing,' I said. 'They're pretty stones.'

He glared at me doubtfully, and he was joined by another similar man who walked across after talking to the now departing girls.

'This guy was asking the girls their names,' he said. 'Looking for Amanda.'

'There's no Amanda.'

'Mandy. He talked to her.'

They both looked at me with narrowed eyes, and I decided it was time to leave. They didn't try to stop me when I headed off in the general direction of the car park. They didn't try to stop me, but they followed along in my wake.

I didn't think much about it, and turned into the short side road which led to the park. Glancing back to see if they were still following I found not only that they were, but there were now four of them. The two new ones were young, like the girls.

It seemed too public a place for much to happen: and I suppose by many standards nothing much did. There was for instance no blood.

There were three more of them loitering around the car park entrance, and all seven of them encircled me outside, before I got there. I pushed one of them to get him out of the way, and got shoved in return by a forest of hands. Shoved sideways along the road a few steps and against a brick wall. If any of the Great British Public saw what was happening, they passed by on the other side.

I stood looking at the seven Colleagues. 'What do you want?' I said.

The second of the two older men said, 'Why were you asking for Mandy?'

'She's my sister.'

It confounded the two elders. They looked at each other. Then the first one decisively shook his head. 'She's got no family. Her mother died years ago. You're lying. How could you possibly think she's your sister?'

'We don't want you nosing round, making trouble,' the second one said. 'If you ask me, he's a reporter.'

The word stung them all into reconciling violence with their strange religion. They banged me against the wall a shade too often, and also pushed and kicked a shade too hard, but apart from trying to shove all seven away like a rugger scrum there wasn't a great deal I could physically do to stop them. It was one of those stupid sorts of scuffles in which no one wanted to go too far. They could have half-killed me easily if they'd meant to, and I could have hurt them more than I did. Escalation seemed a crazy risk when all they were truly delivering was a warning off, so I pushed against their close bodies and hacked at a couple of shins, and that was that.

I didn't tell them the one thing which would have saved me the drubbing: that if they could prove that Mandy was indeed my sister she would inherit a fortune.

Harold watched my arrival outside the weighing room with a scowl of disfavour.

'You're bloody late,' he said. 'And why are you limping?'

'Twisted my ankle.'

'Are you fit to ride?'

'Yes.'

'Huh.'

'Is Victor Briggs here?' I said.

'No, he isn't. You can stop worrying. Sharpener's out to win, and you can ride him in your usual way. None of those crazy damn-fool heroics. Understood? You look after Sharpener or I'll belt the hide off you. Bring him back whole.'

I nodded, smothering a smile, and he gave me another extensive scowl and walked off.

'Honestly, Philip,' said Steve Millace, wandering past. 'He treats you like dirt.'

'No . . . just his way.'

'I wouldn't stand for it.'

I looked at the easy belligerence in the over-young face and realised that he didn't really know about affection coming sometimes in a rough package.

'Good luck, today,' I said neutrally, and he said 'Thanks,' and went on into the weighing room. He would never be like his father, I thought. Never as bright, as ingenious, as perceptive, as ruthless, or as wicked.

I followed Steve inside and changed into Victor Briggs's colours, feeling the effects of the Colleagues attentions as an overall ache. Nothing much. A nuisance. Not enough, I hoped, to make any difference to my riding.

When I went outside the nearest conversation was going on loudly between Elgin Yaxley and Bart Underfield, who were slapping each other on the shoulder and looking the faintest bit drunk. Elgin Yaxley peeled off and rolled away, and Bart, turning with an extravagant lack of coordination, bumped into me.

'Hullo,' he said, giving a spirits-laden cough, 'You'll be the first to know. Elgin's getting some more horses. They're coming to me, of course. We'll make Lambourn sit up. Make the whole of racing sit up.' He gave me a patronising leer. 'Elgin's a man of ideas.'

'He is indeed,' I said dryly.

Bart remembered he didn't much like me and took his good news off to other, more receptive ears. I stood watching him, thinking that Elgin Yaxley would never kill another horse for the insurance. No insurance company would stand for it twice. But Elgin Yaxley believed himself undetected . . . and people didn't change. If their minds ran to fraud once, they would do again. I didn't like the sound of Elgin Yaxley having ideas.

The old dilemma still remained. If I gave the proof of Elgin Yaxley's fraud to the police or the insurance company, I would have to say how I came by the photograph. From George Millace . . . who wrote threatening letters. George Millace, husband of Marie, who was climbing back with frail handholds from the wreck of her life. If justice depended on smashing her deeper into soul-racking misery, justice would still have to wait.

Sharpener's race came third on the card. Not the biggest event of the day, which was the fourth race, a brandy-sponsored Gold Cup, but a well-regarded two mile 'chase. Sharpener had been made favourite because of his win at Kempton and with some of the same joie de vivre he sailed round most of Newbury's long oval in fourth place. We lay third at the third last fence, second at the second last, and jumped to the front over the last. I sat down and rode him out with hands and heels, and my God, I thought, I could do with the muscle-power I lost in Horley.

Sharpener won and I was exhausted, which was ridiculous. Harold, beaming, watched me fumble feebly with the girth buckles in the winner's enclosure. The horse, stamping around, almost knocked me over.

'You only went two miles,' Harold said. 'What the hell's the matter with you?'

I got the buckles undone and pulled off the saddle, and began in fact to feel a trickle of strength flow again through my arms. I grinned at Harold and said, 'Nothing . . . It was a damn good race. Nice shape.'

'Nice shape be buggered. You won. Any race you win is a nice bloody shape.'

I went in to be weighed, leaving him surrounded by congratulations and sportswriters: and while I was sitting on the bench by my peg waiting for vigour to amble back I decided what to do about Elgin Yaxley.

I had grown a habit, over the past two weeks, of taking with me in the car not only my favourite two cameras but also the photographs I seemed to keep on needing. Lance Kinship's reprints were there, although he himself hadn't turned up, and so were the four concerning Yaxley. Straight after the big race I went out and fetched them.

The second horse I was due to ride for Harold was a novice hurdler in the last race: and because there had been so many entries in the novice hurdle that they'd split it into two divisions, the last race on that day was the seventh, not the sixth. It gave me just enough extra time for what I wanted.

Finding Elgin Yaxley wasn't so difficult: it was detaching him from Bart Underfield that gave the trouble.

'Can I talk to you for a moment?' I said to Yaxley.

'You're not having the rides on our horses,' Bart said bossily. 'So don't waste time asking.'

'You can keep them,' I said.

'What do you want, then?'

'I want to give Mr Yaxley a message.' I turned to Yaxley. 'It's a private message, for your ears only.'

'Oh very well.' He was impatient. 'Wait for me in the bar, Bart.'

Bart grumbled and fussed, but finally went.

'Better come over here,' I said to Elgin Yaxley, nodding towards a patch of grass by the entrance gate, away from the huge big-race crowd with their stretched ears and curious eyes. 'You won't want anyone hearing.'

'What the devil *is* all this?' he said crossly.

'A message from George Millace,' I said.

His sharp features grew rigid. The small moustache he wore bristled. The complacency vanished into a furious concentration of fear.

'I have some photographs,' I said, 'which you might like to see.'

I handed him the cardboard envelope. It seemed easier this second time, I thought, to deliver the chop. Maybe I was becoming hardened . . . or maybe I simply didn't like Elgin Yaxley. I watched him open the envelope with no pity at all.

He first went pale, and then red, and great drops of sweat stood out like blisters on his forehead. He checked through the four pictures and found the whole story was there, the café meeting and George's two letters, and the damning note from the farmer, David Parker. The eyes he raised to me were sick and incredulous, and he had difficulty finding his voice.

'Take your time,' I said. 'I expect it's a shock.'

His mouth moved as if practising, but no words came out.

'Any number of copies,' I said, 'could go off to the insurance company and the police and so on.'

He managed a strangled groan.

'There's another way,' I said.

He got his throat and tongue to shape a single hoarse unedifying word. '*Bastard*.'

'Mm,' I said. 'There's George Millace's way.'

I'd never seen anyone look at me with total hatred before, and I found it unnerving. But I wanted to find out just what George had extracted from at least one of his victims, and this was my best chance.

I said flatly, 'I want the same as George Millace.'

'No.' It was more a wail than a shout. Full of horror; empty of hope.

'Yes indeed,' I said.

'But I can't afford it. I haven't got it.'

The anxiety in his eyes was almost too much for me, but I spurred on my flagging resolution with the thought of five shot horses, and said again, 'The same as George.'

'Not ten,' he said wildly. 'I haven't got it.'

I stared at him.

He mistook my silence and gabbled on, finding his voice in a flood of begging, beseeching, cajoling words.

'I've had expenses, you know. It hasn't all been easy. Can't you let me alone? Let me off, won't you? George said once and for all . . . and now *you* . . . Five, then,' he said in the face of my continued silence. 'Will five do? That's enough. I haven't got any more. I haven't.'

I stared once more, and waited.

'All right, then. All *right*.' He was shaking with worry and fury. 'Seven and a half. Will that do? It's all I've got, you bloodsucking leech . . . you're worse than George Millace . . . bastard *blackmailers* . . .'

While I watched he fumbled into his pockets and brought out a cheque book and a pen. Clumsily supporting the cheque book on the photograph envelope, he wrote the date, and a sum of money, and signed his name. Then with shaking fingers he tore the slip of paper out of the book and stood holding it.

'Not Hong Kong,' he said.

I didn't know at once what he meant, so I took refuge in more staring.

'Not Hong Kong. Not there again. I don't like it.' He was beseeching again, begging for crumbs.

'Oh . . .' I hid my understanding in a cough. 'Anywhere,' I said. 'Anywhere out of Britain.'

It was the right answer, but gave him no comfort. I stretched out my hand for the cheque.

He gave it to me, his hand trembling.

'Thank you,' I said.

'Rot in hell.'

He turned and stumbled away, half running, half staggering, utterly in pieces. Serve him right, I thought callously. Let him suffer. It wouldn't be for long.

I meant to tear up his cheque when I'd looked to see how much he thought my silence was worth: how much he'd paid George. I meant to, but I didn't.

When I looked at that cheque something like a huge burst of sunlight happened in my head, a bright expanding delight of awe and comprehension.

I had used George's own cruelty. I had demanded to be given what he himself had demanded. His alternative suggestion for Elgin Yaxley.

I had it. All of it.

Elgin Yaxley was going off into exile, and I held his cheque for seven thousand five hundred pounds.

It was made out not to me, or to Bearer, or even to the estate of George Millace, but to the Injured Jockeys Fund.

SIXTEEN:

I walked around for a while trying to find the particular ex-jockey who had become one of the chief administrators of the Fund, and at length tracked him down in the private entertainment box of one of the television companies. There was a crowd in there, but I winkled him out.

'Want a drink?' he said, holding up his glass.

I shook my head. I was wearing colours, breeches, boots and an anorak. 'More than my life's worth, boozing with you lot before racing.'

He said cheerfully, 'What can I do for you?'

'Take a cheque,' I said, and gave it to him.

'Phew,' he said, looking at it. 'And likewise *wow*.'

'Is it the first time Elgin Yaxley's been so generous?'

'No, it isn't,' he said. 'He gave us ten thousand a few months ago, just before he went abroad. We took it of course, but some of the trustees wondered if it wasn't conscience money. I mean . . . he'd just been paid a hundred thousand by the insurance company for those horses of his that were shot. The whole business looked horribly fishy, didn't it?'

'Mm.' I nodded. 'Well . . . Elgin Yaxley's going abroad again, so he says, and he gave me this cheque for you. So will you take it?'

He smiled. 'If his conscience is troubling him again, we might as well benefit.' He folded the cheque, tucked it away, and patted the pocket which contained it.

'Have you had any other huge cheques like that?' I enquired conversationally.

'People leave big amounts in their wills, sometimes, but no . . . not many like Elgin Yaxley.'

'Would Ivor den Relgan be a generous supporter?' I asked.

'Well yes, he gave us a thousand at the beginning of the season. Some time in September. Very generous.'

I pondered. 'Do you keep lists of the people who donate?'

He laughed. 'Not all of them. Thousands of people contribute over the years. Old age pensioners. Children. Housewives.

Anyone you can think of.' He sighed. 'We never seem to have enough for what we need to do, but we're always grateful for the smallest help . . . and you know all that.'

'Yes. Thanks anyway.'

'Any time.'

He went back to the convivial crowd and I returned to the weighing room and got myself and my saddle weighed out for the last race.

I was as bad as George, I thought. Identically as bad. I had extorted money by threats. It didn't seem so wicked, now that I'd done it myself.

Harold in the parade-ring said sharply, 'You're looking bloody pleased with yourself.'

'Just with life in general.'

I'd ridden a winner. I'd almost certainly found Amanda. I'd discovered a lot more about George. Sundry kicks and punches on the debit side, but who cared. Overall, not a bad day.

'This hurdler,' Harold said severely, 'is the one who ballsed-up the schooling session last Saturday. I know you weren't on him . . . it wasn't your fault . . . but you just mind he gets a good clear view of what he's got to jump. Understand? Go to the front and make the running, so he's got a clear view. He won't last the trip, but it's a big field and I don't want him being jostled and blinded in the pack early on. Got it?'

I nodded. There were twenty-three runners, almost the maximum allowed in this type of race. Harold's hurdler, walking edgily round the parade-ring, was already sweating with nervous excitement, and he was an animal, I knew from experience, who needed a soothing phlegmatic approach.

'Jockeys, please mount,' came the announcement, and I and the hurdler in a decently quiet way got ourselves together and down to the start.

I was thinking only of bowling along in front out of trouble, and when the tapes went up, off we set. Over the first, leading as ordered; good jump, no trouble. Over the second, just out in front; passable jump, no trouble. Over the third . . .

In front, as ordered, at the third. Rotten, disastrous jump, all four feet seeming to tangle in the hurdle instead of rising over it: exactly the mess he'd made over the schooling hurdle at home.

He and I crashed to the turf together, and twenty-two horses came over the hurdle after us.

Horses do their very best to avoid a man or a horse on the

ground, but with so many, so close, going so fast, it would have been a miracle if I hadn't been touched. One couldn't ever tell at those times just how many galloping hooves connected: it always happened too fast. It felt like being rolled like a rag doll under a stampede.

It had happened before. It would happen again. I lay painfully on my side looking at a close bunch of grass, and thought it was a damn silly way to be earning one's living.

I almost laughed. I've thought that before, I thought. Every time I'm down here on the mud, I think it.

A lot of First Aid hands arrived to help me up. Nothing seemed to be broken. Thank God for strong bones. I wrapped my arms round my body, as if hugging would lessen the hurt.

The horse had got up and decamped, unscathed. I rode back to the stands in an ambulance, demonstrated to the doctor that I was basically in one piece, and winced my slow way into ordinary clothes.

When I left the weighing room most people had gone home, but Harold was standing there with Ben, his travelling head lad.

'Are you all right?' Harold demanded.

'Yeah.'

'I'll drive you home,' he said. 'Ben can take your car.'

I looked at the generous worry in both of their faces, and didn't argue. Dug into my pocket, and gave Ben my keys.

'That was a hell of a fall,' Harold said, driving out of the gates. 'A real brute.'

'Mm.'

'I was glad to see you stand up.'

'Is the horse all right?'

'Yes, clumsy bugger.'

We drove in companionable silence towards Lambourn. I felt beaten-up and shivery, but it would pass. It always passed. Always would, until I got too old for it. I'd be too old in my mind, I thought, before my body gave out.

'If Victor Briggs comes down here again,' I said, 'would you tell me?'

He glanced at me sideways. 'You want to see him? Won't do any good, you know. Victor just does what he wants.'

'I want to know . . . what he wants.'

'Why not leave well alone?'

'Because it isn't well. I've left it alone . . . it doesn't work. I want to talk to him . . . and don't worry, I'll be diplomatic. I don't want to lose this job. I don't want you to lose Victor's horses. Don't worry. I know all that. I want to talk to him.'

'All right,' Harold said doubtfully. 'When he comes, I'll tell him.'

He stopped his car beside my front door.

'You're sure you're all right?' he said. 'You look pretty shaken . . . Nasty fall. Horrid.'

'I'll have a hot bath . . . get the stiffness out. Thanks for the lift home.'

'You'll be fit for next week? Tuesday at Plumpton?'

'Absolutely,' I said.

It was already getting dark. I went round in the cottage drawing the curtains, switching on lights, heating some coffee. Bath, food, television, aspirins, bed, I thought, and pray not to feel too sore in the morning.

Ben parked my car in the carport, gave me the keys through the back door, and said goodnight.

Mrs Jackson, the horse-box driver's wife from next door, came to tell me the rating officer had called.

'Oh?' I said.

'Yes. Yesterday. Hope I did right, letting him in, like. Mind you, Mr Nore, I didn't let him out of my sight. I went right round with him, like. He was only in here a matter of five minutes. He didn't touch a thing. Just counted the rooms. Hope it's all right. He had papers from the council, and such.'

'I'm sure it's fine, Mrs Jackson.'

'And your telephone,' she said, 'It's been ringing and ringing. Dozens of times. I can hear it through the wall, you know, when everything's quiet. I didn't know if you'd want me to answer it. I will, any time, you know, if you want.'

'Kind of you,' I said. 'I'll let you know if I do.'

She gave me a bright nod and departed. She would have mothered me if I'd let her, and I guessed she would have been glad to let the rating man in, as she liked looking round in my house. Nosy, friendly, sharp-eyed neighbour, taker-in of parcels and dispenser of gossip and advice. Her two boys had broken my kitchen window once with their football.

I telephoned to Jeremy Folk. He was out: would I care to leave a message? Tell him I found what we were looking for, I said.

The instant I put the receiver down the bell rang. I picked it up again, and heard a child's breathless voice. 'I can tell you where that stable is. Am I the first?'

I regretfully said not. I also passed on the same bad news to ten more children within the next two hours. Several of them checked disappointedly to make sure I'd been told the right place – Zephyr Farm Stables? And several said did I know it had been owned for years and years by some Jesus freaks? I began asking them if they knew how the Colleagues had chanced to buy the stables, and eventually came across a father who did.

'We and the people who kept the riding school,' he said, 'we were pretty close friends. They wanted to move to Devon, and were looking for a buyer for their place, and these fanatics just turned up one day with suitcases full of cash, and bought it on the spot.'

'How did the fanatics hear of it? Was it advertised?'

'No . . .' He paused, thinking. 'Oh, I remember . . . it was because of one of the children who used to ride the ponies. Yes, that's right. Sweet little girl. Mandy something. Always there. She used to stay with our friends for weeks on end. I saw her often. There was something about her mother being on the point of death, and the religious people looking after her. It was through the mother that they heard the stables were for sale. They were in some ruin of a house at the time, I think, and wanted somewhere better.'

'You don't remember the mother's name, I suppose.'

'Sorry, no. Don't think I ever knew it, and after all these years . . .'

'You've been tremendously helpful,' I said. 'I'll send your Peter the tenner, even though he wasn't first.'

The father's voice chuckled. 'That'll please him.'

I took his address, and also the name of the people who had owned the stables, but Peter's father said he had lost touch with them over the years and no longer knew where they lived.

Jeremy could find them, I thought, if he needed to. After I'd bathed and eaten I unplugged the telephone from the kitchen and carried it up to the sitting room, where for another hour it interrupted the television. God bless the little children, I thought, and wondered how many thousands were going to ring up. None of them themselves had ever been inside the high wooden walls: it was always their mummies and daddies who had ridden there when they were young.

By nine o'clock I was thoroughly tired of it. Despite the long hot soak my deeply bruised muscles were beginning to stiffen;

and the best place to take them was bed. Get it over with, I thought. It was going to be lousy. It always was, for about twenty-four hours, after so many kicks. If I went to bed I could sleep through the worst.

I unplugged the telephone and went down to the bathroom in shirtsleeves for a scratch round the teeth; and the front doorbell rang.

Cursing, I went to see who had called.

Opened the door.

Ivor den Relgan stood there holding a gun.

I stared at the pistol, not believing it.

'Back up,' he said. 'I'm coming in.'

It would be untrue to say I wasn't afraid. I was certain he was going to kill me. I felt bodiless. Floating. Blood racing.

For the second time that day I saw into the eyes of hatred, and the power behind den Relgan's paled Elgin Yaxley's into petulance. He jerked the lethal black weapon towards me, insisting I retreated, and I took two or three steps backwards, hardly feeling my feet.

He stepped through my door and kicked it shut behind him.

'You're going to pay,' he said, 'for what you've done to me.'

Be careful, Jeremy had said.

I hadn't been.

'George Millace was bad,' he said. 'You're worse.'

I wasn't sure I was actually going to be able to speak, but I did. My voice sounded strange: almost squeaky.

'Did you . . .' I said, '. . . burn his house?'

His eyes flickered. His naturally arrogant expression, which had survived whatever Lord White had said to him, wasn't going to be broken up by any futile last-minute questions. In adversity his air of superiority had if anything intensified, as if belief in his own importance were the only thing left.

'Burgled, ransacked, burnt,' he said furiously. 'And you had the stuff all the time. You . . . you *rattlesnake*.'

I had destroyed his power base. Taken away his authority. Left him metaphorically as naked as on his St Tropez balcony.

George, I thought, must have used the threat of those photographs to stop den Relgan angling to be let into the Jockey Club. I'd used them to get him thrown out.

He'd had some sort of standing, of credibility, before, in racing men's eyes. Now he had none. Never to be in was one thing. To be in and then out, quite another.

George hadn't shown those photographs to anyone but den Relgan himself.

I had.

'Get back,' he said. 'Back there. Go on.'

He made a small waving movement with the pistol. An automatic. Stupid thought. What did it matter.

'My neighbours'll hear the shot,' I said hopelessly.

He sneered and didn't answer. 'Back past that door.'

It was the door to the darkroom, solidly shut. Even if I could jump in there alive . . . no sanctuary. No lock. I stepped past it.

'Stop,' he said.

I'd have to run, I thought wildly. Had at least to try. I was already turning on the ball of one foot when the kitchen door was smashed open.

I thought for a split second that somehow den Relgan had missed me and the bullet had splintered some glass, but then I realised he hadn't fired. There were people coming into the house from the back. Two people. Two bustling burly young men . . . with nylon stocking masks over their faces.

They were rushing, banging against each other, fast, eager, infinitely destructive.

I tried to fight them.

I tried.

God almighty, I thought. Not three times in one day. How could I explain to them . . . Blood vessels were already severed and bleeding under my skin . . . Too many muscle fibres already crushed and torn . . . too much damage already done. How could I explain . . . and if I had it wouldn't have made any difference. Pleased them, if anything.

Thoughts scattered and flew away. I couldn't see, couldn't yell, could hardly breathe. They wore roughened leather gloves which tore my skin and the punches to my face knocked me silly. When I fell on the ground they used their boots. On limbs, back, stomach, head.

I drifted off altogether.

When I came back it was quiet. I was lying on the white tiled floor with my cheek in a pool of blood. In a dim way I wondered whose blood it was.

Drifted off again.

It's my blood, I thought.

Tried to open my eyes. Something wrong with the eyelids. Oh well, I thought, I'm alive. Drifted off again.

He didn't shoot me, I thought. Did he shoot me? I tried to move, to find out. Bad mistake.

When I tried to move, my whole body went into a sort of rigid spasm. Locked tight in a monstrous cramp from head to foot. I gasped with the crushing, unexpected agony of it. Worse than fractures, worse than dislocations, worse than anything . . .

Screaming nerves, I thought. Telling my brain to seize up. Saying too much was injured, too much was smashed, nothing must move. Too much was bleeding inside.

Christ, I thought. Leave go. Let me go. I won't move. I'll just lie here. Let me go.

After a long time the spasm did pass, and I lay in relief in a flaccid heap. Too weak to do anything but pray that the cramp wouldn't come back. Too shattered to think much at all.

The thoughts I did have, I could have done without. Thoughts like people died of ruptured internal organs . . . kidneys, liver, spleen. Thoughts like what exactly did I have wrong with me, to cause such a fierce reaction. Thoughts like den Relgan coming back to finish the job.

Den Relgan's mid-world voice, 'You'll pay for what you've done to me . . .'

Pay in cuts and internal haemorrhage and wretched pain. Pay in fear that I was lying there dying. Bleeding inside. Bleeding to death. The way people beaten to death died.

Ages passed.

If any of those things were ruptured, I thought . . . liver, kidneys, spleen . . . and pouring out blood, I would be showing the signs of it. Shallow breathing, fluttering pulse, thirst, restlessness, sweat. None of that seemed to be happening.

I took heart after a while, knowing that at least I wasn't getting worse. Maybe if I moved gently, cautiously, it would be all right.

Far from all right. Back into a rigid locked spasm, as bad as before.

It had taken only the intention to move. Only the outward message. The response had been not movement, but cramp. I dare say it was the body's best line of defence, but I could hardly bear it.

It lasted too long, and went away slowly, tentatively, as if threatening to come back. I won't move, I promised. I won't move . . . just let go . . . let me go.

The lights in the cottage were on, but the heating was off. I grew very cold; literally congealing. Cold stopped things bleeding, I thought. Cold wasn't all bad. Cold would contract all those leaking internal blood vessels and stop the red stuff trickling out into where it shouldn't be. Haemorrhage would be finished. Recovery could start.

I lay quiet for hours, waiting. Sore but alive. Increasingly certain of staying alive. Increasingly certain I'd been lucky.

If nothing fatal had ruptured, I could deal with the rest. Familiar country. Boring, but known.

I had no idea of the time. Couldn't see my watch. Suppose I move my arm, I thought. Just my arm. Might manage that, if I'm careful.

It sounded simple. The overall spasm stayed away, but the specific message to my arm produced only a twitch. Crazy. Nothing was working. All circuits jammed.

After another long while I tried again. Tried too hard. The cramp came back, taking my breath away, holding me in a vice, worst now in my stomach, not so bad in my arms, but rigid, fearful, frightening, lasting too long.

I lay on the floor all night and well on into the morning. The patch of blood under my head got sticky and dried. My face felt like a pillow puffed up with gritty lumps. There were splits in my mouth, which were sore, and I could feel with my tongue the jagged edges of broken teeth.

Eventually I lifted my head off the floor.

No spasm.

I was lying in the back part of the hall, not far from the bottom of the stairs. Pity the bedroom was right up at the top. Also the telephone. I might get some help . . . if I could get up the stairs.

Gingerly I tried moving, dreading what would happen. Moved my arms, my legs, tried to sit up. Couldn't do it. My weakness was appalling. My muscles were trembling. I moved a few inches across the floor, still half lying down. Got as far as the stairs. Hip on the hall floor, shoulder on the stairs, head on the stairs, arms failing with weakness . . . the spasms came back.

Oh Christ, I thought, how much more?

In another hour I'd got my haunch up three steps and was again rigid with cramp. Far enough, I thought numbly. No farther. It was certainly more comfortable lying on the stairs than on the floor, as long as I stayed still.

I stayed still. Grateful, wearily, lazily still. For ages.

Somebody rang the front door bell.

Whoever it was, I didn't want them. Whoever it was would make me move. I no longer wanted help, but just peace. Peace would mend me, given time.

The bell rang again. Go away, I thought. I'm better alone.

For a while I thought I'd got my wish, but then I heard someone at the back of the house, coming in through the back door. The broken back door, open to a touch.

Not den Relgan, I thought abjectly. Don't let it be den Relgan . . . not him.

It wasn't, of course. It was Jeremy Folk.

It was Jeremy, coming in tentatively, saying 'Er . . .' and 'Are you there . . .' and 'Philip? . . .' and standing still with shock when he reached the hall.

'Jesus Christ,' he said blankly.

I said 'Hello.'

'*Philip*,' He leaned over me. 'Your face . . .'

'Yeah.'

'What shall I do?'

'Nothing,' I said. 'Sit down . . . on the stairs.' My mouth and tongue felt stiff. Like Marie's, I thought. Just like Marie.

'But what happened? Did you have a fall at the races?'

He did sit down, on the bottom stair by my feet, folding his own legs into ungainly angles.

'Yeah,' I said. 'A fall.'

'But . . . the blood. You've got blood . . . all over your face. In your hair. Everywhere.'

'Leave it,' I said. 'It's dry.'

'Can you see?' he said. 'Your eyes are . . .' He stopped, reduced apparently to silence, not wanting to tell me.

'I can see out of one of them,' I said. 'It's enough.'

He wanted of course to move me, wash the blood off, make things more regular. I wanted to stay just where I was, without having to argue. Hopeless wish. I persuaded him to leave me alone only by confessing to the cramps.

His horror intensified. 'I'll get you a doctor.'

'Just shut up,' I said. 'I'm all right. Talk if you like, but don't *do* anything.'

'Well . . .' He gave in. 'Do you want anything? Tea, or anything?'

'Find some champagne. Kitchen cupboard.'

He looked as if he thought I was mad, but champagne was the best tonic I knew for practically all ills. I heard the cork pop and presently he returned with two tumblers. He put mine on the stair by my left hand, near my head.

Oh well, I thought. May as well find out. The cramps would have to stop sometime. I stiffly moved the arm and fastened the hand round the chunky glass, and tried to connect the whole thing to my mouth: and I got at least three reasonable gulps before everything seized up.

It was Jeremy, that time, who was frightened. He took the glass I was dropping and had a great attack of the dithers, and I said 'Just wait,' through my teeth. The spasm finally wore off, and I thought perhaps it hadn't been so long or so bad that time, and that things really were getting better.

Persuading people to leave one alone always took more energy than one wanted to spend for the purpose. Good friends tired one out. For all that I was grateful for his company, I wished Jeremy would stop fussing and be quiet.

The front door bell rang yet again, and before I could tell him not to, he'd gone off to answer it. My spirits sank even lower. Visitors were too much.

The visitor was Clare, come because I'd invited her.

She knelt on the stairs beside me and said, 'This isn't a fall, is it? Someone's done this to you, haven't they? Beaten you up?'

'Have some champagne,' I said.

'Yes. All right.'

She stood up and went to fetch a glass, and argued on my behalf with Jeremy.

'If he wants to lie on the stairs, let him. He's been injured countless times. He knows what's best.'

My God, I thought. A girl who understands. Incredible.

She and Jeremy sat in the kitchen introducing themselves and drinking my booze, and on the stairs things did improve. Small exploratory stretchings produced no cramps. I drank some champagne. Felt sore but less ill. Felt that some time soon I'd sit up.

The front doorbell rang.

An epidemic.

Clare walked through the hall to answer it. I was sure she intended to keep whoever it was at bay, but she found it impossible. The girl who had called wasn't going to be stopped on the doorstep. She pushed into the house physically past Clare's protestations, and I heard her heels clicking at speed towards me down the hall.

'I must see,' she said frantically. 'I must know if he's alive.'

I knew her voice. I didn't need to see the distraught beautiful face seeking me, seeing me, freezing with shock.

Dana del Relgan.

SEVENTEEN:

'Oh my *God,*' she said.

'I am,' I said in my swollen way, 'alive.'

'He said it would be . . . a toss-up.'

'Came down heads,' I said.

'He didn't seem to care. Didn't seem to realise . . . If they'd killed you . . . what it would mean. He just said no one saw them, they'd never be arrested, so why worry?'

Clare demanded, 'Do you mean you know who did this?'

Dana gave her a distracted look. 'I have to talk to him. Alone. Do you mind?'

'But he's . . .' She stopped, and said, 'Philip?'

'It's all right.'

'We'll be in the kitchen,' Clare said. 'Just shout.'

Dana waited until she had gone, and then perched beside me on the stairs, half sitting, half lying, to bring her head near to mine. I regarded her through the slit of my vision, seeing her almost frantic and deadly anxiety and not knowing its cause. Not for my life, since she could now see it was safe. Not for my silence, since her very presence was an admission that could make things worse. The gold-flecked hair fell softly forward almost to touch me. The sweet scent she was wearing reached my perception even through a battered nose. The silk of her blouse brushed my hand. The voice was soft in its cosmopolitan accent . . . and beseeching.

'Please,' she said. '*Please . . .*'

'Please . . . what?'

'How can I ask you?' Even in trouble, I thought, she had a powerful attraction. I'd only seen it before, not felt it, as before she'd given me only passing and uninterested smiles; but now, with the full wattage switched my way, I found myself thinking that I would help her, if I could.

She said persuadingly, 'Please give me . . . what I wrote for George Millace.'

I lay without answering, closing the persevering eye. She

misread my inaction, which was in truth born of ignorance, and rushed into a flood of impassioned begging.

'I know you'll be thinking . . . how can I ask you, when Ivor's done this to you . . . how can I expect the slightest favour . . . or mercy . . . or kindness.' Her voice was a jumble of shame and despair and anger and cajoling, every emotion rising separately like a wave and subsiding before the next. Asking a favour from someone her father . . . husband? . . . lover . . . had had mauled halfway to extinction wasn't the easiest of errands, but she was having a pretty good stab at it. 'Please, please, I beg of you, give it back.'

'Is he your father?' I said.

'No.' A breath; a whisper; a sigh.

'What, then?'

'We have . . . a relationship.'

You don't say, I thought dryly.

She said, 'Please, please give me the cigarettes.'

The what? I had no idea what she meant.

Trying not to mumble, trying to make my slow tongue lucid, I said, 'Tell me about your . . . relationship . . . with den Relgan . . . and about . . . your relationship with . . . Lord White.'

'If I tell you, will you give it to me? Please, *please*, will you?'

She took my silence to mean that at least she could hope. She scurried into explanations, the words falling over themselves here and there, and here and there coming in faltering pauses: and all of it, overall, apologetic and self-excusing, a distinct flavour of 'poor little me, I've been used, none of it's my fault'.

I opened the slit eye, to watch.

'I've been with him two years . . . not married, it's never been like that . . . not domestic, just . . .'

Just for sex, I thought.

'You talk like him,' I said.

'I'm an actress.' She waited a shade defiantly for me to dispute it, but indeed I couldn't. A pretty good actress, I would have said. Equity card? I thought sardonically, and couldn't be bothered to ask.

'Last summer,' she said, 'Ivor came one day spilling over with a brilliant idea. So pleased with himself . . . if I'd cooperate, he'd see I didn't suffer . . . I mean, he meant . . .' She stopped there, but it was plain what he meant. Won't suffer financially . . . neat euphemism for hefty bribe.

'He said there was a man at the races wanting to flirt. He used not to take me to the races, not until then. But he said, would I go with him and pretend to be his daughter, and see if I could get the man to flirt with *me*. It was a laugh, you see. Ivor said this man had a reputation like snow, and he wanted to play a joke on him . . . Well, that's what he said. He said the man was showing all the signs of wanting a sexual adventure . . . looking at pretty girls in that special way that they do, patting their arms, you know what I mean.'

I thought, how odd it must be to be a pretty girl, to find it normal for middle-aged men to be on the look-out for sex, to expect them to pat one's arms.

'So you went,' I said.

She nodded. 'He was a sweetie . . . John White. It was easy. I mean . . . I liked him. I just smiled . . . and liked him . . . and he . . . well . . . I mean, it was true what Ivor had said, he was on the look-out, and there I was.'

There she was, I thought, beautiful and not too dumb, and trying to catch him. Poor Lord White, hooked because he wanted to be. Fooled by his foolish age, his nostalgia for youth.

'Ivor wanted to use John, of course, I saw it . . . it was plain, but I didn't see all that harm in it. I mean . . . why not? Everything was going fine until Ivor and I went to St Tropez for a week.' The pretty face clouded with remembered rage. 'And that beastly photographer wrote to Ivor . . . saying lay off Lord White, or else he'd show him those pictures of us . . . Ivor and me . . . Ivor was livid, I've never seen him so angry . . . not until this week.'

Each of us, I supposed, thought of the fury we'd witnessed that week in den Relgan.

'Does he know you're here?' I said.

'My God, no.' She looked horrified. 'He doesn't know . . . he hates drugs . . . it's all we have rows about . . . George Millace made me write that list . . . said he'd show the pictures to John if I didn't . . . I *hated* George Millace . . . but you . . . you'll give it back to me, won't you? Please . . . please . . . you must see . . . it would ruin me with anyone who matters . . . I'll pay you. I'll pay you . . . if you'll give it to me.'

Crunch time, I thought.

'What do you expect . . . me to give to you?' I said.

'The packet of cigarettes, of course. With the writing on.'

'Yes . . . why did you write on a cigarette packet?'

'I wrote on the wrapping with the red felt pen . . . George

Millace said write the list and I said I wouldn't whatever he did and he said write it then with this pen on the cellophane wrapper round these cigarettes and you can pretend you haven't done it, because how could anyone take seriously a scrawl on wrapping paper . . .' She stopped suddenly and said with awakening suspicion, 'You have got it, haven't you? George Millace gave it to you . . . with the pictures . . . didn't he?'

'What did you write . . . on the list?'

'My God,' she said. 'You haven't got it: you haven't and I've come here . . . I've told you . . . it's all for nothing . . . you haven't got it . . .' She stood up abruptly, beauty vanishing in fury. 'You beastly *shit*. Ivor should have killed you. Should have made sure. I hope you *hurt*.'

She had her wish, I thought calmly. I felt surprisingly little resentment about den Relgan's tit for tat. I'd clobbered his life, he'd clobbered my body. I'd come off the better, I thought, on the whole. My troubles would pass.

'Be grateful,' I said.

She was too angry, however, at what she had given away. She whisked off through the hall in her silks and her scent, and slammed out of the front door. The air in her wake quivered with feminine impact. Just as well, I thought hazily, that the world wasn't full of Dana den Relgans.

Clare and Jeremy came out of the kitchen.

'What did she want?' Clare said.

'Something I . . . haven't got.'

They began asking what in general was happening, but I said 'Tell you . . . tomorrow,' and they stopped. Clare sat beside me on the stairs and rubbed one finger over my hand.

'You're in a poor way, aren't you?' she said.

I didn't want to say yes. I said, 'What's the time?'

'Half-past three . . . getting on for four.' She looked at her watch. 'Twenty to four.'

'Have some lunch,' I said. 'You and Jeremy.'

'Do you want any?'

'No.'

They heated some soup and some bread and kept life ticking over. It's the only day, I thought inanely, that I've ever spent lying on the stairs. I could smell the dust in the carpet. I ached all over, incessantly, with a grinding stiff soreness, but it was better than the cramps; and movement was becoming possible. Movement soon, I thought, would be imperative. A sign that things were returning to order . . . I needed increasingly to go to the bathroom.

I sat up on the stairs, my back propped against the wall.

Not so bad. Not so bad. No spasms.

A perceptible improvement in function in all muscles. The memory of strength no longer seemed remote. I could stand up, I thought, if I tried.

Clare and Jeremy appeared enquiringly, and without pride I used their offered hands to pull myself upright.

Tottery, but upright.

No cramps.

'Now what?' Clare said.

'A pee.'

They laughed. Clare went off to the kitchen and Jeremy said something, as he gave me an arm for support across the hall, about washing the pool of dried blood off the floor.

'Don't bother,' I said.

'No trouble.'

I hung onto the towel rail in the bathroom a bit and looked into the glass over the washbasin, and saw the state of my face. Swollen, misshapen landscape. Unrecognisable. Raw in patches. Dark red in patches. Caked with dried blood: hair spiky with it. One eye lost in puffy folds, one showing a slit. Cut, purple mouth. Two chipped front teeth.

Give it a week, I thought, sighing. Boxers did it all the time from choice, silly buggers.

Emptying the bladder brought an acute awareness of heavy damage in the abdomen but also reassurance. No blood in the urine. My intestines might have caught it, but not once had those feet, equine or human, landed squarely with exploding force over a kidney. I'd been lucky. Exceptionally lucky. Thanked God for it.

I ran some warm water into the washbasin and sponged off some of the dried blood. Wasn't sure, on the whole, that it was any improvement, either in comfort or visibility. Where the blood had been were more raw patches and clotted cuts. Gingerly I patted the washed bits dry with a tissue. Leave the rest, I thought.

There was a heavy crash somewhere out in the hall.

I pulled open the bathroom door to find Clare coming through from the kitchen, looking anxious.

'Are you all right?' she said. 'You didn't fall?'

'No . . . Must be Jeremy.'

Unhurriedly we went forward towards the front of the house to see what he'd dropped . . . and found Jeremy himself face down on the floor. Half in and half out of the darkroom door. The bowl of water he'd been carrying spilled wetly all around him, and there was a smell . . . a strong smell of bad eggs. A smell I knew. I . . .

'Whatever . . .' Clare began.

Dear Christ, I thought, and it was a prayer, not a blasphemy. I caught her fiercely round the waist and dragged her to the front door. Opened it. Pushed her outside.

'Stay there,' I said urgently. 'Stay outside. It's gas.'

I took a deep lungful of the dark wintry night air and turned back. Felt so feeble . . . so desperate. Bent over Jeremy, grabbed hold of his wrists, one in each hand, and pulled.

Pulled and dragged him over the white tiles, pulling him, sliding him, feeling the deadly tremors in my weak arms and legs. Out of the darkroom, through the hall, to the front door. Not far. Not more than ten feet. My own lungs were bursting for air . . . but not that air . . . not rotten eggs.

Clare took one of Jeremy's arms and pulled with me, and between us we dragged his unconscious form out into the street. I twitched the door shut behind me, and knelt on the cold road, retching and gasping and feeling utterly useless.

Clare was already banging on the house next door, returning with the schoolmaster who lived there.

'Breathe . . . into him,' I said.

'Mouth to mouth?' I nodded. 'Right, then.' He knelt down beside Jeremy, turned him over, and without question began efficient resuscitation, knowing the drill.

Clare herself disappeared but in a minute was back.

'I called the ambulance,' she said, 'But they want to know what gas. There's no gas in Lambourn, they say. They want to know . . . what to bring.'

'A respirator.' My own chest felt leaden. Breathing was difficult. 'Tell them . . . it's sulphur. Some sort of sulphide. Deadly. Tell them to hurry.'

She looked agonised, and ran back into the schoolmaster's house and I leant weakly on my knees against the front wall of my own house and coughed and felt incredibly ill. From the new troubles, not the old. From the gas.

Jeremy didn't stir. Dear God, I thought. Dear Christ, let him live.

Gas in my darkroom had been meant for me, not for him.

Must have been. Must have been in there, somehow, waiting for me, all the hours I'd spent lying outside in the hall.

I thought incoherently: Jeremy, *don't die*. Jeremy, it's my fault. *Don't die*. I should have burned George Millace's rubbish . . . not used it . . . not brought us so near . . . so near to death.

People came out from all the cottages, bringing blankets and shocked eyes. The schoolmaster went on with his task, though I saw from his manner, from glimpses of his face, that he thought it was useless.

Don't die . . .

Clare felt Jeremy's pulse. Her own face looked ashen.

'Is he . . .?' I said.

'A flutter.'

Don't die.

The schoolmaster took heart and tirelessly continued. I felt as if there was a constricting band round my ribs, squeezing my lungs. I'd taken only a few breaths of gas and air. Jeremy had breathed pure gas. And Clare . . .

'How's your chest?' I asked her.

'Tight,' she said. 'Horrid.'

The crowd around us seemed to be swelling. The ambulance arrived, and a police car, and Harold, and a doctor, and what seemed like half of Lambourn.

Expert hands took over from the schoolmaster and pumped air in and out of Jeremy's lungs: and Jeremy himself lay like a log while the doctor examined him and while he was lifted onto a stretcher and loaded into the ambulance.

He had a pulse. Some sort of pulse. That was all they would say. They shut the doors on him, and drove him to Swindon.

Don't die, I prayed. Don't let him die. It's my fault.

A fire engine arrived with men in breathing apparatus. They went round to the back of the cottage carrying equipment with dials, and eventually came out through my front door into the street. What I heard of their reports to the policemen suggested that there shouldn't be any close investigation until the toxic level inside the cottage was within limits.

'What gas is it?' one of the policemen asked.

'Hydrogen sulphide.'

'Lethal?'

'Extremely. Paralyses the breathing. Don't go in until we give the all clear. There's some sort of source in there, still generating gas.'

The policeman turned to me. 'What is it?' he said.

I shook my head. 'I don't know. I've nothing that would.'

He had asked earlier what was wrong with my face.

'Fell in a race.'

Everyone had accepted it. Battered jockeys were commonplace in Lambourn. The whole circus moved up the road to Harold's house, and events became jumbled.

Clare telephoned twice to the hospital for news of Jeremy.

'He's in intensive care . . . very ill. They want to know his next of kin.'

'Parents,' I said despairingly. 'Jeremy's home . . . in St Albans.' The number was in my house, with the gas.

Harold did some work with directory enquiries and got through to Jeremy's father.

Don't die, I thought. Bloody well live . . . *Please live.*

Policemen tramped in and out. An inspector came, asking questions. I told him, and Clare told him, what had happened. I didn't know how hydrogen sulphide had got into my darkroom. It had been a sheer accident that it had been Jeremy who breathed it. I didn't know why anyone should want to put gas in my darkroom. I didn't know who.

The inspector said he didn't believe me. No one had death traps like that set in their houses without knowing why. I shook my head. Talking was still a trial. I'd tell him why, I thought, if Jeremy died. Otherwise not.

How had I known so quickly that there was gas? My reaction had been instantaneous, Clare had said. Why was that?

'Sodium Sulphide . . . used to be used in photographic studios. Still sometimes used . . . but not much . . . because of the smell. I didn't have any. It wasn't . . . mine.'

'Is it a gas?' he said, puzzled.

'No. Comes in crystals. Very poisonous. Comes in sepia toner kits. Kodak made one. Called T – 7 A . . ., I think.'

'But you knew it *was* gas.'

'Because of Jeremy . . . passing out. And I breathed it . . . it felt . . . wrong. You can make gas . . . using sodium sulphide . . . I just knew it was gas . . . I don't know how I knew . . . I just knew.'

'How do you make hydrogen sulphide gas from sodium sulphide crystals?'

'I don't know.'

He was insistent that I should answer, but I truthfully didn't know. And now, sir, he said, about your injuries. Your obvious discomfort and weakness. The state of your face. Are you sure, sir, that these were the result of a fall in a horse race? Because they looked to him, he had to say, more like the result of a severe human attack. He'd seen a few in his time, he said.

A fall, I said.

The inspector asked Harold, who looked troubled but answered forthrightly, 'A wicked fall, inspector. Umpteen horses kicked him. If you want witnesses . . . about six thousand people were watching.'

The inspector shrugged but looked disillusioned. Maybe he had an instinct, I thought, which told him I'd lied on some counts. When he'd gone Harold said, 'Hope you know what you're doing. Your face was O.K. when I left you, wasn't it?'

'Tell you one day,' I said, mumbling.

He said to Clare 'What happened?' but she too shook her head in exhaustion and said she didn't know anything, didn't understand anything, and felt terrible herself. Harold's wife gave us comfort and food and eventually beds; and Jeremy at midnight was still alive.

Several rotten hours later Harold came into the little room where I sat in bed. Sat because I could breathe better that way, and because I couldn't sleep, and because I still ached abominably all over. My young lady, he said, had gone off to London to work, and would telephone that evening. The police wanted to see me. And Jeremy? Jeremy was still alive, still unconscious, still critically ill.

The whole day continued wretchedly.

The police went into my cottage, apparently opening doors and windows for the wind to blow through, and the inspector came to Harold's house to tell me the results.

We sat in Harold's office, where the inspector in daylight proved to be a youngish blond man with sensible eyes and a habit of cracking his knuckles. I hadn't taken him in much as a person the evening before, only his air of hostility; and that was plainly unchanged.

'There's a water filter on the tap in your darkroom,' he said. 'What do you use it for?'

'All water for photographs,' I said, 'has to be clean.'

Some of the worst swelling round my eyes and mouth was beginning to subside. I could see better, talk better: at least some relief.

'Your water filter,' the inspector said, 'Is a hydrogen sulphide generator.'

'It can't be.'

'Why not?'

'Well . . . I use it all the time. It's only a water softener. You regenerate it with salt . . . like all softeners. It couldn't possibly make gas.'

He gave me a long considering stare. Then he went away for an hour, and returned with a box and a young man in jeans and a sweater.

'Now, sir,' the inspector said to me with the studied procedural politeness of the suspicious copper, 'is this your water filter?'

He opened the box to show me the contents. One Durst filter, with, screwed onto its top, the short rubber attachment which was normally pushed onto the tap.

'It looks like it,' I said. 'It looks just like it should. What's wrong with it? It couldn't possibly make gas.'

The inspector gestured to the young man, who produced a pair of plastic gloves from a pocket, putting them on. He then picked up the filter, which was a black plastic globe about the size of a grapefruit, with clear sections top and bottom, and unscrewed it round the middle.

'Inside here,' he said, 'there's usually just the filter cartridge. But as you'll see, in this particular object, things are quite different. Inside here there are two containers, one above the other. They're both empty now . . . but this lower one contained sodium sulphide crystals, and this one . . .' he paused with an inborn sense of the dramatic, '. . . this upper one contained sulphuric acid. There must have been some form of membrane holding the contents of the two containers apart . . . but when the tap was turned on, the water pressure broke or dissolved the membrane, and the two chemicals mixed. Sulphuric acid and sodium sulphide, propelled by water . . . very highly effective sulphide generator. It would have gone on pouring out gas even if the water was turned off. Which it was . . . presumably by Mr Folk.'

There was a long, meaningful, depressing silence.

'So you can see, sir,' the inspector said, 'it couldn't in any way have been an accident.'

'No,' I said dully. 'But I don't know . . . I truthfully don't know . . . who could have put such a thing there . . . They would have to have known what sort of filter I had, wouldn't they?'

'And that you had a filter in the first place.'

'Everyone with a dark room has a filter of some sort.'

Another silence. They seemed to be waiting for me to tell them, but I didn't know. It couldn't have been den Relgan . . . why should he bother with such a device when one or two more kicks would have finished me. It couldn't have been any of the other people George Millace had written his letters to. Two of them were old history, gone and forgotten. One of them was still current, but I'd done nothing about it, and hadn't told the man concerned that the letter existed. It wouldn't anyway be him. He would certainly not kill me.

All of which left one most uncomfortable explanation . . . that somebody thought I had something I didn't have. Someone who knew I'd inherited George Millace's blackmailing package . . . and who knew I'd used some of it . . . and who wanted to stop me using any more of it.

George Millace had definitely had more in that box than I'd inherited. I didn't have, for instance, the cigarette packet on which Dana den Relgan had written her drugs list. And I didn't have . . . what else?

'Well, sir,' the inspector said.

'No one's been into my cottage since I was using the darkroom on Wednesday. Only my neighbour, and the rating officer . . .' I stopped, and they pounced on it. 'What rating officer?'

Ask Mrs Jackson, I said; and they said yes they would.

'She said he didn't touch anything.'

'But he could have seen what type of filter . . .'

'Is it my own filter?' I asked. 'It does look like it.'

'Probably,' the younger man said. 'But our man would have had to see it . . . for the dimensions. Then he would come back . . . and it would take about thirty seconds, I'd reckon, to take the filter cartridge out and put the packets of chemicals in. Pretty neat job.'

'Will Jeremy live?' I said.

The younger man shrugged. 'I'm a chemist. Not a doctor.'

They went away after a while, taking the filter.

I rang the hospital. No change.

I went to the hospital myself in the afternoon, with Harold's wife driving because she insisted I wasn't fit.

I didn't see Jeremy. I saw his parents. They were abstracted with worry, too upset to be angry. Not my fault, they said, though I thought they would think so later. Jeremy was being kept alive by a respirator. His breathing was paralysed. His heart was beating. His brain was alive.

His mother wept.

'Don't worry so,' Harold's wife said, driving home. 'He'll be all right.'

She had persuaded the casualty sister, whom she knew, to get me to have some stitches in my face. The result felt stiffer than ever.

'If he dies . . .'

'He won't die,' Harold's wife said.

The inspector telephoned to say I could go back to the cottage, but not into the darkroom: the police had sealed it.

I wandered slowly round my home feeling no sort of ease. Physically wretched, morally pulverised, neck-deep in guilt.

There were signs everywhere that the police had searched. Hardly surprising, I supposed. They hadn't come across the few prints I still had of George Millace's letters, which were locked in the car. They had left undisturbed on the kitchen dresser the box with the blank-looking negatives.

The box . . .

I opened it. It still contained, beside the puzzles I'd solved, the one that I hadn't.

The black light-proof envelope which contained what looked like a piece of clear plastic and two unused sheets of typing paper.

Perhaps . . . I thought . . . Perhaps it's because I have these that the gas trap was set.

But what . . . *what* did I have?

It was no good, I thought: I would have to find out . . . and pretty fast, before whoever it was had another go at killing me, and succeeded.

EIGHTEEN:

I begged a bed again from Harold's wife, and in the morning telephoned again to Swindon hospital.

Jeremy was alive. No change.

I sat in Harold's kitchen drinking coffee, suicidally depressed.

Harold answered his ringing telephone for about the tenth time that morning and handed the receiver to me.

'It's not an owner, this time,' he said. 'It's for you.'

It was Jeremy's father. I felt sick.

'We want you to know . . . he's awake.'

'Oh . . .'

'He's still on the respirator. But they say that by now if he'd been going to die, he'd have gone. He's still very ill . . . but they say he'll recover. We thought you'd like to know.'

'Thank you,' I said.

The reprieve was almost more unbearable than the anxiety. I gave the receiver to Harold and said Jeremy was better, and went out into the yard to look at the horses. In the fresh air I felt stifled. In relief, overthrown. I stood in the wind waiting for the internal storm to abate, and gradually felt an incredible sense of release. I had literally been freed. Let off a life sentence. You bugger, Jeremy, I thought dishing out such a fright.

Clare telephoned.

'He's all right. He's awake,' I said.

'Thank God.'

'Can I ask you a favour?' I said. 'Can I dump myself on Samantha for a night or two?'

'As in the old days?'

'Until Saturday.'

She swallowed a laugh and said why not, and when did I want to come.

'Tonight,' I said. 'If I may.'

'We'll expect you for supper.'

*   *   *

Harold wanted to know when I thought I'd be fit to race.

I would get some physiotherapy from the Clinic for Injuries in London, I said. By Saturday I'd be ready.

'Not by the look of you.'

'Four days. I'll be fit.'

'Mind you are, then.'

I felt distinctly unfit still for driving, but less than inclined to sleep alone in my cottage. I did some minimal packing, collected George's rubbish box from the kitchen, and set off to Chiswick, where despite wearing sunglass I got a horrified reception. Black bruises, stitched cuts, three-day growth of beard. Hardly a riot.

'But it's *worse,*' Clare said, staring closely.

'Looks worse, feels better.' A good job, I thought, that they couldn't see the rest of me. My whole belly was black with the decaying remains of internal abdominal bleeding. The damage, I'd concluded, which had set off the spasms.

Samantha was troubled. 'Clare said someone had punched you . . . but I never thought . . .'

'Look,' I said, 'I could go somewhere else.'

'Don't be silly. Supper's ready.'

They didn't talk much or seem to expect me to. I wasn't good company. Too drastically feeble. I asked with the coffee if I might telephone to Swindon.

'Jeremy?' Clare said.

I nodded.

'I'll do it. What's the number?'

I told her, and she got through, and consulted.

'Still on the respirator,' she said, 'but progress maintained.'

'If you're tired,' Samantha said calmly, 'go to bed.'

'Well . . .'

They both came upstairs. I walked automatically, without thinking, into the small bedroom next door to the bathroom.

They both laughed. 'We wondered if you would,' Samantha said.

Clare went to work and I spent most of Wednesday dozing in the swinging basket chair in the kitchen. Samantha came in and out, went to her part-time job in the morning, shopped in the afternoon. I waited in a highly peaceful state for energy of any sort to return to brain or limbs and reckoned I was fortunate to have a day like that to mend in.

Thursday took me to the Clinic for Injuries for two long

sessions of electric treatment, massage and general physio, with two more sessions promised for Friday.

On Thursday between the sessions I telephoned to four photographers and one acquaintance who worked on a specialist magazine, and found no one who knew how to raise pictures from plastic or typing paper. Pull the other one, old boy, the specialist said wearily.

When I got back to Chiswick the sun was low on the winter horizon, and in the kitchen Samantha was cleaning the french windows.

'They always look filthy when the sun shines on them,' she said, busily rubbing with a cloth. 'Sorry if it's cold in here, but I won't be long.'

I sat in the basket chair and watched her squirt liquid cleaner out of a white plastic bottle. She finished the outsides of the doors and came in, pulling them after her, fastening the bolts. The plastic bottle stood on a table beside her.

AJAX, it said, in big letters.

I frowned at it, trying to remember. Where had I heard the word Ajax?

I stood up out of the swinging chair and walked over for a closer look. Ajax Window Cleaner, it said in smaller red letters on the white plastic, With Ammonia. I picked the bottle up and shook it. Liquid. I put my nose to the top, and smelled the contents. Soapy. Sweet scented. Not pungent.

'What is it?' Samantha said. 'What are you looking at?'

'This cleaner . . .'

'Yes?'

'Why would a man ask his wife to buy him some Ajax?'

'What a question,' Samantha said. 'I've no idea.'

'Nor did she have,' I said. 'She didn't know why.'

Samantha took the bottle out of my hands and continued with her task. 'You can clean any sort of glass with it,' she said. 'Bathroom tiles. Looking glass. Quite useful stuff.'

I went back to the basket chair and swung in it gently. Samantha cast me a sideways glance, smiling.

'You looked like death two days ago,' she said.

'And now?'

'Now one might pause before calling the undertaker.'

'I'll shave tomorrow,' I said.

'Who punched you?' Her voice sounded casual. Her eyes and attention were on the window. It was, all the same, a serious question. A seeking not for a simple one word answer, but for commitment to herself. A sort of request for payment for shelter unquestioningly given. If I didn't tell her, she wouldn't persist. But if I didn't tell her, we had already gone as far as we ever would in relationship.

What did I want, I thought, in that house that now increasingly felt like home. I had never wanted a family: people always close: permanence. I'd wanted no loving ties. No suffocating emotional dependents. So if I nested comfortably, deeply into the lives lived in that house, wouldn't I feel impelled in a short while to break out with wild flapping freedom-seeking wings. Did anyone ever fundamentally change?

Samantha read into my silence what I expected, and her manner did subtly alter not to one of unfriendliness, but to a cut-off of intimacy. Before she'd finished the window I'd become her guest, not her . . . her what? Her son, brother, nephew . . . part of her.

She gave me a bright surface smile and put the kettle on for tea.

Clare returned from work with gaiety over tiredness, and she too, though not asking, was waiting.

I found myself, halfway through supper, just telling them about George Millace. In the end it was no great hard decision. No cut and dried calculation. I just naturally told them.

'You won't approve,' I said. 'I carried on where George left off.'

They listened with their forks in the air, taking mouthfuls at long intervals, eating peas and lasagne slowly.

'So you see,' I said at the end. 'It isn't finished yet. There's no going back or wishing I hadn't started . . . I don't know that I do wish that . . . but I asked to come here for a few days because I didn't feel safe in the cottage, and I'm not going back there to live permanently until I know who tried to kill me.'

Clare said, 'You might never know.'

'Don't say that,' Samantha said sharply. 'If he doesn't find out . . .' She stopped.

I finished it for her, 'I'll have no defence.'

'Perhaps the police . . .' Clare said.

'Perhaps.'

We passed the rest of the evening more in thoughtfulness than depression, and the news from Swindon was good. Jeremy's lungs were coming out of paralysis. Still on the respirator, but a significant improvement during the past twenty-four hours. The prim voice reading the written bulletin sounded bored. Could I speak to Jeremy himself yet, I asked. They'd check. The prim voice came back; not in intensive care: try on Sunday.

I spent a long time in the bathroom on Friday morning scraping off beard and snipping out unabsorbed ends of the fine transparent thread the casualty sister had used in her stitching. She'd done a neat job, I had to confess. The cuts had all healed, and would disappear probably without scars. All the swelling, also, had gone. There were still the remains of black bruises turning yellow, and still the chipped teeth, but what finally looked out of the mirror was definitely a face, not a nightmare.

Samantha looked relieved over the reemergence of civilisation and insisted on telephoning to her dentist. 'You need caps,' she said, 'and caps you'll have.' And caps I had, late that afternoon. Temporaries, until porcelain jobs could be made.

Between the two sessions in the clinic I drove north out of London to Basildon in Essex, to where a British firm manufactured photographic printing paper. I went instead of telephoning because I thought they would find it less easy to say they had no information if I was actually there; and so it proved.

They did not, they said in the front office politely, know of any photographic materials which looked like plastic or typing paper. Had I brought the specimens with me?

No, I had not. I didn't want them examined in case they were sensitive to light. Could I see someone else?

Difficult, they said.

I showed no signs of leaving. Perhaps Mr Christopher could help me, they suggested at length, if he wasn't too busy.

Mr Christopher turned out to be about nineteen with an anti-social hair-cut and chronic catarrh. He listened, however, attentively.

'This paper and this plastic've got no emulsion on them?'

'No, I don't think so.'

He shrugged. 'There you are, then.'

'There I am where?'

'You got no pictures.'

I sucked at the still broken teeth and asked him what seemed to be a nonsensical question.

'Why would a photographer want ammonia?'

'Well, he wouldn't. Not for photographs. No straight ammonia in any developer or bleach or fix, that I know of.'

'Would anyone here know?' I asked.

He gave me a pitying stare, implying that if he didn't know, no one else would.

'You could ask,' I said persuasively. 'Because if there's a process which does use ammonia, you'd like to know, wouldn't you?'

'Yeah. I reckon I would.'

He gave me a brisk nod and vanished, and I waited a quarter of an hour, wondering if he'd gone off to lunch. He returned, however, with a grey elderly man in glasses who was none too willing but delivered the goods.

'Ammonia,' he said, 'is used in the photographic sections of engineering industries. It develops what the public call blueprints. More accurately, of course, it's the diazo process.'

'Please,' I said humbly and with gratitude, 'could you describe it to me.'

'What's the matter with your face?' he said.

'Lost an argument.'

'Huh.'

'Diazo process,' I said. 'What is it?'

'You get a drawing . . . a line drawing, I'm talking about . . . from the designer. Say of a component in a machine. A drawing with exact specifications for manufacture. Are you with me?'

'Yes.'

'The industry will need several copies of the master drawing. So they make blueprints of it. Or rather, they don't.'

'Er . . .' I said.

'In blueprints,' he said severely, 'the paper turns blue, leaving the design in white. Nowadays the paper turns white and the lines develop in black. Or dark red.'

'Please . . . go on.'

'From the beginning?' he said. 'The master drawing, which is of course on translucent paper, is pinned and pressed tightly by glass over a sheet of diazo paper. Diazo paper is white on the back, and yellow or greenish on the side covered with ammonia-sensitive dye. Bright carbon arclight is shone onto the master drawing for a measured length of time. This light bleaches out all the dye on the diazo paper underneath except for the parts under the lines on the master drawing. The diazo paper is then developed in hot ammonia fumes, and the lines of dye emerge, turning dark. Is that what you want?'

'Indeed it is,' I said with awe. 'Does diazo paper look like typing paper?'

'Certainly it can, if it's cut down to that size.'

'And how about a piece of clear-looking plastic?'

'Sounds like diazo film,' he said calmly. 'You don't need hot ammonia fumes for developing that. Any form of cold liquid ammonia will do. But be careful. I said carbon arc-lights, because that's the method that's used in engineering, but of course a longer exposure to sunlight or any other form of light would also have the same effect. If the piece of film you have looks clear, it means that most of the yellow-looking dye has been already bleached out. If there is a drawing there, you must be careful not to expose it to too much more light.'

'How much more light is too much?' I said anxiously.

He pursed his lips. 'In sunlight, you'd have lost any trace of dye for ever in thirty seconds. In normal room light . . . five to ten minutes.'

'It's in a light-proof envelope.'

'Then you might be lucky.'

'And the sheets of paper . . . they look white on both sides.'

'The same applies,' he said. 'They've been exposed to light. You might have a drawing there, or you might not.'

'How do I make hot ammonia fumes, to find out?'

'Simple,' he said, as if everyone would know items like that. 'Put some ammonia in a saucepan and heat it. Hold the paper over the top. Don't get it wet. Just steam it.'

'Would you,' I said carefully, 'like some champagne for lunch?'

I returned to Samantha's house at about six o'clock with a cheap saucepan, two bottles of Ajax, an anaesthetised top lip, and a set of muscles that had been jerked, pressed and exercised into some sort of resurrection. I also felt dead tired which wasn't a good omen for fitness on the morrow, when, Harold had informed me on the telephone, two 'chasers would be awaiting my services at Sandown Park.

Samantha had gone out. Clare, with work scattered all over the kitchen table, gave me a fast, assessing scrutiny and suggested a large brandy.

'It's in that cupboard with the salt and flour and herbs. Cooking brandy. Pour me some too, would you?'

I sat at the table with her for a while, sipping the repulsive stuff neat and feeling a lot better for it. Her dark head was bent over the book she was working on, the capable hand stretching out now and again for the glass, the mind engrossed in her task.

'Would you live with me?' I said.

She looked up; abstracted, faintly frowning, questioning.

'Did you say . . . ?'

'Yes, I did,' I said. 'Would you live with me?'

Her work at last lost her attention. With a smile in her eyes she said, 'Is that an academic question or a positive invitation?'

'Invitation.'

'I couldn't live in Lambourn' she said. 'Too far to commute. You couldn't live here . . . too far from the horses.'

'Somewhere in between.'

She looked at me wonderingly. 'Are you serious?'

'Yes.'

'But we haven't . . .' She stopped, leaving a clear meaning.

'Been to bed.'

'Well . . .'

'In general,' I said, 'What do you think?'

She took refuge and time with sips from her glass. I waited for what seemed a small age.

'I think,' she said finally, 'why not give it a try.'

I smiled from intense satisfaction.

'Don't look so smug,' she said. 'Drink your brandy while I finish this book.'

She bent her head down again but didn't read far.

'It's no good,' she said. 'How can I work . . . ? Let's get the supper.'

Cooking frozen fish fillets took ages because of her trying to do it with my arms round her waist and my chin on her hair. I didn't taste the stuff when we ate it. I felt extraordinarily light-headed. I hadn't deeply hoped she would say yes, and still less had I expected the incredible sense of adventure since she had. To have someone to care about seemed no longer a burden to be avoided, but a positive privilege.

Amazing, I thought dimly; the whole thing's amazing. Was this what Lord White had felt for Dana den Relgan?

'What time does Samantha get back?' I said.

Clare shook her head. 'Too soon.'

'Will you come with me tomorrow?' I said. 'To the races . . . and then stay somewhere together afterwards.'

'Yes, I will.'

'Samantha won't mind?'

She gave me an amused look. 'No, I don't think so.'

'Why do you laugh?'

'She's gone to the pictures. I asked her why she had to go on your last night here. She said she wanted to see the film. I thought it odd . . . but I believed her. She saw . . . more than I did.'

'My God,' I said. '*Women.*'

While she did try again to finish her work, I fetched the rubbish box and took out the black light-proof envelope.

I borrowed a flat glass dish from a cupboard. Took the piece of plastic film from the envelope. Put it in the dish. At once poured liquid Ajax over it. Held my breath.

Almost instantly dark brownish-red lines became visible. I rocked the dish, sloshing the liquid across the plastic surface, conscious that all of the remaining dye had to be covered with ammonia before the light bleached it away.

It was no engineering drawing, but handwriting.

It looked odd.

As more and more developed, I realised that from the reading point of view the plastic was wrong side up.

Turned it over. Sloshed more Ajax over it, tilting it back and forth. Read the revealed words, as clear as when they'd been written.

They were . . . they had to be . . . what Dana den Relgan had written on the cigarette packet.

Heroin, cocaine, cannabis. Quantities, dates, prices paid, suppliers. No wonder she had wanted it back.

Clare looked up from her work.

'What have you found?'

'What that Dana girl who came last Sunday was wanting.'

'Let's see.' She came across and looked into the dish, reading. 'That's pretty damning, isn't it?'

'Mm.'

'But how did it turn up . . . like this?'

I said appreciatively, 'Crafty George Millace. He got her to write on cellophane wrapping with a red felt-tip pen . . . she felt safer that way, because cigarette packet wrapping is so fragile, so destructible . . . and I expect the words themselves looked indistinct, over the printed packet. But from George's point of view all he wanted was solid lines on transparent material, to make a diazo print.'

I explained to her all that I'd learned in Basildon. 'He must have cut the wrapping off carefully, pressed it flat under glass on top of this piece of diazo film, and exposed it to light. Then with the drugs list safely recorded, it wouldn't matter if the wrapping came to pieces . . . and the list was hidden, like everything else.'

'He was an extraordinary man.'

I nodded. 'Extraordinary. Though, mind you, he didn't mean anyone else to have to solve his puzzles. He made them only to please himself . . . and to save the records from angry burglars.'

'In which he succeeded.'

'He sure did.'

'What about all your photographs?' she said in sudden alarm. 'All the ones in the filing cabinet. Suppose . . .'

'Calm down,' I said. 'Even if anyone stole them or burned them they'd miss all the negatives. The butcher has those down the road in his freezer room.'

'Maybe all photographers,' she said, 'are obsessed.'

It wasn't until much later that I realised I hadn't disputed her classification. I hadn't even *thought* 'I'm a jockey.'

I asked her if she'd mind if I filled the kitchen with the smell of boiling ammonia.

'I'll go and wash my hair,' she said.

When she'd gone I drained the Ajax out of the dish into the saucepan and added to it what was left in the first bottle, and while it heated opened the french windows so as not to asphyxiate. Then I held the first of the sheets of what looked like typing paper over the simmering cleaner, and watched George's words come alive as if they'd been written in secret ink. Ammonia clearly evaporated quickly, because it took the whole second bottle to get results with the second sheet, but it too, grew words like the first.

Together they constituted one handwritten letter in what I had no doubt was George's own writing. He must himself have written on some sort of transparent material . . . and it could have been anything: a polythene bag, tracing paper, a piece of glass, film with all the emulsion bleached off . . . anything. When he'd written, he had put his letter over diazo paper and exposed it to light, and immediately stored the exposed paper in the light-proof envelope.

And then what? Had he sent his transparent original? Had he written it again on ordinary paper? Had he typed it? No way of knowing. But one thing was certain: in some form or other he had despatched his letter.

I had heard of the results of its arrival.

I could guess, I thought, who wanted me dead.

NINETEEN:

Harold met me with some relief on the verandah outside the weighing room at Sandown.

'You at least look better . . . have you passed the doctor?'

I nodded. 'He signed my card.' He'd no reason not to. By his standards a jockey who took a week off because he'd been kicked was acting more self-indulgently than usual. He'd asked me to do a bench-stretch, and nodded me through.

'Victor's here,' Harold said.

'Did you tell him . . . ?'

'Yes, I did. He says he doesn't want to talk to you on a racecourse. He says he wants to see his horses work on the Downs. He's coming on Monday. He'll talk to you then. And, Philip, you bloody well be careful what you say.'

'Mm,' I said non-committally. 'How about Coral Key?'

'What about him? He's fit.'

'No funny business?'

'Victor knows how you feel,' Harold said.

'Victor doesn't care a losing tote ticket how I feel. Is the horse running straight?'

'He hasn't said anything.'

'Because I am,' I said. 'If I'm riding it, I'm riding it straight. Whatever he says in the parade ring.'

'You've got bloody aggressive all of a sudden.'

'No . . . just saving you money. You personally. Don't back me to lose, like you did on Daylight. That's all.'

He said he wouldn't. He also said there was no point in holding the Sunday briefing if I was talking to Victor on Monday, and that we would discuss next week's plans after that. Neither of us said what was in both of our minds . . . after Monday, would there be any plans?

Steve Millace in the changing room was complaining about a starter letting a race off when he, Steve, hadn't been ready, with the consequence that he was left so flat-footed that the other runners had gone half a furlong before he'd got started . . . the owner was angry and said he wanted another jockey next time, and, as Steve asked everyone ad infinitum, was it fair?

'No,' I said. 'Life isn't.'

'It should be.'

'Better face it,' I said smiling. 'The best you can expect is a kick in the teeth.'

'Your teeth are all right,' someone said.

'They've got caps on.'

'Pick up the pieces, huh? Is that what you're saying?'

I nodded.

Steve said, not following this exchange, 'Starters should be fined for letting a race off when the horses aren't pointing the right way.'

'Give it a rest,' someone said: but Steve as usual was still going on about it a couple of hours later.

His mother, he said when I enquired, had gone to friends in Devon for a rest.

Outside the weighing room Bart Underfield was lecturing one of the more gullible of the pressmen on the subject of unusual nutrients.

'It's rubbish giving horses beer and eggs and ridiculous things like that. I never do it.'

The pressman refrained from saying – or perhaps he didn't know – that the trainers addicted to eggs and beer were on the whole more successful than Bart.

Bart's face when he saw me changed from bossy know-all to tight-lipped spite. He jettisoned the pressman and took two decisive steps to stand in my path, but when he'd stopped me he didn't speak.

'Do you want something, Bart?' I said.

He still didn't say anything. I thought that quite likely he couldn't find words intense enough to convey what he felt. I was growing accustomed, I thought, to being hated.

He found his voice. 'You wait,' he said with bitter quiet. 'I'll get you.'

If he'd had a dagger and privacy, I wouldn't have turned my back on him, as I did, to walk away.

Lord White was there, deep in earnest conversation with fellow Stewards, his gaze flicking over me quickly as if wincing. He would never, I supposed, feel comfortable when I was around. Never be absolutely sure that I wouldn't tell. Never like me knowing what I knew.

He would have to put up with it for a long time, I thought.

One way or another the racing world would always be my world, as it was his. He would see me, and I him, week by week, until one of us died.

Victor Briggs was waiting in the parade ring when I went out to ride Coral Key. A heavy brooding figure in his broad-brimmed hat and long navy overcoat: unsmiling, untalkative, gloomy. When I touched my cap to him politely there was no response of any sort, only the maintenance of an expressionless stare.

Coral Key was an oddity among Victor Briggs's horses, a six year old novice 'chaser bought out of the hunting field when he had begun to show promise in point-to-points. Great horses in the past had started that way, like Oxo and Ben Nevis which had both won the Grand National, and although Coral Key was unlikely to be of that class, it seemed to me that he, too, had the feel of good things to come. There was no way that I was going to mess up his early career, whatever my instructions. In my mind and very likely in my attitude I dared his owner to say he didn't want him to try to win.

He didn't say it. He said nothing at all about anything. He simply watched me unblinkingly, and kept his mouth shut.

Harold bustled about as if movement itself could dispel the atmosphere existing between his owner and his jockey; and I mounted and rode out to the course feeling as if I'd been in a strong field of undischarged electricity.

A spark . . . an explosion . . . might lie ahead. Harold sensed it. Harold was worried to the depths of his own explosive soul.

It might be going to be the last race I ever rode for Victor Briggs. I lined up at the start thinking that it was no good speculating about that; that all I should be concentrating on was the matter in hand.

A cold windy cloudy day. Good ground underfoot. Seven other runners, none of them brilliant. If Coral Key jumped as he had when I'd schooled him at home, he should have a good chance.

I settled my goggles over my eyes and gathered the reins.

'Come in, now, jockeys,' the starter said. The horses advanced towards the tapes in a slow line and as the gate flew up accelerated away from bunched haunches. Thirteen fences; two miles. I would find out pretty soon, I thought ruefully, if I wasn't yet fit.

Important, I thought, to get him to jump well. It was what I was best at. What I most enjoyed doing. There were seven fences close together down the far side of the course . . . If one met the first of them just right they all fitted, but a brakes-on approach to the first often meant seven blunders by the end, and countless lengths lost.

From the start there were two fences, then the uphill stretch past the stands, then the top bend, then the downhill fence where I'd stepped off Daylight. No problems on Coral Key: he cleared the lot. Then the sweep round to the seven trappy fences, and if I lost one length getting Coral Key set right for the first, by the end of the seventh I'd stolen ten.

Too soon for satisfaction. Round the long bottom curve Coral Key lay second, taking a breather. Three fences to go . . . and the long hill to home.

Between the last two fences I caught up with the leader. We jumped the last fence alongsides, nothing between us. Raced up the hill, stretching, flying . . . doing everything I could.

The other horse won by two lengths.

Harold said, 'He ran well,' a shade apprehensively, patting Coral Key in the unsaddling enclosure; and Victor Briggs said nothing.

I pulled the saddle off and went in to weigh. There wasn't any way that I could think of that I could have won the race. The other horse had had enough in hand to beat off my challenge. He'd been stronger than Coral Key, and faster. I hadn't felt weak. I hadn't thrown anything away in jumping mistakes. I just hadn't won.

I had needed a strong hand for talking to Victor Briggs; and I hadn't got it.

When life kicks you in the teeth, get caps.

I won the other 'chase, the one that didn't matter so much except to the owners, a junketing quartet of businessmen.

'Bloody good show,' they said, beaming. 'Bloody well ridden.'

I saw Victor Briggs watching from ten paces away, balefully staring. I wondered if he knew how much I'd have given to have those two results reversed.

Clare said, 'I suppose the wrong one won?'

'Yeah.'

'How much does it matter?'

'I'll find out on Monday.'

'Well . . . let's forget it.'

'Shouldn't be difficult,' I said. I looked at the trim dark coat, the white puff-ball hat, the long polished boots. Looked at the large grey eyes and the friendly mouth. Incredible, I thought, to have someone like that waiting for me outside the weighing room. Quite extraordinarily different from going home alone. Like a fire in a cold house. Like sugar on strawberries.

'Would you mind very much,' I said, 'if we made a detour for me to call on my grandmother?'

The old woman was markedly worse.

No longer propped more or less upright, she sagged back without strength on the pillows; and even the eyes seemed to be losing the struggle, with none of the beady aggression glittering out.

'Did you bring her?' she said.

Still no salutation, no preliminaries. Perhaps it was a mistake to expect changes in the mind to accompany changes in the body. Perhaps my feelings for her were different . . . and all that remained immutable was her hatred for me.

'No,' I said. 'I didn't bring her. She's lost.'

'You said you would find her.'

'She's lost.'

She gave a feeble cough, the thin chest jerking. Her eyelids closed for a few seconds and opened again. A weak hand twitched at the sheet.

'Leave your money to James,' I said.

With a faint outer echo of persistent inner stubbornness, she shook her head.

'Leave some to charity, then,' I said. 'Leave it to a dog's home.'

'I hate dogs.' Her voice was weak. Not her opinions.

'How about lifeboats?'

'Hate the sea. Makes me sick.'

'Medical research?'

'Hasn't done me much good, has it?'

'Well,' I said slowly, 'how about leaving it to a religious order of some sort.'

'You must be mad. I hate religion. Cause of trouble. Cause of wars. Wouldn't give them a penny.'

I sat down unbidden in the armchair.

'Can I do anything for you?' I asked. 'Besides, of course, finding Amanda. Can I fetch anything? Is there anything you want?'

She raised a faint sneer. 'Don't think you can soft soap me

into leaving any money to you, because I'm not going to.'

'I'd give water to a dying cat,' I said. 'Even if it spat in my face.'

Her mouth opened and stiffened with affront.

'How . . . dare . . . you?'

'How dare you still think I'd shift a speck of dust for your money?'

The mouth closed into a thin line.

'Can I fetch you anything?' I said again, levelly. 'Is there anything you want?'

She didn't answer for several seconds. Then she said, 'Go away.'

'Well, I will, in a minute,' I said. 'But I want just to suggest something else.' I waited a fraction, but as she didn't immediately argue I continued. 'In case Amanda is ever found . . . why don't you set up a trust for her? Tie up the capital tight with masses of excellent trustees. Make it so that she couldn't ever get her hands on the money herself . . . and nor could anyone who was . . . perhaps . . . after her fortune. Make it impossible for anyone but Amanda herself to benefit . . . with an income paid out only at the direction of the trustees.'

She watched me with half-lowered eyelids.

'Wherever she is,' I said, 'Amanda is still only seventeen or eighteen. Too young to inherit a lot of money without strings. Leave it to her . . . with strings like steel hawsers.'

'Is that all?'

'Mm.'

She lay quiet, immobile.

I waited. I had waited all my life for something other than malevolence from my grandmother. I could wait forever.

'Go away,' she said.

I stood up and said 'Very well.'

Walked to the door. Put my hand on the knob.

'Send me some roses,' my grandmother said.

We found a flower shop still open in the town, though they were sweeping out ready to close.

'Doesn't she realise it's December?' Clare said. 'Roses will cost a fortune.'

'If you were dying, and you wanted roses, do you think you'd care?'

'Maybe not.'

All they had in the flower shop were fifteen very small pink buds on very long thin stems. Not much call for roses. These were left over spare from a wedding.

We drove back to the nursing home and gave them to a nurse to deliver at once, with a card enclosed saying I'd get some better ones next week.

'She doesn't deserve it,' Clare said.

'Poor old woman.'

We stayed in a pub by the Thames which had old beams and good food and bedroom windows looking out to bare willows and sluggish brown water.

No one knew us. We signed in as Mr and Mrs and ate a slow dinner, and went unobtrusively to bed. Not the first time she'd done it, she said: did I mind? Preferred it, I said. No fetishes about virgins? No kinks at all, that I knew of. Good, she said.

It began in friendship and progressed to passion. Ended in breathlessness and laughter, sank to murmurs and sleep. The best it had ever been for me. Couldn't tell about her. She showed no hesitation, however, about a repeat programme in the morning.

In the afternoon, in peaceful accord, we went to see Jeremy.

He was lying in a high bed in a room on his own, with a mass of breathing equipment to one side. He was, though, breathing for himself with his own lungs. Precariously, I guessed, since a nurse came in to check on him every ten minutes while we were there, making sure that a bell-push remained under his fingers the whole time.

He looked thinner than ever, and greyly pale, but there had been no near-execution in his brain. The eyes were as intelligent as ever, and the silly-ass manner appeared strongly as a defence against the indignities of his position. The nurse, on every visit, got a load of weary waffle.

I tried to apologise for what he'd suffered. He wouldn't have it.

'Don't forget,' he said, 'I was there because I wanted to be. No one exactly twisted my arm.' He gave me a travelling inspection. 'Your face looks O.K. How do you heal so fast?'

'Always do.'

'Always . . .' he gave a weak laugh. 'Funny life you lead. Always healing.'

'How long will you be in here?'

'Three or four days.'

'Is that all?' Clare said, surprised. 'You look . . . er . . .'

He looked whiter than the pillows his head lay on. He nodded, however, and said, 'I'm breathing much better. Once there's no danger the nerves will pack up again, I can go. There's nothing else wrong.'

'I'll take you home if you need transport,' I said.

'Might hold you to that.'

We didn't stay very long because talking clearly tired him, but just before we went he said, 'You know, that gas was so quick. Not slow, like gas at the dentist. I'd no time to do anything . . . it was like breathing a brick wall.'

In a short reflective silence Clare said, 'No one would have lived if they'd been there alone.'

'Makes you think . . . what?' said Jeremy cheerfully.

As we drove back towards the pub Clare said, 'You didn't tell him about Amanda.'

'Plenty of time.'

'He came down last Sunday because he'd got your message that you'd found her. He told me while we were in the kitchen. He said your phone was out of order, so he came.'

'I'd unplugged it.'

'Odd how things happen.'

'Mm.'

Our second night was a confirmation of the first. Much the same, but new and different. A tingling, fierce, gentle, intense, turbulent time. A matter, it seemed, as much to her liking as mine.

'Where's this depression one's supposed to get?' she said, very late. 'Post what's-it.'

'Comes in the morning, when you go.'

'That's hours off yet.'

'So it is.'

The morning came, as they do. I drove her to a station to catch a train, and went on myself to Lambourn.

When I got there, before going to Harold's, I called at my cottage. All seemed quiet. All cold. All strangely unfamiliar, as if home was no longer the natural embracing refuge it should be. I saw for the first time the bareness, the emotional chill which had been so apparent to Jeremy on his first visit. It no longer seemed to fit with myself. The person who had made that home was going away, receding in time. I felt oddly nostalgic . . . but there was no calling him back. The maturing change had gone too far.

Shivering a little I spread out on the kitchen table a variety of photographs of different people, and then I asked my neighbour Mrs Jackson to come in and look at them.

'What am I looking for, Mr Nore?'

'Anyone you've seen before.'

Obligingly she studied them carefully one by one, and stopped without hesitation at a certain face.

'How extraordinary!' she exclaimed. 'That's the council man who came about the rates. The one I let in here. Ever so sarcastic, the police were about that, but as I told them, you don't *expect* people to say they're rating officers if they aren't.'

'You're sure he's the one?'

'Positive,' she said, nodding. 'He had that same hat on, and all.'

'Then would you write on the back of the photo, for me, Mrs Jackson?' I gave her a Lumocolor pen that would write boldly and blackly on the photographic paper, and dictated the words for her, saying that this man had called at the house of Philip Nore posing as a rating officer on Friday, November 27th.

'Is that all?' she asked.

'Sign your name, Mrs Jackson. And would you mind repeating the whole message on the back of this other photograph?'

With concentration she did so. 'Are you giving these to the police?' she said. 'I don't want them bothering me again really. Will they come back again with their questions?'

'I shouldn't think so,' I said.

TWENTY:

Victor Briggs had come in his Mercedes, but he went up to the Downs with Harold in the Land Rover. I rode up on a horse. The morning's work got done to everyone's reasonable satisfaction, and we all returned variously to the stable.

When I rode into the yard Victor Briggs was standing by his car, waiting. I slid off the horse and gave it to one of the lads to see to.

'Get in the car,' Victor said.

No waster of words, ever. He stood there in his usual clothes, gloved as always against the chilly wind, darkening the day. If I could see auras, I thought, his would be black.

I sat in the front passenger seat, where he pointed, and he slid himself in beside me, behind the steering wheel. He started the engine, released the brake, put the automatic gear into drive. The quiet hunk of metal eased out of Lambourn, going back to the Downs.

He stopped on a wide piece of grass verge from where one could see half of Berkshire. He switched off the engine, leaned back in his seat, and said, 'Well?'

'Do you know what I'm going to say?' I asked.

'I hear things,' he said. 'I hear a lot of things.'

'I know that.'

'I heard that den Relgan set his goons on you.'

'Did you?' I looked at him with interest. 'Where did you hear that?'

He made a small tight movement of his mouth, but he did answer. 'Gambling club.'

'What did you hear?'

'True, isn't it?' he said. 'You still had the marks on Saturday.'

'Did you hear any reasons?'

He produced the twitch that went for a smothered smile.

'I heard,' he said, 'that you got den Relgan chucked out of the Jockey Club a great deal faster than he got in.'

He watched my alarmed surprise with another twitch, a less successful effort this time at hiding amusement.

'Did you hear how?' I said.

He said with faint regret, 'No. Just that you'd done it. The goons were talking. Stupid bone-headed bull-muscle. Den Relgan's heading for trouble, using them. They never keep their mouths shut.'

'Are they . . . um . . . out for general hire?'

'Chuckers out at a gaming club. Muscle for hire. As you say.'

'They beat up George Millace's wife . . . did you hear that too?'

After a pause he nodded, but offered no comment.

I looked at the closed expression, the dense whitish skin, the black shadow of beard. A secretive, solid, slow-moving man with a tap into a world I knew little of. Gaming clubs, hired bully-boys, underworld gossip.

'The goons said they left you for dead,' he said. 'A week later, you're winning a race.'

'They exaggerated,' I said dryly.

I got a twitch but also a shake of the head. 'One of them was scared. Rattled. Said they'd gone too far . . . with the boots.'

'You know them well?' I said.

'They talk.'

There was another pause, then I said without emphasis, 'George Millace sent you a letter.'

He moved in his seat, seeming almost to relax, breathing out in a long sigh. He'd been waiting to know, I thought. Patiently waiting. Answering questions. Being obliging.

'How long have you had it?' he said.

'Three weeks.'

'You can't use it.' There was a faint tremor of triumph in the statement. 'You'd be in trouble yourself.'

'How did you know I'd got it?' I said.

He blinked. The mouth tightened. He said slowly, 'I heard you had George Millace's . . .'

'George Millace's what?'

'Files.'

'Ah,' I said. 'Nice anonymous words, files. How did you hear I had them? Who from?'

'Ivor,' he said. 'And Dana. Separately.'

'Will you tell me?'

He thought it over, giving me a blank inspection, and then said grudingly, 'Ivor was too angry to be discreet. He said too much about you . . . such as poisonous creep . . . he said you were fifty times worse than George Millace. And Dana . . .

another night . . . she said did I know you had copies of some blackmailing letters George Millace had sent, and were using them. She asked if I could help her to get hers back.'

I smiled in my turn. 'What did you say?'

'I said I couldn't help her.'

'When you talked to them,' I said, 'was it in gaming clubs?'

'It was.'

'Are they . . . your gaming clubs?'

'None of your business,' he said.

'Well,' I said, 'why not tell me?'

He said after a pause, 'I have two partners. Four gaming clubs. The clientele in general don't know I'm a proprietor. I move around. I play. I listen. Does that answer your question?'

I nodded. 'Yes, thank you. Are those goons your goons?'

'I employ them,' he said austerely, 'as chuckers out. Not to smash up women and jockeys.'

'A little moonlighting, was it? On the side.'

He didn't answer directly. 'I have been expecting,' he said, 'that you would demand something from me if you had that letter. Something more than . . . answers.'

I thought of the letter, which I knew word for word:

Dear Victor Briggs,

I am sure you will be interested to know that I have the following information. You did on five separate occasions during the past six months conspire with a bookmaker to defraud the betting public by arranging that your odds-on favourites should not win their races.

There followed a list of the five races, complete with the sums Victor had received from his bookmaker friend. The letter continued:

I hold a signed affidavit from the bookmaker in question.

As you see, all five of these horses were ridden by Philip Nore, who certainly knew what he was doing.

I could send this affidavit to the Jockey Club, in which case you would both be warned off. I will telephone you soon, however, with an alternative suggestion.

The letter had been sent more than three years earlier. For three years Victor Briggs had run his horses straight. When

George Millace died, a week to the day, Victor Briggs had gone back to the old game. Had gone back . . . to find that his vulnerable jockey was no longer reliable.

'I didn't want to do anything about the letter,' I said. 'I didn't mean to tell you I had it. Not until now.'

'Why not? You wanted to ride to win. You could have used it to make me agree. You'd been told you'd lose your job anyway if you wouldn't ride as I wanted. You knew I couldn't face being warned off. Yet you didn't use the letter for that. Why not?'

'I wanted . . . to make you run the horses straight for their own sakes.'

He gave me another of the long uninformative stares.

'I'll tell you,' he said at last. 'Yesterday I added up all the prize money I'd won since Daylight's race at Sandown. All those seconds and thirds, as well as Sharpener's wins. I added up my winnings from betting, win and place. I made more money in the past month with you riding straight than I did with you stepping off Daylight.' He paused, waiting for a reaction, but, catching it from him, I simply stared back. 'I've seen,' he went on, 'that you weren't going to ride any more crooked races. I've understood that. I know you've changed. You're a different person. Older. Stronger. If you go on riding for me, I won't ask you again to lose a race.' He paused once more. 'Is that enough? Is that what you want to hear?'

I looked away from him, out across the windy landscape.

'Yes.'

After a bit he said, 'George Millace didn't demand money, you know. At least . . .'

'A donation to the Injured Jockeys?'

'You know the lot, don't you.'

'I've learned.' I said. 'George wasn't interested in extorting money for himself. He extorted . . .' I searched for the word. '. . . frustration.'

'From how many?'

'Seven, that I know of. Probably eight, if you ask your bookmaker.'

He was astonished.

'George Millace,' I said, 'enjoyed making people cringe. He did it to everybody in a mild way. To people he could catch out doing wrong, he did it with gusto. He had alternative suggestions for everyone . . . disclosure, or do what George wanted. And what George wanted, in general, was to frustrate.

To stop Ivor den Relgan's power play. To stop Dana taking drugs. To stop other people . . . doing other things.'

'To stop me,' Victor said with a hint of dry humour, 'from being warned off.' He nodded. 'You're right, of course. When George Millace telephoned I was expecting straight blackmail. Then he said all I had to do was behave myself. Those were his words. As long as you behave, Victor, he said, nothing will happen. Victor. He called me Victor. I'd never met him. Knew who he was, of course, but that was all. Victor, he said, as if I were a little pet dog, as long as we're a good boy, nothing will happen. But if I suspect anything. Victor, he said, I'll follow Philip Nore around with my motorised telephotos until I have him bang to rights, and then Victor, you'll both be for the chop.'

'Do you remember word for word what he said, after all this time?' I asked, surprised.

'I recorded him. I was expecting his call . . . I wanted evidence of blackmail. All I got was a moral lecture and a suggestion that I give a thousand pounds to the Injured Jockeys Fund.'

'And was that all? For ever?'

'He used to wink at me at the races,' Victor said.

I laughed.

'Yes, very funny' he said. 'Is that the lot?'

'Not really. There's something you could do for me, if you would. Something you know, and could tell me. Something you could tell me in future.'

'What is it?'

'About Dana's drugs.'

'Stupid girl. She won't listen.'

'She will soon. She's still . . . saveable. And besides her . . .'

I told him what I wanted. He listened acutely. When I'd finished I got the twitch of a throttled smile.

'Beside you,' he said, 'George Millace was a beginner.'

Victor drove off in his car and I walked back to Lambourn over the Downs.

An odd man, I thought. I'd learned more about him in half an hour than I had in seven years, and still knew next to nothing. He had given me what I'd wanted, though. Given it freely. Given me my job without strings for as long as I liked . . . and help in another matter just as important. It hadn't all been, I thought, because of my having that letter.

Going home in the wind, out on the bare hills, I thought of the way things had happened during the past few weeks. Not about George and his bombshells, but of Jeremy and Amanda.

Because of Jeremy's persistence, I'd looked for Amanda, and because of looking for Amanda I had now met a grandmother, an uncle, a sister. I knew something at least of my father. I had a feeling of origin that I hadn't had before.

I had people. I had people like everyone else had. Not necessarily loving or praiseworthy or successful, but *there*. I hadn't wanted them, but now that I had them they sat quietly in the mind like foundation stones.

Because of looking for Amanda I had found Samantha, and with her a feeling of continuity, of belonging. I saw the pattern of my childhood in a different perspective, not as a chopped up kaleidoscope, but as a curve. I knew a place where I'd been, and a woman who'd known me, and they seemed to lead smoothly now towards Charlie.

I no longer floated on the tide.

I had roots.

I reached the point on the hill from where I could see down to the cottage, the brow that I looked up to from the sitting room windows. I stopped there. I could see most of Lambourn, stretched out. Could see Harold's house and the yard. Could see the whole row of cottages, with mine in the centre.

I'd belonged in that village, been part of it, breathed its intrigues for seven years. Been happy, miserable, normal. It was what I'd called home. But now in mind and spirit I was leaving that place . . . and soon would in body as well. I would live somewhere else, with Clare. I would be a photographer.

The future lay inside me; waiting, accepted. One day fairly soon I'd walk into it.

I would race, I thought, until the end of the season. Five or six more months. Then in May or June, when summer came, I'd hang up the boots: retire, as every jockey had to, some time or other. I would tell Harold soon, to give him time to find someone else for the autumn. I'd enjoy what was left, and maybe have a last chance at the Grand National. Anything might happen. One never knew.

I still had the appetite, still the physique. Better to go, I supposed, before both of them crumbled.

I went on down the hill without any regrets.

TWENTY-ONE:

Clare came down on the train two days later to sort out what photographs she wanted from the filing cabinet: to make a portfolio, she said. Now that she was my agent, she'd be rustling up business. I laughed. It was serious, she said.

I had no races that day. I'd arranged to fetch Jeremy from hospital and take him home, and to have Clare come with me all the way. I'd also telephoned to Lance Kinship to say I'd had his reprints ready for ages, and hadn't seen him, and would he like me to drop them in as I was practically going past his house.

That would be fine, he said. Afternoon, earlyish, I suggested, and he said 'Right' and left the 't' off. And I'd like to ask you something, I said. 'Oh? All right. Anything you like.'

Jeremy looked a great deal better, without the grey clammy skin of Sunday. We helped him into the back of my car and tucked a rug round him, which he plucked off indignantly saying he was no aged invalid but a perfectly viable solicitor.

'And incidentally,' he said, 'my uncle came down here yesterday. Bad news for you, I'm afraid. Old Mrs Nore died during Monday night.'

'Oh no,' I said.

'Well, you knew,' Jeremy said. 'Only a matter of time.'

'Yes, but . . .'

'My uncle brought two letters for me to give to you. They're in my suitcase somewhere. Fish them out, before we start.'

I fished them out, and we sat in the hospital car park while I read them.

One was a letter. The other was a copy of her will.

Jeremy said, 'My uncle said he was called out urgently to the nursing home on Monday morning. Your grandmother wanted to make her will, and the doctor there told my uncle there wasn't much time.'

'Do you know what's in it?' I asked.

He shook his head. 'My uncle just said she was a stubborn old woman to the last.'

I unfolded the typewritten sheets.

I, Lavinia Nore, being of sound mind, do hereby revoke all previous wills . . .

There was a good deal of legal guff and some complicated pension arrangements for an old cook and gardener, and then the two final fairly simple paragraphs.

'. . . *Half the residue of my estate to my son James Nore . . .*'

'. . . *Half the residue of my estate to my grandson Philip Nore, to be his absolutely, with no strings or steel hawsers attached.*'

'What's the matter?' Clare said. 'You look so grim.'

'The old witch . . . has defeated me.'

I opened the other envelope. Inside there was a letter in shaky handwriting, with no beginning, and no end.

It said:

I think you did find Amanda, and didn't tell me because it would have given me no pleasure.

Is she a nun?

You can do what you like with my money. If it makes you vomit, as you once said . . . then VOMIT.

Or give it to my genes.

Rotten roses.

I handed the will and the letter to Clare and Jeremy, who read them in silence. We sat there for a while, thinking, and then Clare folded up the letter, put it in its envelope, and handed it back to me.

'What will you do?' she said.

'I don't know. See that Amanda never starves, I suppose. Apart from that . . .'

'Enjoy it,' Jeremy said. 'The old woman loved you.'

I listened to the irony in his voice and wondered if it was true. Love or hate. Love and hate. Perhaps she'd felt both at once when she'd made that will.

We drove from Swindon towards St Albans, making a short detour to deliver Lance Kinship's reprints.

'Sorry about this,' I said. 'But it won't take long.'

They didn't seem to mind. We found the house without much trouble . . . typical Kinship country, fake Georgian, large grandiose front, pillared gateway, meagre drive.

I picked the packet of photographs out of the boot of the car, and rang the front doorbell.

Lance opened the door himself, dressed today not in country gent togs but in white jeans, espadrilles, and a red and white horizontally striped T-shirt. International film-director, I diagnosed. All he needed was the megaphone.

'Come inside,' he said. 'I'll pay you for these.'

'O.K. Can't be long though, with my friends waiting.'

He looked briefly towards my car, where Clare and Jeremy's interested faces showed in the windows, and went indoors with me following. He led the way into a large sitting room with expanses of parquet and too much black lacquered furniture. Chrome and glass tables. Art deco lamps.

I gave him the packet of pictures.

'You'd better look at them,' I said, 'to make sure they're all right.'

He shrugged. 'Why shouldn't they be?' All the same, he opened the envelope and pulled out the contents.

The top picture showed him looking straight at the camera in his country gent clothes. Glasses. Trilby hat. Air of bossy authority.

'Turn it over,' I said.

With raised eyebrows he did so: and read what Mrs Jackson had written. *This is the rating officer . . .*

The change in him from one instant to the next was like one person leaving and another entering the same skin. He shed the bumptiously sure-of-himself phoney; slid into a mess of unstable ill-will. The gaudy clothes which had fitted one character seemed grotesque on the other, like gift-wrap round a hand-grenade. I saw the Lance Kinship I'd only suspected existed. Not the faintly ridiculous poseur pretending to be what he wasn't, but the tangled psychotic who would do anything at all to preserve the outward show.

It was in his very inadequacy, I supposed, that the true danger lay. In his estrangement from reality. In his theatrical turn of mind, which had allowed him to see murder as a solution to problems.

'Before you say anything,' I said, 'you'd better look at the other things in that envelope.'

With angry fingers he sorted them out. The regular reprints . . . and also the black and white glossy reproductions of Dana den Relgan's drugs list and the letter I'd found on the diazo paper.

They were for him a fundamental disaster.

He let the pictures of a great film producer fall to the ground around him like ten-by-eight coloured leaves, and stood holding the three black and white sheets in visible horror.

'She said . . .' he said hoarsely, 'she swore you didn't have it. She swore you didn't know what she was talking about. . .'

'She was talking about the drugs you supplied her with. Complete with dates and prices. That list which you hold, which is recognisably in her handwriting, for all that it was originally written on cellophane. And of course, as you see, your name appears on it liberally.'

'I'll kill you,' he said.

'No, you won't. You've missed your chance. It's too late now. If the gas had killed me you would have been all right, but it didn't.'

He didn't say 'What gas?' He said 'It all went wrong. But it didn't matter. I thought . . . it didn't matter.' He looked down helplessly at the black and white prints.

'You thought it didn't matter because you heard from Dana den Relgan that I didn't have the list. And if I didn't have the list, then I didn't have the letter. Whatever else I'd had from George Millace, I didn't after all have the list and the letter . . . Is that what you thought? . . . so if I didn't have them there was no more need to kill me. Was that it?'

He didn't answer.

'It's far too late to do it now,' I said, 'because there are extra prints of those pages all over the place. Another copy of that picture of you, identified by Mrs Jackson. Bank, solicitors, several friends, all have instructions about taking everything to the police if any accidental death should befall me. You've a positive interest in keeping me alive from now on.'

The implication of what I was saying only slowly sank in. He looked from my face to the photographs and back again several times, doubtfully.

'George Millace's letter . . .' he said.

I nodded. George's letter, handwritten, read:

Dear Lance Kinship,

I have received from Dana den Relgan a most interesting list of drugs supplied to her by you over the past few months. I am sure I understand correctly that you are a regular dealer in such illegal substances.

It appears to be all too well known in certain circles that in return for being invited to places which please your ego, you will, so to speak, pay for your pleasure with gifts of cannabis, heroin and cocaine.

I could of course place Dana den Relgan's candid list before the proper authorities. I will telephone you shortly, however, with an alternative suggestion.

Yours sincerely,
George Millace,

'It was typed when I got it,' Lance Kinship said dully. 'I burnt it.'

'When George telephoned,' I said, 'did he tell you his alternative suggestion?'

The shock in Lance Kinship began to abate, with enmity growing in its place.

'I'm telling you nothing.'

I said, disregarding him, 'Did George Millace say to stop supplying drugs . . . and donate to the Injured Jockeys' Fund?'

His mouth opened and snapped shut viciously.

'Did he telephone . . .' I asked, 'or did he tell you his terms when he called here?'

A tight silence.

'Did you put . . . something . . . from your store cupboard into his whisky?'

'Prove it!' he said with sick triumph.

One couldn't, of course. George had been cremated, with his blood tested only for alcohol. There had been no checks for other drugs. Not for perhaps tranquillisers, which were flavourless, and which in sufficient quantity would certainly have sent a driver to sleep.

George, I thought regretfully, had stepped on one victim too many. Had stepped on what he'd considered a worm and never recognised the cobra.

George had made a shattering mistake if he'd wanted for once to see the victim squirm when he came up with his terms. George hadn't dreamt that the inadequate weakling would lethally lash out to preserve his sordid life style: hadn't really understood how fanatically Lance Kinship prized his shoulder-rubbing with a jet-set that at best tolerated him. George must have enjoyed seeing Lance Kinship's fury. Must have driven off laughing. Poor George.

'Didn't you think,' I said, 'that George had left a copy of his letter behind him?'

From his expression, he hadn't. I supposed he'd acted on impulse. He'd very nearly been right.

'When you heard that George had blackmailed other people . . . including Dana . . . is that when you began thinking I might have your letter?'

'I heard,' he said furiously, 'I heard . . . in the clubs . . . Philip Nore has the letters . . . he's ruined den Relgan . . . got him sacked from the Jockey Club . . . Did you think . . . once I knew . . . did you really think I'd wait for you to come around *me*?'

'Unfortunately,' I said slowly, 'whether you like it or not, I now have come around to you.'

'No.'

'Yes,' I said. 'I'll tell you straight away that like George Millace I'm not asking for money.'

He didn't look much reassured.

'I'll also tell you it's your bad luck that my mother died from addiction to heroin.'

He said wildly, 'But I didn't know your mother.'

'No, of course not. And there's no question of your ever having supplied her yourself . . . It's just that I have a certain long-standing prejudice against drug-pushers. You may as well know it. You may as well understand why I want . . . what I want.'

He took a compulsive step towards me. I thought of the brisk karate kick he had delivered to den Relgan at Kempton and wondered if in his rope-soled sandals on parquet he could be as effective. Wondered if he had any real skill . . . or whether it was more window-dressing to cover the vacuum.

He looked incongruous, not dangerous. A man not young, not old, thinning on top, wearing glasses . . . and beach clothes indoors in December.

A man pushed . . . who could kill if pushed too far. Kill not by physical contact, when one came to think of it, but in his absence, by drugs and gas.

He never reached me to deliver whatever blind vengeful blow he had in mind. He stepped on one of the fallen photographs, and slid, and went down hard on one knee. The inefficient indignity of it seemed to break up conclusively whatever remained of his confidence, for when he looked up at me I saw not hatred or defiance, but fear.

I said, 'I don't want what George did. I don't ask you to stop peddling drugs. I want you to tell me who supplies you with heroin.'

He staggered to his feet, his face aghast. 'I can't. I . . . *can't.*'

'It shouldn't be difficult,' I said mildly. 'You must know where you get it from. You get it in sizeable quantities, to sell, to give away. You always have plenty, I'm told. So you must have a regular supplier . . . mustn't you? He's the one I want.'

The source, I thought. One source supplying several pushers. The drug business was like some monstrous tentacled creature: cut off one tentacle and another grew in its place. The war against drugs would never be won . . . but it had to be fought, if only for the sake of silly girls who were sniffing their way to perdition. For the sake of the pretty ones. For Dana. For Caroline . . . my lost butterfly mother, who had saved me from an addiction of my own.

'You don't know . . .' Lance Kinship seemed to be breathless. 'It's impossible. I can't tell you. I'd be . . . dead.'

I shook my head. 'It will be between the two of us. No one will ever know you told me . . . unless you yourself talk, like den Relgan did in the gaming clubs.'

'I can't,' he said despairingly.

'If you don't,' I said conversationally, 'I will first tell the policemen investigating an attempted murder in my house that my neighbour positively identifies you as having posed as a rating officer. This isn't enough on its own to get you charged, but it could certainly get you *investigated* . . . for access to chemicals, and so on.'

He looked sick.

'Secondly,' I said, 'I'll see that it gets known all over the place that people would be unwise to ask you to their parties, despite your little goodies, because they might at any time be raided. Unlawful possession of certain drugs is still an offence, I believe.'

'You . . . you . . .'

I nodded. He couldn't find a word bad enough.

'I know where you go . . . to whose houses. Everyone talks. I've been told. A word in the ear of the drugs squad . . . and you'd be the least welcome guest in Britain.'

'I . . . I . . .'

'Yes, I know,' I said. 'Going to these places is what makes your life worth living. I don't ask you not to go. I don't ask you to stop your gifts. Just to tell me where the heroin comes from. Not the cocaine, not the cannabis, just the heroin. Just the deadly one.'

The faintest of crafty looks crept in round his anguished eyes.

'And don't,' I said, watching for it, 'think you can get away with any old lie. You may as well know that what you tell me will go to the drugs squad. Don't worry . . . by such a round-about route that no one will ever connect it with you. But your present supplier may very likely be put out of business. If that happens, you'll be safe from me.'

He trembled as if his legs would give way.

'Mind you,' I said judiciously, 'with one supplier out of business, you might have to look around for another. In a year or so, I might ask you his name.'

His face was sweating and full of disbelief. 'You mean . . . it will go on . . . and on . . .'

'That's right.'

'But you *can't*.'

'I think you killed George Millace. You certainly tried to kill me. You very nearly killed my friend. Why should you think I shouldn't want retribution?'

He stared.

'I ask very little,' I said. 'A few words written down . . . now and then.'

'Not in my writing,' he said, appalled.

'Certainly, in your writing,' I said matter-of-factly, 'to get the spelling right, and so on. But don't worry, you'll be safe. I promise you no one will ever find out where the tip-offs come from. No one will ever know they come via me. Neither my name nor yours will ever be mentioned.'

'You . . . you're *sure*?'

'Sure.'

I produced a small notebook and a fibre-tipped pen, 'Write now,' I said. 'Your supplier.'

'Not *now*' he said, wavering.

'Why not?' I said calmly. 'May as well get it over. Sit down.'

He sat by one of his glass and chrome coffee tables, looking totally dazed. He wrote a name and address on the notepad.

'And sign it,' I said casually.

'Sign . . .'

'Of course. Just your name.'

He wrote: *Lance Kinship*. And then, underneath, with a flourish, added *'Film Director.'*

'That's great,' I said, without emphasis. I picked up the pad, reading what he'd written. A foreign name. An address in London. One tentacle under the axe.

I stored away in a pocket the small document that would

make him sweat next year . . . and the next, and the next. The document that I would photograph, and keep safe.

'That's . . . all?' he said numbly.

I nodded. 'All for now.'

He didn't stand up when I left him. Just sat on his black lacquer chair in his T-shirt and white trousers, stunned into silence, staring at space.

He'd recover his bumptiousness, I thought. Pseuds always did.

I went out to where Clare and Jeremy were still waiting, and paused briefly in the winter air before getting into the car.

Most people's lives, I thought, weren't a matter of world affairs, but of the problems right beside them. Not concerned portentously with saving mankind, but with creating local order: in small checks and balances.

Neither my life nor George Millace's would ever sway the fate of nations, but our actions could change the lives of individuals; and they had done that.

The dislike I'd felt for him alive was irrelevant to the intimacy I felt with him dead. I knew his mind, his intentions, his beliefs. I'd solved his puzzles. I'd fired his guns.

I got into the car.

'Everything all right?' Clare asked.

'Yes,' I said.

BANKER

My sincere thanks for the
generous help of

JEREMY H. THOMPSON MD FRCPI
Professor of Pharmacology
University of California
Los Angeles

and of
MICHAEL MELLUISH
and
JOHN COOPER

Contents

The First Year

MAY	247
JUNE	261
OCTOBER	286
NOVEMBER	299
DECEMBER	321

The Second Year

FEBRUARY	338
APRIL	351
OCTOBER	368
NOVEMBER	378

The Third Year

APRIL	386
MAY	417
JUNE	448
OCTOBER	486
DECEMBER	493

The First Year

MAY

Gordon Michaels stood in the fountain with all his clothes on.

'My God,' Alec said. 'What is he doing?'

'Who?'

'Your boss,' Alec said. 'Standing in the fountain.'

I crossed to the window and stared downwards: down two floors to the ornamental fountain in the forecourt of the Paul Ekaterin merchant bank. Down to where three entwining plumes of water rose gracefully into the air and fell in a glittering circular curtain. To where, in the bowl, calf-deep, stood Gordon in his navy pin-striped suit . . . in his white shirt and sober silk tie . . . in his charcoal socks and black shoes . . . in his gold cufflinks and onyx ring . . . in his polished City persona . . . soaking wet.

It was his immobility, I thought, which principally alarmed. Impossible to interpret this profoundly uncharacteristic behaviour as in any way an expression of lightheartedness, of celebration or of joy.

I whisked straight out of the deep-carpeted office, through the fire doors, down the flights of gritty stone staircase and across the marbled expanse of entrance hall. The uniformed man at the security desk was staring towards the wide glass front doors with his fillings showing and two arriving visitors were looking stunned. I went past them at a rush into the open air and slowed only in the last few strides before the fountain.

'Gordon!' I said.

His eyes were open. Beads of water ran down his forehead from his dripping black hair and caught here and there on his lashes. The main fall of water slid in a crystal sheet just behind his shoulders with scatterings of drops spraying forwards onto him like rain. Gordon's eyes looked at me unblinkingly with earnest vagueness as if he were not at all sure who I was.

'Get into the fountain,' he said.

'Er . . . why, exactly?'

'They don't like water.'

'Who don't?'

'All those people. Those people with white faces. They don't like water. They won't follow you into the fountain. You'll be all right if you're wet.'

His voice sounded rational enough for me to wonder wildly whether this was not after all a joke: but Gordon's jokes were normally small, civilised, glinting commentaries on the stupidities of mankind, not whooping, gusty, practical affairs smacking of the surreal.

'Come out of there, Gordon,' I said uneasily.

'No, no. They're waiting for me. Send for the police. Ring them up. Tell them to come and take them all away.'

'But *who*, Gordon?'

'All those people, of course. Those people with white faces.' His head slowly turned from side to side, his eyes focused as if at a throng closely surrounding the whole fountain. Instinctively I too looked from side to side, but all I could see were the more distant stone and glass walls of Ekaterin's, with, now, a growing chorus of heads appearing disbelievingly at the windows.

I clung still to a hope of normality. 'They work here,' I said. 'Those people work here.'

'No, no. They came with me. In the car. Only two or three of them, I thought. But all the others, they were here, you know. They want me to go with them, but they can't reach me here, they don't like the water.'

He had spoken fairly loudly throughout so that I should hear him above the noise of the fountain, and the last of these remarks reached the chairman of the bank who came striding briskly across from the building.

'Now, Gordon, my dear chap,' the chairman said authoritatively, coming to a purposeful halt at my side, 'what's all this about, for God's sake?'

'He's having hallucinations,' I said.

The chairman's gaze flicked to my face, and back to Gordon, and Gordon seriously advised him to get into the fountain, because the people with white faces couldn't reach him there, on account of disliking water.

'Do something, Tim,' the chairman said, so I stepped into the fountain and took Gordon's arm.

'Come on,' I said. 'If we're wet they won't touch us. We don't have to stay in the water. Being wet is enough.'

'Is it?' Gordon said. 'Did they tell you?'

'Yes, they did. They won't touch anyone who's wet.'

'Oh. All right. If you're sure.'

'Yes, I'm sure.'

He nodded understandingly and with only slight pressure from my arm took two sensible-seeming paces through the water and stepped over the knee-high coping onto the paving slabs of the forecourt. I held onto him firmly and hoped to heaven that the people with white faces would keep their distance; and although Gordon looked round apprehensively it appeared that they were not so far trying to abduct him.

The chairman's expression of concern was deep and genuine, as he and Gordon were firm and long-time friends. Except in appearance they were much alike; essentially clever, intuitive, and with creative imaginations. Each in normal circumstances had a manner of speaking which expressed even the toughest commands in gentle politeness and both had a visible appetite for their occupation. They were both in their fifties, both at the top of their powers, both comfortably rich.

Gordon dripped onto the paving stones.

'I think,' the chairman said, casting a glance at the inhabited windows, 'that we should go indoors. Into the boardroom, perhaps. Come along, Gordon.'

He took Gordon Michaels by his other sodden sleeve, and between us one of the steadiest banking brains in London walked obediently in its disturbing fog.

'The people with white faces,' I said as we steered a calm course across the marble entrance hall between clearly human open-mouthed watchers, 'are they coming with us?'

'Of course,' Gordon said.

It was obvious also that some of them came up in the lift with us. Gordon watched them dubiously all the time. The others, as we gathered from his reluctance to step out into the top-floor hallway, were waiting for our arrival.

'It's all right,' I said to Gordon encouragingly. 'Don't forget, we're still wet.'

'Henry isn't,' he said, anxiously eyeing the chairman.

'We're all together,' I said. 'It will be all right.'

Gordon looked doubtful, but finally allowed himself to be drawn from the lift between his supporters. The white faces apparently parted before us, to let us through.

The chairman's personal assistant came hurrying along the corridor but the chairman waved him conclusively to a stop and said not to let anyone disturb us in the boardroom until he rang the bell; and Gordon and I in our wet shoes sloshed across the deep-piled green carpet to the long glossy mahogany boardroom table. Gordon consented to sit in one of the comfortable leather arm-chairs which surrounded it with me and the chairman alongside, and this time it was the chairman who asked if the people with white faces were still there.

'Of course,' Gordon said, looking around. 'They're sitting in all the chairs round the table. And standing behind them. Dozens of them. Surely you can see them?'

'What are they wearing?' the chairman asked.

Gordon looked at him in puzzlement, but answered simply enough. 'White suits of course. With black buttons. Down the front, three big black buttons.'

'All of them?' the chairman asked. 'All the same?'

'Oh yes, of course.'

'Clowns,' I exclaimed.

'What?'

'White-faced clowns.'

'Oh no,' Gordon said. 'They're not clowns. They're not funny.'

'White-faced clowns are sad.'

Gordon looked troubled and wary, and kept a good eye on his visitations.

'What's best to do?' wondered the chairman; but he was talking principally to himself. To me directly, after a pause, he said, 'I think we should take him home. He's clearly not violent, and I see no benefit in calling in a doctor here, whom we don't know. I'll ring Judith and warn her, poor girl. I'll drive him in my car as I'm perhaps the only one who knows exactly where he lives. And I'd appreciate it, Tim, if you'd come along, sit with Gordon on the back seat, keep him reassured.'

'Certainly,' I agreed. 'And incidentally his own car's here. He said that when he drove in he thought there were two or three of the white faces with him. The rest were waiting here.'

'Did he?' The chairman pondered. 'He can't have been hallucinating when he actually left home. Surely Judith would have noticed.'

'But he seemed all right in the office when he came in,' I said. 'Quiet, but, all right. He sat at his desk for nearly an hour before he went out and stood in the fountain.'

'Didn't you talk with him?'

'He doesn't like people to talk when he's thinking.'

The chairman nodded. 'First thing, then,' he said, 'see if you can find a blanket. Ask Peter to find one. And . . . er . . . how wet are you, yourself?'

'Not soaked, except for my legs. No problem, honestly. It's not cold.'

He nodded, and I went on the errand. Peter, the assistant, produced a red blanket with Fire written across one corner for no good reason that I could think of, and with this wrapped snugly round his by now naked chest Gordon allowed himself to be conveyed discreetly to the chairman's car. The chairman himself slid behind his wheel and with the direct effectiveness which shaped his whole life drove his still half-damp passengers southwards through the fair May morning.

Henry Shipton, chairman of Paul Ekaterin Ltd, was physically a big-framed man whose natural bulk was kept short of obesity by raw carrots, mineral water and will power. Half visionary, half gambler, he habitually subjected every soaring idea to rigorous analytic test: a man whose powerful instinctive urges were everywhere harnessed and put to work.

I admired him. One had to. During his twenty-year stint (including ten as chairman) Paul Ekaterin Ltd had grown from a moderately successful banking house into one of the senior league, accepted world-wide with respect. I could measure almost exactly the spread of public recognition of the bank's name, since it was mine also: Timothy Ekaterin, great-grandson of Paul the founder. In my schooldays people always said 'Timothy *who*? E-*kat*-erin? How do you spell it?' Quite often now they simply nodded – and expected me to have the fortune to match, which I hadn't.

'They're very peaceful, you know,' Gordon said after a while.

'The white faces?' I asked.

He nodded. 'They didn't say anything. They're just waiting.'

'Here in the car?'

He looked at me uncertainly. 'They come and go.'

At least they weren't pink elephants, I thought irreverently: but Gordon, like the chairman, was abstemious beyond doubt. He looked pathetic in his red blanket, the sharp mind confused with dreams, the well-groomed businessman a pre-fountain memory, the patina stripped away. This was the warrior who dealt confidently every day in millions, this huddled mass of delusions going home in wet trousers. The dignity of man was everywhere tissue-paper thin.

He lived, it transpired, in leafy splendour by Clapham

Common, in a late Victorian family pile surrounded by head-high garden walls. There were high cream-painted wooden gates which were shut, and which I opened, and a short gravelled driveway between tidy lawns.

Judith Michaels erupted from her opening front door to meet the chairman's car as it rolled to a stop, and the first thing she said, aiming it variously between Henry Shipton and myself, was 'I'll throttle that bloody doctor.'

After that she said, 'How is he?' and after that, in compassion, 'Come along, love, it's all right, come along in, darling, we'll get you warm and tucked into bed in no time.'

She put sheltering arms round the red blanket as her child of a husband stumbled out of the car, and to me and to Henry Shipton she said again in fury 'I'll kill him. He ought to be struck off.'

'They're very bad these days about house calls,' the chairman said doubtfully, 'But surely . . . he's coming?'

'No, he's not. Now you lambs both go into the kitchen – there's some coffee in the pot – and I'll be down in a sec. Come on Gordon, my dear love, up those stairs . . .' She helped him through the front door, across a Persian-rugged hall and towards a panelled wood staircase, with me and the chairman following and doing as we were told.

Judith Michaels, somewhere in the later thirties, was a brown-haired woman in whom the life-force flowed strongly and with whom I could easily have fallen in love. I'd met her several times before that morning (at the bank's various social gatherings) and had been conscious freshly each time of the warmth and glamour which were as normal to her as breathing. Whether I in return held the slightest attraction for her I didn't know and hadn't tried to find out, as entangling oneself emotionally with one's boss's wife was hardly best for one's prospects. All the same I felt the same old tug, and wouldn't have minded taking Gordon's place on the staircase.

With these thoughts, I hoped, decently hidden, I went with Henry Shipton into the friendly kitchen and drank the offered coffee.

'A great girl, Judith,' the chairman said with feeling, and I looked at him in rueful surprise and agreed.

She came to join us after a while, still more annoyed than worried. 'Gordon says there are people with white faces sitting all round the room and they won't go away. It's really too bad. It's infuriating. I'm so angry I could *spit*.'

The chairman and I looked bewildered.

'Didn't I tell you?' she said, observing us. 'Oh no, I suppose I didn't. Gordon hates anyone to know about his illness. It isn't very bad, you see. Not bad enough for him to have to stop working, or anything like that.'

'Er . . .' said the chairman. 'What illness?'

'Oh, I suppose I'll have to tell you, now this has happened. I could kill that doctor, I really could.' She took a deep breath and said, 'Gordon's got mild Parkinson's disease. His left hand shakes a bit now and then. I don't expect you've noticed. He tries not to let people see.'

We blankly shook our heads.

'Our normal doctor's just retired, and this new man, he's one of those frightfully bumptious people who think they know better than everyone else. So he's taken Gordon off the old pills, which were fine as far as I could see, and put him on some new ones. As of the day before yesterday. So when I rang him just now in an absolute *panic* thinking Gordon had suddenly gone raving mad or something and I'd be spending the rest of my life visiting mental hospitals he says light-heartedly not to worry, this new drug quite often causes hallucinations, and it's just a matter of getting the dosage right. I tell you, if he hadn't been at the other end of a telephone wire, I'd have *strangled* him.'

Both Henry Shipton and I, however, were feeling markedly relieved.

'You mean,' the chairman asked, 'that this will all just . . . wear off?'

She nodded. 'That bloody doctor said to stop taking the pills and Gordon would be perfectly normal in thirty-six hours. I *ask* you! And after that he's got to start taking them again, but only half the amount, and to see what happens. And if we were *worried,* he said pityingly, as if we'd no right to be, Gordon could toddle along to the surgery in a couple of days and discuss it with him, though as Gordon would be perfectly all right by tomorrow night we might think there was no need.'

She herself was shaking slightly with what still looked like anger but was more probably a release of tension, because she suddenly sobbed, twice, and said 'Oh God,' and wiped crossly at her eyes.

'I was so frightened, when you told me,' she said, half apologetically. 'And when I rang the surgery I got that damned obstructive receptionist and had to argue for ten minutes before she let me even *talk* to the doctor.'

After a brief sympathetic pause the chairman, going as usual to the heart of things, said, 'Did the doctor say how long it would take to get the dosage right?'

She looked at him with a defeated grimace. 'He said that as Gordon had reacted so strongly to an average dose it might take as much as six weeks to get him thoroughly stabilised. He said each patient was different, but that if we would persevere it would be much the best drug for Gordon in the long run.'

Henry Shipton drove me pensively back to the City.

'I think,' he said, 'that we'll say – in the office – that Gordon felt "flu" coming on and took some pills which proved hallucinatory. We might say simply that he imagined that he was on holiday, and felt the need for a dip in a pool. Is that agreeable?'

'Sure,' I said mildly.

'Hallucinatory drugs are, after all, exceedingly common these days.'

'Yes.'

'No need, then, Tim, to mention white-faced clowns.'

'No,' I agreed.

'Nor Parkinson's disease, if Gordon doesn't wish it.'

'I'll say nothing,' I assured him.

The chairman grunted and lapsed into silence; and perhaps we both thought the same thoughts along the well-worn lines of drug-induced side effects being more disturbing than the disease.

It wasn't until we were a mile from the bank that Henry Shipton spoke again, and then he said, 'You've been in Gordon's confidence for two years now, haven't you?'

'Nearly three,' I murmured, nodding.

'Can you hold the fort until he returns?'

It would be dishonest to say that the possibility of this offer hadn't been in my mind since approximately ten-fifteen, so I accepted it with less excitement than relief.

There was no rigid hierarchy in Ekaterin's. Few explicit ranks: to be 'in so and so's confidence', as house jargon put it, meant one would normally be on course for more responsibility, but unlike the other various thirty-two-year olds who crowded the building with their hopes and expectations I lived under the severe disadvantage of my name. The whole board of directors, consistently afraid of accusations of nepotism, made me double-earn every step.

'Thank you,' I said neutrally.

He smiled a shade. 'Consult,' he said, 'whenever you need help.'

I nodded. His words weren't meant as disparagement. Everyone consulted, in Ekaterin's, all the time. Communication between people and between departments was an absolute priority in Henry Shipton's book, and it was he who had swept away a host of small-room offices to form opened-up expanses. He himself sat always at one (fairly opulent) desk in a room that contained eight similar, his own flanked on one side by the vice-chairman's and on the other by that of the head of Corporate Finance. Further senior directors from other departments occupied a row of like desks opposite, all of them within easy talking earshot of each other.

As with all merchant banks, the business carried on by Ekaterin's was different and separate from that conducted by the High Street chains of clearing banks. At Ekaterin's one never actually saw any money. There were no tellers, no clerks, no counters, no paying-ins, no withdrawals and hardly any cheque books.

There were three main departments, each with its separate function and each on its own floor of the building. Corporate Finance acted for major clients on mergers, takeovers and the raising of capital. Banking, which was where I worked with Gordon, lent money to enterprise and industry. And Investment Management, the oldest and largest department, aimed at producing the best possible returns from the vast investment funds of charities, companies, pensions, trusts and trade unions.

There were several small sections like Administration, which did everyone's paperwork; like Property, which bought, sold, developed and leased; like Research, which dug around; like Overseas Investments, growing fast, and like Foreign Exchange, where about ten frenetic young wizards bought and sold world currencies by the minute, risking millions on decimal point margins and burning themselves out by forty.

The lives of all the three hundred and fifty people who worked for Ekaterin's were devoted to making money work. To the manufacture, in the main, of business, trade, industry, pensions and jobs. It wasn't a bad thing to be convinced of the worth of what one did, and certainly there was a tough basic harmony in the place which persisted unruffled by the surface tensions and jealousies and territorial defences of everyday office life.

Events had already moved on by the time the chairman and I returned to the hive. The chairman was pounced upon immediately in the entrance hall by a worriedly waiting figure from Corporate Finance, and upstairs in Banking Alec was giggling into his blotter.

Alec, my own age, suffered, professionally speaking, from an uncontrollable bent for frivolity. It brightened up the office no end, but as court jesters seldom made it to the throne his career path was already observably sideways and erratic. The rest of us were probably hopelessly stuffy. Thank God, I often thought, for Alec.

He had a well-shaped face of scattered freckles on cream-pale skin; a high forehead, a mat of tight tow-coloured curls. Stiff blond eyelashes blinked over alert blue eyes behind gold-framed spectacles, and his mouth twitched easily as he saw the funny side. He was liked on sight by almost everybody, and it was only gradually that one came to wonder whether the examiner who had awarded him a First in law at Oxford had been suffering from critical blindness.

'What's up?' I said, instinctively smiling to match the giggles.

'We've been leaked.' He lifted his head but tapped the paper which lay on his desk. 'My *dear*,' he said with mischievous pleasure, 'this came an hour ago and it seems we're leaking all over the place like a punctured bladder. Like a baby. Like the *Welsh*.'

Leeking like the Welsh . . . ah well.

He lifted up the paper, and all, or at least a great deal, was explained. There had recently appeared a slim bi-monthly publication called *What's Going On Where It Shouldn't*, which had fast caught the attention of most of the country and was reportedly read avidly by the police. Descendant of the flood of investigative journalism spawned by the tidal wave of Watergate, *What's Going On* . . . was said to be positively bombarded by informers telling *precisely* what was going on, and all the investigating the paper had to do was into the truth of the information: which task it had been known to perform less than thoroughly.

'What does it say?' I asked; as who wouldn't.

'Cutting out the larky innuendo,' he said, 'it says that

someone at Ekaterin's has been selling inside information.'

'*Selling* . . .'

'Quite so.'

'About a takeover?'

'How did you guess?'

I thought of the man from Corporate Finance hopping from leg to leg with impatience while he waited for the chairman to return and knew that nothing but extreme urgency would have brought him down to the doorstep.

'Let's see,' I said, and took the paper from Alec.

The piece headed merely 'Tut tut' was only four paragraphs long, and the first three of those were taken up with explaining with seductive authority that in merchant banks it was possible for the managers of investment funds to learn at an early stage about a takeover being organised by their colleagues. It was strictly illegal, however, for an investment manager to act on this private knowledge, even though by doing so he might make a fortune for his clients.

The shares of a company about to be taken over were likely to rise in value. If one could buy them at a low price before even a rumour of takeover started, the gain could be huge.

Such unprofessional behaviour by a merchant bank would be instantly recognised simply *because of* the profits made, and no investment manager would invite personal disaster in that way.

> *However,* [asked the article] *What's Going On in the merchant bank of Paul Ekaterin Ltd? Three times in the past year takeovers managed by this prestigious firm have been 'scooped' by vigorous buying beforehand of the shares concerned. The buying itself cannot be traced to Ekaterin's investment managers, but we are informed that the information did come from within Ekaterin's, and that someone there has been selling the golden news, either for straight cash or a slice of the action.*

'It's a guess,' I said flatly, giving Alec back the paper. 'There are absolutely no facts.'

'A bucket of cold water,' he complained, 'is a sunny day compared with you.'

'Do you *want* it to be true?' I asked curiously.

'Livens the place up a bit.'

And there, I thought, was the difference between Alec and me. For me the place was alive all the time, even though when

I'd first gone there eight years earlier it had been unwillingly; a matter of being forced into it by my uncle. My mother had been bankrupt at that point, her flat stripped to the walls by the bailiffs of everything except a telephone (property of the Post Office) and a bed. My mother's bankruptcy, as both my uncle and I well knew, was without doubt her own fault, but it didn't stop him applying his blackmailing pressure.

'I'll clear her debts and arrange an allowance for her if you come and work in the bank.'

'But I don't want to.'

'I know that. And I know you're stupid enough to try to support her yourself. But if you do that she'll ruin you like she ruined your father. Just give the bank a chance, and if you hate it after three months I'll let you go.'

So I'd gone with mulish rebellion to tread the path of my great-grandfather, my grandfather and my uncle, and within three months you'd have had to prise me loose with a crowbar. I suppose it was in my blood. All the snooty teenage scorn I'd felt for 'money-grubbing', all the supercilious disapproval of my student days, all the negative attitudes bequeathed by my failure of a father, all had melted into comprehension, interest and finally delight. The art of money-management now held me as addicted as any junkie, and my working life was as fulfilling as any mortal could expect.

'Who do you think did it?' Alec said.

'If anyone did.'

'It must have happened,' he said positively. 'Three times in the last year . . . that's more than a coincidence.'

'And I'll bet that that coincidence is all the paper's working on. They're dangling a line. Baiting a hook. They don't even say which takeovers they mean, let alone give figures.'

True or not, though, the story itself was bad for the bank. Clients would back away fast if they couldn't trust, and *What's Going On* . . . was right often enough to instil disquiet. Henry Shipton spent most of the afternoon in the boardroom conducting an emergency meeting of the directors, with ripples of unease spreading outwards from there through all departments. By going home time that evening practically everyone in the building had read the bombshell, and although some took it as lightheartedly as Alec it had the effect of almost totally deflecting speculation from Gordon Michaels.

I explained only twice about 'flu' and pills: only two people asked. When the very reputation of the bank was being rocked, who cared about a dip in the ornamental fountain, even if the bather had had all his clothes on and was a director in Banking.

On the following day I found that filling Gordon's job was no lighthearted matter. Until then he had gradually given me power of decision over loans up to certain amounts, but anything larger was in his own domain entirely. Within my bracket, it meant that I could arrange any loan if I believed the client was sound and could repay principal and interest at an orderly rate: but if I judged wrong and the client went bust, the lenders lost both their money and their belief in my common sense. As the lenders were quite often the bank itself, I couldn't afford for it to happen too often.

With Gordon there, the ceiling of my possible disasters had at least been limited. For him, though, the ceiling hardly existed, except that with loans incurring millions it was normal for him to consult with others on the board.

These consultations, already easy and informal because of the open-plan lay-out, also tended to stretch over lunch, which the directors mostly ate together in their own private dining room. It was Gordon's habit to look with a pleased expression at his watch at five to one and take himself amiably off in the direction of a tomato juice and roast lamb; and he would reurn an hour later with his mind clarified and made up.

I'd been lent Gordon's job but not his seat on the board, so I was without the benefit of the lunches; and as he himself had been the most senior in our own green pasture of office expanse, there was no one else of his stature immediately at hand. Alec's advice tended to swing between the brilliantly perceptive and the maniacally reckless, but one was never quite sure which was which at the time. All high-risk Cinderellas would have gone to the ball under Alec's wand: the trick was in choosing only those who would keep an eye on the clock and deliver the crystal goods.

Gordon tended therefore to allocate only cast-iron certainties to Alec's care and most of the Cinderella-type to me, and he'd said once with a smile that in this job one's nerve either toughened or broke, which I'd thought faintly extravagant at the time. I understood, though, what he meant when I faced without him a task which lay untouched on his desk: a request for financial backing for a series of animated cartoon films.

It was too easy to turn things down . . . and perhaps miss Peanuts or Mickey Mouse. A large slice of the bank's profits came from the interest paid by borrowers. If we didn't lend, we didn't earn. A toss-up. I picked up the telephone and invited the hopeful cartoonist to bring his proposals to the bank.

Most of Gordon's projects were half-way through, his biggest at the moment being three point four million for an extension to a cake factory. I had heard him working on this one for a week, so I merely took on where he had left off, telephoning people who sometimes had funds to lend and asking if they'd be interested in underwriting a chunk of Home-made Heaven. The bank itself, according to Gordon's list, was lending three hundred thousand only, which made me wonder whether he privately expected the populace to go back to eating bread.

There was also, tucked discreetly in a folder, a glossy-prospectus invitation to participate in a multi-million project in Brazil, whereon Gordon had doodled in pencil an army of question marks and a couple of queries: *Do we or don't we? Remember Brasilia! Is coffee enough??* On the top of the front page, written in red, was a jump-to-it memo: *Preliminary answer by Friday.*

It was already Thursday. I picked up the prospectus and went along to the other and larger office at the end of the passage, where Gordon's almost-equal sat at one of the seven desks. Along there the carpet was still lush and the furniture still befitting the sums dealt with on its tops, but the view from the windows was different. No fountain, but the sunlit dome of St Paul's Cathedral rising like a Fabergé egg from the white stone lattice of the City.

'Problem?' asked Gordon's almost-equal. 'Can I help?'

'Do you know if Gordon meant to go any further with this?' I asked. 'Did he say?'

Gordon's colleague looked the prospectus over and shook his head. 'Who's along there with you today?'

'Only Alec. I asked him. He doesn't know.'

'Where's John?'

'On holiday. And Rupert is away because of his wife.'

The colleague nodded. Rupert's wife was imminently dying: cruel at twenty-six.

'I'd take it around,' he said. 'See if Gordon's put out feelers in Research, Overseas, anywhere. Form a view yourself. Then if you think it's worth pursuing you can take it to Val and

Henry.' Val was head of Banking and Henry was Henry Shipton. I saw that to be Gordon was a big step up indeed, and was unsure whether to be glad or sorry that the elevation would be temporary.

I spent all afternoon drifting round with the prospectus and in the process learned less about Brazil than about the tizzy over the report in *What's Going On* . . . Soul-searching appeared to be fashionable. Long faces enquired anxiously, 'Could one possibly . . . without knowing . . . have mentioned a takeover to an interested party?' And the short answer to that, it seemed to me, was No, one couldn't. Secrecy was everywhere second nature to bankers.

If the article in the paper were true there had to be three people involved; the seller, the buyer and the informant; and certainly neither the buyer nor the informant could have acted in ignorance or by chance. Greed and malice moved like worms in the dark. If one were infested by them, one knew.

Gordon seemed to have asked no one about Brazil, and for me it was make-up-your-mind time. It would have been helpful to know what the other merchant banks thought, the sixteen British accepting houses like Schroders, Hambro's, Morgan Grenfell, Kleinwort Benson, Hill Samuel, Warburg's, Robert Fleming, Singer and Friedlander . . . all permitted, like Paul Ekaterin's, to assume that the Bank of England would come to their aid in a crisis.

Gordon's opposite numbers in those banks would all be pursing mouths over the same prospectus, committing millions to a fruitful enterprise, pouring millions down the drain, deciding not to risk it either way.

Which?

One could hardly directly ask, and finding out via the grapevine took a little time.

I carried the prospectus finally to Val Fisher, head of Banking, who usually sat at one of the desks facing Henry Shipton, two floors up.

'Well, Tim, what's your own view?' he said. A short man, very smooth, very charming, with nerves like toughened ice.

'Gordon had reservations, obviously,' I said. 'I don't know enough, and no one else here seems to. I suppose we could either make a preliminary answer of cautious interest and then find out a bit more, or just trust to Gordon's instinct.'

He smiled faintly. 'Which?'

Ah, which?

'Trust to Gordon's instinct, I think,' I said.
'Right.'
He nodded and I went away and wrote a polite letter to the Brazil people expressing regret. And I wouldn't know for six or seven years, probably, whether that decision was right or wrong.
The gambles were all long term. You cast your bread on the waters and hoped it would float back in the future with butter and jam.
Mildew . . . too bad.

The First Year

JUNE

Gordon telephoned three weeks later sounding thoroughly fit and well. I glanced across to where his desk stood mute and tidy, with all the paper action now transferred to my own.

'Judith and I wanted to thank you . . .' he was saying.

'Really no need,' I said. 'How are you?'

'Wasting time. It's ridiculous. Anyway, we've been offered a half-share in a box at Ascot next Thursday. We thought it might be fun . . . We've six places. Would you like to come? As our guest, of course. As a thank-you.'

'I'd love it,' I said. 'But . . .'

'No buts,' he interrupted. 'If you'd like to, Henry will fix it. He's coming himself. He agreed you'd earned a day off, so all you have to do is decide.'

'Then I'd like to, very much.'

'Good. If you haven't a morning coat, don't worry. We're not in the Royal Enclosure.'

'If you're wearing one . . . I inherited my father's.'

'Ah. Good. Yes, then. One o'clock Thursday, for lunch. I'll send the entrance tickets to you in the office. Both Judith and I are very pleased you can come. We're very grateful. Very.' He sounded suddenly half-embarrassed, and disconnected with a click.

I wondered how much he remembered about the white faces, but with Alec and Rupert and John all in earshot it had been impossible to ask. Maybe at the races he would tell me. Maybe not.

Going racing wasn't something I did very often nowadays, although as a child I'd spent countless afternoons waiting around the Tote queues while my mother in pleasurable agony backed her dozens of hunches and bankers and third strings and savers and lost money by the ton.

'I've won!' she would announce radiantly to all about her, waving an indisputably winning ticket: and the bunch of losses on the same race would be thrust into a pocket and later thrown away.

My father at the same time would be standing drinks in the bar, an amiable open-fisted lush with more good nature than sense. They would take me home at the end of the day giggling happily together in a hired chauffeur-driven Rolls, and until I was quite old I never questioned but that this contented affluence was built on rock.

I had been their only child and they'd given me a very good childhood to the extent that when I thought of holidays it was of yachts on warm seas or Christmas in the Alps. The villain of those days was my uncle who descended on us occasionally to utter Dire Warnings about the need for his brother (my father) to find a job.

My father however couldn't shape up to 'money-grubbing' and in any case had no real ability in any direction; and with no habit of working he had quietly scorned people who had. He never tired of his life of aimless ease, and if he earned no one's respect, few detested him either. A weak, friendly, unintelligent man. Not bad as a father. Not good at much else.

He dropped dead of a heart attack when I was nineteen and it was then that the point of the Dire Warnings became apparent. He and mother had lived on the capital inherited from grandfather, and there wasn't a great deal left. Enough just to see me through college; enough, with care, to bring mother a small income for life.

Not enough to finance her manner of betting, which she wouldn't or couldn't give up. A lot more of the Dire Warnings went unheeded, and finally, while I was trying to stem a hopeless tide by working (of all things) for a bookmaker, the bailiffs knocked on the door.

In twenty-five years, it seemed, my mother had gambled away the best part of half a million pounds; all gone on horses, fast and slow. It might well have sickened me altogether against racing, but in a curious way it hadn't. I remembered how much she and father had enjoyed themselves: and who was to say that it was a fortune ill spent?

'Good news?' Alec said, eyeing my no doubt ambivalent expression.

'Gordon's feeling better.'

'Hm,' he said judiciously, 'So he should be. Three weeks off for "flu" . . .' He grinned. 'Stretching it a bit.'

I made a non-committal grunt.

'Be glad, shall we, when he comes back?'

I glanced at his amused, quizzical face and saw that he knew as well as I did that when Gordon reappeared to repossess his kingdom, I wouldn't be glad at all. Doing Gordon's job, after the first breath-shortening initial plunge, had injected me with great feelings of vigour and good health; had found me running up stairs and singing in the bath and showing all the symptoms of a love affair; and like many a love affair it couldn't survive the return of the husband. I wondered how long I'd have to wait for such a chance again, and whether next time I'd feel as high.

'Don't think I haven't noticed,' Alec said, the eyes electric blue behind the gold-rimmed specs.

'Noticed what?' Rupert asked, raising his head above papers he'd been staring blindly at for ninety minutes.

Back from his pretty wife's death and burial poor Rupert still wore a glazed otherwhere look and tended too late to catch up with passing conversations. In the two days since his return he had written no letters, made no telephone calls, reached no decisions. Out of compassion one had had to give him time, and Alec and I continued to do his work surreptitiously without him realising.

'Nothing,' I said.

Rupert nodded vaguely and looked down again, an automaton in his living grief. I'd never loved anyone, I thought, as painfully as that. I think I hoped that I never would.

John, freshly returned also, but from his holidays, glowed with a still-red sunburn and had difficulty in fitting the full lurid details of his sexual adventures into Rupert's brief absences to the washroom. Neither Alec nor I ever believed John's sagas, but at least Alec found them funny, which I didn't. There was an element lurking there of a hatred of women, as if every boasted possession (real or not) was a statement of spite. He didn't actually use the word possession. He said 'made' and 'screwed' and 'had it off with the little cow'. I didn't like him much and he thought me a prig: we were polite in the office and never went together to lunch. And it was he alone of all of us who actively looked forward to Gordon's return, he who couldn't disguise his dismay that it was I who was filling the empty shoes instead of himself.

'Of course, if I'd been here . . .' he said at least once a day; and Alec reported that John had been heard telling Gordon's almost-equal along the passage that now he, John, was back, Gordon's work should be transferred from me to him.

'Did you hear him?' I asked, surprised.

'Sure. And he was told in no uncertain terms that it was the Old Man himself who gave you the green light, and there was nothing John could do about it. Proper miffed was our Lothario. Says it's all because you are who you are, and all that.'

'Sod him.'

'Rather you than me.' He laughed gently into his blotter and picked up the telephone to find backers for a sewage and water purification plant in Norfolk.

'Did you know,' he said conversationally, busy dialling a number, 'that there are so few sewage farms in West Berlin that they pay the East Berliners to get rid of the extra?'

'No, I didn't.' I didn't especially want to know, either, but as usual Alec was full of useless information and possessed by the urge to pass it on.

'The East Berliners take the money and dump the stuff out in the open fields. Untreated, mind you.'

'Do shut up,' I said.

'I saw it,' he said. 'And smelled it. Absolutely disgusting.'

'It was probably fertilizer,' I said, 'and what were you doing in East Berlin?'

'Calling on Nefertiti.'

'She of the one eye?'

'My God, yes, isn't it a shock? Oh . . . hello . . .' He got through to his prospective money-source and for far too long and with a certain relish explained the need for extra facilities to reverse the swamp of effluent which had been killing off the Broads. 'No risk involved, of course, with a water authority.' He listened. 'I'll put you in, then, shall I? Right.' He scribbled busily and in due course disconnected. 'Dead easy, this one. Ecology and all that. Good emotional stuff.'

I shuffled together a bunch of papers of my own that were very far from dead easy and went up to see Val Fisher, who happened to be almost alone in the big office. Henry Shipton, it seemed, was out on one of his frequent walkabouts through the other departments.

'It's a cartoonist,' I said. 'Can I consult?'

'Pull up a chair.' Val nodded and waved hospitably, and I sat beside him, spread out the papers, and explained about the wholly level-headed artist I had spent three hours with two weeks earlier.

'He's been turned down by his own local bank, and so far by

three other firms like ourselves.' I said. 'He's got no realisable assets, no security. He rents a flat and is buying a car on HP. If we financed him, it would be out of faith.'

'Background?' he asked. 'Covenant?'

'Pretty solid. Son of a Sales Manager. Respected at art school as an original talent: I talked to the Principal. His bank manager gave him a clean bill but said that his head office wouldn't grant what he's asking. For the past two years he's worked for a studio making animated commercials. They say he's good at the job; understands it thoroughly. They know he wants to go it alone, they think he's capable and they don't want to lose him.'

'How old?'

'Twenty-four.'

Val gave me an 'Oh ho ho' look, knowing, as I did, that it was the cartoonist's age above all which had invited negative responses from the other banks.

'What he's asking?' Val said, but he too looked as if he were already deciding against.

'A studio, properly equipped. Funds to employ ten copying artists, with the expectation that it will be a year before any films are completed and can expect to make money. Funds for promotion. Funds for himself to live on. These sheets set out the probable figures.'

Val made a face over the pages, momentarily re-arranging the small neat features, slanting the tidy dark moustache, raising the arched eyebrows towards the black cap of hair.

'Why haven't you already turned him down?' he asked finally.

'Um,' I said. 'Look at his drawings.' I opened another file and spread out the riotously coloured progression of pages which established two characters and told a funny story. I watched Val's sophisticated world-weary face as he leafed through them: saw the awakening interest, heard the laugh.

'Exactly,' I said.

'Hmph.' He leaned back in his chair and gave me an assessing stare. 'You're not saying you think we should take him on?'

'It's an unsecured risk, of course. But yes, I am. With a string or two, of course, like a cost accountant to keep tabs on things and a first option to finance future expansion.'

'Hm.' He pondered for several minutes, looking again at the drawings which still seemed funny to me even after a fortnight's close acquaintance. 'Well, I don't know. It's too like aiming at the moon with a bow and arrow.'

'They might watch those films one day on space shuttles,' I said mildly, and he gave me a fast amused glance while he squared up the drawings and returned them to their folder.

'Leave these all here, then, will you?' he said. 'I'll have a word with Henry over lunch.' And I guessed in a swift uncomfortable moment of insight that what they would discuss would be not primarily the cartoonist but the reliability or otherwise of my judgement. If they thought me a fool I'd be back behind John in the promotion queue in no time.

At four-thirty, however, when my inter-office telephone rang, it was Val at the other end.

'Come up and collect your papers,' he said. 'Henry says this decision is to be yours alone. So sink or swim, Tim, it's up to you.'

One's first exposure to the Royal Ascot meeting was, according to one's basic outlook, either a matter of surprised delight or of puritanical disapproval. Either the spirits lifted to the sight of emerald grass, massed flowers, bright dresses, fluffy hats and men elegant in grey formality, or one despised the expenditure, the frivolity, the shame of champagne and strawberries while some of the world starved.

I belonged, without doubt, to the hedonists, both by upbringing and inclination. The Royal meeting at Ascot was, as it happened, the one racing event from which my parents had perenially excluded me, children in any case being barred from the Royal Enclosure for three of the four days, and mother more interested on this occasion in socialising than betting. School, she had said firmly every year, must come first: though on other days it hadn't, necessarily. So it was with an extra sense of pleasure that I walked through the gates in my father's resurrected finery and made my way through the smiling throng to the appointed, high-up box.

'Welcome to the charade,' Gordon said cheerfully, handing me a bubbling glass, and 'Isn't this *fun*?' Judith exclaimed, humming with excitement in yellow silk.

'It's great,' I said, and meant it; and Gordon, looking sunburned and healthy, introduced me to the owner of the box.

'Dissdale, this is Tim Ekaterin. Works in the bank. Tim – Dissdale Smith.'

We shook hands. His was plump and warm, like his body, like his face. 'Delighted,' he said. 'Got a drink? Good. Met my wife? No? Bettina, darling, say hello to Tim.' He put an arm round the thin waist of a girl less than half his age whose clinging white black-dotted dress was cut low and bare at neck and armholes. There was also a wide black hat, beautiful skin and a sweet and practised smile.

'Hello, Tim,' she said. 'So glad you could come.' Her voice, I thought, was like the rest of her: manufactured, processed, not natural top drawer but a long way from gutter.

The box itself was approximately five yards by three, most of the space being filled by a dining table laid with twelve places for lunch. The far end wall was of windows looking out over the green course, with a glass door opening to steps going down to the viewing balcony. The walls of the box were covered as if in a house with pale blue hessian, and a soft blue carpet, pink flowers and pictures lent an air of opulence far greater than the actual expense. Most of the walls of the boxes into which I'd peered on the way along to this one were of builders' universal margarine colour, and I wondered fleetingly whether it was Dissdale or Bettina who had the prettying mind.

Henry Shipton and his wife were standing in the doorway to the balcony, alternately facing out and in, like a couple of Januses. Henry across the room lifted his glass to me in a gesture of acknowledgement, and Lorna as ever looked as if faults were being found.

Lorna Shipton, tall, over-assured, and dressed that frilly day in repressive tailored grey, was a woman from whom disdain flowed outward like a tide, a woman who seemed not to know that words could wound and saw no reason not to air each ungenerous thought. I had met her about the same number of times as I'd met Judith Michaels and mostly upon the same occasions, and if I smothered love for the one it was irritation I had to hide for the other. It was, I suppose, inevitable, that of the two it was Lorna Shipton I was placed next to at lunch.

More guests arrived behind me, Dissdale and Bettina greeting them with whoops and kisses and making the sort of indistinct introductions that one instantly forgets. Dissdale decided there would be less crush if everyone sat down and so took his place at the top of the table with Gordon, his back to the windows, at the foot. When each had arranged their guests around them there were two empty places, one next to Gordon, one up Dissdale's end.

Gordon had Lorna Shipton on his right, with me beside her: the space on his left, then Henry, then Judith. The girl on my right spent most of her time leaning forward to speak to her host Dissdale, so that although I grew to know quite well the blue chiffon back of her shoulder, I never actually learned her name.

Laughter, chatter, the study of race cards, the refilling of glasses: Judith with yellow silk roses on her hat and Lorna telling me that my morning coat looked a size too small.

'It was my father's,' I said.

'Such a stupid man.'

I glanced at her face, but she was merely expressing her thoughts, not positively trying to offend.

'A beautiful day for racing,' I said.

'You should be working. Your Uncle Freddie won't like it, you know. I'm certain that when he bailed you out he made it a condition that you and your mother should both stay away from racecourses. And now look at you. It's really too bad. I'll have to tell him, of course.'

I wondered how Henry put up with it. Wondered, as one does, why he'd married her. He, however, his ear attuned across the table in a husbandly way, said to her pleasantly, 'Freddie knows that Tim is here, my dear. Gordon and I obtained dispensation, so to speak.' He gave me a glimmer of a smile. 'The wrath of God has been averted.'

'Oh.' Lorna Shipton looked disappointed and I noticed Judith trying not to laugh.

Uncle Freddie, ex vice-chairman, now retired, still owned enough of the bank to make his unseen presence felt, and I knew he was in the habit of telephoning Henry two or three times a week to find out what was going on. Out of interest, one gathered, not from desire to meddle; as certainly, once he had set his terms, he never meddled with mother and me.

Dissdale's last guest arrived at that point with an unseen flourish of trumpets, a man making an entrance as if well aware of newsworthiness. Dissdale leapt to his feet to greet him and pumped him warmly by hand.

'Calder, this is great. Calder Jackson, everybody.'

There were yelps of delight from Dissdale's end and polite smiles round Gordon's. 'Calder Johnson,' Dissdale said down the table, 'You know, the miracle-worker. Brings dying horses back to life. You must have seen him on television.'

'Ah yes,' Gordon responded. 'Of course.'

Dissdale beamed and returned to his guest who was lapping up adulation with a show of modesty.

'Who did he say?' Lorna Shipton asked.

'Calder Jackson,' Gordon said.

'Who?'

Gordon shook his head, his ignorance showing. He raised his eyebrows in a question to me, but I fractionally shook my head also. We listened, however, and we learned.

Calder Jackson was a shortish man with a head of hair designed to be noticed. Designed literally, I guessed. He had a lot of dark curls going attractively grey, cut short towards the neck but free and fluffy on top of his head and over his forehead; and he had let his beard grow in a narrow fringe from in front of his ears round the line of his jaw, the hairs of this being also bushy and curly but grey to white. From in front his weathered face was thus circled with curls: from the side he looked as if he were wearing a helmet. Or a coal-scuttle, I thought unflatteringly. Once seen, in any case, never forgotten.

'It's just a gift,' he was saying deprecatingly in a voice that had an edge to it more compelling than loudness: an accent very slightly of the country but of no particular region; a confidence born of acclaim.

The girl sitting next to me was ecstatic. 'How *divine* to meet you. One has heard so *much* . . . Do tell us, now do tell us your secret.'

Calder Jackson eyed her blandly, his gaze sliding for a second beyond her to me and then back again. Myself he quite openly discarded as being of no interest, but to the girl he obligingly said, 'There's no secret, my dear. None at all. Just good food, good care and a few age-old herbal remedies. And, of course . . . well . . . the laying on of hands.'

'But *how,*' asked the girl, 'how do you do that to horses?'

'I just . . . touch them.' He smiled disarmingly. 'And then sometimes I feel them quiver, and I know the healing force is going from me into them.'

'Can you do it infallibly?' Henry asked politely, and I noted with interest that he'd let no implication of doubt sound in his voice: Henry whose gullibility could be measured in micrograms, if at all.

Calder Jackson took his seriousness for granted and slowly shook his head. 'If I have the horse in my care for long enough, it usually happens in the end. But not always. No, sadly, not always.'

'How fascinating,' Judith said, and earned another of those kind bland smiles. Charlatan or not, I thought, Calder Jackson had the mix just right: an arresting appearance, a modest demeanour, no promise of success. And for all I knew, he really could do what he said. Healers were an age-old phenomenon, so why not a healer of horses?

'Can you heal people too?' I asked in a mirror-image of Henry's tone. No doubts. Just enquiry.

The curly head turned my way with more civility than interest and he patiently answered the question he must have been asked a thousand times before. Answered in a sequence of words he had perhaps used almost as often. 'Whatever gift it is that I have is especially for horses. I have no feeling that I can heal humans, and I prefer not to try. I ask people not to ask me, because I don't like to disappoint them.'

I nodded my thanks, watched his head turn away and listened to him willingly answering the next question, from Bettina, as if it too had never before been asked. 'No, the healing very seldom happens instantaneously. I need to be near the horse for a while. Sometimes for only a few days. Sometimes for a few weeks. One can never tell.'

Dissdale basked in the success of having hooked his celebrity and told us all that two of Calder's ex-patients were running that very afternoon. 'Isn't that right, Calder?'

The curly head nodded. 'Cretonne, in the first race, she used to break blood vessels, and Molyneaux, in the fifth, he came to me with infected wounds. I feel they are my friends now. I feel I know them.'

'And shall we back them, Calder?' Dissdale asked roguishly. 'Are they going to win?'

The healer smiled forgivingly. 'If they're fast enough, Dissdale.'

Everyone laughed. Gordon refilled his own guests' glasses. Lorna Shipton said apropos of not much that she had occasionally considered becoming a Christian Scientist and Judith wondered what colour the Queen would be wearing. Dissdale's party talked animatedly among themselves, and the door from the corridor tentatively opened.

Any hopes I might have had that Gordon's sixth place was

destined for a Bettina-equivalent for my special benefit were immediately dashed. The lady who appeared and whom Judith greeted with a kiss on the cheek was nearer forty than twenty-five and more solid than lissom. She wore a brownish pink linen suit and a small white straw hat circled with a brownish pink ribbon. The suit, I diagnosed, was an old friend: the hat, new in honour of the occasion.

Judith in her turn introduced the newcomer: Penelope Warner – Pen – a good friend of hers and Gordon's. Pen Warner sat where invited, next to Gordon and made small-talk with Henry and Lorna. I half listened, and took in a few desultory details like no rings on the fingers, no polish on the nails, no grey in the short brown hair, no artifice in the voice. Worthy, I thought. Well intentioned; slightly boring. Probably runs a church.

A waitress appeared with an excellent lunch, during which Calder could from time to time be heard extolling the virtues of watercress for its iron content and garlic for the treatment of fever and diarrhoea.

'And of course in humans,' he was saying, 'garlic is literally a life saver in whooping-cough. You make a poultice and bind it onto the bottom of the feet of the child every night, in a bandage and a sock, and in the morning you'll smell the garlic on the breath of the child, and the cough will abate. Garlic, in fact, cures almost anything. A truly marvellous life-giving plant.'

I saw Pen Warner lift her head to listen and I thought that I'd been wrong about the church. I had missed the worldliness of the eyes, the long sad knowledge of human frailty. A magistrate, perhaps? Yes, perhaps.

Judith leaned across the table and said teasingly, 'Tim, can't you forget you're a banker even at the races?'

'What?' I said.

'You look at everyone as if you're working out just how much you can lend them without risk.'

'I'd lend you my soul,' I said.

'For me to pay back with interest?'

'Pay in love and kisses.'

Harmless stuff, as frivolous as her hat. Henry, sitting next to her, said in the same vein, 'You're second in the queue, Tim. I've a first option, eh, Judith? Count on me, dear girl, for the last drop of blood.'

She patted his hand affectionately and glowed a little from

the deep truth of our idle protestations: and Calder Jackson's voice came through with 'Comfrey heals tissues with amazing speed and will cause chronic ulcers to disappear in a matter of days, and of course it mends fractures in half the time considered normal. Comfrey is miraculous.'

There was a good deal of speculation after that all round the table about a horse called Sandcastle that had won the 2,000 Guineas six weeks earlier and was hot favourite for the King Edward VII Stakes, the top Ascot race for three-year-old colts, due to be run that afternoon.

Dissdale had actually seen the Guineas at Newmarket and was enthusiastic. 'Daisy-cutter action. Positively eats up the ground.' He sprayed his opinions good naturedly to the furthest ear. 'Big rangy colt, full of courage.'

'Beaten in the Derby, though,' Henry said, judiciously responding.

'Well, yes,' Dissdale allowed. 'But fourth, you know. Not a total disgrace, would you say?'

'He was good as a two-year-old,' Henry said, nodding.

'Glory, yes,' said Dissdale fervently. 'And you can't fault his breeding. By Castle out of an Ampersand mare. You can't get much better than that.'

Several heads nodded respectfully in ignorance.

'He's my banker,' Dissdale said and then spread his arms wide and half-laughed. 'OK, we've got a roomful of bankers. But Sandcastle is where I'm putting my money today. Doubling him with my bets in every other race. Trebles. Accumulators. The lot. You all listen to your Uncle Dissdale. Sandcastle is the soundest banker at Ascot.' His voice positively shook with evangelical belief. 'He simply can't be beaten.'

'Betting is out for you, Tim,' Lorna Shipton said severely in my ear.

'I'm not my mother,' I said mildly.

'Heredity' Lorna said darkly. 'And your father drank.'

I smothered a bursting laugh and ate my strawberries in good humour. Whatever I'd inherited from my parents it wasn't an addiction to their more expensive pleasures; rather a firm intention never again to lose my record collection to the bailiffs. Those stolid men had taken even the rocking horse on which at the age of six I'd ridden my fantasy Grand Nationals. They'd taken my books, my skis and my camera. Mother had fluttered around in tears saying those things were mine, not hers, and they should leave them, and the men had gone on marching out with all our stuff as if they were deaf. About her own disappearing treasures she had been distraught, her distress and grief hopelessly mixed with guilt.

I had been old enough at twenty-four to shrug off our actual losses and more or less replace them (except for the rocking horse) but the fury of that day had affected my whole life since: and I had been silent when it happened, white and dumb with rage.

Lorna Shipton removed her disapproval from me long enough to tell Henry not to have cream and sugar on his strawberries or she would have no sympathy if he put on weight, had a heart attack, or developed pimples. Henry looked resignedly at the forbidden delights which he wouldn't have eaten anyway. God preserve me, I thought, from marrying a Lorna Shipton.

By the coffee-brandy-cigar stage the tranquil seating pattern had broken up into people dashing out to back their hopes in the first race and I, not much of a gambler whatever Mrs Shipton might think, had wandered out onto the balcony to watch the Queen's procession of sleek horses, open carriages, gold, glitter and fluttering feathers trotting like a fairy tale up the green course.

'Isn't it *splendid,*' said Judith's voice at my shoulder, and I glanced at her characterful face and met the straight smiling eyes. Damn it to hell, I thought, I'd like to live with Gordon's wife.

'Gordon's gone to bet,' she said, 'so I thought I'd take the opportunity . . . He's appalled at what happened . . . and we're really grateful to you, you know, for what you did that dreadful day.'

I shook my head. 'I did nothing, believe me.'

'Well, that's half the point. You *said* nothing. In the bank, I mean. Henry says there hasn't been a whisper.'

'But . . . I wouldn't.'

'A lot of people *would,*' she said. 'Suppose you had been that Alec.'

I smiled involuntarily. 'Alec isn't unkind. He wouldn't have told.'

'Gordon says he's as discreet as a town-crier.'

'Do you want to go down and see the horses?' I asked.

'Yes. It's lovely up here, but too far from life.'

We went down to the paddock, saw the horses walk at close quarters round the ring and watched the jockeys mount ready to ride out onto the course. Judith smelled nice. Stop it, I told myself. Stop it.

'That horse over there,' I said, pointing, 'is the one Calder Jackson said he cured. Cretonne. The jockey in bright pink.'

'Are you going to back it?' she said.

'If you like.'

She nodded the yellow silk roses and we queued up in good humour to make the wager. All around us in grey toppers and frothy dresses the Ascot crowd swirled, a feast to the eye in the sunshine, a ritual in make-believe, a suppression of gritty truth. My father's whole life had been a pursuit of the spirit I saw in these Royal Ascot faces; the pursuit and entrapment of happiness.

'What are you thinking,' Judith said, 'so solemnly?'

'That lotus-eaters do no harm. Let terrorists eat lotus.'

'As a steady diet,' she said, 'it would be sickening.'

'On a day like this one could fall in love.'

'Yes, one could.' She was reading her race-card over-intently. 'But should one?'

After a pause I said, 'No, I don't think so.'

'Nor do I.' She looked up with seriousness and understanding and with a smile in her mind. 'I've known you six years.'

'I haven't been faithful,' I said.

She laughed and the moment passed, but the declaration had quite plainly been made and in a way accepted. She showed no awkwardness in my continued presence but rather an increase of warmth, and in mutual contentment we agreed to stay in the paddock for the first short race rather than climb all the way up and find it was over by the time we'd reached the box.

The backs of the jockeys disappeared down the course as they cantered to the start, and I said, as a way of conversation, 'Who is Dissdale Smith?'

'Oh.' She looked amused. 'He's in the motor trade. He loves to make a splash, as no doubt you saw, but I don't think he's doing as well as he pretends. Anyway, he told Gordon he was looking for someone to share the expense of this box here and asked if Gordon would be interested in buying half the box for today. He's sold halves for the other days as well. I don't think he's supposed to, actually, so better say nothing to anyone else.'

'No.'

'Bettina's his third wife,' she said. 'She's a model.'

'Very pretty.'

'And not as dumb as she looks.'

I heard the dryness in her voice and acknowledged that I had myself sounded condescending.

'Mind you,' Judith said forgivingly, 'his second wife was the most gorgeous thing on earth, but without two thoughts to rub together. Even Dissdale got tired of the total vacancy behind the sensational violet eyes. It's all very well to get a buzz when all men light up on meeting your wife, but it rather kicks the stilts away when the same men diagnose total dimness within five minutes and start pitying you instead.'

'I can see that. What became of her?'

'Dissdale introduced her to a boy who'd inherited millions and had an IQ on a par with hers. The last I heard they were in a fog of bliss.'

From where we stood we couldn't see much of the race, only a head-on view of the horses as they came up to the winning post. In no way did I mind that, and when one of the leaders proved to carry bright pink Judith caught hold of my arm and shook it.

'That's Cretonne, isn't it?' She listened to the announcement of the winner's number. 'Do you realise, Tim, that we've damned well won?' She was laughing with pleasure, her face full of sunshine and wonder.

'Bully for Calder Jackson.'

'You don't trust him,' she said. 'I could see it in all your faces, yours and Henry's and Gordon's. You all have the same way of peering into people's souls: you too, though you're so young. You were all being incredibly polite so that he shouldn't see your reservations.'

I smiled. 'That sounds disgusting.'

'I've been married to Gordon for nine years,' she said.

There was again a sudden moment of stillness in which we looked at each other in wordless question and answer. Then she shook her head slightly, and after a pause I nodded acquiescence: and I thought that with a woman so straightforwardly intelligent I could have been content for ever.

'Do we collect our winnings now or later?' she asked.

'Now, if we wait awhile.'

Waiting together for the jockeys to weigh-in and the all-clear to be given for the pay-out seemed as little hardship for her as for me. We talked about nothing much and the time passed in a flash; and eventually we made our way back to the box to find that everyone there too had backed Cretonne and was high with the same success. Calder Jackson beamed and looked modest, and Dissdale expansively opened more bottles of excellent Krug, champagne of Kings.

Escorting one's host's wife to the paddock was not merely acceptable but an expected civility, so that it was with a benign eye that Gordon greeted our return. I was both glad and sorry, looking at his unsuspecting friendliness, that he had nothing to worry about. The jewel in his house would stay there and be his alone. Unattached bachelors could lump it.

The whole party, by now markedly carefree, crowded the box's balcony for the big race. Dissdale said he had staked his all on his banker, Sandcastle; and although he said it with a laugh I saw the tremor in his hands which fidgetted with the raceglasses. He's in too deep, I thought. A bad way to bet.

Most of the others, fired by Dissdale's certainty, happily clutched tickets doubling Sandcastle every which-way. Even Lorna Shipton, with a pink glow on each bony cheekbone, confessed to Henry that just for once, as it was a special day, she had staked five pounds in forecasts.

'And you, Tim?' Henry teased. 'Your shirt?'

Lorna looked confused. I smiled. 'Buttons and all,' I said cheerfully.

'No, but . . .' Lorna said.

'Yes, but,' I said, 'I've dozens more shirts at home.'

Henry laughed and steered Lorna gently away, and I found myself standing next to Calder Jackson.

'Do you gamble?' I asked, for something to say.

'Only on certainties.' He smiled blandly in the way that scarcely warmed his eyes. 'Though on certainties it's hardly a gamble.'

'And is Sandcastle a certainty?'

He shook his curly head. 'A probability. No racing bet's a certainty. The horse might feel ill. Might be kicked at the start.'

I glanced across at Dissdale who was faintly sweating, and hoped for his sake that the horse would feel well and come sweetly out of the stalls.

'Can you tell if a horse is sick just by looking at him?' I enquired. 'I mean, if you just watched him walk round the parade ring, could you tell?'

Calder answered in the way that revealed it was again an often-asked question. 'Of course sometimes you can see at once, but mostly a horse as ill as that wouldn't have been brought to the races. I prefer to look at a horse closely. To examine for instance the colour inside the eyelid and inside the nostril. In a sick horse, what should be a healthy pink may be pallid.' He stopped with apparent finality, as if that were the appointed end of that answer, but after a few seconds, during which the whole huge crowd watched Sandcastle stretch out in the sun in the canter to the post, he said almost with awe, 'That's a superb horse. Superb.' It sounded to me like his first spontaneous remark of the day and it vibrated with genuine enthusiasm.

'He looks great,' I agreed.

Calder Jackson smiled as if with indulgence at the shallowness of my judgement compared with the weight of his inside knowledge. 'He should have won the Derby,' he said. 'He got shut in on the rails, couldn't get out in time.'

My place at the great man's side was taken by Bettina, who threaded her arm through his and said, 'Dear Calder, come down to the front, you can see better than here at the back.' She gave me a photogenic little smile and pulled her captive after her down the steps.

In a buzz that rose to a roar the runners covered their mile and a half journey; longer than the 2,000 Guineas, the same length as the Derby. Sandcastle in scarlet and white was making no show at all to universal groans and lay only fifth as the field swept round the last bend, and Dissdale looked as if he might have a heart attack.

Alas for my shirt, I thought. Alas for Lorna's forecasts. Bang goes the banker that can't lose.

Dissdale, unable to watch, collapsed weakly onto one of the small chairs which dotted the balcony, and in the next-door boxes people were standing on top of theirs and jumping up and down and screaming.

'Sandcastle making his move . . .' the commentator's voice warbled over the loudspeakers, but the yells of the crowd drowned the rest.

The scarlet and white colours had moved to the outside. The daisy-cutter action was there for the world to see. The superb horse, the big rangy colt full of courage was eating up his ground.

Our box in the grandstand was almost a furlong down the course from the winning post, and when he reached us Sandcastle still had three horses ahead. He was flying, though, like a streak, and I found the sight of this fluid valour, this all-out striving, most immensely moving and exciting. I grabbed Dissdale by his despairing shoulder and hauled him forcefully to his feet.

'Look,' I shouted in his ear. 'Watch. Your banker's going to win. He's a marvel. He's a dream.'

He turned with a gaping mouth to stare in the direction of the winning post and he saw . . . he saw Sandcastle among the tumult going like a javelin, free now of all the others, aiming straight for the prize.

'He's won,' Dissdale's mouth said slackly, though amid the noise I could hardly hear him. 'He's bloody won.'

I helped him up the steps into the box. His skin was grey and damp and he was stumbling.

'Sit down,' I said, pulling out the first chair I came to, but he shook his head weakly and made his shaky way to his own place at the head of the table. He almost fell into it, heavily, and stretched out a trembling hand to his champagne.

'My God,' he said, 'I'll never do that again. Never on God's earth.'

'Do what?'

He gave me a flickering glance over his glass and said, 'All on one throw.'

All. He'd said it before. 'All on the banker . . .' He surely couldn't, I thought, have meant literally *all*; but yet not much else could have produced such physical symptoms.

Everyone else piled back into the room with ballooning jollity. Everyone without exception had backed Sandcastle, thanks to Dissdale. Even Calder Jackson, when pressed by Bettina, admitted to 'a small something on the Tote. I don't usually, but just this once.' And if he'd lost, I thought, he wouldn't have confessed.

Dissdale, from near fainting, climbed rapidly to a pulse-throbbing high, the colour coming back to his plump cheeks in a hectic red. No one seemed to have noticed his near-collapse, certainly not his wife, who flirted prettily with the healer and got less than her due response. More wine easily made its way down every throat, and there was no doubt that for the now commingled party the whole day was a riotous success.

In a while Henry offered to take Judith to the paddock. Gordon to my relief invited Lorna, which left me with the mystery lady, Pen Warner, with whom I'd so far exchanged only the thrilling words 'How do you do.'

'Would you like to go down?' I asked.

'Yes, indeed. But you don't need to stay with me if it's too much bother.'

'Are you so insecure?'

There was a quick widening of the eyes and a visible mental shift. 'You're damned rude,' she said. 'And Judith said you were nice.'

I let her go past me out onto the landing and smiled as she went. 'I should like to stay with you,' I said, 'if it's not too much bother.'

She gave me a dry look, but as we more or less had to walk in single file along the narrow passageway owing to people going in the opposite direction she said little more until we had negotiated the lifts, the escalators and the pedestrian tunnel and had emerged into the daylight of the paddock.

It was her first time at Ascot, she said. Her first time, in fact, at the races.

'What do you think of it?'

'Very beautiful. Very brave. Quite mad.'

'Does sanity lie in ugliness and cowardice?' I asked.

'Life does, pretty often,' she said. 'Haven't you noticed?'

'And some aren't happy unless they're desperate.'

She quietly laughed. 'Tragedy inspires, so they say.'

'They can stick it,' I said. 'I'd rather lie in the sun.'

We stood on the raised tiers of steps to watch the horses walk round the ring, and she told me that she lived along the road from Judith in another house fronting the common. 'I've lived there all my life, long before Judith came. We met casually, as one does, in the local shops, and just walked home together one day several years ago. Been friends ever since.'

'Lucky,' I said.

'Yes.'

'Do you live alone?' I asked conversationally.

Her eyes slid my way with inner amusement. 'Yes, I do. Do you?'

I nodded.

'I prefer it,' she said.

'So do I.'

Her skin was clear and still girlish, the thickened figure alone giving an impression of years passing. That and the look in the eyes, the 'I've seen the lot' sadness.

'Are you a magistrate?' I asked.

She looked startled. 'No, I'm not. What an odd thing to ask.'

I made an apologetic gesture. 'You just look as if you might be.'

She shook her head. 'Wouldn't have time, even if I had the urge.'

'But you do do good in the world.'

She was puzzled. 'What makes you say so?'

'I don't know. The way you look.' I smiled to take away any seriousness and said, 'Which horse do you like? Shall we choose one and bet?'

'What about Burnt Marshmallow?'

She liked the name, she said, so we queued briefly at a Tote window and invested some of the winnings from Cretonne and Sandcastle.

During our slow traverse of the paddock crowds on our way back towards the box we came towards Calder Jackson, who was surrounded by respectful listeners and didn't see us.

'Garlic is as good as penicillin,' he was saying. 'If you scatter grated garlic onto a septic wound it will kill all the bacteria . . .'

We slowed a little to hear.

'. . . and comfrey is miraculous,' Calder said. 'It knits bones and cures intractable skin ulcers in half the time you'd expect.'

'He said all that upstairs,' I said.

Pen Warner nodded, faintly smiling. 'Good sound herbal medicine,' she said. 'You can't fault him. Comfrey contains allantoin, a well-known cell proliferant.'

'Does it? I mean . . . do you know about it?'

'Mm.' We walked on, but she said nothing more until we were high up again in the passageway to the box. 'I don't know whether you'd think I do good in the world . . . but basically I dole out pills.'

'Er . . .?' I said.

She smiled. 'I'm a lady in a white coat. A pharmacist.'

I suppose I was in a way disappointed, and she sensed it.

'Well,' she sighed, 'we can't all be glamorous. I told you life was ugly and frightening, and from my point of view that's often what it is for my customers. I see fear every day . . . and I know its face.'

'Pen,' I said, 'forgive my frivolity. I'm duly chastened.'

We reached the box to find Judith alone there, Henry having loitered to place a bet.

'I told Tim I'm a pharmacist,' Pen said. 'He thinks it's boring.'

I got no further than the first words of protestation when Judith interrupted.

'She's not just "a" pharmacist,' she said. 'She owns her own place. Half the medics in London recommend her. You're talking to a walking gold-mine with a heart like a wet sponge.'

She put her arm round Pen's waist and the two of them together looked at me, their eyes shining with what perhaps looked like liking, but also with the mischievous feminine superiority of being five or six years older.

'Judith!' I said compulsively. 'I . . . I . . .' I stopped. 'Oh *damn* it,' I said. 'Have some Krug.'

Dissdale's friends returned giggling to disrupt the incautious minute and shortly Gordon, Henry and Lorna crowded in. The whole party pressed out onto the balcony to watch the race, and because it was a time out of reality Burnt Marshmallow romped home by three lengths.

The rest of the afternoon slid fast away. Henry at some point found himself alone out on the balcony beside me while inside the box the table was being spread with a tea that was beyond my stretched stomach entirely and a temptation from which the ever-hungry Henry had bodily removed himself.

'How's your cartoonist?' he said genially. 'Are we staking him, or are we not?'

'You're sure . . . I have to decide . . . all alone?'

'I said so. Yes.'

'Well . . . I got him to bring some more drawings to the bank. And his paints.'

'His *paints*?'

'Yes. I thought if I could see him at work, I'd know . . .' I shrugged. 'Anyway, I took him into the private interview room and asked him to paint the outline of a cartoon film while I watched; and he did it, there and then, in acrylics. Twenty-five outline sketches in bright colour, all within an hour. Same characters, different story, and terrifically funny. That was on Monday. I've been . . . well . . . dreaming about those cartoons. It sounds absurd. Maybe they're too much on my mind.'

'But you've decided?'

After a pause I said, 'Yes.'

'And?'

With a sense of burning bridges I said, 'To go ahead.'

'All right.' Henry seemed unalarmed. 'Keep me informed.'

'Yes, of course.'

He nodded and smoothly changed the subject. 'Lorna and I have won quite a bit today. How about you?'

'Enough to give Uncle Freddie fits about the effect on my unstable personality.'

Henry laughed aloud. 'Your Uncle Freddie,' he said, 'knows you better than you may think.'

At the end of that splendid afternoon the whole party descended together to ground level and made its way to the exit; to the gate which opened onto the main road, and across that to the car park and to the covered walk which led to the station.

Calder just ahead of me walked in front, the helmet of curls bent kindly over Bettina, the strong voice thanking her and Dissdale for 'a most enjoyable time'. Dissdale himself, not only fully recovered but incoherent with joy as most of his doubles, trebles and accumulators had come up, patted Calder plumply on the shoulder and invited him over to 'my place' for the weekend.

Henry and Gordon, undoubtedly the most sober of the party, were fiddling in their pockets for car keys and throwing their racecards into wastebins. Judith and Pen were talking to each other and Lorna was graciously unbending to Dissdale's friends. It seemed to be only I, with unoccupied eyes, who saw at all what was about to happen.

We were out on the pavement, still in a group, half-waiting for a chance to cross the road, soon to break up and scatter. All talking, laughing, busy; except me.

A boy stood there on the pavement, watchful and still. I noticed first the fixed, burning intent in the dark eyes, and quickly after that the jeans and faded shirt which contrasted sharply with our Ascot clothes, and then finally with incredulity the knife in his hand.

I had almost to guess at whom he was staring with such deadly purpose, and no time even to shout a warning. He moved across the pavement with stunning speed, the stab already on its upward travel.

I jumped almost without thinking; certainly without assessing consequences or chances. Most unbankerlike behaviour.

The steel was almost in Calder's stomach when I deflected it. I hit the boy's arm with my body in a sort of flying tackle and in a flashing view saw the weave of Calder's trousers, the polish on his shoes, the litter on the pavement. The boy fell beneath me and I thought in horror that somewhere between our bodies he still held that wicked blade.

He writhed under me, all muscle and fury, and tried to heave me off. He was lying on his back, his face just under mine, his eyes like slits and his teeth showing between drawn-back lips. I had an impression of dark eyebrows and white skin and I could hear the breath hissing between his teeth in a tempest of effort.

Both of his hands were under my chest and I could feel him trying to get space enough to up-end the knife. I pressed down onto him solidly with all my weight and in my mind I was saying 'Don't do it, don't do it, you bloody fool'; and I was saying it *for his sake*, which seemed crazy to me at the time and even crazier in retrospect. He was trying to do me great harm and all I thought about was the trouble he'd be in if he succeeded.

We were both panting but I was taller and stronger and I could have held him there for a good while longer but for the two policemen who had been out on the road directing traffic. They had seen the melee; seen as they supposed a man in morning dress attacking a pedestrian, seen us struggling on the ground. In any case the first I knew of their presence was the feel of vice-like hands fastening onto my arms and pulling me backwards.

I resisted with all my might. I didn't know they were policemen. I had eyes only for the boy: his eyes, his hands, his knife.

With peremptory strength they hauled me off, one of them anchoring my upper arms to my sides by encircling me from behind. I kicked furiously backwards and turned my head, and only then realised that the new assailants wore navy blue.

The boy comprehended the situation in a flash. He rolled over onto his feet, crouched for a split second like an athlete at the blocks and without lifting his head above waist-height slithered through the flow of the crowds still pouring out of the gates and disappeared out of sight inside the racecourse. Through there they would never find him. Through there he would escape to the cheaper rings and simply walk out of the lower gate.

I stopped struggling but the policemen didn't let go. They had no thought of chasing the boy. They were incongruously calling me 'sir' while treating me with contempt, which if I'd been calm enough for reflection I would have considered fairly normal.

'For God's sake,' I said finally to one of them, 'what do you think that knife's doing on the pavement?'

They looked down to where it lay; to where it had fallen when the boy ran. Eight inches of sharp steel kitchen knife with a black handle.

'He was trying to stab Calder Jackson,' I said. 'All I did was stop him. Why do you think he's gone?'

By this time Henry, Gordon, Laura, Judith and Pen were standing round in an anxious circle continually assuring the law that never in a million years would their friend attack anyone except out of direst need, and Calder was looking dazed and fingering a slit in the waistband of his trousers.

The farce slowly resolved itself into duller bureaucratic order. The policemen relinquished their hold and I brushed the dirt off the knees of my father's suit and straightened my tangled tie. Someone picked up my tumbled top hat and gave it to me. I grinned at Judith. It all seemed such a ridiculous mixture of death and bathos.

The aftermath took half of the evening and was boring in the extreme: police station, hard chairs, polystyrene cups of coffee.

No, I'd never seen the boy before.

Yes, I was sure the boy had been aiming at Calder specifically.

Yes, I was sure he was only a boy. About sixteen, probably.

Yes, I would know him again. Yes, I would help with an Identikit picture.

No. My fingerprints were positively not on the knife. The boy had held onto it until he ran.

Yes, of course they could take my prints, in case.

Calder, wholly mystified, repeated over and over that he had no idea who could want to kill him. He seemed scandalised, indeed, at the very idea. The police persisted: most people knew their murderers, they said, particularly when as seemed possible in this case the prospective killer had been purposefully waiting for his victim. According to Mr Ekaterin the boy had known Calder. That was quite possible, Calder said, because of his television appearances, but Calder had *not* known *him*.

Among some of the police there was a muted quality, among others a sort of defiant aggression, but it was only Calder who rather acidly pointed out that if they hadn't done such a good job of hauling me off, they would now have the boy in custody and wouldn't need to be looking for him.

'You could have asked first,' Calder said, but even I shook my head.

If I had indeed been the aggressor I could have killed the boy while the police were asking the onlookers just who was fighting whom. Act first, ask questions after was a policy full of danger, but getting it the wrong way round could be worse.

Eventually we both left the building, Calder on the way out trying his best with unrehearsed words. 'Er . . . Tim . . . Thanks are in order . . . If it hadn't been for you . . . I don't know what to say.'

'Say nothing,' I said. 'I did it without thinking. Glad you're OK.'

I had taken it for granted that everyone else would be long gone, but Dissdale and Bettina had waited for Calder, and Gordon, Judith and Pen for me, all of them standing in a group by some cars and talking to three or four strangers.

'We know you and Calder both came by train,' Gordon said, walking towards us, 'but we decided we'd drive you home.'

'You're extraordinarily kind,' I said.

'My dear Dissdale . . .' Calder said, seeming still at a loss for words. 'So grateful, really.'

They made a fuss of him; the endangered one, the lion delivered. The strangers round the cars turned out to be gentlemen of the press, to whom Calder Jackson was always news, alive or dead. To my horror they announced themselves, producing notebooks and a camera, and wrote down everything anyone said, except they got nothing from me because all I wanted to do was shut them up.

As well try to stop an avalanche with an outstretched palm. Dissdale and Bettina and Gordon and Judith and Pen did a diabolical job, which was why for a short time afterwards I suffered from public notoriety as the man who had saved Calder Jackson's life.

No one seemed to speculate about his assailant setting out for a second try.

I looked at my photograph in the papers and wondered if the boy would see it, and know my name.

The First Year

OCTOBER

Gordon was back at work with his faintly trembling left hand usually out of sight and unnoticeable.

During periods of activity, as on the day at Ascot, he seemed to forget to camouflage, but at other times he had taken to sitting forwards in a hunched way over his desk with his hand anchored down between his thighs. I thought it a pity. I thought the tremor so slight that none of the others would have remarked on it, either aloud or to themselves, but to Gordon it was clearly a burden.

Not that it seemed to have affected his work. He had come back in July with determination, thanked me briskly in the presence of the others for my stop-gapping and taken all major decisions off my desk and back to his.

John asked him, also in the hearing of Alec, Rupert and myself, to make it clear to us what it was he, John, who was the official next-in-line to Gordon, if the need should occur again. He pointed out that he was older and had worked much longer in the bank than I had. Tim, he said, shouldn't be jumping the queue.

Gordon eyed him blandly and said that if the need arose no doubt the chairman would take every factor into consideration. John made bitter and audible remarks under his breath about favouritism and unfair privilege, and Alec told him ironically to find a merchant bank where there *wasn't* a nephew or some such on the force.

'Be your age,' he said. 'Of *course* they want the next generation to join the family business. Why shouldn't they? It's natural.' But John was unplacated, and didn't see that his acid grudge against me was wasting a lot of his time. I seemed to be continually in his thoughts. He gave me truly vicious looks across the room and took every opportunity to sneer and denigrate. Messages never got passed on, and clients were given the impression that I was incompetent and only employed out of family charity. Occasionally on the telephone people refused to do business with me, saying they wanted

John, and once a caller said straight out, 'Are you that playboy they're shoving ahead over better men's heads?'

John's gripe was basically understandable: in his place I'd have been cynical myself. Gordon did nothing to curb the escalating hate campaign and Alec found it funny. I thought long and hard about what to do and decided simply to work harder. I'd see it was very difficult for John to make his allegations stick.

His aggression showed in his body, which was roundedly muscular and looked the wrong shape for a city suit. Of moderate height, he wore his wiry brown hair very short so that it bristled above his collar, and his voice was loud, as if he thought volume equated authority: and so it might have done in schoolroom or on barrack square, instead of on a civilised patch of carpet.

He had come into banking via business school with high ambitions and good persuasive skills. I sometimes thought he would have made an excellent export salesman, but that wasn't the life he wanted. Alec said that John got his kicks from saying 'I am a merchant banker' to pretty girls and preening himself in their admiration.

Alec was a wicked fellow, really, and a shooter of perceptive arrows.

There came a day in October when three whirlwind things happened more or less simultaneously. The cartoonist telephoned; *What's Going On Where It Shouldn't* landed with a thud throughout the City; and Uncle Freddie descended on Ekaterin's for a tour of inspection.

To begin with the three events were unconnected, but by the end of the day, entwined.

I heard the cartoonist's rapid opening remarks with a sinking heart. 'I've engaged three extra animators and I need five more,' he said. 'Ten isn't nearly enough. I've worked out the amount of increased loan needed to pay them all.'

'Wait,' I said.

He went right on. 'I also need more space, of course, but luckily that's no problem, as there's an empty warehouse next to this place. I've signed a lease for it and told them you'll be advancing the money, and of course more furniture, more materials . . .'

'*Stop*,' I said distractedly, 'You *can't*.'

'What? I can't what?' He sounded, of all things, bewildered.

'You can't just keep on borrowing. You've a limit. You can't go beyond it. Look for heaven's sake come over here quickly and we'll see what can be undone.'

'But you said,' his voice said plaintively, 'that you'd want to finance later expansion. That's what I'm doing. Expanding.'

I thought wildly that I'd be licking stamps for a living as soon as Henry heard. Dear *God* . . .

'*Listen,*' the cartoonist was saying, 'we all worked like hell and finished one whole film. Twelve minutes long, dubbed with music and sound effects, everything, titles, the lot. And we did some rough-cuts of three others, no music, no frills, but enough . . . and I've sold them.'

'You've what?'

'Sold them.' He laughed with excitement. 'It's solid, I promise you. That agent you sent me to, he's fixed the sale and the contract. All I have to do is sign. It's a major firm that's handling them, and I get a big perpetual royalty. World-wide distribution, that's what they're talking about, and the BBC are taking them. But we've got to make twenty films in a year from now, not seven like I meant. Twenty! And if the public like them, that's just the start. Oh heck, I can't believe it. But to do twenty in the time I need a lot more money. Is it all right? I mean . . . I was so sure . . .

'Yes,' I said weakly. 'It's all right. Bring the contract when you've signed it, and new figures, and we'll work things out.'

'Thanks,' he said. 'Thanks, Tim Ekaterin, God bless your darling bank.'

I put the receiver down feebly and ran a hand over my head and down the back of my neck.

'Trouble?' Gordon asked, watching.

'Well no, not exactly . . .' A laugh like the cartoonist's rose in my throat. 'I backed a winner. I think perhaps I backed a bloody geyser.' The laugh broke out aloud. 'Did you ever do that?'

'Ah yes,' Gordon nodded, 'Of course.'

I told him about the cartoonist and showed him the original set of drawings, which were still stowed in my desk: and when he looked through them, he laughed.

'Wasn't that application on my desk,' he said, wrinkling his forehead in an effort to remember, 'just before I was away?'

I thought back. 'Yes, it probably was.'

He nodded. 'I'd decided to turn it down.'

'Had you?'

'Mm. Isn't he too young, or something?'

'That sort of talent strikes at birth.'

He gave me a brief assessing look and handed the drawings back. 'Well,' he said. 'Good luck to him.'

The news that Uncle Freddie had been spotted in the building rippled through every department and stiffened a good many slouching backbones. Uncle Freddie was given to growling out devastatingly accurate judgements of people in their hearing, and it was not only I who'd found the bank more peaceful (if perhaps also more complacent) when he retired.

He was known as 'Mr Fred' as opposed to 'Mr Mark' (grandfather) and 'Mr Paul', the founder. No one ever called me 'Mr Tim'; sign of the changing times. If true to form Uncle Freddie would spend the morning in Investment Management, where he himself had worked all his office life, and after lunch in the boardroom would put at least his head into Corporate Finance, to be civil, and end with a march through Banking. On the way, by some telepathic process of his own, he would learn what moved in the bank's collective mind; sniff, as he had put it, the prevailing scent on the wind.

He had already arrived when the copies of *What's Going On* hit the fan.

Alec as usual slipped out to the local paper shop at about the time they were delivered there and returned with the six copies which the bank officially sanctioned. No one in the City could afford not to know about What Was Going On on their own doorstep.

Alec shunted around delivering one copy to each floor and keeping ours to himself to read first, a perk he said he deserved.

'Your uncle,' he reported on his return, 'is beating the shit out of poor Ted Lorrimer in Investments for failing to sell Winkler Consolidated when even a squint-eyed baboon could see it was overstretched in its Central American operation, and a neck sticking out asking for the comprehensive chop.'

Gordon chuckled mildly at the verbatim reporting, and Alec sat at his desk and opened the paper. Normal office life continued for perhaps five more minutes before Alec shot to his feet as if he'd been stung.

'Jes-us *Christ*,' he said.

'What is it?'

'Our leaker is at it again.'

'What?' Gordon said.

'You'd better read it.' He took the paper across to Gordon whose preliminary face of foreboding turned slowly to anger.

'It's disgraceful,' Gordon said. He made as if to pass the paper to me, but John, on his feet, as good as snatched it out of his hand.

'I should come first,' he said forcefully, and took the paper over to his own desk, sitting down methodically and spreading the paper open on the flat surface to read. Gordon watched him impassively and I said nothing to provoke. When John at his leisure had finished, showing little reaction but a tightened mouth, it was to Rupert he gave the paper, and Rupert, who read it with small gasps and widening eyes, who brought it eventually to me.

'It's bad,' Gordon said.

'So I gather.' I lolled back in my chair and lifted the offending column to eye level. Under a heading of 'Dinky Dirty Doings' it said:

> *It is perhaps not well known to readers that in many a merchant bank two thirds of the annual profits come from interest on loans. Investment and Trust management and Corporate Finance departments are the public faces and glamour machines of these very private banks. Their investments (of other people's money) in the Stock market and their entrepreneurial role in mergers and takeovers earn the spotlight year by year in the City Pages.*
>
> *Below stairs, so to speak, lies the tail that wags the dog, the secretive Banking department which quietly lends from its own deep coffers and rakes in vast profits in the shape of interest at rates they can set to suit themselves.*
>
> *These rates are not necessarily high.*
>
> *Who in Paul Ekaterin Ltd has been effectively lending to himself small fortunes from these coffers at FIVE per cent? Who in Paul Ekaterin Ltd has set up private companies which are NOT carrying on the business for which the money has ostensibly been lent? Who has not declared that these companies are his?*
>
> *The man-in-the-street (poor slob) would be delighted to get unlimited cash from Paul Ekaterin Ltd at five per cent so that he could invest it in something else for more.*
>
> *Don't Bankers have a fun time?*

I looked up from the damaging page and across at Alec, and he was, predictably, grinning.

'I wonder who's had his hand in the cookie jar,' he said.

'And who caught it there,' I asked.

'Wow, yes.'

Gordon said bleakly, 'This is very serious.'

'If you believe it,' I said.

'But this paper . . .' he began.

'Yeah,' I interrupted. 'It had a dig at us before, remember? Way back in May. Remember the flap everyone got into?'

'I was at home . . . with "flu".'

'Oh, yes. Well, the furore went on here for ages and no one came up with any answers. This column today is just as unspecific. So . . . supposing all it's designed to do is stir up trouble for the bank? Who's got it in for us? To what raving nut have we for instance refused a loan?'

Alec was regarding me with exaggerated wonder. 'Here we have Sherlock Holmes to the rescue,' he said admiringly. 'Now we can all go out to lunch.'

Gordon however said thoughtfully, 'It's perfectly possible, though, to set up a company and lend it money. All it would take would be paperwork. I could do it myself. So could anyone here, I suppose, up to his authorised ceiling, if he thought he could get away with it.'

John nodded. 'It's ridiculous of Tim and Alec to make a joke of this,' he said importantly. 'The very reputation of the bank is at stake.'

Gordon frowned, stood up, took the paper off my desk, and went along to see his almost-equal in the room facing St Paul's. Spreading consternation, I thought; bringing out cold sweats from palpitating banking hearts.

I ran a mental eye over everyone in the whole department who could possibly have had enough power along with the opportunity, from Val Fisher all the way down to myself; and there were twelve, perhaps, who could theoretically have done it.

But . . . not Rupert, with his sad mind still grieving, because he wouldn't have had the appetite or energy for fraud.

Not Alec, surely; because I liked him.

Not John: too self-regarding.

Not Val, not Gordon, unthinkable. Not myself.

That left the people along in the other pasture, and I didn't know them well enough to judge. Maybe one of them did believe that a strong fiddle on the side was worth the ruin of discovery, but all of us were already generously paid, perhaps for the very reason that temptations would be more likely to be resisted if we weren't scratching around for the money for the gas.

Gordon didn't return. The morning limped down to lunch-time, when John bustled off announcing he was seeing a client, and Alec encouraged Rupert to go out with him for a pie and pint. I'd taken to working through lunch because of the quietness, and I was still there alone at two o'clock when Peter, Henry's assistant, came and asked me to go up to the top floor, because I was wanted.

Uncle Freddie, I thought. Uncle Freddie's read the rag and will be exploding like a warhead. In some way he'll make it out to be my fault. With a gusty sigh I left my desk and took the lift to face the old warrior with whom I had never in my life felt easy.

He was waiting in the top floor hallway, talking to Henry. Both of them at six foot three over-topped me by three inches. Life would never have been as ominous, I thought, if Uncle Freddie had been small.

'Tim,' Henry said when he saw me, 'Go along to the small conference room, will you?'

I nodded and made my way to the room next to the boardroom where four or five chairs surrounded a square polished table. A copy of *What's Going On* lay there, already dog-eared from many thumbs.

'Now Tim', said my uncle, coming into the room behind me, 'do you know what all this is about?'

I shook my head and said 'No.'

My uncle growled in his throat and sat down, waving Henry and myself to seats. Henry might be chairman, might indeed in office terms have been Uncle Freddie's boss, but the white-haired old tyrant still personally owned the leasehold of the building itself and from long habit treated everyone in it as guests.

Henry absently fingered the newspaper. 'What do you think?' he said to me. '*Who* . . . do you think?'

'It might not be anyone.'

He half smiled. 'A stirrer?'

'Mm. Not a single concrete detail. Same as last time.'

'Last time,' Henry said, 'I asked the paper's editor where he got his information from. Never reveal sources, he said. Useless asking again.'

'Undisclosed sources,' Uncle Freddie said, 'never trust them.'

Henry said, 'Gordon says you can find out, Tim, how many concerns, if any, are borrowing from us at five per cent. There can't be many. A few from when interest rates were low. The few who got us in the past to agree to a long-term fixed rate.' The few, though he didn't say so, from before his time, before he put an end to such unprofitable straitjackets. 'If there are more recent ones among them, could you spot them?'

'I'll look,' I said.

We both knew it would take days rather than hours and might produce no results. The fraud, if it existed, could have been going on for a decade. For half a century. Successful frauds tended to go on and on unnoticed, until some one tripped over them by accident. It might also be easier to find out who had done the tripping, and why he'd told the paper instead of the bank.

'Anyway,' Henry said, 'that isn't primarily why we asked you up here.'

'No,' said my uncle, grunting. 'Time you were a director.'

I thought: I didn't hear that right.

'Er . . . what?' I said.

'A director. A director,' he said impatiently. 'Fellow who sits on the board. Never heard of them, I suppose.'

I looked at Henry, who was smiling and nodding.

'But,' I said, 'so soon . . .'

'Don't you want to, then?' demanded my uncle.

'Yes, I do.'

'Good. Don't let me down. I've had my eye on you since you were eight.'

I must have looked as surprised as I felt.

'You told me then,' he said, 'how much you had saved, and how much you would have if you went on saving a pound a month at four per cent compound interest for forty years, by which time you would be very old. I wrote down your figures and worked them out, and you were right.'

'It's only a formula,' I said.

'Oh sure. You could do it now in a drugged sleep. But at *eight*? You'd inherited the gift, all right. You were just robbed of the inclination.' He nodded heavily. 'Look at your father. My little brother. Got drunk nicely, never a mean thought, but hardly there when the brains were handed out. Look at the way he indulged your mother, letting her gamble like that. Look at the life he gave you. All pleasure, regardless of cost. I despaired of you at times. Thought you'd be ruined. But I knew the gift was there somewhere, might still be dormant, might grow if forced. So there you are, I was right.'

I was pretty well speechless.

'We all agree,' Henry said. 'The whole board was unanimous at our meeting this morning that it's time another Ekaterin took his proper place.'

I thought of John, and of the intensity of rage my promotion would bring forth.

'Would you,' I said slowly, 'have given me a directorship if my name had been Joe Bloggs?'

Henry levelly said, 'Probably not this very day. But soon, I promise you, yes. You're almost thirty-three, after all, and I was on the board here at thirty-four.'

'Thank you,' I said.

'Rest assured,' Henry said. 'You've earned it.' He stood up and formally shook hands. 'Your appointment officially starts as of the first of November, a week today. We will welcome you then to a short meeting in the boardroom, and afterwards to lunch.'

They must both have seen the depth of my pleasure, and they themselves looked satisfied. Hallelujah, I thought, I've made it. I've got there . . . I've barely started.

Gordon went down with me in the lift, also smiling.

'They've all been dithering about it on and off for months,' he said. 'Ever since you took over from me when I was ill, and did OK. Anyway I told them this morning about your news from the cartoonist. Some of them said it was just lucky. I told them you'd now been lucky too often for it to be a coincidence. So there you are.'

'I can't thank you . . .'

'It's your own doing.'

'John will have a fit.'

'You've coped all right so far with his envy.'

'I don't like it, though,' I said.

'Who would? Silly man, he's doing his career no good.'

Gordon straightaway told everyone in the office, and John went white and walked rigidly out of the room.

I went diffidently a week later to the induction and to the first lunch with the board, and then in a few days, as one does, I got used to the change of company and to the higher level of information. In the departments one heard about the decisions that had been made: in the dining room one heard the decisions being reached. 'Our daily board meeting,' Henry said. 'So much easier this way when everyone can simply say what they think without anyone taking notes.'

There were usually from ten to fifteen directors at lunch, although at a pinch the elongated oval table could accommodate the full complement of twenty-three. People would vanish at any moment to answer telephone calls, and to deal. Dealing, the buying and selling of stocks, took urgent precedence over food.

The food itself was no great feast, though perfectly presented. 'Always lamb on Wednesdays,' Gordon said at the buffet table as he took a couple from a row of trimmed lean cutlets. 'Some sort of chicken on Tuesdays, beef wellington most Thursdays. Henry never eats the crust.' Each day there was a clear soup before and fruit and cheese after. Alcohol if one chose, but most of them didn't. No one should deal in millions whose brain wanted to sleep, Henry said, drinking Malvern water steadily. Quite a change, all of it, from a rough-hewn sandwich at my desk.

They were all polite about my failure to discover 'paper' companies to whom the bank had been lending at five per cent, although Val and Henry, I knew, shared my own view that the report originated from malice and not from fact.

I had spent several days in the extra-wide office at the back of our floor, where the more mechanical parts of the banking operation were carried on. There in the huge expanse (grey carpet, this time) were row upon row of long desks whose tops were packed with telephones, adding machines and above all computers.

From there went out our own interest cheques to the depositors who had lent us money for us to lend to things like 'Home-made Heaven cakes' and 'Water Purification' plants in Norfolk. Into there came the interest paid *to* us by cakes and water and cartoonists and ten thousand such. Machines clattered, phone bells rang, people hurried about.

Many of the people working there were girls, and it had often puzzled me why there were so few women among the managers. Gordon said it was because few women wanted to commit their whole lives to making money and John (in the days when he was speaking to me) said with typical contempt that it was because they preferred to spend it. In any case, there were no female managers in Banking, and none at all on the Board.

Despite that, my best helper in the fraud search proved to be a curvy redhead called Patty who had taken the *What's Going*

On article as a personal affront, as had many of her colleagues.

'No one could do that under our noses,' she protested.

'I'm afraid they could. You know they could. No one could blame any of you for not spotting it.'

'Well . . . where do we start?'

'With all the borrowers paying a fixed rate of five per cent. Or perhaps four per cent, or five point seven five, or six or seven. Who knows if five is right?'

She looked at me frustratedly with wide amber eyes. 'But we haven't got them sorted like that.'

Sorted, she meant, on the computer. Each loan transaction would have its own agreement, which in itself could originally range from one single slip of paper to a contract of fifty pages, and each agreement should say at what rate the loan interest was to be levied, such as two above the current accepted base. There were thousands of such agreements typed onto and stored on computer discs. One could retrieve any one transaction by its identifying number, or alphabetically, or by the dates of commencement, or full term, or by the date when the next interest payment was due, but if you asked the computer who was paying at what per cent you'd get a blank screen and the microchip version of a raspberry.

'You can't sort them out by rates,' she said. 'The rates go up and down like seesaws.'

'But there must still be some loans being charged interest at a fixed rate.'

'Well, yes.'

'So when you punch in the new interest rate the computer adjusts the interest due on almost all the loans but doesn't touch those with a fixed rate.'

'I suppose that's right.'

'So somewhere in the computer there must be a code which tells it when not to adjust the rates.'

She smiled sweetly and told me to be patient, and half a day later produced a cheerful-looking computer-programmer to whom the problem was explained.

'Yeah, there's a code,' he said. 'I put it there myself. What you want, then, is a programme that will print out all the loans which have the code attached. That right?'

We nodded. He worked on paper for half an hour with a much-chewed pencil and then typed rapidly onto the computer, pressing buttons and being pleased with the results.

'You leave this programme on here,' he said, 'then feed in

the discs, and you'll get the results on that line-printer over there. And I've written it all out for you tidily in pencil, in case someone switches off your machine. Then just type it all in again, and you're back in business.'

We thanked him and he went away whistling, the aristocrat among ants.

The line-printer clattered away on and off for hours as we fed through the whole library of discs, and it finally produced a list of about a hundred of the ten-digit numbers used to identify an account.

'Now,' Patty said undaunted, 'do you want a complete print-out of all the original agreements for those loans?'

'I'm afraid so, yes.'

'Hang around.'

It took two days even with her help to check through all the resulting paper and by the end I couldn't spot any companies there that had no known physical existence, though short of actually tramping to all the addresses and making an on-the-spot enquiry, one could't be sure.

Henry, however, was against the expenditure of time. 'We'll just be more vigilant,' he said. 'Design some more safeguards, more tracking devices. Could you do that, Tim?'

'I could, with that programmer's help.'

'Right. Get on with it. Let us know.'

I wondered aloud to Patty whether someone in her own department, not one of the managers, could set up such a fraud, but once she'd got over her instinctive indignation she shook her head.

'Who would bother? It would be much simpler – in fact it's almost dead easy – to feed in a mythical firm who has lent *us* money, and to whom we are paying interest. Then the computer goes on sending out interest cheques for ever, and all the crook has to do is cash them.'

Henry, however, said we had already taken advice on that one, and the 'easy' route had been plugged by systematic checks by the auditors.

The paper-induced rumpus again gradually died down and became undiscussed if not forgotten. Life in our plot went on much as before with Rupert slowly recovering, Alec making jokes and Gordon stuffing his left hand anywhere out of sight. John continued to suffer from his obsession, not speaking to me, not looking at me if he could help it, and apparently telling clients outright that my promotion was a sham.

'Cosmetic of course,' Alec reported him of saying on the telephone. 'Makes the notepaper heading look impressive. Means nothing in real terms, you know. Get through to me, I'll see you right.'

'He said all that?' I asked.

'Word for word.' Alec grinned. 'Go and bop him on the nose.'

I shook my head however and wondered if I should get myself transferred along to the St Paul's-facing office. I didn't want to go, but it looked as if John wouldn't recover his balance unless I did. If I tried to get John himself transferred, would it make things that much worse?

I was gradually aware that Gordon, and behind him Henry, were not going to help, their thought being that I was a big boy now and should be able to resolve it myself. It was a freedom which brought responsibility, as all freedoms do, and I had to consider that for the bank's sake John needed to be a sensible member of the team.

I thought he should see a psychiatrist. I got Alec to say it to him lightly as a joke, out of my hearing ('what you need, old pal, is a friendly shrink'), but to John his own anger appeared rational, not a matter for treatment.

I tried saying to him straight, 'Look, John, I know how you feel. I know you think my promotion isn't fair. Well, maybe it is, maybe it isn't, but either way I can't help it. You'll be a lot better off if you just face things and forget it. You're good at your job, we all know it, but you're doing yourself no favours with all this bellyaching. So shut up, accept that life's bloody, and let's lend some money.'

It was a homily that fell on a closed mind, and in the end it was some redecorating which came to the rescue. For a week while painters re-whitened our walls the five of us in the fountain-facing office squeezed into the other one, desks jammed together in every corner, 'phone calls made with palms pressed to ears against the noise and even normally placid tempers itching to snap. Overcrowd the human race, I thought, and you always got a fight. In distance lay peace.

Anyway, I used the time to do some surreptitious persuasion and shuffling, so that when we returned to our own patch both John and Rupert stayed behind. The two oldest men from the St Paul's office came with Gordon, Alec and myself, and Gordon's almost-equal obligingly told John that it was great to be working again with a younger team of bright energetic brains.

The First Year

NOVEMBER

Val Fisher said at lunch one day, 'I've received a fairly odd request.' (It was a Friday: grilled fish.)

'Something new?' Henry asked.

'Yes. Chap wants to borrow five million pounds to buy a racehorse.'

Everyone at the table laughed except Val himself.

'I thought I'd toss it at you,' he said. 'Kick it around some. See what you think.'

'What horse?' Henry said.

'Something called Sandcastle.'

Henry, Gordon and I all looked at Val with sharpened attention; almost perhaps with eagerness.

'Mean something to you three, does it?' he said, turning his head from one to the other of us.

Henry nodded. 'That day we all went to Ascot. Sandcastle ran there, and won. A stunning performance. Beautiful.'

Gordon said reminiscently, 'The man whose box we were in saved his whole business on that race. Do you remember Dissdale, Tim?'

'Certainly do.'

'I saw him a few weeks ago. On top of the world. God knows how much he won.'

'Or how much he staked,' I said.

'Yes, well,' Val said. 'Sandcastle. He won the 2,000 Guineas, as I understand, and the King Edward VII Stakes at Royal Ascot. Also the "Diamond" Stakes in July, and the Champion Stakes at Newmarket last month. This is, I believe, a record second only to winning the Derby or the Arc de Triomphe. He finished fourth, incidentally, in the Derby. He could race next year as a four-year-old, but if he flopped his value would be less than it is at the moment. Our prospective client wants to buy him now and put him to stud.'

The rest of the directors got on with their fillets of sole while listening interestedly with eyes and ears. A stallion made a change, I suppose, from chemicals, electronics and oil.

'Who is our client?' Gordon asked. Gordon liked fish. He could eat it right handed with his fork, in no danger of shaking it off between plate and mouth.

'A man called Oliver Knowles,' Val said. 'He owns a stud farm. He got passed along to me by the horse's trainer, whom I know slightly because of our wives being distantly related. Oliver Knowles wants to buy, the present owner is willing to sell. All they need is the cash.' He smiled. 'Same old story.'

'What's your view?' Henry said.

Val shrugged his well-tailored shoulders. 'Too soon to have one of any consequence. But I thought, if it interested you at all, we could ask Tim to do a preliminary look-see. He has a background, after all, a lengthy acquaintance, shall we say, with racing.'

There was a murmur of dry amusement round the table.

'What do you think?' Henry asked me.

'I'll certainly do it if you like.'

Someone down the far end complained that it would be a waste of time and that merchant banks of our stature should not be associated with the Turf.

'Our own dear Queen,' someone said ironically, 'is associated with the Turf. And knows the Stud Book backwards, so they say.'

Henry smiled. 'I don't see why we shouldn't at least look into it.' He nodded in my direction. 'Go ahead, Tim. Let us know.'

I spent the next few working days alternately chewing pencils with the computer programmer and joining us to a syndicate with three other banks to lend twelve point four million pounds short term at high interest to an international construction company with a gap in its cash-flow. In between those I telephoned around for information and opinions about Oliver Knowles, in the normal investigative preliminaries to any loan for anything, not only for a hair-raising price for a stallion.

Establishing a covenant, it was called. Only if the covenant was sound would any loan be further considered.

Oliver Knowles, I was told, was a sane, sober man of forty-one with a stud farm in Hertfordshire. There were three stallions standing there with ample provision for visiting mares, and he owned the one hundred and fifty acres outright, having inherited them on his father's death.

When talking to local bank managers one listened attentively for what they left out, but Oliver Knowles' bank manager left out not much. Without in the least discussing his client's affairs in detail he said that occasional fair-sized loans had so far been paid off as scheduled and that Mr Knowles' business sense could be commended. A rave notice from such a source.

'Oliver Knowles?' a racing acquaintance from the long past said. 'Don't know him myself. I'll ask around,' and an hour later called back with the news. 'He seems to be a good guy but his wife's just buggered off with a Canadian. He might be a secret wife-beater, who can tell? Otherwise the gen is that he's as honest as any horse-breeder, which you can take as you find it, and how's your mother?'

'She's fine, thanks. She remarried last year. Lives in Jersey.'

'Good. Lovely lady. Always buying us icecreams. I adored her.'

I put the receiver down with a smile and tried a credit rating agency. No black marks, they said: the Knowles credit was good.

I told Gordon across the room that I seemed to be getting nothing but green lights, and at lunch that day repeated the news to Henry. He looked around the table, collecting a few nods, a few frowns and a great deal of indecision.

'We couldn't carry it all ourselves, of course,' Val said. 'And it isn't exactly something we could go to our regular sources with. They'd think us crackers.'

Henry nodded. 'We'd have to canvas friends for private money. I know a few people here or there who might come in. Two million, I think, is all we should consider ourselves. Two and a half at the outside.'

'I don't approve,' a dissenting director said. 'It's madness. Suppose the damn thing broke its leg?'

'Insurance,' Henry said mildly.

Into a small silence I said, 'If you felt like going into it further I could get some expert views on Sandcastle's breeding, and then arrange blood and fertility tests. And I know it's not usual with loans, but I do think someone like Val should go and personally meet Oliver Knowles and look at his place. It's too much of a risk to lend such a sum for a horse without going into it extremely carefully.'

'Just listen to who's talking,' said the dissenter, but without ill-will.

'Mm,' Henry said, considering. 'What do you think, Val?'

Val Fisher smoothed a hand over his always smooth face. 'Tim should go,' he said. 'He's done the groundwork, and all I know about horses is that they eat grass.'

The dissenting director almost rose to his feet with the urgency of his feelings.

'Look,' he said, 'all this is ridiculous. How can we possibly finance a *horse*?'

'Well, now,' Henry answered. 'The breeding of thoroughbreds is big business, tens of thousands of people round the world make their living from it. Look upon it as an industry like any other. We gamble here on shipbuilders, motors, textiles, you name it, and all of those can go bust. And none of them,' he finished with a near-grin, 'can pro-create in their own image.'

The dissenter heavily shook his head. 'Madness. Utter madness.'

'Go and see Oliver Knowles, Tim,' Henry said.

Actually I thought it prudent to bone up on the finances of breeding in general before listening to Oliver Knowles himself, on the basis that I would then have a better idea of whether what he was proposing was sensible or not.

I didn't myself know anyone who knew much on the subject, but one of the beauties of merchant banking was the ramification of people who knew people who knew people who could find someone with the information that was wanted. I sent out the question-mark smoke signal and from distant out-of-sight mountain tops the answer puff-puffed back.

Ursula Young, I was told, would put me right. 'She's a bloodstock agent. Very sharp, very talkative, knows her stuff. She used to work on a stud farm, so you've got it every whichway. She says she'll tell you anything you want, only if you want to see her in person this week it will have to be at Doncaster races on Saturday, she's too busy to spend the time else.'

I went north to Doncaster by train and met the lady at the racecourse, where the last Flat meeting of the year was being held. She was waiting as arranged by the entrance to the Members' Club and wearing an identifying red velvet beret, and she swept me off to a secluded table in a bar where we wouldn't be interrupted.

She was fifty, tough, good-looking, dogmatic and inclined to treat me as a child. She also gave me a patient and invaluable lecture on the economics of owning a stallion.

'Stop me,' she said to begin with, 'if I say something you don't understand.'

I nodded.

'All right. Say you own a horse that's won the Derby and you want to capitalise on your goldmine. You judge what you think you can get for the horse, then you divide that by forty and try to sell each of the forty shares at that price. Maybe you can, maybe you can't. It depends on the horse. With Troy, now, they were queuing up. But if your winner isn't frightfully well bred or if it made little show *except* in the Derby you'll get a cool response and have to bring the price down. OK so far?'

'Um,' I said. 'Why only forty shares?'

She looked at me in amazement. 'You don't know a *thing*, do you?'

'That's why I'm here.'

'Well, a stallion covers forty mares in a season, and the season, incidentally, lasts roughly from February to June. The mares come to *him*, of course. He doesn't travel, he stays put at home. Forty is just about average; physically I mean. Some can do more, but others get exhausted. So forty is the accepted number. Now, say you have a mare and you've worked out that if you mate her with a certain stallion you might get a top-class foal, you try to get one of those forty places. The places are called nominations. You apply for a nomination, either directly to the stud where the stallion is standing, or through an agent like me, or even by advertising in a breeders' newspaper. Follow?'

'Gasping,' I nodded.

She smiled briefly. 'People who invest in stallion shares sometimes have broodmares of their own they want to breed from.' She paused. 'Perhaps I should have explained more clearly that everyone who owns a share automatically has a nomination to the stallion every year.'

'Ah,' I said.

'Yes. So say you've got your share and consequently your nomination but you haven't a mare to send to the stallion, then you sell your nomination to someone who *has* a mare, in the ways I already described.'

'I'm with you.'

'After the first three years the nominations may vary in price and in fact are often auctioned, but of course for the first three years the price is fixed.'

'Why of course?'

She sighed and took a deep breath. 'For three years no one knows whether the progeny on the whole are going to be winners or not. The gestation period is eleven months, and the first crop of foals don't race until they're two. If you work it out, that means that the stallion has stood for three seasons, and therefore covered a hundred and twenty mares, before the crunch.'

'Right.'

'So to fix the stallion fee for the first three years you divide the price of the stallion by one hundred and twenty, and that's it. That's the fee charged for the stallion to cover a mare. That's the sum you receive if you sell your nomination.'

I blinked.

'That means,' I said, 'that if you sell your nomination for three years you have recovered the total amount of your original investment?'

'That's right.'

'And after that . . . every time, every year you sell your nomination, it's clear profit?'

'Yes. But taxed, of course.'

'And how long does that go on?'

She shrugged. 'Ten to fifteen years. Depends on the stallion's potency.'

'But that's . . .'

'Yes,' she said. 'One of the best investments on earth.'

The bar had filled up behind us with people crowding in, talking loudly, and breathing on their fingers against the chill of the raw day outside. Ursula Young accepted a warmer in the shape of whisky and ginger wine, while I had coffee.

'Don't you drink?' she asked with mild disapproval.

'Not often in the daytime.'

She nodded vaguely, her eyes scanning the company, her mind already on her normal job. 'Any more questions?' she asked.

'I'm bound to think of some the minute we part.'

She nodded. 'I'll be here until the end of racing. If you want me, you'll see me near the weighing room after each race.'

We were on the point of standing up to leave when a man whose head one could never forget came into the bar.

'Calder Jackson!' I exclaimed.

Ursula casually looked. 'So it is.'

'Do you know him?' I asked.

'Everyone does.' There was almost a conscious neutrality in her voice as if she didn't want to be caught with her thoughts showing. The same response, I reflected, that he had drawn from Henry and Gordon and me.

'You don't like him?' I suggested.

'I feel nothing either way.' She shrugged. 'He's part of the scene. From what people say, he's achieved some remarkable cures.' She glanced at me briefly. 'I suppose you've seen him on television, extolling the value of herbs?'

'I met him,' I said, 'at Ascot, back in June.'

'One tends to.' She got to her feet, and I with her, thanking her sincerely for her help.

'Think nothing of it,' she said. 'Any time.' She paused. 'I suppose it's no use asking what stallion prompted this chat?'

'Sorry, no. It's on behalf of a client.'

She smiled slightly. 'I'm here if he needs an agent.'

We made our way towards the door, a path, I saw, which would take us closer to Calder. I wondered fleetingly whether he would know me, remember me after several months. I was after all not as memorable as himself, just a standard issue six foot with eyes, nose and mouth in roughly the right places, dark hair on top.

'Hello Ursula,' he said, his voice carrying easily through the general din. 'Bitter cold day.'

'Calder.' She nodded acknowledgement.

His gaze slid to my face, dismissed it, focused again on my companion. Then he did a classic double-take, his eyes widening with recognition.

'Tim,' he said incredulously. 'Tim . . .' he flicked his fingers to bring the difficult name to mind, '. . . Tim Ekaterin!'

I nodded.

He said to Ursula, 'Tim, here, saved my life.'

She was surprised until he explained, and then still surprised I hadn't told her. 'I read about it, of course,' she said. 'And congratulated you, Calder, on your escape.'

'Did you ever hear any more,' I asked him. 'From the police, or anyone?'

He shook his curly head. 'No, I didn't.'

'The boy didn't try again?'

'No.'

'Did you really have no idea where he came from?' I said. 'I know you told the police you didn't know, but . . . well . . . you just might have done.'

He shook his head very positively however and said, 'If I could help to catch the little bastard I'd do it at once. But I don't know who he was. I hardly saw him properly, just enough to know I didn't know him from Satan.'

'How's the healing?' I said. 'The tingling touch.'

There was a brief flash in his eyes as if he had found the question flippant and in bad taste, but perhaps mindful that he owed me his present existence he answered civilly. 'Rewarding,' he said. 'Heartwarming.'

Standard responses, I thought. As before.

'Is your yard full, Calder?' Ursula asked.

'Always a vacancy if needed,' he replied hopefully. 'Have you a horse to send me?'

'One of my clients has a two-year-old which looks ill and half dead all the time, to the despair of the trainer, who can't get it fit. She – my client – was mentioning you.'

'I've had great success with that sort of general debility.'

Ursula wrinkled her forehead in indecision. 'She feels Ian Pargetter would think her disloyal if she sent you her colt. He's been treating him for weeks, I think, without success.'

Calder smiled reassuringly. 'Ian Pargetter and I are on good terms, I promise you. He's even persuaded owners himself sometimes to send me their horses. Very good of him. We talk each case over, you know, and act in agreement. After all, we both have the recovery of the patient as our prime objective.' Again the swift impression of a statement often needed.

'Is Ian Pargetter a vet?' I asked incuriously.

They both looked at me.

'Er . . . yes,' Calder said.

'One of a group practice in Newmarket,' Ursula added. 'Very forward-looking. Tries new things. Dozens of trainers swear by him.'

'Just ask him, Ursula,' Calder said. 'Ian will tell you he doesn't mind owners sending me their horses. Even if he's a bit open-minded about the laying on of hands, at least he trusts me not to make the patient worse.' It was said as a self-deprecating joke, and we all smiled. Ursula Young and I in a moment or two walked on and out of the bar, and behind us we could hear Calder politely answering another of the everlasting questions.

'Yes,' he was saying, 'one of my favourite remedies for a prolonged cough in horses is liquorice root boiled in water with some figs. You strain the mixture and stir it into the horse's normal feed . . .'

The door closed behind us and shut him off.

'You'd think he'd get tired of explaining his methods,' I said. 'I wonder he never snaps.'

The lady said judiciously, 'Calder depends on television fame, good public relations and medical success, roughly in that order. He owns a yard with about thirty boxes on the outskirts of Newmarket – it used to be a regular training stables before he bought it – and the yard's almost always full. Short-term and long-term crocks, all sent to him either from true belief or as a last resort. I don't pretend to know anything about herbalism, and as for supernatural healing powers . . .' she shook her head. 'But there's no doubt that whatever his methods, horses do usually seem to leave his yard in a lot better health than when they went in.'

'Someone at Ascot said he'd brought dying horses back to life.'

'Hmph.'

'You don't believe it?'

She gave me a straight look, a canny businesswoman with a lifetime's devotion to thoroughbreds.

'Dying,' she said, 'Is a relative term when it doesn't end in death.'

I made a nod into a slight bow of appreciation.

'But to be fair,' she said, 'I know for certain that he totally and permanently cured a ten-year-old broodmare of colitis X, which has a habit of being fatal.'

'They're not all horses in training, then, that he treats?'

'Oh no, he'll take anybody's pet from a pony to an event horse. Showjumpers, the lot. But the horse has to be worth it, to the owner, I mean. I don't think Calder's hospital is terribly cheap.'

'Exorbitant?'

'Not that I've heard. Fair, I suppose, if you consider the results.'

I seemed to have heard almost more about Calder Jackson than I had about stallion shares, but I did after all have a sort of vested interest. One tended to want a life one had saved to be of positive use in the world. Illogical, I dare say, but there it was. I was pleased that it was true that Calder cured horses, albeit in his own mysterious unorthodox ways: and if I wished that I could warm to him more as a person, that was unrealistic and sentimental.

Ursula Young went off about her business, and although I caught sight of both her and Calder during the afternoon, I didn't see them again to speak to. I went back to London on the train, spent two hours of Sunday morning on the telephone, and early Sunday afternoon drove off to Hertfordshire in search of Oliver Knowles.

He lived in a square hundred-year-old stark red brick house which to my taste would have been friendlier if softened by trailing creeper. Blurred outlines, however, were not in Oliver Knowles' soul: a crisp bare tidyness was apparent in every corner of his spread.

His land was divided into a good number of paddocks of various sizes, each bordered by an immaculate fence of white rails; and the upkeep of those, I judged, as I pulled up on the weedless gravel before the front door, must alone cost a fortune. There was a scattering of mares and foals in the distance in the paddocks, mostly heads down to the grass, sniffing out the last tender shoots of the dying year. The day itself was cold with a muted sun dipping already towards distant hills, the sky quiet with the greyness of coming winter, the damp air smelling of mustiness, wood smoke and dead leaves.

There were no dead leaves as such to be seen. No flower beds, no ornamental hedges, no nearby trees. A barren mind, I thought, behind a business whose aim was fertility and the creation of life.

Oliver Knowles himself opened his front door to my knock, proving to be a pleasant lean man with an efficient, cultured manner of authority and politeness. Accustomed to command, I diagnosed. Feels easy with it; second nature. Positive, straightforward, self-controlled. Charming also, in an understated way.

'Mr Ekaterin?' he shook hands, smiling. 'I must confess I expected someone . . . older.'

There were several answers to that, such as 'time will take care of it' and 'I'll be older tomorrow', but nothing seemed appropriate. Instead I said 'I report back' to reassure him, which it did, and he invited me into his house.

Predictably the interior was also painfully tidy, such papers and magazines as were to be seen being squared up with the surface they rested on. The furniture was antique, well polished, brass handles shining, and the carpets venerably from Persia. He led me into a sitting room which was also office, the walls thickly covered with framed photographs of horses, mares and foals, and the window giving on to a view of, across a further expanse of gravel, an archway leading into an extensive stable yard.

'Boxes for mares,' he said, following my eyes. 'Beyond them, the foaling boxes. Beyond those, the breeding pen, with the stallion boxes on the far side of that again. My stud groom's bungalow and the lads' hostel, those roofs you can see in the hollow, they're just beyond the stallions.' He paused. 'Would you care perhaps to look round?'

'Very much,' I said.

'Come along, then.' He led the way to a door at the back of the house, collecting an overcoat and a black retriever from a mud room on the way. 'Go on then, Squibs, old fellow,' he said, fondly watching his dog squeeze ecstatically through the opening outside door. 'Breath of fresh air won't hurt you.'

We walked across the stable arch with Squibs circling and zig-zagging nose-down to the gravel.

'It's our quietest time of year, of course,' Oliver Knowles said. 'We have our own mares here, of course, and quite a few at livery.' He looked at my face to see if I understood and decided to explain anyway. 'They belong to people who own broodmares but have nowhere of their own to keep them. They pay us to board them.'

I nodded.

'Then we have the foals born to the mares this past spring, and of course the three stallions. Total of seventy-eight at the moment.'

'And next spring,' I said, 'the mares coming to your stallions will arrive?'

'That's right.' He nodded. 'They come here a month or five weeks before they're due to give birth to the foals they are already carrying, so as to be near the stallion within the month following. They have to foal here, because the foals would be too delicate straight after birth to travel.'

'And . . . how long do they stay here?'

'About three months altogether, by which time we hope the mare is safely in foal again.'

'There isn't much pause then,' I said. 'Between . . . er . . . pregnancies?'

He glanced at me with civil amusement. 'Mares come into use nine days after foaling, but normally we would think this a bit too soon for breeding. The oestrus – heat you would call it – lasts six days, then there's an interval of fifteen days, then the mare comes into use again for six days, and this time we breed her. Mind you,' he added, 'Nature being what it is, this cycle doesn't work to the minute. In some mares the oestrus will last only two days, in some as much as eleven. We try to have the mare covered two or three times while she's in heat, for the best chance of getting her in foal. A great deal depends on the stud groom's judgement, and I've a great chap just now, he has a great feel for mares, a sixth sense, you might say.'

He led me briskly across the first big oblong yard where long dark equine heads peered inquisitively from over half-open stable doors, and through a passage on the far side which led to a second yard of almost the same size but whose doors were fully shut.

'None of these boxes is occupied at the moment,' he said, waving a hand around. 'We have to have the capacity, though, for when the mares come.'

Beyond the second yard lay a third, a good deal smaller and again with closed doors.

'Foaling boxes,' Oliver Knowles explained. 'All empty now, of course.'

The black dog trotted ahead of us, knowing the way. Beyond the foaling boxes lay a wide path between two small paddocks of about half an acre each, and at the end of the path, to the left, rose a fair sized barn with a row of windows just below its roof.

'Breeding shed,' Oliver Knowles said economically, producing a heavy key ring from his trouser pocket and unlocking a door set into a large roll-aside entrance. He gestured to me to go in, and I found myself in a bare concrete-floored expanse surrounded by white walls topped with the high windows, through which the dying sun wanly shone.

'During the season of course the floor in here is covered with peat,' he said.

I nodded vaguely and thought of life being generated purposefully in that quiet place, and we returned prosaically to the outer world with Oliver Knowles locking the door again behind us.

Along another short path between two more small paddocks we came to another small stable yard, this time of only six boxes, with feed room, tack room, hay and peat storage alongside.

'Stallions,' Oliver Knowles said.

Three heads almost immediately appeared over the half-doors, three sets of dark liquid eyes turning inquisitively our way.

'Rotaboy,' my host said, walking to the first head and producing a carrot unexpectedly. The black mobile lips whiffled over the outstretched palm and sucked the goodie in: strong teeth crunched a few times and Rotaboy nudged Oliver Knowles for a second helping. Oliver Knowles produced another carrot, held it out as before, and briefly patted the horse's neck.

'He'll be twenty next year,' he said. 'Getting old, eh, old fella?'

He walked along to the next box and repeated the carrot routine. 'This one is Diarist, rising sixteen.'

By the third box he said, 'This is Parakeet,' and delivered the treats and the pat. 'Parakeet turns twelve on January 1st.'

He stood a little away from the horse so that he could see all three heads at once and said, 'Rotaboy has been an outstanding stallion and still is, but one can't realistically expect more than another one or two seasons. Diarist is successful, with large numbers of winners among his progeny, but none of them absolutely top rank like those of Rotaboy. Parakeet hasn't proved as successful as I'd hoped. He turns out to breed better stayers than sprinters, and the world is mad nowadays for very fast two-year-olds. Parakeet's progeny tend to be better at three, four, five and six. Some of his first crops are now steeplechasing and jumping pretty well.'

'Isn't that good?' I asked, frowning, since he spoke with no great joy.

'I've had to reduce his fee,' he said. 'People won't send their top flat-racing mares to a stallion who breeds jumpers.'

'Oh.'

After a pause he said 'You can see why I need new blood here. Rotaboy is old, Diarist is middle rank, Parakeet is unfashionable. I will soon have to replace Rotaboy, and I must be sure I replace him with something of at least equal quality. The *prestige* of a stud farm, quite apart from its income, depends on the drawing-power of its stallions.'

'Yes,' I said. 'I see.'

Rotaboy, Diarist and Parakeet lost interest in the conversation and hope in the matter of carrots, and one by one withdrew into the boxes. The black retriever trotted around smelling unimaginable scents and Oliver Knowles began to walk me back towards the house.

'On the bigger stud farms,' he said, 'you'll find stallions which are owned by syndicates.'

'Forty shares?' I suggested.

He gave me a brief smile. 'That's right. Stallions are owned by any number of people between one and forty. When I first acquired Rotaboy it was in partnership with five others. I bought two of them out – they needed the money – so now I own half. This means I have twenty nominations each year, and I have no trouble in selling all of them, which is most satisfactory.' He looked at me enquiringly to make sure I understood, which, thanks to Ursula Young, I did.

'I own Diarist outright. He was as expensive in the first place as Rotaboy, and as he's middle rank, so is the fee I can get for him. I don't always succeed in filling his forty places, and when that occurs I breed him to my own mares, and sell the resulting foals as yearlings.'

Fascinated, I nodded again.

'With Parakeet it's much the same. For the last three years I haven't been able to charge the fee I did to begin with, and if I fill his last places these days it's with mares from people who *prefer* steeplechasing, and this is increasingly destructive of his flat-racing image.'

We retraced our steps past the breeding shed and across the foaling yard.

'This place is expensive to run,' he said objectively. 'It makes a profit and I live comfortably, but I'm not getting any further. I have the capacity here for another stallion – enough accommodation, that is to say, for the extra forty mares. I have a good business sense and excellent health, and I feel under-extended. If I am ever to achieve more I must have more capital . . . and capital in the shape of a world-class stallion.'

'Which brings us,' I said, 'to Sandcastle.'

He nodded. 'If I acquired a horse like Sandcastle this stud would immediately be more widely known and more highly regarded.'

Understatement, I thought. The effect would be galvanic. 'A sort of overnight stardom?' I said.

'Well, yes,' he agreed with a satisfied smile. 'I'd say you might be right.'

The big yard nearest the house had come moderately to life, with two or three lads moving about carrying feed scoops, hay nets, buckets of water and sacks of muck. Squibs with madly wagging tail went in a straight line towards a stocky man who bent to fondle his black ears.

'That's Nigel, my stud groom,' Oliver Knowles said. 'Come and meet him.' And as we walked across he added, 'If I can expand this place I'll up-rate him to stud manager; give him more standing with the customers.'

We reached Nigel, who was of about my own age with crinkly light-brown hair and noticeably bushy eyebrows. Oliver Knowles introduced me merely as 'a friend' and Nigel treated me with casual courtesy but not as the possible source of future fortune. He had a Gloucestershire accent but not pronounced, and I would have placed him as a farmer's son, if I'd had to.

'Any problems?' Oliver Knowles asked him, and Nigel shook his head.

'Nothing except that Floating mare with the discharge.'

His manner to his employer was confident and without anxiety but at the same time diffident, and I had a strong impression that it was Nigel's personality which suited Oliver Knowles as much as any skill he might have with mares. Oliver Knowles was not a man, I judged, to surround himself with awkward, unpredictable characters: the behaviour of everyone around him had to be as tidy as his place.

I wondered idly about the wife who had 'just buggered off with a Canadian', and at that moment a horse trotted into the yard with a young woman aboard. A girl, I amended, as she kicked her feet from the stirrups and slid to the ground. A noticeably curved young girl in jeans and heavy sweater with her dark hair tied in a pony tail. She led her horse into one of the boxes and presently emerged carrying the saddle and bridle, which she dumped on the ground outside the box before closing the bottom half of the door and crossing the yard to join us.

'My daughter,' Oliver Knowles said.

'Ginnie,' added the girl, holding out a polite brown hand. 'Are you the reason we didn't go out to lunch?'

Her father gave an instinctive repressing movement and Nigel looked only fairly interested.

'I don't know,' I said. 'I wouldn't think so.'

'Oh, I would,' she said. 'Pa really doesn't like parties. He uses any old excuse to get out of them, don't you Pa?'

He gave her an indulgent smile while looking as if his thoughts were elsewhere.

'I didn't mind missing it,' Ginnie said to me, anxious not to embarrass. 'Twelve miles away and people all Pa's age . . . but they do have frightfully good canapés, and also a lemon tree growing in their greenhouse. Did you know that a lemon tree has everything all at once – buds, flowers, little green knobbly fruit and big fat lemons, all going on all the time?'

'My daughter,' Oliver Knowles said unnecessarily, 'talks a lot.'

'No,' I said, 'I didn't know about lemon trees.'

She gave me an impish smile and I wondered if she was even younger than I'd first thought: and as if by telepathy she said, 'I'm fifteen.'

'Everyone has to go through it,' I said.

He eyes widened. 'Did you hate it?'

I nodded. 'Spots, insecurity, a new body you're not yet comfortable in, self-consciousness . . . terrible.'

Oliver Knowles looked surprised. 'Ginnie isn't self-conscious, are you, Ginnie?'

She looked from him to me and back again and didn't answer. Oliver Knowles dismissed the subject as of no importance anyway and said he ought to walk along and see the mare with the discharge. Would I care to go with him?

I agreed without reservation and we all set off along one of the paths between the white-railed paddocks, Oliver Knowles and myself in front, Nigel and Ginnie following, Squibs sniffing at every fencing post and marking his territory. In between Oliver Knowles explaining that some mares preferred living out of doors permanently, others would go inside if it snowed, others went in at nights, others lived mostly in the boxes, I could heard Ginnie telling Nigel that school this term was a dreadful drag owing to the new headmistress being a health fiend and making them all do jogging.

'How do you know what mares prefer?' I asked.

Oliver Knowles looked for the first time nonplussed. 'Er . . .' he said. 'I suppose . . . by the way they stand. If they feel cold and miserable they put their tails to the wind and look hunched. Some horses never do that, even in a blizzard. If they're obviously unhappy we bring them in. Otherwise they stay out. Same with the foals.' He paused. 'A lot of mares are miserable if you keep them inside. It's just . . . how they are.'

He seemed dissatisfied with the loose ends of his answer, but I found them reassuring. The one thing he had seemed to me to lack had been any emotional contact with the creatures he bred: even the carrots for the stallions had been slightly mechanical.

The mare with the discharge proved to be in one of the paddocks at the boundary of the farm, and while Oliver Knowles and Nigel peered at her rump end and made obscure remarks like 'With any luck she won't slip,' and 'It's clear enough, nothing yellow or bloody,' I spent my time looking past the last set of white rails to the hedge and fields beyond.

The contrast from the Knowles land was dramatic. Instead of extreme tidiness, a haphazard disorder. Instead of short green grass in well-tended rectangles, long unkempt brownish stalks straggling through an army of drying thistles. Instead of rectangular brick-built stable yards, a ramshackle collection of wooden boxes, light grey from old creosote and with tarpaulins tied over patches of roof.

Ginnie followed my gaze. 'That's the Watcherleys' place,' she said. 'I used to go over there a lot but they're so grimy and gloomy these days, not a laugh in sight. And all the patients have gone, practically, and they don't even have the chimpanzees any more, they say they can't afford them.'

'What patients?' I said.

'Horse patients. It's the Watcherleys' hospital for sick horses. Haven't you ever heard of it?'

I shook my head.

'It's pretty well known,' Ginnie said. 'Or at least it was until that razzamatazz man Calder Jackson stole the show. Mind you, the Watcherleys were no great shakes, I suppose, with Bob off to the boozer at all hours and Maggie sweating her guts out carrying muck sacks, but at least they used to be fun. The place was *cosy*, you know, even if bits of the boxes were falling off their hinges and weeds were growing everywhere, and all the horses went home blooming, or most of them, even if Maggie had her knees through her jeans and wore the same jersey for weeks and weeks on end. But Calder Jackson, you see, is the *in* thing, with all those chat shows on television and the publicity and such, and the Watcherleys have sort of got elbowed out.'

Her father, listening to the last of these remarks, added his own view. 'They're disorganised,' he said. 'No business sense. People liked their gypsy style for a while, but, as Ginnie says, they've no answer to Calder Jackson.'

'How old are they?' I asked, frowning.

Oliver Knowles shrugged. 'Thirties. Going on forty. Hard to say.'

'I suppose they don't have a son of about sixteen, thin and intense, who hates Calder Jackson obsessively for ruining his parents' business?'

'What an extraordinary question,' said Oliver Knowles, and Ginnie shook her head. 'They've never had any children,' she said. 'Maggie can't. She told me. They just lavish all that love on animals. It's really grotty, what's happening to them.'

It would have been so neat, I thought, if Calder Jackson's would-be assassin had been a Watcherley son. Too neat, perhaps. But perhaps also there were others like the Watcherleys whose star had descended as Calder Jackson's rose. I said, 'Do you know of any other places, apart from this one and Calder Jackson's, where people send their sick horses?'

'I expect there *are* some,' Ginnie said. 'Bound to be.'

'Sure to be,' said Oliver Knowles, nodding. 'But of course we don't send away any horse which falls ill here. I have an excellent vet, great with mares, comes day or night in emergencies.'

We made the return journey, Oliver Knowles pointing out to me various mares and foals of interest and distributing carrots to any head within armshot. Foals at foot, foals in utero; the fertility cycle swelling again to fruition through the quiet winter, life growing steadily in the dark.

Ginnie went off to see to the horse she'd been riding and Nigel to finish his inspections in the main yard, leaving Oliver Knowles, the dog and myself to go into the house. Squibs, poor fellow, got no further than his basket in the mud room, but Knowles and I returned to the sitting room-office from which we'd started.

Thanks to my telephone calls of the morning I knew what the acquisition and management of Sandcastle would mean in the matter of taxation, and I'd also gone armed with sets of figures to cover the interest payable should the loan be approved. I found that I needed my knowledge not to instruct but to converse: Oliver Knowles was there before me.

'I've done this often, of course,' he said. 'I've had to arrange finance for buildings, for fencing, for buying the three stallions you saw, and for another two before them. I'm used to repaying fairly substantial bank loans. This new venture is of course huge by comparison, but if I didn't feel it was within my scope I assure you I shouldn't be contemplating it.' He gave me a brief charming smile. 'I'm not a nut case, you know. I really do know my business.'

'Yes,' I said. 'One can see.'

I told him that the maximum length of an Ekaterin loan (if one was forthcoming at all) would be five years, to which he merely nodded.

'That basically means,' I insisted, 'That you'd have to receive getting on for eight million in that five years, even allowing for paying off some of the loan every year with consequently diminishing interest. It's a great deal of money . . . Are you sure you understand how much is involved?'

'Of course I understand,' he said. 'Even allowing for interest payments and the ridiculously high insurance premiums on a horse like Sandcastle, I'd be able to repay the loan in five years. That's the period I've used in planning.'

He spread out his sheets of neatly written calculations on his desk, pointing to each figure as he explained to me how he'd reached it. 'A stallion fee of forty thousand pounds will cover it. His racing record justifies that figure, and I've been most carefully into the breeding of Sandcastle himself, as you can imagine. There is absolutely nothing in the family to alarm. No trace of hereditary illness or undesirable tendencies. He comes from a healthy blue-blooded line of winners, and there's no reason why he shouldn't breed true.' He gave me a photocopied genealogical table. 'I wouldn't expect you to advance a loan without getting an expert opinion on this. Please do take it with you.'

He gave me also some copies of his figures, and I packed them all into the brief case I'd taken with me.

'Why don't you consider halving your risk to twenty-one shares?' I asked. 'Sell nineteen. You'd still outvote the other owners – there'd be no chance of them whisking Sandcastle off somewhere else – and you'd be less stretched.'

With a smile he shook his head. 'If I found for any resaon that the repayments were causing me acute difficulty, I'd sell some shares as necessary. But I hope in five years time to own Sandcastle outright, and also as I told you to have attracted other stallions of that calibre, and to be numbered among the world's top-ranking stud farms.'

His pleasant manner took away any suggestion of megalomania, and I could see nothing of that nature in him.

Ginnie came into the office carrying two mugs with slightly anxious diffidence.

'I made some tea. Do you want some, Dad?'

'Yes, please,' I said immediately, before he could answer, and she looked almost painfully relieved. Oliver Knowles turned what had seemed like an incipient shake of the head into a nod, and Ginnie, handing over the mugs, said that if I wanted sugar she would go and fetch some. 'And a spoon, I guess.'

'My wife's away,' Oliver Knowles said abruptly.

'No sugar,' I said. 'This is great.'

'You won't forget, Dad, will you, about me going back to school?'

'Nigel will take you.'

'He's got visitors.'

'Oh . . . all right.' He looked at his watch. 'In half an hour, then.'

Ginnie looked even more relieved, particularly as I could clearly sense the irritation he was suppressing. 'The school run,' he said as the door closed behind his daughter, 'was one of the things my wife always did. Does . . .' He shrugged. 'She's away indefinitely. You might as well know.'

'I'm sorry,' I said.

'Can't be helped.' He looked at the tea-mug in my hand. 'I was going to offer you something stronger.'

'This is fine.'

'Ginnie comes home on four Sundays a term. She's a boarder, of course.' He paused. 'She's not yet used to her mother not being here. It's bad for her, but there you are, life's like that.'

'She's a nice girl,' I said.

He gave me a glance in which I read both love for his daughter and a blindness to her needs. 'I don't suppose,' he said thoughtfully, 'That you go anywhere near High Wycombe on your way home?'

'Well,' I said obligingly, 'I could do.'

I consequently drove Ginnie back to her school, listening on the way to her views on the new headmistress's compulsory jogging programme ('all our bosoms flopping up and down, bloody uncomfortable and absolutely *disgusting* to look at') and to her opinion of Nigel ('Dad thinks the sun shines out of his you-know-what and I dare say he is pretty good with the mares, they all seem to flourish, but what the lads get up to behind his back is nobody's business. They smoke in the feed sheds, I ask you! All that hay around . . . Nigel never notices. He'd make a rotten school prefect') and to her outlook on life in general ('I can't wait to get out of school uniform and out of dormitories and being bossed around, and I'm no good at lessons; the whole thing's a *mess*. Why has everything *changed*? I used to be happy, or at least I wasn't *unhappy*, which I mostly seem to be nowadays, and no, it isn't because of Mum going away, or not especially, as she was never a lovey-dovey sort of mother, always telling me to eat with my mouth shut and so on . . . and you must be bored silly hearing all this.')

'No,' I said truthfully. 'I'm not bored.'

'I'm not even *beautiful*,' she said despairingly. 'I can suck in my cheeks until I faint but I'll never look pale and bony and interesting.'

I glanced at the still rounded child-woman face, at the peach-bloom skin and the worried eyes.

'Practically no one is beautiful at fifteen,' I said. 'It's too soon.'

'How do you mean – too soon?'

'Well,' I said, 'say at twelve you're a child and flat and undeveloped and so on, and at maybe seventeen or eighteen you're a full-grown adult, just think of the terrific changes your body goes through in that time. Appearance, desires, mental outlook, everything. So at fifteen, which isn't much more than halfway, it's still too soon to know exactly what the end product will be like. And if it's of any comfort to you, you do now look as if you may be beautiful in a year or two, or at least not unbearably ugly.'

She sat in uncharacteristic silence for quite a distance, and then she said, 'Why did you come today? I mean, who are you? If it's all right to ask?'

'It's all right. I'm a sort of financial adviser. I work in a bank.'

'Oh.' She sounded slightly disappointed but made no further comment, and soon after that gave me prosaic and accurate directions to the school.

'Thanks for the lift,' she said, politely shaking hands as we stood beside the car.

'A pleasure.'

'And thanks . . .' she hesitated. 'Thanks anyway.'

I nodded, and she half-walked, half-ran to join a group of other girls going into the buildings. Looking briefly back she gave me a sketchy wave, which I acknowledged. Nice child, I thought, pointing the car homewards. Mixed up, as who wasn't at that age. Middling brains, not quite pretty, her future a clean stretch of sand waiting for footprints.

The First Year

DECEMBER

It made the headlines in the *Sporting Life* (OLIVER KNOWLES, KING OF THE SANDCASTLE) and turned up as the lead story under less fanciful banners on the racing pages of all the other dailies.

SANDCASTLE TO GO TO STUD, SANDCASTLE TO STAY IN BRITAIN, SANDCASTLE SHARES NOT FOR SALE, SANDCASTLE BOUGHT PRIVATELY FOR HUGE SUM. The story in every case was short and simple. One of the year's top stallions had been acquired by the owner of a heretofore moderately-ranked stud farm. 'I am very happy,' Oliver Knowles was universally reported as saying. 'Sandcastle is a prize for British bloodstock.'

The buying price, all the papers said, was 'not unadjacent to five million pounds,' and a few of them added 'the financing was private.'

'Well,' Henry said at lunch, tapping the *Sporting Life*, 'not many of our loans make so much splash.'

'It's a belly-flop,' muttered the obstinate dissenter, who on that day happened to be sitting at my elbow.

Henry didn't hear and was anyway in good spirits. 'If one of the foals runs in the Derby we'll take a party from the office. What do you say, Gordon? Fifty people on open-topped buses?'

Gordon agreed with the sort of smile which hoped he wouldn't actually be called upon to fulfil his promise.

'Forty mares,' Henry said musingly. 'Forty foals. Surely one of them might be Derby material.'

'Er,' I said, from new-found knowledge. 'Forty foals is stretching it. Thirty-five would be pretty good. Some mares won't "take", so to speak.'

Henry showed mild alarm. 'Does that mean that five or six fees will have to be returned? Doesn't that affect Knowles' programme of repayment?'

I shook my head. 'For a horse of Sandcastle's stature the fee is all up in front. Payable for services rendered, regardless of results. That's in Britain, of course, and Europe. In America they have the system of no foal, no fee, even for the top stallions. A live foal, that is. Alive, on its feet and suckling.'

Henry relaxed, leaning back in his chair and smiling. 'You've certainly learnt a lot, Tim, since this all started.'

'It's absorbing.'

He nodded. 'I know it isn't usual, but how do you feel about keeping an eye on the bank's money at close quarters? Would Knowles object to you dropping in from time to time?'

'I shouldn't think so. Not out of general interest.'

'Good. Do that, then. Bring us progress reports. I must say I've never been as impressed with any horse as I was that day with Sandcastle.'

Henry's direct admiration of the colt had led in the end to Ekaterin's advancing three of the five million to Oliver Knowles, with private individuals subscribing the other two. The fertility tests had been excellent, the owner had been paid, and Sandcastle already stood in the stallion yard in Hertfordshire alongside Rotaboy, Diarist and Parakeet.

December was marching along towards Christmas, with trees twinkling all over London and sleet falling bleakly in the afternoons. On an impulse I sent a card embossed with tasteful robins to Calder Jackson, wishing him well, and almost by return of post received (in the office) a missive (Stubbs reproduction) thanking me sincerely and asking if I would be interested some time in looking round his place. If so, he finished, would I telephone – number supplied.

I telephoned. He was affable and far more spontaneous than usual. 'Do come,' he said, and we made a date for the following Sunday.

I told Gordon I was going. We were working on an interbank loan of nine and a half million for five days to a competitor, a matter of little more than a few telephone calls and a promise. My hair had almost ceased to rise at the size and speed of such deals, and with only verbal agreement from Val and Henry I had recently on my own lent seven million for forty-eight hours. The trick was never to lend for a longer time than we ourselves were able to borrow the necessary funds: if we did, we ran the risk of having to pay a higher rate of interest than we were receiving on the loan, a process which physically hurt Val Fisher. There had been a time in the past when owing to a client repaying late he had had to borrow several million for eighteen days at twenty-five per cent, and he'd never got over it.

Most of our dealings weren't on such a heavy scale, and next on my agenda was a request for us to lend fifty-five thousand pounds to a man who had invented a waste-paper basket for use in cars and needed funds for development. I read the letter out to Gordon, who made a fast thumbs-down gesture.

'Pity,' I said. 'It's a sorely needed object.'

'He's asking too little.' He put his left hand hard between his knees and clamped it there. 'And there are far better inventions dying the death.'

I agreed with him and wrote a brief note of regret. Gordon looked up from his pages shortly after, and asked me what I'd be doing at Christmas.

'Nothing much,' I said.

'Not going to your mother in Jersey?'

'They're cruising in the Caribbean.'

'Judith and I wondered . . .' he cleared his throat, '. . . if you'd care to stay with us. Come on Christmas Eve, stay three or four days? Just as you like, of course. I daresay you wouldn't find us too exciting . . . but the offer's there, anyway.'

Was it wise, I wondered, to spend three or four days with Judith when three or four *hours* at Ascot had tempted acutely? Was it wise, when the sight of her aroused so many natural urges, to sleep so long – and so near – under her roof?

Most unwise.

'I'd like to,' I said, 'very much'; and I thought you're a bloody stupid fool, Tim Ekaterin, and if you ache it'll be your own ridiculous fault.

'Good,' Gordon said, looking as if he meant it. 'Judith will be pleased. She was afraid you might have younger friends to go to.'

'Nothing fixed.'

He nodded contentedly and went back to his work, and I thought about Judith wanting me to stay, because if she hadn't wanted it I wouldn't have been asked.

If I had any sense I wouldn't go: but I knew I would.

Calder Jackson's place at Newmarket, seen that next Sunday morning, was a gem of public relations, where everything had been done to please those visiting the sick. The yard itself, a three-sided quadrangle, had been cosmetically planted with central grass and a graceful tree, and brightly painted tubs, bare now of flowers, stood at frequent intervals outside the boxes. There were park-bench type seats here and there, and ornamental gates and railings in black iron scroll-work, and a welcoming archway labelled 'Comfort Room This Way'.

Outside the main yard, and to one side, stood a small separate building painted glossy white. There was a large prominent red cross on the door, with, underneath it, the single word 'Surgery'.

The yard and the surgery were what the visitor first saw: beyond and screened by trees stood Calder Jackson's own house, more private from prying eyes than his business. I parked beside several other cars on a stretch of asphalt, and walked over to ring the bell. The front door was opened to me by a manservant in a white coat. Butler or nurse?

'This way, sir,' he said deferentially, when I announced my name. 'Mr Jackson is expecting you.'

Butler.

Interesting to see the dramatic hair-cut in its home setting, which was olde-worlde cottage on a grand scale. I had an impression of a huge room, oak rafters, stone flagged floor, rugs, dark oak furniture, great brick fireplace with burning logs . . . and Calder advancing with a broad smile and outstretched arm.

'Tim!' he exclaimed, shaking hands vigorously. 'This is a pleasure, indeed it is.'

'Been looking forward to it,' I said.

'Come along to the fire. Come and warm yourself. How about a drink? And . . . oh . . . this is a friend of mine . . .' he waved towards a second man already standing by the fireplace, '. . . Ian Pargetter.'

The friend and I nodded to each other and made the usual strangers-meeting signals, and the name tumbled over in my mind as something I'd heard somewhere before but couldn't quite recall.

Calder Jackson clinked bottles and glasses and upon consultation gave me a Scotch of noble proportions.

'And for you, Ian,' he said. 'A further tincture?'

Oh yes, I thought. The vet. Ian Pargetter, the vet who didn't mind consorting with unlicensed practitioners.

Ian Pargetter hesitated but shrugged and held out his glass as one succumbing to pleasurable temptation.

'A small one, then, Calder,' he said. 'I must be off.'

He was about forty, I judged; large and reliable-looking, with sandy greying hair, a heavy moustache and an air of being completely in charge of his life. Calder explained that it was I who had deflected the knife aimed at him at Ascot, and Ian Pargetter made predictable responses about luck, fast reactions and who could have wanted to kill Calder?

'That was altogether a memorable day,' Calder said, and I agreed with him.

'We all won a packet on Sandcastle,' Calder said. 'Pity he's going to stud so soon.'

I smiled. 'Maybe we'll win on his sons.'

There was no particular secret, as far as I knew, about where the finance for Sandcastle had come from, but it was up to Oliver Knowles to reveal it, not me. I thought Calder would have been interested, but bankers' ethics as usual kept me quiet.

'A superb horse,' Calder said, with all the enthusiasm he'd shown in Dissdale's box. 'One of the greats.'

Ian Pargetter nodded agreement, then finished his drink at a gulp and said he'd be going. 'Let me know how that pony fares, Calder.'

'Yes, of course.' Calder moved with his departing guest towards the door and slapped him on the shoulder. 'Thanks for dropping in, Ian. Appreciate it.'

There were sounds of Pargetter leaving by the front door, and Calder returned rubbing his hands together and saying that although it was cold outside, I might care to look round before his other guests arrived for lunch. Accordingly we walked across to the open-sided quadrangle, where Calder moved from box to box giving me a brief resumé of the illness and prospects of each patient.

'This pony only came yesterday . . . it's a prize show pony supposedly, and look at it. Dull eyes, rough coat, altogether droopy. They say it's had diarrhoea on and off for weeks. I'm their last resort, they say.' He smiled philosophically. 'Can't think why they don't send me sick horses as a *first* resort. But there you are, they always try regular vets first. Can't blame them, I suppose.'

We moved along the line. 'This mare was coughing blood when she came three weeks ago. I was her owner's last resort.' He smiled again. 'She's doing fine now. The cough's almost gone. She's eating well, putting on condition.' The mare blinked at us lazily as we strolled away.

'This is a two-year-old filly,' Calder said, peering over a half-door. 'She's had an infected ulcer on her withers for six weeks before she came here. Antibiotics had proved useless. Now the ulcer's dry and healing. Most satisfactory.'

We went on down the row.

'This is someone's favourite hunter, came all the way from Gloucestershire. I don't know what I can do for him, though of course I'll try. His trouble, truthfully, is just age.'

Further on: 'Here's a star three-day-eventer. Came to me with intermittent bleeding in the urine, intractable to antibiotics. He was clearly in great pain, and almost dangerous to deal with on account of it. But now he's fine. He'll be staying here for a while longer but I'm sure the trouble is cured.

'This is a three-year-old colt who won a race back in July but then started breaking blood vessels and went on doing it despite treatment. He's been here a fortnight. Last resort, of course!'

By the next box he said, 'Don't look at this one if you're squeamish. Poor wretched little filly, she's so weak she can't hold her head up and all her bones are sharp under the skin. Some sort of wasting sickness. Blood tests haven't shown what it is. I don't know if I can heal her. I've laid my hands on her twice so far, but there's been nothing. No . . . feeling. Sometimes it takes a long time. But I'm not giving up with her, and there's always hope.'

He turned his curly head and pointed to another box further ahead. 'There's a colt along there who's been here two months and is only just responding. His owners were in despair, and so was I, privately, but then just three days ago when I was in his box I could feel the force flowing down my arms and into him, and the next day he was mending.'

He spoke with a far more natural fluency on his home ground and less as if reciting from a script, but all the same I felt the same reservations about the healing touch as I had at Ascot. I was a doubter, I supposed. I would never in my life have put my trust in a seventh son of a seventh son, probably because the only direct knowledge I had of any human seeking out 'the touch' had been a close friend of mine at college who'd had hopeless cancer and had gone to a woman healer as a last resort, only to be told that he was dying because he wanted to. I could vividly remember his anger, and mine on his behalf: and standing in Calder's yard I wondered if that same woman would also think that *horses* got sick to death because they wanted to.

'Is there anything you can't treat?' I asked. 'Anything you turn away?'

'I'm afraid so, yes.' He smiled ruefully. 'There are some

things, like advanced laminitis, with which I feel hopeless, and as for coryne . . .' He shook his head, '. . . it's a killer.'

'You've lost me,' I said.

'So sorry. Well, laminitis is a condition of the feet where the bone eventually begins to crumble, and horses in the end can't bear the pain of standing up. They lie down, and horses can't live for more than a few days lying down.' He spoke with regret. 'And coryne,' he went on, 'is a frightful bacterial infection which is deadly to foals. It induces a sort of pneumonia which abcesses in the lungs. Terribly contagious. I know of one stud farm in America which lost seventy foals in one day.'

I listened in horror. 'Do we have it in England?' I asked.

'Sometimes, in pockets, but not widespread. It doesn't affect older horses. Foals of three months or over are safe.' He paused. 'Some very young foals do survive, of course, but they're likely to have scar tissue in the lungs which may impair their breathing for racing purposes.'

'Isn't there a vaccine?' I said.

He smiled indulgently. 'Very little research is done into equine diseases, chiefly because of the cost but also because horses are so large, and can't be kept in a laboratory for any controlled series of tests.'

I again had the impression that he had said all this many times before, but it was understandable and I was getting used to it. We proceeded on the hospital round (four-year-old with general debility, show-jumper with festering leg) and came at length to a box with an open door.

'We're giving this one sun treatment,' Calder said, indicating that I should look; and inside the box a thin youth was adjusting the angle of an ultra-violet lamp set on a head-high, wall-mounted bracket. It wasn't at the dappled grey that I looked, however, but at the lad, because in the first brief glimpse I thought he was the boy who had tried to attack Calder.

I opened my mouth . . . and shut it again.

He wasn't the boy. He was of the same height, same build, same litheness, same general colouring, but not with the same eyes or jawline or narrow nose.

Calder saw my reaction and smiled. 'For a split second, when I saw that boy move at Ascot, I though it was Jason here. But it wasn't, of course.'

I shook my head. 'Alike but different.'

Calder nodded. 'And Jason wouldn't want to kill me, would you, Jason?' He spoke with a jocularity to which Jason didn't respond.

'No, sir,' he said stolidly.

'Jason is my right-hand man,' said Calder heartily. 'Indispensable.'

The right-hand man showed no satisfaction at the flattery and maintained an impassive countenance throughout. He touched the grey horse and told it to shift over a bit in the manner of one equal talking to another, and the horse obediently shifted.

'Mind your eyes with that lamp,' Calder said. 'Where are your glasses?'

Jason fished into the breast pocket of his shirt and produced some ultra-dark sun-shades. Calder nodded. 'Put them on,' he said, and Jason complied. Where before there had already been a lack of mobility of expression, there was now, with the obscured eyes, no way at all of guessing Jason's thoughts.

'I'll be finished with this one in ten minutes,' he said. 'Is there anything else after that, sir?'

Calder briefly pondered and shook his head. 'Just the evening rounds at four.'

'Your invalids get every care,' I said, complimenting them.

Jason's blacked-out eyes turned my way, but it was Calder who said 'Hard work gets results.' And you've said that a thousand times, I thought.

We reached the last box in the yard, the first one which was empty.

'Emergency bed,' Calder said, jokingly, and I smiled and asked how much he charged for his patients.

He replied easily and without explanation or apology. 'Twice the training fees currently charged for horses in the top Newmarket stables. When their rates go up, so do mine.'

'*Twice . . .?*'

He nodded. 'I could charge more, you know. But if I charged less I'd be totally swamped by all those "last resort" people, and I simply haven't the room or the time or the spiritual resources to take more cases than I do.'

I wondered how one would ever get to the essence of the man behind the temperate, considerate public face, or indeed if the public face was not a façade at all but the essence itself. I looked at the physical strength of the shoulders below the helmet head and listened to the plain words describing a mystical force, considered the dominating voice and the mild manner, and still found him a man to admire rather than like.

'The surgery,' he said, gesturing towards it as we walked that way. 'My drug store!' He smiled at the joke (how often, I wondered, had he said it?) and produced a key to unlock the door. 'There's nothing dangerous or illegal in here, of course, but one has to protect against vandals. So sad, don't you think?'

The surgery, which had no windows, was basically a large brick-built hut. The internal walls, like the outer, were painted white, and the floor was tiled in red. There were antiseptic-looking glass-fronted cabinets along the two end walls and a wide bench with drawers underneath along the wall facing the door. On the bench, a delicate-looking set of scales, a pestle and mortar and a pair of fine rubber gloves: behind the glass of the cabinets, rows of bottles and boxes. Everything very business-like and tidy: and along the wall which contained the door stood three kitchen appliances, refrigerator, cooker and sink.

Calder pointed vaguely towards the cabinets. 'In there I keep the herbs in pill and powder form. Comfrey, myrrh, sarsaparilla, golden seal, fo-ti-tieng, things like that.'

'Er . . .' I said. 'What do they do?'

He ran through them obligingly. 'Comfrey knits bones, and heals wounds, myrrh is antiseptic and good for diarrhoea and rheumatism, sarsaparilla contains male hormones and increases physical strength, golden seal cures eczema, improves appetite and digestion, fo-ti-tieng is a revitalising tonic second to none. Then there's liquorice for coughs and papaya enzymes for digesting proteins and passiflora to use as a general pacifier and tranquilliser.' He paused. 'There's ginseng also, of course, which is a marvellous rejuvenator and invigorator, but it's really too expensive in the quantities needed to do a horse significant good. It has to be taken continuously, for ever.' He sighed. 'Excellent for humans, though.'

The air in the windowless room was fresh and smelled very faintly fragrant, and as if to account for it Calder started showing me the contents of the drawers.

'I keep seeds in here,' he said. 'My patients eat them by the handful every day.' Three or four of the drawers contained large opaque plastic bags fastened by bull-dog clips. 'Sunflower seeds for vitamins, phosphorus and calcium, good for bones and teeth. Pumpkin seeds for vigour – they contain male hormones – and also for phosphorus and iron. Carrot seeds for calming nervous horses. Sesame seeds for general health.'

He walked along a yard or two and pulled open an extra-large deep drawer which contained larger bags; more like sacks. 'These are hops left after beer-making. They're packed full of all good things. A great tonic, and cheap enough to use in quantity. We have bagfuls of them over in the feed shed to grind up as chaff but I use these here as one ingredient of my special decoction, my concentrated tonic.'

'Do you make it . . . on the stove?' I asked.

He smiled. 'Like a chef.' He opened the refrigerator door. 'I store it in here. Want to see?'

I looked inside. Nearly the whole space was taken with gallon-sized plastic containers full of brownish liquid. 'We mix it in a bran mash, warmed of course, and the horses thrive.'

I knew nothing about the efficiency of his remedies, but I was definitely impressed.

'How do you get the horses to take pills?' I said.

'In an apple, usually. We scoop out half the core, put in the tablet or capsule, or indeed just powder, and replace the plug.'

So simple.

'And incidentally, I make most of my own pills and capsules. Some, like comfrey, are commercially available, but I prefer to buy the dried herbs in their pure form and make my own recipes.' He pulled open one of the lower drawers under the work-bench and lifted out a heavy wooden box. 'This,' he said, laying it on the work surface and opening the lid, 'contains the makings.'

I looked down at a whole array of brass dies, each a small square with a pill-sized cavity in its centre. The cavities varied from tiny to extra large, and from round to oblong.

'It's an antique,' he said with a touch of pride. 'Early Victorian. Dates from when pills were always made by hand – and it's still viable, of course. You put the required drug in powder form into whatever sized cavity you want, and compress it with the rod which exactly fits.' He lifted one of a series of short brass rods from its rack and fitted its end into one of the cavities, tamping it up and down; then picked the whole die out of the box and tipped it right over. 'Hey presto,' he said genially, catching the imaginary contents, 'a pill!'

'Neat,' I said, with positive pleasure.

He nodded. 'Capsules are quicker and more modern.' He pulled open another drawer and briefly showed me the empty tops and bottoms of a host of gelatin capsules, again of varying sizes, though mostly a little larger than those swallowed easily by humans. 'Veterinary size,' he explained.

He closed his gem of a pill-making box and returned it to its drawer, straightening up afterwards and casting a caring eye around the place to make sure everything was tidy. With a nod of private satisfaction he opened the door for us to return to the outside world, switching off the fluorescent lights and locking the door behind us.

A car was just rolling to a stop on the asphalt, and presently two recognised figures emerged from it: Dissdale Smith and his delectable Bettina.

'Hello, hello,' said Dissdale, striding across with ready hand. 'Calder said you were coming. Good to see you. Calder's been showing you all his treasures, eh? The conducted tour, eh, Calder?' I shook the hand. 'Calder's proud of his achievements here, aren't you, Calder?'

'With good reason,' I said civilly, and Calder gave me a swift glance and a genuine-looking smile.

Bettina drifted more slowly to join us, a delight in high heeled boots and cuddling fur, a white silk scarf round her throat and smooth dark hair falling glossily to her shoulders. Her scent travelled sweetly across the quiet cold air and she laid a decorative hand on my arm in an intimate touch.

'Tim the saviour,' she said. 'Calder's hero.'

The over-packaged charm unaccountably brought the contrasting image of Ginnie sharply to my mind, and I briefly thought that the promise was more beckoning than the performance, that child more interesting than that woman.

Calder took us all soon into his maxi-cottage sitting-room and distributed more drinks. Dissdale told me that Sandcastle had almost literally saved his business and metaphorically his life, and we all drank a toast to the wonder horse. Four further guests arrived – a married couple with their two twentyish daughters – and the occasion became an ordinarily enjoyable lunch party, undemanding, unmemorable, good food handed round by the manservant, cigars offered with the coffee.

Calder at some point said he was off to America in the New Year on a short lecture tour.

'Unfortunately,' he said, 'I'll be talking to health clubs, not horse people. American racehorse trainers aren't receptive to me. Or not yet. But then, it took a few years for Newmarket to decide I could make a contribution.'

Everyone smiled at the scepticism of America and Newmarket.

Calder said, 'January is often a quiet month here. We don't take any new admissions if I'm away, and of course my head lad just keeps the establishment routines going until I return. It works pretty well.' He smiled. 'If I'm lucky I'll get some ski-ing; and to be honest, I'm looking forward to the ski-ing much more than the talks.'

Everyone left soon after three, and I drove back to London through the short darkening afternoon wondering if the herbs of antiquity held secrets we'd almost wilfully lost.

'Caffeine,' Calder had been saying towards the end, 'is a get-up-and-go stimulant, tremendously useful. Found in coffee beans of course, and in tea and cocoa and cola drinks. Good for asthma. Vigorous marvellous tonic. A life-saver after shock. And now in America, I ask you, they're casting caffeine as a villain and are busy taking it out of everything it's naturally *in*. You might as well take the alcohol out of bread.'

'But Calder dear,' Bettina said, 'There's no alcohol in bread.'

He looked at her kindly as she sat on his right. 'Bread that is made with yeast definitely does contain alcohol before it's cooked. If you mix yeast with water and sugar you get alcohol and carbon-dioxide, which is the gas which makes the dough rise. The air in a bakery smells of wine . . . simple chemistry, my dear girl, no magic in it. Bread is the staff of life and alcohol is good for you.'

There had been jokes and lifted glasss, and I could have listened to Calder for hours.

The Christmas party at Gordon Michael's home was in a way an echo, because Judith's apothecary friend Pen Warner was in attendance most of the time. I got to know her quite well and to like her very much, which Judith may or may not have intended. In any case, it was again the fairy-tale day at Ascot which had led on to friendly relations.

'Do you remember Burnt Marshmallow?' Pen said. 'I bought a painting with my winnings.'

'I spent mine on riotous living.'

'Oh yes?' She looked me up and down and shook her head. 'You haven't the air.'

'What do I have the air of?' I asked curiously, and she

answered in amusement, 'Of intelligent laziness and boring virtue.'

'All wrong,' I said.

'Ho hum.'

She seemed to me to be slightly less physically solid than at Ascot, but it might have been only the change of clothes; there were still the sad eyes and the ingrained worthiness and the unexpected cast of humour. She had apparently spent twelve hours that day – it was Christmas Eve – doling out remedies to people whose illnesses showed no sense of timing, and proposed to go back at six in the morning. Meanwhile she appeared at the Michaels' house in a long festive caftan with mood to match, and during the evening the four of us ate quails with our fingers, and roasted chestnuts, and played a board game with childish gusto.

Judith wore rose pink and pearls and looked about twenty-five. Gordon in advance had instructed me 'Bring whatever you like as long as it's informal' and himself was resplendent in a plum velvet jacket and bow tie. My own newly bought cream wool shirt which in the shop had looked fairly theatrical seemed in the event to be right, so that on all levels the evening proved harmonious and fun, much more rounded and easy than I'd expected.

Judith's housekeeping throughout my stay proved a poem of invisibility. Food appeared from freezer and cupboard, remnants returned to dishwasher and dustbin. Jobs were distributed when essential but sitting and talking had priority: and nothing so smooth, I reflected, ever got done without hard work beforehand.

'Pen will be back soon after one tomorrow,' Judith said at midnight on that first evening. 'We'll have a drink then and open some presents, and have our Christmas feast at half past three. There will be breakfast in the morning, and Gordon and I will go to church.' She left an invitation lingering in the air, but I marginally shook my head. 'You can look after yourself, then, while we're gone.'

She kissed me goodnight, with affection and on the cheek. Gordon gave me a smile and a wave, and I went to bed across the hall from them and spent an hour before sleep deliberately not thinking at all about Judith in or out of her nightgown – or not much.

Breakfast was taken in dressing gowns. Judith's was red, quilted and unrevealing.

They changed and went to church. Pray for me, I said, and set out for a walk on the common.

There were brightly-wrapped gifts waiting around the base of the silver-starred Christmas tree in the Michaels' drawing room, and a surreptitious inspection had revealed one from Pen addressed to me. I walked across the windy grass, shoulders hunched, hands in pockets, wondering what to do about one for her, and as quite often happens came by chance to a solution.

A small boy was out there with his father, flying a kite, and I stopped to watch.

'That's fun,' I said.

The boy took no notice but the father said, 'There's no satisfying the little bleeder. I give him this and he says he wants roller skates.'

The kite was a brilliant phosphorescent Chinese dragon with butterfly wings and a big frilly tail, soaring and circling like a joyful tethered spirit in the Christmas sky.

'Will you sell it to me?' I asked. 'Buy the roller skates instead?' I explained the problem, the need for an instant present.

Parent and child consulted and the deal was done. I wound up the string carefully and bore the trophy home, wondering what on earth the sober pharmacist would think of such a thing: but when she unwrapped it from gold paper (cadged from Judith for the purpose) she pronounced herself enchanted, and back we all went onto the common to watch her fly it.

The whole day was happy. I hadn't had so good a Christmas since I was a child. I told them so, and kissed Judith uninhibitedly under some mistletoe, which Gordon didn't seem to mind.

'You were born sunny,' Judith said, briefly stroking my cheek, and Gordon, nodding, said, 'A man without sorrows, unacquainted with grief.'

'Grief and sorrow come with time,' Pen said, but not as if she meant it imminently. 'They come to us all.'

On the morning after Christmas Day I drove Judith across London to Hampstead to put flowers on her mother's grave.

'I know you'll think me silly, but I always go. She died on Boxing Day when I was twelve. It's the only way I have of remembering her . . . of feeling I had a mother at all. I usually go by myself. Gordon thinks I'm sentimental and doesn't like coming.'

'Nothing wrong with sentiment,' I said.

Hampstead was where I lived in the upstairs half of a friend's house. I wasn't sure whether or not Judith knew it, and said nothing until she'd delivered the pink chrysanthemums to the square marble tablet let in flush with the grass and communed for a while with the memories floating there.

It was as we walked slowly back toward the iron gates that I neutrally said, 'My flat's only half a mile from here. This part of London is home ground.'

'Is it?'

'Mm.'

After a few steps she said, 'I knew you lived somewhere here. If you remember, you wouldn't let us drive you all the way home from Ascot. You said Hampstead was too far.'

'So it was.'

'Not for Sir Galahad that starry night.'

We reached the gates and paused for her to look back. I was infinitely conscious of her nearness and of my own stifled desire; and she looked abruptly into my eyes and said, 'Gordon knows you live here, also.'

'And does he know how I feel?' I asked.

'I don't know. He hasn't said.'

I wanted very much to go that last half mile: that short distance on wheels, that far journey in commitment. My body tingled . . . rippled . . . from hunger, and I found myself physically clenching my back teeth.

'What are you thinking?' she said.

'For God's sake . . . you know damn well what I'm thinking . . . and we're going back to Clapham right this minute.'

She sighed. 'Yes, I suppose we must.'

'What do you mean . . . suppose?'

'Well, I . . .' she paused. 'I mean, yes we must. I'm sorry . . . it was just that . . . for a moment . . . I was tempted.'

'As at Ascot?' I said.

She nodded. 'As at Ascot.'

'Only here and now,' I said, 'we have the place and the time and the opportunity to do something about it.'

'Yes.'

'And what we're going to do . . . is . . . nothing.' It came out as half a question, half a statement: wholly an impossibility.

'Why do we *care*?' she said explosively. 'Why don't we just get into your bed and have a happy time? Why is the whole thing so tangled up with bloody concepts like honour?'

We walked down the road to where I'd parked the car and I drove southwards with careful observance at every red light; stop signals making round eyes at me all the way to Clapham.

'I'd have liked it,' Judith said as we pulled up outside her house.

'So would I.'

We went indoors in a sort of deprived companionship, and I realised only when I saw Gordon's smiling unsuspicious face that I couldn't have returned there if it had been in any other way.

It was at lunch that day, when Pen had again resurfaced from her stint among the pills that I told them about my visit to Calder. Pen, predictably, was acutely interested and said she'd dearly like to know what was in the decoction in the refrigerator.

'What's a decoction?' Judith asked.

'A preparation boiled with water. If you dissolve things in alcohol, that's a tincture.'

'One lives and bloody well learns!'

Pen laughed. 'How about carminative, anodyne and vermifuge . . . effects of drugs. They simply roll off the tongue with grandeur.'

'And what do they mean?' Gordon asked.

'Getting rid of gas, getting rid of pain, getting rid of worms.'

Gordon too was laughing. 'Have some anodyne tincture of grape.' He poured wine into our glasses. 'Do you honestly believe, Tim, that Calder cures horses by touch?'

'I'm sure *he* believes it.' I reflected. 'I don't know if he will let anyone watch. And if he did, what would one see? I don't suppose with a horse it's a case of "take up your bed and walk." '

Judith said in surprise, 'You sound as if you'd like it to be true. You, that Gordon and Harry have trained to doubt!'

'Calder's impressive,' I admitted. 'So is his place. So are the fees he charges. He wouldn't be able to set his prices so high if he didn't get real results.'

'Do the herbs come extra?' Pen said.

'I didn't ask.'

'Would you expect them to?' Gordon said.

'Well . . .' Pen considered. 'Some of those that Tim mentioned are fairly exotic. Golden seal – that's hydrastis – said in the past to cure practically anything you can mention, but mostly used nowadays in tiny amounts in eye-drops. Has to be imported from America. And fo-ti-teng – which is *Hydrocotyle asiatica minor*, also called the source of the elixir of long life – that only grows as far as I know in the tropical jungles of the far east. I mean, I would have thought that giving things like that to horses would be wildly expensive.'

If I'd been impressed with Calder I was probably more so with Pen. 'I didn't know pharmacists were so clued up on herbs,' I said.

'I was just interested so I learned their properties,' she exclaimed. 'The age-old remedies are hardly even hinted at on the official pharmacy courses, though considering digitalis and penicillin one can't exactly see why. A lot of chemists shops don't sell non-prescription herbal remedies, but I do, and honestly for a stack of people they seem to work.'

'And do you advocate garlic poultices for the feet of babies with whooping-cough?' Gordon asked.

Pen didn't. There was more laughter. If one believed in Calder, Judith said firmly, one believed in him, garlic poultices and all.

The four of us spent a comfortable afternoon and evening together, and when Judith and Gordon went to bed I walked along with Pen to her house, where she'd been staying each night, filling my lungs with the fresh air off the common.

'You're going home tomorrow, aren't you?' she said, fishing out her keys.

I nodded. 'In the morning.'

'It's been great fun.' She found the keys and fitted one in the lock. 'Would you like to come in?'

'No . . . I'll just walk for a bit.'

She opened the door and paused there. 'Thank you for the kite . . . it was brilliant. And goodbye for this time, though I guess if Judith can stand it I'll be seeing you again.'

'Stand what?' I asked.

She kissed me on the cheek. 'Goodnight,' she said. 'And believe it or not, the herb known as passion flower is good for insomnia.'

Her grin shone out like the Cheshire Cat's as she stepped inside her house and closed the door, and I stood hopelessly on her pathway wanting to call her back.

The Second Year

FEBRUARY

Ian Pargetter was murdered at about one in the morning on February 1st.

I learned about his death from Calder when I telephoned that evening on impulse to thank him belatedly for the lunch party, invite him for a reciprocal dinner in London and hear whether or not he had enjoyed his American tour.

'Who?' he said vaguely when I announced myself. 'Who? Oh . . . Tim . . . Look, I can't talk now, I'm simply distracted, a friend of mine's been killed and I can't think of anything else.'

'I'm so sorry,' I said inadequately.

'Yes . . . Ian Pargetter . . . but I don't suppose you know . . .'

This time I remembered at once. The vet; big, reliable, sandy moustache.

'I met him,' I said, 'in your house.'

'Did you? Oh yes. I'm so upset I can't concentrate. Look, Tim, ring some other time, will you?'

'Yes, of course.'

'It's not just that he's been a friend for years,' he said, 'but I don't know . . . I really don't know how my business will fare without him. He sent so many horses my way . . . such a good friend . . . I'm totally distraught . . . Look, ring me another time . . . Tim, so sorry.' He put his receiver down with the rattle of a shaking hand.

I thought at the time that he meant Ian Pargetter had been killed in some sort of accident, and it was only the next day when my eye was caught by a paragraph in a newspaper that I realised the difference.

> *Ian Pargetter, well known, much respected Newmarket veterinary surgeon, was yesterday morning found dead in his home. Police suspect foul play. They state that Pargetter suffered head injuries and that certain supplies of drugs appear to be missing. Pargetter's body was discovered by Mrs Jane Halson, a daily cleaner. The vet is survived by his wife and three young daughters, all of whom were away from home at the time of the attack. Mrs Pargetter was reported last night to be very distressed and under sedation.*

A lot of succinct bad news, I thought, for a lot of sad bereft people. He was the first person I'd known who'd been murdered, and in spite of our very brief meeting I found his death most disturbing: and if I felt so unsettled about a near-stranger, how, I wondered, did anyone ever recover from the murder of someone one knew well and loved. How did one deal with the anger? Come to terms with the urge to revenge?

I'd of course read reports of husbands and wives who pronounced themselves 'not bitter' over the slaughter of a spouse, and I'd never understood it. I felt furious on Ian Pargetter's behalf that anyone should have had the arrogance to wipe him out.

Because of Ascot and Sandcastle my long-dormant interest in racecourses seemed thoroughly to have reawakened, and on three or four Saturday afternoons that winter I'd trekked to Kempton or Sandown or Newbury to watch the jumpers. Ursula Young had become a familiar face, and it was from this brisk well-informed lady bloodstock agent that I learnt most about Ian Pargetter and his death.

'Drink?' I suggested at Kempton, pulling up my coat collar against a bitter wind.

She looked at her watch (I'd never seen her do anything without checking the time) and agreed on a quick one. Whisky-mac for her, coffee for me, as at Doncaster.

'Now tell me,' she said, hugging her glass and yelling in my ear over the general din of a bar packed with other cold customers seeking inner warmth, 'when you asked all those questions about stallion shares, was it for Sandcastle?'

I smiled without actually answering, shielding my coffee inadequately from adjacent nudging elbows.

'Thought so,' she said. 'Look – there's a table. Grab it.'

We sat down in a corner with the racket going on over our heads and the closed-circuit television playing re-runs of the last race fortissimo. Ursula bent her head towards mine. 'A wow-sized coup for Oliver Knowles.'

'You approve?' I asked.

She nodded. 'He'll be among the greats in one throw. Smart move. Clever man.'

'Do you know him?'

'Yes. Meet him often at the sales. He had a snooty wife who left him for some Canadian millionaire or other, and maybe that's why he's aiming for the big-time; just to show her.' She smiled fiendishly. 'She was a real pain and I hope he makes it.'

She drank half her whisky and I said it was a shame about Ian Pargetter, and that I'd met him once at Calder's house.

She grimaced with a stronger echo of the anger I had myself felt. 'He'd been out all evening saving the life of a classic-class colt with colic. It's so beastly. He went home well after midnight, and they reckon whoever killed him was already in the house stealing whatever he could lay his hands on. Ian's wife and family were away visiting her mother, you see, and the police think the killer thought the house would be empty for the night.' She swallowed. 'He was hit on the back of the head with a brass lamp off one of the tables in the sitting room. Just casual. Unpremeditated. Just . . . *stupid*.' She looked moved, as I guessed everyone must have been who had known him. 'Such a waste. He was a really nice man, a good vet, everyone liked him. And all for practically nothing . . . The police found a lot of silver and jewellery lying on a blanket ready to be carried away, but they think the thief just panicked and left it when Ian came home . . . all that anyone can think of that's missing is his case of instruments and a few drugs that he'd had with him that evening . . . nothing worth killing for . . . not even for an addict. Nothing in it like that.' She fell silent and looked down into her nearly empty glass, and I offered her a refill.

'No, thanks all the same, one's enough. I feel pretty maudlin as it is. I liked Ian. He was a good sort. I'd like to *throttle* the little beast who killed him.'

'I think Calder Jackson feels much as you do,' I said.

She glanced up, her good-looking fifty-ish face full of genuine concern. 'Calder will miss Ian terribly. There aren't that number of vets around who'd not only put up with a faith-healer on their doorstep but actually treat him as a colleague. Ian had no professional jealousy. Very rare. Very good man. Makes it all the worse.'

We went out again into the raw air and I lost five pounds on the afternoon, which would have sent Lorna Shipton swooning to Uncle Freddie, if she'd known.

Two weeks later with Oliver Knowles' warm approval I paid another visit to his farm in Hertfordshire, and although it was again a Sunday and still winter, the atmosphere of the place had fundamentally changed. Where there had been quiet sleepy near-hibernation there was now a wakeful bustle and eagerness, where a scattering of dams and foals across the paddocks, now a crowd of mares moving alone and slowly with big bellies.

The crop had come to the harvest. Life was ripening into the daylight, and into the darkness the new seed would be sown.

I had not been truly a country child (ten acres of wooded hill in Surrey) and to me the birth of animals still seemed a wonder and joy: to Oliver Knowles, he said, it meant constant worry and profit and loss. His grasp of essentials still rang out strong and clear, but there were lines on his forehead from the details.

'I suppose,' he said frankly, walking me into the first of the big yards, 'that the one thing I hadn't mentally prepared myself for was the value of the foals now being born here. I mean . . .' he gestured around at the patient heads looking over the rows of half-doors, '. . . these mares have been to the top stallions. They're carrying fabulous blood-lines. They're history.' His awe could be felt. 'I didn't realise, you know, what anxiety they would bring me. We've always done our best for the foals, of course we have, but if one died it wasn't a tragedy, but with this lot . . .' He smiled ruefully. 'It's not enough just owning Sandcastle. I have to make sure that our reputation for handling top broodmares is good and sound.'

We walked along beside one row of boxes with him telling me in detail the breeding of each mare we came to and of the foal she carried, and even to my ignorant ears it sounded as if every Derby and Oaks winner for the past half century had had a hand in the coming generation.

'I had no trouble selling Sandcastle's nominations,' he said. 'Not even at forty thousand pounds a throw. I could even choose, to some extent, which mares to accept. It's been utterly amazing to be able to turn away mares that I considered wouldn't do him justice.'

'Is there a temptation,' I asked mildly, 'to sell more than forty places? To . . . er . . . accept an extra fee . . . in untaxed cash . . . on the quiet?'

He was more amused than offended. 'I wouldn't say it hasn't been done on every farm that ever existed. But I wouldn't do it with Sandcastle . . . or at any rate not this year. He's still young. And untested, of course. Some stallions won't look at as many as forty mares . . . though shy breeders do tend to run in families, and there's nothing in his pedigree to suggest he'll be anything but energetic and fertile. I wouldn't have embarked on all this if there had been any doubts.'

It seemed that he was trying to reassure himself as much as me; as if the size and responsibility of his undertaking had only just penetrated, and in penetrating, frightened.

I felt a faint tremor of dismay but stifled it with the reassurance that come hell or high water Sandcastle was worth his buying price and could be sold again even at this late date for not much less. The bank's money was safe on his hoof.

It was earlier in the day than my last visit – eleven in the morning – and more lads than before were to be seen mucking out the boxes and carrying feed and water.

'I've had to take on extra hands,' Oliver Knowles said matter-of-factly. 'Temporarily, for the season.'

'Has recruitment been difficult?' I asked.

'Not really. I do it every spring. I keep the good ones on for the whole year, if they'll stay, of course: these lads come and go as the whim takes them, the unmarried ones, that is. I keep the nucleus on and put them painting fences and such in the autumn and winter.'

We strolled into the second yard, where the butty figure of Nigel could be seen peering over a half-door into a box.

'You remember Nigel?' Oliver said. 'My stud manager?'

Nigel, I noted, had duly been promoted.

'And Ginnie,' I asked, as we walked over, 'is she home today?'

'Yes, she's somewhere about.' He looked around as if expecting her to materialise at the sound of her name, but nothing happened.

'How's it going, Nigel?' he asked.

Nigel's hairy eyebrows withdrew from the box and aimed themselves in our direction. 'Floradora's eating again,' he said, indicating the inspected lady and sounding relieved. 'And Pattacake is still in labour. I'm just going back there.'

'We'll come,' Oliver said. 'If you'd like to?' he added, looking at me questioningly.

I nodded and walked on with them along the path into the third, smaller quadrangle, the foaling yard.

Here too, in this place that had been empty, there was purposeful life, and the box to which Nigel led us was larger than normal and thickly laid with straw.

'Foals usually drop at night,' Oliver said, and Nigel nodded. 'She started about midnight. She's just lazy, eh, girl?' He patted the brown rump. 'Very slow. Same thing every year.'

'She's not come for Sandcastle, then?' I said.

'No. She's one of mine,' Oliver said. 'The foal's by Diarist.'

We hovered for a few minutes but there was no change in Pattacake. Nigel, running delicately knowledgeable hands over the shape under her ribs, said she'd be another hour, perhaps, and that he would stay with her for a while. Oliver and I walked onwards, past the still closed breeding shed and down the path between the two small paddocks towards the stallion yard. Everything, as before, meticulously tidy.

There was one four-legged figure in one of the paddocks, head down and placid. 'Parakeet,' Oliver said. 'Getting more air than grass, actually. It isn't warm enough yet for the new grass to grow.'

We came finally to the last yard, and there he was, the gilt-edged Sandcastle, looking over his door like any other horse.

One couldn't tell, I thought. True there was a poise to the well-shaped head, and an interested eye and alertly pricked ears, but nothing to announce that this was the marvellous creature I'd seen at Ascot. No one ever again, I reflected, would see that arrow-like raking gallop, that sublime throat-catching valour: and it seemed a shame that he would be denied his ability in the hope that he would pass it on.

A lad, broom in hand, was sweeping scatterings of peat off the concrete apron in front of the six stallion boxes, watched by Sandcastle, Rotaboy and Diarist with the same depth of interest as a bus queue would extend to a busker.

'Lenny,' Oliver said, 'you can take Sandcastle down to the small paddock opposite to the one with Parakeet.' He looked up at the sky as if to sniff the coming weather. 'Put him back in his box when you return for evening stables.'

'Yes, sir.'

Lenny was well into middle age, small, leathery and of obviously long experience. He propped the broom against one of the empty boxes and disappeared into a doorway to reappear presently carrying a length of rope.

'Lenny is one of my most trusted helpers,' Oliver Knowles said. 'Been with me several years. He's good with stallions and much stronger than he looks. Stallions can be quite difficult to handle, but Lenny gets on with them better than with mares. Don't know why.'

Lenny clipped the rope onto the headcollar which Sandcastle, along with every other equine resident, wore at all times. Upon the headcollar was stapled a metal plate bearing the horse's name, an absolute essential for identification. Shuffle all those mares together without their headcollars, I thought, and no one would ever sort them. I suggested the problem mildly to Oliver, who positively blenched. 'God forbid! Don't suggest such things. We're very careful. Have to be. Otherwise, as you say, we could breed the wrong mare to the wrong stallion and never know it.'

I wondered, but privately, how often that in fact had happened, or whether indeed it was possible for two mares or two foals to be permanently swapped. The opportunities for mistakes, if not for outright fraud, put computer manipulation in the shade.

Nigel arrived in the yard, and with his scarcely necessary help Lenny opened Sandcastle's door and led the colt out; and one could see in all their strength the sleek muscles, the tugging sinews, the spring-like joints. The body that was worth its weight in gold pranced and scrunched on the hard apron, wheeling round impatiently and tossing its uncomprehending head.

'Full of himself,' Oliver explained. 'We have to feed him well and keep him fairly fit, but of course he doesn't get the exercise he used to.'

We stepped to one side with undignified haste to avoid Sandcastle's restless hindquarters. 'Has he . . . er . . . started work yet?' I asked.

'Not yet,' Oliver said. 'Only one of his mares has foaled so far. She's almost through her foal-heat, so when she comes into use in fifteen or sixteen days time, she'll be his first. After that there will be a pause – give him time to think! – then he'll be busy until into June.'

'How often . . .?' I murmured delicately.

Oliver fielded the question as if he, like Calder, had had to give the same answer countless times over.

'It depends on the stallion,' he said. 'Some can cover one mare in the morning and another in the afternoon and go on like that for days. Others haven't that much stamina or that much desire. Occasionally you get very shy and choosy stallions. Some of them won't go near some mares but will mate all right with others. Some will cover only one mare a fortnight, if that. Stallions aren't machines, you know, they're individual like everyone else.'

With Nigel in attendance Lenny led Sandcastle out of the

yard, the long bay legs stalking in powerful strides beside the almost trotting little man.

'Sandcastle will be all right with mares,' Oliver said again firmly. 'Most stallions are.'

We stopped for Oliver to give two carrots and a pat each to Rotaboy and Diarist, so that we didn't ourselves see the calamity. We heard a distant clatter and a yell and the thud of fast hooves, and Oliver went white as he turned to run to the disaster.

I followed him, also sprinting.

Lenny lay against one of the white painted posts of the small paddock's rails, dazedly trying to pull himself up. Sandcastle, loose and excited, had found his way into one of the paths between the larger paddocks and from his bolting speed must have taken the rails to be those of a racecourse.

Nigel stood by the open gate of the small paddock, his mouth wide as if arrested there by shock. He was still almost speechless when Oliver and I reached him, but had at least begun to unstick.

'For Christ's sake,' Oliver shouted. 'Get going. Get the Land Rover. He can get out onto the road that way through the Watcherleys'. He ran off in the direction of his own house leaving a partially resurrected Nigel to stumble off towards the bungalow, half in sight beyond the stallion yard.

Lenny raised himself and began his excuses, but I didn't wait to listen. Unused to the problem and ignorant of how best to catch fleeing horses, I simply set off in Sandcastle's wake, following his path between the paddocks and seeing him disappear ahead of me behind a distant hedge.

I ran fast along the grassy path between the rails, past the groups of incurious mares in the paddocks, thinking that my brief January holiday ski-ing down the pistes at Gstaad might have its practical uses after all; there was currently a lot more muscle in my legs than was ever to be found by July.

Whereas on my last visit the hedge between Oliver Knowles' farm and the Watcherleys' run-down hospital for sick horses had been a thorny unbroken boundary, there were now two or three wide gaps, so that passing from one side to the other was easy. I pounded through the gap which lay straight ahead and noticed almost unconsciously that the Watcherleys' dilapidation had been not only halted but partially reversed, with new fencing going up and repairs in hand on the roofs.

I ran towards the stable buildings across a thistly field in which there was no sign of Sandcastle, and through an as yet unmended gate which hung open on broken hinges on the far side. Beyond there between piles of rubble and rusting iron I reached the yard itself, to find Ginnie looking around her with unfocussed anxiety and a man and a girl walking towards her enquiringly.

Ginnie saw me running, and her first instinctively cheerful greeting turned almost at once to alarm.

'What is it?' she said. 'Is one of the mares out?'

'Sandcastle.'

'Oh no . . .' It was a wail of despair. 'He can get on the road.' She turned away, already running, and I ran after her; out of the Watcherleys' yard, round their ramshackle house and down the short weedy gateless drive to the dangerous outside world where a car could kill a horse without even trying.

'We'll never catch him,' Ginnie said as we reached the road. 'It's no use running. We don't know which way he went.' She was in great distress: eyes flooding, tears on her cheeks. 'Where's Dad?'

'I should think he's out in his car, looking. And Nigel's in a Land Rover.'

'I heard a horse gallop through the Watcherleys',' she said. 'I was in one of the boxes with a foal. I never thought . . . I mean, I thought it might be a mare . . .'

A speeding car passed in front of us, followed closely by two others doing at least sixty miles an hour, one of them dicily passing a heavy articulated lorry which should have been home in its nest on a Sunday. The thought of Sandcastle loose in that battlefield was literally goose-pimpling and I began for the first time to believe in his imminent destruction. One of those charging monsters would be sure to hit him. He would waver across the road into their path, swerving, rudderless, hopelessly vulnerable . . . a five million pound traffic accident in the making.

'Let's go this way,' I said, pointing to the left. A motor-cyclist roared from that direction, head down in a black visor, going too fast to stop.

Ginnie shook her head sharply. 'Dad and Nigel will be on the road. But there's a track over there . . .' She pointed slantwise across the road. 'He might just have found it. And there's a bit of a hill and even if he isn't up there at least we might see him from there . . . you can see the road in places . . . I often ride up there.' She was off again, running while she talked, and I fell in beside her. Her face was screwed up with the intensity of her feeling and I felt as much sympathy for her as dismay about the horse. Sandcsatle was insured – I'd vetted the policy myself – but Oliver Knowles' prestige wasn't. The escape and death of the first great stallion in his care would hardly attract future business.

The track was muddy and rutted and slippery from recent rain. There were also a great many hoofprints, some looking new, some overtrodden and old. I pointed to them as we ran and asked Ginnie pantingly if she knew if any of those were Sandcastle's.

'Oh.' She stopped running suddenly. 'Yes. Of course. He hasn't got shoes on. The blacksmith came yesterday, Dad said . . .' She peered at the ground dubiously, '. . . he left Sandcastle without new shoes because he was going to make leather pads for under them . . . I wasn't really listening.' She pointed. 'I think that might be him. Those new marks . . . they could be, they really could.' She began running again up the track, impelled by hope now as well as horror, fit in her jeans and sweater and jodhpur boots after all that compulsory jogging.

I ran beside her thinking that mud anyway washed easily from shoes, socks and trouser legs. The ground began to rise sharply and to narrow between bare-branched scratchy bushes; and the jumble of hoof marks inexorably led on and on.

'Please be up here,' Ginnie was saying. 'Please, Sandcastle, please be up here.' Her urgency pumped in her legs and ran in misery down her cheeks. 'Oh please . . . *please* . . .'

The agony of adolescence, I thought. So real, so overpowering . . . so remembered.

The track curved through the bushes and opened suddenly into a wider place where grass grew in patches beside the rutted mud; and there stood Sandcastle, head high, nostrils twitching to the wind, a brown and black creature of power and beauty and majesty.

Ginnie stopped running in one stride and caught my arm fiercely.

'Don't move,' she said. 'I'll do it. You stay here. Keep still. Please keep still.'

I nodded obediently, respecting her experience. The colt looked ready to run again at the slightest untimely movement, his sides quivering, his legs stiff with tension, his tail sweeping up and down restlessly.

He's frightened, I thought suddenly. He's out here, lost, not knowing where to go. He's never been free before, but his instinct is still wild, still against being caught. Horses were never truly tamed, only accustomed to captivity.

Ginnie walked towards him making crooning noises and holding out her hand palm upwards, an offering hand with nothing to offer. 'Come on, boy,' she said. 'Come on boy, there's a good boy, it's all right, come on now.'

The horse watched her as if he'd never seen a human before, his alarm proclaimed in a general volatile trembling. The rope hung down from the headcollar, its free end curling on the ground; and I wondered whether Ginnie would be able to control the colt if she caught him, where Lenny with all his strength had let him go.

Ginnie came to within a foot of the horse's nose, offering her open left hand upwards and bringing her right hand up slowly under his chin, reaching for the headcollar itself, not the rope: her voice made soothing, murmuring sounds and my own tensed muscles began to relax.

At the last second Sandcastle would have none of it. He wheeled away with a squeal, knocking Ginnie to her knees; took two rocketing strides towards a dense patch of bushes, wheeled again, laid back his ears and accelerated in my direction. Past me lay the open track, down hill again to the slaughtering main road.

Ginnie, seen in peripheral vision, was struggling to her feet in desperation. Without thinking of anything much except perhaps what the horse meant to her family, I jumped not out of his way but at his flying head, my fingers curling for the headcollar and missing that and fastening round the rope.

He nearly tore my arms out of their sockets and all the skin off my palms. He yanked me off my feet, pulled me through the mud and trampled on my legs. I clung all the same with both hands to the rope and bumped against his shoulder and knee, and shortly more by weight than skill hauled him to the side of the track and into the bushes.

The bushes, indeed, acted as an anchor. He couldn't drag my heaviness through them, not if I kept hold of the rope; and I wound the rope clumsily round a stump of branch for leverage, and that was roughly that. Sandcastle stood the width of the bush away, crossly accepting the inevitable, tossing his head and quivering but no longer trying for full stampede.

Ginnie appeared round the curve in the track, running and if possible looking more than ever distraught. When she saw me she stumbled and half fell and came up to me uninhibitedly crying.

'Oh, I'm so glad, so glad, and you should never do that, you can be killed, you should never do it, and I'm so grateful, so glad . . . oh dear.' She leant against me weakly and like a child wiped her eyes and nose on my sleeve.

'Well,' I said pragmatically, 'what do we do with him now?'

What we decided, upon consideration, was that I and Sandcastle should stay where we were, and that Ginnie should go and find Nigel or her father, neither she nor I being confident of leading our prize home without reinforcements.

While she was gone I made an inventory of damage, but so far as my clothes went there was nothing the cleaners couldn't see to, and as for the skin, it would grow again pretty soon. My legs though bruised were functioning, and there was nothing broken or frightful. I made a ball of my handkerchief in my right palm which was bleeding slightly and thought that one of these days a habit of launching oneself at things like fleeing stallions and boys with knives might prove to be unwise.

Oliver, Ginnie, Nigel and Lenny all appeared in the Land Rover, gears grinding and wheels spinning in the mud. Sandcastle, to their obvious relief, was upon inspection pronounced sound, and Oliver told me forcefully that *no one*, should *ever*, repeat *ever*, try to stop a bolting horse in that way.

'I'm sorry,' I said.

'You could have been killed.'

'So Ginnie said.'

'Didn't it occur to you?' He sounded almost angry; the aftermath of fright. 'Didn't you *think*?'

'No,' I said truthfully. 'I just did it.'

'Never do it again,' he said, 'And thanks,' he paused and swallowed and tried to make light of his own shattered state. 'Thanks for taking care of my investment.'

Lenny and Nigel had brought a different sort of headcollar which involved a bit in the mouth and a fierce looking curb chain, and with these in place the captive (if not chastened) fugitive was led away. There seemed to me to be a protest in the stalking hindquarters, a statement of disgust at the injustices of life. I smiled at that fanciful thought; the pathetic fallacy, the ascribing to animals of emotions one felt only oneself.

Oliver drove Ginnie and me back in the Land Rover, travelling slowly behind the horse and telling how Nigel and Lenny had allowed him to go free.

'Sheer bloody carelessness,' he said forthrightly. 'Both of them should know better. They could see the horse was fresh and jumping out of his skin yet Lenny was apparently holding the rope with one hand and stretching to swing the gate open with the other. He took his eyes off Sandcastle so he wasn't ready when Nigel made some sharp movement or other and the horse reared and ran backwards. I ask you! Lenny! Nigel! How can they be so bloody stupid after all these years?'

There seemed to be no answer to that so we just let him curse away, and he was still rumbling like distant thunder when the journey ended. Once home he hurried off to the stallion yard and Ginnie trenchantly said that if Nigel was as sloppy with discipline for animals as he was with the lads, it was no wonder any horse with spirit would take advantage.

'Accidents happen,' I said mildly.

'Huh.' She was scornful. 'Dad's right. That accident *shouldn't* have happened. It was an absolute miracle that Sandcastle came to no harm at all. Even if he hadn't got out on the road he could have tried to jump the paddock rails – loose horses often do – and broken his leg or something.' She sounded as angry as her father, and for the same reason; the flooding release after fear. I put my arm round her shoulders and gave her a quick hug, which seemed to disconcert her horribly. 'Oh dear, you must think me so silly . . . and crying like that . . . and everything.'

'I think you're a nice dear girl who's had a rotten morning,' I said. 'But all's well now, you know; it really is.'

I naturally believed what I said, but I was wrong.

The Second Year

APRIL

Calder Jackson finally came to dinner with me while he was staying in London to attend a world conference of herbalists. He would be glad, he said, to spend one of the evenings away from his colleagues, and I met him in a restaurant on the grounds that although my flat was civilised my cooking was not.

I sensed immediately a difference in him, though it was hard to define; rather as if he had become a figure still larger than life. Heads turned and voices whispered when we walked through the crowded place to our table, but because of television this would have happened anyway. Yet now, I thought, Calder really enjoyed it. There was still no overt arrogance, still a becoming modesty of manner, but something within him had intensified, crystallised, become a governing factor. He was now, I thought, even to himself, the Great Man.

I wondered what, if anything, had specifically altered him, and it turned out to be the one thing I would have least expected: Ian Pargetter's death.

Over a plateful of succulent smoked salmon Calder apologised for the abrupt way he'd brushed me off on the telephone on that disturbing night, and I said it was most understandable.

'Fact is,' Calder said, squeezing lemon juice, 'I was afraid my whole business would collapse. Ian's partners, you know, never approved of me. I was afraid they would influence everyone against me, once Ian had gone.'

'And it hasn't worked out that way?'

He shook his head, assembling a pink forkful. 'Remarkably not. Amazing.' He put the smoked salmon in his mouth and made appreciative noises, munching. I was aware, and I guessed he was, too, that the ears of the people at the tables on either side were almost visibly attuned to the distinctive voice, to the clear loud diction with its country edge. 'My yard's still full. People have faith, you know. I may not get quite so many racehorses, that's to be expected, but still a few.'

'And have you heard any more about Ian Pargetter's death? Did they ever find out who killed him?'

He looked regretful. 'I'm sure they haven't. I asked one of his partners the other day, and he said no one seemed to be asking questions any more. He was quite upset. And so am I. I suppose finding his murderer won't bring Ian back, but all the same one wants to *know*.'

'Tell me some of your recent successes,' I said, nodding, changing the subject and taking a slice of paper-thin brown bread and butter. 'I find your work tremendously interesting.' I also found it about the only thing else to talk about, as we seemed to have few other points of contact. Regret it as I might, there was still no drift towards an easy personal friendship.

Calder ate some more smoked salmon while he thought. 'I had a colt,' he said at last, 'a two-year-old in training. Ian had been treating him, and he'd seemed to be doing well. Then about three weeks after Ian died the colt started bleeding into his mouth and down his nose and went on and on doing it, and as Ian's partner couldn't find out the trouble the trainer persuaded the owner to send the horse to me.'

'And did you discover what was wrong?' I asked.

'Oh no.' He shook his head. 'It wasn't necessary. I laid my hands on him on three succeeding days, and the bleeding stopped immediately. I kept him at my place for two weeks altogether, and returned him on his way back to full good health.'

The adjacent tables were fascinated, as indeed I was myself.

'Did you give him herbs?' I asked.

'Certainly. Of course. And alfalfa in his hay. Excellent for many ills, alfalfa.'

I had only the haziest idea of what alfalfa looked like, beyond it being some sort of grass.

'The one thing you can't do with herbs,' he said confidently, 'is *harm*.'

I raised my eyebrows with my mouth full.

He gave the nearest thing to a grin. 'With ordinary medicines one has to be so careful because of their power and their side effects, but if I'm not certain what's wrong with a horse I can give it all the herbal remedies I can think of all at once in the hope that one of them will hit the target, and it quite often does. It may be hopelessly unscientific, but if a trained vet can't tell exactly what's wrong with a horse, how can I?'

I smiled with undiluted pleasure. 'Have some wine,' I said.

He nodded the helmet of curls, and the movement I made towards the bottle in its ice-bucket was instantly forestalled by a watchful waiter who poured almost reverently into the healer's glass.

'How was the American trip,' I asked, 'way back in January?'

'Mm.' He sipped his wine. 'Interesting.' He frowned a little and went back to finishing the salmon, leaving me wondering whether that was his total answer. When he'd laid down his knife and fork however he sat back in his chair and told me that the most enjoyable part of his American journey had been, as he'd expected, his few days on the ski slopes; and we discussed ski-ing venues throughout the roast beef and burgundy which followed.

With the crepes suzette I asked after Dissdale and Bettina and heard that Dissdale had been to New York on a business trip and that Bettina had been acting a small part in a British movie, which Dissdale hadn't known whether to be pleased about or not. 'Too many gorgeous young studs around,' Calder said, smiling. 'Dissdale gets worried anyway, and he was away for ten days.'

I pondered briefly about Calder's own seemingly non-existent sex-life: but he'd never seen me with a girl either, and certainly there was no hint in him of the homosexual.

Over coffee, running out of subjects, I asked about his yard in general, and how was the right-hand-man Jason in particular.

Calder shrugged. 'He's left. They come and go, you know. No loyalty these days.'

'And you don't fear . . . well, that he'd take your knowledge with him?'

He looked amused. 'He didn't know much. I mean, I'd hand out a pill and tell Jason which horse to give it to. That sort of thing.'

We finished amiably enough with a glass of brandy for each and a cigar for him, and I tried not to wince over the bill.

'A very pleasant evening,' Calder said. 'You must come out to lunch again one day.'

'I'd like to.'

We sat for a final few minutes opposite each other in a pause of mutual appraisal: two people utterly different but bonded by one-tenth of a second on a pavement in Ascot. Saved and saver, inextricably interested in the other; a continuing curiosity which would never quite lose touch. I smiled at him slowly and got a smile in return, but all surface, no depth, a mirror exactly of my own feelings.

In the office things were slowly changing. John had boasted too often of his sexual conquests and complained too often about my directorship, and Gordon's almost-equal had tired of such waste of time. I'd heard from Val Fisher in a perhaps edited version that at a small and special seniors meeting (held in my absence and without my knowledge) Gordon's almost-equal had said he would like to boot John vigorously over St Paul's. His opinion was respected. I heard from Alec one day merely that the mosquito which had stung me for so long had been squashed, and on going along the passage to investigate had found John's desk empty and his bull-like presence but a quiver in the past.

'He's gone to sell air-conditioning to Eskimos,' Alec said, and Gordon's almost-equal, smiling affably, corrected it more probably to a partnership with some brokers on the Stock Exchange.

Alec himself seemed restless, as if his own job no longer held him enthralled.

'It's all right for you,' he said once. 'You've the gift. You've the *sight.* I can't tell a gold mine from a pomegranate at five paces, and it's taken me all these years to know it.'

'But you're a conjuror,' I said. 'You can rattle up outside money faster than anyone.'

'Gift of the old gab, you mean.' He looked uncharacteristically gloomy. 'Syrup with a chisel in it.' He waved his hand towards the desks of our new older colleagues, who had both gone out to lunch. 'I'll end up like them, still here, still smooth-talking, part of the furniture, coming up to *sixty.*' His voice held disbelief that such an age could be achieved. 'That isn't life, is it? That's not *all*?'

I said that I supposed it might be.

'Yes, but for you it's exciting,' he said. 'I mean, you love it. Your eyes *gleam.* You get your kicks right here in this room. But I'll never be made a director, let's face it, and I have this grotty feeling that time's slipping away, and soon it will be too late to start anything else.'

'Like what?'

'Like being an actor. Or a doctor. Or an acrobat.'

'It's been too late for that since you were six.'

'Yeah,' he said. 'Lousy, isn't it?' He put his heart and soul ten minutes later, however, into tracking down a source of a hundred thousand for several years and lending it to a businessman at a profitable rate, knitting together such loan packages all afternoon with diligence and success.

I hoped he would stay. He was the yeast of the office: my bubbles in the dough. As for myself, I had grown accustomed to being on the board and had slowly found I'd reached a new level of confidence. Gordon seemed to treat me unreservedly as an equal, though it was not until he had been doing it for some time that I looked back and realised.

Gordon's hitherto uniformly black hair had grown a streak or two of grey. His right hand now trembled also, and his handwriting had grown smaller through his efforts to control his fingers. I watched his valiant struggles to appear normal and respected his privacy by never making even a visual comment: it had become second nature to look anywhere but directly at his hands. In the brain department he remained energetic, but physically over all he was slowing down.

I had only seen Judith once since Christmas, and that had been in the office at a retirement party given for the head of Corporate Finance, a golden-handshake affair to which all managers' wives had been invited.

'How are you?' she said amid the throng, holding a glass of wine and an unidentifiable canapé and smelling of violets.

'Fine. And you?'

'Fine.'

She was wearing blue, with diamonds in her ears. I looked at her with absolute and unhappy love and saw the strain it put into her face.

'I'm sorry,' I said.

She shook her head and swallowed. 'I thought . . . it might be different . . . here in the bank.'

'No.'

She looked down at the canapé, which was squashy and yellow. 'If I don't eat this damned thing soon it'll drop down my dress.'

I took it out of her fingers and deposited it in an ashtray. 'Invest in a salami cornet. They stay rock-hard for hours.'

'What's Tim telling you to invest in?' demanded Henry Shipton, turning to us a beaming face.

'Salami,' Judith said.

'Typical. He lent money to a seaweed processor last week. Judith, my darling, let me freshen your glass.'

He took the glass away to the bottles and left us again looking at each other with a hundred ears around.

'I was thinking,' I said, 'When it's warmer, could I take you and Gordon, and Pen if she'd like it, out somewhere one Sunday? Somewhere not ordinary. All day.'

She took longer than normal politeness to answer, and I understood all the unspoken things, but finally, as Henry could be seen returning, she said, 'Yes. We'd all like it. I'd like it . . . very much.'

'Here you are,' Henry said. 'Tim, you go and fight for your own refill, and leave me to talk to this gorgeous girl.' He put his arm round her shoulders and swept her off, and although I was vividly aware all evening of her presence, we had no more moments alone.

From day to day when she wasn't around I didn't precisely suffer: her absence was more of a faint background ache. When I saw Gordon daily in the office I felt no constant envy, nor hated him, nor even thought much of where he slept. I liked him for the good clever man he was, and our office relationship continued unruffled and secure. Loving Judith was both pleasure and pain, delight and deprivation, wishes withdrawn, dreams denied. It might have been easier and more sensible to have met and fallen heavily for some young glamorous unattached stranger, but the one thing love never did have was logic.

'Easter,' I said to Gordon one day in the office. 'Are you and Judith going away?'

'We had plans – they fell through.'

'Did Judith mention that I'd like to take you both somewhere – and Pen Warner – as a thank you for Christmas?'

'Yes, I believe she did.'

'Easter Monday, then?'

He seemed pleased at the idea and reported the next day that Judith had asked Pen, and everyone was poised. 'Pen's bringing her kite,' he said. 'Unless it's a day trip to Manchester.'

'I'll think of something,' I said, laughing. 'Tell her it won't be raining.'

* * *

What I did eventually think of seemed to please them all splendidly and also to be acceptable to others concerned, and I consequently collected Gordon and Judith and Pen (but not the kite) from Clapham at eight-thirty on Easter Bank Holiday morning. Judith and Pen were in fizzing high spirits, though Gordon seemed already tired. I suggested abandoning what was bound to be a fairly taxing day for him, but he wouldn't hear of it.

'I want to go,' he said. 'Been looking forward to it all week. But I'll just sit in the back of the car and rest and sleep some of the way.' So Judith sat beside me while I drove and touched my hand now and then, not talking much but contenting me deeply by just being there. The journey to Newmarket lasted two and a half hours and I would as soon it had gone on for ever.

I was taking them to Calder's yard, to the utter fascination of Pen. 'But don't tell him I'm a pharmacist,' she said. 'He might clam up if he knew he had an informed audience.'

'We won't tell,' Judith assured her. 'It would absolutely spoil the fun.'

Poor Calder, I thought: but I wouldn't tell him either.

He greeted us expansively (making me feel guilty) and gave us coffee in the huge oak-beamed sitting room where the memory of Ian Pargetter hovered peripherally by the fireplace.

'Delighted to see you again,' Calder said, peering at Gordon, Judith and Pen as if trying to conjure a memory to fit their faces. He knew of course who they were by name, but Ascot was ten months since, and although it had been an especially memorable day for him he had met a great many new people between then and now. 'Ah *yes,*' he said with relief, his brow clearing. 'Yellow hat with roses.'

Judith laughed. 'Well done.'

'Can't forget anyone so pretty.'

She took it as it was meant, but indeed he hadn't forgotten: as one tended never to forget people whose vitality brought out the sun.

'I see Dissdale and Bettina quite often,' he said, making conversation, and Gordon agreed that he and Judith, also, sometimes saw Dissdale, though infrequently. As a topic it was hardly riveting, but served as an acceptable unwinding interval between the long car journey and the Grand Tour.

The patients in the boxes were all different but their ailments seemed the same; and I supposed surgeons could be excused their impersonal talk of 'the appendix in bed 14', when the occupants changed week by week but the operation didn't.

'This is a star three-day-eventer who came here five weeks ago with severe muscular weakness and no appetite. Wouldn't eat. Couldn't be ridden. He goes home tomorrow, strong and thriving. Looks well, eh?' Calder patted the glossy brown neck over the half-stable door. 'His owner thought he was dying, poor girl. She was weeping when she brought him here. It's really satisfying, you know, to be able to help.'

Gordon said civilly that it must be.

'This is a two-year-old not long in training. Came with an intractably infected wound on his fetlock. He's been here a week, and he's healing. It was most gratifying that the trainer sent him without delay, since I'd treated several of his horses in the past.'

'This mare,' Calder went on, moving us all along, 'came two or three days ago in great discomfort with blood in her urine. She's responding well, I'm glad to say.' He patted this one too, as he did them all.

'What was causing the bleeding?' Pen asked, but with only an uninformed-member-of-the-public intonation.

Calder shook his head. 'I don't know. His vet diagnosed a kidney infection complicated by crystalluria, which means crystals in the urine, but he didn't know the type of germ and, every antibiotic he gave failed to work. So the mare came here. Last resort.' He gave me a wink. 'I'm thinking of simply renaming this whole place "Last Resort".'

'And you're treating her,' Gordon asked, 'with herbs?'

'With everything I can think of,' Calder said. 'And of course . . . with hands.'

'I suppose,' Judith said diffidently, 'that you'd never let anyone watch . . . ?'

'My dear lady, for you, anything,' Calder said. 'But you'd see nothing. You might stand for half an hour, and nothing would happen. It would be terribly boring. And I might, perhaps, be *unable*, you know, if someone was waiting and standing there.'

Judith smiled understandingly and the tour continued, ending as before in the surgery.

Pen stood looking about her with sociable blankness and then wandered over to the glass-fronted cabinets to peer myopically at the contents.

Calder, happily ignoring her in favour of Judith, was pulling out his antique tablet-maker and demonstrating it with pride.

'It's beautiful,' Judith said sincerely. 'Do you use it much?'

'All the time,' he said. 'Any herbalist worth the name makes his own pills and potions.'

'Tim said you had a universal magic potion in the fridge.'

Calder smiled and obligingly opened the refrigerator door, revealing the brown-filled plastic containers, as before.

'What's in it?' Judith asked.

'Trade secret,' he said, smiling. 'Decoction of hops and other things.'

'Like beer?' Judith said.

'Yes, perhaps.'

'Horses do drink beer,' Gordon said. 'Or so I've heard.'

Pen bent down to pick up a small peach-coloured pill which was lying unobtrusively on the floor in the angle of one of the cupboards, and put it without comment on the bench.

'It's all so *absorbing,*' Judith said. 'So tremendously kind of you to show us everything. I'll watch all your programmes with more fervour than ever.'

Calder responded to her warmly as all men did and asked us into the house again for a drink before we left. Gordon however was still showing signs of fatigue and now also hiding both hands in his pockets which meant he felt they were trembling badly, so the rest of us thanked Calder enthusiastically for his welcome and made admiring remarks about his hospital and climbed into the car, into the same places as before.

'Come back any time you like, Tim,' he said; and I said thank you and perhaps I would. We shook hands, and we smiled, caught in our odd relationship and unable to take it further. He waved, and I waved back as I drove away.

'Isn't he amazing?' Judith said. 'I must say, Tim, I do understand why you're impressed.'

Gordon grunted and said that theatrical surgeons weren't necessarily the best; but yes, Calder was impressive.

It was only Pen, after several miles, who expressed her reservations.

'I'm not saying he doesn't do a great deal of good for the horses. Of course he must do, to have amassed such a reputation. But I don't honestly think he does it all with herbs.'

'How do you mean?' Judith asked, twisting round so as to see her better.

Pen leaned forward. 'I found a pill on the floor. I don't suppose you noticed.'

'I did,' I said. 'You put it on the bench.'

'That's right. Well, that was no herb, it was plain straightforward warfarin.'

'It may be plain straightforward war-whatever to you,' Judith said. 'But not to me.'

Pen's voice was smiling. 'Warfarin is a drug used in humans, and I dare say in horses, after things like heart attacks. It's a coumarin – an anticoagulant. Makes the blood less likely to clot and block up the veins and arteries. Widely used all over the place.'

We digested the information in silence for a mile or two, and finally Gordon said 'How do you know it was warfarin? I mean, how can you tell?'

'I handle it every day,' she said. 'I know the dosages, the sizes, the colours, the manufacturers' marks. You see all those things so often, you get to know them at a glance.'

'Do you mean,' I said interestedly, 'that if you saw fifty different pills laid out in a row you could identify the lot?'

'Probably. If they all came from major drug companies and weren't completely new, certainly, yes.'

'Like a wine-taster,' Judith said.

'Clever girl,' Gordon said, meaning Pen.

'It's just habit.' She thought. 'And something else in those cupboards wasn't strictly herbal, I suppose. He had one or two bags of potassium sulphate, bought from Goodison's Garden Centre, wherever that is.'

'Whatever for?' Judith asked. 'Isn't potassium sulphate a fertiliser?'

'Potassium's just as essential to animals as to plants,' Pen said. 'I wouldn't be surprised if it isn't one of the ingredients in that secret brew.'

'What else would you put in it, if you were making it?' I asked curiously.

'Oh heavens.' She pondered. 'Any sort of tonic. Perhaps liquorice root, which he once mentioned. Maybe caffeine. All sorts of vitamins. Just a pepping-up mish-mash.'

The hardest part of the day had been to find somewhere decent to have lunch, and the place I'd chosen via the various gourmet guides turned out, as so often happens, to have changed hands and chefs since the books were written. The resulting repast was slow to arrive and disappointing to eat, but the mood of my guests forgave all.

'You remember,' Gordon said thoughtfully over the coffee, 'that you told us on the way to Newmarket that Calder was worried about his business when that vet was killed?'

'Yes,' I said. 'He was, at the time.'

'Isn't it possible,' Gordon said, 'that the vet was letting Calder have regular official medicines, like warfarin, and Calder thought his supplies would dry up, when the vet died?'

'Gordon!' Judith said. 'How devious you are, darling.'

We all thought about it however, and Pen nodded. 'He must have found another willing source, I should think.'

'But,' I protested, 'would vets really do that?'

'They're not particularly brilliantly paid,' Pen said. 'Not badly by my standards, but they're never *rich*.'

'But Ian Pargetter was very much liked,' I said.

'What's that got to do with it?' Pen said. 'Nothing to stop him passing on a few pills and advice to Calder in return for a fat untaxed fee.'

'To their mutual benefit,' Gordon murmured.

'The healer's feet of clay,' Judith said. 'What a shame.'

The supposition seemed slightly to deflate the remembered pleasure of the morning, but the afternoon's visit put the rest of the day up high.

We went this time to Oliver Knowles' stud farm and found the whole place flooded with foals and mares and activity.

'How *beautiful*,' Judith said, looking away over the stretches of white railed paddocks with their colonies of mothers and babies. 'How speechlessly *great*.'

Oliver Knowles, introduced, was as welcoming as Calder and told Gordon several times that he would never, ever, be out of his debt of gratitude to Paul Ekaterin's, however soon he had paid off his loan.

The anxiety and misgivings to be seen in him on my February visit had all disappeared: Oliver was again, and more so, the capable and decisive executive I had met first. The foals had done well, I gathered. Not one from the mares coming to Sandcastle had been lost, and none of those mares had had any infection, a triumph of care. He told me all this within the first ten minutes, and also that Sandcastle had proved thoroughly potent and fertile and was a dream of a stallion. 'He's tireless,' he said. 'Forty mares will be easy.'

'I'm so glad,' I said, and meant it from the bottom of my banking heart.

With his dog Squibs at his heels he showed us all again through the succession of yards, where since it was approximately four o'clock the evening ritual of mucking out and feeding was in full swing.

'A stud farm is not like a racing stable, of course,' Oliver was explaining to Gordon. 'One lad here can look after far more than three horses, because they don't have to be ridden. And here we have a more flexible system because the mares are sometimes in, sometimes out in the paddocks, and it would be impossible to assign particular mares to particular lads. So here a lad does a particular section of boxes, regardless of which animals are in them.'

Gordon nodded, genially interested.

'Why are some foals in the boxes and some out in the paddocks?' Judith asked, and Oliver without hesitation told her it was because the foals had to stay with their dams, and the mares with foals in the boxes were due to come into heat, or were already in heat, and would go from their boxes to visit the stallion. When their heat was over they would go out into the paddocks, with their foals.

'Oh,' Judith said, blinking slightly at this factory aspect. 'Yes, I see.'

In the foaling yard we came across Nigel and also Ginnie, who ran across to me when she saw me and gave me a great hug and a smacking kiss somewhere to the left of the mouth. Quite an advance in confidence, I thought, and hugged her back, lifting her off her feet and whirling her round in a circle. She was laughing when I put her down, and Oliver watched in some surprise.

'I've never known her so demonstrative,' he said.

Ginnie looked at him apprehensively and held onto my sleeve. 'You didn't mind, did you?' she asked me worriedly.

'I'm flattered,' I said, meaning it and also thinking that her father would kill off her spontaneity altogether if he wasn't careful.

Ginnie, reassured, tucked her arm into mine and said 'Come and look at the newest foal. It was born only about twenty minutes ago. It's a colt. A darling.' She tugged me off, and I caught a fleeting glance of Judith's face which was showing a mixture of all sorts of unreadable thoughts.

'Oliver's daughter,' I said in explanation over my shoulder, and heard Oliver belatedly introducing Nigel.

They all came to look at the foal over the half-door; a glistening little creature half-lying, half-sitting on the thick straw, all long nose, huge eyes and folded legs, new life already making an effort to balance and stand up. The dam, on her feet, alternately bent her head to the foal and looked up at us warily.

'It was an easy one,' Ginnie said. 'Nigel and I just watched.'

'Have you seen many foals born?' Pen asked her.

'Oh, hundreds. All my life. Most often at night.'

Pen looked at her as if she, as I did, felt the imagination stirred by such an unusual childhood: as if she, like myself, had never seen one single birth of any sort, let alone a whole procession by the age of fifteen.

'This mare has come to Sandcastle,' Oliver said.

'And will that foal win the Derby?' Gordon asked, smiling.

Oliver smiled in return. 'You never know. He has the breeding.' He breathed deeply, expanding his chest. 'I've never been able to say anything like that before this year. No foal born or conceived here has in the past won a classic, but now . . .' he gestured widely with his arm, '. . . one day, from these . . .' he paused. 'It's a whole new world. It's . . . tremendous.'

'As good as you hoped?' I asked.

'Better.'

He had a soul after all, I thought, under all that tidy martial efficiency. A vision of the peaks, which he was reaching in reality. And how soon, I wondered, before the glossy became commonplace, the Classic winners a routine, the aristocrats the common herd. It would be what he'd aimed for; but in a way it would be blunting.

We left the foal and went on down the path past the breeding shed, where the main door was today wide open, showing the floor thickly covered with soft brown crumbly peat. Beyond succinctly explaining what went on there when it was inhabited, Oliver made no comment, and we all walked on without stopping to the heart of the place, to the stallions.

Lenny was there, walking one of the horses round the small yard and plodding with his head down as if he'd been doing it for some time. The horse was dripping with sweat, and from the position of the one open empty box I guessed he would be Rotaboy.

'He's just covered a mare,' Oliver said matter-of-factly. 'He's always like that afterwards.'

Judith and Gordon and Pen all looked as if the overt sex of the place was earthier than they'd expected, even without hearing, as I had at one moment, Oliver quietly discussing a vaginal disinfectant process with Nigel. They rallied valiantly however and gazed with proper awe at the head of Sandcastle which swam into view from the inside-box shadows.

He held himself almost imperiously, as if his new role had basically changed his character; and perhaps it had. I had myself seen during my renewed interest in racing how constant success endowed some horses with definite 'presence', and Sandcastle, even lost and frightened up on top of the hill, had perceptibly had it; but now, only two months later, there was a new quality one might almost call arrogance, a fresh certainty of his own supremacy.

'He's splendid,' Gordon exclaimed. 'What a treat to see him again after that great day at Ascot.'

Oliver gave Sandcastle the usual two carrots and a couple of pats, treating the King with familiarity. Neither Judith nor Pen, nor indeed Gordon or myself, tried even to touch the sensitive nose: afraid of getting our fingers bitten off at the wrist, no doubt. It was all right to admire, but distance had virtue.

Lenny put the calming-down Rotaboy back in his box and started mucking out Diarist next door.

'We have two lads looking after the stallions full time,' Oliver said. 'Lenny, here, and another much trusted man, Don. And Nigel feeds them.'

Pen caught the underlying thought behind his words and asked, 'Do you need much security?'

'Some,' he said, nodding. 'We have the yard wired for sound, so either Nigel or I, when we're in our houses, can hear if there are any irregular noises.'

'Like hooves taking a walk?' Judith suggested.

'Exactly.' He smiled at her. 'We also have smoke alarms and massive extinguishers.'

'And brick-built boxes and combination locks on these door bolts at night and lockable gates on all the ways out to the roads,' Ginnie said, chattily. 'Dad's really gone to town on security.'

'Glad to hear it,' Gordon said.

I smiled to myself at the classic example of bolting the stable door after the horse had done likewise, but indeed one could see that Oliver had learned a dire lesson and knew he'd been lucky to be given a second chance.

We began after a while to walk back towards the house, stopping again in the foaling yard to look at the new baby colt, who was now shakily on his feet and searching round for his supper.

Oliver drew me to one side and asked if I would like to see Sandcastle cover a mare, an event apparently scheduled for a short time hence.

'Yes, I would,' I said.

'I can't ask them all – there isn't room,' he said. 'I'll get Ginnie to show them the mares and foals in the paddocks and then take them indoors for tea.'

No one demurred at this suggested programme, especially as Oliver didn't actually mention where he and I were going: Judith, I was sure, would have preferred to join us. Ginnie took them and Squibs off, and I could hear her saying 'Over there, next door, there's another yard. We could walk over that way if you like.'

Oliver, eyeing them amble along the path that Sandcastle had taken at a headlong gallop and I at a sprint, said, 'The Watcherleys look after any delicate foals or any mares with infections. It's all worked out most satisfactorily. I rent their place and they work for me, and their expertise with sick animals comes in very useful.'

'And you were mending their fences for them, I guess, when I came in February.'

'That's right.' He sighed ruefully. 'Another week and the gates would have been up in the hedge and across their driveway, and Sandcastle would never have got out.'

'No harm done,' I said.

'Thanks to you, no.'

We went slowly back towards the breeding shed. 'Have you seen a stallion at work before?' he asked.

'No, I haven't.'

After a pause he said, 'It may seem strong to you. Even violent. But it's normal to them. Remember that. And he'll probably bite her neck, but it's as much to keep himself in position as an expression of passion.'

'All right,' I said.

'This mare, the one we're breeding, is receptive, so there won't be any trouble. Some mares are shy, some are slow to arouse, some are irritable, just like humans.' He smiled faintly. 'This little lady is a born one-nighter.'

It was the first time I'd heard him make anything like a joke about his profession and I was almost startled. As if himself surprised at his own words he said more soberly, 'We put her to Sandcastle yesterday morning, and all went well.'

'The mares go more than once then, to the stallion?' I asked.

He nodded. 'It depends of course on the stud farm, but I'm very anxious as you can guess that all the mares here shall have the best possible chance of conceiving. I bring them all at least twice to the stallion during their heat, then we put them out in the paddocks and wait, and if they come into heat again it means they haven't conceived, so we repeat the breeding process.'

'And how long do you go on trying?'

'Until the end of July. That means the foal won't be born until well on in June, which is late in the year for racehorses. Puts them at a disadvantage as two-year-olds, racing against March and April foals which have had more growing time.' He smiled. 'With any luck Sandcastle won't have any late June foals. It's too early to be complacent, but none of the mares he covered three weeks or more ago has come back into use.'

We reached and entered the breeding shed where the mare already stood, held at the head in a loose twitch by one lad and being washed and attended to by another.

'She can't wait, sir,' that lad said, indicating her tail, which she was holding high, and Oliver replied rather repressively, 'Good.'

Nigel and Lenny came with Sandcastle, who looked eagerly aware of where he was and what for. Nigel closed the door to keep the ritual private; and the mating which followed was swift and sure and utterly primaeval. A copulation of thrust and grandeur, of vigour and pleasure, not without tenderness: remarkably touching.

'They're not all like that,' Oliver remarked prosaically, as Sandcastle slid out and backwards and brought his forelegs to earth with a jolt. 'You've seen a good one.'

I thanked him for letting me be there, and in truth I felt I understood more about horses then than I'd ever imagined I would.

We walked back to the house with Oliver telling me that with the four stallions there were currently six, seven or eight matings a day in the breeding shed, Sundays included. The mind stuttered a bit at the thought of all that rampaging fertility, but that, after all, was what the bank's five million pounds was all about. Rarely, I thought, had anyone seen Ekaterin's money so fundamentally at work.

We set off homewards fortified by tea, scones and whisky, with Oliver and Gordon at the end competing over who thanked whom most warmly. Ginnie gave me another but more composed hug and begged me to come again, and Judith kissed her and offered female succour if ever needed.

'Nice child,' she said as we drove away. 'Growing up fast.'

'Fifteen,' I said.

'Sixeen. She had a birthday last week.'

'You got on well with her,' I said.

'Yes.' She looked round at Pen and Gordon, who were again sitting in the back. 'She told us about your little escapade here two months ago.'

'She didn't!'

'She sure did,' Pen said, smiling. 'Why ever didn't you say?'

'I know why,' Gordon said dryly. 'He didn't want it to be known in the office that the loan he'd recommended had very nearly fallen under a lorry.'

'Is that right?' Judith asked.

'Very much so,' I admitted wryly. 'Some of the board were against the whole thing anyway, and I'd have never heard the end of the horse getting out.'

'What a coward,' Pen said, chuckling.

We pottered slowly back to Clapham through the stop-go end-of-Bank-Holiday traffic, and Judith and Pen voted it the best day they'd had since Ascot. Gordon dozed, I drove with relaxation and so we finally reached the tall gates by the common.

I went in with them for supper as already arranged, but all of them, not only Gordon, were tired from the long day, and I didn't stay late. Judith came out to the car to see me off and to shut the gates after I'd gone.

We didn't really talk. I held her in my arms, her head on my shoulder, my head on hers, close in the dark night, as far apart as planets.

We stood away and I took her hand, lingering, not wanting all contact lost.

'A great day,' she said, and I said 'Mm', and kissed her very briefly.

Got into the car and drove away.

The Second Year

OCTOBER

Summer had come, summer had gone, sodden, cold and unloved. It had been overcast and windy during Royal Ascot week and Gordon and I, clamped to our telephones and pondering our options, had looked at the sullen sky and hardly minded that this year Dissdale hadn't needed to sell half-shares in his box.

Only with the autumn, far too late, had days of sunshine returned, and it was on a bright golden Saturday that I took the race train to Newbury to see the mixed meeting of two jump races and four flat.

Ursula Young was there, standing near the weighing room when I walked in from the station and earnestly reading her racecard.

'Hello', she said when I greeted her. 'Haven't seen you for ages. How's the money-lending?'

'Profitable,' I said.

She laughed. 'Are you here for anything special?'

'No. Just fresh air and a flutter.'

'I'm supposed to meet a client.' She looked at her watch. 'Time for a quick sandwich, though. Are you on?'

I was on, and bought her and myself a thin pallid slice of tasteless white meat between two thick pallid tasteless slices of soggy-crusted bread, the whole wrapped up in cardboard and cellophane and costing a fortune.

Ursula ate it in disgust. 'They used to serve proper luscious sandwiches, thick, juicy handmade affairs which came in a whole stack. I can't stand all this repulsive hygiene.' The rubbish from the sandwiches indeed littered most of the tables around us . . . 'Every so-called advance is a retreat from excellence,' she said, dogmatic as ever.

I totally agreed with her and we chewed in joyless accord.

'How's trade with you?' I said.

She shrugged. 'Fair. The cream of the yearlings are going for huge prices. They've all got high reserves on them because they've cost so much to produce – stallion fees and the cost of keeping the mare and foal to start with, let alone vet's fees and all the incidentals. My sort of clients on the whole settle for a second, third or fourth rank, and many a good horse, mind you, has come from the bargain counter.'

I smiled at the automatic sales pitch. 'Talking of vets,' I said, 'is the Pargetter murder still unsolved?'

She nodded regretfully. 'I was talking to his poor wife in Newmarket last week. We met in the street. She's only half the girl she was, poor thing, no life in her. She said she asked the police recently if they were still even trying, and they assured her they were, but she doesn't believe it. It's been so long, nine months, and if they hadn't any leads to start with, how can they possibly have any now? She's very depressed, it's dreadful.'

I made sympathetic murmurs, and Ursula went on, 'The only good thing you could say is that he'd taken out decent life insurance and paid off the mortgage on their house, so at least she and the children aren't penniless as well. She was telling me how he'd been very careful in those ways, and she burst into tears, poor girl.'

Ursula looked as if the encounter had distressed her also.

'Have another whisky-mac,' I suggested. 'To cheer you up.'

She looked at her watch. 'All right. You get it, but I'll pay. My turn.'

Over the second drink, in a voice of philosophical irritation, she told me about the client she was presently due to meet, a small-time trainer of steeplechasers. 'He's such a fool to himself,' she said. 'He makes hasty decisions, acts on impulse, and then when things go wrong he feels victimised and cheated and gets angry. Yet he can be perfectly nice when he likes.'

I wasn't especially interested in the touchy trainer, but when I went outside again with Ursula he spotted her from a short distance away and practically pounced on her arm.

'There you are,' he said, as if she'd had no right to be anywhere but at his side. 'I've been looking all over.'

'It's only just time,' she said mildly.

He brushed that aside, a short wiry intense man of about forty with a pork-pie hat above a weatherbeaten face.

'I wanted you to see him before he's saddled,' he said. 'Do come on, Ursula. Come and look at his conformation.'

She opened her mouth to say something to me but he almost forcefully dragged her off, holding her sleeve and talking rapidly into her ear. She gave me an apologetic look of long-suffering and departed in the direction of the pre-parade ring, where the horses for the first race were being led round by their lads before going off to the saddling boxes.

I didn't follow but climbed onto the steps of the main parade ring, round which walked several of the runners already saddled. The last of the field to appear some time later was accompanied by the pork-pie hat, and also Ursula, and for something to do I looked the horse up in the racecard.

Zoomalong, five-year-old gelding, trained by F. Barnet.

F. Barnet continued his dissertation into Ursula's ear, aiming his words from approximately six inches away, which I would have found irritating but which she bore without flinching. According to the flickering numbers on the Tote board Zoomalong had a medium chance in the opinion of the public, so for interest I put a medium stake on him to finish in the first three.

I didn't see Ursula or F. Barnet during the race, but Zoomalong zoomed along quite nicely to finish third, and I walked down from the stands towards the unsaddling enclosure to watch the patting-on-the-back post-race routine.

F. Barnet was there, still talking to Ursula and pointing out parts of his now sweating and stamping charge. Ursula nodded non-committally, her own eyes knowledgeably raking the gelding from stem to stern, a neat competent good looking fifty in a rust-coloured coat and brown velvet beret.

Eventually the horses were led away and the whole cycle of excitement began slowly to regenerate towards the second race.

Without in the least meaning to I again found myself standing near Ursula, and this time she introduced me to the pork-pie hat, who had temporarily stopped talking.

'This is Fred Barnet,' she said. 'And his wife Susan.' A rounded motherly person in blue. 'And their son, Ricky.' A boy taller than his father, dark-haired, pleasant-faced.

I shook hands with all three, and it was while I was still touching the son that Ursula in her clear voice said my name, 'Tim Ekaterin.'

The boy's hand jumped in mine as if my flesh had burned him. I was astonished, and then I looked at his whitening skin, at the suddenly frightened dark eyes, at the stiffening of the body, at the rising panic: and I wouldn't have known him if he hadn't reacted in that way.

'What's the matter, Ricky?' his mother said, puzzled.

He said 'Nothing' hoarsely and looked around for escape, but all too clearly he knew I knew exactly who he was now and could always find him however far he ran.

'What do you think, then, Ursula?' Fred Barnet demanded, returning to the business in hand. 'Will you buy him? Can I count on you?'

Ursula said she would have to consult her client.

'But he was third,' Fred Barnet insisted. 'A good third . . . In that company, a pretty good showing. And he'll win, I'm telling you. He'll win.'

'I'll tell my client all about him. I can't say fairer than that.'

'But you do like him, don't you? Look, Ursula, he's a good sort, easy to handle, just right for an amateur . . .' He went on for a while in this vein while his wife listened with a sort of aimless beam meaning nothing at all.

To the son, under cover of his father's hard sell, I quietly said, 'I want to talk to you, and if you run away from me now I'll be telephoning the police.'

He gave me a sick look and stood still.

'We'll walk down the course together to watch the next race,' I said. 'We won't be interrupted there. And you can tell me *why*. And then we'll see.'

It was easy enough for him to drop back unnoticed from his parents, who were still concentrating on Ursula, and he came with me through the gate and out across the track itself to the centre of the racecourse, stumbling slightly as if not in command of his feet. We walked down towards the last fence, and he told me why he'd tried to kill Calder Jackson.

'It doesn't seem real, not now, it doesn't really,' he said first. A young voice, slightly sloppy accent, full of strain.

'How old are you?' I asked.

'Seventeen.'

I hadn't been so far out, I thought, fifteen months ago.

'I never thought I'd see you again,' he said explosively, sounding faintly aggrieved at the twist of fate. 'I mean, the papers said you worked in a bank.'

'So I do. And I go racing.' I paused. 'You remembered my name.

'Yeah. Could hardly forget it, could I? All over the papers.'

We went a few yards in silence. 'Go on,' I said.

He made a convulsive gesture of frustrated despair. 'All

right. But if I tell you, you won't tell *them*, will you, not Mum and Dad?'

I glanced at him, but from his troubled face it was clear that he meant exactly what he'd said: it wasn't my telling the police he minded most, but my telling his parents.

'Just get on with it,' I said.

He sighed. 'Well, we had this horse. Dad did. He'd bought it as a yearling and ran it as a two-year-old and at three, but it was a jumper really, and it turned out to be good.' He paused. 'Indian Silk, that's what it was called.'

I frowned. 'But Indian Silk . . . didn't that win at Cheltenham this year, in March?'

He nodded. 'The Gold Cup. The very top. He's only seven now and he's bound to be brilliant for years.' The voice was bitter with a sort of resigned, stifled anger.

'But he doesn't any longer belong to your father?'

'No, he doesn't.' More bitterness, very sharp.

'Go on, then,' I said.

He swallowed and took his time, but eventually he said, 'Two years ago this month, when Indian Silk was five, like, he won the Hermitage 'Chase very easily here at Newbury, and everyone was tipping him for the Gold Cup *last* year, though Dad was saying he was still on the young side and to give him time. See, Dad was proud of that horse. The best he'd ever trained, and it was his own, not someone else's. Don't know if you can understand that.'

'I do understand it,' I said.

He gave a split-second glance at my face. 'Well, Indian Silk got sick,' he said. 'I mean, there was nothing you could put your finger on. He just lost his speed. He couldn't even gallop properly at home, couldn't beat the other horses in Dad's yard that he'd been running rings round all year. Dad couldn't run him in races. He could hardly train him. And the vet couldn't find out what was wrong with him. They took blood tests and all sorts, and they gave him antibiotics and purges, and they thought it might be worms or something, but it wasn't.'

We had reached the last fence, and stood there on the rough grass beside it while in twos and threes other enthusiasts straggled down from the grandstand towards us to watch the horses in action at close quarters.

'I was at school a lot of the time, see,' Ricky said. 'I was home every night of course but I was taking exams and had a lot of homework and I didn't really want to take much notice of Indian Silk getting so bad or anything. I mean, Dad does go on a bit, and I suppose I thought the horse just had the virus or something and would get better. But he just got slowly worse and one day Mum was crying.' He stopped suddenly, as if that part was the worst. 'I hadn't seen a grown up cry before,' he said. 'Suppose you'll think it funny, but it upset me something awful.'

'I don't think it funny,' I said.

'Anyway,' he went on, seeming to gather confidence, 'It got so that Indian Silk was so weak he could barely walk down the road and he wasn't eating, and Dad was in real despair because there wasn't nothing anyone could do, and Mum couldn't bear the thought of him going to the knackers, and then some guy telephoned and offered to buy him.'

'To buy a sick horse?' I said, surprised.

'I don't think Dad was going to tell him just how bad he was. Well, I mean, at that point Indian Silk was worth just what the knackers would pay for his carcass, which wasn't much, and this man was offering nearly twice that. But the man said he knew Indian Silk couldn't race any more but he'd like to give him a good home in a nice field for as long as necessary, and it meant that Dad didn't have the expense of any more vets' bills and he and Mum didn't have to watch Indian Silk just getting worse and worse, and Mum wouldn't have to think of him going to the knackers for dog meat, so they let him go.'

The horses for the second race came out onto the course and galloped down past us, the jockeys' colours bright in the sun.

'And then what?' I said.

'Then nothing happened for weeks and we were getting over it, like, and then someone told Dad that Indian Silk was back in training and looking fine, and he couldn't believe it.'

'When was that?' I asked.

'It was last year, just before . . . before Ascot.'

A small crowd gathered on the landing side of the fence, and I drew him away down the course a bit further, to where the horses would set themselves right to take off.

'Go on,' I said.

'My exams were coming up,' he said. 'And I mean, they were important, they were going to affect my whole life, see?'

I nodded.

'Then Dad found that the man who'd bought Indian Silk hadn't put him in any field, he'd sent him straight down the road to Calder Jackson.'

'Ah,' I said.

'And there was this man saying Calder Jackson had the gift of healing, some sort of magic, and had simply touched Indian Silk and made him well. I ask you . . . And Dad was in a frightful state because someone had suggested he should send the horse there, to Calder Jackson, while he was so bad, of course, and Dad had said don't be so ridiculous it was all a lot of rubbish. And then Mum was saying he should have listened to her, because she'd said why not try it, it couldn't do any harm, and he wouldn't do it, and they were having rows, and she was crying . . .' He gulped for air, the story now pouring out faster almost than he could speak. 'And I wasn't getting any work done with it all going on, they weren't ever talking about anything else, and I took the first exam and just sat there and couldn't do it, and I knew I'd failed and I was going to fail them all because I couldn't concentrate . . . and then there was Calder Jackson one evening talking on television, saying he'd got a friend of his to buy a dying horse, because the people who owned it would just have let it die because they didn't believe in healers, like a lot of people, and he hoped the horse would be great again some day, like before, thanks to him, and I knew he was talking about Indian Silk. And he said he was going to Ascot on that Thursday . . . and there was Dad screaming that Calder Jackson had stolen the horse away, it was all a filthy swindle, which of course it wasn't, but at the time I believed him . . . and it all got so that I hated Calder Jackson so much that I couldn't think straight. I mean, I thought *he* was the reason Mum was crying and I was failing my exams and Dad had lost the only really top horse he'd have in his whole life, and I just wanted to *kill* him.'

The bed-rock words were out, and the flood suddenly stopped, leaving the echo of them on the October air.

'And did you fail your exams?' I asked, after a moment.

'Yeah. Most of them. But I took them again at Christmas and got good passes.' He shook his head, speaking more slowly, more quietly. 'I was glad even that night that you'd stopped me stabbing him. I mean . . . I'd have thrown my whole life away, I could see it afterwards, and all for nothing, because Dad wasn't going to get the horse back whatever I did, because it was a legal sale, like.'

I thought over what he'd told me while in the distance the horses lined up and set off on their three mile steeplechase.

'I was sort of mad,' he said. 'I can't really understand it now.

I mean, I wouldn't go around trying to kill people. I really wouldn't. It seems like I was a different person.'

Adolescence, I thought, and not for the first time, could be hell.

'I took Mum's knife out of the kitchen,' he said. 'She never could think where it had gone.'

I wondered if the police still had it; with Ricky's fingerprints on file.

'I didn't know there would be so many people at Ascot,' he said. 'And so many gates into the course. Much more than Newmarket. I was getting frantic because I thought I wouldn't find him. I meant to do it earlier, see, when he arrived. I was out on the road, running up and down the pavement, mad, you know, really, looking for him and feeling the knife kind of burning in my sleeve, like I was burning in my mind . . . and I saw his head, all those curls, crossing the road, and I ran, but I was too late, he'd gone inside, through the gate.'

'And then,' I suggested. 'You simply waited for him to come out?'

He nodded. 'There were lots of people around. No one took any notice. I reckoned he'd come up that path from the station, and that was the way he would go back. It didn't seem long, the waiting. Went in a flash.'

The horses came over the next fence down the course like a multi-coloured wave and thundered towards the one where we were standing. The ground trembled from the thud of the hooves, the air rang with the curses of jockeys, the half-ton equine bodies brushed through the birch, the sweat and the effort and the speed filled eyes and ears and mind with pounding wonder and then were gone, flying away, leaving the silence. I had walked down several times before to watch from the fences, both there and on other tracks, and the fierce fast excitement had never grown stale.

'Who is it who owns Indian Silk now?' I asked.

'A Mr Chacksworth, comes from Birmingham,' Ricky answered. 'You see him at the races sometimes, slobbering all over Indian Silk. But it wasn't him that bought him from Dad. He bought him later, when he was all right again. Paid a proper price for him, so we heard. Made it all the worse.'

A sad and miserable tale, all of it.

'Who bought the horse from your father?' I said.

'I never met him . . . his name was Smith. Some funny first name. Can't remember.'

Smith. Friend of Calder's.

'Could it,' I asked, surprised, 'have been *Dissdale* Smith?'

'Yeah. That sounds like it. How do you know?'

'He was there that day at Ascot,' I said. 'There on the pavement, right beside Calder Jackson.'

'Was he?' Ricky looked disconcerted. 'He was a dead liar, you know, all that talk about nice fields.'

'Who tells the truth,' I said, 'when buying or selling horses?'

The runners were round again on the far side of the track, racing hard now on the second circuit.

'What are you going to do?' Ricky said. 'About me, like? You won't tell Mum and Dad. You won't, will you?'

I looked directly at the boy-man, seeing the continuing anxiety but no longer the first panic-stricken fear. He seemed to sense now that I would very likely not drag him into court, but he wasn't sure of much else.

'Perhaps they should know,' I said.

'No!' His agitation rose quickly. 'They've had so much trouble and I would have made it so much worse if you hadn't stopped me, and afterwards I used to wake up sweating at what it would have done to them; and the only good thing was that I did learn that you can't put things right by killing people, you can only make things terrible for your family.'

After a long pause I said 'All right. I won't tell them.' And heaven help me, I thought, if he ever attacked anyone again because he thought he could always get away with it.

The relief seemed to affect him almost as much as the anxiety. He blinked several times and turned his head away to where the race was again coming round into the straight with this time an all-out effort to the winning post. There was again the rise and fall of the field over the distant fences but now the one wave had split into separate components, the runners coming home not in a bunch but a procession.

I watched again the fierce surprising speed of horse and jockey jumping at close quarters and wished with some regret that I could have ridden like that: but like Alec I was wishing too late, even strong and healthy and thirty-three.

The horses galloped off towards the cheers on the grand-stand and Ricky and I began a slow walk in their wake. He seemed quiet and composed in the aftermath of confession, the soul's evacuation giving him ease.

'What do you feel nowadays about Calder Jackson?' I asked.

He produced a lop-sided smile. 'Nothing much. That's

what's so crazy. I mean, it wasn't his fault Dad was so stubborn.'

I digested this. 'You mean,' I said. 'That you think your father should have sent him the horse himself?'

'Yes, I reckon he should've, like Mum wanted. But he said it was rubbish and too expensive, and you don't know my Dad but when he makes his mind up he just gets fighting angry if anyone tries to argue, and he shouts at her, and it isn't fair.'

'If your father had sent the horse to Calder Jackson, I suppose he would still own it,' I said thoughtfully.

'Yes, he would, and don't think he doesn't know it, of course he does, but it's as much as anyone's life's worth to say it.'

We trudged back over the thick grass, and I asked him how Calder or Dissdale had known that Indian Silk was ill.

He shrugged. 'It was in the papers. He'd been favourite for the King George VI on Boxing Day, but of course he didn't run, and the press found out why.'

We came again to the gate into the grandstand enclosure and went through it, and I asked where he lived.

'Exning,' he said.

'Where's that?'

'Near Newmarket. Just outside.' He looked at me with slightly renewed apprehension. 'You meant it, didn't you, about not telling?'

'I meant it,' I said. 'Only . . .' I frowned a little, thinking of the hot-house effect of his living with his parents.

'Only what?' he asked.

I tried a different tack. 'What are you doing now? Are you still at school?'

'No, I left once I'd passed those exams. I really needed them, like. You can't get a half-way decent job without those bits of paper these days.'

'You're not working for your father, then?'

He must have heard the faint relief in my voice because for the first time he fully smiled. 'No, I reckon it wouldn't be good for his temper, and anyway I don't want to be a trainer, one long worry, if you ask me.'

'What do you do, then?' I asked.

'I'm learning electrical engineering in a firm near Cambridge. An apprentice, like.' He smiled again. 'But not with horses, not me.' He shook his head ruefully and delivered his young-solomon judgement of life. 'Break your heart, horses do.'

The Second Year

NOVEMBER

To my great delight the cartoonist came up trumps, his twenty animated films being shown on television every weeknight for a month in the best time-slot for that sort of humour, seven in the evening, when older children were still up and the parents home from work. The nation sat up and giggled, and the cartoonist telephoned breathlessly to ask for a bigger loan.

'I do need a proper studio, not this converted warehouse. And more animators, and designers, and recordists, and equipment.'

'All right,' I said into the first gap. 'Draw up your requirements and come and see me.'

'Do you *realise,*' he said, as if he himself had difficulty, 'That they'll take as many films as I can make? No limit. They said just go on making them for years and years . . . they said *please* go on making them.'

'I'm very glad,' I said sincerely.

'You gave me faith in myself,' he said. 'You'll never believe it, but you did. I'd been turned down so often, and I was getting depressed, but when you lent me the money to start it was like being uncorked. The ideas just rushed out.'

'And are they still rushing?'

'Oh sure. I've got the next twenty films roughed out in drawings already and we're working on those, and now I'm starting on the batch after that.'

'It's terrific,' I said.

'It sure is. Brother, life's amazing.' He put down his receiver and left me smiling into space.

'The cartoonist?' Gordon said.

I nodded. 'Going up like a rocket.'

'Congratulations.' There was warmth and genuine pleasure in his voice. Such a generous man, I thought: so impossible to do him harm.

'He looks like turning into a major industry,' I said.

'Disney, Hanna Barbera, eat your hearts out,' Alec said from across the room.

'Good business for the bank.' Gordon beamed. 'Henry will be pleased.'

Pleasing Henry, indeed, was the aim of us all.

'You must admit, Tim,' Alec said, 'That you're a fairish rocket yourself . . . so what's the secret?'

'Light the blue paper and retire immediately,' I said good humouredly, and he balled a page of jottings to throw at me, and missed.

At mid-morning he went out as customary for the six copies of *What's Going On Where It Shouldn't* and having distributed five was presently sitting back in his chair reading our own with relish.

Ekaterin's had been thankfully absent from the probing columns ever since the five-per-cent business, but it appeared that some of our colleagues along the road weren't so fortunate.

'Did you know,' Alec said conversationally, 'That some of our investment manager chums down on the corner have set up a nice little fiddle on the side, accepting pay-offs from brokers in return for steering business their way?'

'How do you know?' Gordon asked, looking up from a ledger.

Alec lifted the paper. 'The gospel according to this dicky bird.'

'Gospel meaning good news,' I said.

'Don't be so damned erudite.' He grinned at me with mischief and went back to reading aloud, '*Contrary to popular belief the general run of so-called managers in merchant banks are not in the princely bracket.*' He looked up briefly. 'You can say that again.' He went on, '*We hear that four of the investment managers in this establishment have been cosily supplementing their middle-incomes by steering fund money to three stockbrokers in particular. Names will be revealed in our next issue. Watch this space.*'

'It's happened before,' Gordon said philosophically. 'And will happen again. The temptation is always there.' He frowned. 'All the same, I'm surprised their senior managers and the directors haven't spotted it.'

'They'll have spotted it *now*,' Alec said.

'So they will.'

'It would be pretty easy,' I said musingly, 'To set up a computer programme to do the spotting for Ekaterin's, in case we should ever find the pestilence cropping up here.'

'Would it?' Gordon asked.

'Mm. Just a central programme to record every deal in the Investment Department with each stockbroker, with running totals, easy to see. Anything hugely unexpected could be investigated.'

'But that's a vast job, surely,' Gordon said.

I shook my head. 'I doubt it. I could get our tame programmer to have a go, if you like.'

'We'll put it to the others. See what they say.'

'There will be screeches from Investment Management,' Alec said. 'Cries of outraged virtue.'

'Guards them against innuendo like this, though,' Gordon said, pointing to *What's Going On Where . . .*

The board agreed, and in consequence I spent another two days with the programmer, building dykes against future leaks.

Gordon these days seemed no worse, his illness not having progressed in any visible way. There was no means of knowing how he felt, as he never said and hated to be asked, but on the few times I'd seen Judith since the day at Easter, she had said he was as well as could be hoped for.

The best of those times had been a Sunday in July when Pen had given a lunch party in her house in Clapham; it was supposed to have been a lunch-in-the-garden party, but like so much that summer was frustrated by chilly winds. Inside was to me much better, as Pen had written place-cards for her long refectory table and put me next to Judith, with Gordon on her right hand.

The other guests remained a blur, most of them being doctors of some sort or another, or pharmacists like herself. Judith and I made polite noises to the faces on either side of us but spent most of the time talking to each other, carrying on two conversations at once, one with voice, one with eyes; both satisfactory.

When the main party had broken up and gone, Gordon and Judith and I stayed to supper, first helping Pen clear up from what she described as 'repaying so many dinners at one go'.

It had been a day when natural opportunities for touching people abounded, when kisses and hugs of greeting had been appropriate and could be warm, when all the world could watch and see nothing between Judith and me but an enduring and peaceful friendship: a day when I longed to have her for myself worse than ever.

Since then I'd seen her only twice, and both times when she'd come to the bank to collect Gordon before they went on to other events. On each of these times I'd managed at least five minutes with her, stiffly circumspect, Gordon's colleague being polite until Gordon himself was ready to leave.

It wasn't usual for wives to come to the bank: husbands normally joined them at wherever they were going. Judith said, the second time, 'I won't do this often. I just wanted to see you, if you were around.'

'Always here,' I said.

She nodded. She was looking as fresh and poised as ever, wearing a neat blue coat with pearls showing. The brown hair was glossy, the eyes bright, the soft mouth half smiling, the glamour born in her and unconscious.

'I get . . . well . . . thirsty, sometimes,' she said.

'Permanent state with me,' I said lightly.

She swallowed. 'Just for a moment or two . . .'

We were standing in the entrance hall, not touching, waiting for Gordon.

'Just to see you . . .' She seemed uncertain that I understood, but I did.

'It's the same for me,' I assured her. 'I sometimes thing of going to Clapham and waiting around just to see you walk down the street to the bakers. Just to see you, even for seconds.'

'Do you really?'

'I don't go, though. You might send Gordon to buy the bread.'

She laughed a small laugh, a fitting size for the bank; and he came, hurrying, struggling into his overcoat. I sprang to help him and he said to her, 'Sorry, darling, got held up on the telephone, you know how it is.'

'I've been perfectly happy,' she said, kissing him, 'talking to Tim.'

'Splendid. Splendid. Are we ready, then?'

They went off to their evening smiling and waving and leaving me to hunger futilely for this and that.

In the office one day in November Gordon said 'How about you coming over to lunch on Sunday? Judith was saying it's ages since she saw you properly.'

'I'd love to.'

'Pen's coming, Judith said.'

Pen, my friend; my chaperone.

'Great,' I said positively. 'Lovely.'

Gordon nodded contentedly and said it was a shame we couldn't all have a repeat of last Christmas, he and Judith had enjoyed it so much. They were going this year to his son and daughter-in-law in Edinburgh, a visit long promised; to his son by his first long-dead wife, and his grandchildren, twin boys of seven.

'You'll have fun,' I said regretfully.

'They're noisy little brutes.'

His telephone rang, and mine also, and moneylending proceeded. I would be dutiful, I thought, and spend Christmas with my mother in Jersey, as she wanted, and we would laugh and play backgammon, and I would sadden her as usual by bringing no girl-friend, no prospective producer of little brutes.

'*Why*, my love,' she'd said to me once a few years earlier in near despair, 'do you take out these perfectly presentable girls and never marry them?'

'There's always something I don't want to spend my life with.'

'But you do *sleep* with them?'

'Yes, darling, I do.'

'You're too choosy.'

'I expect so,' I said.

'You haven't had a single one that's lasted,' she complained. 'Everyone else's sons manage to have live-in girl friends, sometimes going on for years even if they don't marry, so why can't you?'

I'd smiled at the encouragement to what would once have been called sin, and kissed her, and told her I preferred living alone, but that one day I'd find the perfect girl to love for ever; and it hadn't even fleetingly occurred to me that when I found her she would be married to someone else.

Sunday came and I went to Clapham: bitter-sweet hours, as ever.

Over lunch I told them tentatively that I'd seen the boy who had tried to kill Calder, and they reacted as strongly as I'd expected, Gordon saying, 'You've told the police, of course,' and Judith adding 'He's dangerous, Tim.'

I shook my head. 'No. I don't think so. I hope not.' I smiled wryly and told them all about Ricky Barnet and Indian Silk, and the pressure which had led to the try at stabbing. 'I don't think he'll do anything like that again. He's grown so far away from it already that he feels a different person.'

'I hope you're right,' Gordon said.

'Fancy it being Dissdale who bought Indian Silk,' Pen said. 'Isn't it amazing?'

'Especially as he was saying he was short of cash and wanting to sell box-space at Ascot,' Judith added.

'Mm,' I said. 'But after Calder had cured the horse Dissdale sold it again pretty soon, and made a handsome profit, by what I gather.'

'Typical Dissdale behaviour,' Gordon said without criticism. 'Face the risk, stake all you can afford, take the loot if you're lucky, and get out fast.' He smiled. 'By Ascot I guess he'd blown the Indian Silk profit and was back to basics. It doesn't take someone like Dissdale any longer to lose thousands than it does to make them.'

'He must have colossal faith in Calder,' Pen said musingly.

'Not colossal, Pen,' Gordon said. 'Just twice what a knacker would pay for a carcass.'

'Would *you* buy a sick-to-death horse?' Judith asked. 'I mean, if Calder said buy it and I'll cure him, would you believe it?'

Gordon looked at her fondly. 'I'm not Dissdale, darling, and I don't think I'd buy it.'

'And that is precisely,' I pointed out, 'why Fred Barnet lost Indian Silk. He thought Calder's powers were all rubbish and he wouldn't lash out good money to put them to the test. But Dissdale *did*. Bought the horse and presumably also paid Calder . . . who boasted about his success on television and nearly got himself killed for it.'

'Ironic, the whole thing,' Pen said, and we went on discussing it desultorily over coffee.

I stayed until six, when Pen went off to her shop for a Sunday-evening stint and Gordon began to look tired, and I drove back to Hampstead in the usual post-Judith state; half-fulfilled, half-starved.

Towards the end of November, and at Oliver Knowles' invitation, I travelled to another Sunday lunch, this time at the stud farm in Hertfordshire.

It turned out, not surprisingly, to be one of Ginnie's days home from school, and it was she, whistling to Squibs, who set off with me through the yards.

'Did you know we had a hundred and fifty-two mares here all at the same time, back in May?' she said.

'That's a lot,' I said, impressed.

'They had a hundred and fourteen foals between them, and only one of the mares and three of the foals died. That's a terrifically good record, you know.'

'Your father's very skilled.'

'So is Nigel,' she said grudgingly. 'You have to give him his due.'

I smiled at the expression.

'He isn't here just now,' she said. 'He went off to Miami yesterday to lie in the sun.'

'Nigel?'

She nodded. 'He goes about this time every year. Sets him up for the winter, he says.'

'Always Miami?'

'Yes, he likes it.'

The whole atmosphere of the place was back to where I'd known it first, to the slow chill months of gestation. Ginnie, snuggling inside her padded jacket, gave carrots from her pocket to some of the mares in the first yard and walked me without stopping through the empty places, the second yard, the foaling yard, and past the breeding shed.

We came finally as always to the stallion yard where the curiosity of the residents brought their heads out the moment they heard our footsteps. Ginnie distributed carrots and pats with the aplomb of her father, and Sandcastle graciously allowed her to stroke his nose.

'He's quiet now,' she said. 'He's on a much lower diet at this time of year.'

I listened to the bulk of knowledge behind the calm words and I said, 'What are you going to do when you leave school?'

'This, of course.' She patted Sandcastle's neck. 'Help Dad. Be his assistant.'

'Nothing else?'

She shook her head. 'I love the foals. Seeing them born and watching them grow. I don't want to do anything else, ever.'

We left the stallion and walked between the paddocks with their foals and dams, along the path to the Watcherleys', Squibs trotting on ahead and marking his fence posts. The neighbouring place, whose ramshackle state I'd only glimpsed on my pursuit of the loose five million, proved now to be almost as neat as the parent spread, with much fresh paint in evidence and weeds markedly absent.

'Dad can't bear mess,' Ginnie said when I remarked on the spit-and-polish. 'The Watcherleys are pretty lucky, really, with Dad paying them rent *and* doing up their place *and* employing them to look after the animals in this yard. Bob may still gripe a bit at not being on his own, but Maggie was telling me just last week that she would be everlastingly thankful that Calder Jackson stole their business.'

'He hardly stole it,' I said mildly.

'Well, you know what I mean. Did better at it, if you want to be pedantic.' She grinned. 'Anyway, Maggie's bought some new clothes at last, and I'm glad for her.'

We opened and went into a few of the boxes where she handed out the last of the carrots and fondled the inmates, both mares and growing foals, talking to them, and all of them responded amiably to her touch, nuzzling her gently. She looked at peace and where she belonged, all growing pains suspended.

The Third Year

APRIL

Alec had bought a bunch of yellow tulips when he went out for *What's Going On*, and they stood on his desk in a beer mug, catching a shaft of spring sunshine and standing straight like guardsmen.

Gordon was making notes in a handwriting growing even smaller, and the two older colleagues were counting the weeks to their retirement. Office life: an ordinary day.

My telephone rang, and with eyes still bent on a letter from a tomato grower asking for more time to repay his original loan because of needing a new greenhouse (half an acre) right this minute, I slowly picked up the receiver.

'Oliver Knowles,' the voice said. 'Is that you, Tim?'

'Hello,' I replied warmly. 'Everything going well?'

'No.' The word was sickeningly abrupt, and both mentally and physically I sat up straighter.

'What's the matter?'

'Can you come down here?' he asked, not directly answering. 'I'm rather worried. I want to talk to you.'

'Well . . . I could come on Sunday,' I said.

'Could you come today? Or tomorrow?'

I reviewed my work load and a few appointments. 'Tomorrow afternoon, if you like,' I said. 'If it's bank business.'

'Yes, it is.' The anxiety in his voice was quite plain, and communicated itself with much ease to me.

'Can't you tell me what's the trouble?' I asked. 'Is Sandcastle all right?'

'I don't know,' he said. 'I'll tell you when you come.'

'But Oliver . . .'

'Listen,' he said. 'Sandcastle is in good health and he hasn't escaped again or anything like that. It's too difficult to explain on the telephone. I want your advice, that's all.'

He wouldn't say any more and left me with the dead receiver in my hand and some horrid suspenseful question marks in my mind.

'Sandcastle?' Gordon asked.

'Oliver says he's in good health.'

'That horse is insured against everything – those enormous premiums – so don't worry too much,' Gordon said. 'It's probably something minor.'

It hadn't sounded like anything minor, and when I reached the stud farm the next day I found that it certainly wasn't. Oliver came out to meet me as I braked to a standstill by his front door, and there were new deep lines on his face that hadn't been there before.

'Come in,' he said, clasping my hand. 'I'm seriously worried. I don't know what to do.'

He led the way through the house to the office-sitting room and gestured me to a chair. 'Sit down and read this,' he said, and gave me a letter.

There had been no time for 'nice day' or 'how is Ginnie?' introductory noises, just this stark command. I sat down, and I read, as directed.

The letter dated April 21st, said:

Dear Oliver,

I'm not complaining, because of course one pays one's fee and takes one's chances, but I'm sorry to tell you that the Sandcastle foal out of my mare Spiral Binding has been born with a half of one ear missing. It's a filly, by the way, and I dare say it won't affect her speed, but her looks are ruined.

So sad.

I expect I'll see you one day at the sales.

Yours,

Jane.

'Is that very bad?' I asked, frowning.

In reply he wordlessly handed me another letter. This one said:

Dear Mr Knowles,

You asked me to let you know how my mare Girandette, whom you liked so much, fared on foaling. She gave birth safely to a nice colt foal, but unfortunately he died at six days. We had a post mortem, and it was found that he had malformed heart-valves, like hole-in-heart-babies.

This is a great blow to me, financially as well as all else, but that's life I suppose.

Yours sincerely,

George Page.

'And now this,' Oliver said, and handed me a third.

The heading was that of a highly regarded and well-known stud farm, the letter briefly impersonal.

Dear Sir,

Filly foal born March 31st to Poppingcorn.
Sire: Sandcastle.
Deformed foot, near fore.
Put down.

I gave him back the letters and with growing misgiving asked, 'How common are these malformations?'

Oliver said intensely, 'They happen. They happen occasionally. But those letters aren't all. I've had two telephone calls – one last night. Two other foals have died of holes in the heart. Two more! That's five with something wrong with them.' He stared at me, his eyes like dark pits. 'That's far too many.' He swallowed. 'And what about the others, the other thirty-five? Suppose . . . suppose there are more . . .'

'If you haven't heard, they're surely all right.'

He shook his head hopelessly. 'The mares are scattered all over the place, dropping Sandcastle's foals where they are due to be bred next. There's no automatic reason for those stud managers to tell me when a foal's born, or what it's like. I mean, some do it out of courtesy but they just don't usually bother, and nor do I. I tell the owner of the mare, not the manager of the stallion.'

'Yes, I see.'

'So there may be other foals with deformities . . . that I haven't heard about.'

There was a long fraught pause in which the enormity of the position sank coldly into my banking consciousness. Oliver developed sweat on his forehead and a tic beside his mouth, as if sharing his anxiety had doubled it rather than halved.

The telephone rang suddenly, making us both jump.

'You answer it,' he said. 'Please.'

I opened my mouth to protest that it would be only some routine call about anything else on earth, but then merely picked up the receiver.

'Is that Oliver Knowles?' a voice said.

'No . . . I'm his assistant.'

'Oh. Then will you give him a message?'

'Yes, I will.'

'Tell him that Patrick O'Marr rang him from Limballow, Ireland. Have you got that?'

'Yes,' I said. 'Go ahead.'

'It's about a foal we had born here three or four weeks ago. I thought I'd better let Mr Knowles know that we've had to put it down, though I'm sorry to give him bad news. Are you listening?'

'Yes,' I said, feeling hollow.

'The poor little fellow was born with a sort of curled-in hoof. The vet said it might straighten out in a week or two, but it didn't, so we had it X-rayed, and the lower pastern bone and the coffin bone were fused and tiny. The vet said there was no chance of them developing properly, and the little colt would never be able to walk, let alone race. A beautiful little fella too, in all other ways. Anyway, I'm telling Mr Knowles because of course he'll be looking out for Sandcastle's first crop to win for him, and I'm explaining why this one won't be there. Pink Roses, that's the mare's name. Tell him, will you? Pink Roses. She's come here to be bred to Dallaton. Nice mare. She's fine herself, tell Mr Knowles.'

'Yes,' I said. 'I'm very sorry.'

'One of those things.' The cultured Irish accent sounded not too despairing. 'The owner of Pink Roses is cut up about it, of course, but I believe he'd insured against a dead or deformed foal, so it's a case of wait another year and better luck next time.'

'I'll tell Mr Knowles,' I said. 'And thank you for letting us know.'

'Sorry and all,' he said. 'But there it is.'

I put the receiver down slowly and Oliver said dully, 'Another one? Not another one.'

I nodded and told him what Patrick O'Marr had said.

'That's six,' Oliver said starkly. 'And Pink Roses . . . that's the mare you saw Sandcastle cover, this time last year.'

'Was it?' I thought back to that majestic mating, that moment of such promise. Poor little colt, conceived in splendour and born with a club foot.

'What am I going to do?' Oliver said.

'Get out Sandcastle's insurance policy.'

He looked blank. 'No, I mean, about the mares. We have all the mares here who've come this year to Sandcastle. They've all foaled except one and nearly all of them have already been covered. I mean . . . there's another crop already growing, and suppose those . . . suppose all of those . . .' He stopped as if he simply couldn't make his tongue say the words. 'I was awake all night,' he said.

'The first thing,' I said again, 'is to look at that policy.'

He went unerringly to a neat row of files in a cupboard and pulled out the needed document, a many-paged affair, partly printed, partly typed. I spread it open and said to Oliver, 'How about some coffee? This is going to take ages.'

'Oh. All right.' He looked around him vaguely. 'There'll be some put ready for me for dinner. I'll go and plug it in.' He paused. 'Percolator,' he explained.

I knew all the symptoms of a mouth saying one thing while the mind was locked on to another. 'Yes,' I said. 'That would be fine.' He nodded with the same unmeshed mental gears, and I guessed that when he got to the kitchen he'd have trouble remembering what for.

The insurance policy had been written for the trade and not the customer, a matter of jargon-ridden sentences full of words that made plain sense only to people who used them for a living. I read it very carefully for that reason; slowly and thoroughly from start to finish.

There were many definitions of the word 'accident', with stipulations about the number of veterinary surgeons who should be consulted and should give their signed opinions before Sandcastle (hereinafter called the horse) could be humanely destroyed for any reason whatsoever. There were stipulations about fractures, naming those bones which should commonly be held to be repairable, and about common muscle, nerve and tendon troubles which would not be considered grounds for destruction, unless of such severity that the horse couldn't actually stand up.

Aside from these restrictions the horse was to be considered to be insured against death from any natural causes whatsoever, to be insured against accidental death occurring while the horse was free (such a contingency to be guarded against with diligence, gross negligence being a disqualifying condition) to be insured against death by fire should the stable be consumed, and against death caused maliciously by human hand. He was insured fully against malicious or accidental castration and against such accidental damage being caused by veterinarians acting in good faith to treat the horse. He was insured against fertility on a sliding scale, his full worth being in question only if he proved one hundred per cent infertile (which laboratory tests had shown was not the case).

He was insured against accidental or malicious poisoning and against impotence resulting from non-fatal illness, and against incapacitating or fatal injuries inflicted upon him by any other horse.

He was insured against death caused by the weather (storm, flood, lightning, etc.) and also, surprisingly, against death or incapacity caused by war, riot or civil commotion, causes usually specifically excluded from insurance.

He was insured against objects dropped from the sky and against being driven into by mechanical objects on the ground and against trees falling on him and against hidden wells opening under his feet.

He was insured against every foreseeable disaster except one. He was not insured against being put out of business because of congenital abnormalities among his progeny.

Oliver came back carrying a tray on which sat two kitchen mugs containing tea, not coffee. He put the tray on the desk and looked at my face, which seemed only very slightly to deepen his despair.

'I'm not insured, am I,' he said, 'against possessing a healthy potent stallion to whom no one will send their mares.'

'I don't know.'

'Yes . . . I see you do.' He was shaking slightly. 'When the policy was drawn up about six people, including myself and two vets, beside the insurers themselves, tried to think of every possible contingency, and to guard against it. We threw in everything we could think of.' He swallowed. 'No one . . . no one thought of a whole crop of deformed foals.'

'No,' I said.

'I mean, breeders usually insure their own mares, if they want to, and the foal, to protect the stallion fee, but many don't because of the premiums being high. And I . . . I'm paying this enormous premium . . . and the one thing . . . the one thing that happens is something we never . . . no one ever imagined . . . could happen.'

The policy, I thought, had been too specific. They should have been content with something like 'any factor resulting in the horse not being considered fit for stud purposes'; but perhaps the insurers themselves couldn't find underwriters for anything so open to interpretation and opinion. In any case, the damage was done. All-risk policies all too often were not what they said; and insurance companies never paid out if they could avoid it.

My own skin felt clammy. Three million pounds of the bank's money and two million subscribed by private people were tied up in the horse, and if Oliver couldn't repay, it was we who would lose.

I had recommended the loan. Henry had wanted the adventure and Val and Gordon had been willing, but it was my own report which had carried the day. I couldn't have foreseen the consequences any more than Oliver, but I felt most horribly and personally responsible for the mess.

'What shall I do?' he said again.

'About the mares?'

'And everything else.'

I stared into space. The disaster that for the bank would mean a loss of face and a sharp dip in the profits and to the private subscribers just a painful financial set-back meant in effect total ruin for Oliver Knowles.

If Sandcastle couldn't generate income, Oliver would be bankrupt. His business was not a limited company, which meant that he would lose his farm, his horses, his house; everything he possessed. To him too, as to my mother, the bailiffs would come, carrying off his furniture and his treasures and Ginnie's books and toys . . .

I shook myself mentally and physically and said, 'The first thing to do is nothing. Keep quiet and don't tell anyone what you've told me. Wait to hear if any more of the foals are . . . wrong. I will consult with the other directors at Ekaterin's and see what can be done in the way of providing time. I mean . . . I'm not promising . . . but we might consider suspending repayments while we look into other possibilities.'

He looked bewildered. 'What possibilities?'

'Well . . . of having Sandcastle tested. If the original tests of his fertility weren't thorough enough, for instance, it might be possible to show that his sperm had always been defective in some way, and then the insurance policy would protect you. Or at least it's a very good chance.'

The insurers, I thought, might in that case sue the laboratory that had originally given the fertility all-clear, but that wasn't Oliver's problem, nor mine. What did matter was that all of a sudden he looked a fraction more cheerful, and drank his tea absentmindedly.

'And the mares?' he said.

I shook my head. 'In fairness to their owners you'll have to say that Sandcastle's off colour.'

'And repay their fees,' he said gloomily.

'Mm.'

'He'll have covered two today,' he said. 'I haven't mentioned any of this to Nigel. I mean, it's his job to organise the breeding sessions. He has a great eye for those mares, he knows when they are feeling receptive. I leave it to his judgement a good deal, and he told me this morning that two were ready for Sandcastle. I just nodded. I felt sick. I didn't tell him.'

'So how many does that leave, er, uncovered?'

He consulted a list, fumbling slightly. 'The one that hasn't foaled, and . . . four others.'

Thirty-five more mares, I thought numbly, could be carrying that seed.

'The mare that hasn't yet foaled,' Oliver said flatly, 'Was bred to Sandcastle last year.'

I stared. 'You mean . . . one of his foals will be born *here*?

'Yes.' He rubbed his hand over his face. 'Any day.'

There were footsteps outside the door and Ginnie came in, saying on a rising, enquiring inflection, 'Dad?'

She saw me immediately and her face lit up. 'Hello! How lovely. I didn't know you were coming.'

I stood up to give her a customarily enthusiastic greeting, but she sensed at once that the action didn't match the climate. 'What's the matter?' She looked into my eyes and then at her father. 'What's happened?'

'Nothing,' he said.

'Dad, you're lying.' She turned again to me. 'Tell me. I can see something bad has happened. I'm not a child any more. I'm seventeen.'

'I thought you'd be at school,' I said.

'I've left. At the end of last term. There wasn't any point in me going back for the summer when all I'm interested in is here.'

She looked far more assured, as if the schooldays had been a chrysalis and she were now the imago, flying free. The beauty she had longed for hadn't quite arrived, but her face was full of character and far from plain, and she would be very much liked, I thought, throughout her life.

'What is it?' she said. 'What's happened?'

Oliver made a small gesture of despair and capitulation. 'You'll have to know sometime.' He swallowed. 'Some of Sandcastle's foals . . . aren't perfect.'

'How do you mean, not perfect?'

He told her about all six and showed her the letters, and she went slowly, swaying, pale. 'Oh Dad, no. No. It can't be. Not Sandcastle. Not that beautiful boy.'

'Sit down,' I said, but she turned to me instead, burying her face against my chest and holding on to me tightly. I put my arms round her and kissed her hair and comforted her for an age as best I could.

I went to the office on the following morning, Friday, and with a slight gritting of teeth told Gordon the outcome of my visit to Oliver.

He said 'My God,' several times, and Alec came over from his desk to listen also, his blue eyes for once solemn behind the gold-rimmed spectacles, the blond eyelashes blinking slowly and the laughing mouth grimly shut.

'What will you do?' he said finally, when I stopped.

'I don't really know.'

Gordon stirred, his hands trembling unnoticed on his blotter in his overriding concern. 'The first thing, I suppose,' he said, 'is to tell Val and Henry. Though what any of us can do is a puzzle. As you said, Tim, we'll have to wait to assess quite how irretrievable the situation is, but I can't imagine anyone with a top-class broodmare having the confidence to send her to Sandcastle in future. Can you, really, Tim? Would *you*?'

I shook my head. 'No.'

'Well, there you are,' Gordon said. 'No one would.'

Henry and Val received the news with undisguised dismay and told the rest of the directors at lunch. The man who had been against the project from the beginning reacted with genuine anger and gave me a furious dressing-down over the grilled sole.

'No one could foresee this,' Henry protested, defending me.

'Anyone could foresee,' said the dissenting director caustically, 'that such a scatterbrained scheme would blow up in our faces. Tim has been given too much power too soon, and it's his judgement that's at fault here, his alone. If he'd had the common nous to recognise the dangers, you would have listened to him and turned his proposal down. It's certainly because of his stupidity and immaturity that the bank is facing this loss, and I shall put my views on record at the next board meeting.'

There were a few uncomfortable murmurs round the table, and Henry with unruffled geniality said, 'We are all to blame, if blame there is, and it is unfair to call Tim stupid for not foreseeing something that escaped the imaginations of all the various experts who drew up the insurance policy.'

The dissenter however repeated his 'I told you so' remarks endlessly through the cheese and coffee, and I sat there depressedly enduring his digs because I wouldn't give him the satisfaction of seeing me leave before he did.

'What will you do next?' Henry asked me, when at long last everyone rather silently stood up to drift back to their desks. 'What do you propose?'

I was grateful that by implication he was leaving me in the position I'd reached and not taking the decisions out of my hands. 'I'm going down to the farm tomorrow,' I said, 'to go through the financial situation. Add up the figures. They're bound to be frightful.'

He nodded with regret. 'Such a marvellous horse. And no one, Tim, whatever anyone says, could have dreamt he'd have such a flaw.'

I sighed. 'Oliver has asked me to stay tomorrow night and Sunday night. I don't really want to, but they do need support.'

'They?'

'Ginnie, his daughter, is with him. She's only just seventeen. It's very hard on them both. Shattering, in fact.'

Henry patted my arm and walked with me to the lift. 'Do what you can,' he said. 'Let us know the full state of affairs on Monday.'

Before I left home that Saturday morning I had a telephone call from Judith.

'Gordon's told me about Sandcastle. Tim, it's so terrible. Those poor, poor people.'

'Wretched,' I said.

'Tim, tell Ginnie how sorry I am. Sorry . . . how hopeless words are, you say sorry if you bump someone in the supermarket. That dear child . . . she wrote to me a couple of times from school, just asking for feminine information, like I'd told her to.'

'Did she?'

'Yes. She's such a nice girl. So sensible. But this . . . this is too much. Gordon says they're in danger of losing *everything.*'

'I'm going down there today to see where he stands.'

'Gordon told me. Do please give them my love.'

'I will.' I paused fractionally. 'My love to you, too.'

'Tim . . .'

'I just wanted to tell you. It's still the same.'

'We haven't seen you for weeks. I mean . . . I haven't.'

'Is Gordon in the room with you?' I asked.

'Yes, that's right.'

I smiled twistedly. 'I do hear about you, you know,' I said. 'He mentions you quite often, and I ask after you . . . it makes you feel closer.'

'Yes,' she said in a perfectly neutral voice. 'I know exactly what you mean. I feel the same about it exactly.'

'Judith . . .' I took a breath and made my own voice calm to match hers. 'Tell Gordon I'll telephone him at home, if he'd like, if there is anything that needs consultation before Monday.'

'I'll tell him. Hang on.' I heard her repeating the question and Gordon's distant rumble of an answer, and then she said, 'Yes, he says please do, we'll be at home this evening and most of tomorrow.'

'Perhaps you'll answer when the telephone rings.'

'Perhaps.'

After a brief silence I said, 'I'd better go.'

'Goodbye then, Tim,' she said. 'And do let us know. We'll both be thinking of you all day, I know we will.'

'I'll call,' I said. 'You can count on it.'

The afternoon was on the whole as miserable as I'd expected and in some respects worse. Oliver and Ginnie walked about like pale automatons making disconnected remarks and forgetting where they'd put things, and lunch, Ginnie version, had consisted of eggs boiled too hard and packets of potato crisps.

'We haven't told Nigel or the lads what's happening,' Oliver said. 'Fortunately there is a lull in Sandcastle's programme. He's been very busy because nearly all his mares foaled in mid-March, close together, except for four and the one who's still carrying.' He swallowed. 'And the other stallions, of course, their mares are all here too, and we have their foals to deliver and their matings to be seen to. I mean . . . we have to go on. We have to.'

Towards four o'clock they both went out into the yards for evening stables, visibly squaring their shoulders to face the stable hands in a normal manner, and I began adding the columns of figures I'd drawn up from Oliver's records.

The tally when I'd finished was appalling and meant that Oliver could be an undischarged bankrupt for the rest of his life. I put the results away in my briefcase and tried to think of something more constructive; and Oliver's telephone rang.

'Oliver?' a voice said, sounding vaguely familiar.

'He's out,' I said. 'Can I take a message?'

'Get him to ring me. Ursula Young. I'll give you the number.'

'Ursula!' I said in surprise. 'This is Tim Ekaterin.'

'Really?' For her it was equally unexpected. 'What are *you* doing there?'

'Just staying the weekend. Can I help?'

She hesitated slightly but then said, 'Yes, I suppose you can. I'm afraid it's bad news for him, though. Disappointing, you might say.' She paused. 'I've a friend who has a small stud farm, just one stallion, but quite a good one, and she's been so excited this year because one of the mares booked to him was in foal to Sandcastle. She was thrilled, you see, to be having a foal of that calibre born on her place.'

'Yes,' I said.

'Well, she rang me this morning, and she was crying.' Ursula herself gulped: she might appear tough but other people's tears always moved her. 'She said the mare had dropped the Sandcastle foal during the night and she hadn't been there. She said the mare gave no sign yesterday evening, and the birth must have been quick and easy, and the mare was all right, but . . .'

'But what?' I said, scarcely breathing.

'She said the foal – a filly – was on her feet and suckling when she went to the mare's box this morning, and at first she was overjoyed, but then . . . but then . . .'

'Go on,' I said hopelessly.

'Then she saw. She says it dreadful.'

'Ursula . . .'

'The foal has only one eye.'

Oh my God, I thought: dear *God*.

'She says there's nothing on the other side,' Ursula said. 'No proper socket.' She gulped again. 'Will you tell Oliver? I thought he'd better know. He'll be most disappointed. I'm so sorry.'

'I'll tell him.'

'These things happen, I suppose,' she said. 'But it's so upsetting when they happen to your friends.'

'You're very right.'

'Goodbye then, Tim. See you soon, I hope, at the races.'

I put down the receiver and wondered how I would ever tell them, and in fact I didn't tell Ginnie, only Oliver, who sat with his head in his hands, despair in every line of his body.

'It's hopeless,' he said.

'Not yet,' I said encouragingly, though I wasn't as certain as I sounded. 'There are still the tests to be done on Sandcastle.'

He merely slumped lower. 'I'll get them done, but they won't help. The genes which are wrong will be minute. No one will see them, however powerful the microscope.'

'You can't tell. If they can see DNA, why not a horse's chromosomes?'

He raised his head slowly. 'Even then . . . it's such a long shot.' He sighed deeply. 'I think I'll ask the Equine Research Establishment at Newmarket to have him there, to see what they can find. I'll ring them on Monday.'

'I suppose,' I said tentatively, 'Well, I know it sounds silly, but I suppose it couldn't be anything as simple as something he'd *eaten*? Last year, of course.'

He shook his head. 'I thought of that. I've thought of bloody well everything, believe me. All the stallions had the same food, and none of the others' foals are affected . . . or at least we haven't heard of any. Nigel feeds the stallions himself out of the feed room in that yard, and we're always careful what we give them because of keeping them fit.'

'Carrots?' I said.

'I give carrots to every horse on the place. Everyone here does. Carrots are good food. I buy them by the hundredweight and keep them in the first big yard where the main feed room is. I put handfuls in my pockets every day. You've seen me. Rotaboy, Diarist and Parakeet all had them. It can't possibly be anything to do with carrots.'

'Paint: something like that? Something new in the boxes, when you put in all the security? Something he could chew?'

He again shook his head. 'I've been over it and over it. We did all the boxes exactly the same as each other. There's nothing in Sandcastle's box that wasn't in the others. They're all exactly alike.' He moved restlessly. 'I've been down there to make sure there's nothing Sandcastle could reach to lick if he put his head right over the half-door as far as he could get. There's nothing, nothing at all.'

'Drinking pails?'

'No. They don't always have the same pails. I mean, when Lenny fills them he doesn't necessarily take them back to the particular boxes they come from. The pails don't have the stallions' names on, if that's what you mean.'

I didn't mean anything much: just grabbing at straws.

'Straw . . .' I said. 'How about an allergy? An allergy to something around him? Could an allergy have such an effect?'

'I've never heard of anything like that. I'll ask the Research people, though, on Monday.'

He got up to pour us both a drink. 'It's good to have you here,' he said. 'A sort of net over the bottomless pit.' He gave me the glass with a faint half-smile, and I had a definite impression that he would not in the end go to pieces.

I telephoned then to the Michaels' house and Gordon answered at the first ring as if he'd been passing nearby. Nothing good to report, I said, except that Ginnie sent Judith her love. Gordon said Judith was in the garden picking parsley for supper, and he would tell her. 'Call tomorrow,' he said, 'if we can help.'

Our own supper, left already in the refrigerator by Oliver's part-time housekeeper, filled the hollows left by lunch, and Ginnie went to bed straight afterwards, saying she would be up at two o'clock and out with Nigel in the foal yard.

'She goes most nights,' Oliver said. 'She and Nigel make a good team. He says she's a great help, particularly if three or four mares are foaling at the same time. I'm often out there myself, but with all the decisions and paperwork as well I get very tired if I do it too much. Fall asleep over meals, that sort of thing.'

We ourselves went to bed fairly early, and I awoke in the large high-ceilinged guest room while it was still blackly dark. It was one of those fast awakenings which mean that sleep won't come back easily, and I got out of bed and went to the window, which looked out over the yard.

I could see only roofs and security lights and a small section of the first yard. There was no visible activity, and my watch showed four-thirty.

I wondered if Ginnie would mind if I joined her in the foaling yard; and got dressed and went.

They were all there, Nigel and Oliver as well as Ginnie, all in one open-doored box where a mare lay on her side on the straw. They all turned their heads as I approached but seemed unsurprised to see me and gave no particular greeting.

'This is Plus Factor,' Oliver said. 'In foal to Sandcastle.'

His voice was calm and so was Ginnie's manner, and I guessed that they still hadn't told Nigel about the deformities. There was hope, too, in their faces, as if they were sure that this one, after all, would be perfect.

'She's coming,' Nigel said quietly. 'Here we go.'

The mare gave a grunt and her swelling sides heaved. The rest of us stood silent, watching, taking no part. A glistening half-transparent membrane with a hoof showing within it appeared, followed by the long slim shape of the head, followed very rapidly by the whole foal, flopping out onto the straw, steaming, the membrane breaking open, the fresh air reaching the head, new life beginning with the first fluttering gasp of the lungs.

Amazing, I thought.

'Is he all right?' Oliver said, bending down, the anxiety raw, unstifled.

'Sure,' Nigel said. 'Fine little colt. Just his foreleg's doubled over . . .'

He knelt beside the foal who was already making the first feeble efforts to move his head, and he stretched out both hands gently to free the bent leg fully from the membrane, and to straighten it. He picked it up . . . and froze.

We could all see.

The leg wasn't bent. It ended in a stump at the knee. No cannon bone, no fetlock, no hoof.

Ginnie beside me gave a choking sob and turned abruptly towards the open door, towards the dark. She took one rocky pace and then another, and then was running: running nowhere, running away from the present, the future, the unimaginable. From the hopeless little creature on the straw.

I went after her, listening to her footsteps, hearing them on gravel and then losing them, guessing she had reached the grass. I went more slowly in her wake down the path to the breeding pen, not seeing her, but sure she was out somewhere in the paths round the paddocks. With eyes slowly acclimatising I went that way and found her not far off, on her knees beside one of the posts, sobbing with the deep sound of a wholly adult desperation.

'Ginnie,' I said.

She stood up as if to turn to me was natural and clung to me fiercely, her body shaking from the sobs, her face pressed hard against my shoulder, my arms tightly round her. We stood like that until the paroxysm passed; until, dragging a handkerchief from her jeans, she could speak.

'It's one thing knowing it in theory,' she said, her voice full of tears and her body still shaking spasmodically from after-sobs. 'I read those letters. I did know. But *seeing* it . . . that's different.'

'Yes,' I said.

'And it means . . .' She took gulps of air, trying hard for control. 'It means, doesn't it, that we'll lose our farm. Lose everything?'

'I don't know yet. Too soon to say that.'

'Poor Dad.' The tears were sliding slowly down her cheeks, but like harmless rain after a hurricane. 'I don't see how we can bear it.'

'Don't despair yet. If there's a way to save you, we'll find it.'

'Do you mean . . . your bank?'

'I mean everybody.'

She wiped her eyes and blew her nose, and finally moved away a pace, out of my arms, strong enough to leave shelter. We went slowly back to the foaling yard and found nobody there except horses. I undid the closed top half of Plus Factor's box and looked inside; looked at the mare standing there patiently without her foal and wondered if she felt any fretting sense of loss.

'Dad and Nigel have taken him, haven't they?' Ginnie said.

'Yes.'

She nodded, accepting that bit easily. Death to her was part of life, as to every child brought up close to animals. I closed Plus Factor's door and Ginnie and I went back to the house while the sky lightened in the east to the new day, Sunday.

The work of the place went on.

Oliver telephoned to various owners of the mares who had come to the other three stallions, reporting the birth of foals alive and well and one dead before foaling, very sorry. His voice sounded strong, civilised, controlled, the competent captain at the helm, and one could almost see the steel creeping back, hour by hour, into his battered spirit. I admired him for it; and I would fight to give him time, I thought, to come to some compromise to avert permanent ruin.

Ginnie, showered, breakfasted, tidy in sweater and shirt, went off to spend the morning at the Watcherleys' and came back smiling; the resilience of youth.

'Both of those mares are better from their infections,' she reported, 'and Maggie says she's heard Calder Jackson's not doing so well lately, his yard's half empty. Cheers Maggie up no end, she says.'

For the Watcherlys too, I thought briefly, the fall of Oliver's business could mean a return to rust and weeds, but I said, 'Not enough sick horses just now, perhaps.'

'Not enough sick horses with rich owners, Maggie says.'

In the afternoon Ginnie slept on the sofa looking very childlike and peaceful, and only with the awakening did the night's pain roll back.

'Oh dear . . .' The slow tears came. 'I was dreaming it was all right. That that foal was a dream, only a dream . . .'

'You and your father,' I said. 'Are brave people.'

She sniffed a little, pressing against her nose with the back of her hand. 'Do you mean,' she said slowly, 'that whatever happens, we mustn't be defeated?'

'Mm.'

She looked at me, and after a while nodded. 'If we have to, we'll start again. We'll work. He did it all before, you know.'

'You both have the skills,' I said.

'I'm glad you came.' She brushed the drying tears from her cheeks. 'God knows what it would have been like without you.'

I went with her out into the yards for evening stables, where the muck-carrying and feeding went on as always. Ginnie fetched the usual pocketful of carrots from the feed room and gave them here and there to the mares, talking cheerfully to the lads while they bent to their chores. No one, watching and listening, could ever have imagined that she feared the sky was falling.

'Evening, Chris, how's her hoof today?'

'Hi, Danny. Did you bring this one in this morning?'

'Hello, Pete. She looks as if she'll foal any day now.'

'Evening, Shane. How's she doing?'

'Hi, Sammy, is she eating now OK?'

The lads answered her much as they spoke to Oliver himself, straightforwardly and with respect, and in most cases without stopping what they were doing. I looked back as we left the first big yard for the second, and for a moment took one of the lads to be Ricky Barnet.

'Who's that?' I said to Ginnie.

She followed my gaze to where the lad walked across to the yard tap, swinging an empty bucket with one hand and eating an apple with the other.

'Shane. Why?'

'He reminded me of someone I knew.'

She shrugged. 'He's all right. They all are, when Nigel's looking, which he doesn't do often enough.'

'He works all night,' I said mildly.

'I suppose so.'

The mares in the second yard had mostly given birth already and Ginnie that evening had special eyes for the foals. The lads hadn't yet reached those boxes and Ginnie didn't go in to any of them, warning me that mares with young foals could be protective and snappy.

'You never know if they'll bite or kick you. Dad doesn't like me going in with them alone.' She smiled. 'He still thinks I'm a baby.'

We went on to the foaling yard, where a lad greeted as Dave was installing a heavy slow-walking mare into one of the boxes.

'Nigel says she'll foal tonight,' he told Ginnie.

'He's usually right.'

We went on past the breeding pen and came to the stallions, where Larry and Ron were washing down Diarist (who appeared to have been working) in the centre of the yard, using a lot of water, energy and oaths.

'Mind his feet,' Larry said. 'He's in one of his moods.'

Ginnie gave carrots to Parakeet and Rotaboy, and we came finally to Sandcastle. He looked as great, as charismatic as ever, but Ginnie gave him his tit-bit with her own lips compressed.

'He can't help it all, I suppose,' she said sighing. 'But I do wish he'd never won any races.'

'Or that we'd let him die that day on the main road?'

'Oh no!' She was shocked. 'We couldn't have done that, even if we'd known . . .'

Dear girl, I thought; many people would personally have mown him down with a truck.

We went back to the house via the paddocks, where she fondled any heads that came to the railings and parted with the last of the crunchy orange goodies. 'I can't believe that this will all end,' she said, looking over the horse-dotted acres. 'I just *can't* believe it.'

I tentatively suggested to both her and Oliver that they might prefer it if I went home that evening, but they both declared themselves against.

'Not yet,' Ginnie said anxiously and Oliver nodded forcefully. 'Please do stay, Tim, if you can.'

I nodded, and rang the Michaels', and this time got Judith.

'Do let me speak to her,' Ginnie said, taking the receiver out of my hand. 'I do so want to.'

And I, I thought wryly, I too want so much to talk to her, to hear her voice, to renew my own soul through her: I'm no one's universal pillar of strength, I need my comfort too.

I had my crumbs, after Ginnie. Ordinary words, all else implied; as always.

'Take care of yourself,' she said finally.

'You, too,' I said.

'Yes.' The word was a sigh, faint and receding, as if she'd said it with the receiver already away from her mouth. There was the click of disconnection, and Oliver was announcing briskly that it was time for whisky, time for supper; time for anything perhaps but thinking.

Ginnie decided that she felt too restless after supper to go to bed early, and would go for a walk instead.

'Do you want me to come?' I said.

'No. I'm all right. I just thought I'd go out. Look at the stars.' She kissed her father's forehead, pulling on a thick cardigan for warmth. 'I won't go off the farm. You'll probably find me in the foal yard, if you want me.'

He nodded to her fondly but absentmindedly, and with a small wave to me she went away. Oliver asked me gloomily, as if he'd been waiting for us to be alone, how soon I thought the bank would decide on his fate, and we talked in snatches about his daunting prospects, an hour or two sliding by on possibilities.

Shortly before ten, when we had probably twice repeated all there was to say, there came a heavy hammering on the back door.

'Whoever's that?' Oliver frowned, rose to his feet and went to find out.

I didn't hear the opening words, but only the goose-pimpling urgency in the rising voice.

'She's where?' Oliver said loudly, plainly, in alarm. 'Where?'

I went quickly into the hallway. One of the lads stood in the open doorway, panting for breath, wide-eyed and looking very scared.

Oliver glanced at me over his shoulder, already on the move. 'He says Ginnie's lying on the ground unconscious.'

The lad turned and ran off, with Oliver following and myself close behind: and the lad's breathlessness, I soon found, was owing to Ginnie's being on the far side of the farm, away down beyond Nigel's bungalow and the lads' hostel, right down on the far drive, near the gate to the lower road.

We arrived there still running, the lad now doubling over in his fight for breath, and found Ginnie lying on her side on the hard asphalt surface with another of the lads on his knees beside her, dim figures in weak moonlight, blurred outlines of shadow.

Oliver and I too knelt there and Oliver was saying to the lads, 'What happened, what happened? Did she fall?'

'We just found her,' the kneeling lad said. 'We were on our way back from the pub. She's coming round, though, sir, she's been saying things.'

Ginnie in fact moved slightly, and said 'Dad.'

'Yes, Ginnie, I'm here.' He picked up her hand and patted it. 'We'll soon get you right.' There was relief in his voice, but short-lived.

'Dad,' Ginnie said, mumbling. 'Dad.'

'Yes. I'm here.'

'Dad . . .'

'She isn't hearing you,' I said worriedly.

He turned his head to me, his eyes liquid in the dark of his face. 'Get an ambulance. There's a telephone in Nigel's house. Tell him to get an ambulance here quickly. I don't think we'll move her . . . Get an ambulance.'

I stood up to go on the errand but the breathless lad said, 'Nigel's out. I tried there. There's no one. It's all locked.'

'I'll go back to the house.'

I ran as fast on the way back and had to fight to control my own gulping breaths there to make my words intelligible. 'Tell them to take the lower road from the village . . . the smaller right fork . . . where the road divides. Nearly a mile from there . . . wide metal farm gate, on the left.'

'Understood,' a man said impersonally. 'They'll be on their way.'

I fetched the padded quilt off my bed and ran back across the farm and found everything much as I'd left it. 'They're coming,' I said. 'How is she?'

Oliver tucked the quilt round his daughter as best he could. 'She keeps saying things. Just sounds, not words.'

'Da–' Ginnie said.

Her eyelids trembled and slightly opened.

'Ginnie,' Oliver said urgently. 'This is Dad.'

Her lips moved in a mumbling unformed murmur. The eyes looked at nothing, unfocused, the gleam just reflected moonlight, not an awakening.

'Oh God,' Oliver said. 'What's happened to her? What can have happened?'

The two lads stood there, awkward and silent, not knowing the answer.

'Go and open the gate,' Oliver told them. 'Stand on the road. Signal to the ambulance when it comes.'

They went as if relieved; and the ambulance did come, lights flashing, with two brisk men in uniform who lifted Ginnie without much disturbing her onto a stretcher. Oliver asked them to wait while he fetched the Land Rover from Nigel's garage, and in a short time the ambulance set off to the hospital with Oliver and me following.

'Lucky you had the key,' I said, indicating it in the ignition. Just something to say: anything.

'We always keep it in that tin on the shelf.'

The tin said 'Blackcurrant Coughdrops. Take as Required.'

Oliver drove automatically, following the rear lights ahead. 'Why don't they go faster?' he said, though their speed was quite normal.

'Don't want to jolt her, perhaps.'

'Do you think it's a stroke?' he said.

'She's too young.'

'No. I had a cousin . . . an aneurysm burst when he was sixteen.'

I glanced at his face: lined, grim, intent on the road.

The journey seemed endless, but ended at a huge bright hospital in a sprawling town. The men in uniform opened the rear doors of the ambulance while Oliver parked the Land Rover and we followed them into the brightly lit emergency reception area, seeing them wheel Ginnie into a curtained cubicle, watching them come out again with their stretcher, thanking them as they left.

A nurse told us to sit on some nearby chairs while she

fetched a doctor. The place was empty, quiet, all readiness but no bustle. Ten o'clock on Sunday night.

A doctor came in a white coat, stethoscope dangling. An Indian, young, black-haired, rubbing his eyes with forefinger and thumb. He went behind the curtains with the nurse and for about a minute Oliver clasped and unclasped his fingers, unable to contain his anxiety.

The doctor's voice reached us clearly, the Indian accent making no difference.

'They shouldn't have brought her here,' he said. 'She's dead.'

Oliver was on his feet, bounding across the shining floor, pulling back the curtains with a frantic sweep of the arm.

'She's not dead. She was talking. Moving. She's not dead.'

In dread I followed him. She couldn't be dead, not like that, not so fast, not without the hospital fighting long to save her. She *couldn't* be.

The doctor straightened up from bending over her, withdrawing his hand from under Ginnie's head, looking at us across the small space.

'She's my daughter,' Oliver said. 'She's not dead.'

A sort of weary compassion drooped in the doctor's shoulders. 'I am sorry,' he said. 'Very sorry. She is gone.'

'No!' The word burst out of Oliver in an agony. 'You're wrong. Get someone else.'

The nurse made a shocked gesture but the young doctor said gently, 'There is no pulse. No heartbeat. No contraction of the pupils. She has been gone for perhaps ten minutes, perhaps twenty. I could get someone else, but there is nothing to be done.'

'But *why*?' Oliver said. 'She was talking.'

The dark doctor looked down to where Ginnie was lying on her back, eyes closed, brown hair falling about her head, face very pale. Her jerseys had both been unbuttoned for the stethoscope, the white bra showing, and the nurse had also undone the waistband of the skirt, pulling it loose. Ginnie looked very young, very defenceless, lying there so quiet and still, and I stood numbly, not believing it, unable, like Oliver, to accept such a monstrous change.

'Her skull is fractured,' the doctor said. 'If she was talking, she died on the way here, in the ambulance. With head injuries it can be like that. I am sorry.'

There was a sound of an ambulance's siren wailing outside,

and sudden noise and rushing people by the doors where we had come in, voices raised in a jumble of instructions.

'Traffic accident,' someone shouted, and the doctor's eyes moved beyond us to the new need, to the future, not the past.

'I must go,' he said, and the nurse, nodding, handed me a flat white plastic bottle which she had been holding.

'You may as well take this,' she said. 'It was tucked into the waistband of her skirt, against the stomach.'

She made as if to cover Ginnie with a sheet, but Oliver stopped her.

'I'll do it,' he said. 'I want to be with her.'

The young doctor nodded, and he and I and the nurse stepped outside the cubicle, drawing the curtains behind us. The doctor looked in a brief pause of stillness towards the three or four stretchers arriving at the entrance, taking a breath, seeming to summon up energy from deep reserves.

'I've been on duty for thirty hours,' he said to me. 'And now the pubs are out. Ten o'clock, Sundays. Drunk drivers, drunk pedestrians. Always the same.'

He walked away to his alive and bleeding patients and the nurse pinned a 'Do Not Enter' sign onto the curtains of Ginnie's cubicle, saying she would be taken care of later.

I sat drearily on a chair, waiting for Oliver. The white plastic bottle had a label stuck onto one side saying 'Shampoo'. I put it into my jacket pocket and wondered if it was just through overwork that the doctor hadn't asked how Ginnie's skull had been fractured, asked whether she'd fallen onto a rock or a kerb . . . or been hit.

The rest of the night and all the next day were in their own way worse, a truly awful series of questions, answers, forms and officialdom, with the police slowly taking over from the hospital and Oliver trying to fight against a haze of grief.

It seemed to me wicked that no one would leave him alone. To them he was just one more in a long line of bereaved persons, and although they treated him with perfunctory sympathy, it was for their own paperwork and not for his benefit that they wanted signatures, information and guesses.

Large numbers of policemen descended on the farm early in the morning, and it gradually appeared that that area of the country was being plagued by a stalker of young girls who jumped out of bushes, knocked them unconscious and sexually assaulted them.

'Not Ginnie . . .' Oliver protested in deepening horror.

The most senior of the policemen shook his head. 'It would appear not. She was still wearing her clothing. We can't discount, though, that it was the same man, and that he was disturbed by your grooms. When young girls are knocked unconscious at night, it's most often a sexual attack.'

'But she was on my own land,' he said, disbelieving.

The policeman shrugged. 'It's been known in suburban front gardens.'

He was a fair-haired man with a manner that was not exactly brutal but spoke of long years of acclimatisation to dreadful experiences. Detective Chief Inspector Wyfold, he'd said, introducing himself. Forty-fivish, I guessed, sensing the hardness within him at sight and judging him through that day more dogged than intuitive, looking for results from procedure, not hunches.

He was certain in his own mind that the attack on Ginnie had been sexual in intent and he scarcely considered anything else, particularly since she'd been carrying no money and had expressly said she wouldn't leave the farm.

'She could have talked to someone over the gate,' he said, having himself spent some time on the lower drive. 'Someone walking along the road. And there are all your grooms that we'll need detailed statements from, though from their preliminary answers it seems they weren't in the hostel but down at the village, in the pubs.'

He came and went and reappeared again with more questions at intervals through the day and I lost track altogether of the hours. I tried, in his presence and out, and in Oliver's the same, not to think much about Ginnie herself. I thought I would probably have wept if I had, of no use to anyone. I thrust her away into a defensive compartment knowing that later, alone, I would let her out.

Some time in the morning one of the lads came to the house and asked what they should do about one of the mares who was having difficulty foaling, and Lenny also arrived wanting to know when he should take Rotaboy to the breeding pen. Each of them stood awkwardly, not knowing where to put their hands, saying they were so shocked, so sorry, about Ginnie.

'Where's Nigel?' Oliver said.

They hadn't seen him, they said. He hadn't been out in the yards that morning.

'Didn't you try his house?' Oliver was annoyed rather than alarmed: another burden on a breaking back.

'He isn't there. The door's locked and he didn't answer.'

Oliver frowned, picked up the telephone and pressed the buttons: listened: no reply.

He said to me, 'There's a key to his bungalow over there on the board, third hook from the left. Would you go and look . . . would you mind?'

'Sure.'

I walked down there with Lenny who told me repeatedly how broken up the lads were over what had happened, particularly Dave and Sammy, who'd found her. They'd all liked her, he said. All the lads who lived in the hostel were saying that perhaps if they'd come back sooner, she wouldn't have been attacked.

'You don't live in the hostel, then?' I said.

'No. Down in the village. Got a house. Only the ones who come just for the season, they're the ones in the hostel. It's shut up, see, all winter.'

We eventually reached Nigel's bungalow where I rang the doorbell and banged on the knocker without result. Shaking my head slightly I fitted the key in the lock, opened the door, went in.

Curtains were drawn across the windows, shutting out a good deal of daylight. I switched on a couple of lights and walked into the sitting room, where papers, clothes and dirty cups and plates were strewn haphazardly and the air smelled faintly of horse.

There was no sign of Nigel. I looked into the equally untidy kitchen and opened a door which proved to be that of a bathroom and another which revealed a room with bare-mattressed twin beds. The last door in the small inner hall led into Nigel's own bedroom . . . and there he was, face down, fully clothed, lying across the counterpane.

Lenny, still behind me, took two paces back.

I went over to the bed and felt Nigel's neck behind the ear. Felt the pulse going like a steam-hammer. Heard the rasp of air in the throat. His breath would have anaesthetised a crocodile, and on the floor beside him lay an empty bottle of gin. I shook his shoulder unsympathetically with a complete lack of result.

'He's drunk,' I said to Lenny. 'Just drunk.'

Lenny looked all the same as if he was about to vomit. 'I thought . . . I thought.'

'I know,' I said: and I'd feared it also, instinctively, the one because of the other.

'What will we do, then, out in the yard?' Lenny asked.

'I'll find out.'

We went back into the sitting room where I used Nigel's telephone to call Oliver and report.

'He's flat out,' I said. 'I can't wake him. Lenny wants instructions.'

After a brief silence Oliver said dully, 'Tell him to take Rotaboy to the breeding shed in half an hour. I'll see to things in the yards. And Tim?'

'Yes?'

'Can I ask you . . . would you mind . . . helping me here in the office?'

'Coming straight back.'

The disjointed, terrible day wore on. I telephoned to Gordon in the bank explaining my absence and to Judith also, at Gordon's suggestion, to pass on the heartbreak, and I took countless incoming messages as the news spread. Outside on the farm nearly two hundred horses got fed and watered, and birth and procreation went inexorably on.

Oliver came back stumbling from fatigue at about two o'clock, and we ate some eggs, not tasting them, in the kitchen. He looked repeatedly at his watch and said finally, 'What's eight hours back from now? I can't even *think*.'

'Six in the morning,' I said.

'Oh.' He rubbed a hand over his face. 'I suppose I should have told Ginnie's mother last night.' His face twisted. 'My wife . . . in Canada . . .' He swallowed. 'Never mind, let her sleep. In two hours I'll tell her.'

I left him alone to that wretched task and took myself upstairs to wash and shave and lie for a while on the bed. It was in taking my jacket off for those purposes that I came across the plastic bottle in my pocket, and I took it out and stood it on the shelf in the bathroom while I shaved.

An odd sort of thing, I thought, for Ginnie to have tucked into her waistband. A plastic bottle of shampoo; about six inches high, four across, one deep, with a screw cap on one of the narrow ends. The white label saying 'Shampoo' had been handwritten and stuck on top of the bottle's original dark brown, white-printed label, of which quite a bit still showed round the edges.

'*Instructions*,' part of the underneath label said. '*Shake well.*

Be careful not to get the shampoo in the dog's eyes. Rub well into the coat and leave for ten or fifteen minutes before rinsing.'

At the bottom, below the stuck-on label, were the words, in much smaller print, '*Manufactured by Eagle Inc., Michigan, U.S.A. List number 29931.*

When I'd finished shaving I unscrewed the cap and tilted the bottle gently over the basin.

A thick greenish liquid appeared, smelling powerfully of soap.

Shampoo: what else.

The bottle was to all intents full. I screwed on the cap again and put it on the shelf, and thought about it while I lay on the bed with my hands behind my head.

Shampoo for dogs.

After a while I got up and went down to the kitchen, and in a high cupboard found a small collection of empty, washed, screw-top glass jars, the sort of thing my mother had always saved for herbs and picnics. I took one which would hold perhaps a cupful of liquid and returned upstairs, and over the washbasin I shook the bottle well, unscrewed the cap and carefully poured more than half of the shampoo into the jar.

I screwed the caps onto both the bottle and the jar, copied what could be seen on the original label into the small engagement diary I carried with me everywhere, and stowed the now half full round glass container from Oliver's kitchen inside my own sponge-bag: and when I went downstairs again I took the plastic bottle with me.

'Ginnie had it?' Oliver said dully, picking it up and squinting at it. 'Whatever for?'

'The nurse at the hospital said it was tucked into the waistband of her skirt.'

A smile flickered. 'She always did that when she was little. Plimsols, books, bits of string, anything. To keep her hands free, she said. They all used to slip down into her little knickers, and there would be a whole shower of things sometimes when we undressed her.' His face went hopelessly bleak at this memory. 'I can't believe it, you know,' he said. 'I keep thinking she'll walk through the door.' He paused. 'My wife is flying over. She says she'll be here tomorrow morning.' His voice gave no indication as to whether that was good news or bad. 'Stay tonight, will you?'

'If you want.'

'Yes.'

Chief Inspector Wyfold turned up again at that point and we gave him the shampoo bottle, Oliver explaining about Ginnie's habit of carrying things in her clothes.

'Why didn't you give this to me earlier?' he asked me.

'I forgot I had it. It seemed so paltry at the time, compared with Ginnie dying.'

The Chief Inspector picked up the bottle by its serrated cap and read what one could see of the label, and to Oliver he said, 'Do you have a dog?'

'Yes.'

'Would this be what you usually use, to wash him?'

'I really don't know. I don't wash him myself. One of the lads does.'

'The lads being the grooms?'

'That's right.'

'Which lad washed your dog?' Wyfold asked.

'Um . . . any. Whoever I ask.'

The Chief Inspector produced a thin white folded paper bag from one of his pockets and put the bottle inside it. 'Who to your knowledge has handled this, besides yourselves?' he asked.

'I suppose,' I said, 'the nurse at the hospital . . . and Ginnie.'

'And it spent from last night until now in your pocket?' He shrugged. 'Hopeless for prints, I should think, but we'll try.' He fastened the bag shut and wrote on a section of it with a ball pen. To Oliver, almost as an aside, he said, 'I came to ask you about your daughter's relationship with men.'

Oliver said wearily, 'She didn't have any. She's only just left school.'

Wyfold made small negative movements with head and hands as if amazed at the naiveté of fathers. 'No sexual relationship to your knowledge?'

Oliver was too exhausted for anger. 'No,' he said.

'And you sir?' he turned to me. 'What were your relations with Virginia Knowles?'

'Friendship.'

'Including sexual intercourse?'

'No.'

Wyfold looked at Oliver who said tiredly, 'Tim is a business friend of mine. A financial adviser, staying here for the weekend, that's all.'

The policeman frowned at me with disillusion as if he didn't believe it. I gave him no amplified answer because I simply couldn't be bothered, and what could I have said? That with much affection I'd watched a child grow into an attractive young woman and yet not wanted to sleep with her? His mind ran on carnal rails, all else discounted.

He went away in the end taking the shampoo with him, and Oliver with an immense fortitude said he had better go out into the yards to catch the tail end of evening stables. 'Those mares,' he said. 'Those foals . . . they still need the best of care.'

'I wish I could help,' I said, feeling useless.

'You do.'

I went with him on his rounds, and when we reached the foaling yard, Nigel, resurrected, was there.

His stocky figure leaned against the doorpost of an open box as if without its support he would collapse, and the face he slowly turned towards us had aged ten years. The bushy eyebrows stood out starkly over charcoal shadowed eyes, puffiness in his skin swelling the eyelids and sagging in deep bags on his cheeks. He was also unshaven, unkempt and feeling ill.

'Sorry,' he said. 'Heard about Ginnie. Very sorry.' I wasn't sure whether he was sympathising with Oliver or apologising for the drunkenness. 'A big noise of a policeman came asking if I'd killed her. As if I would.' He put a shaky hand on his head, almost as if physically to support it on his shoulders. 'I feel rotten. My own fault. Deserve it. This mare's likely to foal tonight. That shit of a policeman wanted to know if I was sleeping with Ginnie. Thought I'd tell you . . . I wasn't.'

Wyfold, I reflected, would ask each of the lads individually the same question. A matter of time, perhaps, before he asked Oliver himself; though Oliver and I, he had had to concede, gave each other a rock-solid alibi.

We walked on towards the stallions and I asked Oliver if Nigel often got drunk, since Oliver hadn't shown much surprise.

'Very seldom,' Oliver said. 'He's once or twice turned out in that state but we've never lost a foal because of it. I don't like it, but he's so good with the mares.' He shrugged. 'I overlook it.'

He gave carrrots to all four stallions but scarcely glanced at Sandcastle, as if he could no longer bear the sight.

'I'll try the Research people tomorrow,' he said. 'Forgot about it, today.'

From the stallions he went, unusually, in the direction of

the lower gate, past Nigel's bungalow and the hostel, to stand for a while at the place where Ginnie had lain in the dark on the night before.

The asphalt driveway showed no mark. Oliver looked to where the closed gate sixty feet away led to the road and in a drained voice said, 'Do you think she could have talked to someone out there?'

'She might have, I suppose.'

'Yes.' He turned to go back. 'It's all so *senseless*. And unreal. Nothing feels real.'

Exhaustion of mind and body finally overtook him after dinner and he went grey-faced to bed, but I in the first quiet of the long day went out again for restoration: for a look at the stars, as Ginnie had said.

Thinking only of her I walked slowly along some of the paths between the paddocks, the way lit by a half-moon with small clouds drifting, and stopped eventually at the place where on the previous morning I'd held her tight in her racking distress. The birth of the deformed foal seemed so long ago, yet it was only yesterday: the morning of the last day of Ginnie's life.

I thought about that day, about the despair in its dawn and the resolution of its afternoon. I thought of her tears and her courage, and of the waste of so much goodness. The engulfing, stupefying sense of loss which had hovered all day swamped into my brain until my body felt inadequate, as if it wanted to burst, as if it couldn't hold in so much feeling.

When Ian Pargetter had been murdered I had been angry on his behalf and had supposed that the more one loved the dead person the greater one's fury against the killer. But now I understood that anger could simply be crowded out by something altogether more overwhelming. As for Oliver, he had displayed shock, daze, desolation and disbelief in endless quantities all day, but of anger, barely a flicker.

It was too soon to care who had killed her. The fact of her death was too much. Anger was irrelevant, and no vengeance could give her life.

I had loved her more than I'd known, but not as I loved Judith, not with desire and pain and longing. I'd loved Ginnie as a friend; as a brother. I'd loved her, I thought, right back from the day when I'd returned her to school and listened to her fears. I'd loved her up on the hill, trying to catch Sandcastle, and I'd loved her for her expertise and for her growing adult certainty that here, in these fields, was where her future lay.

I'd thought of her young life once as being a clear stretch of sand waiting for footprints, and now there would be none, now only a blank, chopping end to all she could have been and done, to all the bright love she had scattered around her.

'Oh . . . *Ginnie,*' I said aloud, calling to her hopelessly in tearing body-shaking grief. 'Ginnie . . . little Ginnie . . . come back.'

But she was gone from there. My voice fled away into darkness, and there was no answer.

The Third Year

MAY

On and off for the next two weeks I worked on Oliver's financial chaos at my desk in the bank, and at a special board meeting argued the case for giving him time before we foreclosed and made him sell all he had.

I asked for three months, which was considered scandalously out of the question, but got him two, Gordon chuckling over it quietly as we went down together afterwards in the lift.

'I suppose two months was what you wanted?' he said.

'Er . . . yes.'

'I know you,' he said. 'They were talking of twenty-one days maximum before the meeting, and some wanted to bring in liquidators at once.'

I telephoned Oliver and told him. 'For two months you don't have to pay any interest or capital repayments, but this is only temporary, and it is a special, fairly unusual concession. I'm afraid, though, that if we can't find a solution to Sandcastle's problem or come up with a cast-iron reason for the insurance company to pay out, the prognosis is not good.'

'I understand,' he said, his voice sounding calm. 'I haven't much hope, but thank you, all the same, for the respite – I will at least be able to finish the programmes for the other stallions, and keep all the foals here until they're old enough to travel safely.'

'Have you heard anything about Sandcastle?'

'He's been at the Research Establishment for a week, but so far they can't find anything wrong with him. They don't hold out much hope, I'd better tell you, of being able to prove anything one way or another about his sperm, even though they're sending specimens to another laboratory, they say.'

'They'll do their best.'

'Yes, I know. But . . . I walk around here as if this place no longer belongs to me. As if it isn't mine. I know, inside, that I'm losing it. Don't feel too badly, Tim. When it comes, I'll be prepared.'

I put the receiver down not knowing whether such

resignation was good because he would face whatever came without disintegration, or bad because he might be surrendering too soon. A great host of other troubles still lay ahead, mostly in the shape of breeders demanding the return of their stallion fees, and he needed energy to say that in most cases he couldn't return them. The money had already been lodged with us, and the whole situation would have to be sorted out by lawyers.

The news of Sandcastle's disgrace was so far only a doubtful murmur here and there, but when it all broke open with a screech it was, I suppose predictably, in *What's Going On Where It Shouldn't*.

The bank's six copies were read to rags before lunch on the day Alec fetched them, eyes lifting from the page with anything from fury to a wry smile.

Three short paragraphs headed 'House on Sand', said:

Build not your house on sand. Stake not your banking house on a Sandcastle.

The five million pounds advanced by a certain prestigious merchant bank for the purchase of the stallion Sandcastle now look like being washed away by the tide. Sadly, the investment has produced faulty stock, or in plain language, several deformed foals.

Speculation now abounds as to what the bank can do to minimise its losses, since Sandcastle himself must be considered as half a ton of highly priced dog-meat.

'That's done it,' Gordon said, and I nodded: and the dailies, who always read *What's Going On* as a prime news source, came up in the racing columns the next day with a more cautious approach, asking 'Sandcastle's Progeny Flawed?' and saying things like 'rumours have reached us' and 'we are reliably informed.'

Since our own home-grown leaker for once hadn't mentioned the bank by name, none of the dailies did either, and for them of course the bank itself was unimportant compared with the implications of the news.

Oliver, in the next weekday issues, was reported as having been asked how many, precisely, of Sandcastle's foals were deformed, and as having answered that he didn't know. He had heard of some, certainly, yes. He had no further comment.

A day later still the papers began printing reports telephoned into them by the stud farms where Sandcastle's scattered progeny had been foaled, and the tally of disasters mounted. Oliver was reported this time as having said the horse was at the Equine Research Establishment at Newmarket, and everything possible was being done.

'It's a mess,' Henry said gloomily at lunch, and even the dissenting director had run out of insults, beyond saying four times that we were the laughing-stock of the City and it was all my fault.

'Have they found out who killed Knowles' daughter?' Val Fisher asked.

'No.' I shook my head. 'He says the police no longer come to the house.'

Val looked regretful. 'Such a sadness for him, on top of the other.'

There were murmurs of sympathy and I didn't think I'd spoil it by telling them what the police thought of Oliver's lads.

'That man Wyfold,' Oliver had said on the telephone during one of our almost daily conversations, 'he more or less said I was asking for trouble, having a young girl on the place with all those lads. What's more, it seems many of them were halfway drunk that night, and with three pubs in the village they weren't even all together and have no idea of who was where at what time, so one of Wyfold's theories is that one of them jumped her and Dave and Sammy interrupted him. Alternatively Nigel did it. Alternatively some stranger walking down the road did it. Wyfold's manner is downright abrasive but I'm past caring. He despises my discipline. He says I shouldn't let my lads get drunk – as if anyone could stop them. They're free men. It's their business, not mine, what they do with their money and time on Sunday nights. I can only take action if they don't turn up on Monday morning. And as for Nigel being paralytic!' Words momentarily failed him. 'How can Nigel possibly expect the lads to stay more or less sober if he gets like that? And he says he can't remember anything that happened the night Ginnie died. Nothing at all. Total alcoholic black-out. He's been very subdued since.'

The directors, I felt, would not be any more impressed than the Detective Chief Inspector with the general level of insobriety, and I wondered whether Nigel's slackness with the lads in general had always stemmed from a knowledge of his own occasional weakness.

The police had found no weapon, Oliver said on another day. Wyfold had told him that there was no way of knowing what had been used to cause the depressed fracture at the base of her brain. Her hair over the fracture bore no traces of anything unexpected. The forensic surgeon was of the opinion that there had been a single very heavy blow. She would have been knocked unconscious instantly. She wouldn't even have known. The period of apparent semi-consciousness had been illusory: parts of her brain would have functioned but she would not have been aware of anything at all.

'I suppose it's a mercy,' Oliver said. 'With some girls you hear of . . . how do their parents bear it?'

His wife, he said, had gone back to Canada. Ginnie's death seemed not to have brought mother and father together, but to have made the separation complete.

'The dog shampoo?' Oliver repeated, when I asked. 'Wyfold says that's just what it was, they checked it. He asked Nigel and all the lads if it was theirs, if they'd used it for washing Squibs, but none of them had. He seems to think Ginnie may have seen it lying in the road and picked it up, or that she got into conversation over the gate with a man who gave her the shampoo for Squibs as a come-on and then killed her afterwards.'

'No,' I said.

'Why not?'

'Because he'd have taken the shampoo away again with him.'

'Wyfold says not if he couldn't find it, because of its being dark and her having hidden it to all intents and purposes under her skirt and two jumpers, and not if Dave and Sammy arrived at that point.'

'I suppose it's possible,' I said doubtfully.

'Wyfold says that particular shampoo isn't on sale at all in England, it's American, and there's absolutely no way at all of tracing how it got here. There weren't any fingerprints of any use; all a blur except a few of yours and mine.'

Another day he said, 'Wyfold told me the hardest murders to solve were single blows on the head. He said the case would remain open, but they are busy again with another girl who was killed walking home from a dance, and this time she definitely is one of that dreadful series, poor child . . . I was lucky, Tim, you know, that Dave and Sammy came back when they did.'

There came a fine May day in the office when Alec, deciding

we needed some fresh air, opened one of the windows which looked down to the fountain. The fresh air duly entered but like a lion, not a lamb, and blew papers off all the desks.

'That's a hurricane,' I said. 'For God's sake shut it.'

Alec closed off the gale and turned round with a grin. 'Sorry and all that,' he said.

We all left our chairs and bent down like gleaners to retrieve our scattered work, and during my search for page 3 of a long assessment of a proposed sports complex I came across a severe and unwelcome shock in the shape of a small pale blue sheet off a memo pad.

There were words pencilled on it and crossed out with a wavy line, with other words underneath.

Build your castle not on Sand was crossed out, and so was *Sandcastle gone with the tide,* and underneath was written *Build not your house on Sand. Build not your banking house on a Sandcastle.*

'What's that?' Alec said quickly, seeing it in my hand and stretching out his own. 'Let's see.'

I shook my head and kept it in my own hand while I finished picking up the sportsdrome, and when order was restored throughout the office I said, 'Come along to the interview room.'

'Right now?'

'Right now.'

We went into the only room on our floor where any real privacy was possible and I said without shilly-shallying, 'This is your handwriting. Did you write the article in *What's Going On?*'

He gave me a theatrical sigh and a tentative smile and a large shrug of the shoulders.

'That's just doodling,' he said. 'It means nothing.'

'It means, for a start,' I said, 'that you shouldn't have left it round the office.'

'Didn't know I had.'

'Did you write the article?'

The blue eyes unrepentantly gleamed at me from behind the gold rims. 'It's a fair cop, I suppose.'

'But *Alec* . . .' I protested.

'Yeah.'

'And the others,' I said, 'Those other leaks, was that you?'

He sighed again, his mouth twisting.

'Was it?' I repeated, wanting above all things to hear him deny it.

'Look,' he said, 'What harm did it do? Yes, all right, the stories did come from me. I wrote them myself, actually, like that one.' He pointed to the memo paper in my hand. 'And don't give me any lectures on disloyalty because none of them did us any harm. Did us good, if anything.'

'Alec . . .'

'Yes,' he said, 'but just think, Tim, what did those pieces really do? They stirred everyone up, sure, and it was a laugh a minute to see all their faces, but what else? I've been thinking about it, I assure you. It wasn't why I did it in the first place, that was just wanting to stir things, I'll admit, but *because* of what I wrote we've now got much better security checks than we had before.'

I listened to him open-mouthed.

'All that work you did with the computer, making us safer against frauds, that was because of what I wrote. And the Corporate Finance boys, they now go around with their mouths zipped up like suitcases so as not to spill the beans to the investment managers. I did *good*, do you see, not harm.'

I stood and looked at him, at the tight tow-coloured curls, the cream coloured freckled skin, the eyes that had laughed with me for eight years. I don't want to lose you, I thought: I wish you hadn't done it.

'And what about this piece about Sandcastle? What good has that done?' I said.

He half grinned. 'Too soon to say.'

I looked at the damaging scrap in my hands and almost automatically shook my head.

'You're going to say,' Alec said, 'that I'll have to leave.'

I looked up. His face was wholly calm.

'I knew I'd have to leave if any of you ever found out.'

'But don't you *care*?' I said frustratedly.

He smiled. 'I don't know. I'll miss *you*, and that's a fact. But as for the job . . . well, I told you, it's not my whole life, like it is yours. I loved it, I grant you, when I came here. All I wanted was to be a merchant banker, it sounded great. But to be honest it was the glamour I suppose I wanted, and glamour never lasts once you've got used to something. I'm not a dedicated money-man at heart . . . and there's honesty for you, I never thought I'd admit that, even to myself.'

'But you do it well.'

'Up to a point. We discussed all that.'

'I'm sorry,' I said helplessly.

'Yeah, well, so am I in a way, and in a way I'm not. I've been dithering for ages, and now that it isn't my choice I'm as much relieved as anything.'

'But . . . what will you do?'

He gave a full cherubic smile. 'I don't suppose you'll approve.'

'What, then?'

'*What's Going On,*' he said, 'have offered me a whole-time job.' He looked at my shattered expression. 'I've written quite a bit for them, actually. About other things, of course not us. But in most editions there's something of mine, a paragraph or two or a whole column. They've asked me several times to go, so now I will.'

I thought back to all those days when Alec had bounded out for the six copies and spent his next hour chuckling. Alec, the gatherer of news, who knew all the gossip.

'They get masses of information in,' Alec said, 'but they need someone to evaluate it all properly, and there aren't so many merchant bankers looking for that sort of job.'

'No,' I said dryly. 'I can imagine. For a start, won't your salary be much less?'

'A bit,' he admitted cheerfully. 'But my iconoclastic spirit will survive.'

I moved restlessly, wishing things had been different.

'I'll resign from here,' he said. 'Make it easier.'

Rather gloomily I nodded. 'And will you say why?'

He looked at me thoughtfully. 'If you really want me to, yes,' he said finally. 'Otherwise not. You can tell them yourself, though, after I've gone, if you want to.'

'You're a damned fool,' I said explosively, feeling the loss of him acutely. 'The office will be bloody dull without you.'

He grinned, my long-time colleague, and pointed to the piece of memo paper. 'I'll send you pin-pricks now and then. You won't forget me. Not a chance.'

Gordon, three days later, said to me in surprise, 'Alec's leaving, did you know?'

'I knew he was thinking of it.'

'But why? He's good at his job, and he always seemed happy here.'

I explained that Alec had been unsettled for some time and felt he needed to change direction.

'Amazing,' Gordon said. 'I tried to dissuade him, but he's adamant. He's going in four weeks.'

Alec, indeed, addressed his normal work with the bounce and zealousness of one about to be liberated, and for the rest of his stay in the office was better company than ever. Chains visibly dropped from his spirits, and I caught him several times scribbling speculatively on his memo pad with an anything but angelic grin.

Oliver had sent me at my request a list of all the breeders who had sent their mares to Sandcastle the previous year, and I spent two or three evenings on the telephone asking after those foals we didn't know about. Oliver himself, when I'd asked him, said he frankly couldn't face the task, and I didn't in the least blame him: my enquiries brought forth an ear-burning amount of blasphemy.

The final count came to:

Five foals born outwardly perfect but dead within two weeks because of internal abnormalities.
One foal born with one eye. (Put down.)
Five foals born with deformed legs, deformation varying from a malformed hoof to the absent half-leg of Plus Factor's colt. (All put down.)
Three foals born with part of one or both ears missing. (All still living.)
One foal born with no tail. (Still living.)
Two foals born with malformed mouths, the equivalent of human hare lip. (Both put down.)
One foal born with a grossly deformed head. (Foaled with heart-beat but couldn't breathe; died at once.)

Apart from this horrifying tally, four mares who had been sent home as in foal had subsequently 'slipped' and were barren: one mare had failed to conceive at all; three mares had not yet foaled (breeders' comments incendiary); and fourteen mares had produced live healthy foals with no defects of any sort.

I showed the list to Gordon and Henry, who went shockedly silent for a while as if in mourning for the superb racer they had so admired.

'There may be more to come,' I said, not liking it. 'Oliver says thirty mares covered by Sandcastle this year are definitely in foal. Some of those will be all right . . . and some may not.'

'Isn't there a test you can do to see if a baby is abnormal?' Henry said. 'Can't they do that with the mares, and abort the deformed foals now, before they grow?'

I shook my head. 'I asked Oliver that. He says amniocentesis – that's what that process is called – isn't possible with mares. Something to do with not being able to reach the target with a sterile needle because of all the intestines in the way.'

Henry listened with the distaste of the non-medical to these clinical realities. 'What it means, I suppose,' he said, 'is that the owners of all those thirty-one mares will have the foals aborted and demand their money back.'

'I'd think so, yes.'

He shook his head regretfully. 'So sad, isn't it. Such a shame. Quite apart from the financial loss, a tragedy in racing terms.'

Oliver said on the telephone one morning, 'Tim, I need to talk to you. Something's happened.'

'What?' I said, with misgivings.

'Someone has offered to buy Sandcastle.'

I sat in a mild state of shock, looking at Alec across the room sucking his pencil while he wrote his future.

'Are you there?' Oliver said.

'Yes. What for and for how much?'

'Well, he says to put back into training. I suppose it's possible. Sandcastle's only five. I suppose he could be got fit to race by August or September, and he might still win next year at six.'

'Good heavens.'

'He's offering twenty-five thousand pounds.'

'Um,' I said. 'Is that good or bad?'

'Realistically, it's as much as he's worth.'

'I'll consult with my seniors here,' I said. 'It's too soon, this minute, to say yes or no.'

'I did tell him that my bankers would have to agree, but he wants an answer fairly soon, because the longer the delay the less time there is for training and racing this season.'

'Yes,' I said, understanding. 'Where is he? Sandcastle, I mean.'

'Still in Newmarket. But it's pointless him staying there any longer. They haven't found any answers. They say they just don't know what's wrong with him, and I think they want me to take him away.'

'Well,' I pondered briefly. 'You may as well fetch him, I should think.'

'I'll arrange it,' he said.

'Before we go any further,' I said. 'Are you sure it's a bona-fide offer and not just some crank?'

'I had a letter from him and I've talked to him on the telephone, and to me he sounds genuine,' Oliver answered. 'Would you like to meet him?'

'Perhaps, yes.'

We fixed a provisional date for the following Saturday morning, and almost as an afterthought I asked the potential buyer's name.

'Smith,' Oliver said. 'A Mr Dissdale Smith.'

I went to Hertfordshire on that Saturday with a whole host of question marks raising their eyebrows in my mind, but it was Dissdale, as it so happened, who had the deeper astonishment.

He drove up while I was still outside Oliver's house, still clasping hands in greeting and talking of Ginnie. Dissdale had come without Bettina, and the first thing he said, emerging from his car, was 'Hello, Tim, what a surprise, didn't know you knew Oliver Knowles.'

He walked across, announced himself, shook hands with Oliver, and patted me chubbily on the shoulder. 'How's things then? How are you doing, Tim?'

'Fine,' I said mildly.

Oliver looked from one of us to the other. 'You know each other already?'

Dissdale said, 'How do you mean, already?'

'Tim's my banker,' Oliver said in puzzlement. 'It was his bank, Ekaterin's, which put up the money for Sandcastle.'

Dissdale stared at me in stunned amazement and looked bereft of speech.

'Didn't you know?' Oliver said. 'Didn't I mention it?'

Dissdale blankly shook his head and finally found his voice. 'You just said your banker was coming . . . I never for a moment thought . . .'

'It doesn't make much odds,' Oliver said. 'If you know each other it may simply save some time. Let's go indoors. There's some coffee ready.' He led the way through his immaculate house to the sitting-room office, where a tray stood on the desk with coffee hot in a pot.

Oliver himself had had four weeks by then in that house

without Ginnie, but to me, on my first visit back, she seemed still most sharply alive. It was I, this time, who kept expecting her to walk into the room; to give me a hug, to say hello with her eyes crinkling with welcome. I felt her presence vividly, to an extent that to start with I listened to Dissdale with only surface attention.

'It might be better to geld him,' he was saying. 'There are some good prizes, particularly overseas, for geldings.'

Oliver's instinctive response of horror subsided droopingly to defeat.

'It's too soon,' I said, 'to talk of that.'

'Tim, face facts,' Dissdale said expansively. 'At this moment in time that horse is a walking bomb. I'm making an offer for him because I'm a bit of a gambler, you know that, and I've a soft spot for him, whatever his faults, because of him winning so much for me that day the year before last, when we were all in my box at Ascot. You do remember that, don't you?'

'I do indeed.'

'He saved my life, Sandcastle did.'

'It was partly because of that day,' I said, nodding, 'That Ekaterin's lent the money for him. When the request came in from Oliver, it was because Henry Shipton – our chairman, if you remember – and Gordon and I had all seen the horse in action that we seriously considered the proposition.'

Dissdale nodded his comprehension. 'A great surprise, though,' he said. 'I'm sorry it's you and Gordon. Sorry it's your bank, I mean, that's been hit so hard. I read about the deformed foals in the papers, of course, and that's what gave me the idea of buying Sandcastle in the first place, but it didn't say which bank . . .'

I wondered fleetingly if Alec could claim that omission as a virtue along with everything else.

Oliver offered Dissdale more coffee which he accepted with cream and sugar, drinking almost absentmindedly while he worked through the possible alterations he would need in approach now he'd found he was dealing with semi-friends. Having had time myself over several days to do it, I could guess at the speed he was needing for reassessment.

'Dissdale,' I said neutrally, deciding to disrupt him, 'Did the idea of buying Sandcastle come from your profitable caper with Indian Silk?'

His rounded features fell again into shock. 'How . . . er . . . did you know about that?'

I said vaguely, 'Heard it on the racecourse, I suppose. But didn't you buy Indian Silk for a pittance because he seemed to be dying, and then sent him to Calder?'

'Well . . .'

'And didn't Calder cure him? And then you sold him again, but well this time, no doubt needing the money, as don't we all, since when Indian Silk's won the Cheltenham Gold Cup? Isn't that right?'

Dissdale raised a plump hand palm upwards in a gesture of mock defeat. 'Don't know where you heard it, but yes, there's no secret, that's what happened.'

'Mm.' I smiled at him benignly. 'Calder said on television, didn't he, that buying Indian Silk was his idea originally, so I wondered . . . I'm wondering if this is his idea too. I mean, did he by any chance suggest a repeat of the gamble that came off so happily last time?'

Dissdale looked at me doubtfully.

'There's nothing wrong in it,' I said. 'Is it Calder's idea?'

'Well, yes,' he said, deciding to confide. 'But it's my money, of course.'

'And, um, if you do buy Sandcastle, will you send him too along to Calder, like Indian Silk?'

Dissdale seemed not to know whether to answer or not, but appearing to be reassured by my friendly interest said finally, 'Calder said he could give him a quick pepping-up to get him fit quickly for racing, yes.'

Oliver, having listened restlessly up to this point, said, 'Calder Jackson can't do anything for Sandcastle that I can't.'

Both Dissdale and I looked at Oliver in the same way, hearing the orthodox view ringing out with conviction and knowing that it was very likely untrue.

'I've been thinking these past few days,' I said to Dissdale, 'First about Indian Silk. Didn't you tell Fred Barnet, when you offered him a rock-bottom price, that all you were doing was providing a dying horse with a nice quiet end in some gentle field?'

'Well, Tim,' he said knowingly. 'You know how it is. You buy for the best price you can. Fred Barnet, I know he goes round grousing that I cheated him, but I didn't, he could have sent his horse to Calder the same as I did.'

I nodded. 'So now, be honest, Dissdale, are you planning again to buy for the best price you can? I mean, does twenty-five thousand pounds for Sandcastle represent the same sort of bargain?'

'Tim,' Dissdale said, half affronted, half in sorrow, 'What a naughty suspicious mind. That's not friendly, not at all.'

I smiled. 'I don't think I'd be wise, though, do you, to recommend to my board of directors that we should accept your offer without thinking it over very carefully?'

For the first time there was a shade of dismay in the chubby face. 'Tim, it's a fair offer, anyone will tell you.'

'I think my board may invite other bids,' I said. 'If Sandcastle is to be sold, we must recoup the most we can.'

The dismay faded: man-of-the-world returned. 'That's fair,' he said. 'As long as you'll come back to me, if anyone tops me.'

'Sure,' I said. 'An auction, by telephone. When we're ready, I'll let you know.'

With a touch of anxiety he said, 'Don't wait too long. Time's money, you know.'

'I'll put your offer to the board tomorrow.'

He made a show of bluff contentment, but the anxiety was still there underneath. Oliver took the empty coffee cup which Dissdale still held and asked if he would like to see the horse he wanted to buy.

'But isn't he in Newmarket?' Dissdale said, again looking disconcerted.

'No, he's here. Came back yesterday.'

'Oh. Then yes, of course, yes, I'd like to see him.'

He's out of his depth, I thought abruptly: for some reason Dissdale is very very unsettled.

We went on the old familiar walk through the yards, with Oliver explaining the lay-out to the new visitor. To me there was now a visible thinning out of numbers, and Oliver, with hardly a quiver in his voice, said that he was sending the mares home with their foals in an orderly progression as usual, with in consequence lower feed bills, fewer lads to pay wages to, smaller expenses all round: he would play fair with the bank, he said, matter-of-factly, making sure to charge what he could and also to conserve what he could towards his debt. Dissdale gave him a glance of amused incredulity as if such a sense of honour belonged to a bygone age, and we came in the end to the stallion yard, where the four heads appeared in curiosity.

The stay in Newmarket hadn't done Sandcastle much good, I thought. He looked tired and dull, barely arching his neck to lift his nose over the half-door, and it was he, of the four, who turned away first and retreated into the gloom of his box.

'Is that Sandcastle?' Dissdale said, sounding disappointed. 'I expected something more, somehow.'

'He's had a taxing three weeks,' Oliver said. 'All he needs is some good food and fresh air.'

'And Calder's touch,' Dissdale said with conviction. 'That magic touch most of all.'

When Dissdale had driven away Oliver asked me what I thought, and I said, 'If Dissdale's offering twenty-five thousand he's certainly reckoning to make much more than that. He's right, he is a gambler, and I'll bet he has some scheme in mind. What we need to do is guess what the scheme is, and decide what we'll do on that basis, such as doubling or trebling the ante.'

Oliver was perplexed. 'How can we possibly guess?'

'Hm,' I said. 'Did you know about Indian Silk?'

'Not before today.'

'Well, suppose Dissdale acts to a pattern, which people so often do. He told Fred Barnet he was putting Indian Silk out to grass, which was diametrically untrue; he intended to send him to Calder and with luck put him back in training. He told *you* he was planning to put Sandcastle back into training, so suppose that's just what he *doesn't* plan to do. And he suggested gelding, didn't he?'

Oliver nodded.

'Then I'd expect gelding to be furthest from his mind,' I said. 'He just wants us to believe that's his intention.' I reflected. 'Do you know what I might do if I wanted to have a real gamble with Sandcastle?'

'What?'

'It sounds pretty crazy,' I said. 'But with Calder's reputation it might just work.'

'What are you talking about?' Oliver said in some bewilderment. 'What gamble?'

'Suppose,' I said, 'that you could buy for a pittance a stallion whose perfect foals would be likely to win races.'

'But no one would risk . . .'

'Suppose,' I interrupted. 'There was nearly a fifty per cent chance, going on this year's figures, that you'd get a perfect foal. Suppose Dissdale offered Sandcastle as a sire at say a thousand pounds, the fee only payable if the foal was born perfect and lived a month.'

Oliver simply stared.

'Say Sandcastle's perfect progeny do win, as indeed they should. There are fourteen of them so far this year, don't forget. Say that in the passage of time his good foals proved to be worth the fifty per cent risk. Say Sandcastle stands in Calder's yard, with Calder's skill on the line. Isn't there a chance that over the years Dissdale's twenty-five thousand pound investment would provide a nice steady return for them both?'

'It's impossible,' he said weakly.

'No, not impossible. A gamble.' I paused. 'You wouldn't get people sending the top mares, of course, but you might get enough dreamers among the breeders who'd chance it.'

'Tim . . .'

'Just think of it,' I said. 'A perfect foal by Sandcastle for peanuts. And if you got a malformed foal, well, some years your mare might slip or be barren anyway.'

He looked at his feet for a while, and then into the middle distance, and then he said, 'Come with me. I've something to show you. Something you'd better know.'

He set off towards the Watcherleys', and would say nothing more on the way. I walked beside him down the familiar paths and thought about Ginnie because I couldn't help it, and we arrived in the next-door yard that was now of a neatness to be compared with all the others.

'Over here,' Oliver said, going across to one of the boxes. 'Look at that.'

I looked where directed: at a mare with a colt foal suckling, not unexpected in that place.

'He was born three days ago,' Oliver said. 'I do so wish Ginnie had seen him.'

'Why that one, especially?'

'The mare is one of my own,' he said. 'And that foal is Sandcastle's.'

It was my turn to stare. I looked from Oliver to the foal and back again. 'There's nothing wrong with him,' I said.

'No.'

'But . . .'

Oliver smiled twistedly. 'I was going to breed her to Diarist. She was along here at the Watcherleys' because the foal she had then was always ailing, but she herself was all right. I was along here looking at her one day when she'd been in season a while, and on impulse I led her along to the breeding pen and told Nigel to fetch Sandcastle, and we mated them there and then. That foal's the result.' He shook his head regretfully. 'He'll be sold, of course, with everything else. I wish I could have kept him, but there it is.'

'He should be worth quite a bit,' I said.

'I don't think so,' Oliver said. 'And that's the flaw in your gamble. It's not just the racing potential that raises prices at auction, it's the chance of breeding. And no one could be sure, breeding from Sandcastle's stock, that the genetic trouble wouldn't crop up for evermore. It's not on, I'm afraid. No serious breeder would send him mares, however great the bargain.'

We stood for a while in silence.

'It was a good idea,' I said, 'while it lasted.'

'My dear Tim . . . we're clutching at straws.'

'Yes.' I looked at his calm strong face; the captain whose ship was sinking. 'I'd try anything, you know, to save you,' I said.

'And to save the bank's money?'

'That too.'

He smiled faintly. 'I wish you could, but time's running out.'

The date for bringing in the receivers had been set, the insurance company had finally ducked, the lawyers were closing in and the respite I'd gained for him was trickling away with no tender plant of hope growing in the ruins.

We walked back towards the house, Oliver patting the mares as usual as they came to the fences.

'I suppose this may all be here next year,' he said, 'looking much the same. Someone will buy it . . . it's just I who'll be gone.'

He lifted his head, looking away over his white painted rails to the long line of the roofs of his yards. The enormity of the loss of his life's work settled like a weight on his shoulders and there was a haggard set to his jaw.

'I try not to mind,' he said levelly. 'But I don't quite know how to bear it.'

When I reached home that evening my telephone was ringing. I went across the sitting room expecting it to stop the moment I reached it, but the summons continued, and on the other end was Judith.

'I just came in,' I said.

'We knew you were out. We've tried once or twice.'

'I went to see Oliver.'

'The poor, poor man.' Judith had been very distressed over Ginnie and still felt that Oliver needed more sympathy because of his daughter than because of his bankruptcy, which I wasn't sure was any longer the case. 'Anyway,' she said, 'Pen asked me to call you as she's tied up in her shop all day and you were out when she tried . . . She says she's had the reply from America about the shampoo and are you still interested?'

'Yes, certainly.'

'Then . . . if you're not doing anything else . . . Gordon and I wondered if you'd care to come here for the day tomorrow, and Pen will bring the letter to show you.'

'I'll be there,' I said fervently, and she laughed.

'Good, then. See you.'

I was at Clapham with alacrity before noon, and Pen, over coffee, produced the letter from the drug company.

'I sent them a sample of what you gave me in that little glass jar,' she said. 'And, as you asked, I had some of the rest of it analysed here, but honestly, Tim, don't hope too much from it for finding out who killed Ginnie, it's just shampoo, as it says.'

I took the official-looking letter which was of two pages clipped together, with impressive headings.

Dear Madam,

We have received the enquiry from your pharmacy and also the sample you sent us, and we now reply with this report, which is a copy of that which we recently sent to the Hertfordshire police force on the same subject.

The shampoo in question is our 'Bannitch' which is formulated especially for dogs suffering from various skin troubles, including eczema. It is distributed to shops selling goods to dog owners and offering cosmetic canine services, but would not normally be used except on the advice of a veterinarian.

We enclose the list of active ingredients and excipients, as requested.

'What are exipients?' I asked, looking up.

'The things you put in with the active drug for various reasons,' she said. 'Like for instance chalk for bulk in pills.'

I turned the top page over and read the list on the second.

BANNITCH
EXCIPIENTS
Bentonite
Ethylene glycol monostearate
Citric acid
Sodium phosphate
Glyceryl monoricinoleate
Perfume
ACTIVE INGREDIENTS
Captan
Amphoteric
Selenium

'Terrific,' I said blankly. 'What do they all mean?'

Pen, sitting beside me on the sofa, explained.

'From the top . . . Bentonite is a thickening agent so that everything stays together and doesn't separate out. Ethylene glycol monostearate is a sort of wax, probably there to add bulk. Citric acid is to make the whole mixture acid, not alkaline, and the next one, sodium phosphate, is to keep the acidity level more or less constant. Glyceryl monoricinoleate is a soap, to make lather, and perfume is there so that the dog smells nice to the owner when she's washing him.'

'How do you know so much?' Gordon asked, marvelling.

'I looked some of them up,' said Pen frankly, with a smile. She turned back to me and pointed to the short lower column of active ingredients. 'Captan and Amphoteric are both drugs for killing fungi on the skin, and Selenium is also anti-fungal and is used in shampoos to cure dandruff.' She stopped and looked at me doubtfully. 'I did tell you not to hope too much. There's nothing there of any consequence.'

'And nothing in the sample that isn't on the manufacturer's list?'

She shook her head. 'The analysis from the British lab came yesterday, and the shampoo in Ginnie's bottle contained exactly what it should.'

'What did you expect, Tim?' Gordon asked.

'It wasn't so much expect, as hope,' I said regretfully. 'Hardly hope, really. Just a faint outside chance.'

'Of what?'

'Well . . . the police thought – think – that the purpose of killing Ginnie was sexual assault, because of those other poor girls in the neighbourhood.'

They all nodded.

'But it doesn't *feel* right, does it? Not when you know she wasn't walking home from anywhere, like the others, and not when she wasn't actually, well, interfered with. And then she had the shampoo . . . and the farm was in such trouble, and it seemed to me possible, just slightly possible, that she had somehow discovered that something in that bottle was significant . . .' I paused, and then said slowly to Pen, 'I suppose what I was looking for was something that could have been put into Sandcastle's food or water that affected his reproductive organs. I don't know if that's possible. I don't know anything about drugs . . . I just *wondered*.'

They sat in silence with round eyes, and then Gordon, stirring, said with an inflection of hope, 'Is that possible, Pen? Could it be something like that?'

'Could it *possibly*?' Judith said.

'My loves,' Pen said. 'I don't know.' She looked also as if whatever she said would disappoint us. 'I've never heard of anything like that, I simply haven't.'

'That's why I took the shampoo and gave it to you,' I said. 'I know it's a wild and horrible idea, but I told Oliver I'd try everything, however unlikely.'

'What you're suggesting,' Judith said plainly, 'Is that someone might *deliberately* have given something to Sandcastle to make him produce deformed foals, and that Ginnie found out . . . and was killed for it.'

There was silence.

'I'll go and get a book or two,' Pen said. 'We'll look up the ingredients, just in case. But honestly, don't *hope*.'

She went home leaving the three of us feeling subdued. For me this had been the last possibility, although since I'd heard from Oliver that the police check had revealed only the expected shampoo in the bottle, it had become more and more remote.

Pen came back in half an hour with a thick tome, a piece of paper, and worried creases across her forehead. 'I've been reading,' she said. 'Sorry to be so long. I've been checking up on sperm deformities, and it seems the most likely cause is radiation.'

I said instantly, 'Let's ring Oliver.'

They nodded and I got through to him with Pen's suggestion.

'Tim!' he said. 'I'll see if I can get anyone in Newmarket . . . even though it's Sunday . . . I'll ring you back.'

'Though how a stallion could get anywhere near a radio-active source,' Pen said while we were waiting, 'would be a first-class mystery in itself.' She looked down at the paper she carried. 'This is the analysis report from the British lab, bill attached, I'm afraid. Same ingredients, though written in the opposite order, practically, with selenium put at the top, which means that that's the predominant drug, I should think.'

Oliver telephoned again in a remarkably short time. 'I got the chief researcher at home. He says they did think of radiation but discounted it because it would be more likely to result in total sterility, and there's also the improbability of a horse being near any radio-active isotopes.' He sighed. 'Sandcastle has never even been X-rayed.'

'See if you can check,' I said. 'If he ever was irradiated in any way it would come into the category of accidental or even malicious damage, and we'd be back into the insurance policy.'

'All right,' he said. 'I'll try.'

I put down the receiver to find Pen turning the pages of her large pharmacological book with concentration.

'What's that?' Judith asked, pointing.

'Toxicity of minerals,' Pen answered absentmindedly. 'Ethylene glycol . . .' she turned pages, searching. 'Here we are.' She read down the column, shaking her head. 'Not that, anyway.' She again consulted the index, read the columns, shook her head. 'Selenium . . . selenium . . .' She turned the pages, read the columns, pursed her lips. 'It says that selenium is poisonous if taken internally, though it can be beneficial on the skin.' She read some more. 'It says that if animals eat plants which grow in soil which has much selenium in it, they can die.'

'What is selenium?' Judith asked.

'It's an element,' Pen said. 'Like potassium and sodium.' She read on, 'It says here that it is mostly found in rocks of the Cretaceous Age – such useful information – and that it's among the most poisonous of elements but also an essential nutrient in trace quantities for both animals and plants.' She looked up. 'It says it's useful for flower-growers because it kills insects, and that it accumulates mostly in plants which flourish where there's a low annual rainfall.'

'Is that all?' Gordon asked, sounding disappointed.

'No, there's pages of it. I'm just translating the gist into understandable English.'

She read on for a while, and then it seemed to me that she

totally stopped breathing. She raised her head and looked at me, her eyes wide and dark.

'What is it?' I said.

'Read it.' She gave me the heavy book, pointing to the open page.

I read:

> *Selenium is absorbed easily from the intestines and affects every part of the body, more lodging in the liver, spleen, and kidneys than in brain and muscle. Selenium is teratogenic.*

'What does teratogenic mean?' I asked.

'It means,' Pen said, 'that it produces deformed offspring.'

'*What*?' I exclaimed. 'You don't mean . . .'

Pen was shaking her head. 'It couldn't affect Sandcastle. It's impossible. It would simply poison his system. Teratogens have nothing to do with males.'

'Then what . . . ?'

'They act on the developing embryo,' she said. Her face crumpled almost as if the knowledge was too much and would make her cry. 'You could get deformed foals if you fed selenium *to the mares*.'

I went on the following morning to see Detective Chief Inspector Wyfold, both Gordon and Harry concurring that the errand warranted time off from the bank. The forceful policeman shook my hand, gestured me to a chair and said briskly that he could give me fifteen minutes at the outside, as did I know that yet another young girl had been murdered and sexually assaulted the evening before, which was now a total of six, and that his superiors, the press and the whole flaming country were baying for an arrest? 'And we are no nearer now,' he added with anger, 'than we were five months ago, when it started.'

He listened all the same to what I said about selenium, but in conclusion shook his head.

'We looked it up ourselves. Did you know it's the main ingredient in an anti-dandruff shampoo sold off open shelves all over America in the drug stores? It used to be on sale here too, or something like it, but it's been discontinued. There's no mystery about it. It's not rare, nor illegal. Just ordinary.'

'But the deformities . . .'

'Look,' he said restively, 'I'll bear it in mind. But it's a big jump to decide from one bottle of ordinary dog shampoo that *that*'s what's the matter with those foals. I mean, is there any way of proving it?'

With regret I said, 'No, there isn't.' No animal, Pen's book had inferred, would retain selenium in its system for longer than a day or two if it was eaten only once or twice and in non-fatal amounts.

'And how, anyway,' Wyfold said, 'would you get a whole lot of horses to drink anything as nasty as shampoo?' He shook his head. 'I know you're very anxious to catch Virginia Knowles' killer, and don't think we don't appreciate your coming here, but we've been into the shampoo question thoroughly, I assure you.'

His telephone buzzed and he picked up the receiver, his eyes still turned in my direction but his mind already elsewhere. 'What?' he said. 'Yes, all right. Straightaway.' He put down the reciever. 'I'll have to go.'

'Listen,' I said, 'Isn't it possible that one of the lads was giving selenium to the mares this year also, and that Ginnie somehow found out . . .'

He interrupted. 'We tried to fit that killing onto one of those lads, don't think we didn't, but there was no evidence, absolutely none at all.' He stood up and came round from behind his desk, already leaving me in mind as well as body. 'If you think of anything else Mr Ekaterin, by all means let us know. But for now – I'm sorry, but there's a bestial man out there we've got to catch – and I'm still of the opinion he tried for Virginia Knowles too, and was interrupted.'

He gave me a dismissing but not impatient nod, holding open the door and waiting for me to leave his office ahead of him. I obliged him by going, knowing that realistically he couldn't be expected to listen to any further unsubstantiated theories from me while another victim lay more horribly and recently dead.

Before I went back to him, I thought, I had better dig further and come up with connected, believable facts, and also a basis, at least, for proof.

Henry and Gordon heard with gloom in the bank before lunch that at present we were 'insufficient data' in a Wyfold pigeonhole.

'But you still believe, do you, Tim . . . ?' Henry said enquiringly.

'We have to,' I answered. 'And yes, I do.'

'Hm.' He pondered. 'If you need more time off from the office, you'd better take it. If there's the slightest chance that there's nothing wrong with Sandcastle after all, we must do our absolute best not only to prove it to our own satisfaction but also to the world in general. Confidence would have to be restored to breeders, otherwise they wouldn't send their mares. It's a tall order altogether.'

'Yes,' I said. 'Well . . . I'll do all I can'; and after lunch and some thought I telephoned to Oliver, whose hopes no one had so far raised.

'Sit down,' I said.

'What's the matter?' He sounded immediately anxious. 'What's happened?'

'Do you know what teratogenic means?' I said.

'Yes, of course. With mares one always has to be careful.'

'Mm . . . Well, there was a teratogenic drug in the bottle of dog shampoo that Ginnie had.'

'*What*?' His voice rose an octave on the word, vibrating with instinctive unthinking anger.

'Yes,' I said. 'Now calm down. The police say it proves nothing either way, but Gordon and Henry, our chairman, agree that it's the only hope we have left.'

'But Tim . . .' The realisation hit him, 'That would mean . . . that would mean . . .'

'Yes,' I said. 'It would mean that Sandcastle was always breeding good and true and could return to gold-mine status.'

I could hear Oliver's heavily disturbed breathing and could only guess at his pulse rate.

'No,' he said. 'No. If shampoo had got into a batch of feed, all the mares who ate it would have been affected, not just those covered by Sandcastle.'

'If the shampoo got into the feed accidentally, yes. If it was given deliberately, no.'

'I can't . . . I can't . . .'

'I did tell you to sit down,' I said reasonably.

'Yes, so you did.' There was a pause. 'I'm sitting,' he said.

'It's at least possible,' I said, 'That the Equine Research people could find nothing wrong with Sandcastle because there actually *isn't* anything wrong with him.'

'Yes,' he agreed faintly.

'It is possible to give teratogenic substances to mares.'

'Yes.'

'But horses wouldn't drink shampoo.'

'No, thoroughbreds especially are very choosy.'

'So how would you give them shampoo, and when?'

After a pause he said, still breathlessly, 'I don't know how. They'd spit it out. But when is easier, and that could probably be no more than three or four days after conception. That's when the body tube is forming in the embryo . . . that's when a small amount of teratogenic substance could do a lot of damage.'

'Do you mean,' I said, 'that giving a mare selenium just *once* would ensure a deformed foal?'

'Giving a mare what?'

'Sorry. Selenium. A drug for treating dandruff.'

'Good . . . heavens.' He rallied towards his normal self. 'I suppose it would depend on the strength of the dose, and its timing. Perhaps three or four doses . . . No one could really *know*, because no one would have tried . . . I mean, there wouldn't have been any research.'

'No,' I agreed. 'But supposing that in this instance someone got the dosage and the timing right, and also found a way of making the shampoo palatable, then *who was it*?'

There was a long quietness during which even his breathing abated.

'I don't know,' he said finally. 'Theoretically it could have been me, Ginnie, Nigel, the Watcherleys or any of the lads who were here last year. No one else was on the place often enough.

'Really no one? How about the vet or the blacksmith or just a visiting friend?'

'But there were *eighteen* deformed foals,' he said. 'I would think it would have to have been someone who could come and go here all the time.'

'And someone who knew which mares to pick,' I said. 'Would that knowledge be easy to come by?'

'Easy!' he said explosively. 'It is positively thrust at everyone on the place. There are lists in all the feed rooms and in the breeding pen itself saying which mares are to be bred to which stallion. Nigel has one, there's one in my office, one at the Watcherleys – all over. Everyone is supposed to double-check the lists all the time, so that mistakes aren't made.'

'And all the horses,' I said slowly, 'Wear head-collars with their names on.'

'Yes, that's right. An essential precaution.'

All made easy, I thought, for someone intending mischief towards particular mares and not to any others.

'Your own Sandcastle foal,' I said, 'he's perfect . . . and it may be because on the lists your mare was down for Diarist.'

'Tim!'

'Look after him,' I said. 'And look after Sandcastle.'

'I will,' he said fervently.

'And Oliver . . . is that lad called Shane still with you?'

'No, he's gone. So have Dave and Sammy, who found Ginnie.'

'Then could you send me at the bank a list of the names and addresses of all the people who were working for you last year, and also this year? And I mean *everyone*, even your housekeeper and anyone working for Nigel or cleaning the lads' hostel, things like that.'

'Even my part-time secretary girl?'

'Even her.'

'She only comes three mornings a week.'

'That might be enough.'

'All right,' he said. 'I'll do it straight away.'

'I went to see Chief Inspector Wyfold this morning,' I said. 'But he thinks it's just a coincidence that Ginnie had shampoo with a foal-deforming drug in it. We'll have to come up with a whole lot more, to convince him. So anything you can think of . . .'

'I'll think of nothing else.'

'If Dissdale Smith should telephone you, pressing for an answer,' I said, 'just say the bank are deliberating and keeping you waiting. Don't tell him anything about this new possibility. It might be best to keep it to ourselves until we can prove whether or not it's true.'

'Dear God,' he said fearfully, 'I hope it is.'

In the evening I talked to Pen, asking her if she knew of any way of getting the selenium out of the shampoo.

'The trouble seems to be,' I said, 'That you simply couldn't get the stuff into a horse as it is.'

'I'll work on it,' she said, 'But of course the manufacturer's chemists will have gone to a good deal of trouble to make sure the selenium stays suspended throughout the mixture and doesn't all fall to the bottom.'

'It did say "Shake Well" on the bottle.'

'Mm, but that might be for the soap content, not for the selenium.'

I thought. 'Well, could you get the soap out, then? It must be the soap the horses wouldn't like.'

'I'll try my hardest,' she promised. 'I'll ask a few friends.' She paused. 'There isn't much of the shampoo left. Only what I kept after sending the samples off to America and the British lab.'

'How much?' I said anxiously.

'Half an egg-cupful. Maybe less.'

'Is that enough?'

'If we work in test-tubes . . . perhaps.'

'And Pen . . . Could you or your friends make a guess, as well, as to how much shampoo you'd need to provide enough selenium to give a teratogenic dose to a mare?'

'You sure do come up with some difficult questions, dearest Tim, but we'll certainly try.'

Three days later she sent a message with Gordon, saying that by that evening she might have some answers, if I would care to go down to her house after work.

I cared and went, and with a smiling face she opened her front door to let me in.

'Like a drink?' she said.

'Well, yes, but . . .'

'First things first.' She poured whisky carefully for me and Cinzano for herself. 'Hungry?'

'Pen . . .'

'It's only rolls with ham and lettuce in. I never cook much, as you know.' She disappeared to her seldom-used kitchen and returned with the offerings, which turned out to be nicely squelchy and much what I would have made for myself.

'All right,' she said finally, pushing away the empty plates, 'Now I'll tell you what we've managed.'

'At last.'

She grinned. 'Yes. Well then, we started from the premise that if someone had to use shampoo as the source of selenium then that someone didn't have direct or easy access to poisonous chemicals, which being so he also wouldn't have sophisticated machinery available for separating one ingredient from another – a centrifuge, for instance. OK so far?'

I nodded.

'So what we needed, as we saw it, was a *simple* method that involved only everyday equipment. Something anyone could do anywhere. So the first thing we did was to let the shampoo drip through a paper filter, and we think you could use almost anything for that purpose, like a paper towel, a folded tissue or thin blotting paper. We actually got the best and fastest results from a coffee filter, which is after all specially designed to retain very fine solids while letting liquids through easily.'

'Yes,' I said. 'Highly logical.'

Pen smiled. 'So there we were with some filter-papers in which, we hoped, the microscopic particles of selenium were trapped. The filters were stained bright green by the shampoo. I brought one here to show you . . . I'll get it.' She whisked off to the kitchen taking the empty supper plates with her, and returned carrying a small tray with two glasses on it.

One glass contained cut pieces of green-stained coffee filter lying in what looked like oil, and the second glass contained only an upright test-tube, closed at the top with a cork and showing a dark half-inch of solution at the bottom.

'One of my friends in the lab knows a lot about horses,' Pen said, 'and he reckoned that all race horses are used to the taste of linseed oil, which is given them in their feed quite often as a laxative. So we got some linseed oil and cut up the filter and soaked it.' She pointed to the glass. 'The selenium particles floated out of the paper into the oil.'

'Neat.' I said.

'Yes. So then we poured the result into the test-tube and just waited twenty-four hours or so, and the selenium particles slowly gravitated through the oil to the bottom.' She looked at my face to make sure I understood. 'We transferred the selenium from the wax-soap base in which it would remain suspended into an oil base, in which it *wouldn't* remain suspended.'

'I do understand,' I assured her.

'So here in the test-tube,' she said with a conjuror's flourish, 'we have concentrated selenium with the surplus oil poured off.' She picked the tube out of the glass, keeping it upright, and showed me the brownish shadowy liquid lying there, darkest at the bottom, almost clear amber at the top. 'We had such a small sample to start with that this is all we managed to collect. But that dark stuff is definitely selenium sulphide. We checked it on a sort of scanner called a gas chromatograph.' She grinned. 'No point in not using the sophisticated apparatus when it's there right beside you – and we were in a research lab of a teaching hospital, incidentally.'

'You're marvellous.'

'Quite brilliant,' she agreed with comic modesty. 'We also calculated that that particular shampoo was almost ten per cent selenium, which is a very much higher proportion than you'd find in shampoos for humans. We all agree that this much, in the test-tube, is enough to cause deformity in a foal – or in any other species, for that matter. We found many more references in other books – lambs born with deformed feet, for instance, where the sheep had browsed off plants growing on selenium-rich soil. We all agree that it's the *time* when the mare ingests the selenium that's most crucial, and we think that to be sure of getting the desired result you'd have to give selenium every day for three or four days, starting two or three days after conception.'

I slowly nodded. 'That's the same sort of time-scale that Oliver said.'

'And if you gave too much,' she said, 'Too large a dose, you'd be more likely to get abortions than really gross deformities. The embryo would only go on growing at all, that is, if the damage done to it by the selenium was relatively minor.'

'There were a lot of *different* deformities,' I said.

'Oh sure. It could have affected any developing cell, regardless.'

I picked up the test-tube and peered closely at its murky contents. 'I suppose all you'd have to do would be stir this into a cupful of oats.'

'That's right.'

'Or . . . could you enclose it in a capsule?'

'Yes, if you had the makings. We could have done it quite easily in the lab. You'd need to get rid of as much oil as possible, of course, in that case, and just scrape concentrated selenium into the capsules.'

'Mm. Calder could do it, I suppose?'

'Calder Jackson? Why yes, I guess he could if you wanted him to. He had everything there that you'd need.' She lifted her head, remembering something. 'He's on the television tomorrow night, incidentally.'

'Is he?'

'Yes. They were advertising it tonight just after the news, before you came. He's going to be a guest on that chat show . . . Mickey Bonwith's show . . . Do you ever see it?'

'Sometimes,' I said, thoughtfully. 'It's transmitted live, isn't it?'

'Yes, that's right.' She looked at me with slight puzzlement. 'What's going on in that computer brain?'

'A slight calculation of risk,' I said slowly, 'and of grasping unrepeatable opportunities. And tell me, dearest Pen, if I found myself again in Calder's surgery, what should I look for, to bring out?'

She stared at me literally with her mouth open. Then, recovering, she said. 'You can't mean . . . *Calder*?'

'Well,' I said soberly. 'What I'd really like to do is to make sure one way or another. Because it does seem to me, sad though it is to admit it, that if you tie in Dissdale's offer for Sandcastle with someone deliberately poisoning the mares, and then add Calder's expertise with herbs – in which selenium-soaked plants might be included – you do at least get a *question mark*. You do want to know for sure, don't you think, whether or not Calder and Dissdale set out deliberately to debase Sandcastle's worth so that they could buy him for peanuts . . . So that Calder could perform a well publicised "miracle cure" of some sort on Sandcastle, who would thereafter always sire perfect foals, and gradually climb back into favour. Whose fees might never return to forty thousand pounds, but would over the years add up to a fortune.'

'But they couldn't,' Pen said, aghast. 'I mean . . . Calder and Dissdale . . . we *know* them.'

'And you in your trade, as I in mine, must have met presentable, confidence-inspiring crooks.'

She fell silent, staring at me in a troubled way, until finally I said, 'There's one other thing. Again nothing I could swear to – but the first time I went to Calder's place he had a lad there who reminded me sharply of the boy with the knife at Ascot.'

'Ricky Barnet,' Pen said, nodding.

'Yes. I can't remember Calder's lad's name, and I couldn't identify him at all now after all this time, but at Oliver's I saw another lad, called Shane, who *also* reminded me of Ricky Barnet. I've no idea whether Shane and Calder's lad are one and the same person, though maybe not, because I don't think Calder's lad was called Shane, or I *would* have remembered, if you see what I mean.'

'Got you,' she said.

'But *if* and it's a big if – if Shane did once work for Calder, he might *still* be working for him . . . feeding selenium to mares.'

Pen took her time with gravity in the experienced eyes, and at last said, '*Someone* would have had to be there on the spot to do the feeding, and it certainly couldn't have been Calder or Dissdale. But couldn't it have been that manager, Nigel? It would have been easy for him. Suppose Dissdale and Calder paid him . . . ? Suppose they promised to employ him, or even give him a share in Sandcastle, once they'd got hold of the horse.'

I shook my head. 'I did wonder. I did think of Nigel. There's one good reason why it probably isn't him, though, and that's because he and only he besides Oliver knew that one of the mares down for Diarist was covered by Sandcastle.' I explained about Oliver's impulse mating. 'The foal is perfect, but might very likely not have been if it was Nigel who was doing the feeding.'

'Not conclusive,' Pen said, slowly.

'No.'

She stirred. 'Did you tell the police all this?'

'I meant to,' I said, 'But when I was there with Wyfold on Monday it seemed impossible. It was all so insubstantial. Such a lot of guesses. Maybe wrong conclusions. Dissdale's offer could be genuine. And a lad I'd seen for half a minute eighteen months ago . . . it's difficult to remember a strange face for half an hour, let alone all that time. I have only an impression of blankness and of sunglasses . . . and I don't have the same impression of Oliver's lad Shane. Wyfold isn't the sort of man to be vague to. I thought I'd better come up with something more definite before I went back to him.'

She bit her thumb. 'Can't you take another good look at this Shane?'

I shook my head. 'Oliver's gradually letting his lads go, as he does every year at this time, and Shane is one who has already left. Oliver doesn't know where he went and has no other address for him, which he doesn't think very unusual. It seems that lads can drift from stable to stable for ever with their papers always showing only the address of their last or current employer. But I think we *might* find Shane, if we're lucky.'

'How?'

'By photographing Ricky Barnet, side view, and asking around on racetracks.'

She smiled. 'It might work. It just might.'

'Worth a try.'

My mind drifted back to something else worth a try, and it seemed that hers followed.

'You don't really mean to break into Calder's surgery, do you?' she said.

'Pick the lock,' I said. 'Yes.'

'But . . .'

'Time's running out, and Oliver's future and the bank's money with it, and yes, sure, I'll do what I can.'

She curiously looked into my face. 'You have no real concept of danger, do you?'

'How do you mean?'

'I mean . . . I saw you, that day at Ascot, simply hurl yourself at that boy, at that knife. You could have been badly stabbed, very easily. And Ginnie told us that you frightened her to tears jumping at Sandcastle the way you did, to catch him. She said it was suicidal . . . and yet you yourself seemed to think nothing of it. And at Ascot, that evening, I remember you being *bored* with the police questions, not stirred up high by a brush with death . . .'

Her words petered away. I considered them and found in myself a reason and an answer.

'Nothing that has happened so far in my life,' I said seriously, 'has made me fear I might die. I think . . . I know it sounds silly . . . I am unconvinced of my own mortality.'

The Third Year

JUNE

On the following day, Friday, June 1st, I took up a long-offered invitation and went to lunch with the board of a security firm to whom we had lent money for launching a new burglar alarm on the market. Not greatly to their surprise I was there to ask a favour, and after a repast of five times the calories of Ekaterin's they gave me with some amusement three keys which would unlock almost anything but the crown jewels, and also a concentrated course on how to use them.

'Those pickers are strictly for opening doors in emergencies,' the locksmiths said, smiling. 'If you end up in jail, we don't know you.'

'If I end up in jail, send me another set in a fruit cake.'

I thanked them and left, and practised discreetly on the office doors in the bank, with remarkable results. Going home I let myself in through my own front door with them, and locked and unlocked every cupboard and drawer which had a keyhole. Then I put on a dark roll-neck jersey over my shirt and tie and with scant trepidation drove to Newmarket.

I left my car at the side of the road some distance from Calder's house and finished the journey on foot, walking quietly into his yard in the last of the lingering summer dusk, checking against my watch that it was almost ten o'clock, the hour when Micky Bonwith led his guests to peacock chairs and dug publicly into their psyches.

Calder would give a great performance, I thought: and the regrets I felt about my suspicions of him redoubled as I looked at the outline of his house against the sky and remembered his uncomplicated hospitality.

The reserve which had always at bottom lain between us I now acknowledged as my own instinctive and stifled doubt. Wanting to see worth, I had seen it: and the process of now trying to prove myself wrong gave me more sadness than satisfaction.

His yard was dark and peaceful, all lads long gone. Within the hall of the house a single light burned, a dim point of yellow glimpsed through the bushes fluttering in a gentle breeze. Behind the closed doors of the boxes the patients would be snoozing, those patients with festering sores and bleeding guts and all manner of woes awaiting the touch.

Sandcastle, if I was right, had been destined to stand there, while Calder performed his 'miracle' without having to explain how he'd done it. He never had explained: he'd always broadcast publicly that he didn't know *how* his power worked, he just knew it did. Thousands, perhaps millions, believed in his power. Perhaps even breeders, those dreamers of dreams, would have believed, in the end.

I came to the surgery, a greyish block in the advancing night, and fitted one of the lock-pickers into the keyhole. The internal tumblers turned without protest, much oiled and used, and I pushed the door open and went in.

There were no windows to worry about. I closed the door behind me and switched on the light, and immediately began the search for which I'd come: to find selenium in home-made capsules, or in a filtering device, or in bottles of shampoo.

Pen had had doubts that anyone would have risked giving selenium a second year if the first year's work had proved so effective, but I'd reminded her that Sandcastle had already covered many new mares that year before the deformed foals had been reported.

'Whoever did it couldn't have known at that point that he'd been successful. So to make sure, I'd guess he'd go on, and maybe with an increased dose . . . and if no selenium was being given this year, *why did Ginnie have it*?'

Pen had reluctantly given in. 'I suppose I'm just trying to find reasons for you not to go to Calder's.'

'If I find anything, Chief Inspector Wyfold can go there later with a search warrant. Don't worry so.'

'No,' she'd said, and gone straight on looking anxious.

The locked cabinets at both ends of Calder's surgery proved a doddle for the picks, but the contents were a puzzle, as so few of the jars and boxes were properly labelled. Some indeed had come from commercial suppliers, but these seemed mostly to be the herbs Calder had talked of: hydrastis, comfrey, fo-ti-tieng, myrrh, sarsaparilla, liquorice, passiflora, papaya, garlic; a good quantity of each.

Nothing was obligingly labelled selenium.

I had taken with me a thickish polythene bag which had a zip across one end and had formerly enclosed a silk tie and handkerchief, a present from my mother at Christmas. Into that I systematically put two or three capsules from each bottle, and two or three pills of each sort, and small sachets of herbs: and Pen, I thought, was going to have a fine old time sorting them out.

With the bag almost half full of samples I carefully locked the cabinets again and turned to the refrigerator, which was of an ordinary domestic make with only a magnetic door fastening.

Inside there were no bottles of shampoo. No coffee filters. No linseed oil. There were simply the large plastic containers of Calder's cure-all tonic.

I thought I might as well take some to satisfy Pen's curiosity, and rooted around for a small container, finding some empty medicine bottles in a cupboard below the work bench. Over the sink I poured some of the tonic into a medicine bottle, screwed on the cap, and returned the plastic container carefully to its place in the 'fridge. I stood the medicine bottle on the workbench ready to take away, and turned finally to the drawers where Calder kept things like hops and also his antique pill-making equipment.

Everything was clean and tidy, as before. If he had made capsules containing selenium there, I could see no trace.

With mounting disappointment I went briefly through every drawer. Bags of seeds: sesame, pumpkin, sunflower. Bags of dried herbs, raspberry leaves, alfalfa. Boxes of the empty halves of gelatine capsules, waiting for contents. Empty unused pill bottles. All as before: nothing I hadn't already seen.

The largest bottom drawer still contained the plastic sacks of hops. I pulled open the neck of one of them and found only the expected strong-smelling crop: closed the neck again, moving the bag slightly to settle it back into its place, and saw that under the bags of hops lay a brown leather briefcase, ordinary size, six inches deep.

With a feeling of wasting time I hauled it out onto the working surface on top of the drawers, and tried to open it.

Both catches were locked. I fished for the keys in my trousers pocket and with the smallest of the picks delicately twisted until the mechanisms clicked.

Opened the lid. Found no bottles of dog shampoo, but other things that turned me slowly to a state of stone.

The contents looked at first sight as if the case belonged to a doctor: stethoscope, pen torch, metal instruments, all in fitted compartments. A cardboard box without its lid held four or five small tubes of antibiotic ointment. A large bottle contained only a few small white pills, the bottle labelled with a long name I could scarcely read, let alone remember, with 'diuretic' in brackets underneath. A pad of prescription forms, blank, ready for use.

It was the name and address rubber-stamped onto the prescription forms and the initials heavily embossed in gold into the leather beneath the case's handle which stunned me totally.

I.A.P. on the case.

Ian A. Pargetter on the prescriptions.

Ian Pargetter, veterinary surgeon, address in Newmarket.

His case had vanished the night he died.

This case . . .

With fingers beginning to shake I took one of the tubes of antibiotics and some of the diuretic pills and three of the prescription forms and added them to my other spoils, and then with a heart at least beating at about twice normal speed checked that everything was in its place before closing the case.

I felt as much as heard the surgery door open, the current of air reaching me at the same instant as the night sounds. I turned thinking that one of Calder's lads had come on some late hospital rounds and wondering how I could ever explain my presence; and I saw that no explanation at all would do.

It was Calder himself crossing the threshold. Calder with the light on his curly halo, Calder who should have been a hundred miles away talking to the nation on the tube.

His first expression of surprise turned immediately to grim assessment, his gaze travelling from the medicine bottle of tonic mixture on the workbench to the veterinary case lying open. Shock, disbelief and fury rose in an instantly violent reaction, and he acted with such speed that even if I'd guessed what he would do I could hardly have dodged.

His right arm swung in an arc, coming down against the wall beside the door and pulling from the bracket which held it a slim scarlet fire extinguisher. The swing seemed to me continuous. The red bulbous end of the fire extinguisher in a split second filled my vision and connected with a crash against my forehead, and consciousness ceased with a blink.

* * *

The world came back with the same sort of on-off switch: one second I was unaware, the next, awake. No grey area of daze, no shooting stars, simply on-off, off-on.

I was lying on my back on some smelly straw in an electrically lit horse box with a brown horse peering at me suspiciously from six feet above.

I couldn't remember for a minute how I'd got there; it seemed such an improbable position to be in. Then I had a recollection of a red ball crashing above my eyes, and then, in a snap, total recall of the evening.

Calder.

I was in a box in Calder's yard. I was there because, presumably, Calder had put me there.

Pending? I wondered.

Pending what?

With no reassuring thoughts I made the moves to stand up, but found that though consciousness was total, recovery was not. A whirling dizziness set the walls tilting, the grey concrete blocks seeming to want to lean in and fall on me. Cursing slightly I tried again more slowly and made it to one elbow with eyes balancing precariously in their sockets.

The top half of the stable door abruptly opened with the sound of an unlatching bolt. Calder's head appeared in the doorway, his face showing shock and dismay as he saw me awake.

'I thought,' he said, 'that you'd be unconscious . . . that you wouldn't know. I hit you so hard . . . you're supposed to be out.' His voice saying these bizarre words sounded nothing but normal.

'Calder . . .' I said.

He was looking at me no longer with anger but almost with apology. 'I'm sorry, Tim,' he said. 'I'm sorry you came.'

The walls seemed to be slowing down.

'Ian Pargetter . . .' I said. 'Did *you* . . . kill him? Not you?'

Calder produced an apple and fed it almost absentmindedly to the horse. 'I'm sorry, Tim. He was so stubborn. He refused . . .' He patted the horse's neck. 'He wouldn't do what I wanted. Said it was over, he'd had enough. Said he'd stop me, you know.' He looked for a moment at the horse and then down to me. 'Why did you come? I've liked you. I wish you hadn't.'

I tried again to stand up and the whirling returned as before.

Calder took a step backwards, but only one, stopping when he saw my inability to arise and charge.

'Ginnie,' I said. 'Not Ginnie . . . Say it wasn't you who hit Ginnie . . .'

He simply looked at me, and didn't say it. In the end he said merely, and with clear regret, 'I wish I'd hit you harder . . . but it seemed . . . enough.' He moved another step backwards so that I could see only the helmet of curls under the light and dark shadows where his eyes were; and then while I was still struggling to my knees he closed the half door and bolted it, and from outside switched off the light.

Night-blindness made it even harder to stand up but at least I couldn't *see* the walls whirl, only feel they were spinning. I found myself leaning against one of them and ended more or less upright, spine supported, brain at last settling into equilibrium.

The grey oblong of window gradually detached itself from the blackness, and when my equine companion moved his head I saw the liquid reflection of an eye.

Window . . . way out.

I slithered round the walls to the window and found it barred on the inside, not so much to keep horses in, I supposed, but to prevent them breaking the glass. Five strong bars, in any case, were set in concrete top and bottom, as secure as any prison cell, and I shook them impotently with two hands in proving them immovable.

Through the dusty window panes I had a sideways view across the yard towards the surgery, and while I stood there and held onto the bars and watched, Calder went busily in and out of the open lighted doorway, carrying things from the surgery to his car. I saw what I was sure was Ian Pargetter's case go into the boot, and remembered with discomfiture that I'd left the bunch of picks in one of its locks. I saw him carry also an armful of the jars which contained unlabelled capsules and several boxes of unguessable contents, stowing them in the boot carefully and closing them in.

Calder was busy obliterating his tracks.

I yelled at him, calling his name, but he didn't even hear or turn his head. The only result was startled movement in the horse behind me, a stamping of hooves and a restless swinging round the box.

'All right,' I said soothingly. 'Steady down. All right. Don't be frightened.'

The big animal's alarm abated, and through the window I watched Calder switch off the surgery light, lock the door, get into his car and drive away.

He drove away out of his driveway, towards the main road, not towards his house. The lights of his car passed briefly over the trees as he turned out through the gates, and then were gone: and I seemed suddenly very alone, imprisoned in that dingy place for heaven knew how long.

Vision slowly expanded so that from the dim light of the sky I could see again the outlines within the box: walls, manger . . . horse. The big dark creature didn't like me being there and wouldn't settle, but I could think of no way to relieve him of my presence.

The ceiling was solid, not as in some stables open through the rafters to the roof. In many it would have been possible for an agile man to climb the partition from one box to the next, but not here; and in any case there was no promise of being better off next door. One would be in a different box but probably just as simply and securely bolted in.

There was nothing in my trousers pockets but a handkerchief. Penknife, money and house keys were all in my jacket in the boot of my own unlocked car out on the road. The dark jersey which had seemed good for speed, quiet and concealment had left me without even a coin for a screwdriver.

I thought concentratedly of what a man could do with his fingers that a horse couldn't do with superior strength, but found nothing in the darkness of the door to unwind or unhinge; nothing anywhere to pick loose. It looked most annoyingly as if that was where I was going to stay until Calder came back.

And then . . . what?

If he'd intended to kill me, why hadn't he already made sure of it? Another swipe or two with the fire extinguisher would have done . . . and I would have known nothing about it.

I thought of Ginnie, positive now that that was how it had been for her, that in one instant she had been thinking, and in the next . . . not.

Thought of Ian Pargetter, dead from one blow of his own brass lamp. Thought of Calder's shock and grief at the event, probably none the less real despite his having killed the man he mourned. Calder shattered over the loss of a business friend . . . the friend he had himself struck down.

He must have killed him, I thought, on a moment's ungovernable impulse, for not . . . what had he said? . . . for not wanting to go on, for wanting to stop Calder doing . . . what Calder planned.

Calder had struck at me with the same sort of speed: without pause for consideration, without time to think of consequences. And he had lashed at me as a friend too, without hesitation, while saying shortly after that he liked me.

Calder, swinging the fire extinguisher, had ruthlessly aimed at killing the man who had saved his life.

Saved Calder's life . . . Oh God, I thought, why ever did I do it?

The man in whom I had wanted to see only goodness had after that day killed Ian Pargetter, killed Ginnie: and if I hadn't saved him they would both have lived.

The despair of that thought filled me utterly, swelling with enormity, making me feel, as the simpler grief for Ginnie had done, that one's body couldn't hold so much emotion. Remorse and guilt could rise like dragons' teeth from good intentions, and there were in truth unexpected paths to hell.

I thought back to that distant moment that had affected so many lives: to that instinctive reflex, faster than thought, which had launched me at Ricky's knife. If I could have called it back I would have been looking away, not seeing, letting Calder die . . . letting Ricky take his chances, letting him blast his young life to fragments, destroy his caring parents.

One couldn't help what came after.

A fireman or a lifeboatman or a surgeon might fight to the utmost stretch of skill to save a baby and find he had let loose a Hitler, a Nero, Jack the Ripper. It couldn't always be Beethoven or Pasteur whose life one extended. All one asked was an ordinary, moderately sinful, normally well-intentioned, fairly harmless human. And if he cured horses . . . all the better.

Before that day at Ascot Calder couldn't even have thought of owning Sandcastle, because Sandcastle at that moment was in mid-career with his stud value uncertain. But Calder had seen, as we all had, the majesty of that horse, and I had myself listened to the admiration in his voice.

At some time after that he must have thought of selenium, and from there the wickedness had grown to encompass us all: the wickedness which would have been extinguished before birth if I'd been looking another way.

I knew logically that I couldn't have not done what I did; but in heart and spirit that didn't matter. It didn't stop the engulfing misery or allow me any ease.

Grief and sorrow came to us all, Pen had said: and she was right.

The horse became more restive and began to paw the ground.

I looked at my watch, the digital figures bright in the darkness: twenty minutes or thereabouts since Calder had left. Twenty minutes that already seemed like twenty hours.

The horse swung round suddenly in the gloom with unwelcome vigour, bumping against me with his rump.

'Calm down now, boy,' I said soothingly. 'We're stuck with each other. Go to sleep.'

The horse's reply was the equivalent of unprintable: the crash of a steel-clad hoof against a wall.

Perhaps he didn't like me talking, I thought, or indeed even moving about. His head swung round towards the window, his bulk stamping restlessly from one side of the box to the other, and I saw that he, unlike Oliver's horses, wore no head-collar: nothing with which to hold him, while I calmed him, patting his neck.

His head reared up suddenly, tossing violently, and with a foreleg he lashed forward at the wall.

Not funny, I thought. Horrific to have been in the firing-line of that slashing hoof. For heaven's sake, I said to him mentally, I'll do you no harm. Just stay quiet. Go to sleep.

I was standing at that time with my back to the door, so that to the horse I must have been totally in shadow: but he would know I was there. He could smell my presence, hear my breathing. If he could see me as well, would it be better?

I took a tentative step towards the dim oblong of window, and had a clear, sharp, and swiftly terrifying view of one of his eyes.

No peace. No sleep. No prospect of anything like that. The horse's eye was stretched wide with white showing all round the usual darkness, staring not at me but as if blind, glaring wildly at nothing at all.

The black nostrils looked huge. The lips as I watched were drawing back from the teeth. The ears had gone flat to the head and there was froth forming in the mouth. It was the face, I thought incredulously, not of unrest or alarm . . . but of madness.

The horse backed suddenly away, crashing his hindquarters into the rear wall and rocking again forwards, but this time advancing with both forelegs off the ground, the gleams from thrashing hooves curving in silvery streaks in the gloom, the feet hitting the wall below the window with sickening intent.

I pressed in undoubted panic into the corner made by wall and door, but it gave no real protection. The box was roughly ten feet square by eight feet high, a space even at the best of times half filled by horse. For that horse at that moment it was a strait-jacket confinement out of which he seemed intent on physically smashing his way.

The manger, I thought. Get in the manger.

The manger was built at about waist height diagonally across one of the box's rear corners; a smallish metal trough set into a sturdy wooden support. As a shelter it was pathetic, but at least I would be off the ground . . .

The horse turned and stood on his forelegs and let fly backwards with an almighty double kick that thudded into the concrete wall six inches from my head, and it was then, at that moment, that I began to fear that the crazed animal might not just hurt but kill me.

He wasn't purposely trying to attack; most of his kicks were in other directions. He wasn't trying to bite, though his now open mouth looked savage. He was uncontrollably wild, but not with me . . . though that, in so small a space, made little difference.

He seemed in the next very few seconds to go utterly berserk. With speeds I could only guess at in the scurrying shadows he whirled and kicked and hurled his bulk against the walls, and I, still attempting to jump through the tempest into the manger, was finally knocked over by one of his flailing feet.

I didn't realise at that point that he'd actually broken one of my arms because the whole thing felt numb. I made it to the manger, tried to scramble up, got my foot in . . . sat on the edge . . . tried to raise my other, now dangling foot . . . and couldn't do it fast enough. Another direct hit crunched on my ankle and I knew, that time, that there was damage.

The air about my head seemed to hiss with hooves and the horse was beginning a high bubbling whinny. Surely someone, I thought desperately, someone would hear the crashing and banging and come . . .

I could see him in flashes against the window, a rearing,

bucking, kicking, rocketing nightmare. He came wheeling round, half seen, walking on his hind legs, head hard against the ceiling, the forelegs thrashing as if trying to climb invisible walls . . . and he knocked me off my precarious perch with a swiping punch in the chest that had half a ton of weight behind it and no particular aim.

I fell twisting onto the straw and tried to curl my head away from those lethal feet, to save instinctively one's face and gut . . . and leave backbone and kidney to their fate. Another crushing thud landed on the back of my shoulder and jarred like a hammer through every bone, and I could feel a scream forming somewhere inside me, a wrenching cry for mercy, for escape, for an end to battering, for release from terror.

His mania if anything grew worse, and it was he who was finally screaming, not me. The noise filled my ears, bounced off the walls, stunning, mind-blowing, the roaring of furies.

He somehow got one hoof inside my rolled body and tumbled me fast over, and I could see him arching above me, the tendons like strings, the torment in him too, the rage of the gods bursting from his stretched throat, his forelegs so high that he was hitting the ceiling.

This is death, I thought. This is dreadful, pulverising extinction. Only for this second would I see and feel . . . and one of his feet would land on my head and I'd go . . . I'd go . . .

Before I'd even finished the thought his forelegs came crashing down with a hoof so close it brushed my hair; and then again, as if driven beyond endurance, he reared dementedly on his hind legs, the head going up like a reverse thunderbolt towards the sky, the skull meeting the ceiling with the force of a ram. The whole building shook with the impact, and the horse, his voice cut off, fell in a huge collapsing mass across my legs, spasms shuddering through his body, muscles jerking in stiff kicks, the air still ringing with the echoes of extremity.

He was dying in stages, unconscious, reluctant, the brain finished, the nerve messages still passing to convulsing muscles, turmoil churning without direction in stomach and gut, the head already inert on the straw.

An age passed before it was done. Then the heavy body fell flaccid, all systems spent, and lay in perpetual astonishing silence, pinning me beneath.

The relief of finding him dead and myself alive lasted quite a long time, but then, as always happens with the human race, simple gratitude for existence progressed to discontent that things weren't better.

He had fallen with his spine towards me, his bulk lying across my legs from my knees down; and getting out from under him was proving an impossibility.

The left ankle, which felt broken, protested screechingly at any attempted movement. I couldn't lift my arm for the same reason. There was acute soreness in my chest, making breathing itself painful and coughing frightful; and the only good thing I could think of was that I was lying on my back and not face down in the straw.

A very long time passed very slowly. The crushing weight of the horse slowly numbed my legs altogether and transferred the chief area of agony to the whole of my left arm, which I might have thought totally mangled if I hadn't been able to see it dimly lying there looking the same as usual, covered in blue sweater, white cuff slightly showing, hand with clean nails, gold watch on wrist.

Physical discomfort for a while shut out much in the way of thought, but eventually I began to add up memories and ask questions, and the biggest, most immediate question was what would Calder do when he came back and found me alive.

He wouldn't expect it. No one could really expect anyone to survive being locked in with a mad horse, and the fact that I had was a trick of fate.

I remembered him giving the horse an apple while I'd struggled within the spinning walls to stand up. Giving his apple so routinely, and patting the horse's neck.

I remembered Calder saying on my first visit that he gave his remedies to horses in hollowed-out apples. But this time it had been no remedy, this time something opposite, this time a drug to make crazy, to turn a normal steel-shod horse into a killing machine.

What had he said when he'd first found me conscious? Those bizarre words . . . 'I thought you'd be out. I thought you wouldn't know . . .' And something else . . . 'I wish I'd hit you harder, but it seemed enough.'

He had said also that he was sorry, that he wished I hadn't come . . . He hadn't meant, I thought, that I should be aware of it when the horse killed me. At the very least, he hadn't meant me to see and hear and suffer that death. But also, when he found me awake, it hadn't prevented him from *then* giving the apple, although he knew that I *would* see, *would* hear, would . . . suffer.

The horse hadn't completed the task. When Calder returned, he would make good the deficit. It was certain.

I tried, on that thought, again to slide my legs out, though how much it would have helped if I had succeeded was debatable. It was as excruciating as before, since the numbness proved temporary. I concluded somewhat sadly that dragging a broken ankle from beneath a dead horse was no jolly entertainment, and in fact, given the state of the rest of me, couldn't be done.

I had never broken any bones before, not even ski-ing. I'd never been injured beyond the transient bumps of childhood. Never been to hospital, never troubled a surgeon, never slept from anaesthetic. For thirty-four years I'd been thoroughly healthy and, apart from chicken-pox and such, never ill. I even had good teeth.

I was unprepared in any way for the onslaught of so much pain all at once, and also not quite sure how to deal with it. All I knew was that when I tried to pull out my ankle the protests throughout my body brought actual tears into my eyes and no amount of theoretical resolution could give me the power to continue. I wondered if what I felt was cowardice. I didn't much care if it was. I lay with everything stiffening and getting cold and worse, and I'd have given a good deal to be as oblivious as the horse.

The oblong of window at length began to lighten towards the new day; Saturday, June 2nd. Calder would come back and finish the job, and no reasonable pathologist would swear the last blow had been delivered hours after the first. Calder would say in bewilderment, 'But I had no idea Tim was coming to see me . . . I was in London for the television . . . I have no idea how he came to shut himself into one of the boxes . . . because it's just possible to do that, you know, if you're not careful . . . I've no idea why the horse should have kicked him, because he's a placid old boy, as you can see . . . the whole thing's a terrible accident, and I'm shattered . . . most distressed . . .', and anyone would look at the horse from whose bloodstream the crazing drug would have departed and conclude that I'd been pretty unintelligent and also unlucky, and too bad.

Ian Pargetter's veterinary case had gone to a securer hiding place or to destruction, and there would be only a slight chance left of proving Calder a murderer. Whichever way one considered it, the outlook was discouraging.

I couldn't be bothered to roll my wrist over to see the time. The sun rose and shone slantingly through the bars with the pale brilliance of dawn. It had to be five o'clock, or after.

Time drifted. The sun moved away. The horse and I lay in intimate silence, dead and half dead; waiting.

A car drove up fast outside and doors slammed.

It will be now, I thought. Now. Very soon.

There were voices in the distance, calling to each other. Female and male. *Strangers.*

Not Calder's distinctive, loud, edgy, public voice. Not his at all.

Hope thumped back with a tremendous surge and I called out myself, saying 'Here . . . Come here,' but it was at best a croak, inaudible beyond the door.

Suppose they were looking for Calder, and when they didn't find him, drove away . . . I took all possible breath into my lungs and yelled 'Help . . . Come here.'

Nothing happened. My voice ricocheted off the walls and mocked me, and I dragged in another grinding lungful and shouted again . . . and again . . . and again.

The top half of the door swung outward and let in a dazzle of light, and a voice yelled incredulously, 'He's *here*. He's in here . . .'

The bolt on the lower half-door clattered and the daylight grew to an oblong, and against the light three figures appeared, coming forward, concerned, speaking with anxiety and joy and bringing life.

Judith and Gordon and Pen.

Judith was gulping and so I think was I.

'Thank God,' Gordon said. 'Thank God.'

'You didn't go home,' Pen said. 'We were worried.'

'Are you all right?' Judith said.

'Not really . . . but everything's relative. I've never been happier, so who cares.'

'If we put our arms under your shoulders,' Gordon said, surveying the problem, 'we should be able to pull you out.'

'Don't do that,' I said.

'Why not?'

'One shoulder feels broken. Get a knacker.'

'My dear Tim,' he said, puzzled.

'They'll come with a lorry . . . and a winch. Their job is dead horses.'

'Yes, I see.'

'And an ambulance,' Pen said. 'I should think.'

I smiled at them with much love, my fairly incompetent saviours. They asked how I'd got where I was, and to their horror I briefly told them: and I in turn asked why they'd come, and they explained that they'd been worried because Calder's television programme had been cancelled.

'Micky Bonwith was taken ill,' Pen said. 'They just announced it during the evening. There would be no live Micky Bonwith show, just an old recording, very sorry, expect Calder Jackson at a later date.'

'Pen telephoned and told us where you were going, and why,' Judith said.

'And we were worried,' Gordon added.

'You didn't go home . . . didn't telephone,' Pen said.

'We've been awake all night,' Gordon said. 'The girls were growing more and more anxious . . . so we came.'

They'd come a hundred miles. You couldn't ask for better friends.

Gordon drove away to find a public telephone and Pen asked if I'd found what I'd come for.

'I don't know,' I said. 'Half the things had no labels.'

'Don't talk any more,' Judith said. 'Enough is enough.'

'I might as well.'

'Take your mind off it,' Pen nodded, understanding.

'What time is it?' I asked.

Judith looked at her watch. 'Ten to eight.'

'Calder will come back . . .' And the lads too, I thought. He'd come when the lads turned up for work. About that time. He'd need witnesses to the way he'd found me.

'Tim,' Pen said with decision, 'if he's coming . . . Did you take any samples? Did you get a chance?'

I nodded weakly.

'I suppose you can't remember what they were . . .'

'I hid them.'

'Wouldn't he have found them?' She was gentle and prepared to be disappointed; careful not to blame.

I smiled at her. 'He didn't find them. They're here.'

She looked blankly round the box and then at my face. 'Didn't he search you?' She said in surprise. 'Pockets . . . of course, he would.'

'I don't know . . . but he didn't find the pills.'

'Then where *are* they?'

'I learned from Ginnie about keeping your hands free,' I said. 'They're in a plastic bag . . . below my waistband . . . inside my pants.'

They stared incredulously, and then they laughed, and Judith with tears in her eyes said, 'Do you mean . . . all the time . . . ?'

'All the time,' I agreed. 'And go easy getting them out.'

Some things would be best forgotten but are impossible to forget, and I reckon one could put the next half hour into that category: at the end of it I lay on a table-like stretcher in the open air, and my dead-weight pal was half up the ramp of the knacker's van that Gordon with exceptional persuasiveness had conjured out at that hour of the morning.

The three lads who had at length arrived for work stood around looking helpless, and the two ambulance men, who were not paramedics, were farcically trying to get an answer on a radio with transmission troubles as to where they were supposed to take me.

Gordon was telling the knacker's men that I said it was essential to remove a blood sample from the horse and that the carcass was not to be disposed of until that was done. Judith and Pen both looked tired, and were yawning. I wearily watched some birds wheeling high in the fair blue sky and wished I were up there with them, as light as air; and into this rivetting tableau drove Calder.

Impossible to know what he thought when he saw all the activity, but as he came striding from his car his mouth formed an oval of apprehension and shock.

He seemed first to fasten his attention on Gordon, and then on the knacker's man who was saying loudly, 'If you want a blood sample you'll have to give us a written authorisation, because of calling in a vet and paying him.'

Calder looked from him to the dead horse still halfway up the ramp, and from there towards the horse's normal box, where the door stood wide open.

From there he turned with bewilderment to Judith, and then with horror saw the bag Pen held tightly, the transparent plastic bag with the capsules, pills and other assorted treasures showing clearly inside.

Pen remarkably found her voice and in words that must

have sounded like doom to Calder said, 'I didn't tell you before . . . I'm a pharmacist.'

'Where did you get that?' Calder said, staring at the bag as if his eyes would burn it. 'Where . . .'

'Tim had it.'

Her gaze went to me and Calder seemed finally to realise that my undoubted stillness was not that of death. He took two paces toward the stretcher and looked down at my face and saw me alive, awake, aware.

Neither of us spoke. His eyes seemed to retreat in the sockets and the shape of the upper jaw stood out starkly. He saw in me I dare say the ravages of the night and I saw in him the realisation become certainty that my survival meant his ruin.

I thought: you certainly should have hit harder; and maybe he thought it too. He looked at me with a searing intensity that defied analysis and then turned abruptly away and walked with jerky steps back to his car.

Gordon took two or three hesitant steps towards perhaps stopping him, but Calder without looking back started his engine, put his foot on the accelerator and with protesting tyres made a tight semi-circular turn and headed for the gate.

'We should get the police,' Gordon said, watching him go.

Judith and Pen showed scant enthusiasm and I none at all. I supposed we would have to bring in the police in the end, but the longer the boring rituals could be postponed, from my point of view, the better. Britain was a small island, and Calder too well-known to go far.

Pen looked down at the plastic store-house in her hands and then without actual comment opened her handbag and put the whole thing inside. She glanced briefly at me and smiled faintly, and I nodded with relief that she and her friends would have the unravelling of the capsules to themselves.

On that same Saturday, at about two-thirty in the afternoon, a family of picnickers came across a car which had been parked out of sight of any road behind some clumps of gorse bushes. The engine of the car was running and the children of the family, peering through the windows, saw a man slumped on the back seat with a tube in his mouth.

They knew him because of his curly hair, and his beard.

The children were reported to be in a state of hysterical

shock and the parents were angry, as if some authority, somewhere or other, should prevent suicides spoiling the countryside.

Tributes to Calder's miracle-working appeared on television that evening, and I thought it ironic that the master who had known so much about drugs should have chosen to gas his way out.

He had driven barely thirty miles from his yard. He had left no note. The people who had been working with him on the postponed Micky Bonwith show said they couldn't understand it, and Dissdale telephoned Oliver to say that in view of Calder's tragic death he would have to withdraw his offer for Sandcastle.

I, by the time I heard all this, was half covered in infinitely irritating plaster of paris, there being more grating edges of bone inside me than I cared to hear about, and horse-shoe-shaped crimson bruises besides.

I had been given rather grudgingly a room to myself, privacy in illness being considered a sinful luxury in the national health service, and on Monday evening Pen came all the way from London again to report on the laboratory findings.

She frowned after she'd kissed me. 'You look exhausted,' she said.

'Tiring place, hospital.'

'I suppose it must be. I'd never thought . . .'

She put a bunch of roses in my drinking-water jug and said they were from Gordon and Judith's garden.

'They send their love,' she said chattily, 'and their garden's looking lovely.'

'Pen . . .'

'Yes. Well.' She pulled the visitor's chair closer to the bed upon which I half sat, half lay in my plaster and borrowed dressing gown on top of the blankets. 'You have really, as they say, hit the jackpot.'

'Do you mean it?' I exclaimed.

She grinned cheerfully. 'It's no wonder that Calder killed himself, not after seeing you alive and hearing you were going to get the dead horse tested, and knowing that after all you had taken all those things from his surgery. It was either that or years in jail and total disgrace.'

'A lot of people would prefer disgrace.'

'Not Calder, though.'

'No.'

She opened a slim black briefcase on her knees and produced several typewritten pages.

'We worked all yesterday and this morning,' she said, 'But first I'll tell you that Gordon got the dead horse's blood test done immediately at the Equine Research Establishment, and they told him on the telephone this morning that the horse had been given ethyl isobutrazine, which was contrary to normal veterinary practice.'

'You don't say.'

Her eyes gleamed. 'The Research people told Gordon that any horse given ethyl isobutrazine would go utterly beserk and literally try to climb the walls.'

'That's just what he did,' I said soberly.

'It's a drug which is used all the time as a tranquilliser to stop dogs barking or getting car-sick, but it has an absolutely manic effect on horses. One of its brand names is Diquel, in case you're interested. All the veterinary books warn against giving it to horses.'

'But normally . . . in a horse . . . it would wear off?'

'Yes, in six hours or so, with no trace.'

Six hours, I thought bleakly. *Six hours . . .*

'In your bag of goodies,' Pen said, 'guess what we found? Three tablets of Diquel.'

'Really?'

She nodded. 'Really. And now pin back your ears, dearest Tim, because when we found what Calder had been doing, words simply failed us.'

They seemed indeed to fail her again, for she sat looking at the pages with a faraway expression.

'You remember,' she said at last, 'when we went to Calder's yard that time at Easter, we saw a horse that had been bleeding in its urine . . . crystalluria was what he called it . . . that antibiotics hadn't been able to cure?'

'Yes,' I said. 'Other times too, he cured horses with that.'

'Mm. And those patients had been previously treated by Ian Pargetter before he died, hadn't they?'

I thought back. 'Some of them, certainly.'

'Well . . . you know you told me before they carted you off in the ambulance on Saturday that some of the jars of capsules in the cupboards were labelled only with letters like a+w, b+w, and c+s?'

I nodded.

'Three capsules each with one transparent and one blue end,

did contain c and s. Vitamin C, and sulphanilamide.' She looked at me for a possible reaction, but Vitamin C and sulphanilamide sounded quite harmless, and I said so.

'Yes,' she said, 'separately they do nothing but good, but *together they can cause crystalluria.*'

I stared at her.

'Calder had made those capsules expressly to *cause the horse's illness* in the first place, so that he could "cure" it afterwards. And then the only miracle he'd have to work would be to stop giving the capsules.'

'My God,' I said.

She nodded. 'We could hardly believe it. It meant, you see, that Ian Pargetter almost certainly *knew*. Because it was he, you see, who could have given the horse's trainer or owner or lad or whatever a bottle of capsules labelled "antibiotic" to dole out every day. And those capsules were precisely what was making the horse ill.'

'*Pen*!'

'I'd better explain just a little, if you can bear it,' she said. 'If you give sulpha drugs to anyone – horse or person – who doesn't need them, you won't do much harm because urine is normally slightly alkaline or only slightly acid and you'll get rid of the sulpha safely. But vitamin C is ascorbic acid and makes the urine *more* acid, and the acid works with sulpha drugs to form crystals, and the crystals cause pain and bleeding . . . like powdered glass.'

There was a fairly long silence, and then I said, 'It's diabolical.'

She nodded. 'Once Calder had the horse in his yard he could speed up the cure by giving him bicarbonate of soda, which will make the urine alkaline again and also dissolve the crystals, and with plenty of water to drink the horse would be well in no time. Miraculously fast, in fact.' She paused and smiled, and went on, 'We tested a few more things which were perfectly harmless herbal remedies and then we came to three more homemade capsules, with pale green ends this time, and we reckon that they were your a+w.'

'Go on, then,' I said. 'What's a, and what's w?'

'A is antibiotic, and w is warfarin. And before you ask, warfarin is a drug used in humans for reducing the clotting ability of the blood.'

'That pink pill you found on the surgery floor,' I said. 'That's what you said.'

'Oh yes.' She looked surprised. 'So I did. I'd forgotten. Well . . . if you give certain antibiotics *with* warfarin you increase the effect of the warfarin to the extent that blood will hardly clot at all . . . and you get severe bleeding from the stomach, from the mouth, from anywhere where a small blood-vessel breaks . . . when normally it would clot and mend at once.'

I let out a held breath. 'Every time I went, there was a bleeder.'

She nodded. 'Warfarin acts by drastically reducing the effect of vitamin K, which is needed for normal clotting, so all Calder had to do to reverse things was feed lots of vitamin K . . . which is found in large quantities in alfalfa.'

'And b+w?' I asked numbly.

'Barbiturate and warfarin. Different mechanism, but if you used them together and then stopped just the barbiturate, you could cause a sort of delayed bleeding about three weeks later.' She paused. 'We've all been looking up our pharmacology textbooks, and there are warnings there, plain to see if you're looking for them, about prescribing antibiotics or barbiturates or indeed phenylbutazone or anabolic steroids for people on warfarin without carefully adjusting the warfarin dosage. And you see,' she went on, 'putting two drugs together in one capsule was really brilliant, because no one would think they were giving a horse two drugs, but just one . . . and we reckon Ian Pargetter could have put Calder's capsules into any regular bottle, and the horse's owner would think that he was giving the horse what it said on the label.'

I blinked. 'It's incredible.'

'It's easy,' she said. 'And it gets easier as it goes on.'

'There's more?'

'Sure there's more.' She grinned. 'How about all those poor animals with extreme debility who were so weak they could hardly walk?'

I swallowed. 'How about them?'

'You said you found a large bottle in Ian Pargetter's case with only a few pills in it? A bottle labelled "diuretic", or in other words, pills designed to increase the passing of urine?'

I nodded.

'Well, we identified the ones you took, and if you simply gave those particular thiazide diuretic pills over a long period to a horse you would cause *exactly* the sort of general progressive debility shown by those horses.'

I was past speech.

'And to cure the debility,' she said, 'you just stop the diuretics and provide good food and water. And hey presto!' She smiled blissfully. 'Chemically, it's so elegant. The debility is caused by constant excessive excretion of potassium which the body needs for strength, and the cure is to restore potassium as fast as safely possible . . . with potassium salts, which you can buy anywhere.'

I gazed at her with awe.

She was enjoying her revelations. 'We come now to the horses with non-healing ulcers and sores.'

Always those, too, in the yard, I thought.

'Ulcers and sores are usually cleared up fairly quickly by applications of antibiotic cream. Well . . . by this time we were absolutely bristling with suspicions, so last of all we took that little tube of antibiotic cream you found in Ian Pargetter's case, and we tested it. And lo and behold, it didn't contain antibiotic cream at all.'

'What then?'

'Cortisone cream.'

She looked at my non-comprehension and smiled. 'Cortisone cream is fine for eczema and allergies, but *not* for general healing. In fact, if you scratched a horse and smeared some dirt into the wound to infect it and then religiously applied cortisone cream twice a day you would get a nice little ulcer which would never heal. Until, of course, you sent your horse to Calder, who would lay his hands upon your precious . . . and apply antibiotics at once, to let normal healing begin.'

'Dear God in heaven.'

'Never put cortisone cream on a cut,' she said. 'A lot of people do. It's stupid.'

'I never will,' I said fervently.

Pen grinned. 'They always fill toothpaste from the blunt end. We looked very closely and found that the end of the tube had been unwound and then re-sealed. Very neat.'

She seemed to have stopped, so I asked 'Is that the lot?'

'That's the lot.

We sat for a while and pondered.

'It does answer an awful lot of questions,' I said finally.

'Such as?'

'Such as why Calder killed Ian Pargetter,' I said. 'Ian Pargetter wanted to stop something . . . which must have been this illness caper. Said he'd had enough. Said also that he would stop Calder too, which must have been his death warrant.'

Pen said, 'Is that what Calder actually told you?'

'Yes, that's what he said, but at the time I didn't understand what he meant.'

'I wonder,' Pen said, 'why Ian Pargetter wanted to stop altogether? They must have had a nice steady income going between the two of them. Calder must have recruited him years ago.'

'Selenium,' I said.

'What?'

'Selenium was different. Making horses ill in order to cure them wasn't risking much permanent damage, if any at all. But selenium would be forever. The foals would be deformed. I'd guess when Calder suggested it the idea sickened Ian Pargetter. Revolted him, probably, because he was after all a vet.'

'And Calder wanted to go on with it all . . . enough to kill.'

I nodded. 'Calder would have had his sights on a fortune as well as an income. And but for Ginnie somehow getting hold of that shampoo, he would very likely have achieved it.'

'I wonder how she did,' Pen said.

'Mm.' I shifted uncomfortably on the bed. 'I've remembered the name of the lad Calder had who looked like Ricky Barnet. It was Jason. I remembered it the other night . . . in that yard . . . funny the way the mind works.'

'What about him?' Pen said sympathetically.

'I remembered Calder saying he gave the pills to Jason for Jason to give to the horses. The herb pills, he meant. But with Ian Pargetter gone, Calder would have needed someone else to give those double-edged capsules to horses . . . because he still had horses in his yard with those same troubles long after Ian Pargetter was dead.'

'So he did,' she said blankly. 'Except . . .'

'Except what?'

'Only that when we got to the yard last Saturday, before I heard you calling, we looked into several other boxes, and there weren't many horses there. The place wasn't full, like it had been.'

'I should think,' I said slowly, 'that it was because Jason had been busy working for three months or more at Oliver's farm, feeding selenium in apples.'

A visual memory flashed in my brain. *Apples* . . . Shane, the stable lad, walking across the yard, swinging a bucket and eating an apple. Shane, Jason: one and the same.

'What is it?' Pen said.

'Photos of Ricky Barnet.'

'Oh yes.'

'They say I can leave here tomorrow,' I said, 'if I insist.'

She looked at me with mock despair. 'What exactly did you break?'

'They said this top lot was scapula, clavicle, humerus, sternum and ribs. Down there,' I pointed, 'they lost me. I didn't know there *were* so many bones in one ankle.'

'Did they pin it?'

'God knows.'

'How will you look after yourself?'

'In my usual clumsy fashion.'

'Don't be silly,' she said. 'Stay until it stops hurting.'

'That might be weeks . . . there's some problem with ligaments or tendons or something.'

'What problem?'

'I didn't really listen.'

'*Tim.*' She was exasperated.

'Well . . . it's so boring,' I said.

She gave an eyes-to-heaven laugh. 'I brought you a present from my shop.' She dug into her handbag. 'Here you are, with my love.'

I took the small white box she offered, and looked at the label on its side.

Comfrey, it said.

She grinned. 'You might as well try it,' she said. 'Comfrey does contain allantoin, which helps to knit bones. And you never know . . . Calder really was an absolute expert with all sorts of drugs.'

On Tuesday, June 4th, Oliver Knowles collected me from the hospital to drive me on some errands and then take me to his home, not primarily as an act of compassion but mostly to talk business. I had expected him to accept my temporary disabilities in a straightforward and unemotional manner, and so he did, although he did say dryly when he saw me that when I had invited myself over the telephone I had referred to a 'crack or two' and not to half an acre of plaster with clothes strung on in patches.

'Never mind,' I said. 'I can hop and I can sit and my right arm is fine.'

'Yes. So I see.'

The nurse who had wheeled me in a chair to his car said however, 'He can't hop, it jars him,' and handed Oliver a slip of paper. 'There's a place along that road . . .' she pointed, '. . . where you can hire wheel-chairs.' To me she said, 'Get a comfortable one. And one which lets your leg lie straight out, like this one. You'll ache less. All right?'

'All right,' I said.

'Hm. Well . . . take care.'

She helped me into the car with friendly competence and went away with the hospital transport, and Oliver and I did as she advised, storing the resulting cushioned and chromium comfort into the boot of his car.

'Right,' I said. 'Then the next thing to do is buy a good instant camera and a stack of films.'

Oliver found a shop and bought the camera while I sat in the front passenger seat as patiently as possible.

'Where next?' he said, coming back with parcels.

'Cambridge. An engineering works. Here's the address.' I handed him the piece of paper on which I'd written Ricky Barnet's personal directions. 'We're meeting him when he comes out of work.'

'Who?' Oliver said. 'Who are we meeting?'

'You'll see.'

We parked across the road from the firm's gate and waited, and at four-thirty on the dot the exodus occurred.

Ricky Barnet came out and looked this way and that in searching for us, and beside me I heard Oliver stir and say, 'But that's Shane' in surprise, and then relax and add doubtfully, 'No it isn't.'

'No, it isn't.' I leaned out of the open window and called to him 'Ricky . . . over here.'

He crossed the road and stopped beside the car.

'Hop in,' I said.

'You been in an accident?' he said disbelievingly.

'Sort of.'

He climbed into the back of the car. He hadn't been too keen to have his photograph taken for the purpose I'd outlined, but he was in no great position to refuse; and I'd made my blackmailing pressure sound like honey, which I wasn't too bad at, in my way. He still wasn't pleased however, which had its own virtues, as the last thing I wanted was forty prints of him grinning.

Oliver drove off and stopped where I asked at a suitably neutral background – a grey-painted factory wall – and he said he would take the photographs if I explained what I wanted.

'Ricky looks like Shane,' I said. 'So take pictures of Ricky in the way he *most* looks like Shane. Get him to turn his head slowly like he did when he came out of work, and tell him to hold it where it's best.'

'All right.'

Ricky got out of the car and stood in front of the wall, with Oliver focusing at head-and-shoulder distance. He took the first picture and we waited for it to develop.

Oliver looked at it, grunted, adjusted the light meter, and tried again.

'This one's all right,' he said, watching the colours emerge. 'Looks like Shane. Quite amazing.'

With a faint shade of sullenness Ricky held his pose for as long as it took to shoot four boxes of film. Oliver passed each print to me as it came out of the camera, and I laid them in rows along the seat beside me while they developed.

'That's fine,' I said, when the films were finished. 'Thank you, Ricky.'

He came over to the car window and I asked him without any great emphasis, 'Do you remember, when Indian Silk got so ill with debility, which vet was treating him?'

'Yeah, sure, that fellow that was murdered. Him and his partners. The best, Dad said.'

I nodded non-committally. 'Do you want a ride to Newmarket?'

'Got my motor-bike, thanks.'

We took him back to his engineering works where I finally cheered him up with payment for his time and trouble, and watched while he roared off with a flourish of self-conscious bravado.

'What's now?' Oliver said. 'Did you say Newmarket?'

I nodded. 'I've arranged to meet Ursula Young.'

He gave me a glance of bewilderment and drove without protest, pulling duly into the mid-town car park where Ursula had said to come.

We arrived there first, the photography not having taken as long as I'd expected, and Oliver finally gave voice to a long restrained question.

'Just what,' he said. 'Are the photographs *for*?'

'For finding Shane.'

'But why?'

'Don't explode.'

'No.'

'Because I think he gave the selenium to your mares.'

Oliver sat very still. 'You asked about him before,' he said. 'I did wonder . . . if you thought . . . he killed Ginnie.'

It was my own turn for quiet.

'I don't know if he did,' I said at last. 'I don't know.'

Ursula arrived in her car with a rush, checking her watch and apologising all the same, although she was on time. She, like Oliver and Ricky, looked taken aback at my unorthodox attire, but rallied in her usual no-nonsense fashion and shuffled into the back seat of Oliver's car, leaning forward to bring her face on a level with ours.

I passed her thirty of the forty pictures of Ricky Barnet, who of course she knew immediately.

'Yes, but,' I explained, 'Ricky looks like a lad who worked for Oliver, and it's *that* lad we want to find.'

'Well, all right. How important is it?'

Oliver answered her before I could. 'Ursula, if you find him, we might be able to prove there's nothing wrong with Sandcastle. And don't ask me how, just believe it.'

Her mouth had opened.

'And Ursula,' Oliver said, 'if you find him – Shane, that lad – I'll put business your way for the rest of my life.'

I could see that to her, a middle-rank bloodstock agent, it was no mean promise.

'All right,' she said briskly. 'You're on. I'll start spreading the pictures about at once, tonight, and call you with results.'

'Ursula,' I said. 'If you find where he is now, make sure he isn't frightened off. We don't want to lose him.'

She looked at me shrewdly. 'This is roughly police work?'

I nodded. 'Also, if you find anyone who employed him in the past, ask if by any chance a horse he looked after fell ill. Or any horse in the yard, for that matter. And don't give him a name . . . he isn't always called Shane.'

'Is he dangerous?' she said straightly.

'We don't want him challenged,' I said. 'Just found.'

'All right. I trust you both, so I'll do my best. And I suppose one day you'll explain what it's all about?'

'If he's done what we think,' I said, 'we'll make sure the whole world knows. You can count on it.'

She smiled briefly and patted my unplastered shoulder. 'You look grey,' she said, and to Oliver, 'Tim told me a horse kicked him and broke his arm. Is that right?'

'He told me that, too.'

'And what else?' she asked me astringently. 'How did you get in this state?'

'The horse didn't know it's own strength.' I smiled at her. 'Clumsy brute.'

She knew I was dodging in some way, but she lived in a world where the danger of horse kicks was ever present and always to be avoided, and she made no more demur. Stowing the photographs in her capacious handbag she wriggled her way out of the car, and with assurances of action drove off in her own.

'What now?' Oliver said.

'A bottle of scotch.'

He gave me an austere look which then swept over my general state and softened to understanding.

'Can you wait until we get home?' he said.

That evening, bit by bit, I told Oliver about Pen's analysis of the treasures from Calder's surgery and of Calder's patients' drug-induced illnesses. I told him that Calder had killed Ian Pargetter, and why, and I explained again how the idea of first discrediting, then buying and re-building Sandcastle had followed the pattern of Indian Silk.

'There may be others besides Indian Silk that we haven't heard of,' I said thoughtfully. 'Show jumpers, eventers, even prize ponies. You never know. Dissdale might have gone along more than twice with his offer to buy the no-hoper.'

'He withdrew his offer for Sandcastle the same night Calder died.'

'What exactly did he say?' I asked.

'He was very upset. Said he'd lost his closest friend, and that without Calder to work his miracles there was no point in buying Sandcastle.'

I frowned. 'Do you think it was genuine?'

'His distress? Yes, certainly.'

'And the belief in miracles?'

'He did *sound* as if he believed.'

I wondered if it was in the least possible that Dissdale was an innocent and duped accomplice and hadn't known that his bargains had been first made ill. His pride in knowing the Great Man had been obvious at Ascot, and perhaps he had been flattered and foolish but not wicked after all.

Oliver asked in the end how I'd found out about the drug-induced illnesses and Ian Pargetter's murder, and I told him that too, as flatly as possible.

He sat staring at me, his gaze on the plaster.

'You're very lucky to be in a wheel-chair, and not a coffin,' he said. 'Damn lucky.'

'Yes.'

He poured more of the brandy we had progressed to after dinner. Anaesthesia was coming along nicely.

'I'm almost beginning to believe,' he said, 'that somehow or other I'll still be here next year, even if I do have to sell Sandcastle and whatever else is necessary.'

I drank from my replenished glass. 'Tomorrow we'll make a plan contingent upon Sandcastle's being reinstated in the eyes of the world. Look out the figures, see what the final damage is likely to be, draw up a time scale for recovery. I can't promise because it isn't my final say-so, but if the bank gets all its money in the end, it'll most likely be flexible about when.'

'Good of you,' Oliver said, hiding emotion behind his clipped martial manner.

'Frankly,' I said, 'you're more use to us salvaged than bust.'

He smiled wryly. 'A banker to the last drop of blood.'

Because of stairs being difficult I slept on the sofa where Ginnie had dozed on her last afternoon, and I dreamed of her walking up a path towards me looking happy. Not a significant dream, but an awakening of fresh regret. I spent a good deal of the following day thinking of her instead of concentrating on profit and loss.

In the evening Ursula telephoned with triumph in her strong voice and also a continual undercurrent of amazement.

'You won't believe it,' she said, 'but I've already found three racing stables in Newmarket where he worked last summer and autumn, and in *every case* one of the horses in the yard fell sick!'

I hadn't any trouble at all with belief and asked what sort of sickness.

'They all had crystalluria. That's crystals . . .'

'I know what it is,' I said.

'And . . . it's absolutely incredible . . . but all three were in stables which had in the past sent horses to Calder Jackson, and these were sent as well, and he cured them straight away. Two of the trainers said they would swear by Calder, he had cured horses for them for years.'

'Was the lad called Shane?' I asked.

'No. Bret. Bret Williams. The same in all three places.'

She dictated the addresses of the stables, the names of the trainers, and the dates (approximate) when Shane – Jason – Bret had been in their yards.

'These lads just come and go,' she said. 'He didn't work for any of them for as long as a month. Just didn't turn up one morning. It happens all the time.'

'You're marvellous,' I said.

'I have a feeling,' she said with less excitement, 'that what I'm telling you is what you expected to hear.'

'Hoped.'

'The implications are unbelievable.'

'Believe them.'

'But *Calder*,' she protested. 'He couldn't . . .'

'Shane worked for Calder,' I said. 'All the time. Permanently. Wherever he went, it was to manufacture patients for Calder.'

She was silent so long that in the end I said 'Ursula?'

'I'm here,' she said. 'Do you want me to go on with the photos?'

'Yes, if you would. To find him.'

'Hanging's too good for him,' she said grimly. 'I'll do what I can.'

She disconnected, and I told Oliver what she'd said.

'Bret Williams? He was Shane Williams here.'

'How did you come to employ him?' I asked.

Oliver frowned, looking back. 'Good lads aren't that easy to find, you know. You can advertise until you're blue in the face and only get third- or fourth-rate applicants. But Nigel said Shane impressed him at the interview and that we should give him a month's trial, and of course after that we kept him on, and took him back gladly this year when he telephoned asking, because he was quick and competent and knew the job backwards, and was polite and a good time-keeper . . .'

'A paragon,' I said dryly.

'As lads go, yes.'

I nodded. He would have to have been good; to have taken pride in his deception, with the devotion of all traitors. I considered those fancy names and thought that he must have seen himself as a sort of macho hero, the great foreign agent playing out his fantasies in the day to day tasks, feeling superior to his employers while he tricked them with contempt.

He could have filled the hollowed cores of apples with capsules, and taken a bite or two round the outside to convince, and fed what looked like remainders to his victims. No one would ever have suspected, because suspicion was impossible.

I slept again on the sofa and the following morning Oliver telephoned to Detective Chief Inspector Wyfold and asked him to come to the farm. Wyfold needed persuading; reluctantly agreed; and nearly walked out in a U-turn when he saw me waiting in Oliver's office.

'No. Look,' he protested, 'Mr Ekaterin's already approached me with his ideas and I simply haven't time . . .'

Oliver interrupted. 'We have a great deal more now. Please do listen. We quite understand that you are busy with all those other poor girls, but at the very least we can take Ginnie off that list for you.'

Wyfold finally consented to sit down and accept some coffee and listen to what we had to say: and as we told him in turns and in detail what had been happening his air of impatience dissipated and his natural sharpness took over.

We gave him copies of Pen's analyses, the names of 'Bret's' recent employers and the last ten photographs of Ricky. He glanced at them briefly and said, 'We interviewed this groom, but . . .'

'No, you didn't,' Oliver said. 'The photo is of a boy who looks like him if you don't know either of them well.'

Wyfold pursed his lips, but nodded. 'Fair enough.'

'We do think he may have killed Ginnie, even if you couldn't prove it,' Oliver said.

Wyfold began putting together the papers we'd given him. 'We will certainly redirect our enquiries,' he said, and giving me a dour look added, 'If you had left it to the police to search Calder's surgery, sir, Calder Jackson would not have had the opportunity of disposing of Ian Pargetter's case and any other material evidence. These things are always mishandled by amateurs.' He looked pointedly at my plaster jacket. 'Better have left it to the professionals.'

I gave him an amused look but Oliver was gasping. 'Left to

you,' he said, 'there would have been no search at all . . . or certainly not in time to save my business.'

Wyfold's expression said plainly that saving people's businesses wasn't his prime concern, but beyond mentioning that picking locks and stealing medicinal substances constituted a breach of the law he kept any further disapproval to himself.

He was on his feet ready to go when Ursula rang again, and he could almost hear every word she said because of her enthusiasm.

'I'm in Gloucestershire,' she shouted. 'I thought I'd work from the other end, if you see what I mean. I remembered Calder had miraculously cured Binty Rockingham's utterly brilliant three-day-eventer who was so weak he could hardly totter, so I came here to her house to ask her, and guess what?'

'What?' I asked obligingly.

'That lad worked for her!' The triumph exploded. 'A good lad, she says, would you believe it? He called himself Clint. She can't remember his last name, it was more than two years ago and he was only here a few weeks.'

'Ask her if it was Williams,' I said.

There was some murmuring at the other end then Ursula's voice back again, 'She thinks so, yes.'

'You're a dear, Ursula,' I said.

She gave an unembarrassed laugh. 'Do you want me to go on down the road to Rube Golby's place? He had a show pony Calder cured a fair time ago of a weeping wound that wouldn't heal.'

'Just one more, then, Ursula. It's pretty conclusive already, I'd say.'

'Best to be sure,' she said cheerfully. 'And I'm enjoying myself, actually, now I'm over the shock.'

I wrote down the details she gave me and when she'd gone off the line I handed the new information to Wyfold.

'Clint,' he said with disillusion. 'Elvis next, I shouldn't wonder.'

I shook my head. 'A man of action, our Shane.'

Perhaps through needing to solve at least one murder while reviled for not catching the rapist, Wyfold put his best muscle into the search. It took him two weeks only to find Shane, who was arrested on leaving a pub in the racing village of Malton, Yorkshire, where he had been heard boasting several times about secret exploits of undisclosed daring.

Wyfold told Oliver, who telephoned me in the office, to which I'd returned via a newly installed wheel-chair ramp up the front steps.

'He called himself Dean,' Oliver said. 'Dean Williams. It seems the police are transferring him from Yorkshire back here to Hertfordshire, and Wyfold wants you to come to his police headquarters to identify Shane as the man called Jason at Calder's yard.'

I said I would.

I didn't say that with honesty I couldn't.

'Tomorrow,' Oliver added. 'They're in a hurry because of holding him without a good enough charge, or something.'

'I'll be there.'

I went in a chauffeur-driven hired car, a luxury I seemed to have spent half my salary on since leaving Oliver's house.

I was living nearer the office than usual with a friend whose flat was in a block with a lift, not up stairs like my own. The pains in my immobile joints refused obstinately to depart, but owing to a further gift from Pen (via Gordon) were forgettable most of the time. A new pattern of 'normal' life had evolved, and all I dearly wanted was a bath.

I arrived at Wyfold's police station at the same time as Oliver, and together we were shown into an office, Oliver pushing me as if born to it. Two months minimum, they'd warned me to expect of life on wheels. Even if my shoulder would be mended before then, it wouldn't stand my weight on crutches. Patience, I'd been told. Be patient. My ankle had been in bits and they'd restored it like a jig-saw puzzle and I couldn't expect miracles, they'd said.

Wyfold arrived, shook hands briskly (in advance) and said that this was not a normal identity parade, as of course Oliver knew Shane very well, and I obviously knew him also, because of Ricky Barnet.

'Just call him Jason,' Wyfold told me, 'If you are sure he's the same man you saw at Calder Jackson's.'

We left the office and went along a fiercely-lit institutional corridor to a large interview room which contained a table, three chairs, a uniformed policeman standing . . . and Shane, sitting down.

He looked cocky, not cowed.

When he saw Oliver he tilted his head almost jauntily, showing not shame but pride, not apology but a sneer. On me he looked with only a flickering glance, neither knowing me from our two very brief meetings nor reckoning on trouble from my direction.

Wyfold raised his eyebrows at me to indicate the need for action.

'Hello, Jason,' I said.

His head snapped round immediately and this time he gave me a full stare.

'I met you at Calder Jackson's yard,' I said.

'You never did.'

Although I hadn't expected it, I remembered him clearly. 'You were giving sun-lamp treatment to a horse and Calder Jackson told you to put on your sunglasses.'

He made no effort to deny it. 'What of it, then?' he said.

'Conclusive evidence of your link with the place, I should think,' I said.

Oliver, seeming as much outraged by Shane's lack of contrition as by his sins, turned with force to Wyfold and in half-controlled bitterness said, 'Now prove he killed my daughter.'

'*What*!'

Shane had risen in panic to his feet, knocking his chair over behind him and losing in an instant the smart-alec assurance. 'I never did,' he said.

We all watched him with interest, and his gaze travelled fast from one face to another, seeing only assessment and disbelief and nowhere admiration.

'I didn't kill her,' he said, his voice hoarse and rising. 'I didn't. Straight up, I didn't. It was him. He did it.'

'Who?' I said.

'Calder. Mr Jackson. He did it. It was him, not me.' He looked across us all again with desperation. 'Look, I'm telling you the truth, straight up I am. I never killed her, it was him.'

Wyfold began telling him in a flat voice that he had a right to remain silent and that anything he said might be written down and used in evidence, but Shane wasn't clever and fright had too firm a hold. His fantasy world had vanished in the face of unimaginable reality, and I found myself believing every word he said.

'We didn't know she was there, see. She heard us talking, but we didn't know. And when I carried the stuff back to the hostel he saw her moving so he hit her. I didn't see him do it, I didn't, but when I went back there he was with Ginnie on the ground and I said she was the boss's daughter, which he didn't even know, see, but he said all the worse if she was the boss's daughter because she must have been standing there in the shadow listening and she would have gone straight off and told everybody.'

The words, explanations, excuses came tumbling out in self-righteous urgency and Wyfold thankfully showed no signs of regulating the flow into the careful officialese of a formal statement. The uniformed policeman, now sitting behind Shane, was writing at speed in a notebook, recording, I imagined, the gist.

'I don't believe you,' Wyfold said impatiently. 'What did he hit her with?'

Shane redoubled his efforts to convince, and from then on I admired Wyfold's slyly effective interrogatory technique.

'With a fire extinguisher,' Shane said. 'He kept it in his car, see, and he had it in his hand. He was real fussy about fire always. Would never let anyone smoke anywhere near the stables. That Nigel . . .' the sneer came back temporarily, '. . . the lads all smoked in the feed room, I ask you, behind his back. He'd no idea what went on.'

'Fire extinguisher . . .' Wyfold spoke doubtfully, shaking his head.

'Yeah, it was. It was. One of them red things about this long.' Shane anxiously held up his hands about fifteen inches apart. 'With the nozzle, sort of, at the top. He was holding it by that, sort of swinging it. Ginnie was lying flat on the ground, face down, like, and I said, "What have you gone and done?" and he said she'd been listening.'

Wyfold sniffed.

'It was like that, straight up,' Shane said urgently.

'Listening to what?'

'We were talking about the stuff, see.'

'The shampoo . . .'

'Yeah.' He seemed only briefly to feel the slightest alarm at the mention of it. 'I told him, see, that the stuff had really worked because there'd been a foal born that morning with half a leg, that Nigel he tried to hush it up but by afternoon he was half cut and he told one of the lads so we all knew. So I told Mr Jackson and he said great, because it was time we'd heard and there hadn't been a murmur in the papers and he was getting worried he hadn't got the dose right, or something. So anyway when I told him about the foal with half a leg he laughed, see, he was so pleased, and he said this was probably the last lot I'd have to do, just do the six bottles he'd brought, and then scarper.'

Oliver looked very pale, with sweat along his hair-line and whitely clenched fists. His mouth was rigidly closed with the effort of self control, and he listened throughout without once interrupting or cursing.

'I took the six bottles off to the hostel but when I got there I'd only got five, so I went back to look for the one I'd dropped, but I forgot it, see, when I saw him standing there over Ginnie and him saying she'd heard us talking, and then he said for me to come with him down to the village in his car and he'd drop me at a pub where the other lads were, so as I couldn't have been back home killing the boss's daughter, see? I remembered about the bottle I'd dropped when we were on our way to the village but I didn't think he'd be pleased and anyway I reckoned I'd find it all right when I went back, but I never did. I didn't think it would matter much, because no one would know what it was for, it was just dog shampoo, and anyway I reckoned I'd skip using the new bottles after all because of the fuss there would be over Ginnie. But if it hadn't been for that bottle I wouldn't have gone out again at all, see, and I wouldn't know it was him that killed her, and it wasn't me, it *wasn't.*'

He came to what appeared in his own mind to be a halt, but as far as Wyfold, Oliver and myself were concerned he had stopped short of enough.

'Are you saying,' Wyfold said, 'That you walked back from the village with the other grooms, knowing what you would find?'

'Well, yeah. Only Dave and Sammy, see, they'd got back first, and when I got back there was an ambulance there and such, and I just kept in the background.'

'What did you do with the other five bottles of shampoo?' Wyfold asked. 'We searched all the rooms in the hostel. We didn't find any shampoo.'

The first overwhelming promptings of fear were beginning to die down in Shane, but he answered with only minimal hesitation, 'I took them down the road a ways and threw them in a ditch. That was after they'd all gone off to the hospital.' He nodded in the general direction of Oliver and myself. 'Panicked me a bit, it did, when Dave said she was talking, like. But I was glad I'd got rid of the stuff afterwards, when she was dead after all, with everyone snooping around.'

'You could show me which ditch?' Wyfold said.

'Yeah, I could.'

'Good.'

'You mean,' Shane said, with relief, 'you believe what I told you . . .'

'No, I don't mean that,' Wyfold said repressively. 'I'll need to know what you ordinarily did with the shampoo.'

'What?'

'How you prepared it and gave it to the mares.'

'Oh.' An echo of the cocky cleverness came back: a swagger to the shoulders, a curl to the lip. 'It was dead easy, see. Mr Jackson showed me how. I just had to put a coffee filter in a wash basin and pour the shampoo through it, so's the shampoo all ran down the drain and there was that stuff left on the paper, then I just turned the coffee filter inside out and soaked it in a little jar with some linseed oil from the feed shed, and then I'd stir a quarter of it into the feed if it was for a mare I was looking after anyway, or let the stuff fall to the bottom and scrape up a teasponful and put it in an apple for the others. Mr Jackson showed me how. Dead easy, the whole thing.'

'How many mares did you give it to?'

'Don't rightly know. Dozens, counting last year. Some I missed. Mr Jackson said better to miss some than be found out. He liked me to do the oil best. Said too many apples would be noticed.' A certain amount of anxiety returned. 'Look, now I've told you all this, you know I didn't kill her, don't you?'

Wyfold said impassively, 'How often did Mr Jackson bring you bottles of shampoo?'

'He didn't. I mean, I had a case of it under my bed. Brought it with me when I moved in, see, same as last year. But this year I ran out, like, so I rang him up from the village one night for some more. So he said he'd meet me at the back gate at nine on Sunday when all the lads would be down in the pub.'

'That was a risk he wouldn't take,' Wyfold said sceptically.

'Well, he did.'

Wyfold shook his head.

Shane's panic resurfaced completely. 'He was there,' he almost shouted. 'He was. He *was*.'

Wyfold still looked studiedly unconvinced and told Shane that it would be best if he now made a formal statement, which the sergeant would write down for him to sign when he, Shane, was satisfied that it represented what he had already told us: and Shane in slight bewilderment agreed.

Wyfold nodded to the sergeant, opened the door of the room, and gestured to Oliver and me to leave. Oliver in undiluted grimness silently pushed me out. Wyfold, with a satisfied air, said in his plain uncushioning way, 'There you are then, Mr Knowles, that's how your daughter died, and you're luckier than some. That little sod's telling the truth. Proud of himself, like a lot of crooks. Wants the world to know.' He shook hands perfunctorily with Oliver and nodded briefly to me, and walked away to his unsolved horrors where the papers called for his blood and other fathers choked on their tears.

Oliver pushed me back to the outside world but not directly to where my temporary chauffeur had said he would wait. I found myself making an unscheduled turn into a small public garden, where Oliver abruptly left me beside the first seat we came to and walked jerkily away.

I watched his back, ramrod stiff, disappearing behind bushes and trees. In grief, as in all else, he would be tidy.

A boy came along the path on roller skates and wheeled round to a stop in front of me.

'You want pushing?' he said.

'No. But thanks all the same.'

He looked at me judiciously. 'Can you make that chair go straight, using just one arm?'

'No. I go round in a circle and end where I started.'

'Thought so.' He considered me gravely. 'Just like the earth,' he said.

He pushed off with one foot and sailed away straight on the other and presently, walking firmly, Oliver came back.

He sat on the bench beside me, his eyelids slightly reddened, his manner calm.

'Sorry,' he said after a while.

'She died happy,' I said. 'It's better than nothing.'

'How do you mean?'

'She heard what they were doing. She picked up the shampoo Shane dropped. She was coming to tell you that everything was all right, there was nothing wrong with Sandcastle and you wouldn't lose the farm. At the moment she died she must have been full of joy.'

Oliver raised his face to the pale summer sky.

'Do you think so?'

'Yes, I do.'

'Then I'll believe it,' he said.

The Third Year

OCTOBER

Gordon was coming up to sixty, the age at which everyone retired from Ekaterin's, like it or not. The bustle of young brains, the founder Paul had said, was what kept money moving, and his concept still ruled in the house.

Gordon had his regrets but they were balanced, it seemed to me, by a sense of relief. He had battled for three years now against his palsy and had finished the allotted work span honourably in the face of the enemy within. He began saying he was looking forward to his leisure, and that he and Judith would go on a celebratory journey as soon as possible. Before that, however, he was to be away for a day of medical tests in hospital.

'Such a bore,' he said, 'but they want to make these checks and set me up before we travel.'

'Very sensible,' I said. 'Where will you go?'

He smiled with enthusiasm. 'I've always wanted to see Australia. Never been there, you know.'

'Nor have I.'

He nodded and we continued with our normal work in the accord we had felt together for so many years. I would miss him badly for his own sake, I thought, and even more because through him I would no longer have constant news and contact with Judith. The days seemed to gallop towards his birthday and my spirits grew heavy as his lightened.

Oliver's problems were no longer the day-to-day communiqués at lunch. The dissenting director had conceded that even blue-chip certainties weren't always proof against well-planned malice and no longer grumbled about my part in things, particularly since the day that Henry in his mild-steel voice made observations about defending the bank's money beyond the call of duty.

'And beyond the call of common sense,' Val murmured in my ear. 'Thank goodness.'

Oliver's plight had been extensively aired by Alec in *What's*

Going On Where It Shouldn't, thanks to comprehensive leaks from one of Ekaterin's directors; to wit, me.

Some of the regular newspapers had danced round the subject, since with Shane still awaiting trial the business of poisoning mares was supposed to be sub judice. Alec's paper with its usual disrespect for secrecy had managed to let everyone in the bloodstock industry know that Sandcastle himself was a rock-solid investment, and that any foals already born perfect would not be carrying any damaged genes.

> *As for the mares covered this year,* [the paper continued] *there is a lottery as to whether they will produce deformed foals or not. Breeders are advised to let their mares go to term, because there is a roughly fifty per cent chance that the foal will be perfect. Breeders of mares who produce deformed or imperfect foals will, we understand, have their stallion fees refunded and expenses reimbursed.*
>
> *The bloodstock industry is drawing up its own special guidelines to deal with this exceptional case.*
>
> *Meanwhile, fear not. Sandcastle is potent, fertile and fully reinstated. Apply without delay for a place in next year's programme.*

Alec himself telephoned me in the office two days after the column appeared.

'How do you like it?' he said.

'Absolutely great.'

'The editor says the newsagents in Newmarket have been ringing up like mad for extra copies.'

'Hm,' I said. 'I think perhaps I'll get a list of all breeders and bloodstock agents and personally – I mean anonymously – send each of them a copy of your column, if your editor would agree.'

'Do it without asking him,' Alec said. 'He would probably prefer it. We won't sue you for infringement of copyright, I'll promise you.'

'Thanks a lot,' I said. 'You've been really great.'

'Wait till you get an eyeful of the next issue. I'm working on it now. *Do-it-yourself Miracles,* that's the heading. How does it grab you?'

'Fine.'

'The dead can't sue,' he said cheerfully. 'I just hope I spell the drugs right.'

'I sent you the list,' I protested.

'The typesetters,' he said, 'can scramble eggs, let alone sulphanilamide.'

'See you someday,' I said, smiling.

'Yeah. Pie and beer. We'll fix it.'

His miracle-working column in the next issue demolished Calder's reputation entirely and made further progress towards restoring Sandcastle's and after a third bang on the Sandcastle-is-tops gong in the issue after that, Oliver thankfully reported that confidence both in his stallion and his stud farm was creeping back. Two thirds of the nominations were filled already, and enquiries were arriving for the rest.

'One of the breeders whose mare is in foal now is threatening to sue me for negligence, but the bloodstock associations are trying to dissuade him. He can't do anything, anyway, until after Shane's trial and after the foal is born, and I just hope to God it's one that's perfect.'

From the bank's point of view his affairs were no longer in turmoil. The board had agreed to extend the period of the loan for three extra years, and Val, Gordon and I had worked out the rates at which Oliver could repay without crippling himself. All finally rested on Sandcastle, but if his progeny should prove to have inherited his speed, Oliver should in the end reach the prosperity and prestige for which he had aimed.

'But let's not,' Henry said, smiling one day over roast lamb, 'let's not make a habit of going to the races.'

Gordon came to the office one Monday saying he had met Dissdale the day before at lunch in a restaurant which they both liked.

'He was most embarrassed to see me,' Gordon said. 'But I had quite a talk with him. He really didn't know, you know, that Calder was a fake. He says he can hardly believe, even now, that the cures weren't cures, or that Calder actually killed two people. Very subdued, he was, for Dissdale.'

'I suppose,' I said diffidently, 'You didn't ask him if he and Calder had ever bought, cured and sold sick animals before Indian Silk.'

'Yes, I did, actually, because of your thoughts. But he said they hadn't. Indian Silk was the first, and Dissdale rather despondently said he supposed Calder and Ian Pargetter couldn't bear to see all their time and trouble go to waste, so when Ian Pargetter couldn't persuade Fred Barnet to try Calder, Calder sent Dissdale to buy the horse outright.'

'And it worked a treat.'

Gordon nodded. 'Another thing Dissdale said was that Calder was as stunned as he was himself to find it was Ekaterin's who had lent the money for Sandcastle. There had been no mention of it in the papers. Dissdale asked me to tell you that when he told Calder who it was who had actually put up the money, Calder said 'My God' several times and walked up and down all evening and drank far more than usual. Dissdale didn't know why, and Calder wouldn't tell him, but Dissdale says he thinks now it was because Calder was feeling remorse at hammering Ekaterin's after an Ekaterin had saved his life.'

'Dissdale,' I said dryly, 'is still trying to find excuses for his hero.'

'And for his own admiration of him,' Gordon agreed. 'But perhaps it's true. Dissdale said Calder had liked you very much.'

Liked me, and apologised, and tried to kill me: that too.

Movement had slowly returned to my shoulder and arm once the body-restricting plaster had come off, and via electrical treatment, exercise and massage normal strength had returned.

In the ankle department things weren't quite so good: I still after more than four months wore a brace, though now of removable aluminium and strapping, not plaster. No one would promise I'd be able to ski on the final outcome and meanwhile all but the shortest journeys required sticks. I had tired of hopping up and down my Hampstead stairs on my return there to the extent of renting a flat of my own with a lift to take me aloft and a garage in the basement, and I reckoned life had basically become reasonable again on the day I drove out of there in my car: automatic gear change, no work for the left foot, perfect.

A day or two before he was due to go into hospital for his check-up Gordon mentioned in passing that Judith was coming to collect him from the bank after work to go with him to the hospital, where he would be spending the night so as to be rested for the whole day of tests on Friday.

She would collect him again on Friday evening and they would go home together, and he would have the weekend to rest in before he returned to the office on Monday.

'I'll be glad when it's over,' he said frankly. 'I hate all the needles and the pulling and pushing about.'

'When Judith has settled you in, would she like me to give her some dinner before she goes home?' I said.

He looked across with interest, the idea taking root. 'I should think she would love it. I'll ask her.'

He returned the next day saying Judith was pleased, and we arranged between us that when she left him in the hospital she would come to join me in a convenient restaurant that we all knew well: and on the following day, Thursday, the plan was duly carried out.

She came with a glowing face, eyes sparkling, white teeth gleaming; wearing a blue full-skirted dress and shoes with high heels.

'Gordon is fine, apart from grumbling about tomorrow,' she reported, 'and they gave him almost no supper, to his disgust. He says to think of him during our fillet steaks.'

I doubt if we did. I don't remember what we ate. The feast was there before me on the other side of the small table, Judith looking beautiful and telling me nonsensical things like what happens to a blasé refrigerator when you pull its plug out.

'What, then?'

'It loses its cool.'

I laughed at the stupidity of it and brimmed over with the intoxication of having her there to myself, and I wished she was my own wife so fiercely that my muscles ached.

'You'll be going to Australia . . .' I said.

'Australia?' She hesitated. 'We leave in three weeks.'

'It's so soon.'

'Gordon's sixty the week after next,' she said. 'You know he is. There's the party.'

Henry, Val and I had clubbed together to give Gordon a small sending-off in the office after his last day's work, an affair to which most of the banking managers and their wives had been invited.

'I hate him going,' I said.

'To Australia?'

'From the bank.'

We drank wine and coffee and told each other much without saying a word. Not until we were nearly leaving did she say tentatively 'We'll be away for months, you know.'

My feelings must have shown. 'Months . . . How many?'

'We don't know. We're going to all the places Gordon or I have wanted to see that couldn't be fitted into an ordinary holiday. We're going to potter. Bits of Europe, bits of the

Middle East, India, Singapore, Bali, then Australia, New Zealand, Tahiti, Fiji, Hawaii, America.' She fell silent, her eyes not laughing now but full of sadness.

I swallowed. 'Gordon will find it exhausting.'

'He says not. He passionately wants to go, and I know he's always yearned to have the time to see things . . . and we're going slowly, with lots of rests.'

The restaurant had emptied around us and the waiters hovered with polite faces willing us to go. Judith put on her blue coat and we went outside onto the cold pavement.

'How do you plan to go home now?' I asked.

'Underground.'

'I'll drive you,' I said.

She gave me a small smile and nodded, and we walked slowly across the road to where I'd left the car. She sat in beside me and I did all the automatic things like switching on the lights and letting off the handbrake, and I drove all the way to Clapham without consciously seeing the road.

Gordon's house behind the big gates lay quiet and dark. Judith looked up at its bulk and then at me, and I leaned across in the car and put my arms round her and kissed her. She came close to me, kissing me back with a feeling and a need that seemed as intense as my own, and for a while we stayed in that way, floating in passion, dreaming in deep unaccustomed touch.

As if of one mind we each at the same time drew back and slowly relaxed against the seat. She put her hand on mine and threaded her fingers through, holding tight.

I looked ahead through the windscreen, seeing trees against the stars: seeing nothing.

A long time passed.

'We can't,' I said eventually.

'No.'

'Especially not,' I said, 'in his own house.'

'No.'

After another long minute she let go of my hand and opened the door beside her, and I too opened mine.

'Don't get out,' she said, 'because of your ankle.'

I stood up however on the driveway and she walked around the car towards me. We hugged each other but without kissing, a long hungry minute of body against body; commitment and farewell.

'I'll see you,' she said, 'at the party'; and we both knew how it would be, with Lorna Shipton talking about watching Henry's weight and Henry flirting roguishly with Judith whenever he could, and everyone talking loudly and clapping Gordon on the back.

She walked over the front door and unlocked it, and looked back, briefly, once, and then went in, putting the walls between us in final, mutual, painful decision.

The Third Year

DECEMBER

I felt alone and also lonely, which I'd never been before, and I telephoned to Pen one Sunday in December and suggested taking her out to lunch. She said to come early as she had to open her shop at four, and I arrived at eleven thirty to find coffee percolating richly and Pen trying to unravel the string of the Christmas kite.

'I found it when I was looking for some books,' she said. 'It's so pretty. When we've had coffee, let's go out and fly it.'

We took it onto the common, and she let the string out gradually until the dragon was high on the wind, circling and darting and fluttering its frilly tail. It took us slowly after it across the grass, Pen delightedly intent and I simply pleased to be back there in that place.

She glanced at me over her shoulder. 'Are we going too far for your ankle? Or too fast?'

'No and no,' I said.

'Still taking the comfrey?'

'Religiously.'

The bones and other tissues round my shoulder had mended fast, I'd been told, and although the ankle still lagged I was prepared to give comfrey the benefit of the doubt. Anything which would restore decent mobility attracted my enthusiasm: life with brace and walking stick, still boringly necessary, made even buying groceries a pest.

We had reached a spot on a level with Gordon and Judith's house when a gust of wind took the kite suddenly higher, setting it weaving and diving in bright-coloured arcs and stretching its land-line to tautness. Before anything could be done the string snapped and the dazzling butterfly wings soared away free, rising in a spiral, disappearing to a shape, to a black dot, to nothing.

'What a pity,' Pen said, turning to me with disappointment and then pausing, seeing where my own gaze had travelled downwards to the tall cream gates, firmly shut.

'Let her go,' Pen said soberly, 'like the kite.'

'She'll come back.'

'Take out some other girl,' she urged.

I smiled lop-sidedly. 'I'm out of practice.'

'But you can't spend your whole life . . .' she stopped momentarily, and then said, 'Parkinson's disease isn't fatal. Gordon could live to be eighty or more.'

'I wouldn't want him dead,' I protested. 'How could you think it?'

'Then what?'

'Just to go on, I suppose, as we are.'

She took my arm and turned me away from the gates to return to her house.

'Give it time,' she said. 'You've got months. You both have.'

I glanced at her. 'Both?'

'Gordon and I don't go around with our eyes shut.'

'He's never said anything . . .'

She smiled. 'Gordon likes you better than you like him, if possible. Trusts you, too.' She paused. 'Let her go, Tim, for your own sake.'

We went silently back to her house and I thought of all that had happened since the day Gordon stood in the fountain, and of all I had learned and felt and loved and lost. Thought of Ginnie and Oliver and Calder, and of all the gateways I'd gone through to grief and pain and the knowledge of death. So much – too much – compressed into so small a span.

'You're a child of the light,' Pen said contentedly. 'Both you and Judith. You always take sunshine with you. I don't suppose you know it, but everything brightens when people like you walk in.' She glanced down at my slow foot. 'Sorry. When you limp in. So carry the sunlight to a new young girl who isn't married to Gordon and doesn't break your heart.' She paused. 'That's good pharmacological advice, so take it.

'Yes, doctor,' I said: and knew I couldn't.

On Christmas Eve when I had packed to go to Jersey and was checking around the flat before leaving, the telephone rang.

'Hello,' I said.

There was a series of clicks and hums and I was about to put the receiver down when a breathless voice said, 'Tim . . .'

'Judith?' I said incredulously.

'Yes.'

'Where are you?'

'Listen, just listen. I don't know who else to ask, not at

Christmas . . . Gordon's ill and I'm alone and I don't know, I don't know . . .'

'Where are you?'

'India . . . He's in hospital. They're very good, very kind, but he's so ill . . . unconscious . . . they say cerebral haemorrhage . . . I'm so afraid . . . I do so love him . . .' She was suddenly crying, and trying not to, the words coming out at intervals when control was possible. 'It's so much to ask . . . but I need . . . help.'

'Tell me where,' I said. 'I'll come at once.'

'Oh . . .'

She told me where. I was packed and ready to go, and I went.

Because of the date and the off-track destination there were delays and it took me forty hours to get there. Gordon died before I reached her, on the day after Christmas, like her mother.

My thanks to
MARGARET GILES
of
PANGBOURNE WINES
who taught me her business

and to
BARRY MACKANESS
and
my brother-in-law
DICK YORKE,
wineshippers

and to
LEN LIVINGSTONE-LEARMONTH
long-time friend.

ONE:

Agony is socially unacceptable. One is not supposed to weep. Particularly is one not supposed to weep when one is moderately presentable and thirty-two. When one's wife has been dead for six months and everyone else has done grieving.

Ah well, they say: he'll get over it. There's always another pretty lady. Time's a great healer, they say. He'll marry again one day, they say.

No doubt they're right.

But oh dear God . . . the emptiness in my house. The devastating, weary, ultimate loneliness. The silence where there used to be laughter, the cold hearth that used to leap with fire for my return, the permanent blank in my bed.

Six months into unremitting ache I felt that my own immediate death would be no great disaster. Half of myself had gone; the fulfilled joyful investment of six years' loving, gone into darkness. What was left simply suffered . . . and looked normal.

Habit kept me checking both ways when I crossed the road; and meanwhile I tended my shop and sold my wines, and smiled and smiled and smiled at the customers.

TWO:

Customers came in all possible shapes, from the school children who bought crisps and cola because I was near the bus stop, to the sergeants' mess of the local barracks: from pensioners saving for apologetic half bottles of gin to the knowledgeably lavish laying down port. Customers came once a year and daily, with ignorance and expertise, for happiness and comfort, in gloom and insobriety. Customers ranged from syrup to bitters, like their drinks.

My foremost customer, one Sunday morning that cold October, was a racehorse trainer splashing unstinted fizz over a hundred or so guests in his more or less annual celebration of the Flat races his stable had won during the passing season. Each autumn as his name came high on the winners' list he gave thanks by inviting his owners, his jockeys, his ramifications of friends to share his satisfaction for joys past and to look forward and make plans for starting all over again the following spring.

Each September he would telephone in his perpetual state of rush. 'Tony? Three weeks on Sunday, right? Just the usual, in the tent. You'll do the glasses? And sale or return, of course, right?'

'Right,' I would say, and he'd be gone before I could draw breath. It would be his wife Flora who later came to the shop smilingly with details.

Accordingly on that Sunday I drove to his place at ten o'clock and parked as close as I could to the large once-white marquee rising tautly from his back lawn. He came bustling out of his house the moment I stopped, as if he'd been looking out for me, which perhaps he had: Jack Hawthorn, maybe sixty, short, plump and shrewd.

'Tony. Well done.' He patted me lightly on the shoulder, his usual greeting, as he habitually avoided the social custom of shaking hands. Not, as I had originally guessed, because he feared to catch other people's contagious germs but because, as an acid racing lady had enlightened me, he had 'a grip like a defrosting jellyfish' and hated to see people rub their palms on their clothes after touching him.

'A good day for it,' I said.

He glanced briefly at the clear sky. 'We need rain. The ground's like concrete.' Racehorse trainers, like farmers, were never satisfied with the weather. 'Did you bring any soft drinks? The Sheik's coming, with his whole teetotal entourage. Forgot to tell you.'

I nodded. 'Champagne, soft drinks and a box of oddments.'

'Good. Right. I'll leave you to it. The waitresses will be here at eleven, guests at twelve. And you'll stay yourself, of course? My guest, naturally. I take it for granted.'

'Your secretary sent me an invitation.'

'Did he? Good heavens. How efficient. Right then. Anything you want, come and find me.'

I nodded and he hurried away, taking his life as usual at a trot. Notwithstanding the secretary, a somewhat languid man with a supercilious nose and an indefatigable capacity for accurate detailed work, Jack never quite caught up with what he wanted to do. Flora, his placid wife, had told me, 'It's Jimmy (the secretary) who enters the horses for the races, Jimmy who sends out the bills, Jimmy who runs all the paperwork single-handed, and Jack never so much as has to pick up a postage stamp. It's habit, all this rushing. Just habit.' But she'd spoken fondly, as everyone did, more or less, of Jack Hawthorn: and maybe it was actually the staccato energy of the man which communicated to his horses and set them winning.

He always invited me to his celebrations, either formally or not, partly no doubt so that I should be on the spot to solve any booze-flow problems immediately, but also because I had myself been born into a section of the racing world and was still considered part of it, despite my inexplicable defection into retail liquor.

'Not his father's son,' was how the uncharitable put it. Or more plainly, 'Lacks the family guts.'

My father, a soldier, had won both the Distinguished Service Order and the Military Gold Cup, dashing as valiantly into steeplechase fences as he had into enemy territory. His bravery on all battlefields had been awe-inspiring, and he died from a broken neck on Sandown Park racecourse when I was eleven, and watching.

He had been forty-seven at the time and remained, of

course, at that age in the racing world's memory, a tall, straight, laughing, reckless man, untouched, it still seemed to me, by the world's woes. No matter that he was not an ideal shape for jockeyship, he had resolutely followed in the wake of his own father, my grandfather, a distant Titan who had finished second one year in the Grand National before covering himself with military glory in World War One. My grandfather's Victoria Cross lay beside my father's DSO in the display case I had inherited. It was their dash, their flair, their dare-devilment that they had not passed on.

'Are you going to grow up like your father, then?' had been said to me in friendly, expectant fashion countless times through my childhood, and it had only slowly dawned on everyone, as on me, that no, I wasn't. I learned to ride, but without distinction. I went to Wellington, the school for soldiers' sons, but not in turn to Sandhurst to put on uniform myself. My mother too often said, 'Never mind, dear,' suffering many disappointments nobly; and I developed deep powerful feelings of inferiority, which still lingered, defying common sense.

Only with Emma had they retreated to insignificance, but now that she had gone, faint but persistent, they were back. A discarded habit of mind insidiously creeping into unregarded corners. Miserable.

Jimmy, the secretary, never helped. He sauntered out of the house, hands in pockets, and watched as I lugged three galvanised wash tubs from the rear of my van.

'What are those for?' he said. He couldn't help looking down that nose, I supposed, as he topped six feet four. It was just that his tone of voice matched.

'Ice,' I said.

He said, 'Oh,' or rather 'Ay-oh,' as a dipthong.

I carried the tubs into the tent, which contained a row of trestle tables with tablecloths near one end and clusters of potted chrysanthemums round the bases of the two main supporting poles. The living grass of the lawn had been covered with serviceable fawn matting, and bunches of red and gold ribbons decorated the streaky greyish canvas walls at regular intervals. In one far corner stood a blower-heater, unlit. The day was marginally not cold enough. The tent was almost festive. Almost. Jack and Flora, and who could blame them, never wasted good cash on unnecessaries.

There was no tremble in the air. No shudder. No premonition

at all of the horror soon to happen there. All was quiet and peaceful; expectant certainly, but benign. I remembered it particularly, after.

Jimmy continued to watch while I carted in a case of champagne and unpacked the bottles, standing them upright in one of the tubs on the floor by the tent wall behind the tables. I didn't actually have to do this part of the job, but for Jack Hawthorn, somehow, it was easy to give service beyond contract.

I was working in shirtsleeves, warmed by a pale blue V-necked sleeveless pullover (typical racing world clothes) with my jacket waiting in the van for the metamorphosis to guest. Jimmy was understatedly resplendent in thin fawn polo-necked blazer; plain brass buttons, no crests, no pretentions. That was the trouble. If he'd had any pretentions I could perhaps have despised him instead of suspecting it was the other way round.

I fetched a second box of champagne and began unpacking it. Jimmy bent from his great height and picked up one of the bottles, staring at the foil and the label as if he'd never seen such things before.

'What's this muck?' he said. 'Never heard of it.'

'It's the real thing,' I said mildly. 'It comes from Epernay.'

'So I see.'

'Flora's choice,' I said.

He said 'Ah-oh' in complete understanding and put the bottle back. I fetched ice cubes in large black plastic bags and poured them over and round the standing bottles.

'Did you bring any scotch?' he asked.

'Front seat of the van.'

He strolled off on the search and came back with an unopened bottle.

'Glass?' he enquired.

For reply I went out to the van and fetched a box containing sixty.

'Help yourself.'

Without comment he opened the box, which I'd set on a table, and removed one of the all-purpose goblets.

'Is this ice drinkable?' he said dubiously.

'Pure tap water.'

He put ice and whisky in the glass and sipped the result.

'Very prickly this morning, aren't you?' he said.

I glanced at him, surprised. 'Sorry.'

'Someone knocked off a whole load of this stuff in Scotland yesterday, did you know?'

'Champagne?'

'No. Scotch.'

I shrugged. 'Well . . . it happens.'

I fetched a third case and unpacked the bottles. Jimmy watched, clinking his ice.

'How much do you know about whisky, Tony?' he said.

'Well . . . some.'

'Would you know one from another?'

'I'm better at wine.' I straightened from filling the second tub. 'Why?'

'Would you know for certain,' he said with a bad stab at casualness, 'if you asked for a malt and got sold an ordinary standard, like this?' He raised his glass, nodding to it.

'They taste quite different.'

He relaxed slightly, betraying an inner tension I hadn't until then been aware of. 'Could you tell one malt from another?'

I looked at him assessingly. 'What's all this about?'

'Could you?' He was insistent.

'No,' I said. 'Not this morning. Not to name them. I'd have to practise. Maybe then. Maybe not.'

'But . . . if you learned one particular taste, could you pick it out again from a row of samples? Or say if it wasn't there?'

'Perhaps,' I said. I looked at him, waiting, but he was taking his own troubled time, consulting some inner opinion. Shrugging, I went to fetch more ice, pouring it into the second tub, and then carried in and ripped open the fourth case of champagne.

'It's very awkward,' he said suddenly.

'What is?'

'I wish you'd stop fiddling with those bottles and listen to me.'

His voice was a mixture of petulance and anxiety, and I slowly straightened from putting bottles into the third tub and took notice.

'Tell me, then,' I said.

He was older than me by a few years, and our acquaintanceship had mostly been limited to my visits to the Hawthorn house, both as drinks supplier and as occasional guest. His usual manner to me had been fairly civil but without warmth, as no doubt mine to him. He was the third son of the fourth son of a racehorse-owning earl, which gave him an aristocratic name but no fortune, and his job with Jack Hawthorn resulted directly, it was said, from lack of enough brain to excel in the City. It was a judgement I would have been content to accept were it not for Flora's admiration of him, but I hadn't cared enough one way or the other to give it much thought.

'One of Jack's owners has a restaurant,' he said. 'The Silver Moondance, near Reading. Not aimed at top class. Dinner dances. A singer sometimes. Mass market.' His voice was fastidious but without scorn: stating a fact, not an attitude.

I waited non-committally.

'He invited Jack and Flora and myself to dinner there last week.'

'Decent of him,' I said.

'Yes.' Jimmy looked at me down the nose. 'Quite.' He paused slightly. 'The food was all right, but the drinks . . . Look, Tony, Larry Trent is one of Jack's good owners. He has five horses here. Pays his bills on the nail. I don't want to upset him . . . but what it says on the label of at least one of the bottles in his restaurant is not what they pour out of it.'

He spoke with pained disgust, at which I almost smiled.

'That's not actually unusual,' I said.

'But it's illegal.' He was indignant.

'Sure it's illegal. Are you certain?'

'Yes. Well yes, I think so. But I wondered if perhaps, before I said anything to Larry Trent, you could taste their stuff? I mean, suppose his staff are ripping him off? I mean, er . . . he could be prosecuted, couldn't he?'

I said, 'Why didn't you mention it to him that evening, while you were there?'

Jimmy looked startled. 'But we were his guests! It would have been terribly bad form. Surely you can see that.'

'Hm,' I said dryly. 'Then why don't you just tell him now, and privately, what you thought about his drinks? He might be grateful. He would certainly be warned. Anyway, I can't see him whisking his five horses away in a huff.'

Jimmy made a pained noise and drank some scotch. 'I mentioned this to Jack. He said I must be mistaken. But I'm not, you know. I'm pretty sure I'm not.'

I considered him.

'Why does it bother you so much?' I asked.

'What?' He was surprised. 'Well, I say, a fraud's a fraud, isn't it? It annoys one.'

'Yes.' I sighed. 'What were these drinks supposed to be?'

'I thought the wine wasn't much, considering its label, but you know how it is, you don't suspect anything . . . but there was the Laphroaig.'

I frowned. 'The malt from Islay?'

'That's right,' Jimmy said. 'Heavy malt whisky. My grandfather liked it. He used to give me sips when I was small, much to my mother's fury. Funny how you never forget tastes you learn as a child . . . and of course I've had it since . . . so there it was, on the trolley of drinks they rolled round with the coffee, and I thought I would have some . . . Nostalgia, and all that.'

'And it wasn't Laphroaig?'

'No.'

'What was it?'

He looked uncertain. 'I thought that you, actually, might know. If you drank some, I mean.'

I shook my head. 'You'd need a proper expert.'

He looked unhappy. 'I thought myself, you see, that it was just an ordinary blend, just ordinary, not even pure malt.'

'You'd better tell Mr Trent,' I said. 'Let him deal with it himself.'

He said doubtfully, 'He'll be here this morning.'

'Easy,' I said.

'I don't suppose . . . er . . . that you yourself . . . er . . . could have a word with him?'

'No, I certainly couldn't,' I said positively. 'From you it could be a friendly warning, from me it would be a deadly insult. Sorry, Jimmy, but honestly, no.'

With resignation he said, 'I thought you wouldn't. But worth a try.' He poured himself more scotch and again put ice into it, and I thought in passing that true whisky aficionados thought ice an abomination, and wondered about the trustworthiness of his perception of Laphroaig.

Flora, rotund and happy in cherry red wool, came in her light-stepped way into the tent, looking around and nodding in satisfaction.

'Looks quite bright, doesn't it, Tony dear?'

'Splendid,' I said.

'When it's filled with guests . . .'

'Yes,' I agreed.

She was conventional, well-intentioned and cosy, mother of three children (not Jack's) who telephoned her regularly. She liked to talk about them on her occasional visits to my shop and tended to place larger orders when the news of them was good. Jack was her second husband, mellowing still under her wing but reportedly jealous of her offspring. Amazing the things people told their wine merchants. I knew a great deal about a lot of people's lives.

Flora peered into the tubs. 'Four cases on ice?'

I nodded. 'More in the van, if you need it.'

'Let's hope not.' She smiled sweetly. 'But my dear, I wouldn't bet on it. Jimmy love, you don't need to drink whisky. Open some champagne. I'd like a quick glass before everyone swamps us.'

Jimmy obliged with languid grace, easing out the cork without explosion, containing the force in his hand. Flora smilingly watched the plume of released gas float from the bottle and tilted a glass forward to catch the first bubbles. At her insistence both Jimmy and I drank also, but from Jimmy's expression it didn't go well with his scotch.

'Lovely!' Flora said appreciatively, sipping; and I thought the wine as usual a bit too thin and fizzy, but sensible enough for those quantities. I sold a great deal of it for weddings.

Flora took her glass and wandered down the marquee to the entrance through which the guests would come, the entrance which faced away from the house, towards the field where the cars would be parked. Jack Hawthorn's house and stableyard were built in a hollow high on the eastern end of the Berkshire Downs in a place surrounded by hills, invisible until one was close. Most people would arrive by the main road over the hill which faced the rear of the house, parking in the field, and continuing the downward journey on foot through a gate in the low-growing rose hedge, and onto the lawn. After several such parties, Flora had brought crowd control to a fine art: and besides, this way, no one upset the horses.

Flora suddenly exclaimed loudly and came hurrying back.

'It's really too bad of him. The Sheik is here already. His car's coming over the hill. Jimmy, run and meet him. Jack's still changing. Take the Sheik round the yard. Anything. Really, it's too bad. Tell Jack he's here.'

Jimmy nodded, put down his glass without haste and ambled off to intercept the oil-rich prince and his retinue. Flora hovered indecisively, not following, talking crossly with maximum indiscretion.

'I don't like that particular Sheik. I can't help it. He's fat and horrible and he behaves as if he owns the place, which he doesn't. And I don't like the way he looks at me with those half-shut eyes, as if I were of no account . . . and Tony, dear, I haven't said any of those things, you understand? I don't like the way Arabs treat women.'

'And his horses win races,' I said.

'Yes,' Flora sighed. 'It's not all sweetness and light being a trainer's wife. Some of the owners make me sick.' She gave me a brief half-smile and went away to the house, and I finished the unloading with things like orange juice and cola.

Up on the hill the uniformed chauffeur parked the elongated black-windowed Mercedes, which was so identifiably the Sheik's, with its nose pointing to the marquee, and gradually more cars arrived to swell the row there, bringing waitresses and other helpers, and finally, in a steady stream, the hundred-and-something guests.

They came by Rolls, by Range Rover, by Mini and by Ford. One couple arrived in a horsebox, another by motorcycle. Some brought children, some brought dogs, most of which were left with the cars. In cashmere and cords, in checked shirts and tweeds, in elegance and pearls they walked chatteringly down the grassy slope, through the gate in the rose hedge, across a few steps of lawn, into the beckoning tent. A promising Sunday morning jollification ahead, most troubles left behind.

As always with racing-world parties, everyone there knew somebody else. The decibel count rose rapidly to ear-aching levels and only round the very walls could one talk without shouting. The Sheik, dressed in full Arab robes and flanked by his wary-eyed entourage, was one, I noticed, who stood resolutely with his back to the canvas, holding his orange juice before him and surveying the crush with his half-shut eyes. Jimmy was doing his noble best to amuse, rewarded by unsmiling nods, and gradually and separately other guests stopped to talk to the solid figure in the banded white headgear, but none of them with complete naturalness, and none of them women.

Jimmy after a while detached himself and I found him at my elbow.

'Sticky going, the Sheik?' I said.

'He's not such a bed fellow,' Jimmy said loyally. 'No social graces in western gatherings and absolutely paranoid about being assassinated . . . never even sits in the dentist's chair, I'm told, without all those bodyguards being right there in the surgery . . . but he does know about horses. Loves them. You should have seen him just now, going round the yard, those bored eyes came right to life.' He looked round the gathering and suddenly exclaimed, 'See that man talking to Flora? That's Larry Trent.'

'Of the absent Laphroaig?'

Jimmy nodded, wrinkled his brow in indecision and moved off in another direction altogether, and I for a few moments watched the man with Flora, a middle-aged, dark-haired man with a moustache, one of the few people wearing a suit, in his case a navy pinstripe with the coat buttoned, a line of silk handkerchief showing in the top pocket. The crowd shifted and I lost sight of him, and I talked, as one does, to a succession of familiar half-known people, seen once a year or less, with whom one took on as one had left off, as if time hadn't existed in between. It was one of those, with best intentions, who said inevitably, 'And how's Emma? How's your pretty wife?'

I thought I would never get used to it, that jab like a spike thrust into a jumpy nerve, that positively physical pain. Emma . . . dear God.

'She's dead,' I said, shaking my head slightly, breaking it to him gently, absolving him from embarrassment. I'd had to say it like that often: far too often. I knew how to do it now without causing discomfort. Bitter, extraordinary skill of the widowed, taking the distress away from others, hiding one's own.

'I'm so sorry,' he said, meaning it intensely for the moment, as they do. 'I'd no idea. None at all. Er . . . when . . . ?'

'Six months ago,' I said.

'Oh.' He adjusted his sympathy level suitably. 'I'm really very sorry.'

I nodded. He sighed. The world went on. Transaction over, until next time. Always a next time. And at least he hadn't asked 'How . . . ?', and I hadn't had to tell him, hadn't had to think of the pain and the coma and the child who had died with her, unborn.

A fair few of Jack's guests were also my customers, so that even in that racing gathering I found myself talking as much about wine as horses, and it was while an earnest elderly lady was soliciting my views on Côtes du Rhône versus Côte de Nuits that I saw Jimmy finally talking to Larry Trent. He spotted me too and waved for me to come over, but the earnest lady would buy the better wine by the caseful if convinced, and I telegraphed 'later' gestures to Jimmy, to which he flipped a forgiving hand.

Waitresses wove through the throng carrying dishes of canapés and sausages on sticks, and I reckoned that many more than a hundred throats had turned up and that at the present rate of enthusiasm the forty-eight original bottles would be emptied at any minute. I had already begun to make my way to the tent's service entrance near the house when Jack himself pounced at me, clutching my sleeve.

'We'll need more champagne and the waitresses say your van is locked.' His voice was hurried. 'The party's going well, wouldn't you say?'

'Yes, very.'

'Great. Good. I'll leave it to you, then.' He turned away, patting shoulders in greeting, enjoying his role as host.

I checked the tubs, now empty but for two standing bottles in a sea of melting ice, and went onwards out to the van, fishing in my pocket for the keys. For a moment I glanced up the hill to where all the cars waited, to the Range Rover, the horsebox, the Sheik's Mercedes. No gaps in the line: no one had yet gone home. There was a child up there, playing with a dog.

I unlocked the rear door of my van and leaned in to pull forward the three spare cases which were roughly cooling under more black bags of ice. I threw one of the bags out onto the grass, and I picked up one of the cases.

Movement on the edge of my vision made me turn my head, and in a flash of a second that ordinary day became a nightmare.

The horsebox was rolling down the hill.

Pointing straight at the marquee, gathering speed.

It was already only feet from the rose-hedge. It smashed its way through the fragile plants, flattening the last pink flowers of autumn. It advanced inexorably onto the grass.

I leapt to the doorway of the tent screaming a warning which nobody heard above the din and which was anyway far too late.

For a frozen infinitesimal moment I saw the party still intact, a packed throng of people smiling, drinking, living and unaware.

Then the horsebox ploughed into the canvas, and changed many things for ever.

THREE:

Total communal disbelief lasted through about five seconds of silence, then someone screamed and went on screaming, a high commentary of hysteria on so much horror.

The horsebox had steam-rollered on over the canvas sidewall, burying people beneath; and it had plunged forward into one of the main supporting poles, which snapped under the weight. The whole of the end of the tent nearest me had collapsed inwards so that I stood on the edge of it with the ruin at my feet.

Where I had seen the guests, I now in absolute shock saw expanses of heavy grey canvas with countless bulges heaving desperately beneath.

The horsebox itself stood there obscenely in the middle, huge, dark green, unharmed, impersonal and frightful. There seemed to be no one behind the driving wheel; and to reach the cab one would have had to walk over the shrouded lumps of the living and the dead.

Beyond the horsebox, at the far end of the tent, in the still erect section, people were fighting their way out through the remains of the entrance and rips in the walls, emerging one by one, staggering and falling like figures in a frieze.

I noticed vaguely that I was still holding the case of champagne. I put it down where I stood, and turned and ran urgently to the telephone in the house.

So quiet in there. So utterly normal. My hands were shaking as I held the receiver.

Police and ambulances to Jack Hawthorn's stables. A doctor. And lifting gear. Coming, they said. All coming. At once.

I went back outside, meeting others with stretched eyes intent on the same errand.

'They're coming,' I said. 'Coming.'

Everyone was trembling, not just myself.

The screaming had stopped, but many were shouting, husbands trying to find their wives, wives their husbands, a mother her son. All the faces were white, all the mouths open, all breaths coming in gasps. People had begun making slits in the canvas with penknives to free those trapped underneath. A woman with small scissors was methodically cutting the lacings of a section of side-wall, tears streaming down her face. The efforts all looked puny, the task so immense.

Flora and Jack and Jimmy, I knew, had all been in the part of the tent which had collapsed.

A horse was whinnying nearby and kicking wood, and it was with fresh shock that I realised that the noise was coming from the horsebox itself. There was a horse in there. Inside.

With stiff legs I went along to the standing section of tent, going in through a gap where other people had come out. The second pole stood upright, the potted chrysanthemums bright round its foot. There were many scattered and broken glasses, and a few people trying to lift up the folds of the heavily fallen roof, to let the trapped crawl from under.

'We might make a tunnel,' I said to one man, and he nodded in understanding, and by lifting one section only, but together, and advancing, he and I and several others made a wide head-high passage forward into the collapsed half, through which about thirty struggling people, dazedly getting to their feet, made their way out upright. Many of their faces and hands were bleeding from glass cuts. Few of them knew what had happened. Two of them were children.

One of the furthest figures we reached that way was Flora. I saw the red wool of her dress on the ground under a flap of canvas and bent down to help her: and she was half unconscious with her face to the matting, suffocating.

I pulled her out and carried her down to the free end, and from there gave her to someone outside, and went back.

The tunnel idea gradually extended until there was a ring of humans instead of tent poles holding up a fair section of roof, one or two helpers exploring continuously into the edges until as far as we could tell all the people not near the horsebox itself were outside, walking and alive.

The horsebox . . .

Into that area no one wanted to go, but my original tunneller and I looked at each other for a long moment and told everyone to leave if they wanted to. Some did, but three or four of us made a newer, shorter and lower tunnel, working towards the side of the horsebox facing the standing section of the tent, lifting tautly stretched canvas to free people still pinned underneath.

Almost the first person we came to was one of the Arabs who was fiercely vigorous and at any other time would have seemed comic, because as soon as he was released and mobile he began shouting unintelligibly, producing a repeating rifle from his robes and waving it menacingly about.

All we wanted, I thought: a spray of terrified bullets.

The Sheik, I thought . . . Standing against the side wall, so that his back should be safe.

We found two more people alive on that side, both women, both beyond speech, both white-faced, in torn clothes, bleeding from glass cuts, one with a broken arm. We passed them back into comfort, and went on.

Crawling forward I came then to a pair of feet, toes upwards, then to trouser legs, unmoving. Through the canvas-filtered daylight they were easily recognisable; pinstripe cloth, navy blue.

I lifted more space over him until I could see along to the buttoned jacket and the silk handkerchief and a hand flung sideways holding a glass in fragments. And beyond, where a weight pressed down where his neck should have been, there was a line of crimson pulp.

I let the canvas fall back, feeling sick.

'No good,' I said to the man behind me. 'I think his head's under the front wheel. He's dead.'

He gave me a look as shattered as my own, and we moved slowly sideways towards the horsebox's rear, making our tunnel with difficulty on hands and knees.

Above us, inside the box, the horse kicked frantically and squealed, restless, excited and alarmed no doubt by the smell; horses were always upset by blood. I could see no prospect all the same of anyone lowering the ramps to let him out.

We found another Arab, alive, flat on his back, an arm bleeding, praying to Allah. We pulled him out and afterwards found his rifle lying blackly where he'd been.

'They're mad,' said my companion.

'It didn't save their master,' I said.

On our knees we both looked in silence at what we could see of the Sheik, which was his head, still in its white head-dress with its gold cords. A fold of reddened canvas lay over the rest of him, and my companion, gripping my wrist, said, 'Leave it. Don't look. What's the point.'

I thought fleetingly of the policemen and the ambulance-men who would soon be forced to look, but I did as he asked.

We made our way silently back to the standing section and began a new tunnel round to the other side of the horsebox.

It was there that we came to Jack and also Jimmy, both with pulses, though both were unconscious and pinned to the ground by the thick tent pole, which lay across Jack's legs and Jimmy's chest. We scarcely touched the pole ourselves, but the tremor of our movements brought Jack up to semi-consciousness and to groaning pain.

My companion said 'Hell' through his teeth, and I said, 'I'll stay here if you go and get something to keep the canvas off them,' and he nodded and disappeared, the heavy material falling behind, closing me in.

Jimmy looked dreadful; eyes shut above the long nose, a thread of blood trickling from his mouth.

Jack went on groaning. I held up a bit of tent on my shoulders like Atlas, and presently my fellow tunneller returned, bringing two further helpers and a trestle table for a makeshift roof.

'What do we do?' the first tunneller said, irresolutely.

'Lift the pole,' I said. 'It may hurt Jack . . . but it may be killing Jimmy.'

Everyone agreed. We slowly, carefully, took the weight off the two injured men and laid the pole on the ground. Jack lapsed into silence. Jimmy lay still like a log. But they were both shallowly breathing: I felt their wrists again, one after the other, with relief.

We stood the trestle table over them and gingerly crawled on, and came to a girl lying on her back with one arm up over her face. Her skirt had been ripped away, and the flesh on the outer side of her thigh had been torn open and was sagging away from the bone from hip to knee. I lifted the canvas away from her face and saw that she was to some extent conscious.

'Hello,' I said inadequately.

She looked at me vaguely. 'What's happening?' she said.

'There was an accident.'

'Oh?' She seemed sleepy, but when I touched her cheek it was icy.

'We'll get another table,' the first tunneller said.

'And a rug, if you can,' I said. 'She's far too cold.'

He nodded and said 'Shock,' and they all went away as it needed the three of them to drag the tables through.

I looked at the girl's leg. She was fairly plump, and inside the long wide-gaping wound one could easily identify the cream-coloured bubbly fat tissue and the dense red muscle, open like a jagged book to inspection. I'd never seen anything like it: and extraordinarily she wasn't bleeding a great deal, certainly not as much as one would have expected.

The body shutting down, I thought. The effects of trauma, as deadly as injury itself.

There was little I could do for her, but I did have a penknife in my pocket incorporating a tiny pair of scissors. With a sigh I pulled up my jersey and cut and tore one side from my shirt, stopping a few inches below the collar and cutting across so that from in front it looked as if I had a whole shirt under my sweater; and I thought that my doing that was ridiculous, but all the same I did it.

Torn into two wide strips the shirt front made reasonable bandages. I slid both pieces under her leg and pulled the flesh back into position, tying her leg together round the bone like trussing a joint of meat. I looked anxiously several times at the girl's face, but if she felt what I was doing it must have been remotely. She lay with her eyes open, her elbow bent over her head, and all she said at one point was, 'Where is this?' and later, 'I don't understand.'

'It's all right,' I said.

'Oh . . . Is it . . . ? Good.'

The tunnellers returned with a table and a travelling rug and also a towel.

'I thought we might wrap that wound together, with this,' said the first tunneller, 'but I see you've done it.'

We put the towel round her leg anyway for extra protection, and then wrapped her in the rug and left her under her table roof and crawled apprehensively on; but we found no one else we could help. We found one of the waitresses, dead, lying over her tray of canapés, her smooth young face frosty-white, and we found the protruding legs of a different Arab: and somewhere underneath the horsebox there were dreadful red shapes we couldn't reach even if we'd wanted to.

In accord the four of us retreated, hearing as we emerged into the blessed fresh air the bells and sirens of the official rescuers as they poured over the hill.

I walked along to where Flora was sitting on a kitchen chair that someone had brought out for her: there were women beside her trying to comfort, but her eyes were dark and staring into far spaces, and she was shivering.

'Jack's all right,' I said. 'The pole knocked him out. One leg is maybe broken . . . but he's all right.'

She looked at me blindly. I took my jacket off and wrapped it round her. 'Flora . . . Jack's alive.'

'All those people . . . all our guests . . .' Her voice was faint. 'Are you sure . . . about Jack?'

There was no real consolation. I said yes and hugged her, rocking her in my arms like a baby, and she put her head silently on my shoulder, still too stunned for tears.

Things ran after that into a blur, time passing at an enormous rate but not seeming to.

The police had brought a good deal of equipment and after a while had cut away the marquee from an area round the horsebox, and had set up a head-high ring of screens to hide the shambles there.

Jack, fully conscious, lay on a stretcher with a pain-killer taking the worst off, protesting weakly that he couldn't go to hospital, he couldn't leave his guests, he couldn't leave his horses, he couldn't leave his wife to cope with everything on her own. Still objecting he was lifted into an ambulance and, beside a still unconscious Jimmy, slowly driven away.

The guests drifted into the house or sat in their cars and wanted to go home: but there was an enormous fuss going on somewhere over telephone wires because of the death of the Sheik, and the uniformed police had been instructed not to let anyone leave until other investigators had arrived.

The fuss was nonsense, really, I thought. No one could possibly have told where the Sheik would stand in that tent. No one could possibly have aimed the horsebox deliberately. The brakes had given way and it had rolled down the hill . . . as selective in its victims as an earthquake.

The distraught young couple who had come in it and parked it were both in tears, and I heard the man saying helplessly, 'But I left it in gear, with the brakes on . . . I know I did . . . I'm always careful . . . how could it have happened, how could it?' A uniformed policeman was questioning them, his manner less than sympathetic.

I wandered back to my van, to where I'd dumped the case of champagne. It had gone. So had the sixth and seventh cases from inside. So had the back-up gin and whisky from the front seat.

Disgusting, I thought; and shrugged. After carnage, thieves. Human grade-ten sour age-old behaviour. It didn't seem to matter, except that I would rather have given it away than that.

Flora was indoors, lying down. Someone brought my coat back. It had blood on the sleeves, I noticed. Blood on my shirt cuffs, blood on my pale blue sweater. Blood, dry, on my hands.

A large crane on caterpillar tracks came grinding slowly over the hill and was manoeuvred into position near the horsebox; and in time, with chains, the heavy green vehicle was lifted a few inches into the air, and, after a pause, lifted higher and swung away onto a stretch of cleared grass.

The horse, still intermittently kicking, was finally released down a ramp and led away by one of Jack's lads, and, closing the box again, two policemen took up stances to deter the inquisitive.

There was a small dreadful group of people waiting, unmoving, staring silently at the merciful screens. They knew, they had to know, that those they sought were dead, yet they stood with dry eyes, their faces haggard with persisting hope. Five tons of metal had smashed into a close-packed crowd . . . yet they hoped.

One of them turned his head and saw me, and walked unsteadily towards me as if his feet were obeying different orders from his legs. He was dressed in jeans and a dirty T-shirt, and he neither looked nor sounded like one of the guests. More like one of Jack's lads on his Sunday off.

'You went in there, didn't you?' he said. 'You're the guy who brings the drinks, aren't you? Someone said you went in . . .' He gestured vaguely towards the remains of the tent. 'Did you see my wife? Was she in there? Is she?'

'I don't know.' I shook my head.

'She was carrying things round. Drinks and such. She likes doing that . . . seeing people.'

One of the waitresses. He saw the movement in my face, and interpreted it unerringly.

'She's there . . . isn't she?' I didn't answer for a moment, and he said with pride and despair inextricably mixed. 'She's pretty, you know. So pretty.'

I nodded and swallowed. 'She's pretty.'

'Oh no . . .' He let the grief out in a tearing wail. 'Oh no . . .'

I said helplessly, 'My own wife died . . . not long ago. I do know . . . I'm so . . . so appallingly sorry.'

He looked at me blankly and went back to the others to stare at the screens, and I felt useless and inadequate and swamped with pity.

The horsebox had hit at shortly before one-thirty: it was after five before the new investigators would let anyone leave. Messages were eventually passed that all could go, but that each car would have to stop at the gate for the passengers to give their names.

Tired, hungry, dishevelled, many with bandaged cuts, the guests who had trooped so expectantly down the hill climbed slowly, silently up. Like refugees, I thought. An exodus. One could hear the engines starting in a chorus, and see the first movement of wheels.

A man touched my arm: the fellow tunneller. A tall man, going grey, with intelligent eyes.

'What's your name?' he asked.

'Tony Beach.'

'Mine's McGregor. Gerard McGregor.' He pronounced the G of Gerard soft, like a J, in a voice that was remotely but detectably Scots, 'Glad to know you,' he said. He held out his hand, which I shook.

We smiled slightly at each other, acknowledging our shared experience; then he turned away and put his arm round the shoulders of a good-looking woman at his side, and I watched them thread their way across to the gate through the roses. Pleasant man, I thought; and that was all.

I went into the house to see if there was anything I could do for Flora before I left, and found a shambles of a different sort. Every downstairs room, now empty, looked as if a full-scale army had camped there, which in a way it had. Every cup and saucer in the place must have been pressed into service, and every glass. The bottles on the drinks tray were all empty, open-necked. Ashtrays overflowed. Crumbs of food lay on plates. Cushions were squashed flat.

In the kitchen, locust-like, the lunch-less guests had eaten everything to hand. Empty soup tins littered the worktops, egg shells lay in the sink, a chicken carcass, picked clean, jostled gutted packets of biscuits and crackers. Everything edible had gone from the refrigerator and saucepans lay dirty on the stove.

There was a faint exclamation from the doorway, and I turned to see Flora there, her face heavy and grey above the creased red dress. I made a frustrated gesture at the mess, but she looked at it all without emotion.

'They had to eat,' she said. 'It's all right.'

'I'll straighten it.'

'No. Leave it. Tomorrow will do.' She came into the room and sat wearily on one of the wooden chairs. 'It simply doesn't matter. I told them to help themselves.'

'They might have cleaned up afterwards,' I said.

'You should know the racing world better.'

'Is there anything I can do, then?'

'No, nothing.' She sighed deeply. 'Do you know how many of them are dead?' Her voice itself was lifeless, drained by too much horror.

I shook my head. 'The Sheik and one of his men. Larry Trent. And one of the waitresses, married, I think, to one of your lads. Some others. I don't know who.'

'Not Janey,' Flora said, distressed.

'I don't know.'

'Young and pretty. Married Tom Wickens in the summer. Not her.'

'I think so.'

'Oh dear.' Flora grew if anything paler. 'I don't care about the Sheik. It's a wicked thing to say, and we'll lose those horses, but I've known about him for hours and I simply don't care. But Janey . . .'

'I think you would help Tom Wickens,' I said.

She stared at me for a moment, then rose to her feet and walked out into the garden, and through the window I saw her go over to the man in the T-shirt and put her arms round him. He turned and hugged her desperately in return, and I wondered fleetingly which of them felt the most released.

I chucked all the worst of the litter into the dustbin, but left the rest of it, as she'd said. Then I went out to the van to go home, and found a very young constable by my side as I opened the door.

'Excuse me, sir,' he said, holding pen and notebook ready.

'Yes?'

'Name, sir?'

I gave it, and my address, which he wrote down.

'Where were you in the marquee, sir, when the incident occurred?'

The *incident* . . . ye gods.

'I wasn't in the marquee,' I said. 'I was here, by the van.'

'Oh!' His eyes widened slightly. 'Then would you wait here,

sir?' He hurried away and returned presently with a man out of uniform who walked slowly, with hunched shoulders.

'Mr . . . er . . . Beach?' the newcomer said. A shortish man, not young. No aggression.

I nodded. 'Yes.'

'You were outside, here, is that right, when this happened?'

'Yes.'

'And did you . . . by any chance . . . see the horsebox on its way down the hill?' He had a quiet voice and pronounced every syllable carefully, like talking to a lip-reader.

I nodded again. He said 'Ah,' with deep satisfaction, as if that were the answer he had long been seeking, and he smiled on me with favour and suggested we go into the house (where it would be warmer), accompanied by the constable, to take notes.

Among the litter in the drawing room we sat while I answered his questions.

His name was Wilson, he said. He was disappointed that I hadn't seen the horsebox start down the hill, and he was disappointed that I hadn't seen anyone in or near it before it rolled.

'I'll tell you one thing for certain, though,' I said. 'It was not parked in any prearranged place. I watched quite a few of the cars arrive. I could see them coming over the hill, the horsebox among them. They parked in a row just as they arrived, in the same order.' I paused, then said, 'The Sheik came to the stables a good hour before the other guests, which is why his Mercedes is first in the row. When he arrived he went to look round the yard, to see his horses. Then when several other guests came, he joined them in the marquee. No one manoeuvred him into any particular place. I was in there when he came. He was walking with Jack Hawthorn and Jimmy – Jack's secretary. It was just chance he stood where he did. And he didn't of course stand totally still all the time. He must have moved several yards during the hour he was there.'

I stopped. There was a small silence.

'Did you get all that, constable?' Wilson asked.

'Yes, sir.'

'According to your van, you are a wine merchant, Mr Beach? And you supplied the drinks for the party?'

'Yes,' I agreed.

'And you are observant.' His voice was dry, on the edge of dubious.

'Well . . .'

'Could you describe the position of any other of the guests so accurately? For a whole hour, Mr Beach?'

'Yes, some. But one tends to notice a Sheik. And I do notice where people are when I'm anywhere on business. The hosts, and so on, in case they want me.'

He watched my face without comment, and presently asked, 'What did the Sheik drink?'

'Orange juice with ice and mineral water.'

'And his followers?'

'One had fizzy lemonade, the other two, Coca-Cola.'

'Did you get that, constable?'

'Yes, sir.'

Wilson stared for a while at his toecaps, then took a deep breath as if reaching a decision.

'If I described some clothes to you, Mr Beach,' he said, 'could you tell me who was wearing them?'

'Uh . . . if I knew them.'

'Navy pinstripe suit . . .'

I listened to the familiar description. 'A man called Larry Trent,' I said. 'One of Jack Hawthorn's owners. He was . . . had . . . a restaurant; the Silver Moondance, near Reading.'

'Got that, constable?'

'Yes, sir.'

'And also, Mr Beach, a blue tweed skirt and jacket with a light blue woollen shirt, pearls round the neck, and pearl earrings?'

I concentrated, trying to remember, and he said, 'Greenish slightly hairy trousers, olive-coloured sweater over a mustard shirt. Brown tie with mustard stripes.'

'Oh . . .'

'You know him?'

'Both of them. Colonel and Mrs Fulham. I was talking to them. I sell them wine.'

'Sold, Mr Beach,' Wilson said regretfully. 'That's all, then. I'm afraid all the others have been identified, poor people.'

I swallowed. 'How many . . .?'

'Altogether? Eight dead, I'm afraid. It could have been worse. Much worse.' He rose to his feet and perfunctorily shook my head. 'There may be political repercussions. I can't tell whether you may be needed for more answers. I will put in my report. Good day, Mr Beach.'

He went out in his slow hunched way, followed by the constable, and I walked after them into the garden.

It was growing dark, with lights coming on in places.

The square of screens had been taken down, and two ambulances were preparing to back through the gap the horsebox had made in the hedge. A row of seven totally covered stretchers lay blackly on the horribly bloodstained matting, with the eighth set apart. In that, I supposed, lay the Sheik, as two living Arabs stood there, one at the head, one at the foot, still tenaciously guarding their prince.

In the dusk the small haggard group of people, all hope gone now, watched silently, with Flora among them, as ambulance-men lifted the seven quiet burdens one by one to bear them away; and I went slowly to my van and sat in it until they had done. Until only the Sheik remained, aloof in death as in life, awaiting a nobler hearse.

I switched on lights and engine and followed the two ambulances over the hill, and in depression drove down to the valley, to my house.

Dark house. Empty house.

I let myself in and went upstairs to change my clothes, but when I reached the bedroom I just went and lay on the bed without switching on the lamps; and from exhaustion, from shock, from pity, from loneliness and from grief . . . I wept.

FOUR:

Monday mornings I always spent in the shop restocking the shelves after the weekend's sales and drawing up lists of what I would need as replacements. Monday afternoons I drove the van to the wholesalers for spirits, soft drinks, cigarettes, sweets and crisps, putting some directly into the shop on my return, and the reserves into the storeroom.

Mondays also I took stock of the cases of wines stacked floor to shoulder level in the storeroom and telephoned shippers for more. Mondays the storeroom got tidied by five p.m., checked and ready for the week ahead. Mondays were always hard work.

That particular Monday morning, heavy with the dead feeling of aftermath, I went drearily to work sliding Gordon's gin into neat green rows and slotting Liebfraumilch into its rack; tidying the Teacher's, counting the Bell's, noticing we were out of Moulin à Vent. All of it automatic, my mind still with the Hawthorns, wondering how Jack was, and Jimmy, and how soon I should telephone to find out.

When I first had the shop I had just met Emma, and we had run it together with a sense of adventure that had never quite left us. Nowadays I had more prosaic help in the shape of a Mrs Palissey and also her nephew, Brian, who had willing enough muscles but couldn't read.

Mrs Palissey, generous both as to bosom and gossip, arrived punctually at nine-thirty and told me wide-eyed that she'd seen on the morning television news about the Sheik being killed at the party.

'You were there, Mr Beach, weren't you?' She was agog for gory details and waited expectantly, and with an inward sigh I satisfied at least some of her curiosity. Brian loomed over her, six feet tall, listening intently with his mouth open. Brian did most things with his mouth open, outward sign of inward retardation. Brian worked for me because his aunt had begged me piteously. 'It's giving my sister a nervous breakdown having him mooning round the house all day every day, and he could lift things here for me when you're out, and he'll be no trouble, I'll see to that.'

At first I feared I had simply transferred the imminent breakdown from the sister to myself, but when one got used to Brian's heavy breathing and permanent state of anxiety, one could count on the plus side that he would shift heavy cases of bottles all day without complaining, and didn't talk much.

'All those poor people!' exclaimed Mrs Palissey, enjoying the drama. 'That poor Mrs Hawthorn. Such a nice lady, I always think.'

'Yes,' I said, agreeing: and life did, I supposed, have to go on. Automatic, pointless life, like asking Brian to go into the storeroom and fetch another case of White Satin.

He nodded without closing the mouth and went off on the errand, returning unerringly with the right thing. He might not be able to read, but I had found he could recognise the general appearance of a bottle and label if I told him three or four times what it was, and he now knew all the regular items by sight. Mrs Palissey said at least once a week that she was ever so proud of him, considering.

Mrs Palissey and I remained by common consent on formal terms of Mrs and Mr: more dignified, she said. By nature she liked to please and was in consequence a good saleswoman, making genuinely helpful suggestions to irresolute customers. 'Don't know their own minds, do they, Mr Beach?' she would say when they'd gone and I would agree truthfully that no, they often didn't. Mrs Palissey and I tended to have the same conversations over and over and slightly too often.

She was honest in all major ways and unscrupulous in minor. She would never cheat me through the till, but Brian ate his way through a lot more crisps and Mars bars than I gave him myself, and spare light bulbs and half-full jars of Nescafé tended to go home with Mrs P. if she was short. Mrs Palissey considered such things 'perks' but would have regarded taking a bottle of sherry as stealing. I respected the distinction and was grateful for it, and paid her a little over the norm.

Whenever we were both there together, Mrs Palissey served the shop customers while I sat in the tiny office within earshot taking orders over the telephone and doing the paperwork, ready to help her if necessary. Some customers, particularly men, came for the wine-chat as much as the product, and her true knowledge there was sweet, dry, cheap, expensive, popular.

It was a man's voice I could hear saying, 'Is Mr Beach himself in?' and Mrs Palissey's helpfully answering, 'Yes, sir, he'll be right with you,' and I rose and took the few steps into his sight.

The man there, dressed in a belted fawn raincoat, was perhaps a shade older than myself and had a noticeably authoritative manner. Without enormous surprise I watched him reach into an inner pocket for a badge of office and introduce himself as Detective Sergeant Ridger, Thames Valley police. He hoped I might be able to help him with his enquiries.

My mind did one of those quick half-guilty canters round everything possible I might have done wrong before I came to the more sensible conclusion that his presence must have something to do with the accident. And so it had, in a way, but not how I could have expected.

'Do you know a Mr d'Alban sir?' He consulted his memory. 'The Honourable James d'Alban, sir?'

'Yes I do,' I said. 'He was injured yesterday at the Hawthorn party. He's not . . . dying?' I shied at the last minute away from 'dead'.

'No, sir, he's not. As far as I know he's in Battle Hospital with broken ribs, a pierced lung, and concussion.'

Enough to be going on with, I thought ironically. Poor Jimmy.

Ridger had a short over-neat haircut, watchful brown eyes, a calculator-wristwatch bristling with knobs and no gift for public relations. He said impersonally, 'Mr d'Alban woke up to some extent in the ambulance taking him to hospital and began talking disjointedly but repeatedly about a man called Larry Trent and some unpronounceable whisky that wasn't what it ought to be, and you, sir, who would know for certain if you tasted it.'

I just waited.

Ridger went on, 'There was a uniformed policeman in the ambulance with Mr d'Alban, and the constable reported the substance of those remarks to us, as he was aware we had reason to be interested in them. Mr d'Alban, he said, was totally unable to answer any questions yesterday and indeed appeared not to know he was being addressed.'

I wished vaguely that Ridger would talk more naturally, not as if reading from a notebook. Mrs Palissey was listening hard though pretending not to, with Brian frowning uncomprehendingly beside her. Ridger glanced at them a shade uneasily and asked if we could talk somewhere in private.

I took him into the miniscule office, large enough only for a desk, two chairs and a heater: about five feet square, approximately. He sat in the visitors' chair without waste of time and said, 'We've tried to interview Mr d'Alban this morning but he is in Intensive Care and the doctor refused us entry.' He shrugged. 'They say to try tomorrow, but for our purposes tomorrow may be too late.'

'And your purposes are . . . what?' I asked.

For the first time he seemed to look at me as a person, not just as an aid to enquiries; but I wasn't sure I liked the change because in his warming interest there was also a hint of manipulation. I had dealt in my time with dozens of salesmen seeking business, and Ridger's was the same sort of approach. He needed something from me that called for persuasion.

'Do you verify, sir, that Mr d'Alban did talk to you about this whisky?'

'Yes, he did, yesterday morning.'

Ridger looked almost smug with satisfaction.

'You may not know, sir,' he said, 'that Mr Larry Trent died in yesterday's accident.'

'Yes, I did know.'

'Well, sir . . .' he discreetly cleared his throat, lowering his voice for the sales pitch, softening the natural bossiness in his face. 'To be frank, we've had other complaints about the Silver Moondance. On two former occasions investigations have been carried out there, both times by the Office of Weights and Measures, and by Customs and Excise. On neither occasion was any infringement found.'

He paused.

'But this time?' I prompted obligingly.

'This time we think that in view of Mr Trent's death, it might be possible to make another inspection this morning.'

'Ah.'

I wasn't sure that he liked the dry understanding in my voice, but he soldiered on. 'We have reason to believe that in the past someone at the Silver Moondance, possibly Mr Trent himself, has been tipped off in advance that the investigations were in hand. So this time my superiors in the CID would like to make some preliminary enquiries of our own, assisted, if you are agreeable, by yourself, as an impartial expert.'

'Um,' I said, doubtfully. 'This morning, did you say?'

'Now, sir, if you would be so good.'

'This very minute?'

'We think, sir, the quicker the better.'

'You must surely have your own experts?' I said.

It appeared . . . er . . . that there was no official expert available at such short notice, and that as time was all important . . . would I go?

I could see no real reason why not to, so I said briefly, 'All right', and told Mrs Palissey I'd be back as soon as I could. Ridger drove us in his car, and I wondered on the way just how much of an expert the delirious Jimmy had made me out to be, and whether I would be of any use at all, when it came to the point.

The Silver Moondance, along the valley from the small Thames-side town where I had my shop, had originally been a sprawlingly ugly house built on the highest part of a field sloping up from the river. It had over the years metamorphosed successively into school, nursing home, and general boarding house, adding inappropriate wings at every change. Its most recent transformation had been also the most radical, so that little could now be seen of the original shiny yellow-grey bricks for glossier expanses of plate glass. At night from the river the place looked like Blackpool fully illuminated, and even by day, from the road, one could see 'Silver Moondance' blinking on and off in white letters over the doorway.

'Do they know you here, sir?' Ridger belatedly asked as we turned into the drive.

I shook my head. 'Shouldn't think so. The last time I came here it was the Riverland Guest Home, full of old retired people. I used to deliver their drinks.'

Dears, they had been, I remembered nostalgically, and great topers, on the whole, taking joy in their liquid pleasures.

Ridger grunted without much interest and parked on an acre or two of unpopulated tarmac. 'They should just be open,' he said with satisfaction, locking the car doors. 'Ready, sir?'

'Yes,' I said. 'And Sergeant . . . um . . . let me do the talking.'

'But . . .'

'Best not to alarm them,' I said, persuasively, 'if you don't want them pouring the Laphroaig down the sink.'

'The what?'

'What we're looking for.'

'Oh.' He thought. 'Very well.'

I said, 'Fine,' without emphasis and we walked through the flashing portal into the ritzy plush of the entrance hall.

There were lights on everywhere, but no one in sight. A reception desk; unattended. A flat air of nothing happening and nothing expected.

Ridger and I walked toward a wrought iron and driftwood sign announcing 'Silver Moondance Saloon', and pushed through Western-style swing doors into the room beyond. It was red, black and silver, very large and uninhabited. There were many tables, each with four bentwood chairs set neatly round, and an orthodox bar at one end, open for business.

No bartender.

Ridger walked purposefully across and rapped on the counter, I following him more slowly.

No one came. Ridger rapped again, louder and longer, and was presently rewarded by a young fair-haired man coming through another swinging door at the back of the bar area, sweating visibily and struggling into a white jacket.

'Give us a chance,' he said crossly. 'We've only been open five minutes.' He wiped his damp forehead with his fingers and buttoned his coat. 'What can I get you?'

'Is the restaurant open?' I said.

'What? Not yet. They don't start serving before twelve.'

'And the wine waiter, would he be here?'

The barman looked at the clock and shook his head. 'What do you want him for? Whatever drinks you want, I'll get them.'

'The wine list,' I said humbly. 'Could I see it?'

He shrugged, reached under the bar, and produced a padded crimson folder. 'Help yourself,' he said, handing it across.

He was not actively rude, I thought, just thrown off the rails by the boss's demise. Practised, a touch effeminate, with unfortunate pimples and a silver identification bracelet inscribed with 'Tom'. I could feel Ridger beginning to bristle beside me, so I said mildly, 'Could I have a scotch, please?'

The barman gave a half-exasperated glance at the wine list in my hand but turned away and thrust a regulation glass against the optic measure on a standard-sized bottle of Bell's.

'Something for you?' I said to Ridger.

'Tomato juice. Without Worcester sauce.'

The barman put my whisky on the counter. 'Anything in yours?' he asked.

'No, thanks.'

I paid for the two drinks and we went to sit at one of the tables furthest away from the bar.

'This isn't what we came for,' Ridger said protestingly.

'First things first,' I said, smelling the whisky. 'Start at the bottom and work up. Good wine-tasting tactics.'

'But . . .' He thought better of it, and shrugged. 'All right, then. Your way. But don't take too long.'

I sucked a very small amount of whisky into my mouth and let it wander back over my tongue. One can't judge whisky with the taste buds at the tip, up by the front teeth, but only along the sides of the tongue and at the back, and I let everything that was there in the way of flavour develop to the full before I swallowed, and then waited a while for the aftertaste.

'Well?' said Ridger. 'What now?'

'For a start,' I said. 'This isn't Bell's.'

Ridger looked unexpectedly startled. 'Are you sure?'

'Do you know anything about whisky?' I asked.

'No. I'm a beer man, myself. Drink the odd whisky and ginger now and then, that's all.'

'Do you want to know?' I flicked a finger at the glass. 'I mean, shall I explain?'

'Will it take long?'

'No.'

'Go on, then.'

'Scotch whisky is made of barley,' I said. 'You can malt barley, like is done for beer. You let the grains start to grow, to form shoots about an inch or two long. Then for whisky you smoke the shoots, which are called malts, over burning peat, until they pick up the peat and smoke flavours and are crisp. Then you make a mash of the malts with water and let it ferment, then you distil it and put the distillation in wooden casks to age for several years, and that's pure malt whisky, full of overtones of various tastes.'

'Right,' Ridger said, nodding, his crisp hair-cut clearly concentrating.

'It's much cheaper,' I said, 'to make the barley into a mash without going through the malting and smoking stages, and much quicker because the aging process is years shorter, and that sort of whisky is called grained whisky and is a great deal plainer on the tongue.'

'O.K.' he said. 'Go on.'

'Good standard scotches like Bell's are a mixture of malt and grain whiskies. The more malt, the more varied and subtle the flavour. This in this glass has very little or no malt, which doesn't matter at all if you want to mix it with ginger, because you'd kill the malt flavour anyway.'

Ridger looked round the empty room. 'With this place full, with smoke and perfume and ginger ale, who's to know the difference?'

'It would take a brave man,' I said, smiling.

'What next, then?'

'We might hide the scotch in your tomato juice.' I poured the one into the other, to his horror. 'I can't drink it,' I explained. 'Do you want a drunk expert? No good at all.'

'I suppose not,' he said, weakly for him, and I went over to the bar and asked the barman if he had any malts.

'Sure,' he said, waving a hand along a row of bottles. 'Glenfiddich, down at the other end there.'

'Mm,' I said doubtfully. 'Do you have any Laphroaig?'

'La-what?'

'Laphroaig. A friend of mine had some here. He said it was great. He said as I liked malts I should definitely try it.'

The barman looked at his stock, but shook his head.

'Perhaps it's in the restaurant,' I said. 'I think he did mention drinking it after dinner. Perhaps it's on the drinks trolley.' I pulled out my wallet and opened it expectantly, and with a considering glance at the notes in sight the barman decided to go on the errand. He returned quite soon with a genuine Laphroaig bottle and charged me outrageously for a nip, which I paid without demur, giving him a tip on top.

I carried the glass to the far table to join Ridger.

'What do you do now?' I asked. 'Pray?'

'Taste it,' he said tersely.

I smelled it first, however, and tasted it slowly as before, Ridger sitting forward tensely in his chair.

'Well?' he demanded.

'It's not Laphroaig.'

'Are you certain?'

'Absolutely positive. Laphroaig is as smoky as you can get. Pure malt. There's almost no malt at all in what I've just tasted. It's the same whisky as before.'

'Thanks very much, Mr Beach,' he said with deep satisfaction. 'That's great.'

He stood up, walked over to the bar and asked to see the bottle from which his friend had just drunk. The bartender obligingly pushed it across the counter, and Ridger picked it up. Then with his other hand he pulled out his identification, and the barman, angry, started shouting.

Ridger proved to have a radio inside his jacket. He spoke to some unseen headquarters, received a tinny reply, and told the bartender the police would be prohibiting the sale of all alcohol at the Silver Moondance for that day at least, while tests were made on the stock.

'You're barmy,' the bartender yelled, and to me, viciously, 'Creep.'

His loud voice brought colleagues in the shape of a worried man in a dark suit who looked junior and ineffective, and a girl in a short pert waitress uniform, long fawn legs below a scarlet tunic, scarlet headband over her hair.

Ridger took stock of the opposition and found himself very much in charge. The ineffective junior announced himself to be the assistant manager, which drew looks of scorn and amazement from the waitress and the barman. Assistant to the assistant, I rather gathered. Ridger explained forcibly again that no liquor was to be sold pending investigations, and all three of them said they knew nothing about anything, and we would have to talk to . . . er . . . talk to . . .

'The management?' I suggested.

They nodded dumbly.

'Let's do that,' I said. 'Where's the manager?'

The assistant to the assistant manager finally said that the manager was on holiday and the assistant manager was ill. Head office was sending someone to take over as soon as possible.

'Head office?' I said. 'Didn't Larry Trent own the place?'

'Er . . .' said the assistant unhappily. 'I really don't know. Mr Trent never said he didn't, I mean, I thought he did. But when I got here this morning the telephone was ringing, and it was head office. That's what he said, anyway. He wanted to speak to the manager, and when I explained he said he would send someone along straight away.'

'Who ran things last night?' Ridger demanded.

'What? Oh . . . we're closed, Sunday nights.'

'And yesterday lunchtime?'

'The assistant manager was here, but he'd got 'flu. He went home to bed as soon as we closed. And of course Mr Trent had been here until opening time, seeing that everything was all right before he went to Mr Hawthorn's party.'

All three looked demoralised but at the same time slightly defiant, seeing the policeman as their natural enemy. Relations scarcely improved when Ridger's reinforcements rolled up: two uniformed constables bringing tape and labels for sealing all the bottles.

I diffidently suggested to Ridger that he should extend his suspicions to the wines.

'Wines?' he frowned. 'Yes, if you like, but we've got enough with the spirits.'

'All the same,' I murmured, and Ridger told the assistant to show me where they kept the wine, and to help me and one of his constables bring any bottles I wanted into the bar. The assistant, deciding that helpfulness would establish his driven-snow innocence, put no obstacles in my way, and in due course, and after consulting the wine list, the assistant, the constable and I returned to the bar carrying two large baskets full of bottles.

The spirits bottles all having been sealed, there was at our return a lull of activity in the Silver Moondance Saloon. I unloaded the bottles onto two tables, six white wine on one, six red on another, and from my jacket pocket produced my favourite corkscrew.

'Hey,' the barman protested. 'You can't do that.'

'Every bottle I open will be paid for,' I said, matter-of-factly. 'And what's it to you?'

The barman shrugged. 'Give me twelve glasses,' I said, 'and one of those pewter tankards,' and he did. I opened the six bottles of varying white wines and under the interested gaze of six pairs of eyes poured a little of the first into a glass. Niersteiner, it said on the label: and Niersteiner it was. I spat the tasted mouthful into the pewter tankard, to disgusted reaction from the audience.

'Do you want him to get drunk?' Ridger demanded, belatedly understanding. 'The evidence of a drunk taster wouldn't be acceptable.'

I tasted the second white. Chablis, as it should have been.

The third was similarly O.K., a Pouilly Fuissé.

By the time I'd finished the sixth, a Sauternes, the barman had greatly relaxed.

'Nothing wrong with them?' Ridger asked, not worried.

'Nothing,' I agreed, stuffing the corks back. 'I'll try the reds.'

The reds were a St Emilion, a St Estèphe, a Mâcon, a Valpolicella, a Volnay and a Nuits St Georges, all dated 1979. I smelled and tasted each one carefully, spitting and waiting a few moments in between sips so that each wine should be fresh on the tongue, and by the time I'd finished everyone else was restive.

'Well,' Ridger demanded, 'are they all right?'

'They're quite pleasant,' I said, 'but they're all the same.'

'What do you mean?'

'I mean,' I said, 'that notwithstanding all those pretty labels, the wine in all of these bottles is none of them. It's a blend. Mostly Italian, I would say, mixed with some French and possibly some Yugoslav, but it could be anything.'

'You don't know what you're talking about,' the barman said impatiently. 'We have people every day saying how good the wines are.'

'Mm,' I said neutrally. 'Perhaps you do.'

'Are you positive?' Ridger asked me. 'They're all the same?'

'Yes.'

He nodded as if that settled it and instructed the constables to seal and label the six reds with the date, time and place of confiscation. Then he told the barman to find two boxes to hold all the labelled bottles, which brought a toss of the head, a mulish petulance and a slow and grudging compliance.

I kept my word and paid for all the wine, the only action of mine which pleased the barman from first to last. I got him to itemise every bottle on a Silver Moondance billhead and sign it 'Received in full', and then I paid him by credit card, tucking away the receipts.

Ridger seemed to think paying was unnecessary, but then shrugged, and he and the constable began putting the wine into one of the boxes and the whiskies into the other; and into this sullenly orderly scene erupted the man from head office.

FIVE:

The man from head office was not at first sight intimidating. Short, fortyish, dark-haired, of medium build and wearing glasses, he walked enquiringly into the saloon in a grey worsted business suit as if not sure of the way.

Ridger, taking him, as I did, for a customer, raised his voice and said, 'The bar is closed, sir.'

The man took no notice but advanced more purposefully until he stood near enough to see the bottles in the boxes. He frowned at them and glanced at the policeman, and I could see in him a distinct change of mental gear. A tightening of muscles; a sharpening of attention: cruise to overdrive in three seconds.

'I'm a police officer,' said Ridger firmly, producing his authorisation. 'The bar is closed until further notice.'

'Is it indeed?' said the newcomer ominously. 'Be so good as to explain why.' The first impression was wrong, I thought. This man could intimidate quite easily.

Ridger blinked. 'It's a police matter,' he said. 'It's no concern of yours.'

'Every concern,' said the man shortly. 'I've come from head office to take over. So just what exactly is going on?' His voice had the edge of one not simply used to command but used to instant action when he spoke. His accent, so far as he had one, was straightforward business-English, devoid both of regional vowels and swallowed consonants, but also without timbre. Good plain grain, I thought; not malt.

'Your name, sir?' asked Ridger stolidly, ignoring the sharp tone as if he hadn't heard it, which I was sure he had.

The man from head office looked him up and down, assessing the altogether statement of brushed hair, belted raincoat, polished shoes. Ridger reacted to that aggressively, his spine stiffening, the desire to be the dominator growing unmistakably in the set of his jaw. Interesting, I thought.

The man from head office allowed the pause to lengthen until it was clear to everyone that he was giving his name as a result of thought, not out of obedience to Ridger.

'My name is Paul Young,' he said finally, with weight. 'I represent the company of which this restaurant is a subsidiary. And now, what exactly is going on here?'

Ridger's manner remained combative as he began announcing in his notebook terminology that the Silver Moondance would be prosecuted for contraventions of the Sale of Goods Act.

Paul Young from head office interrupted brusquely. 'Cut the jargon and be precise.'

Ridger glared at him. Paul Young grew impatient. Neither would visibly defer to the other, but Ridger did in the end explain what he was removing in the boxes.

Paul Young listened with fast growing anger, but this time not aiming it at Ridger himself. He turned his glare instead on the barman (who did his best to shelter behind his pimples), and thunderously demanded to know who was responsible for selling substitutions. From the barman, the waitress and the assistant assistant in turn he got weak disclaiming shakes of the head and none of the defiance that they had shown to Ridger.

'And who are you?' he enquired rudely, giving me the up and down inspection. 'Another policeman?'

'A customer,' I said mildly.

Seeing nothing in me to detain him he returned his forceful attention to Ridger, assuring him authoritatively that head office had had no knowledge of the substitutions and that the fraud must have originated right here in this building. The police could be assured that head office would discover the guilty person and prosecute him themselves, ensuring that nothing of this sort could happen again.

It was perfectly clear to Ridger as to everyone else present that Paul Young was in fact badly jolted and surprised by the existence of fraud, but Ridger with smothered satisfaction said that the outcome would be for the police and the courts to decide, and that meanwhile Mr Young could give him the address and telephone number of head office, for future reference.

I watched Paul Young while he wrote the required information onto another billhead provided by the barman and wondered vaguely why he didn't carry business cards to save himself that sort of bother. He had large hands, I noticed, full fleshed, with pale skin, and as he bent his head over the paper I saw the discreet pink hearing aid tucked behind his right ear, below the frame of his glasses. One could get hearing aids built-in with the earpieces of eyeglass frames, I thought, and wondered why he didn't.

What a mess, I thought, for a parent company to walk into unawares. And who, I wondered, had been on the fiddle – the manager, the wine waiter, or Larry Trent himself? Not that I wondered at all deeply. The culprit's identity was to me less interesting than the crime, and the crime itself was hardly unique.

The six corks from the bottles of red were lying where I'd left them on the small table, the constables having sealed the open necks with wide wrappings of sticky tape instead of trying to ram back the original plugs, and I picked the corks up almost absentmindedly and put them in my pocket, tidyminded out of habit.

Paul Young straightened from his writing and handed the sheet of paper to the assistant assistant, who handed it to me, who passed it on to Ridger, who glanced at it, folded it, and tucked it into some inner pocket below the raincoat.

'And now, sir,' he said, 'close the bar.'

The barman looked to Paul Young for instructions and got a shrug and an unwilling nod, and presently an ornamental grille unrolled from ceiling to bar-top, imprisoning the barman in his cage. He clicked a few locks into place and went out through the rear door, not returning to the saloon.

Ridger and Paul Young argued for a while about how soon the Silver Moondance could resume full business, each still covertly manoeuvring for domination. I reckoned it came out about quits because they finally backed off from each other inconclusively, both still in aggressive postures, more snarl than teeth.

Ridger removed his constables, the boxes and myself to the carpark leaving Paul Young to deal with his helpless helpers, and the last I saw of the man from head office, in a backward glance as I went through the western swing doors, was the businesslike glasses turning to survey his large empty-tabled discontinued asset in black and scarlet, the colours of roulette.

Ridger muttered under his breath several times as he drove me back to my shop and broke out into plain exasperation when I asked him for a receipt for the case of wines, which he was transporting in the boot.

'Those twelve bottles do belong to me,' I pointed out. 'I paid for them, and I want them back. You said yourself that you'd got enough with the whisky to prosecute. The wines were my own idea.'

He grudgingly admitted it and gave me a receipt.

'Where do I find you?' I asked.

He told me the address of his station and without the least gratitude for the help he had solicited, drove brusquely away. Between him and Paul Young I thought, definitely not much to choose.

In the shop Mrs Palissey had had a veritable barrage of customers as sometimes happened on Monday mornings, and was showing signs of wear.

'Go to lunch,' I said, although it was early, and with gratitude she put on her coat, took Brian in tow, and departed to the local café for pie and chips and a gossip with her constant friend, the traffic warden.

The customers kept coming and I served them with automatic ease, smiling, always smiling, giving pleasure to the pleasure-seekers. For years, with Emma, I had positively enjoyed the selling, finding my own satisfaction in giving it to others. Without her the warmth I had felt had grown shallow, so that now I dispensed only a surface sympathy, nodding and smiling and hardly listening, hearing only sometimes, not always, the unsaid things in the shopping voices. The power I'd once had had drained away, and I didn't really care.

During a short lull I wrote the list for the wholesaler, planning to go as soon as Mrs Palissey returned, and noticed that Brian, unasked by me, had swept and straightened the store room. The telephone rang three times with good substantial orders and the till, when consulted, showed a healthy profit margin on the morning's trading. Ironic, the whole thing.

Two customers came in together, and I served the woman first, a middle-aged frightened lady who called every day for a bottle of the cheapest gin, tucking it away secretively in a large handbag while taking furtive glances out of the window for passing neighbours. Why didn't she buy it by the case, I'd once long ago asked her teasingly, as it was cheaper by the case, but she'd been alarmed and said no, she enjoyed the walk; and the loneliness had looked out of her eyes along with the fear of being called an alcoholic, which she wasn't quite, and I'd felt remorse for being heartless, because I'd known perfectly well why she bought one private bottle at a time.

'Nice day, Mr Beach,' she said breathlessly, her glance darting to the street.

'Not too bad, Mrs Chance.'

She gave me the exact money, coins warmed by her palm, notes carefully counted, watching nervously while I wrapped her comfort in tissue.

'Thank you, Mrs Chance.'

She nodded dumbly, gave me a half smile, pushed the bottle into her handbag and departed, pausing at the door to reconnoitre. I put the money in the till and looked enquiringly at the man waiting patiently to be served next, and found myself face to face with no customer but the investigator Wilson from the day before.

'Mr Beach,' he said.

'Mr Wilson.'

Externally he wore exactly the same clothes, as if he had never been to bed or to shave, which he had. He looked rested and clean, and moved comfortably in his slow hunchbacked fashion with the knowing eyes and the non-communicating face.

'Do you always know what your customers want without asking them?' he said.

'Quite often,' I nodded, 'but usually I wait for them to say.'

'More polite?'

'Infinitely.'

He paused. 'I came to ask you one or two questions. Is there anywhere we can talk?'

'Just talk,' I said apologetically. 'Would you like a chair?'

'Are you alone here?'

'Yes.'

I fetched the spare chair for him from the office and put it by the counter, and had no sooner done so than three people came in for Cinzano, beer and sherry. Wilson waited through the sales without doing much more than blink, and when the door closed for the third time he stirred without impatience and said, 'Yesterday, during the party, were you at any time talking to the Sheik?'

I smiled involuntarily. 'No, I wasn't.'

'Why does the idea amuse you?'

'Well . . . the Sheik considers all this . . .' I waved a hand around the bottle-lined walls, '. . . as being positively sinful. Forbidden. Pernicious. Much as we regard cocaine. To him I'm a pusher. In his own country I'd be in jail, or worse. I wouldn't have introduced myself to him. Not unless I wanted to invite contempt.'

'I see,' he said, almost nodding, contemplating the Islamic view. Then he slightly pursed his lips, approaching, I guessed, the question he had really come to ask.

'Think back,' he said, 'to when you were outside the tent, when the horsebox rolled.'

'Yes.'

'Why were you out there?'

I told him about fetching more champagne.

'And when you went out, the horsebox was already rolling?'

'No,' I said. 'When I went out I glanced up at the cars and everything was all right. I remembered noting that no one had yet left . . . and hoped I'd taken enough champagne to last out.'

'Was there anyone near the horsebox?'

'No.'

'You're certain?'

'Yes. No one that I could see.'

'You've consulted your memory . . . before this moment?'

I half smiled. 'Yes. You might say so.'

He sighed. 'Did you see anyone at all anywhere near any of the cars?'

'No. Except . . . only a child with a dog.'

'Child?'

'They weren't near the horsebox. Nearer the Sheik's Mercedes, really.'

'Can you describe the child?'

'Well . . .' I frowned. 'A boy.'

'Clothes?'

I looked away from him, gazing vacantly at the racks of wine, thinking back. 'Dark trousers . . . perhaps jeans . . . and a dark blue sweater.'

'Hair?'

'Um . . . light brown, I suppose. Not blond, not black.'

'Age?'

I pondered, looking again at the patient questioner. 'Young. Small. Four, I should think.'

'Why are you so definite?'

'I'm not . . . his head was still big in proportion to his body.'

Wilson's eyes glimmered deeply. 'What sort of dog?' he said.

I stared vaguely once more into the distance, seeing the child on the hill. 'A whippet,' I said.

'On a leash?'

'No . . . running and turning back towards the boy.'

'What sort of shoes did the boy have?'

'For God's sake,' I said, 'I only saw him for a couple of seconds.'

His mouth twitched. He looked down at his hands and then up again. 'No one else?'

'No.'

'How about the Sheik's chauffeur?'

I shook my head. 'He might have been sitting in the car, but one couldn't tell. It had tinted windows, as you saw.'

He stirred and said thank you and began to get to his feet.

'Incidentally,' I said, 'someone stole three cases of champagne and some other bottles out of my van sometime after the accident. I need to report the theft to the police before I claim insurance . . . May I report it to you?'

He gave me a smile. 'I will note that you have reported it.'

'Thanks.'

He held his hand out to me over the counter and I shook it. 'It's I who thank you, Mr Beach,' he said.

'I haven't been much help.'

He smiled his small uncommunicative smile, nodded benignly, and went away.

Good grief, I thought inconsequentially, watching his hunched departing back, one hundred and fifty goblets were lying in splinters in the Hawthorns' back garden, and it was all very well talking of insurance, I was due to supply those very glasses to the Thames Ladies Christmas Charities fundraising wine and cheese party on the following day, Tuesday, which I had forgotten clean about.

Tentatively I rang the Hawthorns' number, not wanting to overload Flora but to ask all the same how many glasses if any remained intact, and I got not Flora but an answering machine with Jimmy's voice, loud, healthy and languid, inviting me to leave my name, number, and message.

I complied, wondering how Jimmy was doing in intensive care, and when Mrs Palissey came back I took Brian with me to the wholesalers, where he helped me shift umpteen cases from the stores onto trolleys, and from those trolleys to other trolleys at the pay desk, for rolling out to the van, and from the second trolleys into the van, and, back at the shop, from the van into the storeroom. My own muscles, after roughly twelve years of such exercise, would have rivalled a fork-lift truck, and Brian's, too, were coming along nicely. He grinned while he worked. He enjoyed lifting the cases. Two-at-a-time he had begun to scorn; he liked me to pile him with three.

Brian never talked much, which I appreciated. He sat placidly beside me in the van on the way back, lips apart as usual, and I wondered what went on in that big vacant head, and how much one could teach him if one tried. He'd learned quite a lot in the three or so months he'd been with me, I reflected. He was brilliantly useful compared with day one.

He unloaded the van by himself when we returned and put everything in the right places in the storeroom, which I had arranged with much more method since his arrival. Mrs Palissey had taken two more orders on the telephone, and I spent some time making up those and the ones from earlier in the day, collecting all the various items together into boxes for Brian to carry out to the van. Being a wine merchant, I often thought, was not a gentle artistic occupation, but thoroughly backbreakingly physical.

The telephone rang yet again while I was sitting in the office writing the bills to go out with the orders and I stretched out one hand for the receiver with my eyes on my work.

'Tony?' a woman's voice said tentatively. 'It's Flora.'

'Dear Flora,' I said. 'How are you? How's Jack? How's everything?'

'Oh . . .' She seemed tired beyond bearing. 'Everything's so awful. I know I shouldn't say that . . . but . . . oh dear.'

'I'll come and fetch the glasses,' I said, hearing the appeal she hadn't uttered. 'I'll come practically at once.'

'There . . . there aren't many left whole . . . but yes, do come.'

'Half an hour,' I said.

She said, 'Thank you,' faintly and disconnected.

I looked at my watch. Four-thirty. Most often at about that time on Mondays Mrs Palissey and Brian set off in the van to do any deliveries which lay roughly on their way home, finishing the round the following morning. Mrs Palissey's ability to drive had been the chief reason I'd originally hired her, and she on her part had been pleased to be given the use of the shop's second string, an elderly capacious Rover estate. We swopped the two vehicles around as required, so I said I would do the deliveries that day, if she would stay until five to close the shop, and go home again in the car.

'By all means, Mr Beach.' She was graciously obliging. 'And I'll be here at nine-thirty, then, in the morning.'

I nodded my thanks and took the bills, the orders, van and myself off up the hill to Jack Hawthorn's stables, where not a great deal had changed since the day before.

I saw, as I came over the hill, that the great green horsebox still stood on the lawn, with, beyond it, the heaped canvas remains of the marquee. The Sheik had gone, and his bodyguards. The mute bloodstained expanse of fawn matting was scattered with trestle tables and sections of tent pole, and glittering here and there in the rays of late afternoon sunshine lay a million pieces of glass.

I parked as before outside the kitchen entrance and locked the van with a sigh. Flora came slowly out of the house to greet me, dressed in a grey skirt and a green cardigan, dark smudges under exhausted eyes.

I gave her a small hug and a kiss on the cheek. We had never before been on those sort of terms, but disasters could work wonders in that area.

'How's Jack?' I said.

'They've just now set his leg . . . pinned it, they say. He's still unconscious . . . but I saw him this morning . . . before.' Her voice was quavery, as it had been on the telephone. 'He was very down. So depressed. It made me so miserable.' The last word came out in a gasp as her face crumpled into tears. 'Oh dear . . . Oh dear . . .'

I put my arm round her shaking shoulders. 'Don't worry,' I said. 'He'll be all right. Truly.'

She nodded mutely, sniffing and fumbling in a pocket for a handkerchief, and after a while, through gulps, said, 'He's alive, and I should be grateful for that, and they say he'll be home quite soon. It's just . . . everything . . . everything . . .'

I nodded. 'Just too much.'

She nodded also and dried her eyes with a re-emergence of spirit, and I asked whether any of her children might not come to help her through this patch.

'They're all so busy . . . I told them not to. And Jack, you know, he's jealous of them really, he wouldn't want them here when he's away, though I shouldn't say that, only I do seem to tell you things, Tony dear, and I don't know why.'

'Like telling the wallpaper,' I said.

She smiled very faintly, a considerable advance.

'How's Jimmy?' I asked.

'I didn't see him. He's conscious, they say, and no worse. I don't know what we'll do if he isn't well soon . . . he runs everything, you know . . . and without them both . . . I feel so lost. I can't help it.'

'Anything I can do?' I said.

'Oh yes,' she said instantly. 'I was so hoping . . . I mean, when you said you'd come . . . Have you got time?'

'For what?' I asked.

'Um . . . Tony dear, I don't know how much I can ask of you, but would you . . . could you possibly . . . walk round the yard with me?'

'Well, of course,' I said, surprised. 'If you want.'

'It's evening stables,' she explained in a rush. 'Jack was so insistent I walked round. He wants me to tell him how everything is, because we've a new head lad, he came only last week, and Jack says he's not sure of him in spite of his references, and he made me promise I'd walk round. And he knows, he really does, that I don't know enough about horses, but he wanted me to promise . . . and he was so depressed, that I did.'

'No problem at all,' I said. 'We'll walk round together, and we'll both listen, and afterwards we'll make notes for you to relay to Jack.'

She sighed with relief and looked at her watch. 'It's time now, I should think.'

'O.K.' I said, and we walked round the house to the stables and to the sixty or so equine inmates.

In Jack's yard there were two big old quadrangles, built of wood mostly, with a preponderance of white paint. Some of the many doors stood wide open with lads carrying sacks and buckets in and out, and some were half closed with horses' heads looking interestedly over the tops.

'We'd better do the colts' yard first,' Flora said, 'and the fillies' yard after, like Jack does, don't you think?'

'Absolutely,' I agreed.

I knew about horses to the extent that I'd been brought up with them, as much after my father's death as before. My mother, wholly dedicated, seldom talked of much else. She had in her time ridden in point-to-point races and also adored to go hunting, which filled her life whenever my father was away on duty, and his as well when he was at home and not that minute racing. I had seen day after day the glowing enjoyment in their faces and had tried hard to feel it myself, but whatever enthusiasm I'd shown had been counterfeit, for their sakes. Galloping after hounds across muddy November fields I had thought chiefly of how soon one could decently go home, and the only part of the ritual I had actually enjoyed had been the cleaning and feeding of the horses afterwards. Those great creatures, tired and dirty, were so uncritical. They never told one to keep one's heels down, one's elbows in, one's head up, one's spine straight. They didn't expect one to be impossibly brave and leap the largest fences. They didn't mind if one sneaked through gates instead. Closed into a box with a horse, humming while I brushed off dried mud and sweat, I'd felt a sort of dumb complete communion, and been happy.

After my father died my mother had hunted on with unfaltering zeal and had for the past ten years been joint master of the local hounds, to her everlasting fulfilment. It had been a relief to her, I often thought, when I had finally left home.

Jack Hawthorn's lads were halfway through the late afternoon programme of mucking out, feeding and watering, a process known throughout the racing world as 'evening stables'. It was the custom for the trainer to walk round, usually with the head lad, stopping at every box to inspect the racer within, feeling its legs for heat (bad sign) and looking for a bright eye (good).

Jack's new head lad had greeted Flora's appearance with an exaggerated obsequiousness which I found distasteful and which seemed also to make Flora even less sure of herself. She introduced him as Howard, and told him Mr Beach would be accompanying her on the rounds.

Howard extending the Uriah Heep manner to myself, we set off on what was clearly the normal pattern, and I listened attentively for Flora's sake to every Howard opinion.

Very little, it seemed to me, could have been different from the morning before, when Jack himself had been there. One horse had trodden on a stone out at exercise and was slightly footsore. Another had eaten only half of his midday feed. A third had rubbed skin off a hock, which would need watching.

Flora said 'I see,' and 'I'll tell Mr Hawthorn,' at regular intervals and Howard ingratiatingly said that Flora could safely leave everything to him, Howard, until Mr Hawthorn's return.

We came in turn to the Sheik's horses, still in residence, and also to Larry Trent's, bursting with health. They had been prolific winners all year, it seemed. Both the Sheik and Larry Trent had been excellent judges of potential, and were lucky as well.

'We'll be losing all of these horses, I suppose,' Flora sighed. 'Jack says it will be a heavy financial loss for us.'

'What will happen to them?' I asked.

'Oh . . . I expect the Sheik's will be sold. I don't know. I don't know if he has any family. And Larry Trent's five, of course, will go back to their owners.'

I raised my eyebrows slightly, but because of Howard's unctuous presence said no more, and it wasn't until Flora and I were at length walking back towards my van that I asked her what she meant.

'Larry Trent's horses?' she repeated. 'They weren't his own property. He leased them.'

'Paid rent for them?'

'My dear, no. A lease is only an agreement. Say someone owns a horse but can't really afford the training fees, and someone else wants to have a horse racing in his name and can afford the training fees but not the cost of the horse itself, then those two people make an agreement, all signed and registered, of course. The usual terms are that when the horse earns any prize-money it's divided fifty-fifty between the two parties. It's done quite often, you know.'

'No, I didn't know,' I said humbly.

'Oh yes. Larry Trent always did it. He was pretty shrewd at it. He would lease a horse for a year, say, and if it turned out all right he might lease it for another year, but if it won nothing, he'd try another. You can lease a horse for as long as you like, as long as you both agree, for a year or a season or three months . . . whatever you want.'

I found it interesting and asked, 'How are the leases fixed up?'

'Jack has the forms.'

'No, I meant, how does anyone know who has a horse they will lease but not sell?'

'Word of mouth,' she said vaguely. 'People just say. Sometimes they advertise. And sometimes one of our owners will ask Jack to find someone to lease their horse so they don't have to pay the training bills. Very often they do it with mares, so that they can have their horse back for breeding afterwards.'

'Neat,' I said.

Flora nodded. 'Larry Trent always liked it because it meant he could run five horses instead of owning only one outright. He was a great gambler, that man.'

'Gambler?'

'A thousand on this, a thousand on that . . . I used to get tired of hearing about it.'

I gave her an amused glance. 'Didn't you like him?'

'I supose he was all right,' she said dubiously. 'He was always friendly. A good owner, Jack always said. Paid regularly and understood that horses aren't machines. Hardly ever blamed the jockey if he lost. But secretive, somehow. I don't really know why I think that, but that's how he seemed to me. Generous, though. He took us to dinner only last week at that place of his, the Silver Moondance. There was a band playing . . . so noisy.' She sighed. 'But of course you know about us going there . . . Jimmy said he told you about that whisky. I told him to forget it . . . Jack didn't want Jimmy stirring up trouble.'

'Mm,' I said. 'The trouble got stirred, all the same, not that it matters.'

'What do you mean?'

I told her of Jimmy's semi-conscious wanderings and my visit with Detective Sergeant Ridger to the Silver Moondance Saloon, and she said 'Good heavens' faintly, with round eyes.

'Someone in that place had a great fiddle going,' I said. 'Whether Larry Trent knew or not.'

She didn't answer directly, but after a long pause said, 'You know, he did something once that I didn't understand. I happened to be at Doncaster sales last year with some friends I was staying with. Jack wasn't there, he was too busy at home. Larry Trent was there . . . He didn't see me, but I saw him across the sale ring, and he was bidding for a horse . . . it was called Ramekin.' She paused, then went on. 'The horse was knocked down to him and I thought good, Jack will be getting it to train. But it never came. Larry Trent never said a word. I told Jack of course, but he said I must have been mistaken, Larry Trent never bought horses, and he wouldn't even ask him about it.'

'So who did train Ramekin afterwards?' I asked.

'No one.' She looked at me anxiously. 'I'm not crazy, you know. I looked it up in the sale prices in the *Sporting Life* and it was sold for more than thirty thousand pounds. They didn't say who had bought it, but I'm absolutely certain it was Larry

Trent because the auctioneer's man went right up to him to ask him his name when it had been knocked down to him, but after that . . . nothing happened.'

'Well . . . someone must have him,' I said reasonably.

'I suppose so. But he's not down in any trainer's list of horses-in-training. I checked, you know, because it would have been so annoying if Larry had sent the horse to someone else after all the races Jack's won for him, but Ramekin wasn't down anywhere, and he hasn't raced the whole season, I've been looking for him. Ramekin just . . . really . . . vanished.'

SIX:

Flora took me into the kitchen to collect the glasses which were left whole: precisely nineteen.

'I'm sorry,' she said.

I shrugged. 'It's a wonder there are as many as that, considering. And don't worry, I'm insured.'

She helped me slot the survivors into the box I'd brought, her kind round face looking worried.

'Insurance!' she said. 'I've been hearing that word all morning. But who, I ask you, insures against such a tragedy? Of course we didn't have any insurance, not special insurance for the party. And those poor young things who own the horsebox . . . I had Sally . . . that's the wife . . . on the telephone at lunch time telling me over and over hysterically that Peter never never never left the hand-brake off and always always always left the horsebox in gear and that they're going to be ruined if the insurance companies can prove negligence. Poor things. Poor things.' She glanced at me. 'He didn't lock the doors, you know. I asked her. I'm afraid I made her angry. She said you don't lock the doors when you're at a friend's house.'

I thought sourly of my stolen champagne and kept quiet.

'She said they came in the horsebox only because they'd been to fetch a new hunter they'd just bought and were on their way home. The hunter's still there, you know, in one of our spare boxes round the back. Sally says she never wants to see it again. She was totally, absolutely, distraught. It's all so awful.'

Flora came with me as I carried the box of empty glasses out to the van, reluctant to let me go. 'We didn't make that list for Jack,' she said; so we returned to the kitchen and made it.

'If you still feel shaky tomorrow I'll come again for evening stables,' I said. 'I enjoyed it, to be honest.'

'You're a dear, Tony,' she said. 'I'd love you to,' and again she came out to the van to say goodbye.

'The police were here all morning swarming around the

horsebox,' she said, looking over to the silent green monster. 'Blowing dust all over it and shaking their heads.'

'Looking for fingerprints, I suppose.'

'I suppose so. Whatever it was they found, they didn't like it. But you know how they are, they didn't tell me a thing.'

'Did you take a look, when they'd gone?' I asked.

She shook her head as if it hadn't occurred to her, but immediately set off towards the horsebox across the grass. I followed, and together we made a rectangular tour, looking at a great deal of pinkish-greyish dust with smudges all over it.

'Hundreds of people must have touched it,' Flora said resignedly.

Including the people with the crane, I thought, and the people who'd released the horse, and any number of people before that.

On impulse I opened the passenger door, which was still not locked, and climbed into the cab.

'Do you think you ought to, dear?' Flora said anxiously.

'They didn't tell you to stay away, did they?'

'No . . . not today.'

'Don't worry, then.'

I looked around. There was a great deal more of the dust inside the cab, and also a great many fingerprints, but those inside were less smudged. I looked at them curiously but without expectation: it was just that I'd never actually seen the real thing, only dozens of representations in films.

Something about many of the prints struck me suddenly with a distinct mental jolt.

They were *tiny*.

Tiny fingerprints all over the vinyl surfaces of both front seats. Tiny fingerprints all over the steering-wheel and on the gear lever and on the brake. Tiny . . .

I climbed down from the cab and told Flora, and I told her also about the investigator Wilson's interest when I'd mentioned a lttle boy and a dog.

'Do you mean,' she said, very distressed, '. . . it was a *child* who caused such horror?'

'Yes, I'd think so. You know how they play. They love cars. They're always climbing into my van when I deliver things. Little wretches, if you don't watch them. I'd guess that that child released the brake and gear. Then when he'd run off with the dog the weight of the van would eventually make it roll if it was on even the slightest incline.'

'Oh dear.' She looked increasingly upset. 'Whose child?'

I described the boy as best I could but she said she didn't know everyone's children by sight, they changed so fast as they grew.

'Never mind,' I said. 'Wilson has addresses for all your guests. He'll find out. And dearest Flora, be grateful. If it was someone else's child who let off the brakes, your friends Peter and Sally won't be ruined.'

'It wasn't their child . . . they haven't any. But that poor little boy!'

'If everyone's got any sense,' I said, 'which you can be sure they haven't, no one will tell him he killed eight people until he's long grown up.'

On my way home from Flora's I got no further than the second delivery because my customer, a retired solicitor, was delighted (he said) that I had brought his order myself, and I must come in straightaway and share a bottle of Château Palmer 1970 which he had just decanted.

I liked the man, who was deeply experienced after countless holidays spent touring vineyards, and we passed a contented evening talking about the small parcels of miraculous fields in Pauillac and Margaux and about the universal virtues of the great grape Cabernet Sauvignon which would grow with distinction almost anywhere on earth. Given poor soil, of course, and sun.

The solicitor's wife, it transpired, was away visiting relatives. The solicitor suggested cold underdone beef with the claret, to which I easily agreed, thinking of my own empty house, and he insisted also on opening a bottle of Clos St Jacques 1982 to drink later.

'It's so seldom,' he said to my protestations, 'that I have anyone here with whom I can truly share my enthusiasm. My dear wife puts up with me, you know, but even after all these years she would as soon drink ordinary everyday Beaujolais or an undemanding Mosel. Tonight, and please don't argue, my dear chap, tonight is a treat.'

It was for me also. I drank my share of the Château Palmer and of the Clos St Jacques, which I had originally tasted when I sold it to him a year earlier; and I greatly enjoyed discovering how that particular wine was satisfactorily changing colour from purplish youth to a smooth deep burgundy red as it matured in excellence and power. It might well improve, I thought, and he said he would put it away for maybe a year. 'But I'm getting old, my dear chap. I want to drink all my treasures, you know, before it's too late.'

What with one thing and another it was nearly midnight before I left. Alcohol decays in the blood at a rate of one glass of wine an hour, I thought driving home, so with luck, after six glasses in five hours, I should be legitimately sober. It wasn't that I was unduly moral; just that to survive in business I needed a driving licence.

Perhaps because of the wine, perhaps because of the tossing and turning I'd done the previous night, I slept long and soundly without bad dreams, and in the morning rose feeling better than usual about facing a new day. The mornings were in any case always better than the nights. Setting out wasn't so bad; it was going home that was hell.

My mother had advised me on the telephone to sell and live somewhere else.

'You'll never be happy there,' she said. 'It never works.'

'You didn't move when Dad died,' I protested.

'But this house was mine to begin with,' she said, surprised. 'Inherited from my family. Quite different, Tony darling.'

I wasn't quite sure where the difference lay, but I didn't argue. I thought she might possibly be right that I should move, but I didn't. All my memories of Emma were alive there in the old renovated cottage overlooking the Thames, and to leave it seemed to be an abandonment of her: an ultimate unfaithfulness. I thought that if I sold the place I would feel guilty, not released, so I stayed there and sweated for her at nights and paid the mortgage and could find no ease.

The morning deliveries were widely scattered which meant a fair amount of zig-zagging, but free home delivering brought me so much extra business that I never minded.

Bad news travels as fast as the thud of jungle drums, and it was at only ten-fifteen, at my last port of call, that I heard about the Silver Moondance.

'Frightful, isn't it?' said a cheerful woman opening her back door to me on the outskirts of Reading. 'Someone broke in there last night and stole every bottle in the place.'

'Did they?' I said.

She nodded happily, enjoying the bad news. 'The milkman just told me, five minutes ago. The Silver Moondance is just along the road from here, you know. He went in there as usual with the milk and found the police standing around scratching their heads. Well, that's what the milkman said. He's not overkeen on the police, I don't think.'

I carried her boxes into the kitchen and waited while she wrote a cheque.

'Did you know the owner of the Silver Moondance was killed in that accident on Sunday, the one with the horsebox?' she asked.

I said that I'd heard.

'Frightful, isn't it, people going in and looting his place as soon as he's dead?'

'Frightful,' I agreed.

'Goodbye, Mr Beach,' she said blithely. 'Wouldn't it be boring if everyone was good?'

The plundered Silver Moondance, so close to her house, lay on my own direct route back to the shop, and I slowed as I approached it, unashamedly curious. There was indeed a police car standing much where Ridger had parked the day before, and on impulse I turned straight into the driveway and pulled up alongside.

There was no one about outside, nor, when I went in, in the entrance hall. There were fewer lights on than before and even less air of anything happening. I pushed through the swinging western doors to the saloon, but the black and scarlet expanse lay dark and empty, gathering dust.

I tried the restaurant on the opposite side of the entrance hall, but that too was deserted. That left the cellars, and I made my way as on the previous day along a passage to a door marked 'Private' and into the staff area beyond. The cellars were not actually in a basement but consisted of two cool interconnecting windowless storerooms off a lobby between the dining room and what had been Larry Trent's office. The lobby opened onto a back yard through a door laden with locks and bolts which now stood wide open, shedding a good deal of physical light onto the hovering figure of Sergeant Ridger, if no enlightenment.

The belted raincoat had been exchanged for an overcoat buttoned with equal military precision, and every hair was still rigidly in place. His brusque manner, too, was unchanged. 'What are you doing here?' he demanded, stiffly, as soon as he saw me.

'Just passing.'

He gave me a dour look but didn't tell me to leave, so I stayed.

'What was in here yesterday?' he asked, pointing to the open doors of the cellars. 'The assistant manager is useless. But you saw what was here. You came here for that wine, didn't you, so what do you remember of the contents?' No 'sir', I noticed, today. I'd progressed in his mind to 'police expert', perhaps.

'Quite a lot,' I said reflectively. 'But what about the wine list? Everything was itemised on that.'

'We can't find any wine lists. They seem to have gone with the wine.'

I was astonished. 'Are you sure?'

'We can't find any,' he said again. 'So I'm asking you to make a list.'

I agreed that I would try. He took me into Larry Trent's office, which was plushly comfortable rather than functional with a busily patterned carpet, several armchairs and many framed photographs on the walls. The photographs, I saw, were nearly all of the finishes of races, the winning post figuring prominently. Larry Trent had been a good picker, Flora had said, and a good gambler . . . whose luck had finally run out.

I sat in his own chair behind his mahogany desk and wrote on a piece of paper from Ridger's official notebook. Ridger himself remained standing as if the original occupant were still there to disturb him, and I thought fleetingly that I too felt like a trespasser on Larry Trent's privacy.

His desk was almost too neat to be believable as the hub of a business the size of the Silver Moondance. Not an invoice, not a letter, not a billhead showing. No government forms, no cash book, no filing cabinets, no typewriter and no readily available calculator. Not a working room, I thought: more a sanctuary.

I wrote what I could remember of bins and quantities of wines and then said I could perhaps add to the list if I went into the cellars and visualised what I'd seen before. We transferred therefore into the first of the rooms, where the bulk of the wines had been kept, and I looked at the empty racks and partitioned shelving and added a couple more names to my list.

From there we went through the sliding inner doors into the second cellar, which had contained stocks of spirits, liqueurs, canned beer and mixers. The beer and mixers remained: brandy, gin, vodka, whisky, rum and liqueurs were absent.

'They did a thorough job,' I remarked, writing.

Ridger grunted. 'They cleared the trolley in the dining room besides.'

'And the bar?'

'That too.'

'Highly methodical,' I said. 'Head office must be fuming. What did your friend Paul Young have to say?'

Ridger looked at me broodingly and then glanced at the list which I still held. 'As a matter of fact,' he said unwillingly, 'the telephone number he gave me is unobtainable. I'm having it checked.'

I blinked. 'He wrote it down himself,' I said.

'Yes, I know that.' He slightly pursed his lips. 'People sometimes make mistakes.'

What ever comment I might have made was forestalled by the arrival at the open door of the lobby of a young man in an afghan jacket who turned out to be a detective constable in plain(ish) clothes. He reported briefly that he'd finished peering into outhouses with the assistant manager, and that there seemed to be nothing missing from those. The assistant manager, he added, would be in the manager's office, if required.

'Where's that?' Ridger asked.

'Near to the front door. Behind the door marked "Staff only" in the entrance hall, so the assistant manager said.'

'Did you search in there?' Ridger asked.

'No, Sergeant, not yet.'

'Get on with it, then,' Ridger said brusquely, and without expression the constable turned and went away.

The radio inside Ridger's coat crackled to life, and Ridger pulled it out and extended its aerial. The metallic voice which came from it reached me clearly in the quiet cellar. It said, 'Further to your enquiry timed ten-fourteen, the telephone number as given does not exist and never has existed. Furthermore the address as given does not exist. There is no such street. This message timed ten-forty-eight. Please acknowledge. Over.'

'Acknowledged,' Ridger said grimly. 'Out.' He pushed the aerial down and said, 'I suppose you heard that?'

'Yes.'

'Shit,' he said forcefully.

'Quite so,' I agreed sympathetically, for which I received an absentminded glare. I handed him the completed list of what had all at once become not just the simple tally of an opportunist break-in but the evidence of a more thorough and purposeful operation. His job, however, not mine. 'I'll be in my shop if you want me again,' I said. 'I'll be glad to help.'

'Very good, sir,' he said vaguely, and then with more attention, 'Right, then. Thanks.'

I nodded and went back through the 'Private' door into the entrance hall, glancing across at the inconspicuous 'Staff only' door which merged chameleon-like with the decor of the walls: and it was while I was supposing that the manager preferred not to be tracked down by grievance-bearing diners that the door itself opened and the assistant assistant manager reeled out backwards through the gap, staring at some sight cut off by the door swinging shut behind him.

The weakly inefficient man of the day before was now in a complete state of non-function, gasping and looking faint. I fairly sprinted across the entrance hall carpet and caught him as he sagged.

'What is it?' I said.

He moaned slightly, his eyes rolling upwards, his weight growing heavier. I let him slide all the way to the carpet until he lay flat and spent a second or two pulling his tie loose. Then with a raised pulse and some shortening of my own breath I opened the door of the manager's office and went in.

It was here, I saw immediately, that the real business was done. Here in this office, very functional indeed, were all the forms, files and untidy heaps of paperwork in progress so conspicuously missing from Larry Trent's. Here there was a metal desk, old and scratched, with a plastic chair behind it and pots of pens among the clutter on its top.

There were stacks of miscellaneous stores in boldly labelled boxes all around: light bulbs, ashtrays, toilet rolls, tablets of soap. There was a floor-to-ceiling cupboard, open, spilling out stationery. There was a view through the single window to the sweep of drive outside, my van and Ridger's car in plain view. There was a sturdy safe the size of a tea-chest, its door wide, its interior bare: and there was the plain clothes constable sitting on the linoleum, his back against a wall, his head down between his knees.

Nothing in that place looked likely at first sight to cause mass unconsciousness. Nothing until one walked round to the chair behind the desk, and looked at the floor; and then I felt my own mouth go dry and my own heart beat suffocatingly against my ribs. There was no blood; but it was worse, much more disturbing than the accidental carnage in the tent.

On the floor, on his back, lay a man in grey trousers with a royal blue padded jacket above. Its zip was fully fastened up the front, I noted, concentrating desperately on details, and there was an embroidered crest sewn on one sleeve, and he was wearing brown shoes with grey socks. His neck was pinkish red above the jacket, the tendons showing tautly, and his arms and hands, neatly arranged, were crossed at the wrists over his chest, in the classic position of corpses.

He was dead. He had to be dead. For a head, above the bare stretched neck, he had a large white featureless globe like a giant puffball, and it was only when one fought down nausea and looked closely that one could see that from the throat up he had been entirely, smoothly and thickly encased in plaster of Paris.

SEVEN:

Retreating shakily I walked out of the office with every sympathy for the constable and the assistant assistant and leaned my back against the wall outside with trembling legs.

How could anyone be so barbaric, I wondered numbly. How could anyone do that, how could anyone think of it?

Sergeant Ridger emerged into the hall from the passage and came towards me, looking with more irritation than concern at the still prostrate assistant.

'What's the matter with him?' he said in his usual forceful way.

I didn't answer. He looked sharply at my face and said with more interest, 'What's the matter?'

'A dead man,' I said. 'In the office.'

He gave me a pitying look of superiority and walked purposefully through the door. When he came out he was three shades paler but still admirably in command and behaving every inch like a detective sergeant.

'Did you touch anything in there?' he asked me sharply. 'Any surface? Would your fingerprints be on anything?'

'No,' I said.

'Certain?'

'Certain.'

'Right.' He pulled out his radio, extended the aerial and said he needed top priority technical teams in connection with the death in suspicious circumstances of a so far unidentified male.

The disembodied voice in reply said that his message was timed at ten fifty-seven and would be acted upon. Ridger collapsed the aerial, put his head through the office door and crisply told his constable to come out of there, refrain from touching things and go outside for fresh air.

As much to himself as to me Ridger said, 'It won't be my case from now on.'

'Won't it?'

'Murder cases go to chief inspectors or superintendents.'

I couldn't tell from his voice whether he was pleased or sorry and concluded he simply accepted the hierarchy without resentment. I said reflectively, 'Is a man called Wilson anything to do with your force?'

'There are about four Wilsons. Which one do you mean?'

I described the hunch-shouldered quiet-mannered investigator and Ridger nodded immediately. 'That's Detective Chief Superintendent Wilson. He's not at our station, of course. He's head of the whole district. Near retirement, they say.'

I said that I'd met him at the Hawthorn accident, and Ridger guessed that Wilson had gone there himself because of the importance of the Sheik. 'Not his job, normally, traffic incidents.'

'Will he be coming here?' I asked.

'Shouldn't think so. He's too senior.'

I wondered in passing why a man of such seniority should come to my shop to ask questions instead of sending a constable, but didn't get to mentioning it to Ridger because at that point the assistant to the assistant manager began to return to life.

He was disorientated after his long faint, sitting up groggily and looking blankly at Ridger and me.

'What happened?' he said; and then without us telling him, he remembered. 'Oh my God . . .' He looked on the point of passing out again but instead pressed his hands over his eyes as if that would shut sight out of memory. 'I saw . . . I saw . . .'

'We know what you saw, sir,' said Ridger without sympathy. 'Can you identify that man? Is he the manager?'

The assistant assistant shook his head and spoke in a muffled voice through his hands. 'The manager's fat.'

'Go on,' Ridger prompted.

'It's Zarac,' said the assistant assistant. 'It's his jacket . . .'

'Who's Zarac?' Ridger said.

'The wine waiter.' The assistant assistant rose unsteadily to his feet and transferred his hands to his mouth before departing with heaving stomach towards the door marked 'Guys'.

'The wine waiter,' Ridger repeated flatly. 'Might have guessed.'

I pushed myself off the wall. 'You don't actually need me here, do you? I should go back to my shop.'

He thought it over briefly and agreed, saying he supposed he could find me easily if I were wanted. I left him standing virtual guard over the office door and went outside to my van, passing the constable who had relieved himself of his breakfast onto the drive.

'Cripes,' he said weakly in an endearing local accent, 'I've never seen anything like that.'

'Not an everyday sight,' I agreed, taking refuge in flippancy: and I thought that I too had seen enough horrors since Sunday to last a lifetime.

I bought more glasses at Tuesday lunchtime and ferried them and the wines to the Thames Ladies for their fund-raising; and little else of note happened for the next three days.

The news media reported briefly on the man with the plaster topping, but no words, I thought, conveyed anything like the shock of actually seeing that football-head lying there blank and inhuman, attached to a human neck.

Cutting off the plaster at the autopsy had confirmed the identity of the victim: Feydor Zaracievesa, British born of Polish descent, succinctly known as Zarac. He had been employed as wine waiter for eighteen months at the Silver Moondance, which had itself been open for business for almost three years. An inquest would shortly be held, it was said, and meanwhile the police were pursuing their enquiries.

Good luck to them, I thought. Pursue away.

On Tuesday, Wednesday and Thursday Mrs Palissey and Brian set off with the deliveries at four o'clock and at approximately four-thirty I stuck a notice on the shop door saying 'Open 6–9 pm' and scooted up the hill to go round the yard with Flora.

Shop hours as far as I was concerned were flexible, and I'd found it didn't much matter what one did as long as one said what one was doing. The pattern of when most customers came and when they stayed away was on the whole constant: a stream in the mornings, predominantly women, a trickle of either sex in the afternoons, a healthy flow, mostly men, in the evenings.

When Emma had been alive we had opened the shop on Friday and Saturday evenings only, but since I'd been alone I'd added Tuesday, Wednesday and Thursday, not simply for the extra trade, but for the company. I enjoyed the evenings. Most of the evening people came for wine, which I liked best to sell: a bottle to go with dinner, champagne for a job promotion, a present on the way to a party.

It was life on a small scale, I dared say. Nothing that would change history or the record books. A passage through time of ordinary mortal dimensions: but with Emma alongside it had contented.

I had never had much ambition, a sadness to my mother and a source of active irritation to my Wellington schoolmasters, one of whom on my last term's report had written acidly, 'Beach's conspicuous intelligence would take him far if only he would stir himself to choose a direction.' My inability to decide what I wanted to be (except not a solider) had resulted in my doing nothing much at all. I passed such exams as were thrust my way but hadn't been drawn to university. French, my best subject, was scarcely in itself a career. I didn't feel like a stockbroker or anything tidy in the City. I wasn't artistic. Had no ear for music. Couldn't face life behind a desk and couldn't ride boldly enough for racing. My only real ability throughout my teens had been a party trick of telling all makes of chocolate blindfold, which had hardly at that time seemed a promising foundation for gainful employment.

Six months after I left school I thought I might go to France for a while, ostensibly to learn the language better, but unhappily admitting to myself that it was to avoid being seen all too clearly as a disappointing failure at home. I could stand being a failure much better on my own.

By total chance, because of friends of friends of my despairing mother's, I was despatched to live as a paying guest with a family in Bordeaux, and it had meant nothing to me at first that my unknown host was a wine shipper. It was Monsieur Henri Tavel himself who had discovered that I could tell one wine from another, once I'd tasted them. He was the only adult I'd ever met who was impressed by my trick with the chocolate. He had laughed loudly and begun to set me tests with wine each evening, and I'd grown more confident the more I got them right.

It had still seemed a game, however, and at the end of the planned three months I'd returned home with still no idea of what to do next. My mother applauded my French accent but said it was hardly to be considered a lifetime's achievement, and I spent my days sneaking out of her sight as much as possible.

She had had to come looking for me the day the letter came, about a month after my return. She held it out in front of her, frowning at it as if it were incomprehensible.

'Monsieur Tavel suggests you go back,' she said. 'He is offering to train you. Train you in what, Tony darling?'

'Wine,' I said, feeling the first pricking of interest for many a long day.

'You?' She was puzzled more than amazed.

'To learn the trade, I expect,' I said.

'Good heavens.'

'Can I go?' I asked.

'Do you want to?' she said, astonished. 'I mean, have you actually found something you'd like to do?'

'I don't seem to be able to do anything else.'

'No,' she agreed prosaically: and she paid my fare again and my board and lodging with the family and a substantial fee to Monsieur Tavel for tuition.

Monsieur Tavel gave me a year's intensive instruction, taking me everywhere himself, showing me every stage of winemaking and shipping, teaching me rapidly what he'd spent a long lifetime learning, expecting me never to need telling twice.

I grew to feel at home in the Quai de Chatrons, where many doors into the warehouses were too narrow for modern lorries as a legacy from an ancient tax and where no wine could still be stored within a hundred yards of the street because it had been thought the vibration from horses' hooves on the quayside would upset it. In the de Luze warehouse, stretching nearly half a mile back, the staff went from end to end by bicycle.

In the city long buses had concertina central sections for turning sharp corners into narrow streets and in the country mimosa trees bloomed fluffily yellow in March, and everywhere, every day, all day, there was the talk and the smell of wine. By the time I left it, Bordeaux was my spiritual home. Henri Tavel hugged me with moist eyes and told me he could place me with de Luze or one of the other top *négociants* if I would stay: and sometimes since then I'd wondered why I hadn't.

On my return to England, armed with a too-flattering Tavel reference, I'd got a job with a wine shipper, but I was too junior for much besides paperwork and after the intensities of Bordeaux grew quickly bored. Impulsively one day I'd walked into a wine shop which said 'Help wanted' and offered my services, and in a short time began a brilliant non-stop career of lugging cases of booze from place to place.

'Tony works in a shop,' my mother would say bravely. My mother was nothing if not courageous. Large fences had to be met squarely. She also, in due course, made me an interest-free loan for basic stock for a shop of my own and had refused to accept repayments once I could afford to start them. As mothers went, in fact, mine wasn't at all bad.

Flora, in essence a more motherly lady, grew day by day less exhausted and depressed. Jack's leg was doing well and Jimmy was tentatively out of danger, although with pierced lungs, it seemed, one couldn't be sure for a fortnight.

Jimmy, Flora said, couldn't remember anything at all of the party. He couldn't remember escorting the Sheik round the yard. The last thing he could remember was talking to me about the Laphroaig; and he had been very shocked to learn that Larry Trent was dead.

'And Jack's spirits?' I asked. 'How are those?'

'Well, you know him, Tony dear, he hates to sit still, and he's growing more bad tempered by the minute, which I suppose I shouldn't say, but you know how he is. He'll be home by the weekend, he says, and he won't sit in a wheelchair, he wants crutches, and he's quite a weight, you know, to support on his arms, and not as young as he was.'

The daily reports, faithfully written by Flora and me, had not unduly cheered Jack, it appeared, because he thought we were keeping disasters from him; but as if in a burst of good luck after bad there had been fewer than usual sprains, knocks and skin eruptions among the string.

By Thursday the horsebox had gone, also the remains of the tent and the matting, only the churned lawn and the gap in the rose-hedge remaining.

'We'll never be able to walk on the grass without shoes,' Flora said. 'not that we ever do, come to that. But everywhere you look there are splinters of glass.'

She'd heard of course about the robbery and murder at the Silver Moondance and listened wide-eyed when I told her I'd been there again on the Tuesday morning. 'How awful,' she said, and 'Poor Larry . . .' and then with confusion, 'Oh dear, I'd forgotten for a minute . . . it's all so dreadful, so dreadful.'

On Wednesday she told me that Sally and Peter now knew who had let off the brakes of their horsebox. Sally had been again on the telephone, almost equally upset, telling Flora that the parents of the little boy were blaming Peter for leaving the doors unlocked and saying it was all Peter's fault, not their son's . They had denied at first that their child could have caused the accident and were very bitter about the fingerprints. Sally was saying they shouldn't have let their beastly brat run around unsupervised and should have taught it never to touch other people's property and especially never to get into strange cars or horseboxes and meddle.

'And who's right?' Flora asked rhetorically, sighing. 'They used to be friends and now they're all so miserable – it's awful.' She shook her head sadly. 'I wish we'd never had that party. We'll never have another, I don't suppose.'

By Thursday afternoon she was almost back to her old cosy self, handling the smarmy Howard on the stable round with sweet-natured assurance, and I said that unless she felt panic-stricken I wouldn't come the next day, Friday.

'Dear Tony, you've been such a rock, I can't tell you . . .' and she gave me a warm kiss on the cheek when I left and said she would see me again, very soon.

Friday proceeded up to a point in the way of most Fridays: morning extra-busy with customers and early afternoon spent making up the big load of orders for week-end delivery. Brian carried countless customers' goods for them personally to their parked cars and received their tips, beaming. Mrs Palissey gave him six Mars bars when she thought I wasn't looking and told me brightly that we were running out of Coca-Cola.

Mrs Chance came for her surreptitious gin. A wine shipper telephoned that he'd reserved me fifty cases of Beaujolais Nouveau for November 15th, and did I want more? (November 15th was to the drinks trade what August 12th was to the food: the race to be first with the new wine, as first with the grouse, was intense. I never waited for the Nouveau to be delivered but fetched it myself from the shipper very early on November 15th so as to be able to open my doors at practically dawn with it already displayed in the window. At least, I had done that for six years. Whether I would bother without Emma I wasn't sure. The fun had all gone. Wait and see.) Fifty cases would be fine, I said, considering Nouveau's short life: it was at its best sold and drunk before Christmas.

Mrs Palissey set off with Brian soon after three on the extra-long delivery round and someone rang up in a great fuss because I'd sent half the amount of beer ordered.

'Do you need it tonight?' I asked, apologising.

'No, Sunday, for after the village football match.'

'I'll bring it myself,' I said. 'Tomorrow morning at nine.'

In order not to forget I carried the beer immediately out of the back door to the Rover estate, and found on my return that I had a visitor in the shop in the quiet shape of Detective Chief Superintendent Wilson.

'Mr Beach,' he said as before, extending his hand.

'Mr Wilson,' I said, trying to smother my surprise and no doubt not succeeding.

'A bottle of wine,' he said with a small smile. 'For dinner. What do you suggest?'

He liked full-bodied red, he said, and I offered him a Rioja of distinction.

'Spanish?' he murmured dubiously, reading the label.

'Very well made,' I said. 'It's excellent.'

He said he would take my word for it and punctiliously paid. I rolled the bottle in tissue and stood it on the counter, but he was not, it appeared, in a hurry to pick it up and depart.

'Your chair . . .' he murmured. 'Would it be available?'

I fetched it at once from the office and he sat gratefully as before.

'A question or two, Mr Beach . . .' His gaze unhurriedly rested on my face and then wandered as if vaguely round the shop. 'I heard that you called in at the Silver Moondance last Tuesday morning, Mr Beach.'

'Yes,' I said.

'And wrote a list of the stolen goods.'

'As much as I could remember, yes.'

'And on Monday last you went there with Detective Sergeant Ridger and tasted various whiskies and wines?'

'Yes,' I said again.

'And you saw a certain Paul Young there?'

'Yes.'

His slow gaze finished its wandering and came to rest tranquilly on my face. 'Can you describe him, Mr Beach?'

That's why he's here, I thought. For that.

'Sergeant Ridger . . .' I began.

'Sergeant Ridger made a full description,' he said, nodding. 'But two sets of eyes . . . Mr Beach?'

I thought back and told him what I could remember of the man from the head office that didn't exist.

'A businessman,' I said. 'About fifty. Thickset, rather short, dark haired, pale skin. Big fleshy hands. No rings. He wore glasses with black frames, but narrow frames, not heavy. He had . . . um . . . the beginnings of a double chin . . . and a hearing aid behind his right ear.'

Wilson received the description benignly without giving me any indication of whether or not it was a carbon copy of Ridger's. 'His voice, Mr Beach?'

'No special accent,' I said. 'Plain English. I doubt if he'd been deaf from birth . . . he didn't sound toneless. He spoke ordinarily and heard everything anyone said. One wouldn't have known he was deaf without seeing the hearing aid.'

'And his manner, Mr Beach?'

'A bull,' I said without hesitation. 'Used to having people jump when he said so.' I thought back. 'He didn't seem like that at first sight, though. I mean, if he came in here now, he wouldn't seem aggressive . . . but he developed aggression very fast. He didn't like Sergeant Ridger's authority . . . he wanted to diminish him somehow.' I smiled faintly. 'Sergeant Ridger was pretty much a match for him.'

Wilson lowered his eyes briefly as if to avoid showing whatever comment lay there and then with a few blinks raised them again. 'Other impressions, Mr Beach?'

I pondered. 'Paul Young was definitely shocked to find so many bottles containing the wrong liquids.'

'Shocked that they did, or shocked that anyone had discovered it?'

'Well . . . at the time I thought it was the first, but now . . . I don't know. He was surprised and angry, that's for sure.'

Wilson rubbed his nose absentmindedly. 'Anything else, Mr Beach? Any insignificant little thing?'

'I don't know . . .'

A customer came in for several items at that point and wanted a detailed receipted bill, which I wrote for her: and the act of writing jogged a few dormant brain cells.

'Paul Young,' I said when she'd gone, 'had a gold coloured ball point with two wide black bands inset near the top. He wrote with his right hand, but with the pen between his first and second fingers and with the fingers curled round so that the pen was above what he was writing, not below. It looked very awkward. It looked how left-handed people sometimes write . . . but I'm sure he was right-handed. He wrote with the hand the same side as his hearing aid, and I was wondering why he didn't have the hearing aid incorporated into the frame of his glasses.'

Wilson incuriously studied the tissue wrapping his waiting bottle.

'Did Paul Young seem genuine to you, Mr Beach?'

'Oh, yes,' I said. 'He behaved very definitely as if the Silver Moondance belonged to an organisation of which he was an executive of the highest rank. He seemed at first only to have come himself to deal with the crisis of Larry Trent's death because the manager was away and the assistant manager had 'flu. The third in line, the assistant to the assistant, was so hopeless that it seemed perfectly natural that head office should appear in person.'

'Quite a long string of command, wouldn't you say?' murmured Wilson. 'Trent himself, a manager, an assistant, an assistant to the assistant?'

'I don't know,' I said, moderately disagreeing. 'A place like that, open long hours, half the night sometimes, they'd need that number. And the assistant assistant struck me as just a general dogsbody in togs above his station . . . poor chap.'

Wilson communed vaguely for a while with the South African sherries and then said, 'Would you know Paul Young again, Mr Beach? Could you pick him out in a roomful of people?'

'Yes,' I said positively. 'As long as I saw him again within a year. After that . . . I don't know. Maybe.'

'And in a photograph?'

'Um . . . it would depend.'

He nodded noncommittally and shifted on his chair.

'I've read Sergeant Ridger's reports. You've been most helpful all along, Mr Beach.'

'Sergeant Ridger did tell me,' I said mildly, 'who you are. I asked him if he knew of you, and he told me. And I've been surprised, you know, that you've come here yourself both times.'

He smiled patiently. 'I like to keep my hand in, Mr Beach, now and again. When I'm passing, you might say, for a bottle of wine.'

He stood up slowly, preparing to go, and I asked him the thing that had been on my mind since Tuesday.

'Was Zarac . . . the wine waiter . . . dead . . . before . . . ?'

I stopped in mid-sentence and he finished it for me. 'Dead before the plaster was applied? Since you asked, Mr Beach, no, he wasn't. Zarac died of suffocation.'

'Oh,' I said numbly.

'It is possible,' Wilson said unemotionally, 'that he had been knocked unconscious first. You may find that thought more bearable perhaps.'

'Is it true?'

'It's not for me to say before the coroner has decided.'

There was a bleakness, I saw, behind his undemanding face. He had been out there for a long time in the undergrowth and found it easy to believe in all manner of horrors.

'I don't think,' I said, 'that I would like your job.'

'Whereas yours, Mr Beach,' he said, his gaze roving the bottles, 'yours I would like very much.'

He gave me the small smile and the unemphatic handshake and went on his way: and I thought of people bandaging all over a live man's head and then soaking the bandage with water to turn it to rock.

EIGHT:

Flora sent Gerard McGregor down to see me: or so he said, that Friday evening, when he came into the shop.

He looked just as he had on Sunday when tunnelling away and hauling trestle tables through under the canvas for roofs. Tall, in his fifties, going grey. Ultra-civilised, with experienced eyes. Gerard with a soft J.

We shook hands again, smiling.

'My wife and I took Flora home to dinner with us yesterday evening,' he said. 'We insisted. She said it was chiefly thanks to you that she was feeling better.'

'No,' I said.

'She talked about you for hours.'

'How utterly boring. She can't have done.'

'You know how Flora talks.' His voice was affectionate. 'We heard all about you and Larry Trent and the goings on at the Silver Moondance.'

'I'm sorry,' I said.

'Whatever for? Fascinating stuff.'

Not for Zarac, I thought.

Gerard McGregor was looking around him with interest.

'We don't live so far from Flora,' he said. 'Five miles or so, but we shop in the opposite direction, not in this town. I've never been here before.' He began to walk down the row of wine racks, looking at labels. 'From what Flora said of the size of the trade you do, I somehow thought your shop would be bigger.' His faintly Scottish voice was without offence, merely full of interest.

'It doesn't need to be bigger,' I explained. 'In fact large brightly-lit expanses tend to put real wine-lovers off, if anything. This is just right, to my mind. There's room to show examples of everything I normally sell. I don't keep more than a dozen of many things out here. The rest's in the storeroom. And everything moves in and out pretty fast.'

The shop itself was about twenty-five feet by thirteen, or eight by four if one counted in metres. Down the whole of one long side there were wine racks in vertical columns, each column capable of holding twelve bottles (one case), the top bottle resting at a slant for display. Opposite the wine racks was the counter with, behind it, the shelves for spirits and liqueurs.

More wine racks took up the furthest wall except for the door through to the office and storeroom, and on every other inch of wall-space there were shelves for sherries, beers, mixers and coke and all the oddments that people asked for.

At the end of the counter, standing at a slight angle into the main floorspace, was a medium sized table covered to the ground with a pretty swagged tablecloth that Emma had made. A sheet of plate glass protected the top, and on it there stood a small forest of liqueur and aperitif and wine bottles, all opened, all available for customers to taste before buying. Coyly out of sight below the tablecloth stood open cartons of the same wines, ready to hand. We'd always sold a great deal because of the table: impulse buys leading to more and more repeat orders. Gerard fingered the bottles with interest, as so many did.

'Would you like to see behind the scenes?' I said, and he answered, 'Very much.'

I showed him my tiny office and also the tiny washroom, and the not-so-tiny storeroom beyond. 'That door,' I said, pointing, 'opens outward to the yard where we park the cars and load and unload deliveries. I usually keep it bolted. Through here is the storeroom.' I switched on the lights as the store had no window, and he looked with interest at the columns of cases ranged all round the walls and in a double row down the centre.

'I didn't always have as much stock as this,' I said. 'It was a terrible struggle to begin with. The storeroom was almost empty. Some weeks I'd buy things one afternoon, sell them the next morning and buy more with the same money again in the afternoon, and so on, round and round. Hair-raising.'

'But not now, I see.'

'Well, no. But it took us a while to get known, because this wasn't a wine shop before. We had to start from utter scratch.'

'We?' he said.

'My wife.'

'Oh yes . . . Flora said . . .'

'Yes,' I said flatly. 'She died.'

He made sympathetic motions with his hands, and we went back to the shop.

'When do you close?' he said, and suggested we might have dinner together.

'Is nine o'clock too late?'

Nine o'clock would do quite well, he said, and he returned at that time and drove me to a restaurant far outside my own catchment area. It seemed a long way to go, but he had reserved a table there, saying the food would be worth it.

We talked on the way about the accident and our excursions in the tent, and over dinner about Flora and Jack, and after that about the Silver Moondance and Larry Trent. We ate trout mousse followed by wild duck and he asked me to choose the wine. It was a pleasant enough evening and seemed purposeless; but it wasn't.

'What would you say,' he said casually over coffee, 'to a consultant's fee?'

'For what?'

'For what you're good at. Distinguishing one whisky from another.'

'I wouldn't mind the fee,' I said frankly. 'But I'm not an expert.'

'You've other qualities.' His eyes, it seemed to me, were all at once concentrating on my face as if he could read every hidden response I might have. 'Observation, resource and leadership.'

I laughed. 'Not me. Wrong guy.'

'I'd like to hire your services,' he said soberly, 'for one particular job.'

I said in puzzlement, 'What sort of job?'

For answer he felt in an inner pocket and drew out a sheet of paper which he unfolded and spread on the tablecloth for me to read: and it was a photostat copy, I saw in some bewilderment, of a page from the Yellow Pages telephone directory.

DETECTIVE AGENCIES, it said in capital letters at the top. Underneath were several boldly outlined box advertisements and a column of small firms. The word 'investigation' figured prominently throughout.

'I am one of the management team of that concern,' McGregor said, pointing to one of the bigger boxes.

'A private detective?' I asked, astounded. 'About the last thing I'd have guessed.'

'Mm.' McGregor's tone was dry. 'We prefer to be known as investigative consultants. Read the advertisement.'

I did as he asked.

'Deglet Ltd', it announced. 'Comprehensive service offered in complete confidence to commercial clients. Experienced consultants in the fields of industrial counter-espionage, fraud detection, electronic security, personnel screening. Business investigations of all sorts. International links.'

At the bottom there was a London box number and telex and telephone numbers, but no plain address. Confidential to the bone, I thought.

'No divorce?' I asked lightly.

'No divorce,' McGregor agreed easily. 'No debt collecting and no private clients. Commercial enquiries only.'

Any image one might have of mean streets didn't fit with McGregor. Boardrooms and country weekends, yes. Fist fights and sleazy night-life, no.

'Do you yourself personally . . .' I flicked a finger at the page, 'go rootling around in factories?'

'Not exactly.' He was quietly amused. 'When we're approached by a prospective client I go along to size up what's happening and what's needed, and then either alone or with colleagues, according to the size of the problem, I plan how to get results.'

There was a pause while I thought over what he had and hadn't so far told me. I evaded all the head-on questions and in the end said only, 'Don't you have any better business cards than photostats of the 'phone book?'

Unruffled, he said, 'We don't advertise anywhere else. We have no pamphlets or brochures and carry only personal cards ourselves. I brought the photostat to show you that we exist, and what we do.'

'And all your business comes from the Yellow Pages?' I asked.

He nodded. 'And from word of mouth. Also, of course, once-satisfied clients call upon us again whenever they need us, which believe me the larger corporations do constantly.'

'You enjoy your job?'

'Very much,' he said. I listened to the quiet assurance in his depths and thought that I wasn't a hunter and never would be. Not I, who ducked through gates to avoid jumping fences, even if the fox escaped.

'Occasionally,' he said conversationally, 'we're asked to

investigate in areas for which none of our regular people are ideal.'

I looked at my coffee.

'We need someone now who knows whisky. Someone who can tell malt whisky from grain whisky, as Flora says you can.'

'Someone who knows a grain from the great grey green greasy Limpopo River?' I said. 'The Limpopo River, don't forget, was full of crocodiles.'

'I'm not asking you to do anything dangerous,' he said reasonably.

'No.' I sighed. 'Go on, then.'

'What are you doing on Sunday?' he said.

'Opening the shop from twelve to two. Washing the car. Doing the crossword.' Damn all, I thought.

'Will you give me the rest of your day from two o'clock on?' he asked.

It sounded harmless, and in any case I still felt considerable camaraderie with him because of our labours in the tent, and Sundays after all were depressing, even without horseboxes.

'O.K.' I said. 'Two o'clock onwards. What do you want me to do?'

He was in no great hurry, it seemed, to tell me. Instead he said, 'Does all grain whisky taste the same?'

'That's why you need a real expert,' I said. 'The answer is no it doesn't quite, but the differences are small. It depends on the grain used and the water, and how long the spirit's been aged.'

'Aged?'

'Newly distilled scotch,' I said, 'burns your throat and scrubs your tongue like fire. It has to be stored in wooden casks for at least three years to become drinkable.'

'Always in wood?'

'Yes. Wood breathes. In wooden casks all spirit grows blander but if you put it in metal or glass containers instead it stays the same for ever. You could keep newly distilled spirits a thousand years in glass and when you opened it it would be as raw as the day it was bottled.'

'One lives and learns,' he said.

'Anyway,' I added after a pause. 'Practically no one sells pure grain whisky. Even the cheapest bulk whisky is a blend of grain and malt, though the amount of malt in some of them is like a pinch of salt in a swimming pool.'

'Flora said you told her some of the scotch at the Silver Moondance was like that,' McGregor said.

'Yes, it was. They were selling it in the bar out of a Bell's bottle, and in the restaurant as Laphroaig.'

McGregor called for the bill. 'This wasn't my case to begin with,' he said almost absentmindedly as he sorted out a credit card. 'One of my colleagues passed it on to me because it seemed to be developing so close to my own doorstep.'

'Do you mean,' I asked, surprised, 'that your firm were already interested in the Silver Moondance?'

'That's right.'

'But how? I mean, in what connection?'

'In connection with some stolen scotch that we were looking for. And it seems, my dear Tony, that you have found it.'

'Good grief,' I said blankly. 'And lost it again.'

'I'm afraid so. We're very much back where we started. But that's hardly your fault, of course. If Jack's secretary had been less fond of Laphroaig . . . if Larry Trent hadn't invited him to dinner . . . One can go back and back saying "if", and it's profitless. We were treading delicately towards the Silver Moondance when the horsebox plunged into the marquee; and it's ironic in the extreme that I didn't know that the Arthur Lawrence Trent who owned that place had horses in training with Jack, and I didn't know he was at the party. I didn't know him by sight . . . and I didn't know that he was one of the men we found dead. If I'd known he was going to be at the party I'd have got Jack or Flora to introduce me.' He shrugged, 'If and if.'

'But you were . . . um . . . investigating him?' I asked.

'No,' McGregor said pleasantly. 'The person we suspected was an employee of his. A man called Zarac.'

I'm sure my mouth physically dropped open. Gerard McGregor placidly finished paying the bill, glancing with dry understanding at my face.

'Yes, he's dead,' he said. 'We really are totally back at the beginning.'

'I don't consider,' I said intensely, 'that Zarac is a matter of no crocodiles.'

I spent most of Saturday with my fingers hovering over the telephone, almost deciding at every minute to ring Flora and ask her for Gerard McGregor's number so that I could cancel my agreement for Sunday. If I did nothing he would turn up at two o'clock and whisk me off heaven knew where to meet his client, the one whose scotch had turned up on my tongue. (Probably.)

In the end I did ring Flora but even after she'd answered I was still shilly-shallying.

'How's Jack?' I said.

'In a vile temper, I'm afraid, Tony dear. The doctors won't let him come home for several more days. They put a rod right down inside his bone, through the marrow, it seems, and they want to make sure it's all settled before they let him loose on crutches.'

'And are you all right?'

'Yes, much better every day.'

'A friend of yours,' I said slowly, 'came to see me. Er . . . Gerard McGregor.'

'Oh yes,' Flora said warmly. 'Such a nice man. And his wife's such a dear. He said you and he together had helped a good few people last Sunday. He asked who you were, and I'm afraid, Tony dear, that I told him quite a lot about you and then about everything that happened at the Silver Moondance, and he seemed frightfully interested though it seems to me now that I did go on and on a bit.'

'I don't think he minded,' I said soothingly. 'Um . . . what does he do, do you know?'

'Some sort of business consultant, I believe. All those jobs are so frightfully vague, don't you think? He's always travelling all over the place, anyway, and Tina . . . that's his wife . . . never seems to know when he'll be home.'

'Have you known them long?' I asked.

'We met them at other people's parties several times before we really got to know them, which would be about a year ago.'

'I mean . . . has he always lived near here?'

'Only about five years, I think. They were saying the other evening how much they preferred it to London even though Gerard has to travel more. He's such a clever man, Tony dear, it just oozes out of his pores. I told him he should buy some wine from you, so perhaps he will.'

'Perhaps,' I said. 'Er . . . do you have his telephone number?'

'Of course,' Flora said happily, and found it for me. I wrote it down and we disconnected, and I was still looking at it indeterminately at nine o'clock when I closed the shop.

* * *

'I half expected you to cry off,' he said, when he picked me up at two the next day.

'I half did.'

'But?'

'Curiosity, I suppose.'

He smiled. Neither of us pointed out that it was curiosity that got the Elephant's Child into deep trouble with the crocodiles in the Limpopo River, though it was quite definitely in my mind, and Gerard, as he had told me to call him, was of the generation that would have had the *Just So Stories* fed to him as a matter of course.

He was dressed that afternoon in a wool checked shirt, knitted tie and tweed jacket, much like myself, and he told me we were going to Watford.

I sensed a change in him immediately I'd committed myself and was too far literally along the road to ask him to turn back. A good deal of surface social manner disappeared and in its place came a tough professional attitude which I felt would shrivel irrelevant comment in the utterer's throat. I listened therefore in silence, and he spoke throughout with his eyes straight ahead, not glancing to my face for reactions.

'Our client is a man called Kenneth Charter,' he said. 'Managing Director and Founder of Charter Carriers, a company whose business is transporting bulk liquids by road in tankers. The company will transport any liquid within reason, the sole limiting factor being that it must be possible to clean the tanker thoroughly afterwards, ready for a change of contents. Today's hydrochloric acid, for instance, must not contaminate next week's crop-sprayer.'

He drove steadily, not fast, but with easy judgement of available space. A Mercedes, fairly new, with velvety upholstery and a walnut dash, automatic gears changing on a purr.

'More than half of their business,' he went on, 'is the transport of various types of inflammable spirit, and in this category they include whisky.' He paused. 'It's of course in their interest if they can arrange to pick up one load near to where they deliver another, the limiting factor again being the cleaning. They have steam cleaning facilities and chemical scrubbing agents at their Watford headquarters, but these are not readily available everywhere. In any case, one of their regular runs has been to take bulk gin to Scotland, wash out the tanker with water, and bring scotch back.'

He stopped talking to navigate through a town of small

streets, and then said, 'While the scotch is in the tanker it is considered to be still in a warehouse. That is to stay, it is still in bond. Duty has not been paid.'

I nodded. I knew that.

'As Charter's tankers carry six thousands imperial gallons,' Gerard said neutrally, 'the amount of duty involved in each load is a good deal more than a hundred thousand pounds. The whisky itself, as you know, is of relatively minor worth.'

I nodded slightly again. Customs and Excise duty, value added tax and income tax paid by the shopkeeper meant that three-quarters of the selling price of every standard bottle of whisky went in one way or another to the inland revenue. One quarter paid for manufacture, bottles, shipping, advertising, and all the labour force needed between the sowing of the barley and the wrapping in a shop. The liquid itself, in that context, cost practically nothing.

'Three times this year,' Gerard said, 'a tanker of Charter's hasn't reached its destination. It wouldn't be accurate to say the tanker was stolen, because on each occasion it turned up. But the contents of course had vanished. The contents each time were bulk scotch. The Customs and Excise immediately demanded duty since the scotch was no longer in the tanker. Charter Carriers have twice had to pay up.'

He paused as if to let me catch up with what he was saying.

'Charter Carriers are of course insured, or have been, and that's where they've run into serious trouble. The insurers, notwithstanding that they rocketed their premiums on each past occasion, now say that enough is enough, they are not satisfied and are withholding payment. They also say no further cover will be extended. Charter's face having to raise the cash themselves, which would be crippling, but more seriously they can't operate without insurance. On top of that the Customs and Excise are threatening to take away their licence to carry goods in bond, which would in itself destroy a large part of their business.' He paused again for appreciable seconds. 'The Excise people are investigating the latest theft, but chiefly because they want the duty, and the police also, but routinely. Charter's feel that this isn't enough because it in no way guarantees the continuation of their licence or the reinstatement of their insurance. They're extremely worried indeed, and they applied to us for help.'

We were speeding by this time along the M40. Another

silence lengthened until Gerard eventually said, 'Any questions?'

'Well . . . dozens, I suppose.'

'Such as?'

'Such as why was it always the scotch that was stolen and not the gin? Such as was it always the same driver and was it always the same tanker? Such as what happened to the driver, did he say? Such as where did the tankers turn up? Such as how did you connect it all with Zarac?'

He positively grinned, his teeth showing in what looked like delight.

'Anything else?' he asked.

'Such as where did the scotch start from and where was it supposed to be going and how many crooks have you turned up at each place, and such as does Kenneth Charter trust his own office staff and why wasn't his security invincible third time around?'

I stopped and he said without sarcasm, 'Those'll do to be going on with. The answers I can give you are that no it wasn't always the same driver but yes it was always the same tanker. The tanker turned up every time abandoned in Scotland in transport café carparks, but always with so many extra miles on the clock that it could have been driven as far as London or Cardiff and back.'

Another pause, then he said, 'The drivers don't remember what happened to them.'

I blinked. 'Don't remember?'

'No. They remember setting off. They remember driving as far as the English border, where they all stopped at a motorway service station for a pee. They stopped at two different service stations. None of them remembers anything else except waking up in a ditch. Never the same ditch.' He smiled. 'After the second theft Kenneth Charter made it a rule that on that run no one was to eat or drink in cafés. The drivers had to take what they wanted with them in the cab. All the same they still had to stop for nature. The police say the thieves must have been following the tanker each time, waiting for that. Then when the driver was out of the cab, they put in an open canister of gas . . . perhaps nitrous oxide, which has no smell and acts fast . . . it's what dentists use . . . and when the driver climbed back in he'd be unconscious before he could drive off.'

'How regular was that run?' I asked.

'Normally twice a week.'

'Always the same tanker?'

'No,' he said contentedly. 'Charter's keep four tankers exclusively for drinkable liquids. One of those. The other three made the run just as often, but weren't touched. It may be coincidence, maybe not.'

'How long ago was the last load stolen?' I asked.

'Three weeks last Wednesday.'

'And before that?'

'One in April, one in June.'

'That's three in six months,' I said, surprised.

'Yes, exactly.'

'No wonder the insurers are kicking up a fuss.'

'Mm.' He drove quietly for a while and then said, 'Every time the scotch was destined for the same place, a bottling plant at Watford, north of London. The scotch didn't however always come from the same distillery, or the same warehouse. The stolen loads came from three different places. The last lot came from a warehouse near Helensburgh in Dunbartonshire, but it set off from there in the normal way and we don't think that's where the trouble is.'

'In the bottling plant?' I asked.

'We don't know, for sure, but we don't think so. The lead to the Silver Moondance looked so conclusive that it was decided we should start from there.'

'What was the lead?' I said.

He didn't answer immediately but in the end said, 'I think Kenneth Charter had better tell you himself.'

'O.K.'

'I should explain,' he said presently, 'that when firms call us in it's often because there are things they don't necessarily want to tell the police. Companies very often like to deal privately, for instance, with frauds. By no means do they always want to prosecute, they just want the fraud stopped. Public admission that a fraud was going on under their noses can be embarrassing.'

'I see,' I said.

'Kenneth Charter told me certain things in confidence which he didn't tell the police or the Customs and Excise. He wants his transport firm to survive, but not at any price. Not if the price in personal terms is too high. He agreed I should bring you in as a consultant, but I'll leave it to him to decide how much he wants you to know.'

'All right,' I said peacefully.

We left the motorway and Gerard began threading his way across the semi-suburban sprawl to the north of London where one town ran into another without noticeable difference.

'You're an undemanding sort of man,' Gerard observed after a while.

'What should I demand?'

'How much a consultancy fee is, perhaps. Conditions, maybe. Assurances.'

'Life's like the weather,' I said wryly. 'What comes, comes. Even with a sunny forecast you can get wet.'

'A fatalist.'

'It rains. You can't stop it.'

He glanced at my face for almost the first time on the journey, but I doubt if he read much there. I'd spoken not bitterly but with a sort of tiredness, result of failing to come to terms with my own private deluge. I was in truth quite interested in the stolen scotch and the tankers, but it was on an upper and minor level, not down where it mattered.

As if sensing it he said, 'You'll do your best for me?'

'Such as it is,' I assured him. 'Yes.'

He nodded as if a doubt had been temporarily stilled and turned off the road into an industrial area where small factories had sprung like recent mushrooms in a concrete field. The fourth on the right bore the words 'Charter Carriers Ltd' in large red letters on a white board attached to the front, while down the side, like piglets to a sow, stretched a long row of silver tankers side by side, engines inwards, sterns out.

NINE:

Kenneth Charter wasn't in the least what I expected, which was, I suppose, a burly North Londoner with a truculent manner. The man who came into the entrance hall to greet us as we pushed through the glass front door was tall, thin, reddish-haired and humorous with an accent distinctly more Scottish than Gerard's faint Highland.

'Is this the consultant?' he said with a lilt. He found my youth more a matter of laughter than concern, it seemed. 'No greybeard, are you?' He shook my hand firmly. 'Come away in, then. And how are you today, Mr McGregor?'

He led the way into a square uninspiring cream-walled office and waved us to two upright armless chairs facing a large unfussy modern desk. There was a brown floor-covering of utilitarian matting, a row of grey filing cabinets, a large framed map of the British Isles and a settled chill in the air which might or might not have been because it was Sunday. Kenneth Charter seemed not to notice it and offered no comment. He had the Scots habit, I suspected, of finding sin in comfort and virtue in thrift and believing morality grew exclusively in a cold climate.

Gerard and I sat in the offered chairs. Kenneth Charter took his place behind his desk in a swivelling chair which he tilted recklessly backward.

'How much have you told this bonny expert?' he said, and listened without visible anxiety to Gerard's recapitulation.

'Well, now,' he said to me cheerfully at the end, 'You'll want to know what liquid you're looking for. Or could you guess, laddie, could you guess?' His very blue eyes were quizzically challenging, and I did a quick flip and a turnover through past occasional nips in customers' houses and sought for a check against the memory from the bar of the Silver Moondance and said on an instinctive, unreasoned impulse, 'Rannoch.'

Charter looked cynical and said to Gerard, 'You told him, then.'

Gerard shook his head. 'I didn't.' He himself was looking

smug. His consultant, it seemed, had come up trumps at the first attempt.

'I guessed,' I said mildly. 'I sell that make. I've tasted it quite a few times. There aren't so many whiskies that would be shipped in bulk and bottled in England. Rannoch . . . just fitted.'

'Very well, then.' He opened a drawer in his desk and produced from it a full bottle of Rannoch whisky, the familiar label adorned with an imposing male kilted figure in red and yellow tartan. The seal, I noticed, was unbroken, and Charter showed no signs of altering that.

'A Christmas gift from the bottling company,' he said.

'Last Christmas?' I asked.

'Of course last Christmas. We'll not be getting one this year, now will we?'

'I guess not,' I said meekly. 'I meant . . . it's a long time for the bottle to be full.'

He chuckled. 'I don't drink alcohol, laddie. Addles your brains, rots your gut. What's more, I can't stand the taste. We need someone like you because I wouldn't recognise that stolen load of firewater if it turned up in the pond in my garden.'

The goldfish would tell him, I thought. They'd die.

'Did you have a profile of that load?' I asked.

'A what?'

'Um . . . its composition. What it was blended from. You could get a detailed list from the distiller, I should think. The profile is a sort of chemical analysis in the form of a graph . . . it looks something like the skyline of New York. Each different blend shows a different skyline. The profile is important to some people . . . the Japanese import scotch by profile alone, though actually a perfect-looking profile can taste rotten. Anyway, profiles are minutely accurate. Sort of like human tissue typing . . . a lot more advanced than just a blood test.'

'All I can tell you is it was fifty-eight per cent alcohol by volume,' Charter said. 'The same strength as always with Rannoch. It's here on the manifest.' He produced from a drawer a copy of the Customs and Excise declaration and pushed it across for me to see. 'I don't ask what's in the stuff, I just ferry it.'

'We'll get on to the profile straight away,' Gerard murmured.

'The Customs people probably have already,' I said. 'They'll have the equipment. A gas chromatograph.'

I had an uncomfortable feeling that Gerard was thinking I should have told him about profiles on the way, but it hadn't crossed my mind.

'I mean,' I said, 'if they took a sample from the distillers and matched it with the sample the police took from the Silver Moondance, they would know for sure one way or another.'

There was a silence. Finally Gerard cleared his throat and said, 'Perhaps you might tell Tony how we were led to the Silver Moondance. Because at this moment,' he looked straight at me, 'there is no reason for the Customs to connect that place to the stolen tanker or to compare the samples. They aren't aware of any link.'

I said 'Oh' fairly vaguely and Kenneth Charter consulted the ceiling, tipping his chair back to where it should surely have overbalanced. He finally let his weight fall forward with a thud and gave me the full blast from his blue eyes.

'Promise of silence, laddie,' he said.

I looked at Gerard, who nodded off-handedly as if such demands were an everyday business fact, which I supposed to him they were.

'Promise of silence,' I said.

Kenneth Charter nodded his long head sharply as if taking it for granted that promises would be kept; then he pulled a bunch of keys from his pocket and unlocked the centre drawer of his desk. The object within needed no searching for. He pulled out a small slim black notebook and laid it on the desk before him, the naturally humorous cast of his face straightening to something like grimness.

'You can trust this laddie?' he said to Gerard.

'I'd believe so.'

Charter sighed, committed, turned to the page that fell open immediately in a way that spoke of constant usage.

'Read that,' he said, turning the notebook round for me to see but retaining it under the pressure of his thumb. 'That' was a long telephone number beginning with 0735, which was the code for the Reading area, with underneath it two lines of writing.

'*Tell Z UNP 786 Y picks up B's Gin Mon 10 a.m. approx.*

'I've read it,' I said, not knowing what exactly was expected.

'Mean anything?'

'I suppose it's the Silver Moondance number, and Z is Zarac?'

'Right. And UNP 786 Y is the registration number of my tanker.' His voice was cold and unemotional.

'I see,' I said.

'Berger's Gin is where it set out from at 10.15 a.m. a month ago tomorrow. It went to Scotland, discharged the gin, was sluiced through in Glasgow and picked up the bulk scotch at Fairley's warehouse near Helensburgh, in Dunbartonshire. Wednesday morning it set off from there. Wednesday evening it didn't arrive at the bottling plant. By Thursday morning we know it was parked outside a drivers' café on the outskirts of Edinburgh, but it wasn't identified until Friday as its registration plates had been changed. The Customs and Excise have impounded it, and we haven't got it back.'

I looked at Gerard and then again at Kenneth Charter.

'And you know,' I said slowly. 'You know who wrote the message.'

'Yes, I do,' he said. 'My son.'

Highly complicating, as Gerard had hinted.

'Um . . .' I said, trying to make my question as non-committal as Charter's own voice. 'What does your son say? Does he know where the bulk in the tanker vanished to? Because . . . er . . . six thousand gallons of scotch can't be hidden all that easily, and the Silver Moondance wouldn't use three times that much in six years, let alone six months . . . if you see.'

The blue eyes if anything grew more intense. 'I haven't spoken to my son. He went to Australia two weeks ago for a holiday and I don't expect him back for three months.'

There was an element of good riddance in that statement, I thought. He wasn't so much grieving over his offspring's treason as finding it thoroughly awkward. I smiled at him faintly without thinking and to my surprise he grinned suddenly and broadly back.

'You're right,' he said. 'The little bugger can stay there, as far as I'm concerned. I'm certainly not trying to fetch him home. I don't want him charged and tried and maybe flung in jail. I don't, I definitely don't want any son of mine behind bars embarrassing the whole family. Making his mother cry, spoiling his sister's wedding next spring, messing up his brother's chances of a degree in law. If I have to sell up here, well, I will. There'll be enough left for me to start something else. And that's the end of the damage that sod will do. I won't have him casting a worse blight on the family.'

'No,' I said slowly. 'When was it, did you say, that he went to Australia?'

'Two weeks ago yesterday, laddie. I took him to Heathrow myself. When I got home I found this notebook on the floor of the car, fallen out of his pocket. I guess he's sweating now, hoping like hell he dropped it anywhere but at my very feet. I opened it to make sure it was his.' Charter shrugged, locking it back into the desk drawer. 'It was his, all right. His writing. Nothing much in it, just a few telephone numbers and lists of things to do. He always made lists of things to do, right from when he was small.'

Something like regret touched Kenneth Charter's mouth. Any son, I supposed, was loved when small, before he grew up a disappointment.

'The tanker's number sort of shouted at me,' he said. 'I felt sick, I'll tell you. My own son! There were the police and the Customs and Excise chasing all over the place looking for the crook who tipped off the thieves, and he'd been right there in my own house.' He shook his head in disgust. 'So then I took advice from a business I knew who'd had their troubles sorted out for them quietly, and I got on to Deglet's, and finally Mr McGregor, here. And there you have it, laddie.'

Kenneth Charter's son, I was thinking, had gone to Australia ten days after the scotch had been stolen and a week before the horsebox had rolled into the marquee. If he was truly in Australia, he'd had nothing to do with the disappearance of the Silver Moondance's liquid assets or the murder of Zarac. For such small crumbs his father could be grateful.

'Would it be easy for your son to find out when exactly the tanker would be going to fetch whisky?' I asked diffidently.

'Back in April, yes, easy. In June, not so easy. Last month, damned difficult. But there you are, I didn't know I had to defend myself so close to home.' Kenneth Charter got to his feet, his big body seeming to rise forever. He grasped the frame of the map of the British Isles and gave it a tug, and the map opened away from the wall like a door, showing a second chart beneath.

The revealed chart was an appointments calendar with registration numbers in a long column down the left hand side, and dates across the top.

'Tankers,' Charter said succinctly, pointing to the registration numbers. 'Thirty-four of them. There's UNP 786 Y, sixth from the top.'

All the spaces across from that number had a line drawn through: tanker out of commission. For many of the others some of the spaces across were filled with stuck on labels of many colours, blue, green, red, yellow, grey, purple, orange, each label bearing a handwritten message.

'We use the labels to save time,' Charter said. 'Purple for instance is always hydrochloric acid. We can see at a glance which tanker is carrying it. On the label it says where from, where to. Grey is gin, yellow is whisky. Red is wine. Blue is sulphuric acid. Green is any of several disinfectants. And so on. My secretary, whom I trust absolutely, she's been with me twenty years, writes the labels and keeps the chart. We don't as a company tell the drivers where they're going or what they're carrying until the moment they set out. They change tankers regularly. We often switch drivers at the last minute. Some of the loads could be dangerous, see, if they fell into the wrong hands. We have an absolute rule that all the tanker doors have to be locked if the drivers so much as set foot out of the cabs, and in all three stolen loads the drivers swore they did that, and found nothing to alarm them when they returned. We've been careful and until this year we've been fortunate.' His voice was suddenly full of suppressed fury. 'It took my own son . . . my own son . . . to crack our system.'

'He could come in here, I suppose,' I said.

'Not often, he didn't. I told him if he wouldn't work in the company, he could stay away. He must have sneaked in here somehow, but I don't know when. He knew about the chart, of course. But since the first two thefts I've not allowed the whisky labels to be written up, just in case the leak was in our own company. Yellow labels, see? All blank. So if he saw the yellow label for that tanker for the Wednesday, it wouldn't say where it was picking up. Grey for gin, on the Monday, that was written up, but only for the pick up, not the destination. If someone wanted to steal the return load of scotch they'd have to follow the tanker all the way from Berger's Gin distillery to find out where it was going.'

I frowned, thinking the theory excessive, but Gerard was nodding as if such dedication to the art of theft was commonplace.

'Undoubtedly what happened,' Gerard said. 'But the question remains, to whom did Zarac pass on that message? He didn't take part in the event himself. He wasn't away from the Silver Moondance long enough, and was definitely at his post both the Tuesday and Wednesday lunchtimes and also in the evening until after midnight. We checked.'

My mind wandered from the problem I didn't consider very closely my own (and in any case unanswerable) and I found my attention fastening on the few red labels on the chart. All the information on them had been heavily crossed out, as indeed it had on the grey labels as well. Kenneth Charter followed my gaze, his hairy Scots eyebrows rising.

'The wine,' I said, almost apologetically. 'Didn't you say red for wine?'

'Aye, I did. All those shipments have had to be cancelled. Normally we fetch it from France and take it direct to the shippers near here, who bottle it themselves. We used to carry a lot more wine once, but they bottle more of it in France now. Half the bottling plants over here have been scratching round for new business. Hard times, laddie. Closures. Not their fault. The world moves on and changes. Always happening. Spend your life learning to make longbows, and someone invents guns.'

He closed the chart into its secrecy behind the map and dusted his hands on his trousers as if wiping off his son's perfidy.

'There's life in tankers yet,' he observed. 'D'you want to see them?'

I said yes, please, as they were clearly his pride, and we left his office with him carefully locking the door behind us. He led the way not to the outside but down a passage lined on either side by office doors and through a heavier door, also locked, at the far end. That door led directly into a large expanse given to the maintenance and cleaning of the silver fleet. There was all the paraphernalia of a commercial garage: inspection pit, heavy-duty jacks, benches with vices, welding equipment, a rack of huge new tyres. Also, slung from the ceiling, chains and machinery for lifting. Two tankers stood in this space, receiving attention from men in brown overalls who from their manner already knew Charter was around on Sunday afternoon and gave Gerard and myself cursory incurious glances.

'Over there,' Charter said, pointing, 'down that side, inside that walled section, we clean the tanks, pumps, valves and hoses. The exteriors go through a carwash outside.' He began walking down the garage, expecting us to follow. The mechanics called him Ken and told him there was trouble with an axle, and I looked with interest at the nearest tanker, which seemed huge to me, indoors.

The tank part was oval in section, resting solidly on its chassis with what I guessed was a low centre of gravity, to make overturning a minor hazard. There was a short ladder bolted on at the back so that one could climb onto the top, where there were the shapes of hatches and loading gear. The silver metal was unpainted and carried no information as to its ownership, only the words 'Flammable Liquid' in small red capitals towards the rear.

The paintwork of the cab, a dark brownish red, was also devoid of name, address and telephone number. The tanker was anonymous, as the whole fleet was, I later saw. Kenneth Charter's security arrangements had kept them safe for years from every predator except the traitor within.

'Why did he do it?' Charter said from over my shoulder, and I shook my head, not knowing.

'He was always jealous as a little boy, but we thought he'd grow out of it.' He sighed. 'The older he got the more bad tempered he was, and sullen, and dead lazy. I tried to speak kindly to him but he'd be bloody rude back and I'd have to go out of the room so as not to hit him sometimes.' He paused, seeking no doubt for the thousandth time for guilt in himself, where there was none. 'He wouldn't work. He seemed to think the world owed him a living. He'd go out and refuse to say where he'd been, and he wouldn't lift a finger to help his mother in the house. He sneered all the time at his brother and sister, who are bonny kids. I offered him his fare to Australia and some money to spend there, and he said he'd go. I hoped, you know, that they'd knock some sense into him over there.' His tall body moved in a sort of shudder. 'I'd no idea he'd done anything criminal. He was a pain in the arse . . . Didn't he know he would ruin me in this business? Did he care? Did he mean to?'

The son sounded irredeemable to me and for the sake of the rest of the Charter family I hoped he'd never come home, but life was seldom so tidy.

'Mr McGregor may save your business,' I said, and he laughed aloud in one of his mercurial changes of mood and clapped me on the shoulder. 'A politician, Mr McGregor, that's what you've brought me here. Aye, laddie, so he may, so he may for the healthy fee I'm paying him.'

Gerard smiled indulgently and we walked on through the

length of the maintenance area and out through the door at the far end. Outside, as Charter had said, there was a tall commercial-sized car wash, but he turned away from that and led us round to the side of the building to where the fleet of tankers nestled in line.

'We've some out on the road,' Charter said. 'And I'm having to arrange huge insurance for every one separately, which is wiping out our profit. I've drivers sitting at home watching television and customers going elsewhere. We can't carry alcohol, the Customs won't let us. It's illegal for this company to operate if it can't pay its workforce and other debts; and I reckon we can keep running on reserves for perhaps two weeks from now, if we're lucky. We could be shut down in five minutes then if the bank foreclosed on the tankers, which they will. Half of these tankers at any one time are being bought on loans, and if we can't service the loans, we're out.' He smoothed a loving hand over one of the gleaming monsters. 'I'll be bloody sorry, and that's a fact.'

The three of us walked soberly along the imposing row until we were back at the entrance, and Gerard's car.

'Two weeks, Mr McGregor,' Kenneth Charter said. He shook our hands vigorously. 'Hardly a sporting chance, would you say?'

'We'll try for results,' Gerard assured him in a stockbroker voice, and we climbed into his car and drove away.

'Any thoughts?' he asked me immediately, before we'd even left the industrial estate.

'Chiefly,' I said, 'why you need me at all.'

'For your knowledge, as I told you. And because people talk to you.'

'How do you mean?'

'Kenneth Charter told you far more about his son than he told me. Flora says she talks to you because you listen. She says you hear things that aren't said. I was most struck by that. It's a most useful ability in a detective.'

'I'm not . . .'

'No. Any other thoughts?'

'Well . . .' I said. 'Did you see the rest of the son's notebook, when you were there before?'

'Yes, I did. Charter didn't want me to take it for some reason, so I used his photocopier to reproduce every page that was written on. As he said, there were just some telephone numbers and a few memos about things to do. We've checked on all the telephone numbers these last few days but they seem to be harmless. Friends' houses, a local cinema, a snooker club and a barber. No lead to how the son knew Zarac, if that's what you're thinking.'

'Yes,' I said.

'Mm. I'll show you the photostats presently. See if you can suggest anything we've missed.'

Unlikely, I thought.

'Is he actually in Australia?' I asked.

'The son? Yes, he is. He stayed in a motel in Sydney the night he arrived. His father made the reservation, and the son did stay there. We checked. Beyond that, we've lost him, except that we know he hasn't used his return ticket. Quite possibly he doesn't know Zarac's dead. If he does know, he's likely to drop even further out of sight. In any case, Kenneth Charter's instructed us not to look for him, and we'll comply with that. We're having to work from the Silver Moondance end, and frankly, since Zarac's murder, that's far from easy.'

I reflected for a while and then said, 'Can you pick the police brains at all?'

'Sometimes. It depends.'

'They'll be looking for Paul Young,' I said.

'Who?'

'Did Flora mention him? A man who came to the Silver Moondance from what he said was head office. He arrived while I was there with Detective Sergeant Ridger, who took me there to taste the Laphroaig.'

Gerard frowned as he drove. 'Flora said one of the managers had come in when you were tasting the whisky and wine, and was furious.'

I shook my head. 'Not a manager.' I told Gerard in detail about Paul Young's visit, and he drove more and more slowly as he listened.

'That makes a difference,' he said almost absently when I'd finished. 'What else do you know that Flora didn't tell me?'

'The barman's homosexual,' I said flippantly. Gerard didn't smile. 'Well,' I sighed, 'Larry Trent bought a horse for thirty thousand pounds, did she tell you that?'

'No . . . Is that important?'

I related the saga of the disappearing Ramekin. 'Maybe the Silver Moondance made that sort of money, but I doubt it,' I said. 'Larry Trent kept five horses in training, which takes some financing, and he gambled in thousands. Gamblers don't win, bookmakers do.'

'When did Larry Trent buy this horse?' Gerard asked.

'At Doncaster Sales a year ago.'

'Before the whisky thefts,' he said regretfully.

'Before those particular whisky thefts. Not necessarily before all the red wines in his cellar began to taste the same.'

'Do you want a full-time job?' he said.

'No thanks.'

'What happened to Ramekin, do you think?'

'I would think,' I said, 'that at a guess he was shipped abroad and sold.'

TEN:

At the rear of the row where my shop was located there was a service road with several small yards opening from it, leading to back doors, so that goods could be loaded and unloaded without one having to carry everything in and out through the front. It was into one of these yards that the bolted door next to my storeroom led, and it was in that yard that we commonly parked the van and the car.

Mrs Palissey, that Sunday, had the van. The Rover estate was standing in the yard where I'd left it when Gerard picked me up. Despite my protestations, when we returned at six he insisted on turning into the service road to save me walking the scant hundred yards from the end.

'Don't bother,' I said.

'No trouble.'

He drove along slowly, saying he'd be in touch with me the following day as we still had things to discuss, turning into the third yard on the left, at my direction.

Besides my car there was a medium-sized van in the yard, its rear doors wide open. I looked at it in vague surprise, as the two other shops who shared the yard with me were my immediate neighbour, a hairdresser, and next to that a dress shop, both of them firmly closed all day on Sundays.

My other immediate neighbour, served by the next yard, was a Chinese takeaway, open always; the van, I thought in explanation, must have driven into my yard in mistake for his.

Gerard slowed his car to a halt . . . and a man carrying a case of wine elbowed his way sideways out of the back door of my shop: the door I had left firmly bolted at two o'clock. I exclaimed furiously, opening the passenger door to scramble out.

'Get back in,' Gerard was saying urgently, but I hardly listened. 'I'll find a telephone for the police.'

'Next yard,' I said over my shoulder. 'Sung Li. Ask him.' I slammed the door behind me and fairly ran across to the intruding van, so angry that I didn't give my own safety the slightest thought. Extremely foolish, as everyone pointed out to me continually during the next week, a view with which in retrospect I had to agree.

The man who had walked from my shop hadn't seen me and had his head in the van, transferring the weight of the case from his arms to the floor, a posture whose mechanics I knew well.

I shoved him hard at the base of the spine to push him off balance forwards and slammed both of the van's doors into his buttocks. He yelled out, swearing with shock and outrage, his voice muffled to all ears but mine. He couldn't do much to free himself: I'd got him pinned into the van by the doors, his legs protruding beneath, and I thought with fierce satisfaction that I could easily hold him there until Gerard returned.

I'd overlooked, unfortunately, that robbers could work in pairs. There was a colossal crunch against the small of my back which by thrusting me into the van doors did more damage still, I should imagine, to the man half in the van, and as I struggled to turn I saw a second, very similar man, carrying another case of wine with which he was trying to bore a hole straight through me, or so it felt.

The man half in half out of the van was practically screaming. The urgency of his message seemed to get through to his pal who suddenly removed the pressure from my back and dropped the case of wine at my feet. I had a flurried view of fuzzy black hair, a heavy black moustache and eyes that boded no good for anybody. His fist slammed into my jaw and shook bits I never knew could rattle, and I kicked him hard on the shin.

No one had ever taught me how to fight because I hadn't wanted to learn. Fighting involved all the scary things like people trying to hurt you, where I considered the avoidance of being hurt a top priority. Fighting led to stamping about with guns, to people shooting at you round corners, to having to kill someone yourself. Fighting led to the Victoria Cross and the Distinguished Service Order, or so it had seemed to my child mind, and the bravery of my father and my grandfather had seemed not only unattainable but alien, as if they belonged to a different race.

The inexpert way I fought that Sunday afternoon had nothing to do with bravery but everything to do with rage. They had no bloody right, I thought breathlessly, to steal my property and they damned well shouldn't, if I could stop them.

They had more to lose than I, I suppose. Liberty, for a start.

Also I had undoubtedly damaged the first one rather severely around the pelvis, and as far as he was able he was looking for revenge.

It wasn't so much a matter of straight hitting with fists: more of clutching and kicking and ramming against hard surfaces and using knees as blunt instruments. At about the instant I ran out of enthusiasm the second man succeeded finally in what I'd been half aware he was trying to do, and reached in through the driver's door of the van, momentarily leaning forward in that same risky posture which I would have taken advantage of if I hadn't had my hands full with robber number one. Too late I kicked free of him and went to go forward.

Number two straightened out of the front of the van, and the fight stopped right there. He was panting a little but triumphantly holding a short-barrelled shotgun which he nastily aimed at my chest.

'Back off,' he said to me grimly.

I backed.

All my feelings about guns returned in a rush. It was suddenly crystal clear that a few cases of wine weren't worth dying for. I walked one step backwards and then another and then a third, which brought me up against the wall beside my rear door. The door tended to close if not propped open, and was at that point shut but on the latch. If I could go through it, I thought dimly, I'd be safe, and I also thought that if I tried to escape through it, I'd be shot.

At the very second it crossed my mind that the man with the gun didn't know whether to shoot me or not, Gerard drove his car back into my yard. The man with the gun swung round towards him and loosed off one of the barrels and I yanked open my door and leaped to go through it. I knew the gun was turning back my way: I could see it in the side of my frantic vision. I knew also that having shot once he'd shoot again, that the moment of inhibition was past. At five paces he was so close that the full discharge would have blown a hole in an ox. I suppose I moved faster in that second than ever before in my life, and I was jumping sideways through the doorway like a streak when he pulled the trigger.

I fell over inside but not entirely from the impact of pellets: mainly because the passage was strewn with more cases of wine. The bits of shot that had actually landed felt like sharp stings in my arm: like hot stabs.

The door swung shut behind me. If I bolted it, I thought, I

would be safe. I also thought of Gerard outside in his car, and along with these two thoughts I noticed blood running down my right hand. Oh well . . . I wasn't dead, was I? I struggled to my feet and opened the door enough to see what I'd be walking out to, and found that it wouldn't be very much, as the two black-headed robbers were scrambling into their van with clear intentions of driving away.

I didn't try to stop them. They rocketed past Gerard's car and swerved into the service road, disappearing with the rear doors swinging open and three or four cases of wine showing within.

The windscreen of Gerard's car was shattered. I went over there with rising dread and found him lying across both front seats, the top of one shoulder reddening and his teeth clenched with pain.

I opened the door beside the steering wheel. One says really such inadequate things at terrible times. I said, 'I'm so sorry . . .' knowing he'd come back to help me, knowing I shouldn't have gone in there, shouldn't have needed help.

Sung Li from next door came tearing round the corner on his feet, his broad face wide with anxiety.

'Shots,' he said. 'I heard shots.'

Gerard said tautly, 'I ducked. Saw the gun. I guess not totally fast enough,' and he struggled into a sitting position, holding on to the wheel and shedding crazed crumbs of windscreen like snow. 'The police are coming and you yourself are alive, I observe. It could fractionally have been worse.'

Sung Li, who spoke competent English, looked at Gerard as if he couldn't believe his ears, and I laughed, transferring his bewilderment to myself.

'Mr Tony,' he said anxiously as if fearing for my reason, 'do you know you are bleeding also?'

'Yes,' I said.

Sung Li's face mutely said that all English were mad, and Gerard didn't help by asking him to whistle up an ambulance, dear chap, if he wouldn't mind.

Sung Li went away looking dazed and Gerard gave me what could only be called a polite social smile.

'Bloody Sundays,' he said, 'are becoming a habit.' He blinked a few times. 'Did you get the number of that van?'

'Mm,' I nodded. 'Did you?'

'Yes. Gave it to the police. Description of men?'

'They were wearing wigs,' I said. 'Fuzzy black wigs, both the same. Also heavy black moustaches, identical. Clip-ons, I should think. Also surgical rubber gloves. If you're asking would I know them again without those additions, then unfortunately I don't think so.'

'Your arm's bleeding,' he said. 'Dripping from your hand.'

'They were stealing my wine.'

After a pause he said, 'Which wine, do you think?'

'A bloody good question. I'll go and look,' I said. 'Will you be all right?'

'Yes.'

I went off across the yard to my back door, aware of the warm stickiness of my right arm, feeling the stinging soreness from shoulder to wrist, but extraordinarily not worried. Elbow and fingers still moved per instructions, though after the first exploratory twitches I decided to leave them immobile for the time being. Only the outer scatterings of the shot had caught me, and compared with what might have happened it did truthfully at that moment seem minor.

I noticed at that point how the thieves had got in: the barred washroom window had been comprehensively smashed inward, frame, bars and all, leaving a hole big enough for a man. I went into the washroom, scrunching on broken glass, and picked up the cloth with which I usually dried the glasses after customers had tasted wines, wrapping it a few times round my wrist to mop up the crimson trickles before going out to see what I'd lost.

For a start I hadn't lost my small stock of really superb wines in wooden boxes at the back of the storeroom. The prizes, the appreciating Margaux and Lafite, were still there.

I hadn't lost, either, ten cases of champagne or six very special bottles of old Cognac, or even a readily handy case of vodka. The boxes I'd fallen over in the passage were all open at the tops, the necks of the bottles showing, and when one went into the shop one could see why.

The robbers had been stealing the bottles from the racks. More peculiarly they had taken all the half-drunk wine bottles standing re-corked on the tasting table, and all the opened cases from beneath the tablecloth.

The wines on and below the table had come from St Emilion, Volnay, Côtes de Roiussillon and Graves, all red. The wines missing from the shop's racks were of those and some from St Estèphe, Nuits St Georges, Mâcon and Valpolicella; also all red.

I went back out into the yard and stooped to look at the

contents of the case robber number two had jabbed me with and then dropped. It contained some of the bottles from the tasting table, four of them broken.

Straightening I continued over to Gerard's car and was relieved to see him looking no worse.

'Well?' he said.

'They weren't ordinary thieves,' I said.

'Go on, then.'

'They were stealing only the sorts of wines I tasted at the Silver Moondance. The wines which weren't what the labels said.'

He looked at me, the effort of concentration showing.

I said, 'I bought those wines, the actual ones, at the Silver Moondance. Paid for them. Got a receipt from the barman. He must have thought I took them away with me . . . but in fact the police have them. Sergeant Ridger. He too gave me a receipt.'

'You are saying,' Gerard said slowly, 'that if you'd brought those wines here to your shop, today they would have vanished.'

'Yeah.'

'Given another half-hour . . .'

I nodded.

'They must be of extraordinary importance.'

'Mm,' I said. 'Be nice to know why.'

'Why did you buy them?'

We were both talking, I saw, so as to give a semblance of normality to the abnormal reality of two ordinary Englishmen quietly bleeding from shotgun wounds in a small town on a Sunday afternoon. I thought 'This is bloody ridiculous' and I answered him civilly, 'I bought them for the labels . . . to see if the labels themselves were forgeries. As a curio. Like collecting stamps.'

'Ah,' he said placidly.

'Gerard . . .'

'Yes?'

'I'm very sorry.'

'So you should be. Stupid behaviour.'

'Yes.'

We waited for a while longer until a police car rolled into the yard without haste, two policemen emerging enquiringly, saying they could see no evidence of any break-in at the wine shop, and did we know who had called them out.

Gerard closed his eyes. I said, 'This is the back of the wine shop. The thieves broke in the back, not the front. If you look closely you'll see they broke the washroom window, climbed in over the loo and unbolted the back door from the inside.'

One of them said 'Oh,' and went to look. The other took out his notebook. I said mildly, 'The thieves had a shotgun and . . . er . . . shot us. They are driving away in a grey Bedford van, brown lines along the sides, licence number MMO 229Y, containing about four cases of red wine . . . and they'll have gone ten miles by now, I shouldn't wonder.'

'Name, sir?' he said blandly.

I wanted to giggle. I told him my name, however, and to do him justice he wasted no time once he realised that red wasn't in the original weave of Gerard's jacket. Gerard and I in due course found ourselves in the casualty department of the local major hospital where he was whisked off to regions unseen and I sat with my bare newly-washed arm on a small table while a middle-aged nursing sister expertly and unemotionally picked pellets out with a glittering instrument reminiscent of tweezers.

'You look as if you've done this before,' I observed.

'Every year during the shooting season.' She paused. 'Can you feel this?'

'No, not really.'

'Good. Some of them have gone deep. If the local anaesthetic isn't enough, tell me.'

'I sure will,' I said fervently.

She dug around for a while until there were eleven little black balls like peppercorns rattling redly in the dish, each of them big enough to kill a pheasant; and to my morbid amusement she said I could take them with me if I liked, many people did.

Carrying my jacket and with a thing like a knitted tube over antiseptic patches replacing the shredded sleeve of my shirt I went to find Gerard, discovering him in a cubicle, sitting in a wheelchair, wearing a hospital-issue fawn dressing-gown over his trousers and looking abysmally bored. He had stopped bleeding both inside and out, it appeared, but several pellets were inaccessible to tweezers and he would have to stay overnight until the theatre staff returned in force in the morning. Life-and-death alone got seen to on Sundays, not small spheres of lead lodged behind collar bones.

He said he had telephoned to Tina, his wife, who was

bringing his pyjamas. Tina also would retrieve his car and get the windscreen fixed; and I wondered whether he had told Tina that the velvety upholstery that was where his head would have been if he hadn't thrown himself sideways was ripped widely apart with the stuffing coming out.

I went back to my shop in a taxi and checked that the police had, as they had promised, sent someone to board up the absent washroom window. I let myself in through the front door, switching on a light, assessing the extent of the mess, seeing it not now with anger but as a practical problem of repair.

For all that it wouldn't be permanently damaged I had an arm not currently of much use. Lifting cases of wine could wait a day or two. Likewise sweeping up broken glass. Thank goodness for Brian, I thought tiredly, and checked that the bolts were once again in position over the door and the sheet of plywood nailed securely in the washroom.

I left everything as it was, switched off the lights and went out again by the front door. Sung Li was emerging reluctantly from his restaurant, his forehead lined with worry.

'Oh, it is you, Mr Tony,' he said with relief. 'No more burglars.'

'No.'

'You want some food?'

I hesitated. I'd eaten nothing all day but felt no hunger.

'It's best to eat,' he said. 'Lemon chicken, your favourite. I made it fresh.' He gave me a brief bow. I bowed courteously in return and went in with him: between us there was the same sort of formality as between myself and Mrs Palissey, and Sung Li, also, seemed to prefer it. I ate the lemon chicken seated at a table in the small restaurant section and after that fried shrimp and felt a good deal less lightheaded. I hadn't known I was lightheaded until then, rather like not knowing how ill one had been until after one felt well again, but, looking back, I imagined I hadn't been entirely ground-based since I'd looked into the business end of a shotgun and found my legs didn't reliably belong to my body. The euphoria of escape, I now saw, accounted for Gerard's and my unconcerned conversation in the yard and for my methodical checking of my losses. It was really odd how the mind strove to pretend things were normal . . . and there were good chemical reasons why that happened after injury. I'd read an article about it, somewhere.

I stood up, making a stiff attempt to pick my wallet out of

my pocket, and Sung Li was at my side instantly, telling me to pay him in the morning. I asked if I could go out to my car in the yard through his kitchen door instead of walking all the way round and he was too polite to tell me I wasn't fit to drive. We bowed to each other again outside in the darkness, and I'd managed to grasp my keys pretty firmly by the time I reached the Rover.

I drove home. I hit nothing. The anaesthetic wore off my arm and the whole thing started burning. I swore aloud, most obscenely, half surprised that I should say such things, even alone. Half surprised I could think them.

I let myself into the cottage. The second Sunday in a row, I thought, that I had gone back there with blood on my clothes and my mind full of horrors.

Emma, I thought, for God's sake help me. I walked through the empty rooms, not really looking for her, knowing perfectly well she wasn't there, but desperately in need all the same of someone to talk to, someone to hold me and love me as she had done.

With the lights all brightly shining I swallowed some aspirin and sat in my accustomed chair in the sitting room and told myself to shut up and be sensible. I'd been robbed . . . so what? Fought . . . and lost . . . so what? Been shot in the arm . . . so what? So Emma . . . my darling love . . . help me.

Get a bloody grip on things, I told myself.

Switch off the lights. Go to bed. Go to sleep.

My arm throbbed unmercifully all night.

The new day, Monday, crept into the world at about the level of my perception of it: dull, overcast, lifeless. Stiffly I dressed and shaved and made coffee, averting my mind from the temptation to go back to bed and abdicate. Mondays were hard at the best of times. The shambles ahead beckoned with all the appeal of a cold swamp.

I put the aspirin bottle in my pocket. The eleven separate punctures, announcing themselves as unready to be overlooked, seemed to be competing against each other for my attention, and various bruises were developing gingerly almost everywhere else. Bugger the lot of you, I thought: to little avail.

I drove to the shop and parked in the yard. Gerard's car stood exactly in the same place where he'd stalled it askew, stamping on the footbrake when he caught sight of the gun swinging round to his face. The keys weren't in the ignition and I couldn't remember who had them. One more problem to shelve indefinitely.

There was a police car already outside my door when I walked round to the front. Inside it, Detective Sergeant Ridger. He emerged from the driver's side at my approach, every button and hair regimentally aligned as before. He stood waiting for me and I stopped when I reached him.

'How are you?' he said. He cleared his throat. 'I'm . . . er . . . sorry.'

I smiled at least a fraction. Sergeant Ridger was becoming quite human. I unlocked the door, let us in and locked it again; then I sat in the tiny office slowly opening the mail while he walked round the place with a notebook, writing painstakingly.

He came to a halt finally and said, 'You weren't trying to be funny, were you, with the list of missing property you dictated to the constable yesterday evening before you went off to the hospital?'

'No.'

'You do realise it was almost identical with the red wines stolen from the Silver Moondance.'

'I do indeed,' I said. 'And I hope you've got my Silver Moondance bottles tucked away safely in your police station. Twelve bottles of wine, all opened. My own property.'

'I haven't forgotten,' he said with a touch of starch. 'You'll get them back in due course.'

'I'd like one of them now,' I said refectively.

'Which one?'

'The St Estèphe.'

'Why that one particularly?' He wasn't exactly suspicious; just naturally vigilant.

'Not that one particularly. It was the first that came to mind. Any would do.'

'What do you want it for?'

'Just to look at it again. Smell it . . . taste it again. You never know . . . it might just be helpful. To you, I mean.'

He shrugged, slightly puzzled but not antagonistic. 'All right. I'll get you one if I can, but I might not be able to. They're evidence.' He looked around the tiny office. 'Did they touch anything in here?'

I shook my head, grateful for that at least. 'They were definitely looking for the wine from the Silver Moondance. The bottles they loaded first and succeeded in taking away with them in the van were all opened and re-corked.' I explained about the bottles missing from on and beneath the tasting table, and he went to have a further look.

'Anything you can add to the description you gave of the thieves?' he asked, coming back.

I shook my head.

'Could one of them have been the barman from the Silver Moondance?'

'No,' I said definitely. 'Not his sort at all.'

'You said they wore wigs,' Ridger said. 'So how can you be sure?'

'The barman has acne. The robbers didn't.'

Ridger wrote it down in his notebook.

'The barman knew exactly what you bought,' he observed. 'He spelled them out item by item on your receipt.'

'Have you asked him about it?' I said neutrally.

Ridger gave me another of the uncertain looks which showed him undecided still about my status: member of the not-to-be-informed public or helpful-consultant-expert.

'We haven't been able to find him,' he said eventually.

I refrained from impolite surprise. I said, 'Since when?'

'Since . . .' he cleared his throat. 'Not actually since you yourself last saw him leaving the bar last Monday after he'd locked the grille. Apparently he drove off immediately in his car, packed his clothes, and left the district entirely.'

'Where did he live?'

'With . . . um . . . a friend.'

'Male friend?'

Ridger nodded. 'Temporary arrangement. No roots. At the first sign of trouble, he was off. We'll look out for him, of course, but he'd gone by early afternoon that Monday.'

'Not suspected of killing Zarac,' I suggested.

'That's right.'

'The assistant assistant and the waitress both knew what I bought,' I said thoughtfully. 'But . . .'

'Too wet,' Ridger said.

'Mm. Which leaves Paul Young.'

'I suppose he wasn't one of the thieves.' Hardly a question, more a statement.

'No,' I said. 'They were both younger and taller, for a start.'

'You would obviously have said.'

'Yes. Have you . . . er . . . found him? Paul Young?'

'We're proceeding with our enquiries.' He spoke without

irony: the notebook jargon came naturally to his tongue. He wasn't much older than myself; maybe four or five years. I wondered what he'd be like off duty, if such a structured and self-disciplined person were ever entirely off duty. Probably always as watchful, as careful, as ready to prickle into suspicion. I was probably seeing, I thought, the real man.

I looked at my watch. Nine-twenty. Mrs Palissey and Brian should be arriving in ten minutes.

I said, 'I suppose it's O.K. with you if I get all this mess cleared up? Replace the window, and so on?'

He nodded. 'I'll just take a look round outside, though, before I go. Come and tell me what's different from before the break-in.'

I got slowly to my feet. We went out into the littered passage and without comment Ridger himself unbolted the heavy door and opened it.

'My car was parked all day yesterday just about where it is now,' I said. 'Gerard McGregor's car wasn't there, of course.'

Ridger looked back through his notebook, found an entry, nodded, and slipped forward again. The door swung shut in its slow way. Ridger pushed it open and went out, looking over his shoulder for me to follow. I stepped after him into the raw cold air and watched him pacing about, measuring distances.

'The thieves' van was there?' he asked, standing still.

'A bit to your right.'

'Where was the man with the shotgun standing when he fired at you?'

'About where you are now.'

He nodded matter-of-factly, swung round towards Gerard's car and raised his arm straight before him. 'He fired at the car,' he said.

'Yes.'

'Then . . .' he turned his body with the arm still outstretched until it was pointing at me. 'He fired again.'

'I wasn't actually standing here by that time.'

Ridger permitted a smile. 'Too close for comfort, I'd say.' He walked the five steps separating us and ran his hand over the outside of the door. 'Want to see what nearly hit you?'

The toughly-grained wood was dark with creosote, the preservative recently applied against the coming winter. I looked more closely to where he pointed, to an area just below the latch, a few inches in from the edge of the door. Wholly embedded in the wood as if they were part of it were dozens and dozens of little black pellets, most of them in a thick cluster, with others making marks like woodworm holes in a wider area all around.

'There are three hundred of those in a normal cartridge,' Ridger observed calmly. 'The report we got from the hospital said they dug eleven of them out of your right arm.'

I looked at the deadly grouping of the little black shots and remembered the frenzied panic of my leap through the door. I'd left my elbow too far out for a split second too long.

The main cluster in the wood was roughly at the height of my heart.

ELEVEN:

Mrs Palissey and Brian arrived on time and fell into various attitudes of horror, which couldn't be helped. I asked her to open the shop for business and asked Brian to start clearing up, and I stayed out in the yard myself knowing it was mostly to postpone answering their eagerly probing questions.

Ridger was still pacing about, estimating and making notes, fetching up finally at a dark red stain on the dirty concrete.

He said, frowning, 'Is this blood?'

'No. It's red wine. The thieves dropped a case of bottles there. Some of them smashed in the case and seeped through onto the ground.'

He looked around. 'Where's the case now?'

'In the sink in the washroom. Your policemen carried it there yesterday evening.'

He made a note.

'Sergeant . . . ?'

'Yes?' He looked up with his eyes only, his head still bent over the notebook.

'Let me know, would you, how things are going?'

'What things, for instance?'

'Whether you find that van . . . Whether you find a lead to Paul Young.'

He looked up fully and soberly, not refusing at once. I could almost feel his hesitation and certainly see it; and his answer when it came was typically ambivalent.

'We could perhaps warn you that you might be needed at some future date for identification purposes.'

'Thank you,' I said.

'Not promising, mind.' He was retreating into the notebook.

'No.'

He finished eventually and went away, and Mrs Palissey enjoyed her ooh/ahh sensations. Mrs Palissey wasn't given to weeping and wailing and needing smelling salts. Mrs Palissey's eyes were shining happily at the newsvalue of the break-in and at the good isn't-it-awful gossip she'd have at lunchtime with the traffic warden.

Brian with little change to his normal anxious expression swept and tidied and asked me what to do about the case in the sink.

'Take out the whole bottles and put them on the draining board,' I said, and presently he came to tell me he'd done that. I went into the washroom to see, and there they were, eight bottles of St Emilion from under the tablecloth.

Brian was holding a piece of paper as if not knowing where to put it.

'What's that?' I said.

'Don't know. It was down in the case.' He held it out to me and I took it: a page from a notepad, folded across the centre, much handled, and damp and stained all down one side with wine from the broken bottles. I read it at first with puzzlement and then with rising amazement.

In a plain strong angular handwriting it read:

FIRST
All opened bottles of wine.
SECOND
All bottles with these names:
St Emilion.
St Estèphe.
Volnay.
Nuits St Georges.
Valpolicella.
Mâcon.
IF TIME
Spirits, etc. Anything to hand.
DARKNESS 6.30. DO NOT USE LIGHTS

'Shall I throw that away, Mr Beach?' Brian asked helpfully.

'You can have six Mars Bars,' I said.

He produced his version of a large smile, a sort of sideways leer, and followed me into the shop for his reward.

Mrs Palissey, enjoyably worried, said she was sure she could cope if I wanted to step out for ten minutes, in spite of customers coming and almost nothing on the shelves, seeing as it was Monday. I assured her I valued her highly and went out along the road to the office of a solicitor of about my age who bought my wine pretty often in the evenings.

Certainly I could borrow his photocopier, he said. Any time.

I made three clear copies of the thieves' shopping list and returned to my own small lair, wondering whether to call Sergeant Ridger immediately and in the end not doing so.

Brian humped cases of whisky, gin and various sherries from storeroom to shop, telling me each time as he passed what he was carrying, and each time getting it right. There was pride on his big face from the accomplishment; job satisfaction at its most pure. Mrs Palissey restocked the shelves, chattering away interminably, and five people telephoned with orders.

Holding a pen was unexpectedly painful, arm muscles stiffly protesting. I realised I'd been doing almost everything left-handedly, including eating Sung Li's chicken, but writing that way was beyond me. I took down the orders right-handedly with many an inward curse, and when it came to the long list for the wholesalers, picked it out left-handed on the typewriter. No one had told me how long the punctures might take to heal. No time was fast enough.

We got through the morning somehow, and Mrs Palissey, pleasantly martyred, agreed to do the wholesalers run with Brian in the afternoon.

When they'd gone I wandered round my battered domain thinking that I should dredge up some energy to telephone for replacement wines, replacement windows . . . replacement self-respect. It was my own silly fault I'd been shot. No getting away from it. It hadn't seemed natural, all the same, to tiptoe off and let the robbery continue. Wiser, of course. Easy in retrospect to see it. But at the time . . .

I thought about it in a jumbled way, without clarity, not understanding the compulsive and utterly irrational urge that had sent me running towards danger when every scared and skin-preserving instinct in my life had been to shy away from it.

Not that I'd been proud of that, either. Nor ashamed of it. I'd accepted that that was the way I was: not brave in the least. Disappointing.

I supposed I had better make a list of the missing wines for the insurance company, who would be getting as fed up with my repeated claims as Kenneth Charter's insurers were with his. I supposed I should, but I didn't do it. Appetite for chores, one might have said, was at an extremely low ebb.

I took some aspirin.

A customer came in for six bottles of port and relentlessly

brought me up to date on the family's inexhaustible and usually disgusting woes. (Father-in-law had something wrong with his bladder.)

Sung Li appeared, bowing, with a gift of spring rolls. He wouldn't be paid for my previous evening's dinner, he said. I was an honoured and frequent customer. When I was in need, he was my friend. I would honour him by not offering payment for yesterday. We bowed to each other, and I accepted.

He had never seen China, but his parents had been born there and had taught him their ways. He was a most punctilious neighbour and because of his roaringly successful but unlicensed take-away I sold much wine in the evenings. Whenever I could without offending him I gave him cigars, which he smoked on sunny afternoons sitting on a wooden chair outside his kitchen door.

At three Sergeant Ridger returned carrying a paper bag from which he produced a bottle, setting it on the counter.

St Estèphe: just as I'd asked. Uncorked and sealed with sticky tape, untouched since its departure from the Silver Moondance.

'Can I keep it?' I said.

He gave one brief sharp nod. 'For now. I said you'd been helpful, that it would be helpful for you to have this. I obtained permission from the Chief Inspector in charge of the Silver Moondance murder investigations.' He dug into a pocket and produced a piece of paper, holding it out. 'Please sign this chit. It makes it official.'

I signed the paper and returned it to him.

'I've something for you, as well,' I said, and fetched for him the thieves' shopping list. The original.

His body seemed to swell physically when he understood what it was, and he looked up from it with sharply bright eyes.

'Where did you find it?'

I explained about Brian clearing up.

'This is of great significance,' he said with satisfaction.

I agreed. I said, 'It would be particularly interesting if this is Paul Young's handwriting.'

His staring gaze intensified, if anything.

'When he wrote his name and address,' I said, 'do you remember, he held his pen so awkwardly? He wrote in short sharp downward strokes. It just seemed to me that this list looked similar . . . though I only saw his name and address very briefly, of course.'

Sergeant Ridger, who had looked at them long and carefully, stared now at the thieves' list, making the comparison in his mind. Almost breathlessly he said, 'I think you're right. I think they're the same. The Chief Inspector will be very pleased.'

'A blank wall, otherwise?' I suggested. 'You can't find him?'

His hesitation was small. 'There are difficulties, certainly,' he said.

No trace at all, I diagnosed.

'How about his car?' I suggested.

'What car?'

'Yes . . . well . . . he didn't come to the Silver Moondance that day on foot, would you think? It's miles from anywhere. But when we went out with the boxes of drinks, there wasn't an extra car in the car park. So . . . um . . . he must have parked round at the back where the cars of the staff were. Round by that door into the lobby where Larry Trent's office is, and the wine cellars. So Paul Young must have been to the Silver Moondance some other time . . . or he would have parked out front. If you see what I mean.'

Detective Sergeant Ridger looked at me long and slowly. 'How do you know the staff parked round at the back?'

'I saw cars through the lobby window when I went to fetch the bottles of wine. It seemed commonsense to assume those were the staff's cars . . . barman, assistant assistant, waitress, kitchen staff and so on. They all had to get to work somehow, and the front car park was empty.'

He nodded, remembering.

'Paul Young stayed there after we left,' I said. 'So maybe the assistant or the waitress . . . or somebody . . . remembers what car he drove away in. Pretty long shot, I suppose.'

Ridger carefully put the folded shopping list into the back of his notebook and then wrote a sentence or two on a fresh page. 'I'm not of course in charge of that investigation,' he said eventually, 'and I would expect this line of questioning has already been thoroughly explored, but . . . I'll find out.'

I didn't ask again if he would tell me the results, nor did he even hint that he might. When he left, however, it was without finality: not so much goodbye as see you later. He would be interested, he said, in anything further I could think of in connection with the bottle of wine he had brought. If I came to any new conclusions, no doubt I would pass them on.

'Yes, of course,' I said.

He nodded, shut the notebook, tucked it into his pocket and collectedly departed, and I took the bottle of St Estèphe carefully into the office, putting it back into the bag in which Ridger had brought it so that it should be out of plain sight.

I sat down at the desk, lethargy deepening. Still a load of orders to make up to go out on the van; couldn't be bothered even to start on them. Everyone would get their delivery a day late. Goblets and champagne needed for a coming-of-age on Thursday . . . by Thursday I mightn't feel so bone weary and comprehensively sore.

Women's voices in the shop. I stood up slowly and went out there, trying to raise a smile. Found the smile came quite easily when I saw who it was.

Flora stood there, short, plump and concerned, her kind eyes searching my face. Beside her, tall and elegant, was the woman I'd seen fleetingly with Gerard after the horsebox accident: his wife, Tina.

'Tony, dear,' Flora exclaimed, coming down the shop to meet me, 'are you sure you should be here? You don't look well, dear. They really should have kept you in hospital, it's too bad they sent you home.'

I kissed her cheek. 'I wouldn't have wanted to stay.' I glanced at Mrs McGregor. 'How's Gerard?'

'Oh dear,' Flora said. 'I should introduce . . . Tina, this is Tony Beach . . .'

Tina McGregor smiled, which was noble considering that her husband's predicament was my fault, and in answer to my enquiry said Gerard had had the pellets removed that morning, but would be staying one more night for recovery.

'He wants to see you,' she said. 'This evening, if you can.'

I nodded. 'I'll go.'

'And Tony, dear,' Flora said, 'I was so wanting to ask you . . . but now I see how dreadfully pale you look I don't suppose . . . It would be too much, I'm sure.'

'What would be too much?' I said.

'You were so frightfully kind coming round the stables with me, and Jack's still in hospital, they still won't let him come home, and every day he gets crosser . . .'

'You want me to visit Jack too, after Gerard?' I guessed.

'Oh no!' She was surprised. 'Though he would love it, of course. No . . . I wondered . . . silly of me, really . . . if you would come with me to the races?' She said the final words in a rush and looked of all things slightly ashamed of herself.

'To the races . . .'

'Yes, I know it's a lot to ask . . . but tomorrow . . . we've a horse running which has a very awkward owner and Jack insists I must be there and honestly that owner makes me feel so flummoxed and stupid, I know it's silly, but you were so good with that horrible Howard and I just thought you might enjoy a day at the races and I would ask you . . . only that was before Tina rang me and told me about last night . . . and now I can see it wouldn't be a pleasure for you after all.'

A day at the races . . . well, why not? Maybe I'd feel better for a day off. No worse, at any rate.

'Which races?' I said.

'Martineau.'

Martineau Park, slightly north east of Oxford, large, popular and not too far away. If ever I went to the races it was either to Martineau Park or to Newbury, because I could reach either track inside forty minutes and combine the trip with shop hours, Mrs Palissey graciously permitting.

'Yes I'll come,' I said.

'But Tony dear . . . are you sure?'

'Yes, sure. I'd like to.'

She looked greatly relieved and arranged to pick me up at one o'clock the next day, promising faithfully to return me by six. Their runner, she explained, was in the big race of the day at three-thirty, and the owner always expected to talk for hours afterwards, analysing every step and consequence.

'As if I can tell him anything,' Flora said despairingly. 'I do so wish the horse would win, but Jack's afraid he won't, which is why I've got to be there . . . Oh dear, oh dear.'

The flat racing season was due end in two or three weeks and none too soon, I judged, from Jack Hawthorn's point of view. No stable could long survive the absence of both its main driving forces, left as it was in the hands of a kind unbusiness-like woman with too little knowledge.

'Listen to the owner with respect and agree with everything he says and he'll think you're wonderful,' I said.

'How very naughty, Tony dear,' she said, but looked more confident all the same.

I took them out to the yard, as Flora had chiefly brought Tina to retrieve Gerard's car. It appeared that Tina herself had the ignition key: Gerard had given it to her the previous evening. Tina gazed without comment for a while at the shattered windscreen and the exploded upholstery and then turned towards me, very tall and erect, all emotions carefully straitjacketed.

'This is the third time,' she said, 'that he's been shot.'

I went to see him in the evening and found him propped against pillows in a room with three other beds but no inmates. Blue curtains, hospital smell, large modern spaces, shiny floors, few people about.

'Utterly boring,' Gerard said. 'Utterly impersonal. A waiting room to limbo. People keep coming to read my notes to see why I'm here, and going away again, never to return.'

His arm was in a sling. He looked freshly shaved, hair brushed, very collected and in control. Hung on the foot of the bed was the clipboard of notes to which he'd referred, so I picked them off and read them also.

'Your temperature's ninety-nine, your pulse seventy-five, you're recovering from birdshot pellets, extracted. No complications. Discharge tomorrow.'

'None too soon.'

'How do you feel?'

'Sore,' he said. 'Like you, no doubt.'

I nodded, put the notes back and sat on a chair.

'Tina said this was the third time for you,' I said.

'Huh.' He smiled lop-sidedly. 'She's never totally approved of my job. An embezzler took a pot at me once. Very unusual, that, they're normally such mild people. I suppose it was true to form that he wasn't altogether successful even at murder. He used too small a pistol and shot me in the thigh. Couldn't hold the thing steady . . . I'd swear he shut his eyes just before he fired.'

'He didn't fire again?'

'Ah. Well I was rushing him, you know. He dropped the pistol and started crying. Pathetic, the whole thing.'

I eyed Gerard respectfully. Rushing someone intent on killing you wasn't my idea of pathos.

'And the other time?' I asked.

He grimaced. 'Mm. Much closer to home. Touch and go, that time. Tina wanted me to promise to do office work only after that, but one can't, you know. If you're hunting out criminals of any sort there's always the outside chance they'll turn on you, even the industrial spies I'm normally concerned with.' He smiled again, ironically. 'It wasn't anyway the disloyal little chemist who sold his company's secrets to their chief rival who shot me, it was his father. Extraordinary. Father wouldn't believe his precious son guilty. He telephoned about six times, shouting I'd sent the most brilliant man of a generation to jail out of spite and ruined his career to cover up for someone else . . . he was obsessed, you know. Mentally disturbed. Anyway, he was waiting for me one day outside the office. Just walked across the pavement and shot me in the chest.' He sighed. 'I'll never forget his face. Evil triumph . . . quite mad.'

'What happened to them?' I asked, riveted.

'The father's in and out of padded cells. Don't know what's happened to the son, though he'll have been out of jail long ago. Sad, you know. Such a clever man. His father's pride and joy.'

I was interested. 'Do you ever try to find out what becomes of the people you catch . . . afterwards?'

'No, not often. On the whole they are vain, greedy, heartless and cunning. I don't care for them. One can feel sorry for them, but it's with their victims my sympathies normally lie.'

'Not like the old joke,' I said.

'What old joke?'

'About the man who fell among thieves, who beat him and robbed him and left him bleeding and unconscious in the gutter. And long came two sociologists who looked down upon him lying there and said, the one to the other, "The man who did this needs our help".'

Gerard chuckled and made a face, putting his free hand to his shoulder.

'You mustn't think,' he said, 'that my record is normal. I've been unlucky. Only one other man in our firm has ever been wounded. And most policemen, don't forget, go through their entire careers uninjured.'

Some didn't, I thought.

'Your bad luck this time,' I apologised, 'was my stupidity.'

He shook his head stiffly, with care. 'Don't blame yourself. I drove back into the yard of my own accord. Let's leave it at that, eh?'

I thought gratefully that he was generous but I felt nonetheless still guilty. Absolution, it had always seemed to me, was a fake. To err was human, to be easily forgiven was to be sentimentally set free to err again. To be repeatedly forgiven destroyed the soul. With luck, I thought, I wouldn't do anything else to incur Gerard's forgiveness.

The word that best described Gerard, I thought, was decent. As a detective he wasn't 'colourful' as understood in fiction: that's to say a womaniser, unshaven and drunk. Goodness, easy enough to perceive, was as quicksilver to define, but that most difficult of virtues lived in the strong lines of his face. Serious, rational, calm, he seemed to be without the mental twitches which afflicted many: the bullying pleasure in petty power, the self regarding pomposity, the devouring anxiety of the insecure, all the qualities I saw at work daily not only among customers but in people to whom others had to go in trust, officials and professional people of all sorts. One never knew for certain: Gerard might indulge secret sins galore, locking his Hyde in a closet; but what I saw, I liked.

I told him about Brian finding the thieves' shopping list and gave him one of the photostats out of my pocket, explaining about it being very likely in Paul Young's own handwriting.

'Great God,' he said, reading it. 'He might as well have signed a confession.'

'Mm.'

'But you can see why the robbers needed a written list,' he said. 'All those French names. They needed a visible check actually in their hand. They'd never have been sure to take the right things without.'

'Not unless they knew the right labels intimately.'

Gerard looked up from the list. 'You mean, the men who broke in are therefore not the designers of the swindle.'

'If they were they wouldn't have needed the list.'

'Right.' He smiled slightly. 'How would they grab you as the murderers of Zarac?'

I opened my mouth and shut it again: then when the small shock had passed, I slowly and undecidedly shook my head.

'I don't know,' I said. 'They were rough . . . but there was a moment, when the bigger one picked the gun out of the van, that he pointed it at me and visibly hesitated. If he'd already helped to kill Zarac . . . wouldn't he have killed me then?'

Gerard considered it. 'We can't tell. Zarac died out of earshot of a Chinese takeaway. The hesitation may have been because of the more public nature of the yard. But people who take shotguns to robberies have at least thought of killing, never forget.'

I wouldn't forget, I thought.

'What made you become a detective?' I asked curiously.

'Don't say detective. Tina doesn't like it.'

'Investigating consultant, then.'

'I was baby-snatched from college while detection still seemed a glamorous idea to my immature mind.' Again the lop-sided self-mocking smile. 'I'd done an accountancy course and was at business school but not much looking forward to living what it taught. Rather dismayed, actually, by my prospects. I mentioned to an uncle of mine one day that I thought I'd like to join the police only the family would have mass heart attacks, and a friend of his who was there said why didn't I join the business police . . . I didn't know what he meant, of course, but he steered me to an agency and I think spoke in their ear. They offered me a trial year and started to teach me how to search . . . It was a different agency, not Deglet's. Deglet's took us over, and I was part of the furniture and fittings.'

'And you've never regretted it?'

He said thoughtfully, 'It's fashionable to explain away all crime as the result of environment and upbringing, always putting the blame on someone else, never the actual culprit. No one's born bad, all that sort of thing. If it weren't for poor housing, violent father, unemployment, capitalism, et cetera, et cetera . . . You'll have heard it all, over and over. Then you get a villain from a good home with normal parents who's in a job and can't keep his fingers out of the till. I've seen far far more of those. They're the ones I investigate. Sometimes there's a particular set of circumstances you can point to as the instigation of their thieving or spying or betraying of confidence, but so many of them, I find, simply have an urge to be dishonest. Often not out of dire need, but because that's how they get their kicks. And whichever way you look at them, as poor little victims of society or as marauding invaders, they damage everyone in their path.' He shifted against his pillows. 'I was brought up to respect that most old-fashioned concept, fair play. Even the present weary world tends not to think all's fair in war . . . I seek to restore fair play. I only achieve a bit here and there and the next trickster with a computer is being born every minute . . . What did you ask me?'

'You've answered it,' I said.

He ran his tongue round his lips as if they were dry. 'Pass me that water, will you?' he said.

I gave him the glass and put it down when he'd drunk.

Be grateful for villainy, I thought. The jobs of millions depended on it, Gerard's included. Police, lawyers, tax inspectors, prison warders, court officials, security guards, locksmiths and people making burglar alarms . . . Where would they be the world over but for the multiple faces of Cain.

'Gerard,' I said.

'Mm?'

'Where does my consultancy start and end?'

'How do you mean?'

'Well . . . there wasn't a tankerful of scotch at the Silver Moondance. That Rannoch scotch is still about somewhere . . . masquerading perhaps as Laphroaig but more likely as Bell's.'

Gerard saw the smile twisting the corners of my mouth and gave another painful chuckle.

'You mean you might find it,' he said, 'if you drank at every hostelry from here to John o'Groats?'

'Just Berkshire and Oxfordshire and all the way to Watford. Say fifty thousand places, for starters . . . A spot of syncopation. Syncopation, as you know, is an uneven movement from bar to bar.'

'Please be quiet,' he said. 'Laughing hurts.'

'Mm,' I said. 'Cirrhosis, I love you.'

'All the same . . .'

'I was only joking.'

'I know. But . . . as you said.'

'Yeah. Well, I'll drink scotch at every opportunity, if not every bar. But I won't find it.'

'You never know. Some dark little pub in a Reading backstreet . . .'

I shook my head. 'Somewhere like the Silver Moondance with smoke and noise and dancing and a huge turnover.'

His glance grew thoughtful. 'It depends how much Kenneth Charter wants to spend. As you say, it's an incredibly long shot . . . but I'll put it to him. Incredibly long shots sometimes pay off, and I've known them happen at worse than fifty thousand to one.'

I hadn't expected him to take me seriously and it made what I had chiefly been going to say sound unimportant. I said, all the same, 'I persuaded Sergeant Ridger to let me have one of the Silver Moondance wine bottles. The label might be informative. I know it's nothing on the face of it to do with

Kenneth Charter's tankers, but . . . er, if you found out more about the wine it might lead you back to the scotch.'

He looked at the photostat lying on the sheet. 'To Paul Young, do you mean?'

'I suppose so . . . yes.'

He said calmly, 'Information about wine labels very definitely comes under the heading of consultancy. Getting too close to Paul Young does not.'

TWELVE:

Henri Tavel in his robust French asked me to give his felicitations to my dear mother.

I said I would.

He said he was delighted to hear my voice after so many months and he again regretted infinitely the death of my so dear Emma.

I thanked him.

He said I would have enjoyed the harvest, it had been an abundant crop of small excellent grapes full of flavour: everyone in Bordeaux was talking of equalling 1970.

I offered congratulations.

He asked if I could spare time to visit. All his family and my many friends would welcome it, he said.

I regretted that my shop prevented an absence at present.

He understood. *C'est la vie.* He hoped to be of help to me in some way, as I had telephoned.

Thus invited and with gratitude I explained about the substitute wine and the existence of various labels.

'Alas,' he said. 'This is unfortunately too common. A matter of great annoyance.'

'If I describe one of the labels, could you find out for me if it's genuine?' I asked.

'Certainly,' he agreed. 'Tomorrow, my dear Tony.'

I was telephoning from the office in the shop with the St Estèphe bottle in front of me.

I said, 'The label is of a château in the region of St Estèphe, a village you know so well.'

'The home of my grandparents. There is no one there of whom I cannot enquire.'

'Yes . . . Well, this label purports to come from Château Caillot.' I spelled it out for him. 'Do you know of it?'

'No, I don't but don't forget there must be two hundred small châteaux in that part of Haut Médoc. I don't know them all. I will find out.'

'Great,' I said. 'The rest of the label reads: "Mis en bouteilles par W. Thiery et Fils, négociants à Bordeaux." '

Henri Tavel's suspicions came clearly down the line. 'I know of no W. Thiery et Fils,' he said. Monsieur Tavel, *négociant à Bourdeaux* himself, was more likely to be aware of a fellow wineshipper than of a château seventy kilometres to the north. 'I'll find out,' he said.

'Also the label bears the year of vintage,' I said.

'Which year?'

'1979.'

He grunted. 'Plentiful and quite good.'

'It's an attractive label altogether,' I said. 'Cream background with black and gold lettering, and a line drawing of an elegant château. The château reminds me of somewhere . . . I wish you could see it, you might recognise it.'

'Soak it off, my dear Tony, and send it.'

'Yes, I might.'

'And the wine under the label?' he asked. 'What of the wine?'

'At a guess, mostly Italian. Blended with maybe Yugoslav, blended again with anything handy. Impossible, I would think, to distinguish its origins, even for a master of wine. It's light. Not much body. No finish. But pleasant enough. Palatable. No one would think it undrinkable. Wherever it came from it wasn't abused too much before it was bottled.'

'Bordeaux bottled . . .' he said thoughtfully.

'If the château doesn't exist, the wine could have been bottled anywhere,' I said. 'I kept the cork. It looks pretty new and there is no lettering on it.'

The row of six corks stood before me on the desk, all identical. When châteaux botled their own wine in their own cellars they stamped the corks with their name and the year of vintage. Anyone ordering a château-bottled wine would expect to see the cork, consequently a swindler would be less likely to present his work as château-bottled: too great a risk of a clued-up customer knowing what he wasn't being given.

Whoever had chosen the Silver Moondance labels had chosen well: all familiar-sounding respected names, all saleable at a substantial price. At a guess the wine itself, part of the great European wine lake, might have cost the bottler one-fiftieth of what Larry Trent's diners had been charged.

I asked Henri Tavel when I could telephone again.

'Tomorrow night, again at this time. I will enquire at once in the morning.'

I thanked him several times and we disconnected, and I

pictured him as I'd so often seen him, sitting roundly at his big dining table with its lace cloth, drinking armagnac alone after the evening meal and refusing to watch television with his wife.

Flora collected me from the shop at one the following day as arranged and drove me in Jack's opulent car to Martineau Park races. She talked most of the way there out of what seemed a compulsive nervousness, warning me mostly about what not to say to Orkney Swayle, the owner she felt cowed by.

Flora, I thought, had no need to be cowed by anybody. She had status in the racing world, she was pleasant to look at in a motherly middle-aged way and she was dressed for action in tailored suit and plainly expensive shoes. Self-confidence had to come from within, however, and within Flora one could discern a paralysed jelly.

'Don't ask him why he's called Orkney,' she said. 'He was conceived there.'

I laughed.

'Yes, but he doesn't like it. He likes the name itself because it has grandeur which he's always looking for, and Tony dear, if you can be a bit grand like Jimmy it will do very well with Orkney. Put on your most upper-class voice like you do sometimes when you aren't thinking, because I know you damp it down a bit in the shop so as not to be intimidating to a lot of people, if you see what I mean.'

I was amused and also rueful at her perception. I'd learned on my first day of sweeping and carrying as general wine shop dogsbody that my voice didn't fit the circumstances, and had altered my ways accordingly. It had been mostly a matter, I'd found, of speaking not far back in the throat but up behind the teeth, a reversal of the way I'd just painstakingly learned to speak French like a Frenchman.

'I'll do my best Jimmy imitation,' I promised. 'And how is he, by the way?'

'Much better, dear, thank goodness.'

I said I was glad.

'Orkney thinks he owns Jack, you know,' she said, reverting to what was more immediately on her mind. 'He hates Jack talking to other owners.' She slowed for a roundabout and sighed. 'Some owners are dreadfully jealous, though I suppose I shouldn't say so, but Orkney gets quite miffed if Jack has another runner in Orkney's race.'

She was driving well and automatically, her mind far from the road. She told me she usually drove Jack to meetings: he liked to read and think on the way there and sleep on the way back. 'About the only time he sits still, dear, so it has to be good for him.'

'How old is this Orkney?' I asked.

'Getting on for fifty, I should think. He manufactures some frantically unmentionable undergarments, but he'll never say exactly what. He doesn't like one to talk about it, dear.' She almost giggled. 'Directoire knickers, do you think?'

I'll be careful not to ask,' I said ironically. 'Directoire knickers! Do even great-grannies wear them any more?'

'You see them in those little advertisements on Saturdays in the newspapers,' Flora said, 'along with things to hold your shoulders back if you're round shouldered and sonic buzzers that don't actually say what they're for, and all sorts of amazing things. Haven't you noticed?'

'No,' I said, smiling.

'I think sometimes of all the people who buy all those things,' she said. 'How different everyone's lives are.'

I glanced at her benign and rounded face, at the tidy greying hair and the pearl earstuds, and reflected not for the first time that the content of what she said was a lot more acute than her manner of saying it.

'I did tell you, dear, didn't I, that Orkney has a box at the races? So we'll be going up there when we get there and of course after the races for ages and ages; he does go on so. He'll probably have a woman there . . . I'm just telling you dear, because she's not his wife and he doesn't like people to ask about that either, dear, so don't ask either of them if they're married, will you dear?'

'There's an awful lot he doesn't like talking about,' I said.

'Oh yes, dear, he's very awkward, but if you stick to horses it will be all right, that's all he likes to talk about and he'll do that all night, and of course that's just what I can't do, as you know.'

'Any other bricks I might drop?' I asked. 'Religion, politics, medical history?'

'Yes, well, Tony dear, you're teasing me . . .' She turned into the entrance of Martineau Park, where the gateman waved her through with welcoming recognition. 'Don't forget his horse is called Breezy Palm and it's a two-year-old colt, and it's run nine times this season and won twice, and once it smashed its way out of the stalls and nearly slaughtered the assistant starter so maybe you'd better not mention that too much either.'

She parked the car but didn't get out immediately, instead pulling on a becoming hat and adjusting the angle in the driving mirror.

'I haven't asked you how your arm is, dear,' she said, 'because it's perfectly obvious it's hurting you.'

'Is it?' I said, slightly dismayed.

'When you move it, dear, you wince.'

'Oh.'

'Wouldn't it be better in a sling, dear?'

'Better to use it, I should think.'

The kind eyes looked my way. 'You know, Tony dear, I think we should go first of all to the first aid room and borrow one of those narrow black wrist-supporting slings that the jumping jockeys use when they've broken things, and then you won't have to shake hands with people, which I noticed you avoided doing with Tina yesterday, and other people won't bang into you if they see they shouldn't.'

She left me speechless. We went to the first aid room, where by a mixture of charm and bullying she got what she wanted, and I emerged feeling both grateful and slightly silly.

'That's better, dear,' she said, nodding. 'Now we can go up to Orkney's box . . .' All her decisiveness in the first aid room vanished. 'Oh dear . . . he makes me feel so stupid and clumsy and as if I'd never stepped out of the schoolroom.'

'You look,' I said truthfully, 'poised, well-dressed and anybody's match. Stifle all doubts.'

Her eyes however were full of them and her nervousness shortened her breath in the lift going up to the fourth floor.

The Martineau Park grandstands were among the best in the country, the whole lot having been designed and built at one time, not piecemeal in modernisation programmes as at many other courses. The old stands having decayed to dangerous levels around 1950, it had been decided to raze the lot and start again, and although one could find fault about wind tunnels (result of schools of architecture being apparently ignorant of elementary physics) the cost-cutting disasters of some other places had been avoided. One could nearly everywhere, for instance, if one wanted to, watch the races from under cover and sitting down, and could celebrate afterwards in bars large enough for the crush. There was a warmed (or cooled) glass walled gallery overlooking the parade ring and a roof above the unsaddling enclosures (as at Aintree) to keep all the back-slapping dry.

The two long tiers of high-up boxes were reached by enclosed hallways along which, when we came out of the lift, waitresses were pushing trolleys of food: a far cry from Ascot where they tottered with trays along open galleries, eclairs flying in the wind. Martineau Park, in fact, was almost too comfortable to be British.

Flora said, 'This way,' and went ahead of me with foreboding. Orkney Swale, I thought, simply couldn't be as intimidating as she made out.

The door of his box stood open. Flora and I reached it together and looked in. A sideboard scarcely groaning with food and drink stood against the wall. Three small tables with attendant chairs filled the rest of the floor space, with glass doors to the viewing balcony beyond. To the right of the entrance door, a small serving pantry, clean and uncluttered. Orkney's, unlike some of the boxes we'd passed, wasn't offering lunch.

A man sat alone at one of the tables, head bent over a racing newspaper and form book, pen at the ready for making notes.

Flora cleared her throat, said 'Orkney?' waveringly and took three tentative steps into the box. The man at the table turned his head without haste, an enquiring expression raising his eyebrows. Even when he saw Flora and clearly knew her he was in no rush to stand up. He finally made it, but as if the politeness were something he'd belatedly thought of, not an instinctive act of greeting.

He was tall, sandy haired, wore glasses over pale blue eyes, smiled with reluctance.

'This is Tony Beach, Orkney,' Flora said.

Orkney looked me calmly up and down, gaze pausing briefly on the sling. 'Jack's assistant?' he asked.

'No, no,' Flora said, 'a friend.'

'How do you do?' I said in my best Jimmy manner, and got a nod for it, which seemed to relieve Flora, although she still tended to shift from foot to foot.

'Jack asked me to tell you he'd had good reports about Breezy Palm from the head lad,' she said valiantly.

'I talked to Jack myself,' Orkney said. After a noticeable pause he added, 'Would you care for a drink?'

I could sense Flora about to refuse so I said. 'Yes, why not?'

in a Jimmy drawl, because a stiffener might be just what Flora needed.

Orkney looked vaguely at the sideboard upon which stood a bottle of gin, a bottle of scotch, an assortment of mixers and several glasses. He picked up an empty glass which had been near him on the small table, transferred it to the sideboard and stretched out his hand to a Seagram's bottle.

'Gin and tonic, Flora?' he offered.

'That would be nice, Orkney.'

Flora bought gin from me to give to visiting owners, saying she didn't much care for it herself. She watched apprehensively as Orkney poured two fingersworth and barely doubled it with tonic.

'Ice? Lemon?' he asked, and added them without waiting for an answer. He handed her the glass while looking at me. 'And you . . . er . . . same for you?'

'Scotch,' I said. 'Most kind.'

It was Teacher's whisky, standard premium. He poured the two fingers and hovered a hand between ginger ale and soda, eyebrows elevated.

'Just as it comes,' I said. 'No ice.'

The eyebrows rose higher. He gave me the glass, recapped the whisky and returned to the gin for himself. Two and a half fingers. Very little tonic. Two chunks of ice.

'To luck,' I said, taking a sip. 'To . . . ah . . . Breezy Palm.'

'Oh yes,' Flora said. 'Breezy Palm.'

The blended flavours trickled back over my tongue, announcing their separate presences, grain, malt and oakwood, familiar and vivid, fading slowly to aftertaste. I maybe couldn't have picked Teacher's reliably from a row of similar blends, but one thing was certain: what I was drinking wasn't Rannoch.

'Hurt your arm?' Orkney asked.

'Er . . .' I said. 'Had an accident with a door.'

Flora's eyes widened but to my relief she refrained from rushing in with details. Orkney merely nodded, acknowledging life's incidental perils. 'Too bad,' he said.

A waitress appeared at the doorway, pushing a trolley. A quick glance at Flora's face showed me one couldn't expect too much from this, and the reality turned out to be three moderately large plates bearing respectively crustless sandwiches, cheese and biscuits and strawberry tartlets, all tautly wrapped in a transparent cling-film. The waitress asked if she could liberate the modest feast but Orkney said no, he would do it later, and there it all sat, mouthwateringly out of reach.

'In the good old days,' Flora told me later, 'one used to be able to take one's own food and drink to one's box, but now the caterers have an absolute stranglehold and everyone has to buy everything from them, and for some things they are frightfully expensive, absolutely exorbitant my dear, and Orkney resents it so much that he buys the absolute minimum. He's not really so mean as he looks today, it's just his way . . . he told us once that the caterers charge bar prices in the boxes, whatever that means, and that made him very angry?'

'Bar prices?' I said. 'Are you sure?'

'Is that so bad, dear?'

'Judging from race meeting bar prices, about a hundred and fifty per cent profit on a bottle of scotch.'

Flora worked it out. 'So Orkney has to pay in his box more than double what the same bottle costs in your shop?'

'Yes, a good deal more than double.'

'My dear,' she said, 'I'd no idea drinks in the boxes cost so much.'

'A pound barely wets the glass.'

'You're teasing me.'

'Not entirely,' I said.

'No wonder Orkney resents having to pay that much when he used to take his own.'

'Mm,' I said reflectively. 'The caterers do have big overheads, of course, but to charge by the tot in the boxes . . .'

'By the tot, dear?'

'Thirty-two tots to a bottle. That's the single measure for spirits in all bars, racing or not. Two centilitres. One large mouthful or two small.'

Flora hardly believed me. 'I suppose I don't often buy drinks in bars, dear,' she said sighing. 'Jack does it, you see.'

In hindsight Orkney Swayle's hand on the bottles had been lavish: generosity well disguised by a cold demeanour. And the external manners, I came to see during the afternoon, were not intentionally rude, but a thoughtless habit, the sort of behaviour one could inherit in ultra-reserved families. He appeared not to be aware of the effect he had on others and would perhaps have been astonished to know he reduced Flora to quivers.

Orkney made inroads in his gin with his regard impassively on my face.

'Are you knowledgeable about horses?' he asked.

I began to say 'marginally' but Flora didn't want any sort of modest disclaimers on my part, she wanted Orkney to be impressed. 'Yes of course he is, Orkney, his mother is a master of hounds and his father was a colonel and the greatest amateur rider of his generation and his grandfather was also a colonel and nearly won the Grand National . . .'

The faintest of gleams entered and left Orkney's eyes and I thought with surprise that somewhere deep down he might have after all a sense of humour.

'Yes, Flora,' he said. 'Those references are impeccable.'

'Oh.' She fell silent, not knowing if he were mocking her, and went pink round the nose, looking unhappily down at her drink.

'Breezy Palm,' Orkney said, oblivious, 'is by Desert Palm out of Breezy City, by Draughty City, which was a half-brother to Goldenburgh whose sire won the Arc de Triomphe, of course.'

He paused as if expecting comment so I obligingly said, 'What interesting breeding,' which seemed to cover most eventualities, including my own absolute ignorance of all the horses involved.

He nodded judiciously. 'American blood, of course. Draughty City was by Chicago Lake out of a dam by Michigan. Good strong hard horses. I never saw Draughty City of course, but I've talked to people who saw him race. You can't do better than mixed American and British blood, I always say.'

'I'm sure you're right,' I said.

Orkney discoursed for several further minutes on Breezy Palm's antecedents with me making appropriate comments here and there and Flora, on the edge of my vision, slowly beginning to relax.

Such progress as she had made was however ruined at that point by the arrival from the powder room of the lady to whom Orkney wasn't married, and it was clear that however much Orkney himself made Flora feel clumsy, his lady did it double.

Compared with Flora she was six inches taller, six inches slimmer and approximately six years younger. She also had strikingly large grey eyes, a long thin neck and luminous make-up, and was wearing almost the same clothes but with distinctly more chic: tailored suit, good shoes, neat felt hat at a becoming angle. An elegant, mature, sophisticated knock-out.

To the eye it was no contest. Flora looked dumpy beside her, and knew it. I put my arm round her shoulders and hugged her and thought for one dreadful second that I'd reduced her to tears.

'Flora,' Orkney said, 'of course you and Isabella know each other . . . Isabella, my dear, this is Flora's walker . . . er . . . what did you say your name was?'

I told him. He told Isabella. Isabella and I exchanged medium hello smiles and Orkney returned to the subject of American forebears.

The races came and went: first, second, third. Everyone went down each time to inspect the horses as they walked round the parade ring, returning to the box to watch the race. Orkney gambled seriously, taking his custom to the bookmakers on the rails. Isabella flourished fistfuls of Tote tickets. Flora said she couldn't be bothered to bet but would rather check to make sure everything was all right with Breezy Palm.

I went with her to find Jack's travelling head lad (not the unctuous Howard but a little dynamo of a man with sharp restless eyes) who said cryptically that the horse was as right as he would ever be and that Mrs Hawthorn wasn't to worry, everything was in order.

Mrs Hawthorn naturally took no heed of his good advice and went on worrying regardless.

'Why didn't you tell Orkney what really happened to your arm, dear?' she asked.

'I'm not proud of it,' I said prosaically. 'Don't want to talk about it. Just like Orkney.'

Flora the constant chatterer deeply sighed. 'So odd, dear. It's nothing to be ashamed of.'

We returned in the lift to the box where Flora wistfully eyed the still-wrapped food and asked if I'd had any lunch.

'No,' I said. 'Did you?'

'I should have remembered,' she sighed, 'but I didn't,' and she told me then about Orkney's hate reaction to the caterers.

Orkney had invited no other guests. He appeared to expect Flora and myself to return to the box for each race but didn't actually say so. An unsettling host, to say the least.

It was out on the balcony when we were waiting for the runners in the third race to canter down to the start that he asked Flora if Jack had found anyone else to lease his mare: he had forgotten to ask him on the hospital telephone.

'He'll do it as soon as he's home, I'm sure,' Flora said placatingly, and to me she added, 'Orkney owns one of the horses that Larry Trent leased.'

Orkney said austerely. 'My good filly by Fringe. A three-year-old, good deep heart room, gets that from her dam, of course.'

I thought back. 'I must have seen her in Jack's yard,' I said. Four evenings in a row, to be precise.

'Really?' Orkney showed interest. 'Liver chestnut, white blaze, kind eye.'

'I remember,' I said. 'Good bone. Nice straight hocks. And she has some cleanly healed scars on her near shoulder. Looks like barbed wire.'

Orkney looked both gratified and annoyed. 'She got loose one day as a two-year-old. The only bit of barbed wire in Berkshire and she has to crash into it. Horses have no sense.'

'They panic easily,' I agreed.

Orkney's manner to me softened perceptibly at that point, which Flora noted and glowed over.

'Your filly did well for Larry Trent,' I said.

'Not bad. Won a nice handicap at Newbury and another at Kempton. Both Larry and I made a profit through the books, but I was hoping for black print, of course.'

I caught Flora starting to look anxious. 'Of course,' I said confidently; and she subsided. 'Black print' had come back just in time as an echo from childhood. Races of prestige and high prizes were printed in heavy black type in auction catalogues: black print earned by a broodmare upped the price of her foals by thousands.

'Will you keep her in training next year?' I asked.

'If I can get someone else to lease her.' He paused slightly. 'I prefer to run two-year-olds myself, of course. I've had four in training with Jack this year. I sell them on if they're any good, or lease them, especially fillies, if they're well bred, so that I can either breed from them later or sell them as broodmares. Larry often took one of my fillies as three- or four-year-olds. Good eye for a horse, Larry had, poor fellow.'

'Yes, so I hear.'

'Did you know him?'

'No.' I shook my head. 'I saw him at the party . . . but that was all.' In my mind's eye I saw him alive and also lifeless, the man whose death had started so many worms crawling.

'I didn't go to the party,' Orkney said calmly. 'Too bad he was killed.'

'You knew him well?' I asked.

'Pretty well. We weren't close friends, of course. Just had the mutual interest in horses.'

Orkney's voice clearly announced what his lips hadn't said: Larry Trent hadn't been, in Orkney's estimation, Orkney's social equal.

'So . . . er . . .' I said, 'you didn't go to his place . . . the Silver Moondance?'

The faintest spasm crossed Orkney's undemonstrative face. 'I met him there, once, yes, in his office, to discuss business. We dined afterwards. A dinner dance, Larry said. Very loud music . . .' He left the sentence hanging, criticism implied but not uttered.

'What did you think of the wine?' I asked.

'Wine?' He was surprised.

'I'm a wine merchant,' I said.

'Oh, really?' Wine merchants, it seemed, were in Orkney's world provisionally O.K., 'Interesting. Well, as far as I remember it was perfectly adequate. For a dinner dance, of course.'

Perfectly adequate for a dinner dance brilliantly summed up the superior plonk in all those suspect bottles. There wasn't any point, I thought, in asking Orkney about the scotch; he was a gin man himself.

The horses for the third race emerged onto the track and cantered past the stands. Orkney raised a massive pair of binoculars and studied his fancy, a flashy looking bay with a bounding impatient stride like an impala and sweat already on his neck.

'Fighting his jockey,' Orkney muttered. 'Losing the race on the way down.' He lowered the race-glasses and scowled.

'Larry Trent sometimes bought horses at the sales,' I said casually, watching the runners. 'Not for you?'

'No, no. For his brother.' Orkney's eyes and attention were anywhere but on me. 'Horses in training. Three-year-olds, or four or five. Shipped them abroad, that sort of thing. No, no, I buy yearlings . . . on bloodstock agents' advice, of course.'

Flora, listening, wore an expression that changed rapidly from surprise to comprehension. The disappearing Ramekin had been explained in the most mundane unmysterious way.

She wasn't exactly disappointed but in the comprehension there was definite anticlimax.

'Look at that!' Orkney exclaimed crossly. 'The damn thing's bolting.'

His fancy had won the battle with his jockey and was departing into the distance at a flat gallop. Orkney raised his binoculars and folded his mouth into a grim and almost spiteful line as if he would have wrung the jockey's neck if he could have caught him.

'Did you know Larry Trent's brother?' I asked.

'What? No. No, never met him. Larry just said . . . Look at that! Bloody fool ought to be fined. I saw Larry buying a good horse for around fifty thousand at the sales. I said if he had that sort of money, why did he prefer leasing? It was his brother's cash, he said. Out of his league. But he could pick horses, he said, and his brother couldn't. The one thing his brother couldn't do, he said. Sounded envious to me. But there you are, that's people. Look at that bloody boy! Gone past the start. It's too bad! It's disgraceful!' Ungovernable irritation rose in his voice. 'Now they'll be late off, and we'll be rushed for Breezy Palm.'

THIRTEEN:

He was right. They were late off. Orkney's fancy finished dead tired and second to last and we were indeed rushed for Breezy Palm.

Orkney was seriously displeased. Orkney became coldly and selfishly unpleasant.

I dutifully walked Flora down to the saddling boxes, though more slowly than our angry host had propelled his lady. ('You didn't mind him calling you my walker, did you, dear?' Flora asked anxiously. 'Not at all. Delighted to walk you anywhere, any time.' 'You're such a comfort, Tony dear.') We reached the saddling boxes as the tiny saddle itself went on over the number cloth, elastic girths dangling.

Breezy Palm, a chestnut with three white socks, looked as if he had a certain amount of growing still to do, particularly in front. Horses, like children, grew at intervals with rests in between: Breezy Palm's forelegs hadn't yet caught up with the last spurt in the hind.

'Good strong rump,' I said, in best Jimmy fashion.

The brisk travelling head lad, busy with girth buckles, glanced at me hopefully but Orkney was in no mood for flattery. 'He's coming to hand again at last,' he said sourly. 'He won twice back in July, but since then there have been several infuriating disappointments. Not Jack's fault, of course . . .' His voice all the same was loaded with criticism. '. . . jockeys' mistakes, entered at the wrong courses, frightened in the starting gate, needed the race, always something.'

Neither the head lad nor Flora looked happy, but nor were they surprised. Orkney's pre-race nerves, I supposed, were part of the job.

'Couldn't you have saddled up sooner?' Orkney said crossly. 'You must have known the last race was delayed.'

'You usually like to see your horses saddled, sir.'

'Yes, yes, but use some commonsense.'

'Sorry, sir.'

'Can't you hurry that up?' Orkney said with increasing

brusqueness as the head lad began sponging the horse's nose and mouth. 'We're damned late already.'

'Just coming, sir.' The head lad's glance fell on the horse's rug, still to be buckled on over the saddle for warming muscles on the October day. There was a pot of oil for brushing gloss onto the hooves . . . and a prize to the lad, it said in the racecard, for the best turned-out horse.

'It's too bad,' Orkney said impatiently. 'We should be in the parade ring already.' He turned away sharply and stalked off in that direction, leaving Isabella, Flora and me to follow as we would.

Isabella looked stoically unaffected. Flora began to scurry after Orkney but I caught her abruptly by the arm, knowing he'd think less of her for hurrying, not more.

'Slow down, slow down, the jockeys aren't out yet.'

'Oh. All right then.' She looked guilty as much as flustered, and walked with small jerky steps between the long-legged Isabella and myself as we joined Orkney in the parade ring, no later than any other owner-trainer group.

Orkney was still in the grip of the outburst of bad temper, which failed to abate when Breezy Palm finally appeared in the ring looking polished. The jockey, approaching it seemed to me unsmilingly out of past experience, was sarcastically told not to leave his winning run as bloody late as last time and not to go to sleep in the stalls, if he didn't mind.

The featherweight jockey listened expressionlessly, his gaze on the ground, his body relaxed. He's heard it all before, I thought, and he simply doesn't care. I wondered, if I'd been a jockey, whether I would have ridden my heart out for owners who spoke in that way, and concluded that possibly not. Breezy Palm's uncertain prospects developed a certainty for me at that moment: and I wondered what Orkney would be like in defeat when he was so obnoxious in hope.

The bell rang for the jockeys to mount. Breezy Palm's jockey nodded to Orkney and went away with Orkney still telling him that if he used his whip too much he'd have him up in front of the stewards.

Flora was standing so close to me she was virtually clinging on. When Orkney turned away and strode out of the parade ring without waiting for Isabella or to see his horse mounted she said to me shakily, 'Jack manages him, but I can't. Jack stops him being so rude to the jockeys. One of them refused to ride his horses . . . can you imagine?'

'Mm,' I said. 'Do we have to go up to the box to watch the race?'

'Oh, my goodness, yes,' she said emphatically. 'At least . . . I mean . . . you don't have to . . . I could go alone.'

'Don't be silly.'

I looked around for the decorative Isabella, but she too had disappeared.

'They've both gone to bet,' Flora said, sighing. 'Jack said the opposition was stiff . . . I'm so afraid Breezy Palm won't win.'

We went up in the lift to the empty box. The sandwiches and tartlets were still wrapped, but the gin level had dropped considerably since we had arrived. Gin itself, I reflected, was a notorious inducer, in some people, of catty ill-humour.

Flora and I went onto the balcony to see the runners go down to the start, and Orkney arrived breathlessly, moving in front of us without apology, raising his binoculars to see what sins his jockey might already be committing. Isabella collectedly arrived with her clutched tickets and I glanced at the flickering light of the Tote board to see Breezy Palm's odds. Seven to one; by no means favourite but fairly well backed.

There were eighteen runners, several of them past winners. Breezy Palm, well drawn, went into the stalls quietly and showed no signs of re-assaulting the assistant starter. Orkney's slightly frantic agitation stilled suddenly to concentration and in the six-furlong distance the dark green starting gates opened in unison and spilled out their brilliant accelerating rainbow cargo.

Flora raised her own small raceglasses but I doubted if she could see much for trembling. Three-quarter-mile straight races were in any case difficult to read in the early stages as the runners were so far away and coming straight towards one, and it took me a fair time myself to sort out Orkney's jockey in red and grey. The commentator, rattling off names, hadn't mentioned Breezy Palm at all by the time they reached half-way but I could see him there, bobbing along in the pack, making no move either forward or backward, proving merely at that stage that he was no better and no worse than his opponents.

Flora gave up the struggle with her raceglasses, lowered them, and watched the last two furlongs simply with anxiety. The bunch of runners which had seemed to be moving slowly was suddenly perceived to be flying, the tiny foreshortened distances from first to last stretching before one's eyes to gaps of a length, to definite possibles and positive losers. The young colts stuck out their necks and strove to be first as they would have done in a wild herd on an unrailed plain, the primaeval instinct flashing there undiluted on the civilised track. The very essence of racing, I thought. The untamed force that made it all possible. Exciting, moving . . . beautiful.

Breezy Palm had the ancient instinct in full measure. Whether urged to the full by his jockey or not he was straining ahead with passion, legs angular beneath the immature body, stride hurried and scratchy, the compulsion to be first all there but the technical ability still underdeveloped.

The trick of race-riding, my father had once said, was to awaken a horse's natural panic fear and then control it. My father, of course, had had no doubt at all that he could do both. It was I, his son, who couldn't do either. Pity . . .

Breezy Palm's natural panic, jockey controlling it to the extent of letting it have its head and keeping it running straight, was still lustily aiming a shade beyond his ability. Orkney watched in concentrated silence. Flora seemed to be holding her breath. Isabella behind me was saying 'Coming on, you bugger, come on, you bugger,' continuously under her breath, her most human reaction to date. Breezy Palm, oblivious, had his eyes fixed on the three horses still in front of him and over the last hundred yards ran as if the great god Pan were at his very heels.

Horses can only do their best. Breezy Palm's best on that day couldn't overhaul the winner, who went ahead by a length, or the second, who left clear space behind him, but he flashed over the line so close to the third of the leaders that from the angle of Orkney's box it was impossible to tell the exact placings. The judge, announced the tannoy, was calling for a photograph.

Orkney, still silent, lowered his glasses and stared up the track to where his hepped-up colt was being hauled back into the twentieth century. Then still saying nothing he turned and hurried away, again leaving his companions to fare for themselves.

'Come on, dear,' Flora said, tugging my sleeve. 'We must go down too. Jack said to be sure to. Oh dear . . .'

The three of us consequently made the downward journey as fast as possible and arrived to find Breezy Palm stamping around in the place allotted to the horse that finished fourth, the jockey unbuckling the girths and Orkney scowling.

'Oh dear . . .' Flora said again. 'The jockeys always know . . . He must have been beaten for third after all.'

The result of the photograph, soon announced, confirmed it: Breezy Palm had finished fourth. Distances: length, two lengths, short head.

Flora, Isabella and I stood beside Orkney, looking at the sweating, tossing skittering two-year-old and making consoling and congratulatory remarks, none of which seemed to please.

'Ran extremely well in a strong field,' I said.

'The wrong race for him,' Orkney said brusquely. 'I've no idea why Jack persists in entering him in this class. Perfectly obvious they were too good for him.'

'Only just,' Isabella said reasonably.

'My dear woman, you know nothing about it.'

Isabella merely smiled; fortitude of an exceptional nature.

It struck me that she herself was totally uncowed by Orkney. He treated her rudely: she ignored it, neither embarrassed nor upset. Subtly, somewhere in their relationship, she was his equal . . . and both of them knew it.

Flora said bravely, 'I thought the horse ran splendidly,' and received a pitying glance from on high.

'He fought to the end,' I said admiringly. 'Definitely not a quitter.'

'Fourth,' Orkney said repressively, as if fourth in itself bespoke a lack of character, and I wondered if he cared in the least how graceless he sounded.

The signal was given for the horses to be led away and Orkney made impatient movements which everyone interpreted as his own type of invitation to the box. There at last he busied himself with removing the wrappings from the overdue sandwiches, but without much method, finally pushing the plates towards Isabella for her to do it. Orkney himself poured fresh drinks as unstintingly as before and indicated that we might all sit down round one of the tables, if we so wished. All of us sat. All of us ate politely, hiding our hunger.

As a post-race jollification it would have done a funeral proud, but gradually the worst of Orkney's sulks wore off and he began to make comments that proved he had at least understood what he'd seen, even if he took no joy in it.

'He's lost his action,' he said. 'Back in July, when he won, he had a better stride. Much more fluent. That's the only trouble with two-year-olds. You think you've got a world beater and then they start developing unevenly.'

'He might be better next year,' I suggested. 'Won't you keep him? He could be worth it.'

Orkney shook his head. 'He's going to the sales next week. I wanted a win today to put his price up. Jack knew that.' The echo of grudge was still strong. 'Larry Trent might have leased him. He thought, as you seem to, that his action might come back once he'd finished growing, but I'm not risking it. Sell, and buy yearlings, that's my preference. Different runners every year . . . more interesting.'

'You don't have time to grow fond of them,' I said neutrally.

'Quite right,' he nodded. 'Once you get sentimental you throw good money down the drain.'

I remembered the friendships my father had had with his steeplechasers, treating each with camaraderie over many years, getting to interpret their every twitch and particularly loving the one that had killed him. Money down the drain, sure, but a bottomless pleasure in return such as Orkney would never get to feel.

'That damned jockey left his run too late,' Orkney said, but without undue viciousness. 'Breezy Palm was still making up ground at the end. You saw that. If he'd got at him sooner . . .'

'Difficult to tell,' I said, drawling.

'I told him not to leave it too late. I told him.'

'You told him not to hit the horse,' Isabella said calmly. 'You can't have it both ways, Orkney.'

Orkney could, however. Throughout the sandwiches, the cheese and the strawberry tartlets he dissected and discussed the race stride by stride, mostly with disapproval. My contention that his colt had shown great racing spirit was accepted. Flora's defence of the jockey wasn't. I grew soundly tired of the whole circus and wondered how soon we could leave.

The waitress appeared again in the doorway asking if Orkney needed anything else, and Orkney said yes, another bottle of gin.

'And make sure it's Seagram's,' he said. The waitress nodded and went away, and he said to me, 'I order Seagram's just because the caterers have to get it in specially. They serve their own brand if you don't ask. They charge disgraceful prices . . . I'm not going to make life easy for them if I can help it.'

Flora's and Isabella's expressions, I saw, were identical in pained resignation. Orkney had mounted his hobby horse and would complain about the caterers for another ten minutes. The arrival of the fresh bottle didn't check him, but at the end he seemed to remember my own job and said with apparently newly-reached decision, 'It's local people like you who should be providing the drinks, not this huge conglomerate. If enough people complain to the Clerk of the Course, I don't see why we couldn't get the system put back to the old ways. Do you?'

'Worth a try,' I said non-committally.

'What you want to do,' he insisted, 'is propose yourself as an alternative. Give these damn monopolists a jolt.'

'Something to think about,' I murmured, not meaning to in the least, and he lectured me at tiresome length on what I ought to do personally for the box-renters of Martineau Park, not to mention for all the other racecourses where the same caterers presided, and what I should do about the other firms of caterers who carved up the whole country's racecourses between them.

'Er . . . Orkney,' Flora said uncertainly, when the tirade had died down, 'I do believe, you know, that at a few courses they really have finished with the conglomerates and called in local caterers, so perhaps . . . you never know.'

Orkney looked at her with an astonishment which seemed to be based less on what she'd said than on the fact of her knowing it. 'Are you sure, Flora?'

'Yes . . . I'm sure.'

'There you are then,' he said to me. 'What are you waiting for?'

'I wouldn't mind shuttling the drinks along,' I said. 'But what about the food? This food is good, you'd have to admit. That's where these caterers excel.'

'Food. Yes, their food's all right,' he said grudgingly.

We'd finished every crumb and I could have eaten the whole lot again. Orkney returned to the subject of Breezy Palm and two drinks later had exhausted even Isabella's long-suffering patience.

'If you want me to drive you home, Orkney, the time is now,' she said. 'You may not have noticed that they ran the last race ten minutes ago.'

'Really?' He looked at his watch and surprisingly took immediate action, standing up and collecting his papers. 'Very well then. Flora, I'll be talking to Jack on the telephone . . . and er . . .' he made an effort to remember my name as the rest of us stood up also. 'Good to have met you . . . er . . . Tony.' He nodded twice in lieu of shaking hands. 'Any time you're here with Flora . . . glad to have you.'

'Thank you, Orkney,' I said.

Isabella bent to give Flora a kiss in the air an inch off her cheek and looked vaguely at my sling, finding like Orkney that hands unavailable for shaking left goodbyes half unsaid.

'Er . . .' she said, 'so nice . . .'

They went away down the hallway and Flora sat down again abruptly.

'Thank goodness that's over,' she said fervently. 'I'd never have got through it without you. Thank goodness he liked you.'

'Liked?' I was sceptical.

'Oh yes, dear, he asked you back, that's practically unheard of.'

'How did Isabella,' I asked, 'get him to go home?'

Flora smiled the first carefree smile of the day, her eyes crinkling with fun. 'My dear, they will certainly have come in her car, and if he didn't go when she says she would drive off and leave him. She did it once . . . there was a terrible fuss and Jack and I had to put him on a train. Because, as you've noticed dear, he likes his gin and a few months ago he was breathalised on the way home and lost his licence . . . but he doesn't like one to talk about that either.'

After the races, during the evening shift in the shop, I telephoned again to Henri Tavel in Bordeaux and listened without much surprise to his news.

'Mon cher Tony, there is no Château Caillot in St Estèphe. There is no Château Caillot in Haut Médoc. There is no Château Caillot in the whole region of Bordeaux.'

'One thought there might not be,' I said.

'As for the *négociant* Thiery et Fils . . .' the heavy gallic shrug travelled almost visibly along the wires, '. . . there is no person called Thiery who is *négociant* in Bordeaux. As you know, some people call themselves *négociants* who work only in paper and never see the wine they sell, but even among these there is no Thiery.'

'You've been most thorough, Henri.'

'To forge wine labels is a serious matter.'

His voice, vibrating deeply, reflected an outrage no less genuine for being unsurprised. To Henri Tavel, as to all the château owners and wineshippers of Bordeaux, wine transcended religion. Conscious and proud of producing the best in the world they worked to stiff bureaucratic criteria which had been laid down in Médoc in 1855 and only fractionally changed since.

They still spoke of 1816, a year of undrinkable quality, as if it were fresh in their memory. They knew the day the grape harvest had started every year back beyond 1795 (September 24th). They knew that wine had been made uninterruptedly in their same vineyards for at least two thousand years.

Every single bottle of the five hundred and fifty million sent out from the region each year had to be certified and accounted for; had to be worthy of the name it bore; had to be able to uphold the reputation for the whole of its life. And the life of a Bordeaux red wine could be amazing . . . With Henri Tavel I had myself tasted one ninety years old which still shone with colour and sang on the palate.

To forge a Bordeaux château label and stick it on an amorphous product of the European wine lake was a heresy of burning-at-the-stake proportions. Henri Tavel wanted assurances that the forgers of Caillot would feel the flames. I could offer only weak-sounding promises that everyone would do their best.

'It is important,' he insisted.

'Yes, I know it is. Truly, Henri, I do know.'

'Give my regards,' he said, 'to your dear mother.'

Life continued normally on the next day, Wednesday, if a disgruntledly itching arm could be considered normal. I was due to take it back to the hospital for inspection the following afternoon and meanwhile went on using the sling much of the time, finding it comfortable and a good excuse for not lifting the cases. Brian had become anxiously solicitous at the sight of it and carefully took even single bottles out of my grasp. Mrs Palissey was writing down the telephone orders to save me the wincing. I felt cossetted and amused.

She and Brian left early with the deliveries because there were so many: some postponed and some in advance, including the glasses and champagne for the next day's coming-of-age. I kept shop, smiling, ever smiling as usual, and thinking, when I could.

Shortly after eight in the evening Gerard walked in looking grey and tired and asking if I could shut the damned place and come out and eat. Somewhere quiet. He wanted to talk.

I looked at the fatigued lines in his face and the droop of his normally erect body. I was twenty years younger than he and I hadn't had a general anaesthetic, and if in spite of taking things fairly easy I still felt battered and weak, then he must feel worse. And maybe the cause wasn't simply the profusion of little burning stab wounds but the residue also from the horsebox . . . the *frissons* of nearness to death.

'We could take Sung Li's food home to my house,' I suggested diffidently, 'if you'd like.'

He would like, he said. He would also buy the food while I fiddled with the till and locked up, and how soon would that be?

'Half an hour,' I said. 'Have some wine.'

He sighed with resignation, sat on the chair I brought from the office and ruefully smiled at our two slings.

'Snap,' he said.

'Flora's idea, mine.'

'Sensible lady.'

'I'll get the wine.'

In the office I poured some genuine wine from St Estèphe and some of the Silver Moondance version into two glasses and carried them out to the counter.

'Taste them both,' I said. 'Say what you think.'

'What are they?'

'Tell you later.'

'I'm no expert,' he protested. He sipped the first, however, rolling it round his gums and grimacing as if he'd sucked a lemon.

'Very dry,' he said.

'Try the other.'

The second seemed at first to please him better, but after a while he eyed it thoughtfully and put the glass down carefully on the counter.

'Well?' I asked.

He smiled. 'The first is demanding. The second is pleasant . . . but light. You're going to tell me that the first is more expensive.'

'Pretty good. The second one, the pleasant but light one, came from the Silver Moondance. The first is near enough what it should have tasted like, according to the label.'

He savoured the various significances. 'Many might prefer the fake. People who didn't know what to expect.'

'Yes. A good drink. Nothing wrong with it.'

He sipped the genuine article again. 'But once you know this one, you grow to appreciate it.'

'If I had any just now I'd give you one of the great St Estèphes . . . Cos d'Etournel, Montrose, Calon-Ségur . . . but this is a good cru bourgeois . . . lots of body and force.'

'Take your word for it,' he said amiably. 'I've often wished I knew more about wine.'

'Stick around.'

I tasted both the wines again myself, meeting them as old friends. The Silver Moondance wine had stood up pretty well to being opened and refastened, but now that I'd poured the second sample out of the bottle what was left would begin to deteriorate. For wine to remain perfect it had to be in contact with the cork. The more air in the bottle the more damage it did.

I fetched and showed him both of the bottles, real and fake, and told him what Henri Tavel had had to say about forgeries.

He listened attentively, thought for a while, and then said, 'What is it about the fake wine that seems more significant to you than the fake whisky? Because it does, doesn't it?'

'Just as much. Equally.'

'Why, then?'

'Because . . .' I began, and was immediately interrupted by a row of customers wanting to know what to drink inexpensively with Sung Li's crispy duck and Peking prawn and beef in oyster sauce. Gerard listened with interest and watched them go one by one with their bottles of Bergerac and Soave and Côtes du Ventoux.

He said, 'You sell knowledge, don't you, as much as wine?'

'Yeah. And pleasure. And human contact. Anything you can't get from a supermarket.'

A large man with eyes awash shouldered his way unsteadily into the shop demanding beer loudly, and I sold him what he wanted without demur. He paid clumsily, belched, went on his weaving way: and Gerard frowned at his departing back.

'He was drunk,' he said.

'Sure.'

'Don't you care?'

'Not as long as they're not sick in the shop.'

'That's immoral.'

I grinned faintly. 'I sell escape also.'

'Temporary,' he objected disapprovingly, sounding austerely Scots.

'Temporary is better than nothing,' I said. 'Have an aspirin.'

He made a noise between a cough and a chuckle. 'I suppose you've lived on them since Sunday.'

'Yes, quite right.' I swallowed two more with some St Estèphe, in itself a minor heresy. 'I'm all for escape.'

He gave me a dry look which I didn't at first understand, and only belatedly remembered my rush down the yard.

'Well . . . as long as I'm not being robbed.'

He nodded sardonically and waited through two more sales and a discussion about whether Sauternes would go with lamb chops, which it wouldn't; they would each taste dreadful.

'What goes with Sauternes then? I like Sauternes.'

'Anything sweet,' I said. 'Also perhaps curry. Or ham. Also blue cheese.'

'Good heavens,' said Gerard when he'd gone. 'Blue cheese with sweet wine . . . how odd.'

'Wine and cheese parties thrive on it.'

He looked round the shop as if at a new world. 'Is there anything you can't drink wine with?' he said.

'As far as I'm concerned . . . grapefruit.'

He made a face.

'And that's from one,' I said, 'who drinks wine with baked beans . . . who practically scrubs his teeth in it.'

'You really love it?'

I nodded. 'Nature's magical accident.'

'What?'

'That the fungus on grapes turns the sugar in grape juice to alcohol. That the result is delicious.'

'For heaven's sake . . .'

'No one could have invented it,' I said. 'It's just there. A gift to the planet. Elegant.'

'But there are all sorts of different wines.'

'Oh, sure, because there are different sorts of grapes. But a lot of champagne is made from black-skinned grapes . . . things may not be as they seem, which should please you as a detective.'

'Hm,' he said dryly. His glance roved over the racks of bottles. 'As a detective what pleases me is proof . . . so what's proof?'

'If you mix a liquid with gunpowder and ignite it, and it burns with a steady blue flame, that's proof.'

He looked faintly bemused. 'Proof of what?'

'Proof that the liquid is at least fifty percent alcohol. That's how they proved a liquid was alcohol three centuries ago when they first put a tax on distilled spirits. Fifty percent alcohol, one hundred percent proved. They measure the percentage now with hydrometers, not gunpowder and fire. Less risky, I dare say.'

'Gunpowder,' he said, 'is something you and I have had too much of recently.' He stood up stiffly. 'Your half-hour is up. I'll get the food.'

FOURTEEN:

Gerard followed me home in his mended Mercedes and came into the house bearing Sung Li's fragrant parcels.

'You call this a cottage?' he said sceptically, looking at perspectives. 'More like a palace.'

'It was a cottage beside a barn, both of them falling to pieces. The barn was bigger than the cottage . . . hence the space.'

We had joyfully planned that house, Emma and I, shaping the rooms to fit what we'd expected to be our lives, making provision for children. A big kitchen for family meals; a sitting room, future playroom; a dining room for friends; many bedrooms; a large quiet drawing room, splendid for parties. The conversion, done in three stages as we could afford it, had taken nearly five years. Emma had contentedly waited, wanting the nest to be ready for the chicks, and almost the moment it was done she had become pregnant.

Gerard and I had come into the house through the kitchen, but I seldom ate there any more. When the food was re-heated and in dishes we transferred it to the sitting room, putting it on a coffee table between two comfortable chairs and eating with our plates balanced on our knees.

It was in that warm looking room with its bookshelves, soft lamplight, television, photographs and rugs that I mostly lived, when I was there at all. It was there that I now kept a wine rack and glasses lazily to hand and averted my mind from chores like gardening. It was there, I dare say, that my energy was chronically at its lowest ebb, yet it was to there also that I instinctively returned.

Gerard looked better for the food, settling deep into his chair when he'd finished with a sigh of relaxation. He put his arm back in its sling and accepted coffee and a second glass of Californian wine, a 1978 Napa Cabernet Sauvignon I'd been recently selling and liked very much myself.

'It's come a long way,' Gerard observed, reading the label.

'And going further,' I said. 'California's growing grapes like crazy, and their best wine is world class.'

He drank a little and shook his head. 'It's pleasant enough but I honestly couldn't tell it from any old plonk. A terrible admission, but there you are.'

'Just what the Silver Moondance ordered . . . customers like you.'

He smiled. 'And I'd guess I'm in the majority.'

'It doesn't matter. Liking wine at all is the main thing.'

He said, 'You were going to tell me why the substitute wines were equally as important as the substitute scotch at the Silver Moondance.'

I glanced at him, hearing the hardening tone in the sub-Scottish voice and seeing the same change in him as there had been in the car the previous Sunday: the shedding of the social shell, the emergence of the investigator. His eyes were steady and intent, his face concentrated, his mouth unsmiling: and I answered to this second man with recognition and relief, dealing in facts and guesses dispassionately.

'People who steal scotch whisky,' I said, 'usually go for a shipment of bottles in cases. The proceeds are ready to sell . . . the receiver's probably already lined up. There's no difficulty. It's all profit. But if you steal a tankerful of the liquid in bulk you have the trouble and expense in bottling it. Cost of bottles, cost of labour, all sorts of incidentals.'

'Right,' he said nodding.

'There were six thousand gallons of scotch at roughly fifty-eight per cent alcohol content in each of Kenneth Charter's three lost loads.'

'Right.'

'Each load was of a higher concentration than is ever sold for drinking. When they received the tankerload the Rannoch people would have added water to bring the scotch down to retail strength, around forty per cent alcohol by volume.'

Gerard listened and nodded.

'At that point they'd have enough scotch to fill approximately fifty thousand bottles of standard size.'

Gerard's mouth opened slightly with surprise. 'Kenneth Charter never said that.'

'He shifts the stuff, he doesn't bottle it. He maybe never did the arithmetic. Anyway, with three tankersful we're talking about one hundred and fifty thousand bottles in six months, and that's not something you can mess about with in the back yard.'

He was silent for a while thinking about it, and then said merely, 'Go on.'

'On each occasion the whole load was pumped out of the tanker pretty fast, as the tanker was found empty on the following day.'

'Right.'

'So unless the point of the operation was simply to ruin Kenneth Charter, in which case it's conceivable the loads were dumped in ditches like the drivers, the scotch was pumped from the tanker into some sort of storage.'

'Yes, of course.'

'So the logical place for the tanker to be unloaded was at a bottling plant.'

'Yes, but it never reached there.'

'It never reached Rannoch's bottling plant. There's a difference.'

'All right.' His eyes smiled. 'Go on.'

'Fifty thousand bottles three times over isn't going to keep any reasonable plant in operation for anything like six months. Small châteaux bottle that much themselves in a few weeks without blinking. So . . . um . . . what if in between times the whisky bottling changed over to wine . . . to Silver Moondance wine, to be precise.'

'Ah.' It was a deep note, an acknowledgement that we'd arrived at the centre of things. 'Carry on.'

'Well . . . with a bottling plant it would be easy to fill any shape of bottle from a single source of wine . . . and the shapes of the bottles at the Silver Moondance fitted the labels: claret bottles for claret labels, burgundy bottles for burgundy labels and so on. The very fact that there were both scotch and wine under false labels at the Silver Moondance . . . well, for the simplest explanation I'd bet you a pea to a case of Krug they were bottled in the same place.'

Gerard drank some of his wine absentmindedly.

'Where?' he said succinctly.

'Mm . . . that's the rub.'

'Any ideas?'

'It did occur to me that it might be in one of those plants that Kenneth Charter described, that got into difficulties or went bust when the French started bottling more of their own wines. I mean . . . suppose someone came to you if you were on the verge of bankruptcy and offered you work. Even if you knew it was crooked you might do it and keep quiet. Or suppose a bottling plant was for sale or lease at a ridiculous price, which they're bound to have been . . . if the game looked worth it . . . if it was going to go on maybe for years . . .'

'Yes,' Gerard said. 'It's possible.' He gave it about five seconds' thought. 'So provisionally we're looking for a bottling plant. Now let's shelve that for a moment.' He paused again, considering, and then said, 'In Deglet's we often work in pairs, discussing a case, bouncing ideas off each other, coming up sometimes with things neither of us had considered on our own. It's a way that I'm used to, that I like . . . but my usual partner's in London, and frankly I'm too tired to go there . . . and you're here on the doorstep loaded to the hairline with specialist knowledge . . . so do you mind letting me talk my ideas to you? And be sure to speak out if I start something in your thoughts. That's where the value of these sessions lies. Bouncing ideas back. Do you mind?'

'No, of course not. But I . . .'

'Just listen,' he said. 'Stop me if you've a comment. That's all there is to it.'

'All right.'

'And honestly . . . do you have any brandy?'

I smiled. 'Yes, I do. What would you like?'

'Anything.'

I gave him some Hine Antique, which he sighed over as if putting on friendly old shoes. I poured some for myself also on the grounds that people who said it had medicinal qualities weren't joking. If queasy, drink brandy, if tired, drink brandy, if suffering from green shivers and cold shakes . . . drink brandy.

'All right, then,' he said, cradling his glass in the palm of one hand. 'First, review the status quo. Under that heading we have the prime and never-to-be-forgotten fact that our number one aim is to save Kenneth Charter's business without landing his son in jail. That's what we're being paid for. Justice and other considerations are secondary.'

He sipped his drink.

'Fact number two,' he went on, 'Kenneth Charter's son . . . whose name is also Kenneth, to be awkward, so we'll call him Kenneth Junior . . . Kenneth Charter Junior made the theft of the scotch possible by telling Zarac of the Silver Moondance where to find the tanker.' He paused. 'We still have the unanswered question.'

'How did Kenneth Junior know Zarac?'

'Yes. Anyway, I've brought the photostats of the pages of Kenneth Junior's notebook.' He pulled a well-filled business-sized envelope from an inner pocket and laid it on the table. 'I'll leave these with you . . . see if you make anything from them that we haven't.'

He saw the doubt in my face. 'You'll try?' he said almost severely, and I without apology said, 'Yes.'

'Right, then. Fact three: Zarac passed on the message and wasn't present when the tanker was stolen. Fact four: scotch was being sold under the wrong labels at the Silver Moondance, which Zarac as head waiter must have known. Supposition arising: the substitute scotch was part of an earlier load stolen from Charter's tankers. Any comment?'

I shook my head.

'Second supposition arising: Larry Trent knew his whisky and wines were cheating the customers.'

He stopped, waiting for an opinion. I said, 'I agree with that, yes. I'd say it was definite.'

'Supposition three: Larry Trent organised the theft of the tankers.'

I frowned.

'You don't think so?'

'I don't know,' I said. 'I never talked to him . . . can't make a first-hand guess. He certainly did have in his hands a great deal more cash than he would have made out of the Silver Moondance, but he said it was his brother's.' I told Gerard precisely what Orkney Swayle had told me at Martineau Park. 'Larry Trent was buying horses and shipping them abroad to be sold. As sweet a way as one can imagine of turning illegal money pure white.'

Gerard drank some brandy.

'Did you believe in the brother?' he asked.

'You mean, was it a case of the hypothetical friend? My friend has a problem, give me advice?'

He nodded.

'I would have thought so,' I said, 'except for one thing which rang humanly true. Orkney said that Larry Trent said he, Larry, was buying the horses for his brother because his brother couldn't tell good from bad. About the only thing his brother couldn't do, he said. Orkney Swayle said Larry was envious. That sort of grudge sounds like a real brother to me. Or at any rate a real person. Partner, maybe.'

A small silence. We both thought about the partner who might or might not be a brother, and finally Gerard gave him his name. The name, anyway, that we knew him by.

'Paul Young.'

I agreed.

'Supposition four,' Gerard said. 'When Larry Trent was killed, Paul Young came to the Silver Moondance to take over, unaware that the police were investigating the drinks and unaware that Charter's tanker thefts had been linked with Zarac.'

'Those are certainties, not suppositions. I saw him arrive myself . . . he had no idea he was walking into trouble.'

'Right. And I'll add in a few certainties of my own at this point. I've spent all day interviewing people from the Silver Moondance, especially the waitress and the wet little assistant who were both there with you in the bar. They say that soon after you left, Paul Young told them to go home, the waitress until told to return and the assistant until the following day. Paul Young said he would discuss with the police about a re-opening date, and run the place himself until the manager returned from holiday. After that, Head Office would appoint a replacement for poor Mr Trent. None of the staff saw anything odd in his manner or proposals. Very sensible, they thought him, considering how angry he was about the drinks. He then sent the kitchen staff home, telling them also to return when told. The waitress said Zarac arrived for work just as she was leaving, and Paul Young told him to go into Larry Trent's office and wait for him.'

I was fascinated. 'Did she remember exactly what they said to each other?'

Gerard smiled thinly. 'She's used to remembering orders. An excellent ear. She said they knew each other . . . Paul Young called him Zarac without being told.'

'And the other way round?'

'She said Paul Young said "I'm Paul Young" which she thought silly because Zarac looked as if he knew him perfectly well.'

'Telling Zarac his alias.'

'Exactly. The waitress said Paul Young looked very angry with Zarac, which she thought natural, and she thought Zarac was going to get a right ticking off, which she was sorry about because Zarac was all right with the waitresses and kept his hands to himself, unlike some others she could mention.'

I appreciated the verbatim reporting. 'And who were those?'

'The manager, mostly.'

'Not Larry Trent?'

'No. Always the perfect gent, she said.' He paused. 'She said the police sergeant had been round before me, asking the same questions. She said he asked her about Paul Young's car.'

I was amused. 'What else did she say?'

'She said it was a Rolls.'

'Really?'

'Her exact words were "a black Roller with them tinted windows." She said it had to be Paul Young's because it was in the staff car park and it didn't belong to the regular staff, and it hadn't been there when she came to work an hour earlier.'

'Observant girl.'

Gerard nodded. 'I went to the wet assistant's home after I left the waitress and asked him mostly the same questions. He said he didn't know what car Paul Young had come in. He couldn't even describe Paul Young. Useless.'

'And the barman hoofed it.' I relayed Ridger's half-hearted search. 'I guess he knew he wasn't selling the right stuff, but you wouldn't get him to admit it, even if you found him.'

'No,' he agreed. 'So now we come to supposition . . . where are we? five? . . . supposition five: that Paul Young and Zarac spent the afternoon deciding what to do and organising the removal of all the wines and spirits to look like burglary.'

'It would have taken them hours if they did it themselves.'

'And they would have needed a van.'

'Large,' I said, nodding. 'There were dozens of cases.'

He put his head on one side. 'They had all day and all night, I suppose.'

'Do we know when Zarac actually died?' I asked.

Gerard shook his head. 'There was an opening inquest last Friday, adjourned for a week. The police aren't giving out much publicity on Zarac, but I've found a friend behind the forensic scenes and I'll hear everything the police know about times and so on by this Friday.'

'He suffocated . . .' I said with revulsion.

'It bothers you?'

'Like bricking up someone alive.'

'Much quicker,' he said prosaically. 'Supposition six: Paul Young and Zarac weren't the greatest of buddy-buddies.'

'A fair conclusion,' I said dryly.

'Supposition seven: Zarac was in some way a terrible threat to Paul Young.'

'Who solved the problem permanently.'

'Mm,' he reflected. 'So far, that seems reasonable. Any questions?'

'Yes . . . How did Paul Young happen to have plaster of Paris bandage with him on what he expected to be simply an organisational outing?'

'You mean it might be significant?'

'Something to add to what we know of him, anyway.'

'And why use it? Why not smash in his head?'

'Well, why?' I said.

'A warning to others, perhaps. Or genuine psychosis. Very nasty, in any case.' He drank some brandy. A brain alive above a flagging body. 'Our Mr Young is a middle-aged businessman with a hearing aid, a black Rolls and a reason for carrying plaster of Paris. Pity we can't, as they say, run that lot through the computer.'

'Any self-respecting computer would come up with a consultant surgeon, ear, nose and throat.'

Gerard was startled. 'You don't suppose . . .? No, most unlikely.'

'Computers only spit out what you feed in.'

'Whereas you can feed countless facts into a human being and get no connections at all.' He sighed resignedly. 'All right, then. Work arising. Find out if Larry Trent had a brother. Search further to know how Kenneth Junior knew Zarac. Sort out bottling plants. And Rannoch, by the way, have posted to us profile analyses of the loads they sent in Charter's tankers. If you can wheedle a sample from the Silver Moondance out of your pal Ridger, I can get the comparisons made. For proof rather than speculation.' He paused. 'Anything else?'

'Well . . .' I hesitated.

'Go on.'

'Ramekin, then. The horse Flora saw Larry Trent buy at Doncaster Sales a year ago. If Ramekin was shipped abroad, someone shipped it. There aren't so very many shippers. They'd have Ramekin in their records . . . racehorses have passports, like people. Masses of export documents, besides. If we could find the shipper we'd know the destination. Larry Trent might always have used the same shipper and sold all the horses through one agent at the same destination . . . If you've set up a line, so to speak, you carry on using it. The agent at the far end might know . . . just might know . . . whose cash had bought the horses. The real owner, for whom Larry Trent was acting.'

He listened intently, but he said, 'That's stretching it.'

'I suppose so.'

'I'll see how much is involved.'

'Do you want me to do it?'

He shook his head. 'We'll do it in the office, if at all. We have country-wide 'phone books and our staff are used to that sort of routine. They make it sound enormously official and get the most surprising results. They'll do the bottling plant sales and leases first; a long job but more promising.'

'I suppose it would be too simple . . .' I began diffidently.

'What would?'

'I mean . . . you could try them first . . . there's nothing to lose . . .'

'Do get on,' he said.

I felt foolish. I said, 'The plants to which Kenneth Charter took red wine in his tankers.'

Gerard looked at me levelly for a while with unblinking eyes. 'Right,' he said eventually, without inflection. 'We'll start with those. As you say, nothing to lose.' He looked at his watch and took the second-to-last mouthful of brandy. 'Tina will be locking me out.'

'Come any time,' I said.

I didn't mean to sound lonely, but maybe that's what he heard. He looked at the photograph of Emma and myself on our wedding day which stood on a table near him in a silver frame. We were laughing in a shower of bubbles from a shaken-up champagne bottle in the hands of my best man, and Emma had liked the picture for its informality. 'Most brides and grooms look like waxworks,' she'd said. 'At least you can tell we were alive.'

'You were a good-looking couple,' Gerard said neutrally. 'And happy.'

'Yes.'

'How did she die?'

He asked it straightforwardly, without emotion, and after a moment I answered him similarly, as I had learned to do, as if it happened to someone else.

'She had a sub-arachnoid haemorrhage. Something called Berry's aneurism. In effect a blood vessel split in her brain.'

'But . . .' His gaze slid to the photograph, '. . . how old was she?'

'Twenty-seven.'

'So young.'

'Apparently it can happen at any age.'

'I'm so sorry.'

'She was pregnant,' I said, and surprised myself. I normally didn't say that. Normally I said the absolute minimum. But to Gerard, after months of silence, I found myself slowly telling it all, wanting to and not wanting to, trying to keep my voice steady and not cry . . . for God's sake don't cry.

'She'd been having headaches on and off for ages. Then she had backaches. Nothing specific. Just aches in her spine. Everyone put it down to her being pregnant. And it passed off . . . until next time. Every week or so, for a day or two. One Sunday when she was nearly six months pregnant she woke up with one of those headaches, a fairly bad one. She took some aspirins but they never did much good. It got worse during the morning and when I went to do the midday stint in the shop she said she would go to bed and sleep it off. But when I got back she was crying . . . moaning . . . with pain. I tried to get a doctor . . . but it took ages . . . it was Sunday afternoon . . . Sunday . . . an ambulance finally came for her but by then she was begging me . . . begging me somehow to knock her out . . . but how could I? I couldn't. We were both terrified . . . more than frightened . . . it was so implacable . . . she was in awful agony in the ambulance . . . hitting her head with her fists . . . nothing I could do . . . I couldn't even hold her . . . she was yelling, rolling, jerking with pain. At the end of the journey she went slowly unconscious, and I was glad for her, even though by then I feared . . . well, I feared.'

'My dear man.'

I sat for a while looking back to the past, and then swallowed and told him the rest of it coldly.

'She was in a coma for four days, going deeper . . . I stayed with her. They let me stay. They said they couldn't save the baby, it was too soon. In another month, perhaps . . . They told me the blood vessel had been leaking for ages . . . it was the blood leaking into her brain and down her spinal nerves that had given her the headaches and backaches . . . but even if they'd diagnosed the trouble earlier they couldn't have done much . . . it would have split open more one day, as it did . . . so perhaps it was better we didn't know.'

I stopped. No tears. All I couldn't have borne at that point was sympathy, and Gerard didn't offer it.

'Life's most unfair,' he said calmly.

'Yes.'

He didn't say I would get over it, or that time was a great healer. He didn't say I would find another girl. Marry again . . . I approved of Gerard more and more.

'Thank you for telling me,' he said.

'I don't usually,' I said apologetically.

'No. Flora told me. You clam up, she said, if anyone asks.'

'Flora chatters.'

'Chattering does good, sometimes.'

I was silent. What I felt, having told him about Emma, was a sort of release. Chattering helped. Sometimes.

He finished his brandy and stood up to go. 'If you have any more thoughts, telephone.'

'O.K.'

He walked towards the door and stopped by a side table upon which stood three or four more photo frames among Emma's collection of shells.

'Your mother?' he asked, picking up the lady on horseback with hounds. 'Most handsome.'

'Mother,' I nodded.

He put her down. Picked up another. 'Father?'

'Father.'

He looked at the strong amused face above the colonel's uniform with its double row of medal ribbons, at the light in the eyes and the tilt of the chin, at the firm half-smiling mouth.

'You're like him,' Gerard said.

'Only in looks.' I turned away. 'I loved him when I was small. Adored him. He died when I was eleven.'

He put the picture down and peered at the others. 'No brothers or sisters?'

'No.' I grinned faintly. 'My birth interfered with a whole season's hunting. Once was enough, my mother said.'

Gerard glanced at me. 'You don't mind?'

'No, I never did. I never minded being alone until I got used to something else.' I shrugged abruptly. 'I'm basically all right alone. I will be again, in the end.'

Gerard merely nodded and moved on out into the hall and from there to the kitchen and beyond to the rear door, where neither of us shook hands because of the slings.

'A most productive and interesting evening,' he said.

'I enjoy your company.'

He seemed almost surprised. 'Do you? Why?'

'You don't expect too much.'

'Like what?'

'Like . . . er . . . Chinese takeaway on your knees.' It wasn't what I truly meant, but it would do.

He made an untranslatable noise low in his throat, hearing the evasion and not agreeing with it. 'I expect more than you think. You underestimate yourself.' He smiled sardonically. 'Good night.'

'Good night.'

He drove away and I locked the doors and went back through the house to fetch the supper dishes, to stack them in the dishwasher. I thought of what I'd said to him about being all right alone, hearing in memory in the accumulated voices of years of customers the sighs and sadnesses of the bereaved. They talked of the common experience that was freshly awful for each individual. Two years, they said, was what it took. Two years before the sun shone. After two years the lost person became a memory, the loss itself bearable. I'd listened to them long before I thought of needing their wisdom, and I believed them still. Grief couldn't be escaped, but it would pass.

I finished tidying downstairs and went up to bed, to the room where Emma and I had made love.

I still slept there. She often seemed extroardinarily near. I woke sometimes in the early hours and stretched out for her, forgetting. I heard the memory of her giggle in the dark.

We had been lucky in love; passionate and well matched, equal in satisfaction. I remembered chiefly her stomach flat, her breasts unswollen, remembered the years of utter fun, her gleeful orgasms, the sharp incredible ecstasy of ejaculation. It was better to remember that.

The room was quiet now. No unseen presence. No restless spirit hovering.

If I lived with ghosts, they were within me: Emma, my father and the titanic figure of my grandfather, impossibly brave. They lived in me not condemning but unconsoling. I struggled forever to come to terms with them, for if I didn't I was sunk, but all three of their shadows fell long.

Pregnancy might recently have raised Emma's blood pressure, they'd said. It was quite common. Higher blood pressure would have put too much strain on the slow leak, opening it wider . . . too wide.

Pregnancy itself, they'd said, had tipped the scales towards death. Although we had both wanted children, the seed that I'd planted had killed her.

FIFTEEN:

I let myself into the shop the next morning wondering what I could trade with Sergeant Ridger for a sample of the Silver Moondance scotch, and he solved the problem himself by appearing almost immediately at my door as if transported by telekinesis.

'Morning,' he said, as I let him in. Raincoat belted, shoes polished, hair brushed. Hadn't he heard, I wondered, that plain clothes policemen these days were supposed to dress in grubby jeans and look unemployed?

'Good morning,' I replied, shutting the door behind him. 'Can I sell you something?'

'Information.' He was serious, as always, coming into the centre of the shop and standing solidly there with his feet apart.

'Ah. Yes, well fire away.'

'Is your arm worse? You didn't have a sling last time I came.'

'No worse.' I shook my head. 'More comfortable.'

He looked not exactly relieved but reassured. 'Good. Then . . . I'm making an official request to you to aid us in our enquiries.'

'What aid? What enquiries?'

'This is a direct suggestion from Detective Chief Superintendent Wilson.'

'Is it?' I was interested. 'To me personally?'

'He suggested you himself, yes.' Ridger cleared his throat. 'It is in connection with our enquiries into complaints received about goods supplied by licensed premises other than the Silver Moondance.'

'Er . . .' I said. 'Sergeant, would you drop the jargon?'

Ridger looked surprised. What he'd said had been obviously of crystal clarity to his notebook mind. He said, 'In the course of our investigations into the murder of Zarac it was suggested that we should follow up certain other complaints of malpractice throughout the whole area. There was a top level regional conference yesterday, part of which I attended as the officer first on the spot in the drinks fraud, and Chief Superintendent Wilson requested me directly to enlist your help as before. He said if we could find another place passing off one whisky as another, and if such whisky were similar or identical to that in the Silver Moondance, we might also find a lead to Zarac's supplier and murderer. It was worth a try, he said, as there were so few other lines of enquiry. So, er, here I am.'

I gazed at him in awe. 'You're asking me to go on a pub crawl?'

'Er . . . if you must put it like that, yes.'

Beautiful, I thought. Stunning. Fifty thousand bars between home and Watford . . . with the known bad apples offered on the platter of a police list.

'Would you be driving me, like last time?' I asked.

'I've been assigned to that duty.' He showed no feelings either for or against. 'Can I take it you will be available?'

'You can,' I said. 'When?'

He consulted his bristling wristwatch. 'Ten-fifteen.'

'This morning?'

'Of course. I'll go back now and report and return for you later.'

'All right,' I said. 'And Sergeant, when you return, would you bring with you the Bell's whisky bottle from the Silver Moondance bar?'

He looked concentratedly doubtful.

'I'd like to taste its contents again,' I explained. 'It's ten days since that morning in the Silver Moondance. If more of that scotch is what you're looking for in these enquiries, I'll have to learn it well enough to know it anywhere.'

He saw the logic. 'I'll request it.'

'Mm . . . say it's a requirement. I can't do what you're asking without it.'

'Very well.' He pulled out the notebook and wrote in it, rolling his wrist for another time check and adding nine-fourteen punctiliously.

'How many places are we going to?' I asked.

'It's quite a long list.' He spoke matter-of-factly. 'It's a big area, of course. My Chief Inspector's hoping we can complete the enquiry within two weeks.'

'Two weeks!'

'Working from ten-thirty to two o'clock daily in licensing hours.'

'Is this an official appointment with pay?'

He checked internally before he answered. 'It was being discussed.'

'And?'

'They used to have an available consultant expert, but he's just retired to live in Spain. He was paid. Sure to have been.'

'How often was he . . . consulted?'

'Don't rightly know. I only saw him once or twice. He could tell things by taste like you. The Customs and Excise people use instruments, same as the Weights and Measures. They're concerned with alcohol content, not flavour.'

'Did they check any of the places on your list?'

He said, 'All of them,' disapprovingly, and I remembered what he'd said before about someone in one of those two departments tipping off the Silver Moondance that investigators were on their way.

'With no luck?' I asked.

'No prosecutions have resulted.'

Quite so. 'All right, Sergeant. You drive, I'll drink, and I've got to be sober and back here by three to get my arm checked at the hospital.'

He went away looking smug and at nine-thirty to the half-minute Mrs Palissey arrived with Brian. I explained that I would be away every mid-day for a while and said I would get her some help by tomorrow if she could possibly manage that morning on her own.

'Help?' She was affronted. 'I don't need help.'

'But your lunch-hour . . .'

'I'll bring our lunch and we'll eat in the back,' she said. 'I don't want strangers in here meddling. Brian and I will see to things. You go off and enjoy yourself, you're still looking peaky.'

I was about to say that I wasn't doing police work to enjoy myself but then it occurred to me that I probably was. I'd had no hesitation at all in accepting Ridger's – or Wilson's – invitation. I was flattered to be thought an expert. Deplorable vanity. Laugh at yourself, Tony. Stay human.

For an hour the three of us restocked the shop, made lists, took telephone orders, served customers, swept and dusted. I looked back when I left with Ridger: to a clean, cosy, welcoming place with Mrs Palissey smiling behind the counter and Brian arranging wine boxes with anxious care. I wasn't an empire builder, I thought. I would never start a chain. That one prosperous place was enough.

Prosperous, I knew, against the odds. A great many small businesses like mine had died of trying to compete with chains and supermarkets, those giants engaged in such fierce undercutting price wars that they bled their own profits to death. I'd started that way and began losing money, and, against everything believed and advised in the trade, had restored my position by going back to fair, not suicidal prices. The losses had stopped, my customers had multiplied, not deserted, and I'd begun to enjoy life instead of waking up at night sweating.

Ridger had brought the Bell's bottle with him in his car; it sat upright on the back seat in the same box in which it had left the Silver Moondance, two-thirds full, as before.

'Before we go,' I said, 'I'll take that whisky into the shop and taste it there.'

'Why not here?'

'The car smells of petrol.' A gift, I thought.

'I've just filled up. What does it matter?'

'Petrol smells block out scotch.'

'Oh. All right.' He got out of his car, removed the box and methodically locked his doors although the car was right outside the shop and perfectly visible through the window: then he carried the box in and set it on the counter.

Casually I slipped my wrist out of the sling, picked up the Bell's bottle, took it back to the office, and with a clink or two poured a good measure through a funnel into a clean small bottle I'd put ready, and then a very little into a goblet. The small bottle had a screw-on cap which I caught against the thread in my haste, but it was closed and hidden with the funnel behind box-files in an instant, and I walked unhurriedly back into the shop sipping thoughtfully at the glass, right wrist again supported.

Ridger was coming towards me. 'I'm not supposed to let that bottle out of my sight,' he said.

'Sorry.' I gestured with the glass. 'It's just on the desk in the office. Perfectly safe.'

He peered into the recess to make sure and turned back nodding. 'How long will you be?'

'Not long.'

The liquid in my mouth was definitely Rannoch, I thought. Straightforward Rannoch. Except that . . .

'What's the matter?' Ridger demanded; and I realised I'd been frowning.

'Nothing,' I said, looking happier. 'If you want to know if I'll recognise it again, then yes, I will.'

'You're sure?'

'Yes.'

'Why are you smiling?'

'Sergeant,' I said with exasperation, 'this is a collaboration not an inquisition. Let's take the bottle and get the show on the road.'

I wondered if Sergeant Ridger ever achieved friendship; if his suspicious nature ever gave him a rest. Certainly after all our meetings I found his porcupine reflexes as sensitive as at the beginning, and I made no attempt to placate him, as any such attempt would in itself be seen as suspicious.

He drove away from the kerb saying that he would visit the nearest places first, with which I could find no quarrel, and I discovered that by nearest he meant nearest to the Silver Moondance. He turned off the main road about a mile before we reached it, and stopped in a village outside a country pub.

As an inn it had been old when Queen Anne died, when coaches had paused there to change horses. The building of the twentieth century highway had left the pub in a backwater, the old coaching road a dead end now, an artery reduced to an appendix. Emma and I had drunk a few times there, liking the old bulging building with the windows leaning sideways and the Stuart brickwork still in the fireplaces.

'Not here!' I said, surprised, as we stopped.

'Do you know it?'

'I've been here, but not for a year.'

Ridger consulted a clipboard. 'Complaints of whisky being watered, gin ditto. Complaints investigated, found to be unfounded. Investigations dated August 23rd and September 18th last.'

'The landlord's a retired cricketer,' I said. 'Generous. Loves to talk. Lazy. The place needs a facelift.'

'Landlord: Noel George Darnley.'

I turned my head, squinting down at the page. 'Different man.'

'Right.' Ridger climbed out of the car and carefully locked it. 'I'll have a tomato juice.'

'Who's paying?'

Ridger looked blank. 'I haven't much money . . .'

'No instructions?' I asked. 'No police float?'

He cleared his throat. 'We must keep an account,' he said.

'O.K.,' I said. 'I'll pay. We'll write down at each place what I spend and you'll initial it.'

He agreed to that. Whether the police would reimburse me or not I didn't know, but Kenneth Charter very likely would, if not. If neither did, no great matter.

'And what if we find a match?' I asked.

He was on surer ground. 'We impound the bottle, sealing it, labelling it, and giving a receipt.'

'Right.'

We walked into the pub as customers, Ridger as relaxed as guitar strings.

The facelift, I saw at once, had occurred, but I found I preferred the old wrinkles. True, the worn Indian rugs with threadbare patches had needed renewing, but not with orange and brown stripes. The underpolished knobbly oak benches had vanished in favour of smooth leather-look vinyl, and there were shiny modern brass ornaments on the mantel instead of antique pewter platters.

The new landlord's new broom had resulted, however, in a much cleaner looking bar, and the landlord himself, appearing from the rear, wasn't fat, sloppily dressed and beaming, but neat, thin and characterless. In the old days the pub had been full: I wondered how many of the regulars still came.

'A Bell's whisky, please,' I said. I looked at his row of bottles. 'And a second Bell's whisky from that bottle over there, and a tomato juice, please.'

He filled the order without conversation. We carried the glasses to a small table and I began on the unlikely task with a judicious trial of the first tot of Bell's.

'Well?' Ridger asked, after fidgeting a full minute. 'What have we got?'

I shook my head. 'It's Bell's all right. Not like the Silver Moondance.'

Ridger had left his clipboard in the car, otherwise I was sure he would have crossed off mine host there and then.

I tried the second Bell's. No luck there either.

As far as I could tell, neither bottle had been watered: both samples seemed full strength. I told Ridger so while he was making inroads into the tomato juice, which he genuinely seemed to enjoy.

I left both whiskies on the table and wandered to the bar.

'You're new here?' I said.

'Fairly.' He seemed cautious, not friendly.

'Settling in well with the locals?' I asked.

'Are you here to make trouble?'

'No.' I was surprised at the resentment he hadn't bothered to hide. 'What do you mean?'

'Sorry, then. It was you ordering two whiskies from different bottles and tasting them carefully, as you did. Someone round here made trouble with the Weights and Measures, saying I gave short measures and watered the spirits. Some of them round here don't like me smartening the place up. But I ask you, trying to get me fined or lose my licence . . . too much.'

'Yes,' I agreed. 'Malicious.'

He turned away, still not sure of me, which was fair enough, considering. I collected Ridger who was wiping red stains from his mouth and we went outside leaving the unfinished whiskies on the table, which probably hardened the landlord's suspicions into certainty, poor man.

Ridger ticked off the pub on the clipboard and read out the notes of our next destination, which proved to be a huge soulless place built of brick in the thirties and run for a brewery by a prim-looking tenant with a passion for fresh air. Even Ridger in his raincoat shivered before the thrown-open windows of the bar and muttered that the place looked dull. We were the first customers, it was true, but on a greyly chilly morning there were no electric lights to warm and welcome thirsty strangers.

'Tomato juice, please,' I said. 'And a Bell's whisky.'

The puritan landlord provided them, stating the price in a tight-lipped way.

'And could we have the windows closed, please?'

The landlord looked at his watch, shrugged, and went round closing October out with ill grace. I wouldn't sell much in my shop, I reflected, with that scowl: everyone sought to buy more than the product they asked for and it was the intangible extra that repelled or attracted a return. The whisky in that place might be fine, but I'd never go back out of choice.

'Well?' Ridger said, initialling the cost on our list. 'What is it?'

'Bell's.'

Ridger nodded, drinking this time barely a mouthful from his glass. 'Shall we go, then?'

'Glad to.'

We left the landlord bitterly reopening his windows and Ridger consulted his clipboard in the car.

'The next place is a hotel, the Peverill Arms, on the Reading to Henley road. Several complaints of thin or tasteless whisky. Complaints investigated, September 12th. Whisky found to be full strength in random samples.'

His voice told something more than the usual dry information: a reservation, almost an alarm.

'You know the place?' I asked.

'I've been there. Disturbances.' He fell silent with determination and started the car, driving with disapproval quivering in the stiffness of his neck. I thought from these signs that we might be on the way to a rowdy rendezvous with Hell's Angels, but found to my amusement on arrival that Ridger's devil was a woman.

A woman moreover of statuesque proportions, rising six feet tall with the voluptuous shape of Venus de Milo, who had forty-two inch hips.

'Mrs Alexis,' Ridger muttered. 'She may not remember me.'

Mrs Alexis indeed gave our arrival scarcely a glance. Mrs Alexis was supervising the lighting of logs in the vast fireplace in the entrance lounge, an enterprise presently producing acid smoke in plenty but few actual flames.

Apart from the heavyside layer floating in a haze below the ceiling the hall gave a lift to the entering spirit: clusters of chintz-covered armchairs, warm colours, gleaming copper jugs, an indefinable aura of success. Across the far end an extensive bar stood open but untended, and from the fireplace protruded the trousered behind of the luckless firelighter, to the interest and entertainment of scattered armchaired guests.

'For God's sake, Wilfred, fetch the bloody bellows,' Mrs Alexis said distinctly. 'You look idiotic with your arse in the air puffing like a beetroot.'

She was well over fifty, I judged, with the crisp assurance of a natural commander. Handsome, expensively dressed, gustily uninhibited. I found myself smiling in the same instant that the corners of Ridger's mouth turned down.

The unfortunate Wilfred removed his beetroot-red face from the task and went off obediently, and Mrs Alexis with bright eyes asked what we wanted.

'Drinks,' I said vaguely.

'Come along then.' She led the way, going towards the bar.

'It's our first fire this winter. Always smokes like hell until we get it going.' She frowned upwards at the drifting cloud. 'Worse than usual, this year.'

'The chimney needs sweeping,' Ridger said.

Mrs Alexis gave him a birdlike look from an eye as sharp and yellow as a hawk's. 'It's swept every year in the spring. And aren't you that policeman who told me if I served the local rugger team when they'd won I should expect them to swing from the chandeliers and put beer into my piano?'

Ridger cleared his throat. I swallowed a laugh with difficulty and received the full beam from the hawk eyes.

'Are you a policeman too?' she asked with good humour. 'Come to cadge for your bloody ball?'

'No,' I said. I could feel the smothered laugh escaping through the eyes. 'We came for a drink.'

She believed the simple answer as much as a declaration of innocence from a red-handed thief, but went around behind her bar and waited expectantly.

'A Bell's whisky and a tomato juice, please.'

She pushed a glass against the Bell's optic and waited for the full measure to descend. 'Anything else?'

I said no thank you and she steered the whisky my way and the tomato juice towards Ridger, accepting my money and giving change. We removed ourselves to a pair of armchairs near a small table, where Ridger again initialled our itemised account.

'What happened with the rugger club?' I asked interestedly.

His face showed profound disapproval. 'She knew there'd be trouble. They're a rowdy lot. They pulled the chandeliers clean out of the ceiling with a lot of plaster besides and she had them lined up against the wall at gunpoint by the time we go here.'

'Gunpoint?' I said, astonished.

'It wasn't loaded, but the rugger club weren't taking chances. They knew her reputation against pheasants.'

'A shotgun?'

'That's right. She keeps it there behind the bar. We can't stop her, though I'd like to, personally, but she's got a licence for it. She keeps it there to repel villains, she says, though there isn't a local villain who'd face her.'

'Did she send to you for help with the rugger club?'

'Not her. Some of the other customers. She wasn't much pleased when we turned up. She said there wasn't a man born she couldn't deal with.' Ridger looked as if he believed it. 'She wouldn't bring charges for all the damage, but I heard they paid up pretty meekly.'

It would be a brave man, I reflected, who told Mrs Alexis that her Bell's whisky was Rannoch: but in fact it wasn't. Bell's it was: unadulterated.

'Pity,' Ridger said, at the news.

I said thoughtfully, 'She has some Laphroaig up there on the top shelf.'

'Has she?' Ridger's hopes were raised. 'Are you going to try it?'

I nodded and returned to the bar, but Mrs Alexis had departed again towards the fireplace where Wilfred with the bellows was merely adding to the smog.

'The chimney seems to be blocked,' he said anxiously, exonerating himself.

'Blocked?' Mrs Alexis demanded. 'How could it be?' She thought for barely two seconds. 'Unless some bloody bird has built a nest in it, same as three years ago.'

'We'd better wait until it's swept again,' Wilfred suggested.

'Wait? Certainly not.' She strode towards the bar. 'I'll be with you in a moment,' she said, seeing me waiting there. 'Bird's nest. Birds building their bloody nests in my chimney. They did it once before. I'll shift the little buggers. Give them the shock of their lives.'

I didn't bother to point out that nests in October were bound to be uninhabited. She was certain to know. She was also smiling with reckless mischief and reappeared from behind the bar carrying the fabled shotgun and feeding a cartridge into the breach. My own feelings at the sight seemed to be shared by most of the people present as she walked towards the fireplace, but no one thought of stopping her.

Ridger's mouth opened in disbelief.

Mrs Alexis thrust the whole gun up inside the vast chimney and at arm's length unceremoniously pulled the trigger. There was a muffled bang inside the brickwork and a clatter as she dropped the gun on the recoil onto the logs. The eyes of everyone else in the place were popping out but Mrs Alexis calmly picked up her fallen property and returned to the bar.

'Another Bell?'s' she asked, stowing the shotgun lengthways under the counter. 'Another tomato juice?'

'Er . . .' I said.

She was laughing. 'Fastest way to clear a chimney. Didn't you know?'

'No.'

'It's an old gun . . . the barrel's not straight. I wouldn't treat a good gun like that.' She looked towards the fireplace. 'The damn smoke's clearing, anyway.'

It appeared that she was right. Wilfred, again on his knees with the bellows, was producing smoke which rose upwards, not out into the room. The eyes of the onlookers retreated to their accustomed sockets and the mouths slowly closed: even Ridger's.

'Laphroaig,' I said. 'Please. And could I look at your wine list?'

'Anything you like.' She stretched for the Laphroaig bottle and poured a fair measure. 'You and the policeman . . . what are you in here for?' The bright eyes searched my face. 'That policeman wouldn't come here just for a drink. Not him. Not tomato juice. Not early.'

I paid for the Laphroaig and took the wine list that she held out. 'We're looking for some scotch that turned up in a Bell's bottle at the Silver Moondance,' I said. 'More of the same, that is.'

The sharp gaze intensified. 'You won't find any here.'

'No, I don't suppose so.'

'Is this because of those complaints last month?'

'We're here because of them, yes.'

'You've shown me no authority.' No antagonism, I thought: therefore no guilt.

'I haven't any. I'm a wine merchant.'

'A wine . . . ?' She considered it. 'What's your name?'

I told her, also the name of my shop.

'Never heard of you,' she said cheerfully. 'Would you know this scotch if you tasted it?'

'That's the general idea. Yes.'

'Then good luck to you.' She gave me an amused and shining glance and turned away to another customer, and I carried my glass across to Ridger expecting the Laphroaig to be Laphroaig and nothing else.

'She's disgraceful,' Ridger said. 'I should arrest her.'

'On what charge?'

'Discharging a firearm in a public place.'

'The inside of a chimney is hardly a public place.'

'It's no laughing matter,' he said severely.

'The smoke's clearing,' I said. 'The shot worked.'

'I would have thought you'd had enough shooting for one lifetime.'

'Well, yes.'

I drank the Laphroaig: smoky, peaty, oak-aged historic Laphroaig, the genuine thing.

Ridger bit on his disappointment, complained about the price and fidgeted unhelpfully while I read the wine list, which was handwritten and extensive. All the familiar Silver Moondance names were there along with dozens of others, but when I pointed this out to him he said stiffly that his brief was for whisky only.

I took the wine list thoughtfully back to the bar and asked Mrs Alexis for a bottle of St Estèphe.

She smiled. 'By all means. Do you want it decanted?'

'Not yet.' I went through the rest of the list with her, picking out St Emilion, Mâcon, Valpolicella, Volnay and Nuits St Georges.

'Sure,' she said easily. 'Do you want all of them?'

'Yes, please.'

She disappeared briefly and came back with a partitioned basket containing the six asked for wines. I picked each bottle up in turn to read the labels: all the right names but none from the right year.

'We've sold all we had of 1979,' she explained patiently when I pointed it out. 'We constantly update the wine list, which is why we don't have it printed. We're writing another at the moment. These present wines are better. Do you want them, then, or not?'

'Sorry,' I said. 'Not.'

She put the basket of bottles without comment on the floor near her feet and smiled at me blandly.

'Do you know the Silver Moondance?' I asked.

'Heard of it. Who hasn't, round here? Never been there. Not my style. I'm told it's a tube job, anyway.'

'A tube . . . ?'

'Down the tubes,' she said patiently. 'The bank's foreclosing on the mortgage. As of this morning the staff have been sacked. I had one of the chefs telephoning to ask for a job.' She spoke with amusement as if the closure were comic, but she'd worn the same expression all the time we'd been there, her cheek muscles seeming to be permanently set in tolerant mockery.

'At the Silver Moondance,' I said mildly, 'they were selling one single wine under six different labels.'

Her expression didn't change but she glanced down at her feet.

'Yes, those,' I said. 'Or rather, not those.'
'Are you insulting me?'
'No, just telling you.'
The brilliant eyes watched me steadily. 'And you're looking for that wine as well as the scotch?'
'Yes.'
'Sorry I can't help you.'
'Perhaps it's as well,' I said.
'Why?'
'Well . . . I don't think it's too utterly safe to know much about that wine. The head waiter of the Silver Moondance undoubtedly knew what he was selling . . . and he's dead.'
Nothing altered in her face. 'I'm in no danger,' she said. 'I can promise you that. Do you want anything else?'
I shook my head. 'We'll be on our way.'
Her gaze slid past me to rest on Ridger and still without any change of expression she said, 'Give me a man who'll swing from a chandelier. Give me a goddamn man.' Her glance came back to my face, the mockery bold and strong. 'The world's a bloody bore.'
Her abundant hair was a dark reddish brown gleaming with good health and hair dye, and her nails were hard and long like talons. A woman of vibrating appetite who reminded me forcibly of all the species where the female crunched her husband for breakfast.
Wilfred (currently on the menu?) was still on his knees to the fire god when Ridger and I eventually made our way to the door. As Ridger went out ahead of me there was a sort of soft thudding *flump* from the direction of the chimney and a cloud of dislodged shot-up soot descended in a sticky billowing mass onto logs, flames and man beneath.
Transfixed, the armchair audience watched Wilfred rise balefully to his feet like a fuzzily inefficient demon king, scattering black rain and blinking great eyes slowly like a surprised owl on a dark night.
'I'll sue that bloody sweep,' Mrs Alexis said.

SIXTEEN:

We went to four more pubs on that first day and I grew tired of the perpetual taste of neat Bell's whisky. Ridger methodically annotated his clipboard and showed not the slightest disappointment as glass after glass proved genuine. The pub crawl was a job to him like any other, it seemed, and he would phlegmatically continue until instructed otherwise.

He was a man without rebellion, I thought, never questioning an order nor the order of things; living at the opposite end of the spectrum from that mean kicker-over-of-traces, Kenneth Charter's son. Somewhere between the two lay the rest of us, grousing, lobbying, enduring and philosophical, making what best we could of our imperfect evolution.

Towards the end I asked him if they'd found any trace of the Bedford van used in the robbery at my shop, and perhaps because by that time he had provisionally accepted me as a full colleague he answered without his usual reservations.

'No, we haven't found it,' he said. 'And we don't expect to.'

'How do you mean?' I asked.

'It belonged to a firm called Quality House Provisions who hadn't noticed it was missing until one of our PCs went there early Monday asking about it. Dozy lot. They'd got several vans, they said. It's now on the stolen-vehicle list marked urgent because of its tie-in with Zarac's murder, but a hot van like that's sure to be dumped somewhere already, probably in a scrap yard miles away with the number plates off. No one will find it except by luck, I shouldn't think.'

'Cheerful.'

'Fact of life.'

He drove me back towards the shop, saying he would return in the morning with tomorrow's list of suspicious premises.

'Can't you bring the whole list instead of in bits?' I asked.

'It's still being compiled. We started today with our own patch, but we may have to wait for information from others.'

'Mm – Do you have a first name, Sergeant?'

He looked faintly surprised. 'John,' he said.

'In the pubs tomorrow, do you mind if I use it? I damn nearly called you Sergeant twice in front of barmen today.'

He considered it. 'Yes. All right. Do you want me to call you Tony?'

'It would make more sense.'

'All right.'

'What do you do off duty?' I asked.

'Garden,' he said. 'Grow vegetables, mostly.'

'Married?'

'Yes, been married fourteen years. Two daughters, proper little madams.' An indulgence in his face belied the sharpness in his voice. 'Your wife died, they say.'

'Yes.'

'Sorry about that.'

'Thank you, Sergeant.'

He nodded. John was for business, a temporary intimacy that wouldn't commit him to friendship. I could sense his approval, almost his relief, at my avoidance of John in private.

He left me outside my door and drove tidily away, indicator blinking, carefully efficient to the last. Mrs Palissey had been rushed off her feet, she was glad to say, and was I sure I was fit to drive myself to the hospital because to be honest, Mr Beach, I did smell a wee bit of drink.

I reflected that I'd ordered, paid for and swallowed a good deal of a dozen neat whiskies and if I still felt sober it was an illusion. I went to the hospital by taxi and received disgusted sniffs from the nursing sister (the same one), who stripped off the tube bandage to see what was cooking underneath.

'People who drink heal more slowly,' she said severely.

'Do they?'

'Yes.'

With her head not far from mine she one by one unstuck the antiseptic patches she'd applied the previous Sunday, and I tried to breathe shallowly through my nose in the opposite direction. Without much success, it seemed, judging from the offended twitch of her nostrils.

'Most of these are healing better than you deserve,' she said finally. 'Three are inflamed and another looks troublesome . . . Do they hurt?'

'Well . . . sort of.'

She nodded. 'One should expect it. Several were more than an inch deep.' She began sticking on new patches. 'I'll put a stich in this bad one up here on your biceps, to hold it together. And keep off alcohol. There are much better pain killers.'

'Yes, ma'am,' I said dryly, and thought of the boozy tomorrow and of fifty thousand pubs to Watford.

Back in the shop I saw Mrs Palissey and Brian off with the deliveries and dealt with some paperwork, and in the lull between late afternoon customers eventually got dutifully around to looking at the photostats of Kenneth Junior's notebook.

Gerard's firm had made a good job of their deciphering and checking and my respect for his organisation consolidated from vague expectation into recognition that Deglet's were experienced experts in a way I hadn't appreciated.

Gerard's fat envelope contained an explanatory note and about fifteen sheets of typing paper. The centre of each sheet bore the stat of one page of the small notebook, and from each entry in the notebook a fine straight line led to explanation in the margin.

Gerard's note was typewritten:

> Tony,
>
> All the enquiries were done by telephone, not in person. Answers were given freely by Kenneth Charter himself, also by his wife and daughter and elder son, although with them as with friends and shops our questions had to be cautious, as Kenneth Charter forbade us to represent Kenneth Junior in a criminal light.
>
> The sheets are numbered in the order in which the pages occurred in the notebook. Kenneth Charter dates the first page as having been written at the beginning of August as it refers to Mrs Charter's birthday on August 8th. One may assume that the entries were written consecutively after that, but it is not certain, and there are no other positive dates, as you will see.
>
> Please write down immediately any thoughts which cross your mind as you read. Don't leave such thoughts until afterwards as they are apt to evaporate.
>
> G

I turned to the first of the notebook pages and found that the first entry of all read:

Buy card for Mum's birthday next week.

A fine straight line led to the marginal note: *August 8th.*

Kenneth Junior's handwriting was inclined to shoot off at both forward and backward sloping angles in the same word, but was otherwise distinctly formed and easy to read. The Deglet's annotator had written in neat fine black script, utterly different but equally legible. I could hardly complain that Gerard had set me a technically difficult task.

The second entry on the first page read:

Go to D.N.'s for w.g.

The marginal note said: *D.N. is David Naylor, Kenneth Junior's only close friend. It is thought the letters w.g. stand for war games, as they are David Naylor's hobby.*

The first page also read:

Collect trousers from cleaners.

Ask Dad for cash.

Tell B.T. to fuck off.

The line from the last entry led to: *B.T. is probably Betty Townsend, a girl Kenneth Junior had been seeing. Mrs Charter says she was a nice girl but clinging.*

Poor Betty Townsend.

I turned to page two and found a list of telephone numbers, each with an identification in the margin, along with an address.

Odeon cinema (local)

Diamond snooker club (local)

David Naylor (Friend. Unemployed)

Clipjoint (Barber's shop, local)

Lisa Smithson (Occasional girlfriend. Unemployed)

Ronald Haleby (Friend. Works as doorman at local disco)

The next many pages contained entries which were only understandable because of the telephone numbers and spoke eloquently of a drifting purposeless life. Kenneth Junior's lists were almost a diary, embracing such revelations as '*Snort with R.H. Sunday, take cash*' and '*Get abortion number for L.S.*' but were mainly on the more mundane level of '*Tell Mum to buy toothbrush*', '*Play snooker at Diamond's*' and '*Rewire plug on stereo*'.

One later page read:

Haircut.

Go to Halifax.

Buy tank for w.g., Phone D.N.

Get keys of N.T. for duplicates.

Meet R.H. in Diamond's.

Pay L.S. for abortion.

Deglet's annotations were:

(1) Clipjoint say Kenneth Junior went there at about ten day intervals for shampoo and styling. He bought expensive products and tipped lavishly.

(2) Kenneth Junior is most unlikely to have been to the town of Halifax. Suggest this reference means Halifax Building Society, though his parents don't know if he had an account there. Kenneth Charter thought that apart from unemployment benefit his son had no money except what he himself gave him, but this cannot be right as Charter did not give him enough extra for cocaine and abortions.

(3) Tank must be toy tank for war games.

(4) Not traced.

I frowned for a while over the letters N.T. but could make no more of them than Deglet's had. What did one need keys for? House, car, suitcase, drawer, locker, desk, mail box, deposit box . . . infinitum. N.T. was perhaps a person. Person unknown.

On the next page there was a single entry, the one which had started the bushfire.

The Reading telephone number followed by:

Tell Z UNP 786Y picks up B's Gin Mon 10 a.m. approx.

I made a wry face over the bald and still disturbing treachery and turned over to what was left: three more pages very much like the others, with only a few new themes.

Go with D.N. for w.g. with S.N! bore the Deglet explanation: *S.N. is Stewart Naylor, David Naylor's father. Stewart Naylor lives apart after divorce. David Naylor visits his father occasionally. Stewart Naylor is noted for skill in war games, which probably accounts for the exclamation mark.*

On the last page of all it said:

Get visa for Australia.

Ask R.H. about pushers in Sydney.

Pay L.S. That's her lot.

Go to Halifax.

Remember to ask Dad for cash.

Collect keys from Simpers and send them off.

There was a final Deglet explanation: *Simpers is a hardware shop which duplicates keys. They have no record of work done for Kenneth Junior or anyone else in the family. They normally cut keys immediately, while you wait, but not if they don't keep the blanks in stock and have to send away for them. In that case they ask for an address and a deposit. If Kenneth Junior obtained keys in that way from Simpers he gave a name and address not his own.*

I shuffled the pages together and put them back in the envelope, looking dubiously at the very few thoughts and comments I'd jotted down for Gerard; and half an hour later, when he telephoned, I offered them reluctantly and apologetically.

'Just say what occurred to you,' he said a touch impatiently. 'Anything at all may be useful.'

'Well . . . those keys.'

'What about them?'

'Well . . . what sort of keys do the tankers have?'

There was utter silence from Gerard.

'Are you still there?' I asked.

'Yes, I am.' Another pause. 'Go on talking.'

'Um . . . I wondered at the beginning about it always being the same tanker which was stolen, and I thought it might be because of something dead simple, like that one being the only tanker the thieves had the keys for. Because they would have needed the keys to unlock the cab door when the driver was in the service stations, in order to put the gas in there, and lock the door again so the driver found nothing suspicious when he got back.'

'Hm,' Gerard said. 'The police assumed the thieves used lock-pickers.'

'The right key would be quicker.'

'I agree.'

'Kenneth Junior had easy access to Charter's office and everywhere else in the place before the first theft. You might ask Charter Senior where the tanker keys are kept.'

'Yes, I will.'

'It struck me that maybe it was keys to a second tanker that Kenneth Junior was having cut. I mean, N.T. might stand for Next Tanker or New Tanker or something. Anyway, it might be worth taking some tanker keys to Simpers and seeing if they keep those blanks in stock or if they'd need to send away for them. And it might be as well to warn Kenneth Charter that someone, somewhere, might have the keys to another of his tankers . . . if any of this is right, of course.'

'Right or wrong, I'll warn him.'

'I'm afraid that's all,' I said. 'I didn't think of much else. Except . . .'

'Except?'

'Except that to himself Kenneth Junior didn't seem so bad. He sold information for presumably spot cash and he banked it in something ultra-conservative like a building society. He might have enjoyed his snort with the disco doorman but he wasn't addicted. He paid for the girl's abortion. That's none of it heavy villainy.'

'No. A moderately stable personality, I thought so too. Staying at home, buying a birthday card for his mother, being impressed by his friend's father . . . but totally without loyalty to his own.'

'Teenage rebellion gone a step too far.'

'Right,' Gerard said. 'Untrustworthy little bugger. But there you are, he's earning us money. Life's full of such ironies.'

I said with a smile in my voice, 'Want another? We're now looking for that scotch courtesy of the police.'

I told him about my day's journeyings with Ridger and raised a chuckle on account of Mrs Alexis.

'I wasn't sure about Mrs Alexis,' I said. 'She did have all those wines on her list. She says she's sold them all. She wears such a knowing expression the whole time that you can't tell if she knows anything specific. Maybe I'll go back.'

'She sounds an utter dragon.'

'Very good value,' I said. 'She likes men who swing from chandeliers.'

'But you don't. You're not the type.'

'No . . . I should be safe.'

He laughed. 'How was your arm? I have to go myself tomorrow.'

'Not bad. And good luck.'

Ridger returned punctually in the morning and we set off to cover a territory in and around Henley-on-Thames, where in July each year the rowing regatta brought the sleepy town to bulging expensive life. In late October, in a cold drizzle, it was quiet. Ducks swam silently on the grey river and shoppers huddled head-down under umbrellas. Ridger and I went into bar after bar brushing off raindrops and I lost count after a while of the Bell's.

All of the Bell's rang true. Not a cracked note among them.

One of the barmen gave us short change, slapping down coins in a handful while sloshing water onto the counter top, so that I should snatch them up without checking, but Ridger said that that didn't rate a clipboard entry. He produced his badge, however, and warned the barman, who scowled. As the high spot of the morning it didn't rate much, but one couldn't expect a Mrs Alexis every day of the week.

Some of the pubs had two bars. One had three. My friend John insisted on making sure of every Bell's bottle in sight.

Awash with tomato juice he returned me to my shop at two-thirty and I sat heavy-headed in my office regretting the whole enterprise. I would simply have to take something to spit into, I thought, even if spitting alerted the barman and disgusted the other customers. Getting half cut every lunchtime was no joke.

Mrs Palissey drove Brian away with a big load of deliveries and between each sporadic afternoon customer I sat down and felt thick with sleep. When the door buzzer roused me for the fifth time I went into the shop yawning.

'That's no way to greet manna from heaven,' my customer said.

Mrs Alexis stood there, larger than life, bringing out her own sun on a wet afternoon. I shut my mouth slowly, readjusted it to a smile, and said, 'I was coming to see you again at the first opportunity.'

'Were you now?' she said, mockery in full swing. 'So this is where our little wine merchant dwells.' She peered about her good-humouredly, oblivious to the fact that her 'little' wine merchant stood a fraction under six feet himself and could at least look her levelly in the eyes. Nearly all men, I guessed, were 'little' to her.

'I was passing,' she said.

I nodded. Amazing, the number of people who said that. 'No, I bloody well wasn't,' she amended explosively. 'I came here on purpose.' She lifted her chin almost defiantly. 'Does that surprise you?'

'Yes,' I said truthfully.

'I liked the look of you.'

'That surprises me too.'

'Bloody cool, aren't you?'

I was still half drunk, I thought. Almost a third of a bottle of scotch on an empty stomach, whichever way you looked at it. Ulcer land.

'How's the chimney?' I asked.

She grinned, showing teeth like a shark.

'Bloody Wilfred hasn't forgiven me.'

'And the fire?'

'Burning like Rome.' She eyed me assessingly. 'You're young enough to be my bloody son.'

'Just about.'

'And do you want to know about those bloody wines or don't you?'

'Yes, I do indeed.'

'I wasn't going to tell that police sergeant. Wouldn't give him the satisfaction. Pompous little killjoy.'

I said 'Mm' non-committally.

'I bought them, all right,' she said. 'But I damn soon sent them back.'

I breathed in deeply, trying to do nothing to distract her.

'I ran short of Bell's,' she said. 'So I 'phoned across to the pub opposite to borrow some. Nothing odd in that, we always help each other out. So he brings a whole unopened bloody case over, saying it came from a new supplier who offered good discounts, especially on wine, which was more my sort of thing than his. He gave me a 'phone number and told me to ask for Vernon.'

I looked at her.

'Should have known better, shouldn't I?' she said cheerfully. 'Should have suspected it had all fallen off the back of a bloody lorry.'

'But you telephoned?'

'That's right. Very good wines, just under normal price. So I said right, shunt along a case of each, I'd put them on the wine list and see if anyone liked them.'

'And did they?'

'Sure.' She gave me the shark smile. 'Shows how much some of these so-called buffs really know.'

'And then what?'

'Then I got someone in the bar one day kicking up a fuss and saying he'd been given the wrong whisky. I'd given it to him myself out of a Bell's bottle, one I'd got from my neighbour. I tasted it but I don't like the stuff, can't tell one from another. Anyway I gave him some Glenlivet free to placate him and aplogised and when he'd gone I rang up my neighbour pretty damn quick, but he said he was certain it was O.K., Vernon worked for a big firm.'

'Which big firm?'

'How the hell do I know? I didn't ask. But I'll tell you, I wasn't taking any risks so I poured the rest of the case of Bell's down the drain and chalked it up to experience. Damn good thing I did, because the next bloody day I got the Weights and Measures people round with their little measuring instruments following a strong complaint from a customer. And that damned man drank my Glenlivet, too, and still reported me.'

'And I don't suppose he's been back,' I said, smiling.

'I'd've strangled him.'

'If it hadn't been him, it would have been someone else.'

'You don't have to be so bloody right. Anyway, after that I asked a man I know who buys for a wine society to come out straight away and taste those splendid wines, and when he told me they were all the same I rang up that bloody Vernon and told him to collect what was left and repay me for the whole lot or I'd give his bloody 'phone number to the police.'

'And what happened?' I asked, fascinated.

'The same man who delivered them came back with my cash and took his wines away, what wasn't already drunk. He said he wasn't Vernon, just a friend of his, but I'll bet it was Vernon himself. He said Vernon hoped I'd keep my word about the 'phone number because if not something very nasty would happen to me.' She grinned, superbly unconcerned. 'I told him if Vernon tried anything with me, I'd eat him.'

I laughed. 'And that was that?'

'That was bloody that. Until you came round yesterday snooping.'

'Well,' I said, 'Do you still have the 'phone number?'

Her brilliant eyes shone yellowly. 'Yes, I do. How much is it worth to you? A case of Krug? Case of Pol Roger? Dom Pérignon?'

I reflected. 'Case of Bell's?' I suggested.

'Done.' She picked a piece of paper without ceremony out of her handbag and gave it to me.

'If you carry it,' I said.

She glanced at the sling I still wore. 'Hurt your arm?'

'Shotgun pellets . . . I wouldn't tell anyone, if I were you, that you'd been here to see me. I got shot at because of that wine. Vernon might not be pleased to know you'd given me his 'phone number.'

Her eyes opened wide and the mockery for once died right out of her face.

'I came here,' she said flatly, 'because of the head waiter at the Silver Moondance. Murder's going too far. But you didn't say . . .'

I shook my head. 'I'm sorry. There seemed no need. I had no idea you would come here. And I'm sure you'll be O.K. if you just keep quiet. After all, others must have Vernon's number. Your neighbour, for one.'

'Yes.' She thought it over. 'You're damn right.' Her face lightened back into its accustomed lines. 'Any time you're passing, my little wine merchant, call in for dinner.'

She came with me into the storeroom to collect her trophy which she bore easily away under her arm, diving out into the drizzle with the teeth and eyes gleaming against the grey sky.

Gerard said, 'That's great,' and promised to ring back as soon as his firm had traced the number.

'It's somewhere near Oxford,' I said.

'Yes,' he agreed. 'Oxford code.'

His voice for all his enthusiasm sounded tired and when I asked after his shoulder he merely grunted without comment, which I took to mean no good news.

'I'll call you back,' he said, and within half an hour did so, but not to say he had located Vernon's number.

'Thought you'd like to know . . . the office has checked with the Doncaster auctioneers. Ramekin was bought for actual cash. Banknotes. They've no record of who bought it. The office did a quick check also on transporters and sure enough, as you said, Ramekin was in their books. He was shipped to California to a well-known bloodstock agent. The agent is away travelling in Japan and no one in his office will release information in his absence. He's expected home next Thursday night. Ramekin's shipment costs were paid in cash by a Mr A. L. Trent, who has sent several other horses to California via the same shipper to the same agent. So there we are. The laundered cash is in California, either banked or still on the hoof.'

'Banked, I'd bet a million.'

'Yes, I'd think so. But a dead end until Friday.'

'Pity.'

'We're making progress,' he said. 'And you might also like to know about the tanker keys.'

'What about them?'

'I talked to Kenneth Charter. He says there's nothing exceptional about the keys to the cab or the ignition keys but he has special keys for the valves into the segments in his tankers. Part of his security arrangements. There are nine separate segments in those big tankers. He says it's so the tanker can carry several different liquids in small loads on the same journey, if necessary. Anyway, each segment has its own particular key, to avoid mistakes with unloading, so the scotch tankers each have a bunch of nine valve keys. With goods in bond Charter has always posted a set of keys in advance to both shipper and destination so that they are never carried on the tanker itself, for security.'

'Most prudent,' I said.

'Yes. So Kenneth Charter went to the Simpers shop himself this afternoon, and sure enough they said they'd twice made a set of nine keys like that, and both times they'd had to send away for the blanks. The young man who'd ordered them had given his name as Harrison each time. Kenneth Charter is spitting mad as of course the shop has no record of the shapes they cut into the blanks, and he doesn't know which of his tankers is now at risk.'

'Awkward.'

'He says if he loses the whole business it won't matter a damn. What upset him most was Kenneth Junior going to such lengths.'

'Does he know how Kenneth Junior got hold of the keys?' I asked.

'He says they're usually kept in his office, but when the tankers' valves are being steam cleaned the keys are out in the workshop. He reckons Kenneth Junior took them from there.'

'Cunning little beast.'

'Absolutely. Incidentally, both Kenneth Charter and Deglet's have now received from Rannoch the profile analysis of all three of the stolen loads of scotch. Apparently they are all slightly different because they were blends from more than one distillery. Too technical for me. Anyway, they're in our office ready, if we find anything to match.'

'Mm. I wonder if Mrs Alexis's neighbour still has any.'

'What a thought! Get onto her pronto.'

'Pity she poured hers down the drain.'

Gerard and I disconnected and I got through to Mrs Alexis who sounded breezily unaffected and said she would find out at once; but she called back within ten minutes to say her neighbour had sold the lot some time ago and couldn't get any more at that price because Vernon had discontinued the discount, but she thought Vernon must have got the wind up after his brush with her and had closed down altogether in her area.

Damn, I thought, and told Gerard.

'Whenever we get near that stuff it seems to recede from us like a phantom,' he said wearily.

'Maybe I'll find it tomorrow.'

He sighed. 'It's a very big haystack.'

SEVENTEEN:

Flora came breathlessly into the shop soon after I'd opened it on the Saturday morning, saying she was on her way to fetch Jack home and wanted to thank me again for my help with Howard and Orkney Swayle.

'There's no need. I enjoyed it.'

'All the same, Tony dear, I want you to have this.' She put a gift-wrapped parcel on the counter, and when I opened my mouth to protest said, 'Now don't argue, Tony dear, it's for you and it's not enough, it's very small and I expect you have one already, but I'll have my hands full when Jack's home so I thought I'd bring it for you now.'

She patted my hand in motherly fashion and I bent to kiss her cheek.

'You're very naughty,' I said. 'But thank you.'

'That's right dear. Where's your sling?'

'I forgot it this morning. It's at home.'

'Don't tire yourself, dear, will you? And we'll need some more drinks whenever you've time.' She fished in her handbag and produced a list. 'After Jack's home the owners will start coming again and some of them drink like fish, though I shouldn't say it, and Jack says he's going to add it on their bills as medicine for the horses, which you can't blame him for, can you, dear?'

'Er . . . no.'

She put the list on the counter beside the present, and, saying she had a thousand things to see to on her way to the hospital, went lightfootedly away.

I unwrapped the parcel curiously and found that although it was small in size it couldn't have been in price. The box inside the glazed white paper had come from a jeweller in Reading, and it contained, in a nest of red velvet, a silver penknife.

Not one that would necessarily gladden the hearts of Boy Scouts. Not knobbly with thirteen blades and a hook for taking stones out of horses' hooves, like the one which had been the pride of my childhood. A slim elegantly tooled affair with a sharp steel cutting blade tucked into one side and a second blade on the other which turned out to be a screwdriver. I liked both the look and the feel, and although it was true I already had a knife, it was old and blunt. I took the old knife out of my pocket and replaced it with the new, and thought friendly thoughts of Flora all morning.

Ridger added to my pleasure by telephoning to say there would be no more pub crawls for a few days as he had been assigned to other duties, but we would resume on Wednesday and he would be along for me then at ten-fifteen.

I suppose I should have told him about Mrs Alexis and the mysterious Vernon with his telephone number, but I didn't. It seemed odd to me to find that my allegiance was to Gerard rather than to the police. I had caught from him quite thoroughly, it seemed, the belief that the paying client's interests came first, with public justice second.

I did actually half jokingly ask Ridger who I should tell if I came across the suspect scotch when I wasn't in his own company, and he answered seriously, after earnest thought, that I'd probably better tell Chief Superintendent Wilson straight away, as Ridger himself along with many of the county's police was having to go up north to help deal with some ugly picketing, which made a change, and he couldn't tell who'd be on duty while he was away.

'How would I reach the Chief Superintendent?' I asked.

He told me to wait a moment and came back with a number which would reach the Zarac investigation room direct. Night or day, he said. Priority.

'Would the Silver Moondance scotch be priority?'

'Of course,' he said. 'Anything would.'

'O.K., Sergeant. See you on Wednesday.'

He said he hoped so, and goodbye.

Relieved at being let off the drinking I sold a lot of wine to a flood of customers, with Mrs Palissey busily beaming and Brian carrying the loads out to the cars, and it seemed as if it would be for once a normal day until Tina McGregor telephoned at eleven.

'Gerard's gone up to the office,' she said. 'I wish he wouldn't on Saturdays and particularly as he's not right yet from last Sunday, but it's like arguing with a bulldozer . . . Anyway, he asked me to tell you they've traced the number you gave him yesterday and it doesn't look too promising. It's the number of the big caterers at Martineau Park racecourse. He says if you'd care to go along there you might ask them if Vernon – is that right? – still works for them. He says if you should see Vernon yourself he'll leave it up to you to decide whether or not to ask him where he got the scotch and wines from. Is that all right?'

'Yes, fine,' I said. 'How's the shoulder?'

'He's being utterly tight-lipped about it and they've put him on antibiotics.'

'It's infected?' I asked, alarmed.

'He didn't say. I just wish he'd slow down.'

She sounded neither anxious nor angry, but one could never tell Tina's reactions from her voice. I said weakly, 'I'm sorry,' and she answered, 'No need to be,' in the same calm tone, and said Gerard would like me to telephone him at his home later to let him know how I got on at Martineau Park.

It was odd, I reflected, putting down the receiver, to think that I had been at Martineau Park races so long on Tuesday afternoon totally oblivious of the existence of Vernon among the caterers Orkney Swayle so much detested. Life, as Gerard said, was full of ironies.

Mrs Palissey, geared to my planned absence with Ridger, took my substitute trip to Martineau Park in her stride. 'Of course, Mr Beach. No trouble at all.'

Grudge-and-spite might be the prevailing social climate but Mrs Palissey rose gloriously above it. Mrs Palissey was a non-interfering do-gooder, heaven reward her. I said I would make it up to her later, and she said, 'Yes, Yes,' as if it didn't matter one way or the other.

I drove to Martineau Park wondering if in fact there would be anyone there. It wasn't a race day. There would be no crowds. I hadn't before been to a racecourse on a non-racing day and didn't know what level of activity to expect in the way of managers, maintenance, groundsmen or cleaners. The whole catering department would very likely be locked. I would quite likely be turning round to drive straight back.

The gates into the members' car park at least stood open, unguarded. I drove through them and across the unpopulated expanses of cindery grass, leaving the Rover at the end of the short row of cars near the entrance to the paddock. The gate too was open and unattended, where on race days watchful officials checked the admittance badges of the throng streaming through.

It was eerie, I thought, to see the place so deserted. Without people the bulky line of buildings seemed huge. Bustling human life somehow reduced their proportions, filled their spaces, made them friendlier, brought them to comfortable size. I hadn't realised how big the place was in all the days I'd been there.

There was no one about around the weighing room area, though the doors there too were open. I went curiously inside, looking at the holies from where racegoers were normally barred, peering with interest at the scales themselves and at the flat pieces of lead used for packing weight-cloths. I went on into the jockeys' changing rooms and looked at the rows of empty pegs, empty benches, empty racks for saddles: all echoingly bare with no scrap of personal life remaining. When the racing circus moved on, it took all with it but the dust.

Gerard might consider the detour a waste of time, but I would probably never get such an opportunity again. I peered for good measure into a room marked 'Stewards' which contained merely a table, six undistinguished chairs and two pictures ditto. No mementos, no records of the make-or-break enquiries held there.

Returning to fresh air and the allotted task I came to a door marked 'Clerk of the Course' which stood slightly ajar. I pushed it open tentatively and found a man sitting at a desk, writing. He raised a smooth head and bushy eyebrows and said in a civilised voice, 'Can I help you?'

'I'm looking for the caterers,' I said.

'Delivery entrance?'

'Er . . . yes.'

'You'll want to go along the back of the stands to the far end. You'll find the Tote building facing you. Turn right. You'll see the Celebration Bar there alongside the Tote, but the door you want is to your right again before you get there. A green door. Not conspicuous. There are some empty beer crates just outside, unless they've moved them as I asked.'

'Thank you.'

He nodded civilly and bent to his writing, and I walked to the far end of the stands and found the green door and the beer crates, as he'd said.

I found also that deliveries were at that moment taking place. A large dark van had been drawn up outside the closed front of the Celebration Bar, a van with its rear doors opened wide and two workmen in brown overalls unloading a shipment of gin from it onto a pallet on a fork-lift truck.

The green door itself stood open, propped that way by a

crate. I walked through it behind the two men in overalls as they trundled inwards the make of gin which Orkney had refused to have in his box.

The door, I saw, represented the outward end of a very dimly lit passage about six feet wide which stretched away into the distance as far as one could see, and I realised that it must run under the whole length of the main bank of stands, an inner spinal thoroughfare, the gut life of the building, unseen from outside.

The gin-handlers walked onwards past three closed green painted doors marked Stores A, Stores B, and Stores C, and past an open one, Stores D, which revealed only a half dozen of the sort of deep trays used by bakers.

A few paces beyond that the gin turned abruptly to the left, and I, turning after it, found myself in a wider side passage aiming for an open but heavy and purposeful-looking door. Beyond the door were brighter lights and more people in what was clearly a larger area and I went in there wondering whether Vernon was a first name or surname, and whether there was the slightest chance of his being at work on a Saturday.

Immediately through the heavy door there was a large storeroom stacked head high with dense-packed beer crates like those outside, only these were full. To the left was a partitioned section, walls of wood to waist height, glass above, containing a desk, files, calendar, paperwork. To the right an inner door led into a still larger storeroom, a mini-warehouse where the ranks of cases of drink rose nearly to the ceiling and advanced into the central space in deep blocks. Martineau Park, I reflected, was due to hold its Autumn Carnival jump-racing meeting near the beginning of November and was stocking up accordingly. At the Cheltenham Festival in March, one wine merchant had told me, the jump-racing crowd had in three days, apart from beer by the lakeful, despatched six thousand bottles of champagne in addition to nine thousand bottles of other wines and four thousand bottles of spirits. At Martineau, by the look of things, at least double that was expected.

The gin went through into the inner warehouse to be added to a huge stack already growing there, and I again followed. One large man with a clipboard was checking off quantities and another with a black felt pen put a mark on each box as it was unloaded.

No one paid me any attention. I stood there as if invisible to all of them, and it slowly struck me that each set thought I belonged to the other. The two delivery men disengaged the fork-lift from the pallet they'd brought in, picked up an empty one from a low stack and began wheeling back to the door. The man with the pen heaved the cases into their new positions, putting his mark on each, and the man with the clipboard watched and counted.

I thought I'd better wait until they'd finished before I interrupted, and looking back it seems possible that that brief hesitation saved my life.

The telephone rang in the office section, raucously loud.

'Go and answer that, Mervyn,' the man with the clipboard said, and his henchman with the marker went off to obey. Then the clipboard man frowned as if remembering something, looked sharply at his watch, and called out, 'Mervyn, I'll answer it. You go and shift those beer cases like the man says. Put them in store D. Wait outside until I tell you to come back. And tell those men not to bring in the next load until I'm off the 'phone, right?' His gaze flicked over me, scarcely reaching my face. 'Your job, of course,' he said. 'You tell them.'

He strode away fast in the direction of the office leaving me flat-footed in his wake, and presently I could hear his voice answering the telephone and could see a portion of his backview through the glass.

'Yes, speaking. Yes, yes. Go on.'

Before I'd consciously decided whether to retire or eavesdrop another and different voice spoke loudly from the passage outside, a voice accompanied by firm approaching footsteps.

'Vernon? Are you there?'

He came straight through the doorway and veered immediately to his left towards the office: and to my startled eyes he was unmistakable.

Paul Young.

'Vernon!'

'Yes, look, I'll be with you . . .' Vernon of the clipboard put the palm of his hand over the telephone and began to turn towards the newcomer, and while neither of them was looking my way I stepped backwards out of their line of sight.

Paul Young.

My mind seemed stuck; my body of lead.

To reach the outside world I would have to go past the office section and with all that glass around Paul Young would be sure to see me. He might not have taken particular note of me on that Monday morning in the Silver Moondance Saloon but he'd certainly thought of me a good deal since. The assistant assistant would have told him who I was. He'd sent the thieves to my shop with his list. He must know how that sortie had ended. He must also know it hadn't achieved its main purpose. I thought that if he saw me now he would know me, and the idea of that filled me with numbing, muscle-paralysing fright.

Neither Vernon nor Paul Young at that exact moment seemed to be moving, but impelled no doubt by the atavistic burrowing instincts of the hunted and trapped I sought in that brightly-lit warehouse for a dark place to hide.

There were no soft nooks or crannies, just solid blocks and columns of cases of drink. There were narrow spaces between some of the blocks into which I could squeeze . . . and where anyone glancing in as they walked past would easily see me. Down the far end, I thought in panicky fashion. They might not go right down there.

But I'd have to get there, and at any second, any second . . . It was too far. Something else . . . something fast . . .

I climbed.

I climbed the highest and most extensive stack, which happened to be of non-vintage champagne. I lay flat on my stomach along the top of it, at the back against the wall. The ceiling was eighteen inches above my head. The cases stretched beyond my feet at one end and beyond my head at the other. I could see nothing but cardboard. No floor. No people. My heart bounced around like a rubber ball and I wanted to shut my eyes on the ostrich principle that if I didn't look I wouldn't be seen.

Consultancy did not include getting too close to Paul Young.

What a hollow bloody laugh.

If he found me on top of the champagne it would be a crocodile job for sure. Did he take plaster of Paris with him always in his Rolls?

Why hadn't I run for it? If I'd run, he might not have caught me. I ought simply to have sprinted. It would have been better. There were people around . . . I'd have been safe. And now here I was, marooned eight feet up on a liquid mountain and feeling more frightened than I'd ever been in my life.

They left the office and came into the main storeroom. I clenched my teeth and sweated.

If they searched for me . . . if they knew I was there . . . they would certainly find me.

'I'm not satisfied. I want to see for myself.'

It was Paul Young's own hard voice, full of aggressive determination and so close that he might have been speaking to me directly. I tried not to tremble . . . not to rustle against the cardboard . . . not to breathe.

'But I've told you . . .' the clipboard man said.

'I don't give a sod what you've told me. You're a twisty bastard, Vernon. You'd lie as soon as spit. I've warned you twice and I don't trust you. By my reckoning you should still have twenty-four cases of scotch left here and I've written down on this list how much you should have under each label. And I'm telling you, Vernon, you'd better show me just that much because if I find you've been selling any more on your own account and pocketing the proceeds, you're out.'

Vernon said suddenly, 'Your list won't be up to date. I sold a lot to that wine bar in Oxford.'

'How many labels?' Paul Young asked sharply.

'Two.'

'That'd better be right. You can show me the invoices.'

Vernon said combatively, 'You make selling them too difficult, not letting more than two go to each place. No one ever says they're the same. How many complaints have we had, tell me that? Your brother's been selling all six for years and no one's ever said they aren't what's on the labels.'

Paul Young said heavily, 'Someone must have complained, otherwise why was that snooping wine-merchant there tasting everything and telling the police? I'm not risking all six together any more, not for anyone. If you want to stay in business, Vernon, you'll do what I tell you and don't you forget it. Now let's check on the stocks, and you'd better not have been cheating me, Vernon, you'd better not.'

'It's all down the far end,' Vernon said glumly, and their voices faded and became less distinct as they moved away down the long room.

At the far end . . . and I'd have gone down there to hide, if I'd had time. Great God Almighty . . .

I wondered if they would see my feet. I thought of escape but knew my first movement would alert them. I thought that if the worst came to the worst I could defend myself by throwing champagne bottles. Champagne bottles were reinforced because if they broke they were like mini-grenades exploding with gas into cutting knives of glass. Flying glass was lethal, which people tended to forget because of actors crashing out harmlessly through windows in television sagas: but that fictional glass was made of sugar to safeguard the stuntmen . . . and little children had been killed by dropping fizzy-drink bottles . . . and I'd fight with champagne if I had to.

They were down at the far end for several minutes, their voices still muffled. When they came back, nothing between them had improved.

'You had all the Silver Moondance scotch back here,' Paul Young said furiously. 'I brought it myself. What have you done with it?'

Silence from Vernon.

'I put a red circle on every box from there when Zarac and I loaded it. You didn't notice that, I suppose? I didn't trust you, Vernon. I was sodding right not to trust you. You've been useful to me, I'm not saying different. But you're not the only stores manager who can shuffle a bit of paper. You're greedy and you're not safe. The party's over, Vernon. You're short a total of twenty-eight cases by my reckoning and I won't have people steal from me. You've had a fair cut. Very fair. But enough's enough. We're through. I'll remove the rest of my stock tomorrow afternoon in one of the vans, and you'll be here with the keys of this place to see to it.'

With defensive anger and no caution at all Vernon said explosively, 'If you break with me I'll see you regret it.'

There was a small intense silence, then in a deadly voice Paul Young said, 'The last person who threatened me in that way was Zarac.'

Vernon made no reply. I felt my own hairs rising, my breath stifling, my skin chilling to cold.

I had heard too much.

If I'd been at risk before, it was now redoubled. And it wasn't just the threat that terrified, but the manner of it . . . the nightmare of a soft white bandage over one's nose and mouth, turning to rock, chocking off breath . . . coming my way if Paul Young knew what I'd heard . . . or so it seemed to me, lying in fear, trying to prevent tremor or twitch from creaking through the unstable columns of boxes.

Vernon must have known what had become of Zarac. He made no reply at all, nor did Paul Young find it necessary to spell out his meaning at more length. I heard his strong gritty footsteps move away towards the doorway to the office, and after them, hesitant, shuffling, the footfalls of Vernon.

I heard Vernon's voice saying loudly, angrily, 'What are you doing? I told you not to bring that lot in until I was ready,' and with the sublime disrespect for orders shown by a certain type of British workman the two men in brown overalls pushed their fork-lift truck resolutely past him into the warehouse.

I couldn't see them, but I heard them plainly. One of them said truculently, 'Time and a half or no time and a half, we knock off at twelve-thirty, and if this isn't unloaded by then we'll take it back with us. We can't ponce about waiting for your private 'phone calls.'

Vernon was flustered. I heard him outside calling, 'Mervyn, Mervyn, get back here'; and when Mervyn returned it was with news that made my precarious position much worse.

'Did you know Bakerton's van's here? They've brought fifty more cases of Pol Roger White Foil.'

Pol Roger White Foil was what I was lying on.

If they were busy with Pol Roger someone would be bound to see me. They could hardly avoid it. Delivery men wouldn't exactly ignore a man lying on top of their boxes . . . they would for instance remark on it . . . who wouldn't?

Vernon said disorganisedly, 'Well if they've brought it . . . Go out and count what they unload, they left us short two cases last time . . . And you there with the gin, stack that lot separately, it's not checked . . .'

Paul Young's decisive voice cut through the hurrying orders. 'Tomorrow afternoon, Vernon. Two o'clock sharp.'

Vernon's reply was drowned as far as I was concerned by the gin handlers heating up an argument about football six paces from my toes. I could no longer hear Paul Young either. I heard too much about a questionable foul and the eyesight of the ref.

Staying on top of the champagne was hopeless, though the temptation to remain invisible was almost overwhelming. Discovery on my stomach, discovery on my feet . . . one or the other was inevitable.

There must be a safety of sorts, I thought, in the presence of all those delivery men.

On my feet, then.

I slithered backwards and dropped down into the narrow gap between the bulk of the Pol Roger and the smaller block of Krug beyond.

I was trembling. It wouldn't do. I stepped from the champagne shelter numb with fright and went down to the men with the gin.

One of them broke off his denunciation of a deliberate kick at a knee cap and said, 'Blimey, where did you come from?'

'Just checking,' I said vaguely. 'Have you finished?'

'Near enough.' They expertly off-loaded the last few cases. 'That's the lot. You want to sign our chit?'

One of them picked a yellow folded paper from his top overall pocket and held it out.

'Er . . .' I said, fishing for a pen. 'Yes.'

I opened the yellow paper, leaned it against a case of gin, signed it illegibly in the space provided and gave it back to them.

'Right. We'll be off.'

They left the fork-lift truck where it was in the middle of the wide central aisle, and set off for the door. Almost without thought I grasped the truck's handle and pushed it along in their wake, and it was in that way that I came face to face with Vernon.

There was sweat on his forehead. He looked harassed, small eyes anxious above a flourishing moustache, mouth open, breath hurried and heavy.

He gave me the smallest frown. He was accompanying an incoming load of white boxes. I let go of the truck I was pushing and walked past Vernon and the Pol Roger and was out into the passage with no sign of Paul Young, no shouts, no scalding pursuit.

I followed the brown-overalled gin men round the turn into the main passage with only a short way to go to the free open air . . . and there he was, Paul Young, outside the green entrance, lit by daylight, standing as if waiting, solid, shortish, unremarkable, a man without pity.

I glanced back the way I'd come. Vernon had peeled off from the champagne and was advancing after me, appearing undecided, enquiring, on the verge of suspicious.

'You, there,' he said. 'I didn't see you come in.'

'Maintenance,' I said briskly. 'Just checking.'

Vernon's frown deepened. Paul Young remained at the outer door motionless and in plain sight, watching something outside.

I turned towards the only alternative, the long passage leading deep under the stands. Vernon glanced to where I'd been looking and saw Paul Young, and his mouth tightened. I gave him no more time to crystallise his suspicions of me but set off down the long passage as if every step of the way was familiar. When I looked back after about fifteen places Vernon was still there, still staring after me. I gave him a wave. Beyond him Paul Young still filled the way out. I continued to walk onwards, trying to control a terrible urge to run. At all costs, I told myself, don't look back again. Vernon would begin to follow.

Don't look back.

Don't actually run.

I went faster and deeper to I didn't know where.

EIGHTEEN:

The passage ended in kitchens: vast cavernous halls with stainless steel growing everywhere in monstrous mixing bowls and sink-like trays.

Empty, cold, clean, greyly gleaming: a deserted science-fiction landscape which on Tuesday must have been alive with warmth and smells and food and bustle. There were a few lights on, inadequate for the area, but no sign that anyone was working. I glanced back against all my good intentions as I turned away from the passage and saw that Vernon had indeed followed; that he was almost half way along.

I waved again as I stepped out of his sight, a brief and I hoped reassuring signal.

Vernon was not apparently reassured. I heard his voice shouting loudly from the distance, 'Hey!'

He didn't know who I was, but he was alarmed that I could have overheard what I had. His unease sprang from guilt and his persistence in following me from a wholly accurate instinct. If he thought I was a danger to him, he was right.

Damn him, I thought. He was a better prospect than Paul Young, but not much. I might be able to talk myself free of him with something like saying I was checking electric wiring . . . or I might not. Better by far to vanish as inexplicably as I'd appeared.

The ovens were big enough to crawl into . . . but they had glass doors . . . and gas jets inside . . . What else?

Another way out . . . There had to be a way out for food. They wouldn't push it along that passage out into possible rain. There would be a way into bars, into dining rooms. Exit doors, somewhere.

I sped round two corners. More stainless steel monsters. Sinks like bathtubs for dishwashing. Floor to ceiling stacks of trays. No doors out.

Nowhere to hide.

'Are you there?' Vernon's voice shouted. 'Hey you. Where are you?' He was much nearer. He sounded determined now, and more belligerent. 'Come out of there. Show yourself.'

I went desperately round the furthest possible corner into a small space which looked at first like a short blank corridor leading nowhere. I began to turn to go back the way I'd come, feverishly trying to remember electricians' terms to flourish around like interrupted resistance and circuit overload and other such nonsense when I saw that one wall of the blank corridor wasn't blank.

One wall contained a row of four small lifts, each about a yard high, a yard wide, a yard deep. Constructed without fronts, they were of the sort especially designed for transporting food upwards from downstairs cooks. Dumb waiters the Victorians had called them. Beside each lift, selector buttons: 1, 2, 3.

I scrambled into the nearest lift, pressed button 3, not by choice but because my unsteady fingers hit it first, and wondered what on earth I would say now if Vernon at that moment appeared.

He didn't. I heard him still round a corner or two, calling angrily, 'Hey, you. Answer me.': and the food lift rose smoothly, quietly, taking me far upwards like a sandwich.

When it stopped I spilled hurriedly out, finding myself in a serving area high up in the stands. There was daylight from large windows and a row of food trolleys parked end to end along a wall.

No one about. No sound from below . . . but Vernon might have heard the lift's electric hum and be on his way . . . he knew every cranny . . . he belonged there. Out of a muddled thought that if the lift returned to the kitchens before he saw it had gone he might not think I'd used it, I pressed the down button and saw it disappear as fast as I'd come up.

Then I scorched out of the serving area and at any other time might have laughed, because I was up on the level of Orkney Swayle's box. Up where the waitresses had ferried the food whose origins I hadn't imagined.

I ran at last: softly but with terrible fear still at my heels. Ran past the big passenger lifts that might go down from there to the ground floor, but would go slowly with flashing lights announcing their progress and which might deliver me to Vernon waiting in anticipation at the doors . . . Ran past them to Orkney's box, because I knew it. Prayed the door wouldn't be locked.

None of the boxes was locked.

Marvellous.

Orkney's was ten or more along the glassed-in gallery, and I reached it at an Olympic sprint. I went in there and stood in the corner that couldn't be seen from the passage because of the out-jutting service section just inside the door, and I made my breathing shallow and almost silent, and couldn't stop the noisy thump of my heart.

Nothing happened for a long long time.

Nothing at all.

There was no more voice shouting, 'Hey . . .'

No Vernon appeared like Nemesis in the doorway.

I couldn't bring myself to believe he'd given up. I thought that if I took a step into the gallery he would pounce on me. That somewhere, round a turning, he would be lying in wait. As in a childhood game I strained deep into a hiding place cringing from the heartstopping moment of capture . . . but this time for real, with a penalty beyond facing.

I wasn't good at this sort of thing, I thought miserably. I felt sick. Why couldn't I have courage like my father?

I stood in my corner while time stretched agonisingly and silently out . . . and I'd almost got to the point of thinking it would perhaps be safe to move, when I saw him. He was down below in front of the stands out on the far edge of the tarmac where the bookmakers raised their tempting racket on racedays. He had his back to the racecourse rails. He was scanning the length of stands, searching for movement . . . searching for a sight of me.

Beside him, looking upward, was Paul Young.

If I could see them they could see me . . . but to them I must be in darkness . . . I could see them through glass, through the glass of the doors leading from the box to the steps on the balcony.

I stood frozen, afraid almost to blink. It was movement they would see, not a stock-still shadow in the angle of two walls.

Why ever, I thought hopelessly, had I dived into such a small dead end so close to the lifts, so easy to track down and find? Why hadn't I searched for a staircase and run downwards? Going upwards was fatal . . . one could run out of up. I'd always thought it stupid for fugitives in films to start climbing, and now I'd done it myself. Escape always lay downwards. I thought it and knew it, and couldn't bring myself to move even though if I ran fast enough and if I could find the way, I might escape down the stairs and be away through some exit before they came in from the tarmac . . .

Very slowly I turned my head to look along to where my car was parked by the paddock entrance. I could see it all right, elderly and serviceable, ready to go. I could see also a car parked next to it, where no car had stood when I arrived.

My eyes ached with looking at the newly arrived car with its noble unmistakable lines and its darkened glass and sable paint.

Black Rolls-Royce . . . 'a black Roller with them tinted windows' . . . next to my way out.

Reason told me that Paul Young didn't know the car next to his was mine. Reason said he didn't know it was I he was looking for, and that the urgency of his search must be relative. Reason had very little to do with lurching intestines.

The two men gave up their raking inspection and walked towards the stands, going out of my line of sight below the outer edge of the balcony. If I'd been rushing downstairs I could have run straight into them . . . If they started searching methodically, and I didn't move, they would find me. Yet I didn't move. I couldn't.

For a whole hour I saw nothing, heard nothing.

They were waiting for me, I thought.

Listening for my footfall on a stairway, for the whine of a lift, for a door stealthily opening. The tension in my body went screaming along like a roller-coaster, winding up as soon as it began to die down, kept going only by my own wretched thoughts.

Cat and mouse . . .

This mouse would stay a long time in his hole.

Orkney's box, I thought; where the tartlets had waited so long in their wrapping and Flora had flushed uncomplainingly for Jack's sake. The sideboard was emptier than ever. Orkney's bad temper rested sourly in the memory. Breezy Palm had run in panic and lost. Dear heavens . . .

When I'd been in Orkney's box for two hours, Paul Young returned to his Rolls and drove it out of the car park.

I should have been reassured that it no longer stood next to my Rover, but I wasn't. I feared that he'd driven out, round and back through a service entrance from the main road, where the delivery vans must come in and out. I feared that he was still down there below me, claws ready.

When I moved in the end it was out of a sort of shame. I couldn't stand there quivering forever. If the cat was waiting right outside Orkney's door . . . then all the same I'd have to risk it.

I looked most delicately out . . . and there was no one in sight. Breathing shallowly with a racing pulse I stepped slowly into the gallery and looked down from the windows there into the wide tarmacked area behind the stands along which I'd walked to find the green door.

The green door itself was round a corner out of sight, and from my angle I couldn't see any delivery vans . . . or any Rolls-Royce.

No one was out in the rear area looking up to the gallery, but I crabbed along it with my back against the walls of the boxes, sliding past their open doors nervously, ready at any moment to stop, to dive into any shelter, to freeze.

No sound. I reached the place where the gallery opened into a wider concourse, and in the last yard of window and with my last glance downwards I saw Vernon walk into sight.

He was still looking around him. Still looking upward. Still unsatisfied, still worried, still persistent.

I watched him breathlessly until he began to walk back towards the buildings, then I ran through the concourse because at least he couldn't see me at that point, and at the far end with trepidation approached the stairs to the next lower level; and I went down them in a blue funk and from there out to the huge viewing balcony where tiered rows of seats stretched away on each side, turning their blank tipped-up bottoms to the empty track.

I walked along behind the top row of seats in the direction of the winning post and saw no one, and at the end hopped over a railing into a similar enclosure labelled firmly 'Owners and Trainers Only'. Not an owner or trainer in sight. Nor Vernon, nor Paul Young.

From the 'Owners and Trainers' a small staircase led downwards into the main bulk of the stands, and down there I went, heart thudding, trying to make myself believe that the smaller the place I was in, the less likely it was that I would be spotted from a distance.

The Owners and Trainers' staircase led into the Owners and Trainers' bar. There were rattan armchairs, small glass-topped tables, sporting murals, not a bottle or glass in sight: and at the far end, a wide tier of steps allowed one to see through a wall of glass to the parade ring. Outside and to the left, before one reached the parade ring, lay the weighing room and the office of the Clerk of the Course. Beyond the parade ring lay the gate to the car park and to freedom.

I was there. Nearly there. A door at the bottom of the Owners and Trainers' enclosed viewing steps led straight out to the area in front of the weighing room, and if only that door like every one else in the building were unlocked, I'd be out.

I approached the steps thinking only of that, and along from behind the stands, barely twenty paces away from me, marched Vernon.

If he had walked up to the glass and looked through he would have seen me clearly. I could see even the brown and white checks of his shirt collar over his zipped jacket. I stood stock still in shuddering dismay and watched him walk along to the Clerk of the Course's office and knock on the door.

The man who had been writing there came outside. I watched them talking. Watched them both look across to the stands. The man from the office pointed to the way he'd told me to go to find the caterers. Vernon seemed to be asking urgent questions but the office man shook his head and after a while went back indoors; and with clearly evident frustration Vernon began to hurry back the way he'd come.

The door at the bottom of the Owners and Trainers' Bar steps proved to be bolted on the inside, top and bottom. I undid the bolts, fumbling. The door itself . . . the knob turned under my hand and the door opened inward towards me when I pulled, and I stepped out feeling that if Vernon or Paul Young jumped on me at that moment I would scream, literally scream with hysterics.

They weren't there. I shut the door behind me and started walking with unsteady knees, and the man from the office came out of his door and said, 'I say, do you know the caterer's store manager is looking for you?'

'Yes,' I said. It came out as a croak. I cleared my throat and said again, 'Yes. I just met him along there.' I pointed to the way Vernon had gone . . . and feared he would come back.

'Did you? Righto.' He frowned at me, puzzled. 'He wanted to know your name. Most odd, what? I said I didn't know, but mentioned that it was hours since you'd asked the way to his door. I'd have thought he would have known.'

'Most odd,' I agreed. 'Anyway, he knows now. I told him. Er . . . Peter Cash. Insurance.'

'Ah.'

'Not a bad day,' I said, looking at the sky. 'After yesterday.'

'We needed the rain.'

'Yes. Well . . . good day.'

He nodded benignly over the civility and returned to his lair, and I went shakily onwards past the parade ring, down the path, through the still open entrance gate and out to the Rover; and no one yelled behind me, no one ran to pounce and clutch and drag me back at the last moment. No one came.

The keys went tremblingly into the locks. The engine started. There were no flat tyres. I pushed the old gear level through the ancient gears, reverse and forward, and drove away over the cindery grass and through the main gates and away from Martineau Park with Pan at my shoulder fading slowly into the shadows on the journey.

When I went into the shop it was still only twenty-one minutes to four, although I felt as if I had lived several lifetimes. I headed straight through to the washroom and was sick in the washbasin and spent a long time wretchedly on the loo and felt my skin still clammy with shivers.

I splashed water on my face and dried it, and when I eventually emerged it was to worried enquiries from Mrs Palissey and open-mouthed concern from Brian.

'Something I ate,' I said weakly, and took a brandy miniature from the shelves, and despatched it.

Mrs Palissey and Brian had been too busy with customers to make even a start on the telephone orders. I looked at the pile of numbered lists carefully written in Mrs Palissey's handwriting and felt absolutely incapable of the task of collecting each customer's requirements into cartons for delivery.

'Are any of these urgent?' I asked helplessly.

'Don't you worry,' Mrs Palissey said comfortingly. 'Only one . . . and Brian and I will see to it.'

'I'll make it up to you.'

'Yes, yes,' she said, nodding. 'I know that. I do really.'

I went and sat in the office and dialled Gerard's number.

Tina answered. Gerard had left his office to go home but would still be on his way to the train. He would telephone, she said, when he came in; and could it wait until after a shower and a drink?

'Preferably not.'

'All right. I'll tell him. He'll be tired.' It was more a warning than a plea, I thought.

'I'll be brief,' I said, and she said, 'Good,' and put her receiver down decisively.

Mrs Palissey and Brian left at four-thirty and I locked the shop door behind them, retreating out of sight to my desk while I returned physically to normal and mentally to the accustomed morass of no self-respect.

Gerard, when he telephoned, sounded very tired indeed.

'How did you get on?' he said, stifling a yawn. 'Tina said it wouldn't wait.'

I told him what I'd heard of the conversation between Vernon and Paul Young and where I'd been when I heard it: everything in detail to that point but very little after.

'Paul Young?' he said aghast.

'Yes.'

'Good grief. Look, I'm sorry.'

'Whatever for?'

'I shouldn't have sent you there.'

'You couldn't have known,' I said, 'but I'm afraid we're no nearer discovering who Paul Young is or where he came from. Vernon didn't call him by name from start to finish.'

'We now know for sure he's Larry Trent's brother,' Gerard pointed out. 'And that's not much help. Someone in our office traced Larry Trent's birth certificate yesterday afternoon. He was illegitimate. His mother was a Jane Trent. Father unknown.'

'What are you going to do?' I asked. 'Do you want me to tell the police?'

'No, not yet. Let me think it over and call you back. Will you be in your shop all evening?'

'Until nine, yes.'

'Right.'

I opened my doors again at six, trying and failing to raise genuine interest in the customers' needs. I felt limp and unsteady as if after illness and wondered how Gerard had survived a working lifetime of chasing villains with every nerve coolly intact.

He didn't telephone again until almost closing time, and by then he sounded exhausted.

'Look . . . Tony . . . can you meet me in the morning at nine at Martineau Park?'

'Er . . .' I said feebly. 'Well . . . yes.' Going back there, I thought, was so low on my priority list as to have dropped off the bottom.

'Good,' Gerard said, oblivious. 'I've had a good deal of trouble running to ground the proprietor of the caterers at Martineau. Why does everyone go away at weekends? Anyway, he's meeting us there tomorrow morning. We both agree it's best to find out just what's been going on there in the stores before we say anything to the police. I said I'd bring you because you'd know the scotch and the wine if you tasted them, and he agreed you were essential. He himself is no expert, he says.'

Gerard made the expedition sound perfectly regular. I said, 'You won't forget Paul Young's going there tomorrow afternoon, will you?'

'No. That's why we must go early, before he removes anything.'

'I meant . . . the police could arrest him and find out who he is.'

'Once we're sure the whisky is at Martineau, we'll alert them.' He spoke patiently but there were reservations in his voice. He would do the police's work only when his own was completed.

'Can I count on you?' he said, after a pause.

'Not to tell them anyway?'

'Yes.'

'I won't,' I said.

'Good.' He yawned. 'Goodnight, then. See you in twelve hours.'

He was waiting in his Mercedes outside the main gates when I arrived, and sleep had clearly done a poor job on restoration. Grey shadows lay in his lean cheeks, with puffed bags under his eyes and lines of strain everywhere, ageing him by years.

'Don't say it,' he said as I approached. 'Antibiotics make me feel lousy.' He was still wearing his sling, I saw, for everything except actual driving. He yawned. 'How do we get into this place?'

We went in the way I'd gone the day before, all the gates again standing open, and walked as far as the Clerk of the Course's office before being challenged. At that point the same man as on the previous day came out with bushy eyebrows rising and asked civilly if he could help us.

'We've come to meet Mr Quigley . . . the caterer.'

'Ah.'

'I'm Gerard McGregor,' Gerard said. 'This is Tony Beach.'

The eyebrows frowned. 'I thought you said Cash,' he said to me. 'Peter Cash.'

I shook my head. 'Beach.'

'Oh.' He was puzzled, but shrugged. 'Well, you know the way.'

We smiled, nodded, walked on.

'Who's Peter Cash?' Gerard asked.

'No one.' I explained about Vernon still searching for me the day before. 'I didn't want him to know it was Tony Beach who was there. Peter Cash was the first name which came into my head.'

'Do you mean,' he said, alarmed, 'that this Vernon chased you all over the stands?'

'Hardly chased.'

'It must have felt like it to you.'

'Mm.'

We reached the green door, which on this occasion was firmly locked. Gerard looked at his watch, and almost immediately a proprietor-sized car appeared from behind the far end of the Tote building, pulled up near us outside the Celebration Bar, and disgorged a proprietor-shaped occupant.

He had black hair, a moustache and a paunch. First impressions also included an air of importance, a touch of irritability and a liking for white silk scarves worn cravat-style under nautical blazers.

'Miles Quigley,' he announced briefly. 'Gerard McGregor?'

Gerard nodded.

'Tony Beach,' I said.

'Right.' He looked us over without cordiality. 'Let's see what all this is about, shall we? Although I'll tell you again as I told you last night, I'm certain you're wrong. Vernon has worked for our family for years.'

I could almost feel Gerard thinking of a hundred clients who had said and believed much the same.

'Vernon who?' he said.

'What? No, Vernon's his last name. He's always called Vernon.'

The keyhole in the green door was round and uninformative. The key Miles Quigley produced was six inches long. The one inside the other turned with a good deal of pressure and the multiple click of a heavy mortice lock.

'That's the first locked door I've seen on this racecourse,' I said.

'Really?' Miles Quigley raised his eyebrows. 'They do tend to open everything for easy maintenance between meetings in the daytime but I assure you everything's locked at night. A security guard comes on duty after dark. We're very security conscious of course because of all the alcohol stored here.'

The green door opened outwards like that by my own storeroom: more difficult to break in. Miles Quigley pulled it wide and we went into the passage, where he importantly turned on the lights by slapping a double row of switches with his palm. Yesterday's all too familiar scene sprang to life, the long corridor stretching away dimly to the bowels of the kitchens.

In the wider passage leading to the drinks store Quigley opened a small cupboard marked First Aid and applied to the contents a second key, not as large as the first but equally intricate.

'Security alarm,' he explained with superiority. 'A heat-sensitive system. If anyone goes into the store when the system is on, an alarm rings in the security office here on the racecourse and also in the main police station in Oxford. We test the system regularly. I assure you it works.'

'Who has keys?' Gerard asked, and Quigley's irritated look was its own reply.

'I'd trust Vernon with my life,' he said.

Not me, I thought. I wouldn't.

'Only Vernon and yourself have keys?' Gerard persisted.

'Yes, that's right. Keys to the alarm and the store, that is. The racecourse has a key to the outer door, the green one.'

Gerard nodded non-committally. Quigley turned his back on the problem and produced a third and a fourth key to undo the heavy door into the actual store, each key having to be turned twice, alternately: and considering the value of the liquor stacked inside, I supposed the vault-like precautions weren't unjustified.

'Can your keys be duplicated?' Gerard asked.

'What? No, they can't. They can be obtained only from the firm who installed the system, and they wouldn't issue duplicates without my say-so.'

Quigley was younger than I first thought. Not mid-forties, I judged, standing near him in the brighter storeroom lights: more like mid-thirties aping the manner of fifty.

'A family firm, did you say?' I asked.

'Basically, yes. My father's retired.'

Gerard gave him a dry look. 'He's still chairman, I believe, your father?'

'Presides over board meetings, yes,' Quigley said patronisingly. 'Makes him feel wanted. Old people need that, you know. But I run things. Have done for three years. This is a big firm, you know. We don't cater only for this racecourse, but for many other sporting events and also for weddings and dances. Very big, and growing.'

'Do you keep everything here?' I asked. 'Your linen, tableware, glasses, things like that?'

He shook his head. 'Only the liquor here, because of the high security of this place. Everything else is at our central depot two miles away. Equipment, food stores and offices. We ship everything from there by van daily as required. It's a very big operation, as I said.' He sounded vastly self-satisfied. 'I have streamlined the whole business considerably.'

'Were spirits by the tot in the private boxes here your own idea?' I asked.

'What?' His eyebrows rose. 'Yes, of course. Got to fall in line with other racecourse caterers. Much more profitable. Got to answer to shareholders, you know. Shareholders are always with us.'

'Mm,' I said.

He heard doubt in my tone. He said sharply, 'Don't forget it's to the box-holder's advantage. When only a little has been used, we don't insist on them buying the whole bottle.'

'True,' I said neutrally. A Quigley-Swayle face-to-face could draw blood: diverting prospect. 'Your strawberry tartlets are excellent.'

He looked at me uncertainly and explained to Gerard that all the paperwork to do with wines, beer and spirits passed through the small office to our left. Vernon, he said without happiness, was wholly in charge.

'He chooses and orders?' Gerard said.

'Yes. He's done it for years.'

'And pays the bills?'

'No. We have a computerised system. The checked invoices go from here to the office two miles away to be paid through the computer. Saves time. I installed it, of course.'

Gerard nodded, ignoring the smugness.

'We keep beer in here, as you see,' Quigley said. 'This is just back-up. Normally we get suppliers to deliver on the day of need.'

Gerard nodded.

'Outside in the passage . . . we've just passed it . . . is the one passenger lift which comes down here . . . in this part of the stands the ground floor as far as the public is concerned is above our heads. We transfer from here to the bars and the boxes using that lift: to the bars on all floors. Early on racedays we are extremely busy.'

Gerard said he was sure.

'Through here are the wines and spirits,' Quigley said, leading the way into the main storeroom. 'As you see.'

Gerard saw. Quigley walked a few steps ahead of us and Gerard said quietly, 'Where were you yesterday?'

'Lying up here . . . on the Pol Roger.'

He looked at me with curiosity. 'What's the matter?'

'What do you mean?'

'You look . . . it can't be right . . . you look of all things ashamed.'

I swallowed. 'When I was up there . . . I was frightened sick.'

He looked round the storeroom; at the possibilities and limitations of concealment; and he said judiciously, 'You'd have been a fool not to be scared stiff. I don't think there's much doubt Paul Young would have killed you if he'd found you. Killing the second time is easier, I'm told. Fear in a fearful situation is normal. Absence of fear is not. Keeping one's nerve in spite of fear is courage.'

He had a way, I thought, of speaking without sympathy while giving incredible comfort. I didn't thank him, but profoundly in my heart I was grateful.

'Shall we start?' he said as we rejoined Quigley. 'Tony, you said the suspect cases are somewhere at the far end?'

'Yes.'

We all moved through the central canyon between the piled-high city blocks of cartons until we reached the end wall.

'Where now?' Quigley demanded. 'I see nothing wrong. This all looks exactly the same as usual.'

'Always Bell's whisky at the end here?'

'Of course.'

The size of the Bell's block would have shamed the wholesalers I regularly bought from. Even Gerard looked daunted at the possibility of having to open the whole lot to find the bad apples, which was nothing to the vision of paralytic drunkenness crossing my own imagination.

'Er . . .' I said. 'There may be marks of some sort on the

boxes. Someone was putting black felt tip squiggles on the gin when it was being checked in.'

'Mervyn, probably,' Quigley said.

'Yes, that's right.'

I walked back to the gin and looked at Mervyn's handiwork: a hasty curling cross with two diagonals almost joined in a circle on the right side. The only problem was that it appeared also on every Bell's case in sight. No other distinguishing mark seemed to be on any that we could see without dismantling the whole mountain.

'Vernon must have been able to tell one from another, easily,' Gerard said. 'He wouldn't risk not knowing his stuff at a glance.'

'I don't believe all this,' Quigley announced irritably. 'Vernon's a most efficient manager.'

'I don't doubt it,' Gerard murmured.

'Perhaps we could find the wine,' I suggested. 'It might be less difficult.'

Wine was stacked in narrower blocks on the opposite wall from the spirits, the quantity in each stack less but the variety more: and I found St Estèphe and St Emilion six deep behind a fronting wall of unimpeachable Mouton Cadet.

Quigley consented to the opening of a case of St Estèphe, which laid bare the familiar false label in all its duplicity.

'This is it,' I said. 'Shall we taste it to make sure?'

Quigley frowned. 'You can't be right. It's come from a respectable supplier. Vintners Incorporated. There's their name stamped on the box.'

'Taste the wine,' Gerard said.

I produced my corkscrew, opened a bottle and went back to the office section to search for a glass. All I could find were throwaway expanded polystyrene beakers which would have given Henri Tavel a fit: but even in the featherweight plastic the bottle's contents were unmistakable.

'Not St Estèphe,' I said positively. 'Shall I try the St Emilion?'

Quigley shrugged. I opened a case and a bottle, and tasted.

'It's the same,' I said. 'Shall we look for the other four?'

They were all there, all hidden behind respectable façades of the same sort of wine: the Mâcon behind Mâcon, and so on. The contents of all were identical, as at the Silver Moondance: and all six wines had been supplied, according to the cases, by Vintners Incorporated.

'Um,' Gerard said thoughtfully, 'do Vintners Incorporated supply Bell's whisky also?'

'But they're a well-known firm,' Quigley protested.

'Anyone,' Gerard pointed out, 'can cut a stencil and slap the name Vintners Incorporated onto anything.'

Quigley opened his mouth and then slowly closed it. We returned to the Bell's and immediately found a section at the back of the block with Vintners Incorporated emblazoned obviously on the side.

'I can't believe it,' Quigley said. Then, 'Oh, very well. Taste it.'

I tasted it. Waited. Let aftertaste develop. Beyond that let nuances linger in mouth, throat and nose.

'He can't tell,' Quigley said impatiently to Gerard. 'There's nothing wrong with it. I told you.'

'Have you ever had complaints?' I asked eventually.

'Of course we have,' he said. 'What caterer hasn't? But none of them has been justified.'

I wondered if Martineau Park would turn up on Ridger's lists. No hope of finding out until he came back on Wednesday.

'This isn't Bell's,' I said. 'Too much grain, hardly any malt.'

'Sure?' Gerard said.

'It's what we're looking for,' I said, nodding.

'What do you mean?' Quigley asked, and then without waiting for an answer said aggrievedly, 'How could Vernon possibly be so disloyal?'

His reply came through the doorway in the shape of the man himself: Vernon in his leather jacket, large, angry and alarmed.

'What the bloody hell is going on here?' he shouted, advancing fast down the storeroom. 'What the hell do you think you're doing?'

He stopped dead when Gerard moved slightly, disclosing the presence of Quigley.

He said, 'Oh . . . Miles . . . I didn't expect . . .'

He sensed something ominous in our stillness. His gaze shifted warily from Quigley to Gerard and finally to me: and I was a shock to him of cataclysmic proportions.

NINETEEN:

'Let's straighten this out,' Gerard said matter of factly in the office section, to which we had all moved. 'The fraud as I see it is as follows.'

His voice was as unhurried and unemotional as an accountant summing up an unexciting audit and was having a positively calming effect on Quigley if not on Vernon.

'It appears to me from a preliminary inspection of the invoices at present to hand in this office that the following sequence of events has been taking place. And perhaps I should explain to you,' he said directly to Vernon, 'that the unravelling of commercial fraud is my normal and constant occupation.'

Vernon's small intense eyes stared at him blankly and under the large drooping moustache the mouth moved in twitches, tightening and loosening with tension. He half stood, half sat, his bulk supported by the desk on which he had done his constructive paperwork, and he had folded his arms across his chest as if not accepting in the least the accusations now coming his way. The fine dew, however, stood again on his forehead, and I guessed that all he could be grateful for was that this present inquisitor was not his dangerous friend Paul Young.

'A supplier proposed to you the following scheme,' Gerard said. 'You as liquor manager here would order extensively from him and in return receive a sizeable commission. A kick-back. You were to sell what he provided as if it were part of your firm's regular stock. However, what he provided was not as described on the invoice. Your firm was paying for Bell's whisky and fine wines and receiving liquor of lower quality. You certainly knew this. It considerably increased your pay off.'

Quigley, standing by the doorway, rocked slowly on his heels as if disassociating himself from the proceedings. Gerard, seated on the only chair, dominated the proceedings absolutely.

'Your provider,' he said, 'chose the name of a respectable supplier with whom you didn't already do business and sent you everything stencilled "Vintners Incorporated". You received normal-looking invoices from your supplier with that heading and your treasurer's department sent cheques normally in return. They were perhaps negligent in not checking that the address printed on the invoice heading was truly that of Vintners Incorporated, as you have just heard me doing on the telephone, but no doubt Mr Quigley's firm as a whole deals with dozens of different suppliers and has no habit of checking each one.' He broke off and turned his head towards Quigley. 'I always advise firms to check and keep checking. Such a simple matter. When an address has been entered once into a computerised system such as yours, it's seldom ever checked. The computer goes on sending payments without question. Invoices may indeed be routinely paid without the goods ever being delivered.' He turned back to Vernon. 'On how many occasions did that happen?'

'Rubbish,' Vernon said.

'Vernon,' Quigley said, and it was a shattered word of disillusion, not of disbelief. 'Vernon, how could you? You've been with the family for years.'

Vernon gave him a look in which contempt was clearly a component. Vernon might have remained loyal to the father, I thought, but had been a pushover under the son.

'Who is this provider?' Quigley said.

I saw Gerard wince internally: it wasn't a question he would have asked except obliquely, trying to squeeze out a name by finesse.

Vernon said, 'No one.'

'He's coming here this afternoon,' I said.

Vernon stood up compulsively and unfolded his arms.

'You bloody spy,' he said intensely.

'And you're afraid of him,' I said. 'You don't want to follow Zarac to the cemetery.'

He glared at me. 'You're not Peter Cash,' he said suddenly. 'I know who you are. You're that interfering bloody wine merchant, that's who you are. Beach, bloody Beach.'

No one denied it. No one asked him, either, how he knew anything about any bloody interfering wine merchant called Beach. He could only have known if Paul Young had told him.

'Who's Peter Cash?' Quigley asked, lost.

'He told the racecourse people his name was Peter Cash,' Vernon said violently. 'Insurance.' He nearly spat. 'He didn't want us knowing who he was.'

'Us?' Gerard asked.

Vernon shut his mouth tight under the curtain of moustache.

'I'd guess,' I said slowly, 'that you turned up this early today because you intended to take all the "Vintners Incorporated" cases out of here and be long gone before your provider arrived at two.'

Vernon said, 'Rot,' but without conviction, and Quigley shook his head despairingly.

'It's possible,' Gerard said with authority, 'that Mr Quigley wouldn't himself press charges against you, Vernon, if you cared to answer some questions.'

Quigley stiffened. I murmured 'Shareholders?' at his elbow and felt his opposition falter and evaporate. With the faintest twitch of humour to his mouth Gerard said, 'For instance, Vernon, how close were your ties with Zarac at the Silver Moondance?'

Silence. The dew on Vernon's forehead coagulated into visible drops and he brushed the back of one hand over the moustache in evident nervousness. The struggle within him continued for a lengthening time until his doubts forced a way out.

'How can I know?' he said. 'How can I be sure he wouldn't get the force here the minute I said anything?' He, it appeared, was Miles Quigley. 'Keep the trap shut and stay out of trouble, that's what I say,' Vernon said.

'Wise advice, if we were the police,' Gerard said. 'But we're not. Whatever you say here won't be taken down and used in evidence. Mr Quigley can give you an assurance and you can believe it.'

Mr Quigley looked as if he were well on the way from injured sorrow to vengeful fury at Vernon's defection, but still had enough of an eye to the annual general meeting to see that swallowing the unpalatable now could save him corporate indigestion later on.

'Very well,' he said rigidly. 'No prosecutions.'

'On condition,' Gerard added, 'that we consider your answers to be frank.'

Vernon said nothing. Gerard neutrally repeated his question about Zarac, and waited.

'I knew him,' Vernon said at length, grudgingly. 'He used to come here for wine if they ran out at the Silver Moondance.'

'Your provider's wine?' Gerard said. 'The "Vintners Incorporated" labels?'

'Yes, of course.

'Why of course?'

Vernon hesitated. Gerard knew the answer: testing him, I thought.

Vernon said jerkily, 'Larry Trent was his brother.'

'Zarac's brother?'

'No, of course not. My . . . well . . . provider's.'

'His name?'

'Paul Young.' Vernon had less trouble with that answer, not more. He sounded glib, I thought. He was lying.

Gerard didn't press it. He said merely, 'Paul Young was Larry Trent's brother, is that it?'

'Half-brother.'

'Did you know Zarac before this Paul Young persuaded you to join his scheme?'

'Yes, I did. He came here for regular wine like restaurants do sometimes and said he knew of a good fiddle, no risks, for someone in my position. If I was interested, he would let me in.'

Gerard pondered. 'Did the Silver Moondance normally get its wine straight from, er, Paul Young?'

'Yes, it did.'

'Did you know Larry Trent?'

'I met him.' Vernon's voice was unimpressed. 'All he cared about was horses. His brother was bloody good to him, letting him strut about pretending to own that place, giving him money by the fistful for his training fees and gambling. Too bloody good to him by half, Zarac said.'

I heard in memory Orkney Swayle saying Larry Trent was jealous of his brother; the brother who gave him so much. Sad world; ironic.

'What was the relationship between Larry Trent and Zarac?'

'They both worked for his brother. For Paul Young.' Again the unfamiliarity over the name. Gerard again let it go.

'Equal footing?'

'Not in public, I don't suppose.'

'Why did Paul Young kill Zarac?'

'I don't know,' Vernon said, indistinctly, very disturbed. 'I don't know.'

'But you knew he did kill him?'

'Jesus . . .'

'Yes,' Gerard went on. 'Go on. You do know, and you can tell us.'

Vernon spoke suddenly as if compelled. 'He said Zarac wanted the Silver Moondance. Wanted it given to him on a plate. Given to him or else. Sort of blackmail.'

Vernon was a sweating mixture of fear, indignation, sympathy and candour and had begun to experience the cathartic release of confession.

I watched in fascination. Gerard said smoothly, 'He justified the killing to you?'

'Explained it,' Vernon said. 'He came here with the Silver Moondance liquor piled up in his Rolls. He said he was loading it with Zarac's help. He made three trips. There was so much. The third time he came he was different. He was flushed . . . excited . . . very strong. He said I would hear Zarac was dead, and to keep my mouth shut. He said Zarac had wanted power over him, and he couldn't have that . . . and then I heard later how he'd killed him . . . made me vomit . . . Zarac wasn't a bad guy . . . Jesus, I never meant to get mixed up in murder. I didn't. It was supposed to be just an easy fiddle for good money . . .'

'And for how long,' Gerard said flatly, 'has the fiddle been in progress?'

'About fifteen months.'

'Wine and whisky all the time?'

'No. Just wine to start with. Whisky these past six months.'

'Always Bell's?'

'Yes.'

'Where did the fake Bell's whisky go from here?'

'Where?' Vernon took a moment to understand. 'Oh. We sold it in the bars here all the time. Sometimes in the boxes too. Also it went to the other sports fixtures Quigley's cater for, and weddings and dances in halls everywhere. All over.'

Quigley's face went stiff and blank with almost comical shock.

'Anywhere you thought no one would notice the difference?' Gerard asked.

'I suppose so. Most people can't. Not in a crowded place, they can't. There's too many other smells. Zarac told me that, and he was right.'

Wine waiters, I knew, were cynics. I also thought that but

for Orkney's anti-caterer obsession and his refusal to accept what they routinely offered, I might even have found the Rannoch/Bell's in his box.

'Do you know what precise whisky you were selling in Bell's bottles?' Gerard asked.

Vernon looked as if he hadn't considered it closely. 'It was scotch.'

'And have you heard of a young man called Kenneth Charter?'

'Who?' Vernon said, bewildered.

'Return to Paul Young,' Gerard said without visible disappointment. 'Did he plan with you the robbery at Mr Beach's shop?'

Vernon wasn't so penitent as not to be able to afford me a venomous glance. 'No, not really. He just borrowed one of our vans. I lent him the keys.'

'What?' Quigley exclaimed. 'The van that was stolen?'

Quigley . . . Quality House Provisions. I picked up one of the printed catering pricelists from the desk beside Gerard and belatedly read the heading: Crisp, Duval and Quigley Ltd, incorporating Quality House Provisions. Quigley's own van outside my back door.

'They meant to bring it back,' Vernon said defensively. 'They didn't expect that bloody man to turn up on a Sunday teatime.' He glared at me balefully. 'They said he might have seen the number plate and they'd keep the van for a while but we'd get it back eventually. When the heat died down they'd dump it somewhere. They told me to report it missing, but I didn't get a chance, the police were round at the office before you could sneeze.'

'They,' Gerard said calmly. 'Who are they?'

'They work for . . . Paul Young.'

'Names?'

'Don't know.'

'Try again.'

'Denny. That's all I know. One's called Denny. I was just told Denny would pick up the van. They were going to bring the wines here from the shop for me to sort through but they didn't come although I waited until nine. Then I heard *he* turned up,' Vernon jerked his head in my direction, 'and something happened to put them off so they never came here. I heard later they got the wrong stuff anyway, so it was all a bloody muddle for nothing.'

'Did anyone tell you what it was that happened to put them off?' Gerard asked casually.

'No, except they panicked or something because something happened they didn't expect, but I didn't hear what.'

Both Gerard and I believed him. He couldn't have stood there so unconcernedly disclaiming knowledge in front of us if he'd known that the something that had happened was our being shot.

'How well do you know them?' Gerard asked.

'I don't. Denny drives the delivery van which brings the stuff here. The other comes sometimes. They never talk much.'

'How often do they deliver?'

'About once a week. Depends.'

'On how much you've sold?'

'Yes.'

'Why didn't they use that van to rob Mr Beach's shop?'

'It's big . . . it's got Vintners Incorporated on the door . . . it was in for repairs, or something.'

'And can you describe Denny and his mate?'

Vernon shrugged. 'They're young.'

'Hair style?'

'Nothing special.'

'Not frizzy black Afro?'

'No.' Vernon was positive and slightly puzzled. 'Just ordinary.'

'Where do they come from? Where do they bring the wine from?'

'I don't know,' Vernon said. 'I never asked. They wouldn't have said. They're not friendly. They work for Paul Young . . . that's all I know.'

He said Paul Young this time far more easily. Getting accustomed, I thought.

'When did you first meet Paul Young?'

'Right when I started. When I told Zarac I was interested. He said the boss would come to check me out and explain what he wanted, and he came. He said we'd get on well together, which we did mostly.'

Until Vernon started in business on the side, stealing from his master: but he wasn't confessing that, I noticed.

'And what is Paul Young's real name?' Gerard asked.

The open doors of the confessional slammed rapidly shut.

Vernon said tightly, 'His name is Paul Young.'

Gerard shook his head.

'Paul Young,' Vernon insisted. 'That's what his name is.'

'No,' Gerard said.

Vernon's sweat ran from his forehead across his temple and down to his jaw. 'He told me the police had seen him in the Silver Moondance when he went there unawares after his brother died, and that was the name he gave them because he didn't want to be investigated because of the drinks, and he said they'd be looking for him now because of Zarac, they'd be looking for Paul Young who didn't exist, he just said the first name that came into his head . . . He said if ever, if ever anyone came here asking, which he said he was certain they wouldn't, but if ever . . . I was to call him Paul Young. And my God, my God, that's what I'm calling him and I'm not telling you his real name, he'd kill me somehow . . . and I'm not joking, I know it. I'll go to jail . . . but I'm not telling you.'

He'd spoken with total conviction and in understandable fear, but all the same I was slightly surprised when Gerard didn't press him, didn't lean on him further.

He said merely, 'All right.' And after a pause, 'That's all, then.'

Vernon for a wild moment seemed to think he had been let off all hooks, straightening up with a returning echo of burly authority.

Quigley instantly deflated him, saying in pompous outrage, 'Give me your keys, Vernon. At once.' He held out his hand peremptorily. 'At once.'

Vernon silently brought a ring of keys from his pocket and handed them over.

'Tomorrow you can look for another job,' Quigley said. 'I'll stick to my agreement. I won't prosecute. But you'll get no reference. I'm disappointed in you, Vernon, I don't understand you. But you'll have to go, and that's it.'

Vernon said blankly, 'I'm forty-eight.'

'And you had a good job here for life,' Gerard said, nodding. 'You blew it. Your own fault.'

As if for the first time Vernon seemed to be looking realistically at his doubtful future. New lines of worry deepened round his eyes.

'Do you have a family?' Gerard said.

Vernon said faintly, 'Yes.'

'Unemployment is preferable to imprisonment,' Gerard said austerely, as no doubt he had said to many a detected cheat: and Quigley as well as Vernon and myself heard the iron in his voice. Actions had to be accounted for and responsibility accepted. Consequences had to be faced. Constant forgiveness destroyed the soul . . .

Vernon shivered.

With Quigley's permission, after Vernon had gone, Gerard and I loaded into his Mercedes (driven round to the green door) a case of 'Vintners Incorporated' Bell's and a case each of the 'Vintners Incorporated' wines. In effect Gerard and Quigley watched while I shifted the cases. Back to my normal occupation, I thought with a sigh, and let the fork-lift truck take most of the strain off my mending muscles.

'What do I do with the rest?' Quigley said helplessly. 'And how are we going to cope with the Autumn Carnival without Vernon? No one else knows the routine. He's been here so long. He *is* the routine . . . he developed it.'

Neither Gerard nor I offered solutions. Quigley gloomily set about double-double-locking his treasure house and switching on the alarm, and we made the final reverse trip to the outer world.

'What should I do?' Quigley asked, fastening the green door. 'I mean . . . about that murder?'

Gerard said, 'Vernon told you his version of what Paul Young told him, which was itself no doubt only a version of the facts. That's a long way from first-hand knowledge.'

'You mean . . . I could do nothing?'

'Act as your judgment dictates,' Gerard said pleasantly and unhelpfully, and for once in his life I guessed Quigley was searching his self-importance and finding only doubt and irresolution.

Gerard said, 'Tony and I will tell the police that Paul Young may arrive here at any time from now on. After that, it's up to them.'

'He said he was coming at two o'clock,' Quigley corrected.

'Mm. But he might suspect Vernon would do what Vernon did mean to do, in other words clear off with the loot before Paul Young got here. Paul Young could be here at any minute.' Gerard seemed unconcerned but he was alone in that. Quigley made his mind up to leave us as soon as possible and I felt very much like following.

'He won't be able to get in as I have all the keys,' Quigley said. 'I suppose I must thank you, Mr McGregor. I don't like any of this. I can only hope that with Vernon gone we'll have no more trouble.'

'Certainly hope not,' Gerard said blandly, and we both watched Quigley drive away with hope already straightening the shoulders and throwing forward the chin. 'He might be lucky, he might not,' Gerard said.

'I don't want to be here when Paul Young gets here,' I said.

He half smiled. 'More prudent not. Get in my car and we'll fetch your car first and then find a telephone box.'

We both drove for five miles and stopped in a small village where he made the call from the public telephone outside the post office. I gave him the priority number Ridger had told me, and I listened to his brief message.

'It's possible,' he said to the police, 'that the man known as Paul Young may arrive at the caterers' entrance in the grandstands of Martineau Park racecourse at any time today from now onwards.' He listened to a reply and said, 'No. No names. Goodbye.'

Smiling, he replaced the receiver. 'O.K., he said. 'Duty done.'

'To some extent,' I said.

'Everything's relative.' He was cheerful although still looking far from well. 'We know where Kenneth Charter's scotch is.'

'Some of it,' I said.

'Enough.'

'But not where it went between the tanker and the Vintners Incorporated deliveries.'

'To a bottling plant, as you said.'

He was leaning against his car, arm in sling, looking frail, a recuperating English gentleman out for a harmless Sunday morning drive in the country. There was also a glimmer of humour about him and the steel core looking out of the eyes, and I said abruptly, 'You know something you haven't told me.'

'Do you think so? What about?'

'You've found the bottling plant!'

'Found *a* bottling plant, yes. Somewhere to start from anyway. I thought I'd go and take a look this afternoon. Preliminary recce.'

'But it's Sunday. There'll be no one there.'

'That's sometimes an advantage.'

'You don't mean . . . break in?'

'We'll see,' he said. 'It depends. Sometimes there's a caretaker. I'm good at government inspectors, even on Sundays.'

Slightly aghast I said, 'Well . . . where is it?'

'Roughly twenty-five miles this side of Kenneth Charter's headquarters.' He smiled slightly. 'By Friday afternoon we had concluded in the office that your idea of looking first at the plants to which Charter's tankers took wine had been good but wrong. There were five of them. We screened them at first, and all of them were rock-solid businesses. Then some time during last night . . . you know how things float into your head while you're half asleep . . . I remembered that one of them had had two links with Charter, not just one, and that maybe, just maybe, that second link is more important than we thought.'

'Tell me,' I said.

'Mm. I don't want to be too positive.'

'For heaven's sake . . .'

'All right then. We established right at the beginning of our bottle-plant enquiries that one of the plants is owned by a man called Stewart Naylor. It was at the top of the list that Charter gave us, and the first we checked.'

'Stewart Naylor?' I thought. 'He's . . . he's . . . um . . . isn't he mentioned in Kenneth Junior's notebook? Oh yes . . . the father who plays war games . . . David Naylor's father.'

'Top of the class. Stewart Naylor owns Bernard Naylor Bottling. Started by his grandfather. Old respectable firm. I woke up with that word Naylor fizzing like a sparkler in my head. I telephoned Kenneth Charter himself early this morning and asked him about his son's friendship with David Naylor. He says he's known the father, Stewart Naylor, for years: they're not close friends but they know each other quite well because of their business connection and because their sons like each other's company. Kenneth Charter says David Naylor is the only good thing in Kenneth Junior's lazy life, he keeps Kenneth Junior off the streets. War games, Kenneth Charter thinks, are a waste of time, but better than glue-sniffing.'

'His words?' I asked amused.

'Aye, laddie.'

'Do you really think . . .'

'Kenneth Charter doesn't. Grasping at straws, he thinks it. He says Bernard Naylor Bottling is twenty-four carat. But we've found no other leads at all, and we've been checking bottling plants up and down the country until the entire staff are sick at the sound of the words. Three days' concentrated work, fruitless. A lot of them have gone out of business. One's a library now. Another's a boot and shoe warehouse.'

'Mm,' I said. 'Could Stewart Naylor have an illegitimate half-brother?'

'Anyone can have an illegitimate half-brother. It happens to the best.'

'I mean . . .'

'I know what you mean. Kenneth Charter didn't know of one.' He shrugged. 'Naylor's plant's a long shot. Either a bullseye or a case for apology. I'll go and find out.'

'Right now?'

'Absolutely right now. If Stewart Naylor is by any chance also Paul Young, he should be going to or from Martineau Park this afternoon, not stalking about among his bottles.'

'Did you ask Kenneth Charter what he looked like?'

'Yes . . . ordinary, he said.'

All these ordinary men . . . 'Is he deaf?' I asked.

Gerard blinked. 'I forgot about that.'

'Ask him,' I said. 'Telephone now, before you go.'

'And if Steward Naylor is deaf . . . don't go?'

'Quite right. Don't go.'

Gerard shook his head. 'All the more reason to go.'

'It's flinging oneself into the Limpopo,' I said.

'Perhaps. Only perhaps. Nothing's certain.' He returned to the telephone, however, and dialled Kenneth Charter's house and then his office, and to neither attempt was there a reply.

'That's it, then,' he said calmly. 'I'll be off.'

'Have you ever been in a bottling plant?' I said despairingly. 'I mean . . . do you know what to look for?'

'No.'

I stared at him. He stared right back. In the end I said, 'I spent a year in and out of bottling plants in Bordeaux.'

'Did you?'

'Yes.'

'Tell me, then, what to look for.'

I thought of pumps and machinery. I thought of vats and what might be in them. I said hopelessly, 'You need me with you, don't you?'

'I'd like it,' he said. 'But I won't ask. It's on the very edge of consultancy . . . and maybe beyond.'

'You wouldn't know the wine if you fell into it, would you?' I said. 'Nor the scotch?'

'Not a chance,' he agreed placidly.

'Bloody sodding hell,' I said. 'You're a bugger.'

He smiled. 'I thought you'd come, really, if I told you.'

TWENTY:

I put a notice on my shop door saying, 'Closed. Very sorry. Staff illness. Open Monday 9.30 a.m.'

I'm mad, I thought. Crazy.

If I didn't go, he would go on his own.

My thoughts stopped there. I couldn't let him go on his own when it was I who had the knowledge he needed. When he felt tired and ill and I was well and almost as strong as ever.

I sat at my desk and wrote a note to Sergeant John Ridger saying I'd been told to look in the Bernard Naylor bottling plant for the Silver Moondance scotch, and I was going there with Gerard McGregor (I gave his address) to check. I sealed the note in an envelope and wrote on it an instruction to Mrs Palissey: Take this to the police station if you haven't heard from me by ten this morning and tell them to open it.

I wedged the envelope on the till where she couldn't miss it and hoped she would never read it. Then with a last look round I locked my door and drove away, and tried not to wonder if I would ever come back.

Half the time I thought Kenneth Charter must know his man. Stewart Naylor was true blue. Half the time I trusted Gerard's fizzler in the night. Intuition existed. Solutions came in sleep.

It would probably turn out to be an anticlimax of a journey not worth melodramatic notes to policemen or all this soul-searching. We would drive to the bottling plant, we would not break in, there would be plentiful evidence of legal prosperity and we would drive sedately home. It would not be another day of Sunday bloody horrors.

Gerard met me in a car park we had agreed on, he having meanwhile been home to leave the Martineau Park spoils in his garage. From there we went towards London in his Mercedes, but with me driving this time.

'Suppose you were Stewart Naylor,' Gerard said. 'Suppose you'd spent your entire working life learning to run the family bottling business and then because of the French changing their regulations found the wine flood drying to a trickle.'

'Longbows,' I said nodding.

'What? Oh yes. Kenneth Charter was wrong, you know, in point of fact. It was the crossbow which put paid to the longbow . . . well, never mind. Crossbows, guns, whatever, from no fault of your own you're going out of business. Kenneth Charter confirmed this morning that he hardly takes a fifth of what he used to to the Naylor plant, but it's still quite a lot. More than to anywhere else. He says that's how he knows that Naylor's is healthy while others struggle.'

'Huh.'

'Yes, indeed. Suppose you are Stewart Naylor and you look anxiously around for other things to bottle . . . tomato sauce, cleaning fluid, whatever . . . and you find everyone else in your line of business is in the same boat and doing the same. Ruin raises its ugly head and gives you a good long threatening glare.' He paused as I passed a lorry, then went on, 'We supposed earlier that at that point a convenient crook came along offering salvation in return for dishonesty and that our beleaguered bottler accepted. But suppose it wasn't like that. Suppose Stewart Naylor needed no seducing but without help thought up his own crooked scheme?'

'Which was,' I said, 'to buy wine himself instead of bottling for others. To bottle it and label it as better than it was, and then sell it.' I frowned. 'And at that point you get discovered and prosecuted.'

'Not if you have a half-brother who likes horses. You set him up . . . on bank money . . . in a Silver Moondance, and you take him your wine to sell. It sells well and for about twenty times more than it cost you, even including the bottles. Money starts flowing in, not out . . . and that's when the greed complex hits you.'

'The greed complex?' I asked.

'Addiction,' Gerard said. 'The first step is the huge one. The decision. To snort cocaine or not to. To borrow the Christmas Club's money, just once. To sell the first secret. To design a label for a non-existent château and stick it on a bottle of wine-lake. The first step's huge, the second half the size, by the sixth step it's a habit. Suppose our Stewart Naylor begins to think that if he could arrange other outlets he could double and redouble his receipts?'

'O.K.' I said. 'Suppose.'

'At this point we have to suppose a henchman called Zarac, whom one conveniently instals as head waiter at the Silver Moondance. One of his duties is to cast about for possibilities of expansion and in due course he arrives on Vernon's doorstep at Martineau Park. He reports back to Paul Young . . . er . . . Paul Young query Stewart Naylor . . . who goes to see Vernon and hey presto, the fake wine business takes a deep breath and swells to double size. Money now rolls in to the extent that concealing it is a problem. Never mind. Half-brother Larry is a whiz at horses. Pass Larry the embarrassing cash, magic-wand it into horseflesh, ship it to California, convert it again at a profit if possible and bank it . . . intending, I dare say, to collect it one day and live in the sun. In my experience the last chapter seldom happens. The addiction to the crime becomes so integral to the criminal that he can't give it up. I've caught several industrial spies because they couldn't kick their taste for creeping about with cameras.'

'Clean up and clear out,' I suggested.

'Absolutely. Almost never done. They come back for a second bite, and a third, and just once more . . . and whammo, one too much.'

'So Stewart Naylor turned his ideas to scotch?'

'Ah,' Gerard said. 'Suppose when your son visits his divorced father one day he brings his friend Kenneth Junior with him? Or suppose he's often brought him? Stewart Naylor knows Kenneth Junior's father quite well . . . Kenneth Charter's tankers have brought wine to Naylor's plant for many years. Suppose our crime-addicted Stewart casts an idle eye on Kenneth Junior and reflects that Charter's tankers carry scotch and gin as well as wine, and that whereas the wine profits are healthy, from stolen scotch they would be astronomical.'

'But he couldn't ask Kenneth Junior outright to sell his dad's tankers' routes and destinations and time-tables. Kenneth Junior might have gone all righteous and buzzed home to spill the beans . . .'

'But he does think Kenneth Junior is ripe for a spot of treason as he's probably heard him bellyaching about his life with father . . .'

'So he sends Zarac to recruit him,' I said. 'Sends Zarac perhaps to the Diamond snooker hall? Or the disco? Somewhere like that? And Zarac says here's a lot of money, kid. Get me a tanker's keys, get me a tanker's route, and I'll give you some more cash. And three months later he pays again. And again. And then says get me another tanker's keys, kid, the first one's too hot . . .'

'Don't see why not, do you?'

'No,' I said. 'I don't.'

'Zarac,' Gerard said thoughtfully, 'held a very strong hand anyway when it came to blackmail.'

I nodded. 'Too strong for his own good.'

We came to the end of the motorway and turned off into narrower streets to thread the way to Ealing.

'Do you know how to find this plant?' I said. 'Or do we ask a policeman?'

'Map,' Gerard said succinctly, producing one from the glove compartment. 'It shows the roads. When we reach the road, drive slowly, keep the eyes skinned.'

'Fair enough.'

'And drive straight past,' he said. 'When we see what's what, we'll decide what to do.'

'All right.'

'If you turn left a mile ahead we'll be about five miles from target. I'll steer you.'

'Right.'

We turned left at a major intersection onto a dual carriageway through sleepy suburbs where in countless ovens Sunday roasts spluttered to lunchtime.

'We'll get a profile done tomorrow of that scotch we took from Martineau,' Gerard said.

'And of the sample I took from the Silver Moondance bottle.'

'They should be the same.'

'They will be.'

'You're exceedingly positive.'

I grinned. 'Yes.'

'Go on, then. What's the joke?'

'Well . . . you know that the tankerful set off from Scotland every time at fifty-eight per cent alcohol? And that at Rannoch's own bottling plant they would have added water to dilute it to forty?'

'Yes,' he nodded.

'Have you any idea how much water that entails?'

'No, of course not. How much?'

'About two thousand seven hundred gallons. More than ten tons by weight.'

'Good grief!'

'Well,' I said, 'Rannoch's would be careful about that water. They'd use pure spring water of some sort, even if it hadn't actually come from a Scottish loch. But I'll swear that Charter's stolen loads have been diluted from an ordinary tap.'

'Is that bad?'

I laughed. 'It sure is. Any Scottish distiller would have a fit. They say that Scotch whisky is only the way it is because of the softness and purity of loch water. When I tasted the Silver Moondance scotch again in my shop I could sort of smell chemicals very faintly in the aftertaste. A lot of tap water isn't too bad, but some is awful. Makes disgusting tea. Ask the residents around here.'

'Here?' he exclaimed.

'Western parts of London. Notorious.'

'Good grief.'

'It will turn up in the profile, too.'

'Water?'

'Mm. Purifying chemicals. There shouldn't be any in neat scotch.'

'But won't tap water spoil the scotch profile? I mean . . . will we still be able to prove our samples are identical with the original sent off from Scotland?'

'Yes, don't worry. Tap water won't affect the whisky profile, it'll just show up as extra components.'

'Will it matter that the scotch is diluted?'

'No,' I said. 'The gas chromatograph just shows up the presence of things, not their quantity.'

He seemed relieved. 'Turn right at the next traffic lights. Could the gas chromatograph tell where any particular sample of tap water came from?'

'I don't know.'

'Amazing.'

'What is?'

'There's something you don't know.'

'Yeah . . . Well, I don't know the dynasties of China or how to say no thanks in fifteen languages or the way to this bottling plant.' And I'd like to turn straight round and go home, I thought. The nearer we got to Naylor's the more my nervousness increased . . . and I thought of my father, brave as brave, setting off into battlefields, inspiring his men . . . and why couldn't I be like him instead of feeling my mouth go dry and my breath shorten before we were even in the heartland of deepest Ealing.

'Turn left here,' Gerard said. 'Then the third on the right. That's our road.'

He was totally calm. No strain or anxiety in voice or face. I consciously unclenched my fingers from their grip on the steering wheel and tried without noticeable success to relax to Gerard's level.

Hopeless. Even my teeth were tightly together when we turned into the third on the right and went slowly along.

'There it is,' Gerard said matter of factly. 'See?'

I glanced to where he indicated and saw a pair of very tall entrance gates, shut, set in a length of very tall brick wall. On the gates in faded white lettering were the words 'Bernard Naylor Bottling', with below them a padlock the size of a saucer.

We wouldn't be able to get in, I thought. Thank goodness for that.

'Turn left at the end,' Gerard said. 'Park there if you can.'

It was one of those suburbs built before zoning where light industries sat among dwelling houses as an integral part of the community. When I'd parked the Mercedes at a kerbside among a row of residents' wheels we walked past lace curtains and shrubby front gardens to get back to the high wall. Eating their roast beef, I thought, and the Yorkshire puddings and the gravy . . . ten minutes past lunchtime and my stomach fluttering with enough butterflies to stock a Brazilian rain forest.

We walked slowly as if out for a stroll and in the short street there was only one other pedestrian, an elderly man waiting patiently for his dog at lampposts.

When we reached the gates, eight feet high, dark green sun-faded paint Gerard stopped and faced them, head back as if reading the big white letters spreading across.

'There's broken glass embedded in the top of those walls,' I said. 'Barbed wire along the top of the gates. Don't tell me you can pick that half-ton padlock.'

'No need,' Gerard said placidly. 'Open your eyes. In many massive gates conspicuously bolted there's a smaller door inset, wide enough for one person only. There's one right ahead of us in the left hand gate with quite an ordinary looking spring lock, and if I can't let us in through there I've been wasting the best years of my life.'

He stopped his apparent reading of the legend on the gates and resumed his stroll, glancing as if casually at the small gate cut in the large.

'Do you smoke?' he said.

'No,' I said in surprise.

'Tie a shoelace.'

'Sure,' I said, understanding, and bent down obligingly to pretend to tie bows on my laceless slip-ons.

'A doddle,' Gerard said, above my head.

'What?'

'Step in.'

I saw to my astonishment that the narrow door was already swinging open. He'd been so fast. He was tucking a piece of clear plastic into his top pocket and glancing down to where the dog was again detaining his master.

Gerard stepped through the gate as if belonging there and with a rapid acceleration of heartbeats I went after him. He pushed the gate shut behind me and the spring lock fell into place with a click. He smiled faintly, and I saw with incredulity that beneath the tiredness and the malaise he was quietly enjoying himself.

'There may be people in here,' I said.

'If there are . . . we found the gate open. Curiosity.'

We both looked at the insides of the very large gates. The padlock outside had been at least partly for show: on the inside there were thick bolts into the ground and a bar let into sockets waist high so that no amount of direct pressure from outside could force the gates open.

'Factories often cut that hole in their defences,' Gerard said, waving at the way we had come in. 'Especially old ones like this, built in the age of innocence.'

We were in a big concreted yard with a high brick building running the whole length of it on our right: small square barred windows pierced the walls in two long rows, one up, one down. At the far end of the yard, facing us, was a one-storey modern office building of panel-like construction, and on our immediate left was a gate-house which on busy days would have contained a man to check people and vehicles in and out.

No gatekeeper. His door was shut. Gerard twisted the knob, but to no avail.

Alongside the door was a window reminiscent of a ticket office, and I supposed that on working days that was where the gate-house keeper actually stood. Gerard peered through it for some time at all angles, and then readdressed himself to the door.

'Mortice lock,' he said, inspecting a keyhole. 'Pity.'

'Does it matter?' I said. 'I mean, there wouldn't be much of interest in a gate-house.'

Gerard glanced at me forgivingly. 'In old factories like this it's quite common to find the keys to all the buildings hanging on a board in the gate-house. The gatekeeper issues keys as needed when employees arrive.'

Silenced, I watched with a parched mouth while he put a steel probe into the keyhole and concentrated on feeling his way through the tumblers, his eyes unfocused and unseeing, all the consciousness in his fingers.

The place was deserted. No one came running across the yard demanding impossible explanations. There was a heavy click from the gate-house door and Gerard with a sigh of satisfaction put his steel probe away and again twisted the doorknob.

'That's better,' he said calmly, as the door opened without protest. 'Now let's see.'

We stepped into a wooden floored room which contained a chair, a time-punch clock with barely six cards in a slot-holder designed for a hundred, a new-looking fire extinguisher, a poster announcing Factory Act regulations and a shallow unlocked wall-cupboard. Gerard opened the cupboard and it was just as he'd said: inside there were four rows of labelled hooks, and upon all the hooks, labelled keys.

'All there,' Gerard said with immense satisfaction. 'There really is no one here. We have the place to ourselves.' He looked along the labels, reading. 'We'll start with the offices. I know more about those. Then . . . what?'

I read the labels also. 'Main plant. Bottle store. Label room. Vats. Dispatch. How long have we got?'

'If Stewart Naylor is Paul Young and does what he said, he'll be on his way now to Martineau Park. If the police detain him there we've at least two or three hours.'

'It doesn't feel like that,' I said.

'No. Always scary, the first few times.'

He left me again speechless. He took the keys he wanted from the hooks and indicated that I should do the same. Then we left the gate-house, closing the door (unnecessarily I thought) behind us and walked on into the main part of the yard.

Another large brick building was revealed to the left; and any residual hopes I might have had of our establishing Stewart Naylor's innocence and retreating in prudence were cancelled at that point. Tucked into the left hand corner of the yard stood a grey Bedford van, brown lines down the sides, devoid of number plates. I went across and looked through its windows but it held nothing: no wine, no fuzzy wigs, no shotgun.

'God in heaven,' Gerard said. 'That's the very one, isn't it?'

'Identical, if not.'

He sighed deeply and glanced round the yard. 'There's no big delivery van here marked Vintners Incorporated. It's probably on its way to Martineau. Let's take the offices, then, and . . . er . . . try not to leave any trace of our having been here.'

'No,' I said weakly.

We walked across the concrete, our shoes scrunching it seemed to me with alarming noise, and Gerard unlocked the door of the office building as if he were the manager arriving in pinstripes.

As revealed by the time-punch cards, the plant for its size was almost unstaffed. There were six small offices in the office block, four of them empty but for desk and chair, two of them showing slight paperwork activity: beyond those a locked suite of rooms marked 'Managing Director' on the outer door said in smaller letters underneath, 'Knock and Enter'.

We entered without knocking, using the appropriate key from the gate-house. Inside, first of all, was a pleasant looking office, walls lined with calendars, charts, and posters of wine districts in France. There were two desks, one managerial, one secretarial, both clearly in everyday use. In-trays bore letters, receipts were spiked, an african violet bloomed next to a pot of pens.

I left Gerard reading invoices with concentration and went through into the next room which was furnished with an expensive leather-topped desk, green leather armchairs, carpet, brass pot with six foot high evergreen, cocktail cabinet, framed drawings of Bernard Naylor and his bottling plant fifty years earlier and a door into a luxurious washroom.

On the far side of the plushy office another door led into what had probably been designed as a boardroom, but in there, with daylight pouring through the skylights, the whole centre space was taken up by a table larger than a billiard table upon which someone appeared to have been modelling a miniature terrain of hills, valleys, plains and plateaux, all of it green and brown like the earth, with a winding ribbon of pale blue stuck on in a valley as a river.

I looked at it in awe. Gerard poked his head round the door, glanced at the table, frowned and said 'What's that?'

'War games,' I said.

'Really?' He came closer for a look. 'A battlefield. So it is. Where are the soldiers?'

We found the soldiers in a cupboard against one wall, tidily stacked in trays, hundreds of them in different uniforms, many hand-painted. There were also ranks of miniature tanks and gun carriages of all historical ages and fierce looking missiles in pits. There were troop-carrying helicopters and First-World-War biplanes, baby rolls of barbed wire, ambulances and small buildings of all sorts, some of them bombed-looking, some painted red as if on fire.

'Incredible,' Gerard said. 'Just as well wars aren't fought on the throw of dice. I've thrown a six, I'll wipe out your bridgehead.'

We closed the cupboard and in giving the table a last interested look I brushed my hand lightly over the contours of the nearest range of mountains.

They moved.

Slightly horrified I picked them up to put them back into place and stood looking at the hollowed out interior in absolute surprise. I picked up another hill or two. Same thing.

'What is it?' Gerard said.

'The mountains are white inside.'

'What of it?'

'See what they're made of?'

I held the mountains hollow side up so that he could see the hard white interior. 'Its plaster of Paris,' I said. 'Look at the edges . . . like bandage. I should think he's modelled that whole countryside in it.'

'Good grief.'

'Not an ear nose and throat surgeon. A war games fanatic. Simple material . . . easily moulded, easily coloured, sets hard as rock.'

I put the hills and the mountains carefully back in position. 'There must be a fair few rolls of the stuff on this table. And if you don't mind . . . let's get out of here.'

'Yes,' Gerard agreed. 'I suppose he'd just bought some more, the day he went to the Silver Moondance. Just happened to have it in his Rolls.'

People didn't just happen to wrap people's heads in it. To do that, people had to have seriously vengeful thoughts and psychotic malice. Paul Young had gone a long way from where Stewart Naylor set out.

We closed the war games room door, crossed the green leather office, returned to the business sector.

'There's just enough legitimate trade going on to give an appearance of tottering a fraction this side of bankruptcy,' Gerard said. 'I can't find anything out of place. There were deliveries via Charter Carriers up to a month ago. Nothing since. No invoices as from Vintners Incorporated, no delivery notes, nothing. This office is for accountants and inspectors. Depressingly clean except for many samples of the Young-Naylor handwriting. Let's try the plant itself.'

He locked our way out of the office block and raised his eyebrows for a decision from me.

'Let's try over there,' I said, pointing to the building by the Bedford van. 'See what's in there first.'

'Right.'

There were two sets of double doors set into the long blank wall, and having tried 'bottle store' and 'vats' I found the key marked 'dispatch' opened one of them.

The hinges creaked as I pulled the door open. My body had almost given up on separate nervous reactions: how could one sweat in some places while one's mouth was in drought? We went into the building and found it was the store for goods already bottled and boxed ready for sending out.

There was a great deal more space than merchandise. There were three lonely pallets laden with cases marked 'House Wine – Red', addressed to a restaurant in Surrey and four other pallets for the same place marked 'House Wine – White': and that was all.

'The paperwork for that lot is in the office,' Gerard said. 'The restaurant bought and shipped the wine, Naylor bottled it. Regular consignments, it looked like.'

We went back into the yard and locked the dispatch doors.

'Main plant,' I said, looking at the high building opposite. 'Well . . . let's see what it's like.'

The key duly let us in. The building was old, it was clear at once, built by grandfather Naylor sturdily to last for generations. Internal walls were extensively tiled in white to shoulder height, cream-painted (long ago) above. From the central entrance some stairs on the left wound upwards, and Gerard chose to go that way first as his paper-oriented mind looked instinctively for most enlightenment aloft: so we went upstairs and to a great extent he was right.

Upstairs, among much unused and dusty space, we found a locked door to further reaches, a door that opened like Sesame to the 'label room' key.

'Great heavens,' Gerard said. 'Is all this usual?'

We stood looking at an expanse of floor covered with heaps of bundles of labels, thousand upon thousand of them altogether, in an apparent muddle but no doubt in some sort of order.

'Quite usual,' I said. 'No one ever tries to order exactly the right number of labels needed for any particular job. You always have to have more, for contingencies. The unused ones just tend to be dumped, and they pile up.'

'So they do.'

'Labels in constant use are probably in those small drawers over there. The ones looking like safe deposit boxes. Some of those drawers have labels on the front . . . they'll have those labels in the drawers.'

'What we want are St Estèphe and all the rest, and Bell's.'

'Mm.'

We both set to, but none of the fake labels turned up, very much to our dismay.

'We need something,' Gerard said. 'We need proof.'

We didn't find it in the label room.

At the back of the label room a closed door led presumably to another room beyond, and I suggested taking a look through there, on the off chance.

'All right,' Gerard said, shrugging.

The door was locked and the 'label room' key didn't fit. Gerard diagnosed another mortice job and took what seemed to be an age with his probe turning the mechanism, but eventually that door too yielded to him, and we went through.

Inside that room there was a printing press. A clean, oiled, sleek modern machine capable of turning out impeccable labels.

Some of the press's recent work was still in uncut sheets: rows and rows of Bell's upon Bell's, brilliant in colour, indistinguishable from the real thing.

Neither Gerard nor I said a word. We turned instead to the

cupboards and boxes stacked around the walls, and we found them all, the neatly printed oblongs saying St Estèphe, St Emilion, Valpolicella, Mâcon, Volnay and Nuits St Georges.

'It's the Château de Chenonceaux,' I said suddenly.

'What is?'

'On this St Estèphe label. I knew I'd seen it somewhere. It's the Château de Chenonceaux on the Loire, without its bridge.'

'I'm glad you know what you're talking about.'

He was taking one each of all the fake labels and stowing them tenderly in his wallet, tucking them away in his jacket. We left everything else as it was but on the way out to my relief he didn't stop to relock the door. We went down again to the hall and from there to a door on the left which unlocked to 'vats'.

One could immediately smell the wine; a warm rosy airfilling aroma like a lungful of earthy fruit. Gerard lifted his head in surprise and to me it felt like coming home.

'I'd no idea,' he said.

A small lobby opened into two long halls, the larger, on the left, containing a row of ten huge round vats down each side. Each vat, painted dark red, was eight feet high, six feet in diameter, and sat eighteen inches above ground level on thick brick pillars. Each vat, on its front, had large valves for loading and unloading, a small valve for testing, a quantity gauge, and a holder into which one could slot a card identifying the present contents.

'They're vast,' Gerard said.

'Kenneth Charter's tanker would fill four of these. That size vat holds fifteen hundred gallons. You can get them bigger.'

'Thanks.'

I smiled. 'Let's see what's in them.'

We read the contents cards. Most of them said 'EMPTY', the quantity gauges reading zero. The three nearest the entrance on the left side bore 'Keely house wine, shipped October 1st', and another further along, 'Dinzag private cuve, shipped Sept. 24th'. Two together on the opposite side said 'Linakket, shipped Sept. 10th'; and all of the occupied vats were only three-quarters full.

'They're all in the office paperwork,' Gerard said regretfully.

'Let's try the empties, then,' I said. 'Quantity gauges can be disconnected.'

I started at the far end under the premise that if Paul Young stacked his loot as far from the entrance as possible at

Martineau Park then he might have done so on his own territory: and he had. The very first trickle which came out onto my fingers as I turned the small testing valve bore the raw volatile smell of scotch.

'Bloody bingo,' I said. 'I'll find a bottle and we'll take a sample, if you like.'

'Later. Try the others.'

'All of them?'

'Yes.'

I loosed the small valves on all the 'EMPTY' monsters, and we found scotch in five of them and wine in three. There was no way of telling how many gallons were in each, but to neither of us did that seem to matter. The wine, as far as I could tell from sucking it from my palm, was similar to our old friend 'St Estèphe', and the scotch was Rannoch already mixed with tap. Gerard looked like a cat in cream as I straightened from testing the last 'EMPTY' (which was in fact empty) and said we'd seen everything now except the actual bottling department, and where would that be?

'Follow the hoses,' I said.

He looked at the three or four hoses which were lying on the ground, fat lightweight grey ridged plastic hoses like giant earthworms as thick as a wrist, some in coils, some straightened out and running the length of the room between the vats.

I said, 'Those connectors at the end of the hoses lock into the valves on the vats. One of them is connected to one of the so called "empty" vats we found the wine in, see? The wine is pumped from the vats to the bottling plant . . . so to find the plant, follow the hoses.'

The hoses snaked round a corner into another wide hall which this time contained only two vats, both painted a silvery white, taller, slimmer, and with several upright pipes attached from top to bottom of their sides.

'White wine?' Gerard said flippantly.

'Not really. They're refrigeration vats.'

'Go on then, what are they for?'

I went over to the nearest, but it was switched off, and so was the other, as far as I could see. 'They use them to clear cloudy particles out of spirits and white wine. If you drop the temperature, the bits and pieces fall to the bottom, and you run off the cleared liquid from higher up.'

The hoses ran straight past the refrigeration vats and through another wide doorway, and through there were found what Gerard was looking for, the long light and airy hall, two storeys high, where the liquids were fed into the bottles and stoppered by corks, where the caps and the labels were applied and the bottles packed into cases.

There were four separate lines of filling, corking, labelling and capping machines, a capacity way beyond the jobs in hand. The machines themselves, like the vats and hoses, were new compared with the buildings. It all looked bright, clean, orderly, spacious and well run.

'I somehow expected something dark and Dickensian,' Gerard said. 'Where do we look?'

'Those big wooden slatted crates standing around probably contain empty bottles,' I said, 'but some might have full ones ready for labelling. Look in those.'

'What are those glass booth things?'

'The actual bottling machines and corking machines and automatic labellers are enclosed with glass for safety and they don't work unless the glass doors are shut. One set of the machines looks ready to go. See the corks in that transparent hopper up there? And up there,' I pointed, 'on that bridge, see those four vats? The wine or whatever is pumped along from those huge storage vats in the long hall through the hoses up into these vats on the bridge, then it feeds down again by gravity into the bottles. The pumps for those vats look as if they're up on the bridge. I'll go up and see if there's anything in those feeder vats, if you like.'

Gerard nodded and I went up the stairs. The bridge, stretching from side to side of the bottling hall, was about twelve feet wide, railed at the sides, with four feeder vats on it standing taller than my head, each with a ladder bolted to its side so that one could go up to the entry valves on top.

There were four electric pumps on the bridge, one for each feeder vat, but only one was connected to hoses. In that one case a hose came up from the floor below and a second hose ran from the pump to the top of one of the feeder vats. In that vat I thought I might find more of the 'St Estèphe', and I squatted at the base of it and released a few drops through the small valve there.

Gerard was rattling bottles in the slatted wooden crates, looking for full ones. The crates were about five feet square, four feet high, very heavy, constructed of rows of timber rather like five barred gates. One could see the bottles inside glinting between the slats, hundreds in each crate.

I had become so at home in my more or less natural surroundings that I'd forgotten to be frightened for the past ten minutes: and that was a fundamental mistake because a voice suddenly spoke from directly beneath me, harsh, fortissimo and threatening.

'What the hell do you think you're doing? Back off, put your hands up and turn round.'

TWENTY-ONE:

He was speaking not to me but to Gerard.

He advanced from below the bridge into my vision, young, bullish, dressed in jeans and padded jacket, carrying a short-barrelled shotgun. He had his back to me and he hadn't seen me, and I crouched on the bridge in a frozen state, incapable of movement, muscles locked, with the old clammy chill of abject fear sweeping over my skin and setting in my gut.

He was the one, I was intuitively certain, who had shot us before.

He was probably Denny. I called him Denny in my mind.

Gerard turned slowly towards him and raised one hand, the other being still in its sling. He didn't look up to the bridge. He could have seen me perhaps if he had, even though I was down behind the railings and between two vats. He did nothing, said nothing, then or later, to let Denny suspect I was there.

'Stand still,' Denny said, 'or I'll blast you.'

Another voice said, 'Who is it? Is it Beach?'; and that was worse. I knew the voice too well.

Paul Young's voice. Stewart Naylor.

'That's not Beach,' he said.

He appeared from below me and stood beside Denny.

I could see the black hair, the heavy shoulders, the glint of glasses, the hearing aid behind his ear.

'Who is it, then?' Denny said.

'The one who was with him. Older, greyer, wearing a sling. That's him. Some name like Gregg, Lew said.'

Who was Lew . . .

'What's the sling for?' Stewart Naylor demanded.

Gerard didn't answer. After a silence Naylor said, 'You said you hit someone in a car at Beach's shop. Was this him?'

Denny said, 'I couldn't see who it was.'

'I don't want him shot in here,' Naylor said forcefully. 'Too much sodding mess. You can keep your sodding finger off the trigger. And you, Gregg, take your arm out of that sling and turn your back to me and put both your hands on the top rail of that bottle-container crate, and you do just what I tell you or you'll get shot again, mess or not.'

Gerard did as he was told. I've got to do something, I thought, and couldn't think what. Couldn't think. Listened in hopeless horror.

Stewart Naylor walked to Gerard and patted him all over, looking for weapons. Gerard didn't move. Naylor reached round into Gerard's jacket and pulled out his wallet, stepping back a few paces to look at the contents.

'Gerard McGregor,' Naylor said, reading. 'Where's your friend Beach?'

'Don't know,' Gerard said, shrugging.

'How the hell did he turn up here?' Denny said. 'I don't like it.'

With suddenly spurting alarm and anger Naylor viciously said, 'He'll sodding wish he hadn't!'

I watched in despair. He had found in the wallet the fake labels from upstairs. He was holding them out as if in disbelief.

'He's seen the press,' he said furiously. 'He knows too bloody much. We'll kill him and dump him. He'll have had no chance yet to tell what he's seen. We'll be all right.' He sounded convinced of it.

Gerard's apparently untroubled voice rose as if in courteous discussion. 'I did of course leave word of where I was going. If I don't return safely you'll find the police at your door.'

'They always say that in movies,' Denny said. 'It's never bloody true.'

After a pause Naylor said, 'Hold him there, Denny. I'll be straight back,' and he turned and walked under the bridge and out of the bottling hall, and I thought about trying to jump onto Denny . . . who was too far away for it to be practicable. He would whirl when he heard me move and he would shoot while I was climbing the railings to launch myself far enough out to have a hope of reaching him in one jump . . . he would shoot either Gerard or me for sure before we could overpower and disarm him. I didn't see what else to do and I was certain that that jump would be literally fatal perhaps for both of us, and I was worrying also and cringing inside with fear that the reason I didn't move was fear . . . Not caution, just cowardice. One could fling one's life away trying to prove to oneself one was brave . . . and maybe for some people it was worth it, but not to me.

Stewart Naylor came back carrying a small package which he zipped open as he walked.

The contents were wide white bandage.

I felt sick.

I should have jumped, I thought. I should have risked it while I had the chance. Why hadn't I?

Commonsense, emotion, logic, bravado . . . they could whirl through the mind in a jumbled mess, and how could one tell which was right.

Naylor walked over to Gerard and with great speed tied the wrist of his injured arm to the rail with the bandage. A strong tremor ran visibly through Gerard's body and he turned away from the crate, trying to tug himself free, trying to escape. The lines of his face were set rigid, the eyes hollowly dark.

He's afraid too, I thought. He knows what that bandage is. He's as human as I am . . . and he's terrified.

He didn't look up at the bridge.

Something, I thought. I must do something. I had no weapon. Nothing. Gerard. Plaster of Paris.

What did I have . . .

I had knowledge.

Naylor hit Gerard's face a swiping blow with his fist and when he had him off balance he tied the second wrist to the railing, and although I could then see only his back the desperation in Gerard's body was like a shout.

In my mind I was begging, 'No, don't do it, no, no . . .' and Naylor wound the bandage once round Gerard's neck.

Knowledge.

The bandage went round twice and three times. Naylor was intent on the work. So was Denny, his back to me, the barrel of the gun drooping.

Gerard was kicking backwards and not reaching Naylor's legs, yelling to him, screaming that what he was doing was useless, useless, people knew he was there and would come looking.

Neither Naylor nor Denny believed him. They were intent . . . enjoying . . . the wrapping of a living head . . . to turn it to rock.

The weapon I had was knowledge.

I moved. My muscles felt stiff. I slid jerkily round the vat I'd tested for St Estèphe and climbed its ladder.

Go on yelling, Gerard, I thought. Go on filling the hearing aid of the deaf man. Go on kicking. Keep them looking your way.

My hands grasped the locking nut which connected the hose to the valve at the top of the feeder vat. Usually I could turn them easily without a wrench. My hands slipped with sweat. I'd got to unlock it. Only chance. Had to have the hose off the vat.

Had to have the hose free at that end.

On top of the vat I strained with almost fury and felt the locking nut turn and turn again and come loose. I lifted the hose off the vat and carried the end of it with me down the short ladder, trying to do it all silently, making small noises that sounded frightful to me but brought no dreaded shouts from the floor.

I was down the ladder. By the pump. From the pump the main long hose ran down to the ground and away into the distance, going to the great storage vat in the main hall. Long hose, holding a good deal of wine.

I switched on the pump. Begging. Praying. Sick.

The pump went smoothly about its business, efficient beyond dream. Wine gushed out of the hose I held like red force-driven water out of a fire hose. I directed it straight at Naylor, drenching Denny on the way. I propped the spurting nozzle between the railings. I climbed over the railings myself and made the flying leap that had been so illogical, so impossible, so deadly. I landed on Denny who couldn't see for wine, and grabbed his shotgun from him and hit him hard with it on the head.

Naylor, totally surprised, tried to clutch me. I felt such anger for him that he would have needed twice his strength. I caught him by his clothes and pushed him until he was under the gushing wine, and I pulled his head back by the hair until the wine was running full onto his face, onto his glasses and up his nose and into his opening mouth until he was beginning to choke.

I was drowning him, I thought.

Perhaps I shouldn't.

He was gagging for breath. Waving his arms about. Helpless.

I half pulled, half pushed him back to the crate Gerard was tied to and propped him chest forwards against it, holding him there by leaning on his back.

He really was choking. Not breathing.

I hit him very hard with my palm below the shoulder blades and the air trapped in his lungs rushed out through the wine blockage in his trachea, and he began to breathe again in whooping gasps like whooping cough, air fighting against wine in all his bronchial tubes.

He had dropped the plaster of Paris bandage at Gerard's feet. I picked up the roll, wet and soggy and pink now with wine, and unwound the layers from Gerard's throat.

Naylor hadn't had any scissors. The bandage led from Gerard's neck down to one wrist and from there to the other. Tight knots on his wrists beyond undoing.

Something to cut with, to free him.

Old blunt penknife. I felt in my pocket for it and with some astonishment came up with Flora's new sharp silver present. Blessed Flora.

I cut the roll of bandage off Gerard's wrist and then cut the bandages tying his wrists to the crate. Even when his wrists were no longer fixed there he held onto the rail for a few moments, and in that time I'd wound the end of the bandage roll about eight times around one of Naylor's wrists instead, and fastened it similarly to the crate.

Naylor leaned over the crate, retching, coughing, his glasses opaque with wine, his body jerking with the effort of drawing breath. He seemed hardly to notice, much less fight, when I fastened his other wrist to the rail.

Denny on the floor returned to life. I looked down from tying knots and watched fuzzy thoughts begin to straighten out in his eyes, and I took one of the empty bottles out of the crate and hit him again with it on the head.

The bottle broke. A claret bottle, I remotely noticed. The pieces fell into the wine that was still flooding out in a red lake all over the floor, curling round corners, making rivers, pulsating down from the open hose. The smell of it filled the senses; heavily sensuous, headily potent.

So much wine . . . The main valve on the huge storage vat must be open, I thought. The whole thing must be emptying through the pump. Fifteen hundred gallons . . .

Denny was lying face down in it. I hauled him over to the crate, turned him onto his back, pulled his arms up, and with soggy pink bandage tied each of his wrists separately to one of the sturdy lower slats.

Wine swirled through his hair. If there was blood there also, I couldn't see.

Gerard watched, leaning against the crate.

When I'd finished the essential tying there was still some bandage left in the roll. I wound some more of it round each of

Naylor's wrists, joining them in more and more layers to the crate, and then used the last of it to do the same for Denny.

The gypsum in the bandage had been already released to some extent by the wine so that my fingers were covered with pale pink slime. I picked an empty bottle from the crate and held it under the spurting hose until it was half filled and then I carefully poured wine over each tied wrist until the bandages were soaked right through.

Gerard watched throughout, speechless.

Finally I went up the stairs and switched off the pump.

The gusher stopped. The only sound suddenly was the laboured wheezing of Naylor fighting for breath.

I looked down for a moment at the scene below: at so much floor redly awash, at Denny lying on his back with his hands tied above his head, at Naylor heaving over the crate, at the shotgun lying in the wine, and the broken claret bottle . . . and the bottles in the crates.

The only thing that might cut through hardening plaster of Paris was broken glass.

I went down the stairs and carefully removed the broken bottle from anywhere near Denny, and took enough bottles out of the crate to make sure Naylor couldn't reach any.

I pushed the shotgun well out of their reach with my foot.

What else?

Nothing else.

I was myself, like Naylor and Denny, soaked from head to foot with wine: jacket, trousers, shirt, socks, shoes, all dark red against dark red skin. Gerard alone, though copiously splashed, was relatively dry.

I said to him, 'Could you fetch your car to the gate? I'll drive from there, but I'm not quite sure that I'm what they'd expect in this neighbourhood.'

'What about them?' he said, looking at our captives.

'We'll send the posse. I'd like to get away from here first. Denny has a partner somewhere.'

'Right. Yes, I'll get the car.' He sounded exhausted and very subdued, and looked anywhere but at my face.

Denny stirred and groaned. Naylor wheezed. In a very few minutes the bandages round their wrists would be pink rock, and it would take a saw to release them.

We left without locking anything. Gerard brought the car to the gates and I drove from there on, apologising as I got in for the stains I would be leaving on the upholstery. He said stains were secondary. He said little else.

We stopped again as in the morning at a nearby public telephone and this time I got through myself to the priority number, reversing the charges. I said to the answering voice that I wanted an urgent message to reach Detective Chief Superintendent Wilson from Tony Beach.

Hold on, he said. I held. A smooth well-known voice came on the line and said, 'Mr Beach? Is that you?'

'Yes, Mr Wilson.'

'And was it you earlier, who directed us to Martineau Park?'

'Not exactly.'

'Mr McGregor, was it?'

'Yes. How do you know?'

'A man at the racecourse . . . the deputy clerk of the course who is present there on Saturdays and Sundays while the gates and doors are unlocked . . . he told our men that a Mr Beach had been to the caterer's section yesterday and again today with a Mr McGregor.'

'What happened?' I asked.

'Paul Young hasn't gone there, Mr Beach.' He spoke partly regretfully, partly with faint reproof.

'Has anyone?' I asked.

'A man called Lew Smith arrived a short while ago in a van from Vintners Incorporated. Our men surrounded him, accompanied by the deputy clerk of the course. Lew Smith could give no good reason for being there, but neither was he Paul Young. There seemed to be no grounds for detaining him on the basis of an anonymous telephone call, and our men let him go. And now Mr Beach, could you give me an explanation? Why did you expect Paul Young to go to Martineau Park?'

'Mr Wilson,' I said. 'I do know where Paul Young is now. Do you want him?'

'Don't be facetious, Mr Beach.'

I told him exactly where to find his quarry. I said, 'You'll find a printing press if you go upstairs, complete with Bell's labels and also the same fake wine labels found in the Silver Moondance. You'll find stolen whisky in the vats . . . if you apply to Rannoch whisky distillers you'll get a profile match. The scotch was stolen from tankers belonging to a firm called Charter Carriers . . . you'll find another branch of the police investigating those thefts. You'll find plaster of Paris in Paul Young's office . . . and he's Larry Trent's half-brother and his name is Stewart Naylor.'

'Mr Beach . . .'

'Goodbye, Mr Wilson,' I said. 'Please don't waste time. Lew Smith might drive there and free him. And oh, yes, you remember Gerard McGregor and I were shot at by the robbers outside my shop? You'll find one of those thieves tied up with Naylor. Also his gun's there. I think his name's Denny. Lew Smith was probably his partner. Worth a try, anyway.'

I put the receiver down although I could hear him still talking and got back into the car with Gerard.

'There will be endless questions,' he said.

'Can't be helped.'

I restarted the engine and we angled our way sedately out of Ealing, crossed the hinterland, made it safely back to the high road home.

Neither of us talked again for a long way. There was none of the euphoria of the Sunday before with the pellets burning in our bodies and our spirits high with escape. Today had been grimmer, dark with real horror, dark as wine.

Gerard shifted in his seat and sighed and said eventually, 'I'm glad you were with me.'

'Mm.'

Five minutes later he said, 'I was afraid.'

'Yes, I know. Well, so was I.'

He turned his head, glanced finally at my face and then looked forward again through the windscreen.

'That plaster . . .' He shuddered. 'I was screaming . . . I've never been so craven in my life.'

'Fear in a fearful situation is normal. Absence of fear is not.'

He swallowed. 'I also feared you wouldn't rescue me.'

'Wouldn't? Do you mean couldn't, or wouldn't try?'

'Couldn't, of course.' He seemed surprised at the question. 'It would have been pointless to do anything useless like throwing your life away to make a gesture.'

'Die in the attempt?'

'Dying in the attempt,' he said sombrely, 'has always seemed to me the height of incompetence.'

'Or plain bad luck.'

'All right,' he said. 'I'll allow bad luck.'

Another silence lengthened. We turned off the motorway and would soon be back where we'd left my car.

'Are you all right to drive home?' I said.

'Yes, perfectly.'

He looked no better than when we'd set off, but not worse either. Still grey, still strained, but still also with apparently endless reserves of stamina.

I had known him for two weeks. Fifteen days, to be accurate, since we had made tunnels under the tent at Flora's party. With him and through him I had looked newly into many internal mirrors and was coming to understand what I saw there. I owed him a great deal and didn't know how to tell him.

I stopped his car beside mine. We both got out. We stood looking at each other, almost awkwardly. After such intensity there seemed to be no suitable farewell.

'I'm in your debt,' he said.

I shook my head. 'Other way round.'

He smiled faintly, ruefully. 'Call it quits.'

He stepped quietly into his wine-stained car, gave me the briefest of waves, drove away.

I watched him go until he was out of sight. Then in similar peace I unlocked my own door and motored ordinarily home.

The sun was breaking through clouds when I reached the cottage, shining with the heavy golden slant of a late October tea-time.

I went into the hall and looked into the real mirror there. My hair was spiky and sticky with wine. The stains all over my head and face had dried to purple, but in the sun's rays they still seemed to glow red. My eyes shone pale grey in a burnished landscape.

I smiled. My teeth gleamed. I looked like a red devil, I thought. A bloody red devil from the far side of terror.

I was filled quite suddenly with a sort of restless exultation.

I went through my sun-filled house shouting aloud, 'Emma . . . Emma . . . Emma . . . Emma . . .' and my voice bounced off the walls, reverberating.

I didn't shout for lack of her but from wanting to tell her . . . wanting to shout to her to make her hear . . . that for once I felt I had done what I should, that I hadn't been for ever a coward, that I knew I hadn't failed her memory . . . or myself . . . or anything I thought I ought to be . . . and that I felt comforted and whole and at one with her, and that if I wept for her from now on it would be for what she had missed . . . the whole of life . . . the unborn child . . . and not for my own loss, not from loneliness . . . not from guilt.

TWENTY-TWO:

Fragments of information floated my way for days like debris from a shipwreck.

Chief Superintendent Wilson came to tell me the police had had to saw through the crate and transport Naylor and Denny to a hospital to get their unorthodox handcuffs removed. He seemed deeply amused and also content, and took away a bottle of wine for dinner.

Sergeant Ridger returned with a cut forehead from his scuffle with the pickets and told me that the racecourse bars at Martineau Park had been on the police list of whisky complaints. He said we would have gone there on the next raceday and our pub crawl would have been successful: and I didn't like to tell him that it already had been, thanks to Mrs Alexis.

Mrs Alexis asked me to lunch. I went, laughed a lot, and came away with a commission to choose and supply wine for her restaurant. Wilfred had survived the soot and the sweep got the sack.

Gerard fed me with constant news, mostly good.

The scotch in the big storage tanks had been profile-matched and had proved to be the third load stolen from the tanker. The Martineau Park and Silver Moondance scotch was all from the second load. The first load had presumably been sold and drunk.

Rannoch's were refusing to collect or accept their scotch because of the tap water. Customs and Excise were pressing all and sundry for the duty. Kenneth Charter's insurers were insisting that as the whisky was Rannoch's, Rannoch's should pay. Rannoch's said Naylor should pay. Kenneth Charter's suggestion that they run the stuff away down a drain and forget it was not being treated seriously.

The best news was that the insurers had agreed to reinstate Charter's policies in full: the tanker fleet would stay in business.

Kenneth Junior's part was so far unknown to the police and

would with luck remain so. Kenneth Junior wrote to his father from Australia asking for more money, which Kenneth Senior sent him along with advice to stay far away until parental disgust had abated.

Mission accomplished, Gerard said with satisfaction. Deglet's was sending Charter their account.

Into Deglet's office came news also from the Californian bloodstock agent: he regularly sold the horses shipped by Larry Trent and paid the proceeds as instructed into three bank accounts in the name of Stewart Naylor.

He had met Mr Naylor, who had been over once to open the accounts. The horses were good and had won races for their new owners. Everything was straightforward, he was sure.

Flora came to tell me she and Jack were going to Barbados for a month to lie in the sun.

'We go every year, dear, but you know Jack, never still for five minutes except that this time his leg will slow him up nicely, won't it? Of course half the racing world goes to Barbados in the winter . . . did you know they call it Newmarket-on-Sea?' And later she sent me a postcard saying Orkney Swayle and Isabella were staying in the same hotel and one couldn't have everything, dear, could one?

Miles Quigley telephoned, full of importance, to offer me Vernon's job, starting immediately, as liquor manager to his firm. Double Vernon's salary, he said, and managerial status and a seat on the board; and I reflected while politely declining that if he'd given Vernon those rewards Vernon might have stayed loyal for life.

Quigley said he was sticking to his agreement not to prosecute and Vernon was co-operating with the police. Co-operating? I asked. Vernon, Quigley said, would be a prosecution witness, chattering in return for immunity. Was I sure about the job?

I was sure. Perfectly certain, thanks all the same.

I would stay with my shop, I thought, because for me it was right. The scale of its life was my scale. We fitted.

I would stay with good-natured Mrs Palissey and maybe one day teach Brian to write his own name. I would eat Sung Li's dinners and bow to him; and I would listen to my customers and sell them comfort.

Ordinary life would go on.

I went home one night after closing at nine and found the postman had left a package from my mother.

She seldom wrote; mostly telephoned. The note inside the package was characteristically short.

Darling,
Turned out some very old boxes. Found these oddments of your father's. If you don't want them, throw them away.

The oddments were from a long way back, I thought, looking through them. One of a pair of military gold cuff links. A bronze belt buckle with his regimental crest. A leather jotter with a slot for a pencil, but no pencil.

I riffled through the pages of the jotter. Nothing but memos about things like duty rosters; notes about the day-to-day running of the regiment. It was only by chance that I came upon the page where he had written something else.

I stared at the page, transfixed. It was a scrawl, a *cri de coeur*, hurried, barely punctuated, ending without a question mark. I knew my mother wouldn't have sent it, if she'd seen it. It too nearly destroyed the myth.

I felt nearer to him than ever before. I felt his true son.

He had written . . . at not quite my present age, he had written:

The battle must be soon now. It is essential not to show fear to the men, but God, I fear
Why can't I have the courage of my father

Somewhere in the battle, I thought, he had found it.